Susan Hoply attacked by the Robbers in the Forest.

SUSAN HOPLY;

OR, THE

TRIALS AND VICISSITUDES OF A SERVANT GIRL.

A TALE OF DEEP INTEREST.

BY THE AUTHOR OF "KATHLEEN," "HEBREW MAIDEN," &c.

" Ye good distrest!
Ye noble few! who here unbending stand
Beneath life's pressure; yet bear up awhile;
And what your bounded view, which only saw
A little part, deemed evil, is no more!
The storms of wintry time will quickly pass,
And one unbounded spring encircle all."—ANON.

LONDON:
PRINTED AND PUBLISHED BY E. LLOYD, 231, SHOREDITCH.

PREFACE.

THE domestic nature of the present work has ensured for it a popularity and wide circulation almost unprecedented in the annals of publishing. As the reader will observe, there are several distinct plots in the course of the tale, each of them apparently unconnected with the other, yet terminating in one, and thus affording various instances in which circumstantial evidence has brought punishment upon the guilty parties.

It has, however, been the aim of the Author to introduce nothing that is improbable; and, numerous as the incidents are, he trusts it will be acknowledged that each and every one of them might have occurred in real life. Some, indeed, founded upon facts, and consequently, though the present work is in the form of a fiction, it may be said to contain more truths than most others of a similar description.

Having said thus much for ourselves and the labours we have thus brought to a conclusion, it would be unpardonable were we omit to returning our thanks for the very liberal patronage that has been bestowed on us, and to repeat our former promises, that the kindness of our friends shall urge us on to renewed exertions in our endeavours to convey intruction and amusement to those who have encouraged us with their smiles.

May 15th, 1842.

SUSAN HOPLY;

OR, THE TRIALS AND VICISSITUDES OF A

SERVANT GIRL.

CHAPTER I.

THE FALSE FRIEND.

"Tut, tut, girl, am I never to hear an end of these complaints against Mr. Gravestow? One would think he was a devil incarnate at the very least, from all the idle reports that are raised to his prejudice, and I am sure, whatever people may choose to say to the contrary, he is a worthy creature, and in every way deserving the esteem in which I hold him."

Thus spoke Mr. Langton Wentford, a retired city merchant, to his young housekeeper, Susan Hoply, who had ventured to express an opinion anything but favourable to the person their conversation referred to. It must be acknowledged, that Susan had formed a very great dislike towards Walter Gravestow, but there was some reason for her antipathy, for he was an artful hypocrite, and there were not wanting persons, besides Susan Hoply, who thought him capable of committing any crime so long as it would serve a particular purpose. Susan had never before ventured to ex-

No. 1

press herself quite so freely, but finding that she had not given any great offence, she said :—

"You will pardon me, sir, I hope, for saying anything against a friend of yours; but really, in this instance, I can see so much art and hypocrisy, that it is impossible to hold my tongue any longer."

"Psha!" retorted the old gentleman; "he has given you some sort of offence I suppose, and so you take this method to revenge yourself. But I'll hear nothing you have to say against Mr. Gravestow, and so I desire the subject may never be mentioned in my presence again."

"I'll endeavour to obey you, sir," replied Susan; "but I believe you love little Edwin, the poor orphan child that you have brought up from infancy, and I have a notion Mr. Gravestow is jealous of the favours you have bestowed upon him; and if my suspicions are correct, there is but too much reason to fear the boy is in danger."

"Why, you don't mean to insinuate that my friend Gravestow would do aught to injure the boy ?"

"I am afraid there is not much doubt of it," answered Susan. "I have watched the evil looks with which he regards the poor child, and I am much mistaken indeed if he is not scheming some plan or other to get rid of him."

"Nonsense, girl!" exclaimed the old gentleman; "your prejudice against a very worthy man is most unjust. It is true I have brought Edwin up, and intend to leave him a portion of my fortune, but Mr. Gravestow is about to marry my daughter, and, of course, by far the greater share will go to him. Besides, he always appears to be very fond of the child, and frequently caresses him, which he would hardly do if he had formed such a dislike as you think."

"Ah, sir, you are deceived, depend on it," said Susan. "He can pretend to be very fond of Edwin in your presence, but you know not the cruel thoughts he entertains towards him when no one is by to guess what his mind is running on."

"And pray why have you taken this dislike to a man that I should suppose has never offended you ?"

"Because I have pretty good reason for believing the very worst of him," replied Susan. "There is no one in the house that likes him, for he's one of those downcast-looking fellows that have always got mischief running in their heads."

"On the contrary, Susan," replied Mr. Wentford, "I have ever been a friend to the man we are speaking of, and, therefore, it is hardly likely he would attempt anything that might serve to bring him into disgrace. Besides, I have never yet seen cause to believe that he is unworthy the kindness I have bestowed on him, and, you may depend upon it, Susan, that I will never turn my back upon a man, till I see sufficient reasons for doing so."

"Perhaps you are offended with me, sir, for speaking my mind a little too plainly in the present instance ?"

"I am not offended with you in the present instance," returned the old gentleman, "but in future I would be glad if you spoke less disrespectfully of those I call my friends. Mr. Gravestow is shortly about to be closely connected with me; and you may, of course, suppose I hold him in the highest esteem, since I do not hesitate to entrust him with a daughter whom I fondly love."

"I am very sorry my young lady is about to have such a husband," exclaimed Susan Hoply; "she is a great deal too good for him, and I am afraid you will one of these days find him out, when it's too late."

"And are you aware," cried Mr. Wentford, "that the person you are speaking of was once my partner, and is now my successor, in a business which has engaged by far the greater portion of my life? I have, in fact, ever found Mr. Gravestow a strictly honourable man; and should he turn out otherwise, I shall be candid enough to acknowledge that for once in my life I have been most wofully deceived in a man's character."

" And that you will have to confess it I am very certain," answered Susan. " I have not been watching him all this time for nothing, and, take my word for it, sir, the first bad turn he does you will be to injure poor Edwin, who never did him any harm in his life."

" Psha!" cried Mr. Wentworth, "all your thoughts seem to run upon that boy, as if it would be worth any one's while to do anything against him. So once for all, I tell you Edwin has nothing to fear from him, and you will remember, that it is my wish you ever treat him with the same attention and respect that you do all the rest of my friends."

" I'll try my best to be civil to him, sir," answered Susan Hoply, "but it will come with a very bad grace, seeing that I am quite convinced that he is one of the greatest vil——."

" You forget yourself, girl," interrupted Mr. Wentford. " I have this moment desired you to change this course, and yet you were about to apply an epithet to him that I should be sorry to know was deserved by any person with whom I am on terms of intimacy."

" Well, sir," replied the girl, " I only hope you may never have reason to be sorry for the hour that first made you acquainted with Mr. Walter Gravestow; he is pretty well seen through by everybody else, and if I may have been rather bold in expressing my thoughts upon the subject, it was only that you might be upon your guard against him before it is too late. At any rate, it would be worth while looking after him a bit, so as to find out what sort of a man he is before he becomes the husband of my young lady."

" Aye, aye, I shall not fail to do that, you may depend on it," answered the old gentleman. " Her happiness is bound up with my own so closely, that I shall hardly think of bestowing her upon any man till I am thoroughly convinced that he is in every way deserving of her. But where is little Edwin all this time, that I have not seen him since the hour of breakfast?"

" He said nothing about where he was going to," answered Susan; " but as he took his rod and lines with him, I suppose he has gone to fish in the lake."

" And did no one go with him?" asked Mr. Wentworth, in a tone of uneasiness.

" No one, sir."

" Indeed!—where is Mr. Gravestow?"

" That," replied the girl, " is more than anybody knows. It is certain, however, that he left the house shortly after Edwin; and, it is said, he was seen making his way towards the lake."

" Aye, a favourite walk of his, I believe," observed her master. " He is fond of retirement, and where else can I find it in such perfection as in the neighbourhood of that lovely spot?"

" Very true, sir; but if he should happen to meet with poor Edwin there?"

" They would then be companions together, and the boy would, at least, have a protector at hand in case he should chance to meet with any accident."

" He'll have a better protector than him, I am thinking, in case he should happen to need one," answered Susan.

" And who may that be?"

" My brother Andrew, sir."

¶ " Why, you don't mean to say that Andrew has been foolish enough to neglect his work, that he may act the spy upon a friend of mine ?"

" He would not meanly act the spy, sir," answered Susan, " but he has a notion that some mischief is intended; and so, loving the boy as he does, he took the road that leads towards the lake, just to see what was going on."

"And for which I shall severely reprimand him," exclaimed Mr. Wentford. " It is not to be endured that my friends are to be treated thus by those in my employ, and should Andrew ever do such a thing again, I shall most assuredly discharge him from my service. But stay; what is the meaning of that crowd I see coming down the avenue ?—Run and ascertain the cause, Susan, and return here as quickly as you can, that I may know what has occasioned this unusual assemblage of persons."

Without waiting for a second bidding, Susan Hoply ran off, leaving her master a prey to feelings of anxiety that he could not account for. The girl's expressions of dislike towards Walter Gravestow, had made some little impression upon his mind, in spite of his endeavours to put the most favourable construction upon every thing. But in a brief space of time he discarded the thoughts as unworthy of him, and with some impatience he waited for the return of his domestic with the news he was so anxious to hear. Taking this opportunity, we will explain, as shortly as possible, a few circumstances, that may be necessary for the development of our story.

Mr. Langton Wentford, formerly an opulent merchant of the City of London, had risen by his own unaided industry, from a very humble situation in life, to a station that all men were willing to admit was richly deserved. He had attained the summit of his ambition by the acquirement of a handsome fortune; and when age crept upon him with slow and stealthy footsteps, he resolved to quit the more active duties of his life, and seek that retirement which his former habits of diligence had rendered so necessary. Arrangements were accordingly made, and quitting town with his only daughter, he left the future management of his business to Mr. Walter Gravestow, who, from having been his head clerk, he now admitted as a partner in the business, which he was not yet inclined to re-linquish. But in this instance the confidence of the good merchant had been sadly misplaced; for Gravestow was a smooth-tongued villain, who, by hypocrisy, had succeeded in winning the regard of his master, whilst he was, in fact, contriving the destruction of him, who had thus raised him to a point of comfort and respectability that he little deserved. Yet, as we have seen, Walter Gravestow continued to maintain the esteem of his former master, who, as an act of still further friendship and confidence, was now about to bestow upon him his only daughter in marriage.

With this brief explanation we will now return to Mr. Wentworth, who, having waited some time patiently for the return of Susan, rang the bell furiously, in order that he might learn the cause of the crowd which he had seen coming down the avenue. The summons was quickly answered, and the domestic, pale and agitated, presented herself before her master.

" Now, Susan," he exclaimed, " what is the meaning of all this ?—you look terrified, girl; but I will know all, even though my worst anticipations should prove correct. Who are those people, and what is the object that has brought them here ?"

" Ah ! sir," cried the girl, " poor little Edwin has—"

′ " Met with some accident, you would tell me," interrupted her master, impatiently. " Speak !—is he alive ?"

" He is, sir, but that is almost as much as you can say."

" Poor child !—poor child !" he exclaimed; " this comes of his fondness for the dangerous amusement of fishing. But I will not be angry with him just now, so take me to him, that I may know the worst without delay."

"I believe he is no longer in danger, sir," answered Susan; "and as he has been put to bed, the doctor says he must, on no account, be disturbed for the present."

"How!—am I to be debarred seeing the poor child when his life is [in danger?"

"He is not in danger now, sir," replied the girl;—"at least, the doctor says he is going on very favourable, and that all he requires is, a few hours rest and quietness."

"Well, well," cried the old gentleman, "it is hard to be denied seeing him, but if it is for the poor boy's advantage I will e'en submit to it, since, it seems, he is no longer in peril; and now tell me, Susan, how this accident occurred?"

"In my opinion, sir, it was no accident at all."

"Nay, speak to me not in riddles," exclaimed her master, "but tell me as briefly as you can, how this affair happened."

"To tell you the truth, then," she replied, "I believe, he was pushed into the water."

"Oh!—by some of his playmates, I suppose?"

"He had no playmates with him."

"Who, then, could have pushed him into the water?"

"That I hardly like to say, for fear of offending you," replied Susan, with hesitation.

"Nay," exclaimed the old gentleman, "I have asked you a plain question, and expect an answer. Speak, girl, and tell me who you think could have been so base as to have committed so cowardly an act upon a helpless child, like my poor little Edwin?"

"Well, then, sir," replied Susan, "to speak the truth, this deed could have been done by no one but Mr. Gravestow!"

"Hah!" cried the old man, startled by the name she had pronounced, "again is my friend to be cruelly sacrificed to the unjust prejudices that exist against him. But, explain yourself, girl, for surely you would not venture on such an assertion without having some cause for making it."

"I told you, sir, that Mr. Gravestow followed the child almost as soon as he had left the house."

"You did;—but that is no proof of his having done so with a guilty intention."

"Perhaps not," she replied, "but I, also, told you that my brother Andrew went out that he might see whether any mischief was going forward."

"Which was an act of impertinence," exclaimed Mr. Wentford, "that I shall not fail to punish him for. However, you have not yet told me whether he witnessed anything to confirm the suspicions you have told me of."

"He saw quite enough to convince everybody that heard him," replied Susan.

"Did he see Mr. Gravestow push the child into the water?"

"No," answered the girl; "he was not there in time for that, but he saw Edwin struggling in the lake, and just as he was rushing to his rescue, he met Mr. Gravestow hurrying away as fast as his legs would carry him."

"And did he say anything?"

"Nothing more than that he was running off to fetch a doctor!—A likely thing, forsooth, that he should be going to fetch a doctor whilst the child was struggling for its life in the water!"

"Nay," cried Mr. Wentford, "you judge him far too harshly; all men are not endowed alike with self-possession, and it is not at all improbable, that, in his alarm, he might have done as you have described. At any rate, I will not believe anything against him, and it is my desire, that you say no more about a suspicion that I feel quite certain is both unfounded and unjust. So now go to Mr. Gravestow, and say I wish to see him immediately."

"He has not returned yet."

"That is strange, too," observed the old gentleman, "for one would have thought his natural anxiety for the child's safety would have prompted his immediate return. But, perhaps, no one has sought him in his own chamber?"

"He has been sought for all over the house," replied Susan, "but no one has been able to find him. Indeed, it's most likely he is ashamed to show his face, and no wonder at it after what he has done."

"Am I again to warn you against these unjust expressions?" said Mr. Wentword. "You offend me, girl, by thus charging my friend with a crime that I am certain he would never be guilty of."

"Indeed, sir," answered Susan, "I should be most sorry to offend so good a master, but——"

"I will hear no more," interrupted her master; "my friend's character should be as free from suspicion as my own, and with respect to Mr. Gravestow, I feel quite assured that he is utterly incapable of the base act which evil minded people would charge him. You may now leave me, Susan, and do not let me hear that any of the persons in my employ recur to a subject so painful to me."

"I can promise for myself," she replied, "but it may not be so easy to stop the tongues of others; besides, Edwin may be able to throw some light on the affair when he recovers, and if he should say that Mr. Gaveston threw him into the lake, of course it would be in vain to deny it any longer."

"Edwin's testimony is all we have to rely on," answered Mr. Wentford. "The boy will, no doubt, speak the truth, and, in my own mind, I feel perfectly satisfied that he will completely exonerate Mr. Gravestow from all blame. So now, girl, go to the servant's hall, and should any of my people persist in this abominable story of theirs, tell them I will not permit a word to be said that may in any way be injurious to my friend."

Susan, however, was not to be thus easily convinced of the innocence of a man whose actions had long been the subject of conversation, and hurrying down to the hall, she found a number of servants congregated, all of whom were talking over the event of the last hour. Here at least unanimity prevailed, for whatever might be the opinion of the master, they had but one notion about the subject, and that was anything but favourable to the person in question. Nay, she was more convinced than ever by the few words she heard on entering the room, but remembering the injunctions of her master, she delivered his commands, and entreated them, whatever their own notions might be, to say no more about it till they had further evidence to bring against the object of their doubt.

"At present," she said, "we can bring forward no proof that will satisfy our master, however certain we may be in our own minds of Mr. Gravestow's guilt. Let us, therefore, think it possible that we may have suspected him unjustly, and though we may not be able to convince ourselves, it will at least give us time to look about for further evidence against the guilty party. Besides, poor little Edwin may recollect something about the affair, though I dare say care enough was taken to prevent his knowing who it was that made the attempt upon his life."

" But they can't deny what I saw with my own eyes," exclaimed Andrew Hoply, who at that moment presented himself among them. " Mr. Gravestow was near the spot when nobody else was, and when I spoke to him he was confused, and made a lame excuse that only served to convince me the more of his guilt."

" Nay, brother, say no more about it," interposed Susan. " Our master has strictly forbidden us to connect the name of Mr. Gravestow with this mysterious affair, and if we are heard speaking of it we shall seriously offend him."

" Well, I have no wish to do that," answered Andrew, " but it's a hard thing to close a man's mouth when he is quite convinced that he has spoken nothing but the truth."

" And especially," observed the gardener, " when it's to let off a chap that every body believes to be guilty of a cowardly attempt to murder a poor innocent child."

" But if he is guilty," cried Susan, " he shall not escape the punishment he deserves. I will, myself, keep a close and careful watch upon him, and, take my word for it, something or other will one day come out to fix him with the crime."

" Aye, aye," exclaimed her brother, " it's in very good hands now, and though he may escape a little while longer, he may make up his mind to be found out in time. Why, all the neighbours are up in arms against him, and I don't believe there's a person but would cheerfully sacrifice all he possessed to bring the affair home to the right party."

" But what puzzles me most of all is," observed the gardener, " that our master should be so blind as to side with a man that every body else looks upon as a villain. For my own part, I have the very worst notion of this Mr. Gravestow, and sorry enough I should be to meet him alone in a dark road."

" Yes, if you had ever offended him," exclaimed Andrew. " At all events, he has very few friends, I believe, except our master, and he is one of those men that will never turn his back upon any one till he's quite convinced that they are unworthy of any further regard. This fellow, Gravestow, has somehow or other contrived to sneak into his favour, and it will not be a very easy task to set him against him, whilst a doubt remains in his favour."

" That's very true," replied Susan Hoply, " but in my opinion, the worst of it is, that Miss Fanny is to be his wife. Only think of her marrying a murderer !"

" Horrible !" groaned every one present.

" And yet there seems to be no doubt of it," continued Susan, " for he is now here on a visit to make arrangements for their union, and I have heard it said the ceremony is to take place very shortly."

" But your young mistress don't like him a bit, I've heard say," observed Andrew.

" Then you have heard exactly the truth," answered his sister :—" she dislikes him very much, and has even ventured to tell her father so ; but the old gentleman,—though he loves her very dearly,—is rather obstinate in this affair, and tells her not to be prejudiced, because a parcel of foolish people have taken a dislike to his intended son-in-law."

" And will she marry him ?"

" Most assuredly she will," replied Susan ;—" the poor dear young lady thinks herself bound to obey her father's wishes in all things, and so she receives the wishes of Mr. Gravestow with civility, in spite of her dislikes for him."

" In that case there's pretty certain to be a life of misery for her," observed Andrew ; " and yet it's a sad thing to see young folks made unhappy through the blind obstinacy of self-willed old fathers."

" Nay," cried Susan, " I must not hear a word said against our master. We have all experienced his goodness, and it becomes not those who live upon his bounty to speak disrespectfully of him. To Mr. Gravestow, however, we owe no thanks, and, therefore, there is no great harm in saying just what we please of him, though Mr. Wentworth had so positively forbidden our doing so."

" Mr. Gravestow is a villain," exclaimed Andrew, " and I should like to have the strangling of him, if it was only for the dislike he has taken to a poor boy that never did him any harm in his life."

" The truth is, he is jealous of Edwin," answered Susan.   " He thinks, I dare say, the child will come in for some share of the property after the old gentleman's death, and I have no doubt nothing would please him half so well as to hear of Edwin's death.   That it is which makes me think it was him that threw him into the water, and never will I give up my object till I have brought the affair completely home."

" Well," cried Andrew' " I am not very fond of such things, but nothing in the world would give me so much pleasure as to go and see the execution of this Mr. Gravestow."

" Indeed !" exclaimed a voice near them, and turning round they discovered to their no little dismay, that it had proceeded from the very person they had been speaking of. Some of the more timid among them ran away through terror, but Susan and her brother with four or five others remained as if scorning to shield themselves from a tempest which they had themselves assisted in raising. Walter Gravestow eyed them with a look of hatred, but quickly changing it for an appearance of his usual forced calmness, he said,—

" It appears, my friends, that, for some reason or other, I am not regarded among you with much favour.   This I am the more concerned at as I know not of any reason why you should have formed so unfounded a prejudice against me."

" And yet," observed Andrew, " since you have thought it worth your while to play the part of a listener, it would be easy to guess what it is that makes us all look upon you as a man that ought to be shunned."

" Humph ! and so your master's guest is to be offended because you choose to believe him to be a monster of iniquity ?"

" We are not the only people that think strange things about you," replied Andrew.   " Besides, there is a good deal of doubt as to how the child came in the water, and we think you could explain it better than anybody else."

" And what reason have you for thinking so ?"

" Because you were near the spot at the time, and instead of assisting to get him out, you ran away under the pretence that you was going to fetch a doctor.   In fact the whole affair looks very black against you, and so now you have got the whole of the truth from me."

" I know nothing whatever about the circumstance you have been speaking of," exclaimed Gravestow.   " The boy went from this house alone, and it was by mere accident that I happened to see him struggling in the lake, into which, I suppose, he had unfortunately slipped."

" And wouldn't it have been a Christian act," asked Andrew, " to have helped him out of it instead of suffering him to run the chance of perishing for want of a friendly hand to save the life of a fellow creature ?"

" There are few of us that are prepared for these sudden emergencies,"
answered the other ;—" in my terror I ran away for assistance, though I
willingly grant it would have been better, had I thought of it, to have used
my endeavours to extricate him from his perilous situation."

" Almost any one would have done so," cried Susan ; " but the truth is
you never liked the child, and would not have been sorry if he had perished."

" Do you think, then, that I would have stood by to see him perish, had
I not been alarmed and lost all power over myself."

" To speak my mind freely," answered Susan, " I do not think you would
have taken much trouble to save one that you have no great liking for."

" And to speak mine still more freely," added Andrew, " I have a pretty
strong notion, that the boy would never have been in the lake at all if it had
not been for you."

" Or, in other words," observed Gravestow, " you suspect that I threw
him in ?"

" I do, indeed."

" And why should not I believe that you did it yourself, and thus try to
shift all the blame from your own shoulders to mine ?"

" For a very good reason," answered Andrew ;—" I never had any reason
to dislike the boy as you have. He never stood between me and sundry
pounds, shillings, and pence, and so its hardly likely I should have been
guilty of such a base crime. Besides, everybody knows that I love the
child as if he was my own, and that I risked my own life in saving his when
he was about to sink for ever beneath the waters."

" You can make up a good story for yourself, no doubt," exclaimed Gravestow. " This may be all very well till the case comes to be enquired into,
but, rely on it, there is as much cause for suspicion against you as there is

No. 2

against myself, and if you dare to whisper these foul culamnies to my injury, I shall not fail in my own defence to charge you as the person who really committed the deed."

"Villain!" cried Susan, "you surely would not dare to accuse my brother of a crime that his heart was never base enough to contemplate."

"And who shall say," demanded Gravestow, "that he was not quite as likely to have done it as myself? I bore the youth no malice, in spite of the assertions you have made, and even if I had, the deed was too base, ever to have been entertained for a moment."

"Well," exclaimed Andrew, "it is to be hoped we shall be able to get at the truth by and by. The child is likely enough to recover, and I dare say he will recollect who it was that stole upon him unawares for the purpose of putting him out of the way."

"Let him do so if he can," cried Gravestow, "for I, at least, can defy him to say a word that will injure me. The boy cannot say he saw me near the spot, and that, I should imagine, will be quite enough to prove that your vile suspicions are unfounded."

"That may be," replied Andrew, "but I saw you though, and in a pretty hurry you seemed to be in to get out of the way as quickly as possible. Why there was guilt pictured in your face, and any one might have sworn that you had been doing some foul deed, by the agitation and tremor you were in."

"The agitation was caused by my fright," answered the other ;—"I saw a fellow creature in a situation of great peril, and that was quite sufficient to cause the alarm you speak of. But why do I thus offer an explanation to persons who have no right to ask me a question, and who have previously wronged me by harbouring such a suspicion?"

"The truth is, Mr. Gravestow, you have got yourself into a dilemma that it will not be very easy to get out of," exclaimed Andrew. "You may deny this affair as much as you please, but there is no one will believe you, and for my own part I am determined never to rest satisfied till I have sifted the whole affair to the very bottom."

"Nor will I, either," cried Susan, "and from this time forward I will devote myself as much as possible to the task of discovering who it was that committed the cowardly act of attempting the life of a poor helpless child."

"You can do as you please about it," replied Gravestow, with affected coolness. "At any rate I have little to fear from such enemies as you, but on the other hand, I would advise you to beware of the man you have thus wronged with your suspicions. I can be terrible in my wrath, and you shall yet feel the vengeance you have both been mad enough to provoke."

And so saying, Gravestow strode eagerly away to join Mr. Wentford, whose favour he had determined to gain by giving his own version of the story.

CHAPTER II.

THE MURDER PLAN.

MR. WENTFORD was highly indignant as he listened to the narrative of his friend, and feeling certain in his own mind that the charges were utterly without foundation, he consoled Gravestow with an assurrance that nothing should ever induce him to give credit to a report so monstrous and improbable. In fact, he treated the affair very lightly, expressing it as his opinion that the whole thing had been the result of accident, and that the boy had fallen into the lake during the excitement of the sport he had gone to enjoy.

" I am quite convinced of their being no blame attached to you," he said, " and, therefore, it is quite unnecessary to continue the painful subject any longer. Indeed I desired to see you upon a very different affair, for as I find old age making rapid inroads upon my constitution, it has become necessary to make arrangements for quitting a world that I shall not be permitted much longer to enjoy. You are almost the only friend I can consult, and, as I suppose, we shall be more nearly connected before long, I was about to take the opportunity to speak to you about the disposal of my property."

" I should be proud to be of service to you, my dear sir," answered the hypocrite, but really, under present circumstances, I know not what to say; my character, as you are aware, has been attacked, and there are people who would be wicked enough to accuse me of interested motives, were I to give you my counsel in so delicate an affair as this."

" Psha!" exclaimed Mr. Wentford, "what have you to care about them, so long as I continue to entertain a favourable opinion of you. The world is made up of many dispositions, amongst which, the ill-natured hold no trifling place. Such persons may have said things to your injury, but thinking men, like myself, Mr. Gravestow, are not to be carried away by the words of mischief-makers."

" You have removed a great weight from my mind, sir, by assuring me that I still hold a place in your esteem," cried Walter Gravestow, with assumed gratitude."

" You have done nothing to forfeit my regard, my dear sir," answered the other;—" I have heard an idle rumour, but it has been treated with the contempt it merits."

" The plain fact is," exclaimed Gravestow, " that your little favourite, Edwin, has had the misfortune to fall into the lake, I, however, have been accused of throwing him in, and I therefore ask you ——"

" There is no occasion to ask me anything," interrupted the old gentleman;—" I have heard all you are about to tell me, and am quite able to from my own opinion, without being led by the folly of others."

" I may understand then that you entirely acquit me of having any hand in so base an affair."

" If that had not been my notion, sir," answered Mr. Wentford, " I should not have troubled you with the present interview. You may rest assured that I treat the rumour with the scorn it merits, and if I should hear anything more of it, the persons so offending will fall under my severest displeasure."

" But it would be more satisfactory to myself, sir, if my innocence could be clearly manifested," exclaimed Gravestow, who could speak out more boldly now that he found one friend on his side. " As your future son-in-law, I should feel more at rest were this matter placed beyond a doubt."

" Aye, aye, that shall be done another time," replied the old gentleman, " but you were speaking at breakfast time of returning shortly to London, and there were two or three things that I wish to consult you about previously to your departure. We have already spoken upon the subject of your marriage with my daughter, and the more I have considered the matter, the more disposed am I that the nuptials shall take place at an early opportunity. Your steady habits and knowledge of business have served to raise you very high in my estimation, and I believe my daughter is so far obedient to her father's wishes, that she will not oppose him in the wish that is nearest to his heart."

" I have ventured to speak to Fanny upon the subject, sir," replied Gravestow.

"Well, and what answer did she give you?"

"She requested time for consideration, and in the meanwhile referred me to you, in order that your pleasure might be known on the subject."

"She already knows my wishes," exclaimed Mr. Wentford; "however, Fanny is a good girl, and will, doubtless, prove her obedience in an affair that my heart is so much set on. I can rely on her, Mr. Gravestow, and, therefore, you may make your mind quite easy on that matter."

"And I, for my own part," replied the other, obsequiously, "shall be most flattered by being received into the family of my generous friend and patron."

"You have deserved much from me, sir, and I am well pleased at the chance that offers of securing my daughter's happiness," answered the old gentleman. "Immediately upon your union, I shall retire from the firm; you will then have the largest share of my business, besides, the sum of ten thousand pounds on the day that makes Fanny yours. Nor has the boy, Edwin, been forgotten, for at a proper age he will be received as a partner in the business, and it is my intention to bestow upon him one thousand pounds in money, to be free from all deductions, and which it will be your duty, as my executor, to give him on the day when he becomes of age. Thus, you see, I have provided for all whom I regard, and may however reward those upon whom I have endeavoured to raise above the wants and vicissitudes of this life."

Walter Gravestow was not much pleased at hearing that Edwin was to be thus provided for, but he was a consummate hypocrite, and thus contrived to hide the real feelings of a malignant heart. He remained silent, as if listening with the most profound attention, and Mr. Wentford, deceived as he was, thus proceeded:—

"You have now heard, my dear sir, the determination I have come to, and it therefore only remains for me to observe that my will has been made in exact conformity with the resolution I have just expressed. In fact, the document is put under my pillow every night when I retire to rest, so that whenever I die it will easily be found by those who are most interested in its contents. And now, having thus far explained myself on business affairs, let me enquire if it is your intention to accompany myself and Fanny to the ball at Upton? I go merely as a sort of protector to the girl, though, to confess the truth, it is hardly necessary, as you will be there."

"When is the ball to take place?" asked Gravestow.

"To-night;—the carriage will be at the door at dusk, and there will be sufficient room in it for you, should you think proper to oblige us with your company."

"I should be most happy to do so," replied Walter Gravestow, "but first of all I should wish to know whether such an arrangement will be agreeable to your daughter."

"Oh, I can answer for Fanny," returned the old gentleman, "she is always obedient to any wish of mine, and, in this instance, I am certain she would not refuse the society of her father's most esteemed friend."

"But I am not certain," exclaimed Gravestow, "that I am quite so agreeable to the daughter as I am to the father. In fact, Fanny has always seemed to avoid my company, and I should be sorry to intrude myself where my presence might prove disagreeable."

"Nonsense, man!" cried Mr. Wentford, "you are quite mistaken about it. However, to prevent a misunderstanding I'll send for my daughter, and you shall hear from herself how happy she will be to have you with us."

And so saying, he rang for one of the servants, who he desired to inform Miss Wentford that he wished to see her immediately in the drawing-room.

It was not long before this mandate was obeyed by the young lady, who presented herself before them, without manifesting any of that dislike towards Mr. Gravestow which she had exhibited on former occasions. The truth is, she had been seriously reflecting on her father's wishes, and as there was no absolute proof of anything against the person that had been selected as her husband, she determined to submit to the will of her father, and in answer to his question upon that subject, candidly admitted that she could offer no further objection to the addresses of Walter Gravestow.

"There!" exclaimed Mr. Wentford, "I knew we should find Fanny reasonable enough, and you have now heard from her own lips that she is willing to admit you as her lover. I have already mentioned the fortune it is my intention to give with her, and it may be almost unnecessary to say that it will be very considerably increased at my death. Edwin will receive the sum I have named, but in the event of his dying before reaching the years of maturity, that also will come into your hands."

"Your liberality, sir, overwhelms me," cried Gravestow.

"Tush, man!" exclaimed Mr. Wentford, "you little think how much pleasure it affords me to bestow my wealth upon a man whom I so much esteem. As a servant, you were always remarkable for the strictest integrity; and, as a friend, I esteem you far beyond all others whom I have ever met with. By the by I had a thought of making you the boy's guardian, but upon second thoughts, I shall relieve you from that trouble, and place him under the care of Mr. Smithson, our chief clerk. He is an older man than yourself, Gravestow, and consequently the duty will be less irksome than it would be to one who, like yourself, may probably mix in the gaieties of life to which your wealth will introduce you."

"Believe me, sir," answered Gravestow, with well-feigned sincerity, "any duty you may be pleased to impose upon me shall be most rigidly and faithfully performed."

"I know it, my dear sir," replied the old gentleman, "and the consciousness that my good opinion will not be abused adds greatly to the happiness and serenity which should ever accompany us to the grave. We will now, however, drop the subject for the present, and return to one of which we were just now speaking. You will accompany me and my daughter to-night to Upton, where a ball is to take place, and which, I understand, will be fully attended."

"Do you return home to-night, sir?" asked the hypocrite, with an appearance of unconcern.

"Why, I believe we must do so," replied Mr. Wentford. "I have made enquiries whether we could have beds in the town, but it seems they are all engaged; and, consequently, though the hour will be very late, we must come back, I suppose. However, I intend to take Andrew Hoply with us, and as there will be five male persons, including ourselves, I think Fanny need entertain very little fear of being stopped by highwaymen."

"Do persons of that description ever visit this neighbourhood?" asked Walter Gravestow.

"Not very often, I believe," replied the old man; "but a suspicious character has been seen lurking about this house a good deal of late, and, at one time, I took it into my head that he had planned a robbery. Since then, however, there is reason to believe that his visits are paid to my dairy-maid, Dolly Pratt, who everybody thought, a little while ago, was rather fond of Andrew Hoply. But let that be as it may, the fellow's looks are not much in his favour, and I have, therefore, given orders for him to be watched, and warned off my premises, should he ever take it into his head to honour us with another visit."

Gravestow was rather disconcerted at this piece of information; but,

skilled as he was in duplicity, he contrived to pass it off without exciting
any notice.   He was, however, glad to make his escape, and as it was beginning to grow dark, he made an excuse that he was going to prepare himself for the ball, he left the room, brooding on the mischief he was concoct-
ing against his generous, warm-hearted friend.   But instead of going to
his own chamber, Gravestow hurried towards the back part of the house,
and entered the gardens, where he walked uneasily up and down, ruminating upon the dark plot in which he was engaged, and endeavouring to devise some means by which he might speedily possess himself of the old
gentleman's property.   Even the thought of blood did not deter him from
the purpose that occupied his mind, and he had half resolved to assassinate
with his own hands the friend whose hospitality he was now enjoying;
when steps were heard approaching him, and, raising his eyes from the
ground, he perceived a man of ragged and miserable appearance, who
seemed to be following him, as if for the purpose of seeking an interview.
This, he had no doubt, was the fellow of whom Mr. Wentford had just before been speaking; and he was about to turn away that he might avoid
an interview, when the other called him by name, and he at once recognized
the well-remembered voice of George Ransley, a profligate youth of his
acquaintance, who, having dissipated a considerable property which he had
formerly possessed in the neighbourhood, was now reduced to a state of the
most abject poverty.   This recognition was far from pleasant to Walter
Gravestow, and his first thought was to flee from the wretched being who
had thus presented himself before him; but recollecting that he might be
of service to him in the business that occupied his mind, he thought better
of it, and greeted him with a semblance of friendship; and, appearing to be
affected at the alteration that had taken place in him since they had last
met, demanded the nature of the business which had occasioned this unexpected meeting.

"Can't you guess?" demanded the ruffian.

"Indeed I cannot," replied Walter; "unless, indeed, you require money
from me."

"You have pretty nearly guessed it," replied Ransley, with a self-ap-
proving chuckle: "the truth is, old friend, I have been left without a feather to fly with,—I am regularly cleaned out, and unless you think proper
to give me a little assistance, I shall be compelled to do something very desperate."

"Why, surely," cried Walter, "your desperation will not prompt you to
make an attempt upon your own life?"

"No, but it will compel me to *work*, though," answered the other; "and
that, to a gentleman like me, is an alternative that is not to be thought of
without a shudder.   So come, Walter, tell me whether you mean to relieve
me, that I may know the worst of it at once."

"What!" exclaimed Gravestow, "are you really so very poor that you
are driven to ask for charity?"

"Charity be d——d," growled George, indignantly: "I merely use the
privilege of an old acquaintance, and surely you can give a plain answer to
my demand."

"But I can scarcely believe you are in earnest."

"A man in my situation," replied the other, "is not much given to jest-
ing.   Look at my ragged attire, and then judge for yourself whether I speak
the truth or not.   I want money, I say; and you, who have it in your
power, must assist me before it is too late."

"You are peremptory in your demands, at any rate," exclaimed Walter
Gravestow, regarding him with a look of surprise.   "It sounds somewhat
like a command, and I am not to be intimidated because a desperate man

insolently desires me to open my purse-strings. However, there are certain conditions, perhaps, on which I may relieve you; but it must be understood that I shall require a service in return for it."

" Indeed !—and what may that service consist of ?"

" Promise me secresy, and you shall know."

" Oh, I'll not blab anything, you may depend on it ; so speak out, Walter Gravestow, and I dare say you and I shall understand one another well enough."

" Are you inclined then," demanded Walter, " to earn a handsome sum of money easily, by aiding me in a little affair that I have just now on hand ?"

" I dare say," answered George Ransley, carelessly, " there will be no objection, when I know what is to be done. So speak out boldly, man, and I am much mistaken if you and I don't understand each other perfectly well."

" May I depend on your assistance, then, in securing a will which I have set my mind on obtaining ?"

" Securing a will, eh ?" ejaculated Ransley ; " oh, ho !—then I begin to suspect there's a bit of a robbery in the wind."

" You may call it a robbery," exclaimed Walter, " or by any other name you please ; but the will must be got possession of, so be as brief as possible in saying whether I may depend on your assistance."

" Why, to be sure you may," answered the other ;—" that is to say, if I receive a fair consideration for the service."

" In that respect," cried Gravestow, " you shall not have to call me a niggard. I will pay you handsomely, George ; but let it be understood between us, that the affair ends not merely in a robbery : the old man to whom the will belongs must die, or the possession of the document I am so anxious to get hold of would be of little service to me."

" Humph !" muttered Ransley ; " this seems likely to turn out a very ugly business."

" You begin to be afraid, then, already ?"

" It takes a good deal to make me afraid," replied the ruffian ; " but murder is an awkward thing to have to deal with, and it seems you don't mean to stop short of it."

" I have told you there is no way of avoiding it."

" There is not, eh ? Well, then, in that case, as a desperate man, I don't mind joining you in it. But I must be well paid for it, you understand."

" You shall."

" Then now tell me who is to be the victim ?"

" Mr. Wentford, the owner of this mansion."

" Your friend and patron ! Phew !—this is an ugly job, Gravestow ; but never mind, I want money, and so give us your hand to the bargain. I'll assist you, Walter ; and if you name the time and place, you may be sure I will be there."

" It must be done this night," replied the other. " You must remain lurking about the place till we return from a ball to which we are going, and when all is quiet, I will give you admittance to the place. The old man will then be asleep : you and I can enter his chamber, secure the will, and——"

" Finish the matter by murdering your best friend."

" Hah !" cried Gravestow, " do you reproach me ?"

" No," answered the other, carelessly, " it was only a passing thought ; and now, having given vent to it, I am ready to engage in the affair, on condition that I receive something very handsome for the share I shall have in it."

"You shall find me a man of my word, George," returned the other; "so fail not to meet me at the time and place appointed. And now, as our arrangement is complete, I must leave you, lest my absence from the house should happen to give rise to enquiries after me."

"Stay," exclaimed Ramsden, as the other was about to leave him; "when the thing is done, you know there is a pretty good chance that we may be suspected. That might lead to a very awkward dilemma, and, as I have no wish to put the country to any expence, I should like to know what sort of a story we are to trump up in case any foolish questions should be asked."

"We have only to keep our own counsel," replied Gravestow, "and all will be right enough. Besides, I have an idea that we may manage matters so as to throw the suspicion upon another party."

"Upon my life, Gravestow," exclaimed the other, "you are one of the cunningest rascals I ever met with."

"How! do you reproach me?"

"Not I," answered the other, "but I couldn't help paying you a little passing compliments, that's all. And now, as its not worth while quarreling about trifles, perhaps you'll tell me who it is that we can throw the suspicion on?"

"A favourite servant of the old gentleman's, one Andrew Hoply."

"Ha! I should know something of the young fellow," exclaimed Ramsden; he has the presumption to love a wench in this establishment, to whom I flatter myself I am not altogether disagreeable, and as I am not inclined to have a rival in my way, I don't know but this may be as good a plan to get rid of him as any other."

"Psha!" muttered his associate in crime, "why think of a woman at such a moment as this?"

"Because I rather fancy the affair may be turned to our advantage," replied George. "The fact is, one life must be taken to night, and while our hands are in, I don't see why we should not finish the business for my rival."

"But if we do that," exclaimed Gravestow, "there's an end of my project for throwing the blame of his master's murder upon him."

"Not a bit of it; in fact it will rather serve us than otherwise."

"How so?"

"Why, by concealing Andrew's body, to be sure," answered the ruffian. "It will then appear that he has fled, and as his sweetheart, Dolly Pratt, has agreed to elope with him to-night, it will be supposed that they have fled together, and thus you and I shall escape suspicion."

"Your idea is an excellent one," exclaimed Walter; "this Andrew Hoply has ever been in my way, and I shall thus rid myself of a fellow who has made himself too busy in my affairs. He shall die, and thus shall we secure ourselves by throwing all the suspicion of his master's murder upon him."

"For once, then, you will admit that I have furnished you with a bright thought?"

"You have," replied Walter Gravestow, "but now let me ask for the last time whether I may rely upon your faithfully performing your share of the contract?"

"To be sure you may," answered the other; "am I not reduced to the lowest state of misery, and where's the man that will reject a good offer, merely because the business is not exactly such as the world in general might approve of?"

"And you will remain about this place till we return from the ball?"

"Aye, Dolly expects me, and we can have a stroll about the grounds til

you want my assistance. When the job is over, I'll take her off, and everybody will then believe that Andrew Hoply is the murderer, and that the girl has escaped with him. All I shall then have to do will be to keep her out of the way, and, if there should be any fear of her letting the cat out of the bag, why I can take her abroad, or dispose of her in any other way that will make us the more safe."

" If there is any fear of the girl," observed Walter, " the only way will be to serve her as we intend to do by the others."

" Yes, knock her on the head, you mean ?"

" I do."

" At any rate that will keep her quiet enough," exclaimed the ruffian, with a grin of delight. " We must not let any one live that may have it in their power to injure us, and though Dolly Pratt and I are very good friends at present, I should not hesitate to sacrifice her, in case it should be for our own advantage. But hush ! I hear a carriage coming this way, and if we are seen together, it may afterwards be remembered and give rise to certain awkward suspicions."

" It would, indeed," cried Walter Gravestow, " so good night for the present, and fail not to meet me at the time and place that has been appointed."

Upon this they separated, and Walter entering the house unperceived, proceeded to his own chamber, and prepared himself to accompany his patron and Fanny to the scene of gaiety they were about to visit. In half an hour afterwards, he descended with a calm countenance, as if no crime had ever haunted his brain, and following his two companions into the carriage, they drove off for the ball at Upton.

Susan Hoply, the servant girl, had, however, witnessed their departure
No. 3

with a feeliug of disquietude that she in vain endeavoured to account for. A presentiment of evil filled her mind, and without knowing why or wherefore, she felt assured that some terrible catastrophe was about to take place. A foreboding of some terrible event pressed like a heavy weight upon her heart, and long after their departure she stood at the entrance gate listening to the retreating carriage which, till the last faint sound was entirely lost in distance. It seemed to her that some danger hung over her master, and in spite of every effort that she made to get rid of the feeling, it still clung to her as if certainty had taken the place of doubt. At length with an oppressed and sorrowful heart, she turned away to re-enter the house, when a shadow seemed to cross her path, and looking up she discovered the dark outline of a man gliding away as if to seek for concealment among the trees in the shrubbery. Alarmed at this unexpected circumstance, she paused to ascertain whether the cause of her fears was real or imaginary, and having waited some time, she was beginning to believe that she had been mistaken, when the same figure was seen gliding in another direction. Resolving to satisfy herself, she waited a little longer, and when the figure for the third time crossed her path, she addressed it, and demanded of the person who he was, and why he had thus intruded himself upon her master's grounds at that late hour of the evening. George Ramsden, for he it was that stood before her, then thought it necessary to put on an appearance of easy confidence, and advancing a few steps nearer to her, though with his face concealed as much as possible by means of a handkerchief, he said :—

"Don't be alarmed, my dear, for it's only a friend that has the honour of standing. before you. The fact is, there's a lovely creature of a woman in this house that I come to visit, and—and—the fact is, a—a—"

"The fact is," interrupted Susan, "neither you nor anybody else has a right to be in this place at unreasonable hours."

"But, my charmer," cried the fellow with insolent familiarity, "what time is so fitting a man to make love as night? Did you never happen, in the course of your life, to hear of a gentleman serenading his mistress, and if you should ever have heard of such a thing, did you ever know it to have been done in the broad open light of day.

"I know nothing of the folly you are talking about," answered Susan Hoply, "but I am very certain that you have no business to be creeping and crawling about my master's premises at such a time as this."

"Psha! I am here by appointment to see my own sweet, adorable, Dolly Pratt."

"Then Dolly Pratt ought to be ashamed of herself for suffering anything of the sort," cried Susan, pettishly. "However, I am not going to let anybody remain in this place during my master's absence, and so I'll be obliged to you to go before I am compelled to call those that will put you out."

"My love," exclaimed George Ramsden, "there's no occasion for you to put yourself at all out of the way. A lady's commands are at all times sufficient for me, and since it is your desire, I shall wish you a very good evening."

With this he turned suddenly round and pretended to direct his footsteps towards the gate; but taking his way towards the shrubbery, he darted into it with the speed of lightning, and thus succeeded in cheating her into a belief that he had quitted the premises. Satisfied that she had got rid of the intruder, Susan Hoply next secured the gates, and then returning to the house, pondered over the alarm she had experienced until she almost convinced herself that her worst fears were about to be realized.

CHAPTER III.

THE DREAM FULFILLED.

Occupied with these thoughts hour after hour passed away wearily enough, for it grew late, and those who had gone to the ball returned not at the hour at which they had said it was probable they would be at home. This, however, did not occasion much surprise to Susan, because she knew that they were likely to forget the time in the festive scene they had gone to visit; but her mind was depressed by the thoughts that had so long harassed her, and in spite of all her efforts to chace them away, her terror increased to the highest pitch. The stranger, too, that she had seen in the garden had filled her with suspicion and distrust, and though he professed to have come on a very different object, she felt convinced in her own mind that mischief was brooding which it would be out of her power to prevent. Every sound startled her, and even the moaning of the wind among the trees seemed to her excited imagination like the death-cry of some unfortunate victim in his last extremity. Fifty times at least did she rise from her seat and approach the window, where she stood listening for the long expected carriage; but all was in vain, and each time did she return to her chair more convinced than ever that some accident had happened to her master and Miss Fanny. She thought, too, of Gravestow and his recent attempt upon the life of Edwin, for still she could think no otherwise than that the boy had been plunged purposely into the lake, and in spite of her master's commands to the contrary, she still felt quite satisfied in her own mind that the affair had not been the result of chance. Then her mind wandered to the anticipated union of her young lady with Walter Gravestow, and she could not restrain a shudder at the probable misery that would follow so ill-fated a marriage. All these reflections served to make her more and more wretched, and each hour that was struck upon the distant village clock served but to wake up in her heart fresh cause for terror and apprehension.

At length nature yielded to fatigue and long watching, and trusting to her own wakefulness on the slightest noise, she threw herself upon her bed to snatch a brief interval of rest and a cessation of those painful thoughts that had haunted her imagination. But in this she was sadly mistaken, for she was haunted by a fearful dream that appeared to chain up all her faculties and deprive her of the power of either speaking or moving.

First of all the apparition of her brother, who, from the blood that gushed from his throat, seemed to have been murdered, presented himself to her view, and by the mournful looks with which he regarded her implored vengeance upon those who had sent him to an untimely grave. Then on a sudden she was transported to the chamber of her master who was calmly sleeping in his bed unconscious of the dreadful fate that awaited him; and as she was approaching to warn him of his danger, the door was gently opened, and the figures of two men stealthily entered the room; they wore crape over their faces, and yet she fancied that she could recognize in them the forms and features of Walter Gravestow and the stranger whom she had that night seen prowling about the garden. Horrified as she was, it was in vain that she attempted to raise an alarm, for all power of utterance was denied her, and whilst she was thus under the dominion of terror, the two villains approached the bed-side of her master and secured the will, which, it appeared, was the object of their deadly visit. At this moment the old man started from his sleep, and by his cry of horror seemed to recognize one of the villains, but ere he could repeat the alarm so as to make himself heard, a knife was plunged into his heart, and he sank back upon his bed a lifeless and blood-stained corse !   At that moment she fancied she saw her brother rush in to the assistance of his master, but he also was stabbed, and his body placed for concealment behind a sliding panel in the wainscot.

Unable to endure these horrors any longer, Susan started from her sleep and gazed around her with horror as if expecting to behold a realization of the dreadful vision which had haunted her imagination.   All, however, was as she had left it scarcely half an hour before, and smiling at the strong hold which terror had taken upon her mind, she endeavoured to convince herself that all which she had seen in her dream was merely the effect of her previous waking thoughts.   Just at that moment, too, she heard the voices of her master and Miss Fanny, who were bidding each other good night on the landing place, and being thus quite satisfied of her safety, she began to laugh at her fears, and with more serenity than she had possessed for some time, sank into a calm and gentle sleep.

Through long watching, it was late on the following morning when Susan was awakened by one of the servants, but she soon found by the anxious tone in which she was called, that something was wrong, and hastily throwing on her clothes, she opened the door, and enquired with the most intense anxiety, whether anything particular had occurred.   But the messenger informed her that she had been strictly desired to answer no questions, and bidding her follow without delay, she led her down to a room, in which Gravestow and a great number of persons were assembled.   She could perceive that something serious had occurred, and remembering the horrible vision of last night, earnestly implored them to tell her whether Mr. Wentford was alive or not.

"You hear, gentlemen !" exclaimed Gravestow, pointedly addressing himself to the persons he was surrounded by.   " This girl without any intimation of what has taken place, has made an enquiry that affords ample proof of her having a guilty knowledge of the terrible tragedy that has been enacted beneath this roof.   She knows something about it, or——"

" In heaven's name, what mean you ?" cried the terrified girl ; " there is some dreadful mystery to be revealed, and my heart already assures me that my master has been murdered."

" This pretended distress will not serve you here," exclaimed Walter Gravestow,—" your master *has* been murdered, and you know more than you think proper to reveal."

" I know of his murder !" cried Susan, overwhelmed with grief ; " can any here believe me guilty of so foul a crime ?"

" At any rate," answered Walter, " there is strong suspicion that you must know something about this business : your enquiry on entering the room proves that you are not so innocent as you would make it appear, and however painful it may be to us, it will be our duty to prevent your leaving this place till a short investigation has been gone into."

" I am innocent," cried Susan, falling upon her knees, " indeed, indeed I am innocent."

" Let us hope that you will be able to satisfy us upon that point," exclaimed Mr. Downing, an attorney, who had been sent for to advise upon the proceedings that ought to be adopted.   " For my own part, I see very little grounds for suspecting you, though, of course, it is necessary under these distressing circumstances, to adopt every means in our power for the discovery of the real perpetrators."

" Perhaps, Susan, you will answer me one question," said Walter Gravestow, with as much confidence as if he had been perfectly free from guilt. " Did you not know before you entered this room, that your master had been murdered ?"

" Alas ! I knew it not," she replied, " but my heart sorely misgave me when I saw so many persons assembled in this room."

" But there might have been other causes for our meeting, besides the one you have mentioned."

" True," she replied, " but I had a dream last night that seemed sent as a forewarning of the dreadful tragedy that was to take place."

" A dream !" exclaimed Gravestow, contemptuously ; " and do you imagine that we can give credit to such an assertion as you have just made ?"

" I ask no favourable opinion from *you*," answered Susan, with firmness. " I have been accused of the horrible deed, but you, Mr. Gravestow, can tell better than any one else that I am innocent."

" And, how, pray, can I answer for your innocence ?"

" Ask your own heart," she replied, " and then tell me whether you really believe me guilty of the foul deed that has been charged against me ?"

" I have already told you," he replied, " that, though the proof is not very strong at present, there are circumstances that induce me to believe you must be implicated in some way or other."

" Again I most solemnly declare that I am entirely free from all share in it."

" Of course, we expected to hear nothing else," answered Walter Gravestow. " However, there is one question which I now wish to put ;—is there any person that you suspect as being the murderer of poor Mr. Wentford ?"

" There is."

" Will you name him ?" asked Gravestow, fixing his eyes upon her's threateningly. " I repeat it, girl ;—will you say who you believe to have been the perpetrator of this deed ?"

" Another time," she replied, " I may be better able to answer your questions."

" And why not now ?"

" Because my assertion rests only upon the dream I had."

" Indeed ! and, in this singular vision of yours, did you, in your imagination, see the murder of my friend ?"

" I did."

" And did you observe the countenances of the assassins ?"

" There were two of them," she replied, " but their faces were covered with black crape, and I could only conjecture who they were by their figures."

It was here observed, that the countenance of Walter Gravestow underwent a marked change, and that his whole manner became very different to what it had been before. He himself could not fail to perceive that his agitation had not passed unnoticed, and pretending to be much agitated, he said :—

" You will pardon me, my friends, for the slight interruption my trepidation has occasioned, but I feel deeply for the loss of a dearly-valued friend, and the emotion had well nigh overpowered me." Then addressing himself to Susan Hoply, he said :—" you have just told us, girl, that in this vision of yours, you beheld two assassins."

" I did, sir."

" Then it proves how little reliance is to be placed in dreams," he continued, " for we have good reason to believe that there was but one person concerned in the murder."

" And that person was——"

" Your own brother."

" 'Tis false!—by Heaven 'tis false!" cried Susan, vehemently; "Andrew is innocent, and this foul charge has been brought against him only that the guilty may escape the punishment due to their crimes."

" That you seek to shield your brother, is natural enough," observed Walter Gravestow; "we are all sorry that so serious a crime should be brought against him, but the truth is, there happens to be strong circumstantial evidence to connect him with the murder, and our present object is, to discover whether you had any guilty knowledge of his treacherous designs against the life of his master."

" This is a base conspiracy to punish the innocent, that the guilty may escape," answered Susan. " My brother Andrew loved his master, and would have shed the last drop of his blood to have preserved him from such a fate as he has met with."

" You mean to tell us, then, that you know nothing of your brother's disappearance?"

" Ah!" cried Susan, wildly,—" is Andrew missing?"

" He is," replied Mr. Downing, " and favourably as we wish to think of him, I grieve to say, his disappearance, at such a moment as this, affords but too much ground for believing that he is the assassin of his master."

" Oh, judge him not so harshly, I implore you," cried Susan, " he is no assassin, and now, I remember, that in my last night's dreadful vision, he also, fell a victim to the murderer's knife, and that they concealed his mangled body——"

" Where ?" exclaimed Gravestow, eagerly, as she paused, seemingly to recollect herself.

" Alas !" she replied, " all that part of my vision is dark and indistinct, but, I remember, they raised the bleeding corse, and—— and; but it is in vain that I try to recollect the place where they concealed him."

" Really, gentlemen," exclaimed Walter Gravestow, appealing to those about him, " I think you must all acknowledge that this story is too absurd to obtain any credit. It is evident the story she has told about the dream is a mere fabrication, and, perhaps, she may be excused for it, seeing that her brother's life is placed in jeopardy."

" Indeed I have uttered nothing but the truth," cried Susan, in an agony of despair.

" We believe nothing of it," returned Walter;—" in fact, your brother was missing immediately after the murder, and that circumstance alone is quite sufficent to assure us that he is guilty of the murder. Besides, the dairymaid, Dolly Pratt has also disappeared within the last few hours, and as it is well-known that your brother paid his addresses to her, it is likely they have fled together."

" The girl you speak of has not fled with him," answered our grief-stricken heroine. " I remember now, that a stranger last night intruded himself into the garden. I spoke to him, and from what escaped him, it seemed that he came to pay a clandestine visit to the dairymaid."

" Have you ever mentioned that circumstance before?" asked Walter Gravestow.

" I have not."

" Did any one else see the stranger ?"

" Not that I am aware of."

" In that case we have reason to suppose this to be another fabrication of yours, to shield Andrew Hoply," exclaimed the other. " No one but yourself seems to know anything about this stranger, and had such a person been seen lurking in the garden, it would have been your duty to have mentioned it."

" I thought there was no occasion to do so," answered Susan; " for at my request he left the premises, and having fastened the gates, I returned into the house, perfectly well assured that everything was quite safe."

" Well, then, even upon your own showing," exclaimed Walter Gravestow, " it is very evident the girl could not have escaped with him; the gates, it seems, were locked, and, therefore, the stranger—if, indeed, there was such a person—must have been shut out."

" You're rather premature, sir," interposed the attorney, " in forming a judgment upon this case. The girl may, as she says, have seen a stranger lurking about the place, and she may have locked him out, but when people are bent upon an evil design, there are ways and means to accomplish it, that you and I may not think of. At any rate a strict enquiry must be made in the neighbourhood, whether such a person has been seen, and if there has, it will remove one portion of the doubt with which you receive this girl's assertions."

" There is sufficient reason to doubt her," replied Gravestow, with evident vexation, " when we know how natural it is that a sister should try to clear the character of her brother."

" Are there any persons present," asked the lawyer, " who happened to have seen such a person as has been described?"

" Yes, I did," exclaimed William Dain, a young miller, who had long paid his addresses to Susan, and who had been standing at the further part of the room during the latter part of the scene we have been describing. Hitherto the servants had forbidden him to approach Susan, but his feelings were no longer to be controled, and rushing forward, he placed himself by her side. This interruption was a source of uneasiness to Walter Gravestow, who pettishly demanded who the intruder was.

" My name," replied the young man, " is William Dain, and I came here to protect this girl from the artful villains that are endeavouring to effect her destruction."

" You must be more moderate, sir, in the expressions you make use of," interposed the attorney;—" we are assembled to make a most important enquiry, and I am here to watch the interests of all parties, so that no one who is really innocent shall labour under suspicion. I will now hear what you have to say, young man;—it seems you saw a stranger lurking about the neighbourhood."

" I did."

" When was it?"

" Yesterday."

" Did you speak to him?"

" I should have passed him," replied William, " but he stopped me to ask a question."

" And what was it he asked?"

" He wanted to know if I could inform him about a Mr. Walter Gravestow, of whom, it seems, he was in search."

" Humph!" exclaimed the lawyer, " and did you give him the information he required?"

" Yes, I told him he was residing at Mr. Wentford's, and then he left me, taking his way towards this house."

" At what time did this occur?"

" A little before dusk last evening."

" Really," exclaimed Gravestow, who was growing more and more uneasy as these questions proceeded, " it appears to me that very little reliance can be placed upon this man's word. He professes to be the lover of this girl, and, therefore, it is to be expected that he would confirm the very improbable story she has told."

"And yet," observed the attorney, "there is no reason to doubt the evidence of the young man who has answered my question in a very candid, straight-forward manner. In fact, the only part that appears to be worthy of discredit is, that in which he says the stranger enquired for you."

"I can assure you," replied Walter Gravestow, with unblushing effrontery, I know not any such person as the one we have been speaking of." Then addressing himself to William, he said, "What sort of man was it that you say accosted you last night?"

"As hang-dog a looking fellow as ever I set eyes on," replied the young man, bluntly.

"Indeed!—then I can only say that I have not the honour of his acquaintance."

"Perhaps," observed William Dain, "you are like many other persons that deny their acquaintances when they happen to be down in the world."

"Sirrah!" exclaimed Walter, furiously, "this insolence shall be punished. Nay, I am not quite sure but that you may have had a hand in this murder, and that the story you have been telling has been invented to direct suspicion into another channel."

"You may think what you like about me," replied the young man, "but I am no more likely to have committed the foul deed than yourself.— Aye, you may frown upon me as much as you please; but in this neighbourhood I am well known, and there is no other man besides yourself that would have dared to throw out an insinuation against William Dain."

"Enough of this," interposed the lawyer; "this is no time for disputing when we are engaged in making an enquiry for the purpose of bringing the guilty to punishment."

"And have you any clue to the villains?" asked William.

"Yes; Andrew Hoply has disappeared most strangely, and there are other circumstances, that cannot fail to throw a great deal of suspicion on him."

"Suspect Andrew Hoply!" cried the young man, with indignant astonishment; "why you might as well suspect his sister, who, I can answer for it, is innocent."

"The truth is," said Walter Gravestow, in his peculiar insinuating way, "Susan Hoply is not altogether free from suspicion."

"Show me, then, the man," exclaimed William, "who will dare, in my presence, say that she is guilty of the black crime that has just been committed."

"You are too impatient, my good friend," cried the lawyer; "no one has directly charged her with being a party in the murder of Mr. Wentford; but there are little matters to be explained, and when this is done, no one will be more happy than myself to congratulate her on clearing herself from so serious a charge."

"Why, Susan," exclaimed her lover, "do I hear right, or is this some horrible dream?"

"It is but too true, William," she replied. "They say there are suspicious circumstances against me; but I rely on Heaven for support and protection under the heavy afflictions that have thus fallen on me. You, however, will not believe their falsehoods, and in that consciousness I can be content to await the issue of this enquiry."

"Who is it that first thought of throwing any blame on you," exclaimed William Dain;—"point him out to me, I say, and I'll tear him limb from limb, even if it should be my own brother."

"If you wish to know who it was that started this subject," returned Walter Gravestow, "you need look no further than myself."

"I thought so," cried the other; "and since it has been confirmed, I shall not fail to punish your villany as it deserves. At present you are safe among your friends, but it will not be very long before an opportunity presents itself, and, depend on it, I shall not fail to revenge the evil you have sought to do a poor harmless girl."

"You forget yourself, young man," exclaimed the lawyer, "we are now in the house of mourning, and should Miss Wentford chance to hear the unseemly brawling, it will only serve to aggravate the sufferings she already endures."

"I know it," replied William Dain, "and if it had not been for thinking of that yonder *gentleman*, as I suppose he calls himself, should he have felt before now that Susan has got a protector that will not see her trampled on."

"You mistake our motives altogether," exclaimed the attorney, "for the girl has nothing to fear from any of us, if she can only prove her own innocence."

"And that," observed William, "every one must be quite convinced of, without taking the trouble to make much further enquiries about it."

"At any rate," said Walter Gravestow, "nobody can imagine that I feel any ill-will towards the girl, for my only motive in acting as I have is to punish those who are really deserving of it. Susan may be innocent, perhaps, but I believe there are few persons who can dare to assert that her brother is so."

"I can dare assert it, at all events," exclaimed William. "We were

No. 4

playmates as children, and from that time to the present no one has ever been base enough to say that he was guilty of an unworthy action."

" And yet," observed Gravestow, with a sneer, " it will require something more than your bare assertion to prove that he had no hand in this murder of my good friend."

" And it will require something more than your word for it to prove that he was engaged in the deed," retorted William Dain.

" If he had been innocent," exclaimed the accuser, " why has he absconded at such a moment as this ?"

" It is false to say that my brother has absconded," cried Susan, resentfully. " He, alas! has fallen by the same assassin that slew Mr. Wentford ; and I swear before Heaven never to desist till I have brought this crime home to those who committed it."

" But is it true," asked the young man, " that Andrew Hoply is at present missing ?"

" They tell me so," sighed our heroine.

" And has search been made for him ?"

" We have sent in every direction, but without hearing any tidings of him," answered the attorney. He is known to have been in the house after the family returned from the ball at Upton, and was supposed to have retired to his own bed-room, which was situated near that occupied by his master. This morning his chamber-door was found open, and there is every reason to suppose that he has decamped, after committing one of the most foul murders I ever heard of."

" Well, you may say what you please about him," retorted William Dain, " but you must bring forward a great deal more proof before I can be satisfied of his guilt. Besides, I have seen how much he was attached to his master ; and the poor fellow would rather have shed every drop of his own blood than any harm should have happened to the old gentleman."

" We can easily understand how this is," observed Gravestow—" he is the brother of Susan Hoply, and, of course, you feel bound to shield him from so serious a charge as this is."

" You are quite mistaken in me, there," exclaimed William Dain, " for I would never shield guilt, even though my own father should chance to be the criminal. I can, however, speak for Andrew Hoply, who, though he is absent at this time, will soon return to vindicate his own character and honour."

" Alas !" groaned Susan, " that can never be."

" Never be, Susan !" exclaimed her lover ; " and why are you so despairing about it ?"

" Because I feel assured he has been murdered."

" And upon what a baseless foundation has that assurance been formed !" cried Walter Gravestow. " The fact is, the girl had a dream last night, and upon that rests the charge she has thus made."

" And yet how awfully has one portion of my dream been fulfilled !" cried Susan, with a shudder : " Mr. Wentford has been murdered, and nothing will ever convince me that my brother Andrew has not shared the same fate."

" And your sole ground for thinking so," exclaimed Walter, " is that the revelation was made in a dream."

" But that dream was heaven-directed," exclaimed our heroine ; " it was sent to bring conviction upon the murderers ; and be assured it will, one day or other, serve to complete the ends of justice. At present, the chain of my vision is broken and disjointed, for though I saw my brother slain, I cannot now remember in what place it was that they concealed his body."

" And was all this seen in a dream?" asked William.

" It was," she replied. " In imagination, I saw him rush into the chamber immediately after his master had been assassinated; but ere he could seize upon the villain nearest to him, the other had raised the fatal knife, and he fell dead at the feet of his murderer! This, they tell me, was but a dream, but it seemed terribly real, William; and, alas! part of it has already turned out but too true."

" And should you know the villains again, should they ever come in your way?"

" One of them, I feel almost certain, was the stranger that was about the house last night, and the other——"

"This is really most ridiculous," interrupted Walter Gravestow, alarmed lest his name should be pronounced. " The girl has been haunted by a vision, and yet she would denounce persons upon no better grounds than you have heard."

" Mr. Gravestow is perfectly right in what he has said," exclaimed the attorney. " It would be doing a great injustice, were we to hear anything further upon such a proof as this girl has brought forward; and even if she mentioned the name of the parties that she saw in this dream, it would not be sufficient to warrant us in ordering the persons to be arrested on so serious a charge. Besides, it might subject innocent people to suspicion; and, therefore, the only advice I can give, is to make diligent enquiries, so that we may bring the guilty to punishment."

" And what is to become of Susan?" demanded her lover.

" Why, at present there is no evidence whatever against her," replied the lawyer; " and, therefore, she is free to go whenever she pleases. I should, however, advise her not to leave the neighbourhood till after the inquest, which will take place to-morrow, as we may gather fresh information by that time, or it may so happen that we shall require her evidence on some point or other."

" It seems, then," said William Dain, addressing himself to Gravestow, " that your evil intentions towards Susan have not been so successful as you could have wished."

" You are mistaken, young man," answered the other, " in supposing that I had any ill feeling towards this girl. I thought it possible she might have had some share in the guilt, but you may take my word that no one will rejoice more than myself at finding that I was mistaken."

" At any rate," exclaimed William, looking sternly towards Gravestow, " the real perpetrators of this crime will not escape if I can do anything towards discovering them. I will do my best to hunt them out, and thus entirely remove every suspicion that has been raised against this poor girl."

With this he led Susan from the room, and, having entreated her to keep up her spirits, he retired, with a promise to see her again on the following day at noon.

CHAPTER IV.

THE CORONER'S INQUEST.

AFTER a restless night, Susan Hoply rose at an early hour on the next day, and went, as usual, into the servants' hall: but she soon saw enough to convince her that she was not esteemed in the same light as she had been previously to the recent melancholy occurrence. Their looks seemed to reproach her for being the sister of a man who could commit a cold-blooded murder on so good a master as they had just lost; and the poor

girl felt that she was now left alone in the world, to endure the taunts and
ill-nature of those who judged her thus harshly.   She could not forbear
weeping at the marked difference with which she was received, for all regarded her with coldness, and seemed to shun her, as if they thought her
unworthy of associating with them any longer.   It was indeed a sad change
for one who had lately been so happy, yet she affected to take no notice of
it ; and, without making any observation, she returned to her own little
room, to give a free vent to the sorrows that afflicted her.   There she remained till after breakfast-time, and then, quitting the house, she proceeded
alone to place the where the inquest was to be held.

On arriving there, however, she found that she was too early for the
melancholy business that was about to take place, and hurrying out she
stationed herself nearer the door, where several females were congregated,
all of whom were speaking of the murder, and the mystery that enveloped
it.   It then took a change, and they began to speak of the Manor House,
which had been deserted for a long time past, except a domestic or] two,
and was now falling rapidly to decay.

" Aye," exclaimed an old woman, " evil luck has attended that place
ever since the family grew proud, and turned their backs upon the poor.
I remember the time when every cottager hereabouts might take her pitcher
and draw water from a beautiful spring that gushed out near the house.
But, at length, a fine madam began to think that poor folks had no business
to have pure water, as the gates were closed against us, and we were obliged
to go near half a mile for every drop we used."

" You are speaking of a former Mrs. Ramsden, I suppose ?" observed a
younger female.

" I am," answered the first speaker ; " but heavy was the blow that came
upon her soon after she had shut us out of the place.   Her only child, a
boy, of about two years of age, fell into the water they had deprived us of,
and though it was scarcely a foot in depth, the poor lad was drowned.   It
was a heavy blow, as I said, for the mother ; and they reported that she
looked upon it as a judgment upon her for the accursed sins of pride and
covetousness.   Be that as it may, however, she was never a happy woman
afterwards ; and, within three months from the death of her boy, she was
carried into the chancel of our church yonder, where she lies under a fair
marble monument.   Then her husband could no longer bear to live in the
house, so he went abroad ; and, at last, news arrived that he had died
somewhere in foreign parts."

" And this estate came to a nephew of his, if I have heard right ?" observed another of the party.

" It did," answered the woman who had spoken previously, " and a rare
wild fellow he is by all accounts ; he never comes down here though,
for they say he has ran through all his property except this estate,
which he can't sell, and as its so ruinous as not to be fit for anybody
to live in, of course he gets nothing out of it.   So you see, neighbours,
what pride does !—the Ramsdens' perished miserably ; and the one that
succeeded them is now wandering about worse off than any of ourselves
are.   But see, the coroner and jury are coming this way from the house of
the murdered man, where they have been to view the body ; and now, I
suppose, they are going to examine the witnesses, and try if they can't get
to the bottom of this mysterious affair."

Susan followed them into the room where the inquest was to take place,
and, stationing herself at one end of the table, she heard the different witnesses as they were brought forward to give their evidence.   The facts
drawn forth on this occasion were to the following effect :—On their arrival
at home from the ball, they separated, to retire to their several rooms ; but

it was remarked, that Mr. Wentford was more serious than usual, as i labouring under great depression of spirits. After that time he was never again seen alive!

From the evidence of Mr. Gravestow, it appeared that he went at an early hour, and from certain indications, he immediately suspected that some one had been in his room during the time he had been asleep. By his own account, he directly jumped out of bed, and having searched the chamber, he discovered that money, and a few articles of jewelery, had been taken away, which he was positive he had placed on a table just before he went to bed. On this discovery, he ran to the apartment occupied by Mr. Wentford, but though he knocked repeatedly, no answer was given from within. Alarmed, he said, at this, he went and procured assistance, and having broken open the door, they discovered the horrible spectacle of the old man's mangled body as it lay on the bed weltering in blood! This latter part of his evidence was confirmed by the men who had assisted in breaking open the room. Upon further examination of the witnesses, it appeared, that they next proceeded to the sleeping room of Andrew Hoply, but, to their astonishment, they discovered that he had left it, and that the place was in the greatest disorder and confusion; the window, too, had been thrown open, leaving little doubt that he had used that means to effect his escape from the house. Thus, as far as circumstantial evidence went, the affair wore a very dark aspect against Andrew, and there were very few persons present in the room but were quite convinced that he had committed the murder, and had subsequently escaped with the dairy-maid, to whom it was known he was greatly attached.

Most of the witnesses, however, concurred in giving him an excellent character, previous to the melancholy occasion they were met to enquire into. No one had a bad word to say against him, except Gravestow, and he was particularly cautious in his replies on that subject, contenting himself with merely saying, that he had always formed a very indifferent opinion of the young man, but refusing to give any reason for forming the notion. He also said, that he had rode out to make enquiries whether any persons answering the description of Andrew Hoply and the supposed companion of his flight, and that he had discovered that a man and woman had been seen on the road to London; that they seemed to be afraid of being pursued, and were particularly cautious to avoid observation. All this afforded a chain of evidence that could leave no doubt on the minds of the jurymen, and without a moment's hesitation, they returned a verdict of " Wilful Murder" against the unfortunate brother of our heroine.

It was in vain that Susan endeavoured to obtain a hearing in favour of her relative;—the affair appeared to be so conclusive, that no denial or argument could remove this impression that had been formed against him, and she retired from the room, well nigh broken-hearted. William Dain, who was there according to promise, sought to console her with an assurance that the truth would yet be revealed in spite of the present threatening aspect; but his kindness was of no avail, for she thus saw all her fairest prospects blighted, and taking leave of her lover when they came within sight of the house, she pursued the remainder of her journey in solitude and grief. At one time, she could scarcely refrain from throwing herself into a pond near which she was passing, but she reflected, that, by so doing, she would prevent all chance of rescuing her brother's name from dishonour, and for his sake, she resolved to live and devote herself to the task of tracing out the real perpetrators of the deed.

On reaching home, she again retired to the solitude of her own chamber, intending to make preparations for leaving a house where most of the inmates regarded her with scorn and contempt as being the sister of the man

who had been pronounced guilty of a cold blooded-murder. She had not,
however, been long there before a message was brought from her young
lady, desiring to see her immediately in her own apartment. The mandate
Susan promptly obeyed, and found her young mistress absorbed in the
most intense grief for the death of her father. But she received Susan with
all her wonted goodness, and perceiving that the poor girl was broken-
hearted by her own sorrows, she said :—

"I have not seen you, Susan, since the sad event that has so unexpectedly made this a house of mourning. I am aware too of the strong
prejudice that exists against your brother, and that he is suspected of the
crime which has deprived me of a parent."

"Indeed, indeed Miss, he is innocent," cried Susan, in a tone of the
greatest earnestness.

"I would fain think so," answered Miss Wentford, "but I fear it will
be difficult to make others think as favourably in this instance as myself.
A prejudice has been formed against your brother, and weighty as the
evidence is, I almost despair of seeing an opinion more favourable to him.
You, I dare say, will be made to endure the scorn of those whose esteem
and confidence you once enjoyed, and I have sent for you that I may know
what step you intend taking under these circumstances."

"I have been thinking of it myself, Miss; "for I can already perceive a
difference in the manner of people towards me, and I had therefore made
up my mind to leave this place as soon as it may be convenient to yourself."

"I was myself about to propose it, Susan," answered the young lady.
"In this neighbourhood I fear there is very little prospect of your enjoying
that happiness which once fell to your lot. People, I know, are too apt to
condemn with injustice, and though I may myself continue to bestow upon
you as much confidence as ever, I fear there is too much reason to believe
that your former friends will become cool and insulting in their behaviour
towards you."

"You would advise me then to leave the neighbourhood?"

"For the present it would be better for you to do so, I think," replied
Miss Wentford. "In time we may discover who were really the perpetrators of this dreadful tragedy, and should we succeed in removing the odium
from your brother, we may hope to see you back among us, and as happy
as you used to be."

"And yet," sighed our heroine, "it is hard to be compelled to leave a
place as if I had been hunted out for some foul crime."

"It is indeed hard," replied the young lady, "but we have all of us our
trials to endure, and perhaps this of yours may terminate sooner than you
anticipate."

"Then your advice is that I leave this place, and seek a situation somewhere else?"

"I think it will be better for you to do so," answered Miss Wentford;—
"not, however, that I wish you to go away against your own inclination,
but for your own sake I believe it would be advisable."

"And will not ill-natured people say that I left because I was aware of
my brother's guilt, and was ashamed to remain where I am known?"

"It is likely some few may think so," answered her mistress, "but you
will at any rate be conscious of not deserving such ill-nature, and you may
rely on it I shall ever be ready to check it, should such things ever come to
my ears. Besides, time will serve to remove a great deal of the prejudice,
and whenever that is the case, I shall be happy to show my regard for a
faithful servant, by receiving you again in my house."

"Perhaps, then," observed Susan, "it would be better to follow the
plan I was thinking of when you sent for me. I came home from the

inquest with a sad and heavy heart; and, believing that all the world was against me, I had resolved to leave the place before night."

"That, I think, would be too sudden," answered Miss Wentford; "you can remain here for a few days, and then leave for London, or any other place, where you may be able to obtain a situation."

"Oh, Miss," cried Susan, "but there is the difficulty I am so much afraid of. My name will be notorious; and who will take into their house the sister of Andrew Hoply, who is accused of murdering his master."

"It is, indeed, likely you may have to endure some trouble in that respect," answered the young lady, "and for that reason I have desired the steward to give you fifteen pounds beyond the wages you have to receive. That sum will support you for a little time, and should more be required, it shall be sent immediately, upon hearing from you to that effect."

"Oh, my kind, indulgent benefactress," cried Susan, "what gratitude do I owe you for the generous interest you have taken in my behalf. But for you, I should at this moment have been without a friend in the world."

"Not so, Susan," replied her mistress, kindly, "for I have been told that you have gained the regards of William Dain, the miller's son, and report speaks of him as being endowed with many very excellent qualities. He, I am sure, will never forsake you, nor think the worse of you for being the sister of a man who, after all, has not been proved guilty of the crime laid to his charge."

"William does not believe it, Miss," answered Susan; "he has told me that he is sure poor Andrew is innocent, and that he will never rest satisfied till he has proved it. At any rate, I shall have the cheering consolation of knowing that there are two persons in the world who will still regard me with all their former kindness."

"And is there no other person," asked Miss Wentford, who might, with greater justice, be suspected of the cruel deed that has deprived me of a father?"

"There is one, at least, who, I feel confident, was deeply concerned in it," replied Susan. "You have, perhaps, heard of the stranger that I saw in the garden on the night of the ball at Upton. I spoke to him, and, in answer to my questions, he told me that he had come to visit the dairy-maid."

"The girl that has since been missing?"

"Yes, Miss."

"Then it is likely she has eloped with this stranger, and not, as suspected, with your brother."

"In my own mind," replied Susan, "I am quite certain of it. There is every reason to believe he is a bad character, and I trust that by and by the honour of my poor brother will be vindicated."

"It certainly does seem likely that the girl has run away with this stranger," observed Miss Wentford, "and if we could only prove that, it would go far to clear your brother from this horrible charge."

"Alas!" cried Susan, sorrowfully, "I fear it will now come too late, for there is little doubt that my brother Andrew fell by the same hands that slew his master."

"And what ground have you for thinking so?" asked the young lady, eagerly.

"I had a dream, Miss," replied the girl, "and in it was revealed all the fearful tragedy that afterwards took place."

"But a dream will not do to place much confidence in," answered Miss Wentford;—"they are mere shadows, and those who rely upon them, will most certainly be deceived."

"And yet," observed Susan, with a shudder, "all the other part of it has turned out exactly as I saw it in my sleep. In my terror I woke up, and at that moment I heard you and my poor master return from the ball. I could distinguish the voice of Mr. Gravestow, too, and, though I cannot tell why, I trembled, as if I felt certain that he was about to do some very terrible action."

" You are prejudiced against Mr. Gravestow, as I must acknowledge, I once was myself," exclaimed the young lady ; " I, however, conquered my dislike, by remembering that he was an esteemed friend of my dear father's, and, as you are aware, I was about speedily to become his wife, had not this mournful event taken place."

" May you never be united to that man !" cried Susan, earnestly. " I should grieve to see the sacrifice, for should you be united to him, I feel confident that you will for ever throw away every chance of happiness."

" Let us hope your anticipations are unfounded," answered Miss Wentford ; " at all events, it was my father's wish to see us married, and having once permitted Mr. Gravestow to visit me as a lover, it would be most ungenerous to break off the engagement merely because an opinion has been formed against him."

" I am not the only one that has taken a dislike to him," said Susan. " He is looked upon by almost everybody with suspicion, and I think all the worse of him since William Dain says he met the stranger on that fatal night, and that he enquired where he could find Mr. Gravestow."

" But he might have sought him as an enemy," observed Miss Wentford ;—" nay, it is even probable that he intended to murder him as well as my hapless father."

" It might be so," answered the girl, in a tone that betrayed her doubt upon the subject ; " but I am almost afraid they are more closely connected than they ought to be. Mr. Gravestow is said to have mixed in very indifferent society, though he took care not to let every body know it ; and that being the case, it is but too likely that he and the stranger have been acquainted with each other before."

" All this is nothing but surmise, Susan," cried her young mistress, " and can only tend to injure a man without serving in any way to clear up this dreadful mystery. Mr. Gravestow has undertaken to use every exertion to discover the assassin, and most sincerely do I hope he may succeed, though Heaven knows I seek not for vengeance. But it would be a satisfaction to all of us, and would, I have no doubt, clear your brother Andrew from the foul suspicion he lies under."

" I would willingly lay down my life the next moment, could I but bring proof of my brother's innocence," cried Susan Hoply. " In my own mind I am well assured that he is so, but, unfortunately, the world in general is too apt to condemn persons unheard."

" Do not make yourself uneasy about your brother's absence, my good girl," exclaimed Miss Wentford, " because, I dare say, come when he may, he will be able to give a satisfactory reason for his absence. It is certain, however, that you will be regarded with coolness till the mystery is cleared up, and for that reason I have proposed your leaving the place for the present. You can, however, remain in this house a few days longer, and when you feel inclined I will pay your fare up to London by the coach, and whenever you think proper to return, there will always be a home at this place ready to receive you."

" And you will not believe poor Andrew to be the guilty wretch that circumstances at present make him appear to be ?"

" Heaven will, no doubt, in its own good time remove the mystery that at present involves this melancholy business," replied Miss Wentford. " Andrew has always been a favourite in this house up to this time

and if he is innocent—as I firmly believe he is—there is no fear but he will be cleared from these heavy charges. In the meantime you will be away from the scene where all this misfortune has occurred, and let me entreat you to forget the source that has produced such evil consequences."

"It is impossible that I can ever forget it, even for a moment," answered Susan;—"my very thoughts will be directed to the one object that occupies my soul, in the hope that by and by I may be able to discover those who have done the cruel deed that has involved us in this sorrow."

"But you will, at all events, remain in this house for a few days longer?"

"If you wish it I will," replied Susan, "but it is hard to endure the cold looks of those that were wont to regard me with affection. Even the housekeeper, who was like a mother to me before this happened, seems to have changed her conduct, and I feel that I have lost a friend, whose good opinion I was so proud to have obtained."

"Mrs. Judson," answered the young lady, "possesses too kind a heart to do you an injustice. At first she may be misled by appearances, but depend on it she will be as kind a friend as ever when she comes to reflect on the sufferings you have already endured. I would, therefore, have you go to your own room, and I will send her to you presently, when you will have an opportunity of convincing yourself that the prejudice has been removed. So you may leave me now, Susan, for my heart is sorely oppressed, and I would be alone to indulge in those griefs which recent events have plunged me in."

Earnestly entreating her young mistress to endure her misfortunes with firmness, Susan retired and went to her own room, where, in solitude, she could think over the vicissitudes that had fallen upon her. Again she
No. 5.

thought of the dream that had haunted her on the night of the murder, and almost every portion of it was as distinct as at the moment when the vision occurred. The murder of the old gentleman and her brother she could vividly remember, but though she could recollect one of the assassins bore a close resemblance to the stranger whom she had seen in her master's garden, she could not bring it to her mind who it was that the other was like. Sometimes she fancied it was Walter Gravestow, but upon that point she could not be quite certain, and rather than do him an injustice by mentioning such a suspicion, she resolved to say nothing about it till circumstances should give her more reason for the belief. She knew also that in the same vision she had seen the murderers secrete the body of her unfortunate brother Andrew, but in spite of all her efforts, she could not then remember the place. Under these circumstances, she determined to remain silent for the present, and trust to time for a complete revelation of the mystery that involved the whole fearful transaction.

While she was still occupied with these thoughts, a gentle rap was heard at the door, and ere she could run to open it, Mrs. Judson entered the room, wearing the good humoured expression of countenance with which she had been wont to greet her young favourite.

"I am come, Susan," she said, "by the desire of our young mistress, who tells me you fancy I look coldly upon you, because everybody else does so. But it is all a mistake, for you may depend on it, I, for one, should never turn my back on you, even if it was a proved fact that your brother Andrew was guilty of the crime charged against him."

"Thank Heaven I have one more friend than I counted on," cried Susan, pressing the hand of the housekeeper. "An hour or two ago I believed that all were against me, but, since you and my young lady and William Dain support me with your regard, I can endure the ill nature of those whom prejudice has urged to look frowningly upon me."

"You may depend upon it, Susan," exclaimed the old woman, "that all will be set right sooner than may be expected. A reward has been offered for the apprehension of your brother, and if we could only see him, the thing would soon be explained to the satisfaction of everybody."

"Andrew will never be seen again alive," cried Susan, with the deepest despondency.

"Ah, you think so on account of that strange dream of yours," returned Mrs. Judson; "but there's no dependence to be placed on such things, and you may take my word for it, that your brother Andrew will come back again, and give a very good reason for his absence."

"I pray Heaven he may," cried our heroine, earnestly, "and that he may be able to throw some light upon an affair, that, at present, is involved in so much darkness."

"Why, child," observed the housekeeper, "it's the most foolish thing in the world to give way to despair, for my own part, I always look on the bright side of things, and some how it strikes me, that, perhaps, Andrew was roused by the cries of his master, and that, though he was too late to prevent the crime, he may have pursued the murderers, which, of course, would account for his absence."

"You are very kind, Mrs. Judson, to try and give me hopes," cried Susan;—"I know it is all done for the best, and most sincerely do I thank you for it. But my own heart tells me that it is in vain to look for Andrew, since I feel an inward consciousness that he perished in endeavouring to save the life of his master."

"And, in that case," asked Mrs. Judson, "who could have been the villains that committed the deed?—I know you have said a stranger was lurking about the place, and that your words have been confirmed by

William Dain, but everybody hereabouts, seems to doubt it, and that it is which makes people look the more coldly on you."

"They are cruel to suspect me of a falsehood," cried Susan, "for, even if it had been to save my brother, I could not have stooped to such a meanness. That which I have spoken is the truth, and one day or other, my words will be confirmed."

"For my own part, I have no doubt of it," returned the old lady. "I have never yet known you tell a falsehood, and, in this instance, your assertions about a stranger being in the neighbourhood, have been completely borne out by the miller's son. Mr. Gravestow, however, says he may have done that to save you."

"Mr. Gravestow is a bitter enemy both to me and my poor brother," answered the girl; he knew that we both suspected his intentions towards little Edwin, and from that moment I could see that he took the greatest dislike to us."

"Perhaps you are mistaken, then, Susan," observed the housekeeper, "for he was much respected by our master; and, surely, he would not have esteemed the man unless he had been assured of his worth."

"But Mr. Gravestow possesses a smooth tongue that would deceive anybody that his not aware of him," returned Susan. "He was about to marry our young mistress, and as there was a great deal of money depending on it, he would, of course, try his best to conceal his real disposition. Be that as it may, however, he was certainly jealous of Edwin; and there are other people besides myself, who suspect that he threw him purposely into the water, though he endeavoured to make it appear that it was a mere accident. Poor Andrew spoke his mind openly upon the subject, and now you have seen that Mr. Gravestow was the very first to accuse him of being the murderer of his master; but I will find out the truth, if it takes my whole lifetime to do it."

"And what plan do you think of following to do so?"

"Why, in the first place," answered Susan, "I should like to go over the room in which the murder was committed; some clue might be found there which would lead to the discovery I am anxious to make."

"That is impossible," returned the housekeeper, "for orders have been given to lock-up the room, and not to suffer any person to enter it except in presence of the police. I have, however, been looking about the rooms near to it, and found this gold locket. It is marked, as you see, with the initials 'W. G.;' and, no doubt, is one of the articles that Mr. Walter Gravestow says was stolen from him on the night of the murder."

"This," cried Susan, "may be important evidence by and by; give it into my custody, and should the locket ever be demanded from you, I promise to restore it immediately."

"Well, on that condition, you may keep it for the present;" answered Mrs. Judson. "And so now I must leave you for the present; but keep up your courage, Susan, for though it may run a little cross at present, I dare say every thing will turn out better than you expect by and by."

With these words the housekeeper bustled out of the room, leaving Susan to reflect alone on the course she should next adopt as to the discovery of the murder.

CHAPTER V.

THE MARKED COIN.

MORE than a week passed away, in the course of which time the funeral of Mr. Wentford took place, amidst the general grief of the whole neighbourhood. During this period the one engrossing subject of conversation, was the mystery which still continued to involve the dark transaction, for though no one ventured to doubt that Andrew Hoply was guilty of the crime, yet it seemed strange that nothing had been seen or heard of him, in spite of the large reward that had been offered for his apprehension, and the vigilant search that had been made after him. As may be imagined, this was an interval of the severest affliction to Susan, who still remained in the solitude of her own room, except when at the request of her young mistress, she visited her on some matter of moment. But nothing could be heard to throw any light upon the subject; and in the absence of any proof of his innocence, Andrew was regarded as the assassin of his master.

Two days after the funeral, Susan was visited by William Dain, who has thus long abstained from calling on her, least his presence should serve to remind her of the past. He, however, found her calm and resigned under the afflictions with which she had been oppressed, and seeing that he might venture to speak upon it, he informed Susan that he had exerted himself to the utmost, to discover some trace by which the murderers might be brought to justice, but that hitherto his efforts had proved unavailing.

"However," he continued, "I do not despair yet, but we shall by and by succeed, and if I do but obtain even the slightest guide, you may rely on it I will risk every thing, rather than be foiled in my designs."

"For your kindness, William," she replied, "I know not how to express half the gratitude I feel. You have refused to listen to the idle tales that have been spread abroad to my disadvantage, and still continue to esteem me as if this horrible affair had never happened."

"I regard you more dear, Susan," he replied, "for I have seen you suffering for no crime of your own, and with eagerness I look forward to the day that will make you mine for ever."

"That," she replied, firmly, "under present circumstances can never be."

"Susan," he exclaimed, with alarm, "surely my ears deceive me, for you never can mean to break your engagement with one who has given you no cause for it?"

"To speak the truth," she replied, "I see more reason to regard you now than ever I did. But circumstances have occurred that render it necessary for me to come to this determination, and, therefore, with deep sorrow, I repeat it, we must never again meet each other as lovers."

"Nay, you cannot mean it, Susan," he exclaimed, "for there is no reason why we should part in this way."

"There are many causes for it," she replied; "your father has never been favourable to the match, and now that I am forsaken by almost all the world, he will regard me with more dislike than ever."

"Indeed, Susan, you are mistaken," exclaimed William. "My father was, as you say, at one time opposed to our union, but since we last met, I have spoken to him upon the subject, and though he has not positively said he will agree to our marriage, I have every reason to believe he will not offer any further opposition to it."

"But when all the world is forsaking me," she cried, "it would be unjust were I to enter a family that is so much beloved and respected."

"It is because so many are against you, that I wish to offer you a home and a protector," answered William. "This is the time when you have most need of a friend, and, depend upon it, I am most sincere in making the proposition."

"I am sure of that," replied our heroine, "but at present I would rather give no other answer than that you have already heard. A short time may serve to clear my brother's character from the foul stain that has been cast upon it, and should you then regard me as much as now, I will no longer hesitate to become your wife."

"And is that the only answer you will at present give me?" asked the young man.

"For a time, it is," she replied;—"a few weeks, however, may make a most important alteration, and should I then find that I can become your wife without bringing shame upon you, I will freely give you my hand, and with it a heart that is truly grateful for the kindness and affection you have ever manifested towards me."

William was about to urge her yet more earnestly to consent to an immediate union, but ere he could do so, the door opened, and Mr. Cornish, the steward, entered the room, with all the pomp and dignity belonging to so great a personage. The young man perceiving that he was rather in the way, now took his departure, and thereupon Mr. Cornish broke forth.

"Upon my life, this is a most mysterious affair!—A very mysterious affair, indeed, for here have we been searching all over the house, and though no corner has been overlooked, it can't be found any where."

"Of what are you speaking, sir?" asked Susan, puzzled to understand his meaning.

"Ah!" he exclaimed, "I forgot that you have been shutting yourself up here for the last ten or twelve days, and know nothing about it; so I'll explain myself, girl:—the truth is, everybody in the house is very certain that our late poor dear master made a will;—he told me so himself only a day or two before he was murdered, and yet,—would you believe it!—there's not such a thing to be found in the house."

"Perhaps," observed Susan, "he destroyed it with the intention of making another."

"That's not at all a likely thing," replied the steward; "Mr. Wentford was not a fickle man on business affairs, and so the only conclusion I can come to is, that the will must have been stolen by whoever it was that murdered him."

"That is likely enough," answered Susan, thoughtfully, "and if so, it will go far to prove that my brother Andrew had nothing to do with the dreadful crime."

"And how will it prove that?" asked the steward.

"Because no one would have taken it who had not an interest of his own to serve," she replied.

"Humph!" muttered the steward, "there's something in that, to be sure. And yet, if we come to that conclusion, the only person who had an important interest, and whom we could suspect of the murder and robbery, would be Mr. Walter Gravestow."

"Well, sir!" cried Susan, with breathless haste.

"Well, girl," he resumed, "you might just as well suspect me as him, for who, I should like to know, would ever think for a moment that such a gentleman as he is could commit so foul a deed?"

"Very true," sighed our heroine, "and yet there is much deceit in the world, and it is impossible to say who would do such a thing, or who would not."

"Why, you must be crazed, girl, to let such a thought ever enter your head !" cried Mr. Cornish, fairly gasping with astonishment. "Mr. Grave-stow a murderer !—Psha ! the most preposterous thing I ever heard of in my life !"

" You mistake me, sir," replied Susan, who began to find she had gone rather too far ;—" I have not accused Mr. Gravestow of this dreadful act, but where all is uncertainty, I repeat, we may as well suspect one person as another."

" But there's no reason to suppose that he had any hand in it," exclaimed the steward.

" And yet you say the will has been stolen ?"

" It certainly is not anywhere about the house," returned Mr. Cornish, " but whither it has been stolen or not, I am unable to say."

" But you are sure Mr. Wentford made a will ?"

" Oh yes, I am quite certain about that."

" And you are equally sure that it is not anywhere about the house ?"

" Bless your soul, girl, we've hunted everywhere, and not been able to find it. Mr. Gravestow has assisted us, and he, poor man, seems as much concerned about the loss as anybody."

" And yet it will not matter much to him," answered Susan, " for as he is about to marry our dear young lady, he will, of course, come in for almost all the property."

" That's very true, girl, but it would have been a very great satisfaction to him if the will had been found."

" I wish it had, with all my heart," replied our heroine; for " little Edwin was, no doubt, mentioned in it, and the poor boy may lose all that was left him, or depend on the generosity of Mr. Gravestow."

" It will be upon Miss Wentford that the boy will have to depend," answered the steward, " and you may be sure she will do justice by him. Why, she loves the child almost as much as if he was her own brother, and I dare say when she is married she will take Edwin into the house to live with her."

" Yes," replied Susan, significantly, " if her husband will allow her to do so."

" There, again," cried the steward, " you are doubting the justice of Mr. Gravestow's intentions."

" Because I fear there is but too much reason to do so," exclaimed Susan ;—" the person you have just named has never had any very great liking for the boy, and it's my opinion he would be pleased enough to have an opportunity to vent his spite upon him. I have not forgot that affair of the water, and shall always suspect that Mr. Gravestow threw him in purposely, unless he can ever prove to the contrary."

" Psha !—it is impossible."

" And yet, whenever the subject is mentioned in his presence," answered Susan, " he turns pale, and contrives to shift the conversation to something else."

" That," replied Mr. Cornish, " may be because he has heard the slanders that have been whispered about him."

" Nothing would ever shame him," cried Susan ;—" he does not seem to have any heart, and as for Miss Wentford taking care of the boy, as you hinted just now, I am afraid it will not be in her power to do so for some time to come."

" And why so ?" demanded the steward.

" Because she is not of age yet, and if she marries Mr. Gravestow before she is twenty-one, he will take care to prevent her making use of her own money. And as for Edwin, I feel quite certain he will take care not to have him in the house longer than he can help."

"Ah! I see you are prejudiced against him," exclaimed the old man, "and so the better way will be for you and I to say no more about it."

"But the will," observed Susan, "is no further trouble to be taken to find it?"

"Oh, yes," replied the steward, "we shall not let that affair drop very quietly, I can tell you. Advertisements are to be put into all the newspapers, offering a reward to any one that can give information upon the subject. I dare say that may answer the purpose, though, perhaps, it will be some time before we hear anything about it."

"And what will be the use of it?" asked Susan.

"Why," replied the old man, "it will most likely give Mr. Gravestow a very considerable sum of money."

"But that he will have without the will," said our heroine, "for on his marriage with Miss Wentford, of course he must become possessed of nearly all the property."

"That's true enough," answered Mr. Cornish, "and having admitted that, you must allow he could have had no interest in getting rid of the will."

"I don't know that," replied Susan, "for no doubt, as I said before, something handsome was left to Edwin, and if the will is lost, Mr. Gravestow will have an opportunity to satisfy his malice of depriving the poor boy of everything."

"Well," exclaimed the steward, "I see it's no use of arguing this matter any further,—you are determined to believe the worst of Mr. Gravestow, and so I shall leave you for the present, with a hope that you may think better of him in future."

Upon this, Mr. Cornish took leave of her, and went his way, wondering how Susan could take a dislike to such a worthy, excellent creature, as he esteemed Walter Gravestow. He never could see any harm in the future husband of his young mistress, and he could not but mutter his astonishment that any one should entertain an evil thought against him.

But the more Susan weighed these matters over in her mind the more positive she felt that her suspicions were but too well founded. The loss of the will, which was known to have been in existence only a few days before the murder of Mr. Wentford, still further confirmed the notion that had taken possession of her mind. Who else, she reasoned within herself, would have thought it worth their while to carry away a document that would prove utterly valueless to them? Was it likely that a piece of useless paper would have been carried away by strangers when there was a large sum of money in the old gentleman's room that could have been easily carried off? To be sure some few articles of jewellery and a little money were missing, but the probability was that it had been taken merely to give a colour to the assertion that the murder had been committed for the sake of plunder. At least Susan could come to no other conclusion, and she would have told her young mistress as much, only that she feared lest by so doing she might defeat the ends of justice she had in view. At any rate, every circumstance served more and more to convince her that Andrew was innocent, and in that assurance her mind grew easier and she looked forward with greater certainty to the period when she might be able to rescue the character of a beloved brother from the ignominy that at present rested upon it.

It was this thought which had detained her so much longer than she had intended in the service of Miss Wentford. She was anxious to seize every opportunity that offered to obtain information that might serve to bring affairs to a crisis, and for that reason she submitted to remain in a house where it was but too evident she had many enemies. There was something abhorrent to her feelings in being thus near Walter Gravestow, who she could not but regard as a murderer, and when they met, as occasionally they did, she shrunk from him as from a monster whose crimes had rendered him hideous in her sight.   Nor were these meetings more agreeable to Gravestow himself, for he knew well enough that he was, to her, an object of suspicion, and he felt his heart sink whenever he chanced to approach the sister of that man whom he had murdered, and whose name he had covered with ignominy and reproach.   Still, however, he found it necessary to carry it off with a high hand when anybody was present; but in moments of privacy and seclusion he devoted all his thoughts to the means by which he might rid himself of one who, he was but too well aware, remained passive only till she could find an opportunity to plunge him into irretrievable ruin and ignominy.   This was the one engrossing object that filled his mind, and since no other means were left he determined to get rid of her by the same means that he had employed in removing Mr. Wentford.   To this end he resolved once more to secure the services of George Ramsden, who, having squandered away the money he received for his share in the former crime, had written three or four pressing letters, threatening him with a disclosure of all that had taken place unless he received as much gold as his extravagance required.   Finding himself thus thrown into the power of a hungry villain, he thought he might quiet him with a large sum of money on condition that he assisted in getting rid of Susan Hoply.   Thus he began to feel the wretched situation to which he had brought himself, and he found that his own preservation from a disgraceful end depended on his adding another crime to that which he had already committed.

We must now return to Susan, who, shortly after the departure of Mr. Cornish, was agreeably surprised by a visit from her little favourite Edwin, who, taking the first opportunity that offered itself after leaving his room, ran to her to ask her why she shut herself up so, instead of mixing with the other domestics as she had been used to do.

"They have tried to make me believe," he said, "that your brother Andrew is a bad man, and that he is the murderer of Mr. Wentford; but I would not believe them, for Andrew was always so kind, that I am sure he never could have been the wretch they make him out."

"You do my brother no more than justice, my dear boy," cried Susan. "He is, indeed, innocent, though circumstances at present have been made to throw some suspicion on him.   But he shall yet have justice done him, if heaven will but permit me to live a short time longer."

"And where is he?" asked the boy.

"In his grave!"

"Andrew dead!—nay, tell me not so, dear Susan, for I loved him as my own brother, and I should weep bitterly were I to know that he was lost to me for ever."

"I fear it is but too true," answered Susan; "for, had he been alive, he would, long ere this, have come forward to deny the foul charges that have been brought against him."

"But he may be alive, for all that," replied Edwin.   "I have a notion that they have hid him somewhere or other, and that he cannot come till the gaolers choose to set him at liberty."

"I have had such an idea as that myself," sighed our heroine, "but on reflection I believe he is dead."

"Then what caused his death?" asked the child.

"It would be dangerous even to hint my suspicions," replied Susan; "but I cannot help telling you that I fear he has perished by the hands of an assassin."

"Ah! I understand you now," cried the boy, sorrowfully: "Poor Andrew Hoply died in defence of his master, when the murderers attacked him."

"I have thought so," replied Susan, "but in our present uncertainty it is almost dangerous to say so."

"You may depend on it I will not give a hint about such a thing," exclaimed Edwin. "But I think you are quite right, Susan, for Andrew dearly loved his master, and, I know, would have defended him to the very last."

"Such, at any rate, is my opinion," cried our heroine, "and I am determined to find out the truth, if it takes me a whole life-time to do it."

"But does any one suspect who were the murderers of poor Mr. Wentford?"

"At present," replied Susan, "the whole affair is involved in the greatest mystery."

"Ah!" exclaimed the boy, " so everybody tells me. Just now I asked Mr. Gravestow if he knew who were the assassins, and he flew into such a terrible passion that I shall never enquire of him again."

"It would be better not to do so," returned Susan, "for such a question might excite his anger, and might deprive you of a protector. I have myself seen him very cross with people when the subject was mentioned before him, and I believe there are very few persons who would introduce it when Mr. Gravestow is present."

"And why should he be angry?" asked the boy.

"That we will not talk about at present, my dear Edwin," she replied. "It is sufficient for us to know that he does not like to hear it mentioned,

No. 6

and, therefore, we must rest satisfied till circumstances reveal secrets which are at present hidden in mystery."

"I don't know how it is," said the boy, "but, for some reason or other, Mr. Gravestow don't seem to like me at all. He always frowns upon me, and says such ill-natured things that sometimes I wish I was a few years older, that I might punish him for it as he deserves."

"Nay, my love," answered Susan, "you should bear these things with more patience. Mr. Gravestow is much older than yourself, and may, perhaps, think he now stands in the place of your late kind protector."

"Oh, but he'll never be like him, though," returned Edwin. "I have already found a great difference between them, for Mr. Wentford was always kind and affectionate, and the other never knows how to be ill-natured enough."

"Has he been so very cross to you then?" asked Susan.

"Oh, yes; and then he speaks of you in a way that vexes me very much; and as for Andrew, it seems that he can never speak a word half bad enough for him."

"For the present he may do so," replied Susan Hoply, "but he may depend upon it the time will come when I shall be enabled to hurl back upon himself the foul charges he has so unjustly brought against my poor brother."

"I told him, a little while ago," replied Edwin, "that no one should ever make me believe Andrew Hoply was guilty of the murder; and then he said, with a sneer, that it would be much more to my credit if I was to think less of a low-born fellow who I had always made a companion of, though he was so far inferior to myself. But I said that Andrew was a kind friend to me, and that he had saved my life when somebody else that I could mention ran away under the pretence of looking for a doctor. And, oh! if you had seen him at that moment, Susan, you never would have forgotten him as long as you live! He would have killed me, I do verily believe, if Miss Wentford had not fortunately have happened to have been in the room."

"Indeed, Edwin," cried Susan, "you must not venture to speak so plainly to a person of violent temper like Mr. Gravestow. You have seen how his anger was excited, and had it not been for the presence of my young lady, you might have suffered severely for it."

"But I don't care for him a bit, in spite of the ill-natured things he said when he found that he could not have his vengeance on me," replied the boy. "He rolled his eyes and gnashed his teeth, and, as well as his rage would suffer him, said that if I chose to take part with such low-bred people, it should be somewhere else than under his roof. Then he called me a pauper, and said I was existing upon his charity! My heart was almost ready to burst at hearing him speak so, for Mr. Wentford never told me such a thing in his life, and it seemed hard that a stranger should call me a beggar. However, there is one thing I am glad of—I never shed so much as a single tear till I was out of his sight."

"And has he treated you in this way ever since the death of your generous patron?" asked Susan.

"No," replied the boy, "he was rather kind to me at first, but I could see plainly enough that he was only trying to make friends with me because I should not say anything about my falling into the lake. He was always offering me presents, but I never took anything from him except this half-guinea, which he put into my hands before I was aware of what he was going to do. And now, dear Susan, as I have no use for it, do take it from me, and you have no idea how happy it will make me."

As he said this he put the gold into her hand, but she would not accept of it, and as she was about to return it, her eye caught a mark upon the money which made her look at it more closely. She then saw that it was stamped with an inscription besides that which is usual on coins, and could plainly perceive the words and figures, "April 3, 1781." It seemed to have been done with a stamp, and the more Susan looked at it, the more certain she was that she had seen the coin in Mr. Wentford's possession a very short time previous to the fatal night which had terminated his existence. She remembered having entered his room at a moment when he was seated at a table counting over a large sum of gold which he had just received, and that, whilst he was thus occupied, a pile was accidentally knocked from the table on to the floor. She assisted him in gathering up the gold, and on again counting it over, he expressed himself quite satisfied that all had been picked up. After that, however, Susan found just beneath the fender, where it had rolled, a half-guinea, which she immediately gave him. He then observed that it was one which he had dropped from his pocket at an earlier hour of the morning; and as she saw that he appeared to set considerable store on that particular coin, she remarked that it bore the very same inscription which she now detected on the half-guinea that had been offered to her by Edwin.

This circumstance opened a fresh channel for enquiry. It was strange, she thought, how this coin, which she knew had been in the possession of her master just before his death, should have come into the hands of Mr. Gravestow so shortly afterwards; for it so happened that the piece of gold was kept as a relic in the purse which was said to have been stolen on the night of the assassination; and hence arose a question, as to how he could have had the coin, unless he was himself one of the murderers. At any rate, it afforded another link to the chain of evidence that she hoped one day or other to complete against Walter Gravestow; and, taking another half-guinea from her pocket, she gave it to Edwin in exchange for the one he had offered her.

"I will not accept your well-meant gift, my dear boy," she said; "but if it makes no difference, I will give you this other piece of money in exchange for it."

"If you will not take it," he replied, it can make no difference which one I have. But why, Susan, do you seem so anxious to possess that coin, when both of them are of the same value?"

"There is no particular reason, dear Edwin, she replied, with hesitation; "none whatever. But I am about to leave this place, you know, and it would be some consolation when we are parted to have something that I can keep by me in remembrance of you."

"And will you indeed think of me, Susan?"

"Aye, child, to the latest hour of my life."

"But you will come back again before long?"

"I hope so," she replied; "but it will not be till I can bring with me evidence to clear the character of poor Andrew from the stain that has been cast on it."

"You think, then, it will be possible to prove to the world that he is innocent!"

"There is no doubt of it," she replied; "I myself know that he is guiltless of the crime, and it only requires a little perseverance to collect sufficient evidence to prove it to the satisfaction of every disinterested person."

"Oh, what a pleasure," cried Edwin, "that would be to all those who loved Andrew as I did!"

"Be assured I will not fail for want of a good heart to proceed fearlessly in the task I have undertaken,' exclaimed our heroine, resolutely. "It is a cause for which I could cheerfully lay down my life, if it should be necessary ; and no thoughts of the consequences that may happen to myself should ever deter me from going on with it to the very last. Andrew has been publicly dishonoured, and equally public shall be his acquittal."

"And if I was a man," cried Edwin, you should see with what a good heart I would assist you."

"I know you would, dear boy," answered Susan, gratefully : "you, at all events, do not believe the wicked falsehoods that have been told against my brother, and or that I thank you. There are a few others to whom my gratitude is due, and those that believe him guilty shall yet acknowledge that they have done him an injustice. But you must leave me now, Edwin, and it is likely we may not meet each other again till I return with tidings that will fill your young heart with joy."

"Are you going to leave us so soon, then ?" asked Edwin.

"This very day," she replied. "Here I shall never be happy whilst the mystery is unexplained ; and by going to London I may meet with other friends who will assist me in the task I have undertaken."

At this juncture the voice of Mr. Gravestow was heard calling for Edwin, and the poor boy was obliged to take a hasty farewell of his favourite, who, being now left alone, put the marked coin along with the locket which she already possessed, and, sewing them up in her dress for fear of accident, proceeded to the room usually occupied by the steward, and received from him the fifteen pounds over and above her wages, which had been promised by Miss Fanny. With this sum in her possession, she went to bid good bye to her young lady, who would fain have prevailed on her to remain where she was till she heard of a situation that would suit her. But Susan's resolution was not to be shaken ; and having repeatedly expressed her gratitude for the many acts of kindness she had received, she left the house, intending to walk across the fields to the road where she was to meet the London coach.

CHAPTER VI.

A VISIT TO THE CHURCHYARD.

IT was with a sorrowful heart that our heroine left the scene of so many joyous and happy hours, for it seemed to her as if she had been banished for some crime of her own, and, innocent as she was, she left the place in which she had once been respected, carrying with her the suspicions of those who, in former times, had loved and esteemed her. With such melancholy thoughts as these crowding upon her mind, she entered the village churchyard, and took the path which led towards the grave in which, scarcely twelve months since, her parents had been laid. The green turf that flourished over those who had so fondly loved her, formed a sad contrast to the work of destruction that was going on beneath, and as she thought of the happy hours that had fled never more to return, she threw herself upon the ground and wept in all the agony and anguish of an almost broken heart.

How long she had remained in this situation Susan knew not, but on recovering her recollection, she found herself supported in the arms of William Dain, her still faithful lover, who, it appeared, had found her, by mere accident, as she was lying, almost insensible, on the grave of her beloved parents.

"Why, how is this, dear Susan?" he exclaimed, as soon as she had sufficiently recovered herself to recognize him; "how is it that I find you exposing yourself to the chill evening air, and mourning over those who have long since passed into a far happier world than the one they have left?"

"Would to Heaven I was with them," groaned Susan, and burying her face in the bosom of her lover, she burst into a flood of bitter tears.

"Nay, this melancholy is uncalled for," exclaimed the young man, "your grief should long, ere this, have been forgotten, and yet I find you mourning over the grave of your parents, as if their death had taken place only a few days since."

"You are mistaken, William," she replied, "for, instead of grieving for their loss, I have cause rather to rejoice that Heaven has removed them from me, for, had they lived till this period, the suffering of their daughter, and the suspicion that is attached to Andrew, would have sent them despairing and broken-hearted to their grave."

"And, has nothing yet been heard," asked William, "that may serve to prove the innocence of your brother?"

"Nothing."

"That is, indeed, unfortunate," answered her lover, "and yet I would not have you despair, for time, I dare say, will clear up the mystery, and release him from the foul imputation that have been cast upon his character."

"Alas!" cried Susan, "I cannot forget that he has been accused of being an assassin. You have heard it, William, and, therefore, the love that has hitherto existed between us, must now be forgotten for ever."

"And think you, Susan," he asked, "that I believe the slanders they have cast upon your brother's name, or, that I can love you the less because it happens that falsehoods have been uttered against one, whose only crime consists in being related to the man they have wrongfully accused?"

"Aye, William," she replied, "but Andrew must be proved to be innocent, ere I give my hand to one who loves me as you do. Besides, I have determined to prosecute this enquiry to a successful termination, and, though I am now about to leave this neighbourhood for a time, it will be that I may banish myself from the society of those, who, for motives of their own, will not fail to persecute me, even though it should be to death."

"What is it you say?" cried William, with alarm;—"am I to understand, Susan, that you are going to leave us?"

"I have no other alternative left," she replied;—"you now see me on my way to London, but I still hope my absence from this place will not be for any long time. At present, people regard me with coldness, because they persist in believing that poor Andrew is guilty of shedding the blood of his master. Yet I again tell you, William, he is innocent, and I will prove it ere long, to the satisfaction of those even who are at present inclined to believe in his guilt."

"I, for one, have the most perfect confidence that the mystery will be cleared up in his favour," answered William. "I am sure he loved his master too well to shed his blood, though the fact of his disappearance immediately after the murder may give rise to doubts in the minds of those who never look to more than one side of a question. But he will, I dare say, return again ere long, and from his own lips we shall have an explanation of the motives that induced him to leave the place at such a moment."

"My brother Andrew will never be seen alive again," replied Susan, mournfully.

"Ah!" exclaimed her lover, "you still fancy, then, that he has been murdered?"

"I feel confident of it," replied Susan,—"nay, more; I can almost venture to affirm, that he was assassinated by those who slew my late unfortunate master."

"Have you any evidence to prove this?" asked the young man.

"Nothing more than the dream I have already told you of."

"And that," observed William, "will go but a little way towards convincing people that your suspicions are correct. Dreams, you know, are merely the effect of imagination, and cannot be relied on in so serious an affair as this is."

"But, in the same vision," answered our heroine, "I saw the whole dreadful tragedy that terminated in the death of my master."

"Yet that, you may believe me," he replied, "was nothing more than the effect of chance."

"Do you, then," she said, reproachfully, "believe that Andrew is guilty of the crime?"

"On the contrary," he replied, " I could willingly stake my existence on his innocence. Andrew and I were playmates from early infancy; and, knowing him as I did, I can venture to say that, however appearances may at present be against him, he would rather have perished in defence of his master, than have raised a hand to injure him."

"You have spoken truly, William," she exclaimed, "for it was in defence of his master's life that my brother fell."

"You speak confidently upon the subject," answered William, "and I pray to Heaven your words, in this instance, may prove unfounded. For my own part, I believe he is still alive, and that, return when he may, he will be able to give a very satisfactory reason for his absence."

"Indeed, indeed he has been killed!" exclaimed Susan, wound up to the highest pitch of energy. " In my vision, I saw him stabbed to the heart, and then the villains concealed the body, though where I cannot now remember."

"And did you not mark the countenances of those who did the deed?"

"It was impossible to do so," she replied, "for they wore crape upon their faces, and were, probably, otherwise disguised, in case they should be disturbed in their unholy deed. But circumstances may yet enable me to recollect where it was they concealed the body, and should that be the case, it will at any rate remove all suspicion from Andrew."

"And, perhaps," observed William Dain, "the force of conscience may then compel the real perpetrators of the crime to avow their share in the transaction."

"Such things have occurred before now," she replied, "and it may be so in the present instance. This it is that alone sustains me through my heavy afflictions, and in that reliance I patiently submit to the misery by which I am at present surrounded. The hour of retribution must and will arrive, and till then I will endure all without a murmur."

"But surely," cried her lover, "there can be no occasion for you to leave this neighbourhood?"

"I cannot endure to meet scorn where once I met nothing but kindness," she replied. " I feel myself a marked and degraded being whilst I remain here, and, perhaps, when I find myself in a strange place, I may meet with friends to support me under my afflictions."

"And have you not friends here, Susan?" he asked.

"Yes," she replied, "I have a few who still regard me, in spite of the cruel coldness with which others have shown towards me. "You, William, have proved yourself to be above the prejudices that others have conceived against me, and that thought alone will cheer me in many an hour, when I might, perhaps, give myself up to despair."

"Then why leave me?" he exclaimed. "I have already told you that my father is inclined to consent to our union, and you will then have a protector, who will fearlessly shield you against the shafts of the malevolent."

"Nay, you already know my mind upon that subject," she replied. "My heart is yours, William, but my hand you never can possess, till the foul stain has been removed which at present rests upon my family."

"But I am willing to endure all," he replied, "for the sake of affording you a shelter from the enmity that circumstances have raised up against you."

"And why should I bring dishonour upon one who has hitherto lived respected?" asked our heroine; "is it not enough that I must myself endure these calumnies, but I should seek to bring the tongue of slander upon one whose generosity would prompt him to make so great a sacrifice?—No, William; dear as you are to me, I would rather perish than be guilty of so great injustice."

"Indeed, Susan, you are mistaken in this instance," replied her lover. "People would cease to regard you with coldness after you became my wife, and thus you would secure yourself against the annoyance you at present complain of."

"Urge me no more," she cried, "for my mind is made up; and, though, from my heart I thank you for your kindness, yet will I pursue the course I have resolved on."

"You are determined then to go to London?"

"I am, William."

"In that case I will urge you no further," he replied; "but you will require a good deal of money, Susan, in a strange place; and if you will accept this purse and its contents, you know not how happy it will make me."

"Dear William," she exclaimed, "this is indeed a most kind and considerate offer of yours, but I have no occasion to tax your generosity, since my young lady has liberally given me fifteen pounds beyond the wages I had to receive. With that I shall be rich enough till I get a situation, which I dare say will not be very long, as I have a female acquaintance in London who will assist me in obtaining one."

"And is Miss Fanny aware that you have made up your mind to leave her?"

"She is," replied Susan; "but we part upon the best terms, since she thinks it will be better that I leave the place till I can return under happier circumstances."

"Well," exclaimed her lover, "I don't know but you are right; "yet, it is hard to part with you, Susan, especially as my father would make no further objection to our marriage."

"But he might afterwards repent that he had sanctioned it," he replied; "and I could never be happy if ever I should discover that our union had sown dissension between you and your father. Besides, I have told you that all my thoughts and energies must be directed to one object; and till that is obtained I will never marry."

"But have you reflected on the difficulties you may have to encounter in a strange place?" asked William. "You will be thrown entirely among strangers, and there are villains in London who are ever seeking to make a prey of those who are too innocent to suspect them."

" And there are also many good people there, upon whose kindness I may rely with some confidence, answered Susan.   " The friend I shall seek on my arrival there has often expressed a wish that I would go to town, and even Miss Fanny, who knows her well, thinks I shall be perfectly safe whilst under her protection."

" Which cannot be for any long time, since your object in going to London is to obtain a situation."

" I see, William," she cried, " you would fain persuade me against undertaking this journey. That it is against my own wish you may be certain, but circumstances have compelled me to adopt the alternative ; and let the consequences be what they may, I leave this place till I can return to it with news of my brother's innocence."

" Which may take years ere you can accomplish it," exclaimed William Dain.

" Nay," she answered, " I am sanguine enough to hope a very short time may serve to unravel the mystery. The perpetrators of murder can seldom escape the punishment due to their crimes ; and, depend on it, something or other will ever turn up by which I may obtain a clue that will lead to their apprehension."

" At any rate," exclaimed William, " there is very little doubt that the stranger you saw in the garden was one of them."

" Of that I am convinced," she replied ; " but he has escaped, and at present we know not where he is to be found. In London, however, I may chance to see him, and should that be the case, I shall not fail to make the best use of my advantage."

" But though there is good ground to believe that he was concerned in the murder," exclaimed William, " we have no direct evidence by which to bring the crime home to him."

" Yet we soon may have," cried our heroine. " Already I have a slight clue which, well followed up, may lead to the discovery of his accomplice."

" You have some idea then who he is ?"

" My suspicions have been awakened," she replied.

" And may I ask who it is ?"

" Not at present, dear William," she replied ; " for a time I must act with caution, and should my chain of evidence be completed, you, as well as many others, will be surprised at the discovery I shall make."

" And yet you will not trust me with this secret," he exclaimed, " though it is likely I might be able to assist you so materially in bringing about the discovery."

" Blame me not," cried Susan, " and the time will come when I can give a good reason for the caution I have found it necessary to adopt. But I must now leave you, William, for the coach I am going by will pass before long, and I would not lose my opportunity of reaching London on any consideration."

" You will let me walk with you to the place where you are to be overtaken by the coach ?"

" Indeed I would rather go alone," she said. " Do not think me unkind in thus refusing your offer, but I have reasons to prefer going alone."

" In that case I will urge my request no further," replied her lover, " so farewell, dear Susan, and may Heaven watch over and protect you from the snares and dangers which lurk around the innocent."

Susan could not forbear weeping at taking leave of William Dain, and once more thanking him for the generous interest he had taken in her

behalf, she tore herself away, and crossing the style which separated the churchyard from a bye lane, she resumed the journey which had been thus interrupted. William observed the direction she had taken, and then slowly following, he ascended an elevated point from whence he could watch her for some distance along the road.

Scarcely had they left the churchyard when a couple of ruffians who had been secretly observing them and listening to their conversation, came forward from their lurking place, and with a chuckle of satisfaction congratulated each other on the prospect of obtaining booty.

"I say, Larkins," exclaimed one of them to his comrade, "this affair will turn out better than we expected. The girl has got money it seems, and it will be our own fault if it don't change hands before long."

"What you say's very true," replied the other, "but if we stop here much longer we shall let the prize slip through our fingers; so come along, Gomm, and let's finish the business with execution and despatch."

"Bah! there's no occasion to be in such a confounded hurry about it," answered Gomm; "I know the road she's taken well enough, and as there's a near cut across the fields that will bring us out to a place where she must pass, there's very little fear of her escaping from us. So now tell me what Mr. Gravestow said when he was whispering to you a little time back?"

"He was only talking about the girl that's just gone away," replied Larkins. "He's a little bit afraid of her, you must know, for she suspects too much about the murder of the old gentleman, and so he's taken it into his head that she must be got rid of."

"That fellow's a born devil," exclaimed Gomm, "if people offend him he thinks no more of taking their lives than you or I do of taking a purse."

No. 7

"What's that to either you or I?" demanded the other, sullenly; "he don't mind paying us handsomely for the job, and as we both want money we should be fools to stand out about trifles."

"Do you call shedding blood a trifle?" asked Gomm.

"At any rate I don't think much of it," answered his comrade; "it's a thing that's soon over, and the gold one earns is a capital salve for an uneasy conscience."

"To be sure there's something in that," replied the other, "but I think we might just as well spare her life and take the gold, which is all either you or I want."

"But that won't satisfy Mr. Gravestow," exclaimed Larkins. "He's afraid she'll be too much for him by and by, for he says the girl suspects that he had a hand in the murder of old Mr. Wentford, and so to make all safe, he's willing to give us a good handsome sum, on condition that we make away with her."

"Or, in other words, that we cut her throat."

"Exactly so, Gomm, only you've always such an ugly way of speaking of these things."

"I like to call things by their right names," replied the other; "we are expected to commit a murder,—for that's the plain English of it,—and as he's afraid to do it himself, he don't mind paying others to do his dirty work."

"Humph! perhaps you'll not help me then?"

"Why, as far as the robbery goes I don't mind joining you in it, because that's all in the way of our profession," replied Gomm; "but a murder is quite another thing, and especially when the victim is a young and innocent girl like that."

"Yet innocent as she is," returned Larkins, "she may do a deal of mischief; she's only quiet a little while, just till she can rake a little evidence together, and then who knows what she may say to get him into a hobble that he won't know how to get out of?"

"Depend on it he's frightened about nothing," answered the other. "She can't know who it was that committed the murder, or she'd have let the cat out of the bag long before this time."

"Mr. Gravestow thinks differently," replied Larkins;—"the girl is always talking about a dream that she had on the night of the murder, and it may happen by and by that she'll take it into her head to accuse him of being one of the assassins."

"Which won't be very far from the truth," observed Gomm.

"But it will be very far from being pleasant though," returned his companion. "Mr. Gravestow says he lives in continual danger, and so to make himself safe he has made up his mind that Susan Hoply shall die."

"And suppose we satisfy ourselves with taking what money she has and then let her off with her life," said Gomm. "He'll not know any difference if we tell him she's dead, and so we may earn the reward he's promised without having her blood to answer for."

"Are you afraid of a little blood then?"

"I'd rather not spill any," replied his companion. "It's apt to lay confoundedly heavy upon a man's soul, and hang me if I like the risk just for the sake of a purse full of gold that would be spent almost as soon as it was earnt."

"Then you'd better say at once that you'll have nothing at all to do with it, then I shall know what I've got to expect."

"Why, you don't think I'd leave an old comrade, do you?" exclaimed Gomm. "No, no, we generally manage these matters in partnership, and I'm not going to desert you in a moment like this."

" Tell me what you mean to do then ?"

" Do ! why rob the girl and let her go on her journey, to be sure."

" And what would be the use of that ?"

" A good deal in my opinion ; you heard her tell the young fellow just now that she had fifteen pounds in her pocket besides the wages she had received, and if we get possession of that, it will be a very tidy day's work."

" But will it satisfy our employer, think you ?"

" That'll depend upon ourselves," replied Gomm. " We have only to tell him the girl is dead, and how will he be able to say anything to the contrary ?"

" Why, of course, he must hear of it before long."

" And what will it matter if he does ?" demanded the other ;—" by that time we shall have got the money from him, and he can't say anything about it, you know, for fear of his own neck."

" I don't know that," exclaimed his comrade ; " this Mr. Gravestow is a desperate sort of character, and there's no saying what he might do to be revenged for any scurvy trick we take it in our heads to play him. He's got his eye upon us, depend on it, and we should have a poor chance with him if he happened to suspect that we meant anything on the cross."

" 'Psha ! are you afraid of him ?"

" Not a bit ; but I like to keep out of danger for all that. Once offend him, Gomm, and, take my word for it, it would soon be all up."

" Why, he's as much in our power as we are in his."

" Very likely," replied Larkins ; " but it would be very poor satisfaction to know that he must come to the gallows because we are on the road to it. For my own part I don't feel at all inclined to offend him, and so come what may, I'm determined the girl shall die according to the bargain we've made."

" Well," returned Gomm, " I know it's no use arguing when once you've made up your mind ; but what if the young chap we saw here just now has taken into his head to follow her ? We should find him an awkward customer, I'm thinking ; and who knows but we might find ourselves in a scrape before we are aware of it ?"

" If he should interfere," replied Larkins, " the only way will be to put an end to him. He must die, too, and thus your difficulty is soon got rid of."

" Aye, if words will do it, I grant the trouble would be nothing," replied Gomm. " But it strikes me we should find this young miller a very awkward customer,—and, therefore, I'd advise you to think well before we go any further."

" He'd be just as bad if we only robbed her of the money she's got," answered the other ; " so I say let's put her out of the way by all means, and the thing may be done without her making any disturbance."

" I'll tell you what, Larkins," says his comrade, " let's try if she'll give up the money quietly ; and if she'll do that, we may let her go on without doing anything worse ; but if she chooses to make a noise about it, why then I shall be as much inclined for mischief as yourself, and she must die to make ourselves secure. Do you agree to that ?"

" I do ; but you must make an excuse to Mr. Gravestow : for hang me if I can meet him with a lie on my tongue. He'd be sure to find me out, and then we may pretty well guess what the end of it would be."

" Oh, I'll manage all that comfortably enough," replied Gomm ; " I'm pretty well at telling a lie, and especially when it happens to be in a case like this."

" And if the young miller interferes with us, of course, it's understood that he must be despatched ?"

" Yes, yes," replied the other ; " in that case we must take care of our-

selves. It wouldn't puzzle a conjuror to tell what would be the consequence of being found out; and as every man thinks of taking care of
number one, why he must die if we should be hard pressed."

"And the girl as well?"

"Yes;" answered Gomm, "they are lovers, it seems, and it would be
cruel, you know, to kill one and leave the other to lament the loss."

"So far we are agreed then," answered Larkins; "and now I suppose
you are ready to follow the wench?"

"The sooner the better," replied Gomm, "for if she gets too far on the
road, we shall lose all chance of overtaking her; so come along, and
remember we are not kill her if she will quietly give up her money."

Larkins nodded an assent to this, and leaping the wall of the churchyard,
they took a path across the fields, which led by a much nearer way into the
lane down which Susan Hoply had gone, and by which means they expected
to intercept her before she reached the main road.

CHAPTER VII.

AN ENCOUNTER WITH ROBBERS.

OCCUPIED as her mind was with a variety of conflicting thoughts, Susan
Hoply scarcely observed the fast approaching darkness of the night, nor did
she feel any alarm as she passed along the secluded way that was to conduct her to the place she desired to reach. Her chief thoughts were directed to the unfortunate turn that had taken place in her situation, and
which had made her a wanderer from the happy scenes of her childhood.
Yet there was one consolation still left to her, for she had still a few friends
whose confidence no evil reports could shake; and among those was William Dain, the companion of her early youth, and her chief support under
the severe afflictions which recent events had plunged her into. Miss
Welford, too, had proved that she was above the prejudices that had rendered her the mark of scorn among so many of her former acquaintances;
and there was a cheering consolation that the day would yet arrive when
she would be able to return to her native place with ample proof of her
brother's innocence, and evidence sufficient to procure the punishment of
those who had been guilty of the tragic deed that had brought suspicion
upon the unfortunate Andrew. It is true, she foresaw that all this must be
the result of much time and patient investigation; but William Dain, and
other kind friends, had promised to assist her, and there could be little
doubt, therefore, that in the end their efforts would prove successful.

With her mind thus occupied, Susan had nearly reached the end of the
lane where it joined the high road which led towards London, and at which
place she intended to await the arrival of the coach that was to convey her
to the great metropolis. But, by this time, other enemies were at hand,
whose presence she little suspected; and in the midst of her rumination,
she was startled by a noise in the hedge, and ere she could run forward to
escape the danger a couple of ruffians sprang into the lane, and with horrible denunciations, commanded her to stop. Terrified as she was, Susan
summoned firmness enough to ask why her progress had been thus im-
peded; but her enquiry was answered by a volley of oaths,—and Larkins,
seizing her by the arms, demanded her money.

"Come, come," he said, roughly, as he perceived that she hesitated,
"we have no time to waste in nonsense;—we want your money, girl, and
must have it too, or it may chance that we shall not leave this place without bloodshed."

"Villains!" she cried, "would you rob me of the trifle that I so much need to carry me to the end of my journey?"

"A trifle do you call it!" exclaimed Larkins; "you've got fifteen pounds besides your wages, and that's more than you will want to carry you to London."

"How know you I have money?" asked Susan, endeavouring to gain time so as to give a chance for the arrival of succour.

"By making a good use of our ears to be sure," replied Gomm,—"we overheard you in the churchyard when you were taking leave of your sweetheart, and so as we know all about the matter, it will save trouble, and perhaps a life, if you hand over the money without more fuss."

"Ah!" she said, "would you then take my life if I resist the demand you made?"

"Why, there ain't much doubt about that," answered Larkins; "we have taken the trouble to follow you all this evening for the sake of your money; and as we don't mean to be cheated out of it, you had best give it up without giving us reasons to make you repent your obstinacy, One blow with this bludgeon would be enough to do the business, and then the prize we seek would be sure, in spite of your being so unwilling to give it up."

"Alas! there is no alternative, and I must submit," said Susan, taking out the pocket-book and handing it to the ruffians, who eagerly snatched it from her; "It is all I have," she exclaimed, "and the only favour I ask is that you will give me a small sum that will be just sufficient to carry me to London."

"Not so much as a farthing will I give you," replied Larkins. "It's ours now, and if you want money for your journey you must beg your way up to town, as many a one has been obliged to do before you."

"Besides," exclaimed Gomm, "you may think yourself lucky to have got off with your life, for we meant to have knocked your brains out, and so, if you're wise, you'll make yourself scarce before we take second thoughts about it."

"I've a great mind to do it now," muttered Larkins, raising his bludgeon, as if preparing to strike her down. "It would prevent her raising a hue and cry after us, and we should be sure to get well paid for it by a certain party that must be nameless."

"Ah!" cried Susan, catching at these words, "you have been employed then to murder me!"

"Ask no questions and you will hear no lies," exclaimed Larkins; "we know what we are about, and it's all owing to that pretty face of your's that we haven't settled your business before."

"He says right enough there," observed Gomm, "so now I'll make a bargain with you,—give me a kiss, lass, and you shall go on your way as soon as you please."

"Unhand me, villain, or my cries shall bring those to my assistance who will not fail to punish you for the insult you have offered a defenceless woman. Release me, I say, or—"

"Psha!" interrupted Gomm, "what a fuss you're making about nothing. Give me a kiss, girl; for I'm a resolute chap, and not be foiled by a squalling woman."

Susan struggled violently to release herself from the ruffian's firm hold, but finding that her efforts were useless, she uttered a loud and piercing scream that was answered by a thousand echoes. Still, however, Gomm persisted in his determination in spite of the remonstrances of his comrade.

"Come, come, leave off this fooling," he exclaimed; "she has screamed loud enough to wake the dead ; and if we stop here much longer we shall find ourselves in a scrape that we shan't like. D'ye hear, Gomm, leave the wench alone, and let's cut while the coast is clear."

"I tell you I'll have one kiss before I go," said Gomm, resolutely, and resuming his attack more violently than ever, he would probably have succeeded, had not a tremendous blow nearly struck him to the earth ; and relinquishing his hold upon our heroine, he reeled like a drunken man towards his comrade. In a moment or two, however, he recovered himself a little, and turning round to see who his assailant was, he beheld William Dain, supporting the almost fainting girl in one arm, and with the other flourishing a stout cudgel, as if in defiance of any attack they might make upon him,

"You brace of unmanly scoundrels," he exclaimed ; "if this poor girl was not requiring my support, I would teach you what it is to insult a defenceless woman. But I may have a chance with you yet, and if you don't make yourself scarce in quick time, by the heaven that's above us, I'll so maul your hides that you shall remember this day to the very last hour of your lives."

"Humph !" muttered Larkins, "you forget that there's two to one, and that you'd have no chance against us, if we'd a mind to put you to the proof."

"I see two cowards," replied William Dain, indignantly, "and, by George, I only wish my hands were free, that I might show you how a man can fight against odds, when it's in a good cause like this."

"For my sake, dear William," cried our heroine, "do not engage yourself in a quarrel with these ruffians ;—they are robbers, and your life might be sacrificed to their fury."

"Robbers, eh !" exclaimed the young man ;—"then, I suppose, the villains were for taking your money from you?"

"They have done so."

"Why didn't you tell me that before, Susan?" he whispered ; "but never mind, it's not too late now, so if you will just sit yourself down upon this bit of a bank for a few minutes, I'll soon see whether they are going to walk off with their prize quite as easily as they expected."

Saying this, he supported her to the place he had mentioned, and then hurrying after the villains, who were beginning to move off, he seized the nearest one by the throat, and in a resolute tone, said :—

"It seems, sirrah, that you and your comrade have had the baseness to rob a poor girl of the little pittance that was to support her in the strange place she is going to. Now, I'm a resolute chap, mind you, and in a case like this can fight like a lion, so return the money this instant, or take such a punishment from my hands as your villany deserves. Come, out with it, fellow, before I let you feel the weight of this bludgeon on your shoulders."

"Why, you wouldn't murder me, would you?" muttered Larkins, struggling to release himself from the powerful grasp of his antagonist. "And you, Gomm," he continued, addressing himself to his associate in crime, "what do you stand looking on for, when your friend wants your assistance?"

"Your villanous comrade knows better than to come again within reach of a bludgeon that he has already felt the weight of," exclaimed Dain. "But come, I've no time to lose over this affair, as you know what I want, and I'll have it back, or one of us shall die in seeing who is to be master."

"Take your hand from my throat, then," cried Larkins, in a voice that was scarcely audible ;—"I'm choking, and you'll have my death to answer for."

"Will you give up the money then?"

" I will;—here it is, and may ten thousand curses light upon you for foiling us as you have !"

With this the ruffian produced the pocket-book and its contents, and handed it to William Dain, who having got secure possession of it, released his hold, exclaiming :—

" It's well for you that I was not kept in suspense much longer about this matter, and that there's a female present who I did not wish to terrify by any act of violence. Had it been otherwise, we should not have parted upon quite such easy terms, as it appears we now shall."

" I'll tell you what it is, young fellow," said Gomm ;—" you've got a little bit of a victory over us, it seems, and we've lost the booty that tempted us to follow yonder girl. But we ain't fellows to be trifled with in this sort of way, and, as we owe you something for th... ... ... pend on it it will not be long before we pay off old scor... ... ... won't like."

" You'll waylay me, I suppose ?"

' I won't say what we may do," answered Gomm ;—... ... ... stand very nice for a shade or two, and when we meet again, I'd advise you to look out, for there's something in store for you, that will prevent your ever interfering with us again."

" Why, you white-livered villain," exclaimed William, " do you mean to threaten me ?"

" It ain't our business to tell you what we mean to do," answered the ruffian ; " but I'd have you beware of us, that's all, because from this time you've got enemies to deal with that will not be very particular as to the way they make you smart for this night's work. Beware of us, I say, and tremble for the fate that will be yours."

William Dain merely smiled at this threat of the fellows he had so easily overcome, and having watched their retreating forms till they were no longer in sight, he returned to Susan, who by this time had recovered from the terror into which she had been thrown.

" Here is your money, dear Susan," he said, returning the pocket-book into her hands ; " the rascals thought to have made a good night's work of this, but thanks to my timely arrival, they have been completely foiled in their attempt to rob you of the little store that is to support you on your arrival in town. One of them, it seems, would have polluted your lips with a kiss, yet he has paid dearly for his insolence, and will remember it to the latest day of his life."

" Your arrival was indeed most fortunate," cried Susan, " and yet I heard them threaten you with their vengeance, and desperate as they are, I almost fear they will not fail to carry their evil designs into execution."

" The scoundrels know better than to do anything of the sort," answered William. " In this place they will dare not remain much longer, for upon my report of what has taken place, they will be glad to escape from the hot pursuit that will be made after them, and you may rely on it, they will leave the neighbourhood without waiting to fulfil the threat you heard them utter."

" I fear you are too sanguine on that subject," cried Susan. " At any rate we know they are desperate characters, and what will not such men do to revenge themselves after the disappointment which they have met with ?"

" But not when their own necks are in jeopardy," replied her lover. " These fellows know well enough that if once they come within the gripe of the law, they will have a poor chance of escaping with their lives. So the wisest course they can adopt will be to get off whilst they can, and afterwards keep out of danger till their time comes for the gallows."

" Have you ever seen either of them before?" asked Susan.

" Never—why do you ask the question?"

" I was merely thinking," she replied, " they might be in the employ of Mr. Gravestow. He has kept such 'company ere now, and a thought struck me whether they might be the persons who murdered poor Mr. Wentford."

" It is possible enough," replied William Dain : " the rascals looked as if they were quite capable of committing the horrible crime you speak of, and I am half sorry now that I didn't keep them in custody till they had an opportunity of explaining before a magistrate the business that brought them into this part of the country."

" Nay, it is, perhaps, better as it is," replied Susan. " At present I would have the affair remain quiet, in order that the guilty parties may imagine that all further enquiry is at an end. They will then rest in fancied security, and I shall then be the better able to pursue my object to a successful termination."

" And, depend on it, I shall not fail to lend my aid towards bringing about so desirable an end," answered William. " I shall keep a strict watch upon certain parties that I think know more about the murder than they would like to have it suspected ; and should I see anything that would afford the least clue, they may depend on it I should never give it up while there was a chance of bringing them to justice."

" But you be careful," exclaimed Susan, " not to let Mr. Gravestow suspect your intentions."

" He shall not," replied the young man. " He, of all others, must be kept most in the dark with respect to what we are doing, and as I still fancy he knows something about the murder, it will, of course, be necessary for us to be very careful in keeping our suspicions from him. But hark! I hear the coach rattling along on its way to London. Lean on my arm, Susan, and we shall reach the end of the lane just in time to meet it."

Our heroine readily accepted the offer of her lover, and, with his assist- ance, reached the destined spot just as the vehicle came up. As very little time was thus left them, they took a hasty farewell of each other, and as Susan took her seat, the coach drove off at its former rapid pace towards London.

We shall not attempt to describe the journey which passed off without requiring particular comment, and shall merely content ourselves with ob- serving that our heroine arrived safely at the coach office in town, from whence she had to find her way to Piccadilly, where her friend, Mrs. Cheerlie, was housekeeper to a family of distinction. Enquiring her way from some of the people about the place, she took her bundle from the guard, and proceeded in the direction she had pointed out ; but scarcely had she gone a hundred yards from the place when her mind became con- fused at the number of streets that met her view, and the crowds of per- sons that were passing and repassing in every direction. In the midst of all this wonder she turned down a street where there seemed to be but few people ; but she had not gone any very great distance when her arms were suddenly seized from behind, and before she could raise an alarm, a man rushed forward, seized the bundle she was carrying, and then darted away, followed by the rascal who had evidently acted as an accomplice. Stupe- fied by the rapidity with which all this had taken place, Susan could only gaze after the retreating forms of the two villains, and when they had turned down another street and were completely lost to her view, she burst

into a flood of tears at finding herself thus deprived of the little stock of clothes she had brought to town with her. As people passed by, they looked at her as if wondering what could be the matter, but no one offered to speak or render her the least assistance till a lady-like young female approached, and, in a voice of much kindness, enquired what she was crying for.

"Alas, madam!" returned Susan, "I am a stranger, just arrived in town, and, short as the time is that I have been in it, some villains have robbed me, and I find myself destitute and among strangers."

"Your's is a sad plight, indeed, my dear," replied the lady. "And have you no friends in town to whom you can apply for shelter?"

"There is one," she replied, "but I fear the place where she lives is far off, and I am afraid to ask any one to direct me to it, lest they should deceive me."

"It is likely enough they would," answered the lady; "but in what part of the town is it your friend lives?"

"In Piccadilly."

"Ah! that is indeed a long way off," cried the lady. "Unfortunately, too, it lies quite out of my way; but if you are not afraid to trust yourself with a stranger, you shall go home with me and have a lodging for the night. You will be rested by the morning, and perhaps by that time I may be able to go and assist you in finding your friend."

"Oh, madam!" exclaimed the grateful girl, "that is indeed most kind of you; for as a stranger I know not where to seek for a resting-place amidst the countless houses that surround me on every side."

"And yet," said the lady, "you should be very careful how you trust a person that you have never seen in your life before. However, you have

No. 8

been fortunate enough to meet with one who means you well, and whose motives in thus offering you an asylum are those of kindness. And now, my girl, let me ask your name?"

"Susan Hoply, ma'am."

"And where did you come from?"

"From a place called Summerfield."

"And what induced you to leave the place?"

"I wished to see my friend in town," replied Susan, who, of course, could not give a full explanation of the events that had compelled her to leave the place of her birth.

"Do you think of returning to the country, or is it your intention to seek for a situation in town?"

"I should prefer remaining in town. . . . . place that will suit me," answered Susan.

"And yet one would think," answered the lady, "you have already seen enough of its people to convince you that it is not exactly the place for young and simple country people."

During the latter part of the conversation they had walked on at a brisk pace, and just at this period they paused at a respectable little house at a short distance from the more bustling streets of the metropolis. Here she knocked, and presently the door was opened: and then, beckoning for Susan to follow, she led her up-stairs to a drawing-room that was furnished with an appearance of much neatness and comfort: a lamp was burning on the table, and a few articles of needlework were lying about. Susan knew not what to make of the situation in which she found herself, and began to regret that she had accepted the offer of a perfect stranger; but the lady evidently guessed her thoughts, and with much kindness said—

"I can readily understand that you feel somewhat perplexed at finding yourself thus under the protection of one who cannot be supposed to feel much interest in your behalf. I, however, have reason to pity those whom circumstances bring to town without a friend to look after them; and as you have received my offer in confidence, you shall not be deceived in me."

"From my very soul," cried Susan, earnestly, "I thank you for your kindness."

"It seems," said the lady, without heeding these latter words, "that my husband has not yet returned. It would, perhaps, be better that he should not know of your being in the house, and, to avoid seeing him, I would have you retire to the chamber where you are to sleep. You will take part of a bed with my little girl, and in the morning I will assist you in finding out where your friend lives."

Susan was about to return thanks for the kindness with which this offer had been made, but a slight motion enjoined her to be silent, and following her conductress to the chamber she had spoken of, she was soon left to the reflections which her singular adventure had called up. But the fatigue she had undergone rendered rest absolutely necessary, and, without undressing herself, she threw herself upon the bed beside the child, who had not been disturbed from the gentle slumber into which it had sunk. How long Susan had slept she knew not, but it seemed to her many hours when she awoke, and there was a noise in the adjoining room that she could not at first make out. At length, however, she could hear the voice of the female who had given her shelter; and presently she could plainly make out a few words by which it appeared that she was talking to her husband, who appeared to be intoxicated, and who, it seemed, she was endeavouring to pacify with gentle words of kindness. All, however, would not do, for it was evident he was growing more boisterous than ever, and in a voice hoarse with rage, he demanded what money she had in the house.

"None, George," she replied.

"No money!—I'll not believe it," he exclaimed; "this morning you had five pounds, and all that can't have been spent upon finery, I am certain."

"Not a farthing," she replied; "but there were many people to pay, and I parted with it among them, that you might be relieved from their continual annoyance."

"Then you must go to the father of your brat," exclaimed the other; "he can't refuse you, for fear of exposure; and if he should hesitate, I know a way that will soon bring him to account, if everything else should fail."

"Alas!" exclaimed his wife, "would you have me extort money by means of a threat?"

"To be sure I would," answered the man. "When people are hard up, they must not be too proud to beg; and if they can't get it by begging, they must make use of threats, or anything else that will answer their purpose. But you were always a fool, and I suppose will continue so to the end of your days."

"You did not always think so, George," answered the female, in a melancholy tone.

"Yes I did," he replied; "I always thought so, only I never spoke my mind quite so freely before. And now, because money runs short, and I've more need of it, you won't do the most trifling thing to help me."

"Name any honourable means," she exclaimed, "and I will work my fingers to the very bones to serve you."

"Work!" he cried, with a sneer, "and what occasion is there for you or I to work, when money is to be made without it? We ought to live handsomely, and so we should, if you were only of my way of thinking."

"What would you have me do, George?"

"Why, go to sleep, to be sure, if you can't guess my meaning better than that," replied the brute. "However, you seem to cross me in everything, so I shall leave you for a little while, and see how you'll like that."

"Leave me, did you say?"

"Aye, it's plain English, I believe;—I shall go out of town for a little while;—a month or two, perhaps, and in that time you'll be obliged to do something, if it was only to keep your brat from starving."

"I will do nothing unworthy of myself, George."

"That's more than I know, or care about," he replied. "It seems you won't ask for money, though you could have it for demanding, and as I have no more just now than I want, I shall go away and spend it myself."

"You will at least give me a trifle," she said; "a few pounds would be sufficient to put me into some small way of business, and by industry I might afterwards be able to maintain myself and child without ever taxing your pocket again."

"What!" he exclaimed, "do you suppose I'm going to rob myself to support you?—No, no, what I've got I shall keep, and'if you want money, you know where to apply for it. Go to him, and he'll give you some, I dare say."

"I cannot ask him for more, just yet," she cried;—"I have received all that I have any right to expect, and it would be most unjust to demand more than my allowance."

"Then tell him you'll take a sum of money down, and release him from all other liabilities."

"You know I never wish to see him again," replied the female. "You, perhaps, will name the subject to him, and if he will consent to pay me a certain sum, I will embark it in some little business, and, with Heaven's

assistance, procure a living for myself and little one. Will you do this for
me, George? It is perhaps the last, and certainly will be the greatest
favour you can bestow upon me."

"Perhaps I may," replied the other;—"anything to get rid of a woman
that's always annoying me."

"Alas!" groaned the unhappy woman, "the truth is at length spoken;
you no longer regard me with the love you once did, and would now break
my heart with your unkindness. Yet I can endure much from you,
George, and would to heaven the meekness with which I put up with your
bad treatment, would soften your heart towards one who even now cannot
regard you with any other feeling than that of love."

"Will you leave off this eternal nonsense of yours?" exclaimed the man;
"haven't I told you I want to get a little rest, and yet you keep boring me
about a parcel of things that I don't want to hear."

"Answer me the question I have asked," she replied, "and I will have
done. Will you try to get me the money, and thus provide for me and my
helpless child, without taking anything from your own pocket?"

"Aye, aye, perhaps I may trouble myself as far as that goes," replied
the man. "You begin to be an annoyance to me now, and I don't mind
putting myself a little out of the way, so that I can fairly get rid of you
altogether."

"Your unkindness kills me!" sighed the woman.

"It's a pity it hasn't done so before," exclaimed the brute. "I hate you
from my very soul, and yet you live on as if to spite me. If you're tired of
life, why don't you die, and release me from your eternal complaints?"

"Nay, George," she cried, "you surely cannot mean what you say?"

"But I do mean it, though," he replied, sullenly; "it's just what I
want, but as you don't die, why the best way is to cut the matter short,
by leaving you, as I'm going to do! So now hold your tongue, woman,
for I'm tired, and want to get a little sleep."

A dead stillness succeeded, and Susan, who was compelled to hear the
conversation, soon afterwards fell into a profound slumber, from which she
woke not till broad day-light on the following morning, when the female
who had so kindly befriended her, entered the room. It was evident
enough that the poor creature had passed the night in weeping, and that she
still felt the bitter pang which brutality had inflicted upon her heart. She,
however, put on a forced smile, and enquiring whether her guest had slept
well, told her that breakfast was quite ready, and that when they had
finished it, she would see her to the house where her friend lived, according
to the promise she had made on the night before. After the conversation
she had overheard, Susan would have refused the offer of a meal, but she
was fearful of giving offence to one whose kindness had been so seasonable,
and with many expressions of gratitude she followed her hostess into the
other room, where the breakfast was laid out with the greatest attention to
comfort and neatness. During the repast, not a word was uttered that
would have been equally painful to them both, and when the meal was concluded, Amelia,—for that was the name of her generous friend,—insisted
upon seeing her to the house of her friend. They accordingly set out, and as
Susan Hoply could afford some little clue upon the subject, they succeeded,
more easily than had been expected, in finding the place they were in search
of. On arriving at the door, Amelia took her leave of our heroine with
many expressions of kindness, and within a minute or two afterwards, Susan
was warmly greeted Mrs. Cheerlie, who, as a friend of her mother, had
undertaken to protect her at any time when circumstances might need it.
She was immediately taken to the apartment which was exclusively devoted
to the use of the worthy housekeeper, and as briefly as possible Susan

related the sad events that had driven her from a once happy home, and the determination she had formed to exert every means in her power to discover the real perpetrators of a crime with which her brother had been unjustly charged.

CHAPTER VIII.

THE RIVAL LOVERS.

Susan had not been in the house many days before she became the envy of the female domestics, and the admiration of all the men. In fact, her beauty and artlessness served to raise some little discord in the house, for her admirers grew wondrously jealous of each other if by word or look she seemed to show any preference, and those who had been tolerably good friends before, now regarded each other with distrust, as fearing to lose a prize upon which each had set his heart. Susan herself could not help seeing the great attention that was paid her, and being no coquet she took every care to let them know that her heart was already engaged. But this, instead of allaying the evil, served rather to increase it; for they thought her lover must be some country bumpkin who had no right to aspire to the possession of such a prize, and who, as a matter of course, it would be very easy to cut out and then laugh at him for his disappointment. They still saw, however, that Susan's heart was not to be taken by storm as they imagined; for though she was kind and affable towards them, it was plain enough, even to the most sanguine, that her thoughts were still turned towards home and the rival who had succeeded in gaining her affection. This occasioned no little chagrin among them, but as they thought it quite impossible she could remain faithful to her rustic lover, they were not without hope that, in the course of time, she would select a husband from among themselves. Mrs. Cheerlie could not help smiling at all this, but she kept a watchful eye over her young charge, and occasionally gave her a little advice upon an affair that, if not carefully managed, might give rise to a good deal of bickering and jealousy.

"These menfolks," she said to her one day, "have had their heads turned ever since you came into the house, and I verily believe if their stations in life had been a little higher, there would, before now, have been more than one duel fought on your account."

"And yet," replied Susan, "I am sure I have never given even the slightest encouragement to any of them."

"But when people are in love, my dear, they are not apt to see very distinctly," answered the old lady. "They each fancy that a preference is given to another, and hence arises the jealousy that has set them all by the ears."

"In that case," cried our heroine, "perhaps you would be kind enough to tell them that my heart is already engaged, and that their attentions, though flattering enough, can never divert my thoughts from him who possesses my love."

"Why, I should only get laughed at for my pains," answered Mrs. Cheerlie; "they would never believe that you can seriously love this country youth when you have an opportunity of marrying a spruce Londoner, who can introduce you to all the gaieties and follies of town. Besides, my dear, they have each vanity enough to think themselves irresistible, and, therefore, I must leave it to yourself to convince them of the mistake they have fallen into."

"What can I do more," asked Susan, "than tell them my heart is already given to another?"

"Upon my word I can hardly tell you how to act," answered the house-keeper. "The fact is, you have got into an awkward dilemma, and the best advice I can give, is to get out of it in the best way you can."

"The only way I know of is to leave the house."

"And what good would that do you?" asked Mrs. Cheerlie. "Go where you may they would follow you, and the annoyance would be even greater than it is now."

"And yet," sighed our heroine, "I have never given the slightest encouragement to any of them."

"That's true enough, my dear, but they, I dare say, think differently. Your lovers are strange kinds of animals, and I believe you must be downright rude to them before they can see how disagreeable they have been making themselves."

"At any rate," answered Susan, "I have tried what coolness will do, and I have shunned their society even at the risk of being thought proud and disdainful. That is as much as I can do, and now I must throw myself on your generosity, to extricate me from a disagreeable situation."

"In that case," observed Mrs. Cheerlie, "there is only one plan that I think will prove effectual."

"And what is it?"

"To marry your rustic lover at once, and thus put an end to the hopes of his rivals."

"Alas!" cried Susan, "that is impossible."

"Indeed! and why so?"

"Because I have vowed never to marry till I have discovered the murderers of my poor master, and thus rescue my brother's name from infamy."

"In my opinion, then," exclaimed Mrs. Cheerlie, "you have made a very rash and foolish vow. You need a protector, my dear, and in the event of your marrying this young man, I can see no reason why you should not prosecute your inquiries as well as now that you are single."

"The affair, my dear madam," answered Susan, "requires all my thought and attention, and my heart being set upon it, I can never marry till the dreadful mystery has been revealed. William Dain knows my resolution, and has consented to wait till I have fulfilled my task."

"But perhaps he may grow tired of waiting, and you will thus lose a husband who, it seems, you are strongly attached to."

"Oh, madam," cried our heroine, "you know not William, or such a thought would never have entered your head."

"You think him a paragon of perfection no doubt," answered Mrs. Cheerlie, with a smile; "nay, I am willing enough to believe that he is all that you imagine, and will give him the full credit of being a most excellent young man. Yet for all that, Susan, even a lover's patience may wear out in time, and it is by no means impossible but you may lose the man upon whom your affections are fixed."

"Indeed you wrong him," cried Susan earnestly.

"Perhaps I may," replied her friend, "but I have gained more experience in the world than you have, and I know that when lovers are separated they are very apt to forget each other after a time. This William of yours that you talk so much about may begin to think you care very little for him, and should he see a girl that takes his fancy, it is likely enough he would marry her."

"In that case," answered Susan, "I should have every reason to believe he cared little about me, and though my heart might be deeply wounded by his inconstancy, I should endure the blow without complaining."

" And in revenge, I suppose," observed Mrs. Cheerlie, " you would choose a husband from among your numerous admirers in this house?"

" Indeed, madam, you have mistaken me," replied Susan, " for if William Dain deceived me I would never again place confidence in the word of man. But why do I entertain a thought so unworthy of him whom no circumstances will ever change? He will remain faithful to me, and you, my dear madam, will own by and by that you have wronged him by such a suspicion."

" But why do you torture the young man by keeping him so long in suspense?" asked Mrs. Cheerlie. " You have told me he is in good circumstances, and is willing to make you his wife immediately, and in that case I should say your wisest course would be to get rid of your other lovers by marrying him without any more delay."

" I have explained my reason," answered Susan.

" You have," returned the housekeeper, " but the young man of course knows all the circumstances, and yet it appears they are no obstacles in the way of your marriage."

" William Dain," replied our heroine, " has hitherto borne an irreproachable character, and never will I consent to a union with him till this foul stain has been taken from my unfortunate brother's name."

" But surely people cannot seriously believe that Andrew is guilty of taking away his master's life?"

" Unhappily but too many persons give credit to the base assertion," replied our heroine. " Mr. Gravestow has directly charged him with it, and circumstances unhappily assist to support the falsehood. His absence immediately after the murder seems to prove that he is guilty of shedding the blood of his master."

" But let us hope he will return and refute the calumnies that have been uttered against him."

" Andrew will never be seen again alive," answered Susan mournfully; " he has fallen by the same hands that took the life of the unfortunate Mr. Wentford."

" Perhaps you are deceived in that respect," exclaimed Mrs. Cheerlie; " I know you place great reliance on the dream you had on the night of the murder, but for my own part I have no faith in it, and take my word for it Andrew is still alive and will appear among us again when least we expect his return."

" It is impossible," replied Susan; " for, had he been alive, nothing could have prevented his coming forward to answer the base calumnies that have been uttered against him."

" And yet there may be reasons for his absence that will be quite satisfactory when thoroughly explained," answered Mrs. Cheerlie. " You are convinced that the murder was committed by some other persons, and how do we know but they may have concealed him somewhere or other in order that his absence may throw suspicion upon him. At any rate, that is the only reason I can see for his sudden disappearance; and you may depend on it, my notion will be found to be pretty nearly correct. As for your dream, I think nothing of it, because many persons besides yourself have been deceived through placing too much reliance on them."

" So many persons would fain persuade me," replied Susan; " but since one part of my terrible vision was realized, why should I not believe the other to be equally true?"

" I shall not attempt to convince you to the contrary," answered the old lady; "but my own opinion remains just as it was,—and, therefore, as there can be no doubt of Andrew's innocence, I can see no reason why your union with this William Dain should bring any disgrace upon him."

"He argues in the same way," exclaimed Susan; "but I cannot consent to wed him under these circumstances, nor shall I return to my native village till I can do so with honour to myself."

"And what says Miss Wentford to this report?"

"She believes my brother to be guiltless."

"And yet you left her house?"

"I did so," replied Susan; "because I could both see and hear that other people were not so charitable in their opinions. Even some of them who were my best friends began to look coldly on me at least, and then I thought it better to leave the place and come to London, where I might have leisure to prosecute my enquiry."

"And there you got robbed upon your arrival, and then found shelter for the night at a perfect stranger's?"

"But that stranger," answered our heroine, "proved herself to be a most kind friend."

"Aye," exclaimed Mrs. Cheerlie, "you were lucky enough, certainly, to fall into very good hands. It was, however, a great chance, and most sincerely do I congratulate you on escaping the snares that are laid in London for the destruction of unsuspecting innocence. The woman who gave you shelter did it from motives of pure kindness, and we must seek her out in order that I may thank her for the service she was generous enough to perform."

"I would gladly take you there," replied Susan, "but, unfortunately, I have forgotten the name of the street where she lives."

"In that case we must wait till chance throws her in our way," answered the old lady, "you may meet her by accident; and, should you do so, be sure to inquire where we may call upon her. But I must now leave you, Susan, for a little while, and during the time you are alone, just think over the advice I have been giving you; either make up your mind to marry William Dain without any further delay, or accept the offer of one of the numerous lovers that are dying for you in this house."

This was said with so much good humour, that Susan could not be offended; and when her friend left the room, she sat herself down to needle-work, and indulged herself with the thoughts of her native place, and the few kind friends she had left there. Of course, William Dain was the principal subject of her reflections, and glad would she have been could she have followed the counsel given by Mrs. Cheerlie; but she had pledged herself to remain single till her inquiries had terminated successfully, and she was determined nothing should ever induce her to break the vow. Occupied in these thoughts, Susan was not aware that any one had entered the room; but, at length, a very heavy sigh startled her from the reverie into which she had fallen,—and, raising her eyes, she saw Mr. Jonathan, the footman, who was amongst the foremost of the numerous lovers. Poor Jonathan looked rather confused at first; but, on finding that she was not absolutely angry at his having intruded upon her, he ventured to approach a step or two nearer, and gave utterance to another sigh, that was was even more tremendous than the last. Susan felt vexed enough at the fellow's presence,—but, concealing it as well as she could, she said, with apparent unconcern,

"You have been sent, I suppose, with a message from Mrs. Cheerlie?"

"No," he replied, "I've not been sent by anybody; but I've come on my own account, Susan, to ask if you see anything very disagreeable about me?"

"Why, what a strange question that is to ask, Mr. Jonathan," exclaimed Susan, almost ready to laugh in his face.

"And yet it ain't so very strange neither when you come to think of it," he replied. "The thing is this, I want to know from yourself whether you can take a fancy for a chap that believes there's worse looking fellows than himself in the world?"

"Of course you are alluding to yourself?"

"To be sure I am; so, as the truth is now out, perhaps you'll have the goodness to give me an answer."

"I will, and a very short one it will be; the fact is, I have no idea of marrying just yet."

"Never mind," replied Jonathan, "I can wait a bit if that's all; a few months won't be an object; and so, if you'll only say the word, I shall be the happiest fellow alive."

"Really I'm quite bewildered, Mr. Jonathan; this is so unexpected, that I must request a little time to recover myself."

"There's no occasion to be at all nervous about it," returned the foot-man;—"these are things that happen to every one in the course of a life time, and as you know what I've come for, you've only got to say the little word 'yes,' and the affair is settled."

"But I am not prepared to give any such answer," replied Susan. "The fact is, sir, my heart was given long since to another, and I trust there will never be any reason to regret the choice I have made."

"Why, you don't mean to say that you love another?"

"Indeed but I do mean to say it."

"Then," groaned Jonathan, "I'm a lost, unhappy individual!"

"There is no occasion for you to be either lost or unhappy," replied

Susan. "There are thousands of girls in the world more worthy of your love than I am, and surely among them you may find one to your liking."

"Impossible!" exclaimed the footman, throwing himself into a theatrical attitude; "there ain't your equal in the whole world, and I must either have Susan Hoply for a wife, or pine out the remainder of my days in single wretchedness."

"I am really very sorry, Mr. Jonathan, that you should have been so unfortunate in making your selection; but you have heard me, and, therefore, I hope you will say no more upon this subject."

"Say no more?" exclaimed the footman;—"why you surely don't mean to say that I've no hope?"

"Indeed I do."

"Then tell me who it is you love, and I'll go directly and blow his brains out!"

"Upon my word," laughed Susan, "you have given me a very sufficient reason to keep his name a secret. I have told you I love him, and it is hardly likely I should mention his name to the man that has threatened to put him out of the way by violence."

"Is it any of the chaps belonging to this house?"

"Certainly not," she replied; "and now, having satisfied you so far, I hope you will not ask me any further questions upon the subject."

"How can I help it?" exclaimed the footman;—"ain't I desperately in love, and haven't you thwarted me, and made me a miserable wretch?"

"I am sorry for it, if you are made miserable on my account," replied Susan;—"it seems, however, that the fault is certainly your own, and now that you have had a plain answer, the only advice that I can give you is, to think of me no more."

"But how can I forget you?" asked Jonathan;—"ain't your lovely image always before me, and don't I dream of you every night?—and can I forget you Susan?"

"I have never given you any reason to imagine that your regard would be returned."

"Perhaps not," he replied, "but I thought it might, for all that. A man can't help falling in love, you know, and I didn't expect you was going to tell me there was some other chap in the way."

"Enough has now been said on this subject," answered Susan; "I have told you my affections are already engaged, and you should, therefore, spare both yourself and me the pain of returning to it again."

"You won't tell me then who my rival is?"

"I will not."

"Perhaps you are afraid he might get the worst of it, if you did."

"I believe there is very little to fear on that account," answered Susan, "for the person you speak of has at least a fair share of courage, and would not fail to punish any one who attempted to rob him of my affection."

"What a savage he must be!" drawled the footman.

"He is an estimable man," replied Susan, "and, therefore, you cannot offend me more than by speaking disrespectfully of him. And now, Mr. Jonathan, having said thus much, I must again request you to leave me."

"Won't you give me any hope then?"

"Not the slightest."

"Cruel girl, you have broken my heart, and if you should happen to hear of a body being picked up in the river, you may pretty well guess whose it is."

"There is very little fear of anything of that sort happening," replied Susan, "for when people intend to make away with themselves, they generally keep the secret to themselves. And even if you were foolish enough to mean such a thing, it would be no reason why I should break my word to the man I have bestowed my affections on."

" You ain't to be frightened then ?"

" Certainly not by unmeaning threats such as you have uttered," replied our heroine. " I have, however, suffered this foolery to go too far, and, therefore, you will oblige me by leaving the room."

" Hear me, Susan," exclaimed the footman, throwing himself upon his knees ;—" I'm a lost man, if you cast me off ;—my love for you ain't to be controlled, and if you are obstinate, I shall be obliged to take you off by force, and compell you to marry me whether you like it or not."

",I'll hear no more of this," cried Susan, indignantly ; " leave me instantly, or I shall seek for means to punish your insolence as it deserves."

" Hoity toity !" exclaimed Mrs. Cheerlie, who at that moment entered the room ; " why, what's all the matter now ?—Mr. Jonathan on his knees, and Susan angrily reprimanding him, as if his conduct had not been very pleasing to her."

" It's no fault of mine," replied the footman ;—" I offered the young woman fairly enough, and she won't have anything to say to me, because there's a rival in the way."

" And I suppose she has a right to love who she pleases, without asking your leave," answered Mrs. Cheerlie.

" And I suppose," retorted the footman, " that I've a right to try if I can cut him out. He's a rustic booby, it seems, and I wanted to convince her how much better it would be to marry a smart chap like myself, than a country fellow that has no more brains than a clod."

" Brains, or no brains, he's a man of her choice," replied the house-keeper, " and I must say it's like your impertinence to insult a person that is in this house under my protection."

" Do you call my love for her an insult ?"

" Yes, after you find she rejects your offer."

" But she hasn't yet heard half that I had to say."

" At any rate she seems to have heard quite enough," replied Mrs. Cheer-lie, " and, therefore, I must desire you to leave this room without saying anything more on a subject that is so disagreeable to the person you profess to admire."

" Very well," exclaimed Jonathan, resentfully ;—" I'll go, Mrs. Cheer-lie, because it's your wish ;—but I sharn't give up all hope yet, and if I can only find out who my rival is, I'll exterminate him,—that's what I will."

And with this doughty resolution, Mr. Jonathan strutted out of the room with as much pomp as if he had been one of the first lords of the land. Susan could only smile at a threat which she knew foreboded no mischief, and having explained to Mrs. Cheerlie the conversation that had taken place, she asked whether it would not be better for her to leave the house, after the rupture that had just taken place. But the old lady would not listen to this, as she had a situation for Susan in view, and a short time longer might place her in a comfortable house, where she would be safe from the annoyance she had just experienced. This made her anxious for her young friend to remain under her protection, and as she had permission to give her shelter, she easily prevailed on Susan to stop with her till the arrangements respecting her new situation were satisfactorily completed.

" As for Mr. Jonathan," she said, " I believe you have no occasion to fear any more of his love making. He has been repulsed, and, stupid as he is, I believe he has just sense enough to know that he has not the slightest chance of succeeding in his suit."

" But it seems," replied Susan, " that he is not the only one in this house who has taken it into his head to honour me with his particular regard."

"True," answered her friend, "but he will be sure to tell the others the sort of reception he has met with, and if that don't damp their courage a bit, I know not what will. They must see how little chance they have whilst a successful lover is in the way, and no doubt you will in future be spared the annoyance you complain of."

"At all events," exclaimed Susan, "there is reason to hope Mr. Jonathan will rest contented with the answer he has had, and as for his threats about William Dain, I suppose they are ——"

"As empty as his own head," cried Mrs. Cheerlie;—"the simpleton has made a greater fool himself than ever, and now that you have taken some of the conceit out of him, there is some ground for believing he may henceforth become something more like a rational being. The poor fellow looked crest-fallen enough at being found on his knees before you, and I dare say he expects to have a fine laugh raised at his exposure."

"Nothing could have been more fortunate than your arrival," cried Susan; "for I knew not how to get rid of him, and when he went down upon his knees, I began to be afraid there would be quite a scene. However, your coming into the room, threw him into no little confusion, and, that added to the lecture you gave him, may, perhaps, teach him to be wiser in future."

"By the by," exclaimed Mrs. Cheerlie, "I had almost forgotten what I came to tell you. A rough-looking fellow is down stairs who calls himself a constable, and he has been making enquiries if a person of your description lives here."

"Oh!" cried Susan, with terror, "what fresh evil is this that is about to befal me?"

"None whatever—so you need not alarm yourself," replied the housekeeper. "It seems that he succeeded in following the fellows that stole your bundle the other evening, and he has come to see you about prosecuting them."

"Did he say how he discovered where I was to be found?" asked Susan, anxiously.

"Yes," replied Mrs. Cheerlie; "it seems he succeeded in tracing you afterwards to the house of your friend who gave you a night's lodging, and from her he gathered the information that has brought him here. Your loss, however, was so trifling that it was scarcely worth all the trouble that has been taken about it."

"And will they want me to prosecute the man?" asked Susan, with alarm.

"I dare say they will," replied the housekeeper; "the thieves, it seems, are well known to the police, and this will give a fair opportunity to get them out of the country. At all events, you will be obliged to appear against them, however unwilling you may be to prosecute for the small amount of your loss."

"The constable knows, then, that I am in the house?"

"He does—in fact, there was no denying it when the question was fairly put; and, therefore, the only thing I can recommend you to do, is to keep up your courage. So come with me, and you shall see the man who was so officious in securing your property from the depredators."

As there was no alternative, Susan followed the old lady to a room down stairs, where she saw a course, vulgar-looking fellow, whose very countenance betrayed the sort of business he was engaged in. Smoothing down his hair with one hand, he gave a familiar nod of the head, and jumping up from his seat, exclaimed—

"Ah! you're the young woman as I wants, I 'spose."

"I know not," replied Susan, with hesitation. "Indeed, I hope there will be no necessity for my appearing in a court of justice against these men."

"Oh, won't there though!" exclaimed the fellow. "there'll be every 'cessity for it, I should think, for the chaps is taken, and we can't lag 'em without you."

"She don't understand your cant terms," interposed Mrs. Cheerlie, who saw our heroine's perplexity.

"Well, then, to speak classically," answered the constable, "we can't manage to send 'em over the herring pond, unless the young 'oman swears to their being the men that run off with her bundle."

"And that I cannot do," replied Susan, "for one of them held my arms behind me whilst the other snatched the bundle from me, and then they both ran away before I had an opportunity to see the faces of either of them."

"Well, but you can swear to their figures?"

"Indeed I cannot."

"Not their dress?"

"No—except that they were both of them very ragged."

"That'll do; the fellows we've got is both on 'em werry ragged. Besides, we found the bundle in their possession, and if that don't do their business for 'em, I don't know what the law is."

"Perhaps," observed Susan, "you may be able to proceed against them without me."

"Not by no manner of means," replied the fellow; "this is a case that the law can't wink at. The men must be punished, and you must prosecute. So now, perhaps, you'll have the perliteness to tell me your name, that I may go back and have the charge entered properly."

"But I repeat it is no wish of my own that any further steps are taken in this affair."

"Your name, young 'oman?"

"Susan Hoply."

"Hoply! Hoply!" repeated the fellow; "let's see, where have I heard that name lately? Oh, I remember—a reward has been offered for a young chap named Andrew Hoply, that bolted away after murdering his master."

"No! no!" cried Susan, "he is innocent!—indeed, indeed, he is innocent."

"Holloa! how do you know so much about it?" demanded the constable, with surprise.

"He is my brother," she replied.

"Oho!—then that's what makes you so afraid of going to the police-office," exclaimed the fellow. "You don't like to be known, I dare say, as the sister of a murderer."

"He is no murderer," cried the indignant girl.

"Well, I don't know whether he is or not," replied the other, with indifference. "Howsumdever, people says he did it, and a reward's been offered for him, and what's more, if he happens to come in my way, it's likely enough he'll find himself in Queer-street."

"He will never come in your way," sighed our heroine.

"And how do you know that?"

"Because those who murdered the old gentleman took the life of my brother at the same time."

"Ah!" exclaimed the fellow; "that's a very fine story to tell, but it won't do for me; I'm not to be put off the scent in that way, and as sure as eggs is eggs, we shall nab him before long. I dare say he's lurking somewhere about London, but be where he may, he'll be a cunning chap if he keeps out of my reach."

"You came here," said Susan, anxious to change the conversation, "on a very different business to that you are now speaking about. The men who robbed me you say are in custody?"

"Yes; but they wouldn't have been though, if it hadn't been for me."

"And it is absolutely necessary, I suppose, that I appear to prosecute them?"

"Why, in course you must."

"Must I go with you now?"

"Oh no, to-morrow will do for that. I only came to see what sort of a charge we could make of it, and as it's all right as ninepence, I'll toddle off, and come to-morrow morning and take you down to the p'lice-office. So good-by to you, Miss Susan Hoply, and, I say, if you should see anything of your brother, give my compliments to him, and say I should be glad to meet him. D'ye hear? Ha! ha! ha!"

And with this explosion of wit and laughter, the constable took his departure, much to the relief of those who had been compelled to endure his company.

CHAPTER IX.

AN AFFAIR OF GALLANTRY.

WE must now request the reader to accompany us to the town of Havre, in France, where, for the present, the course of our narrative takes us. At the place we have just named, resided a certain Count de Marceau, whom poverty at an earlier period of his life had compelled to join a mercantile house of high respectability, but who, at the time of which we write, had advanced considerably in years, and retiring from the more active part of the business, resided at his country chateau, a little way out of the town. The Count—for he had inherited a title from his father, though very little property—had always been notorious for his gallantry, and now that he was in the enjoyment of ease and retirement, he devoted himself almost entirely to making conquests among the females who were either ignorant of his gaieties, or careless of their characters. Age seemed to have no effect upon him, for the number of his amours increased as he advanced towards his dotage, and in these affairs he was ably assisted by Boulet, his valet, who was ever ready to aid him in the pursuit of his pleasures. But just at the time we speak of, the Count de Marceau had been rather crossed by a little coquet to whom he had been vowing all sorts of nonsense, and who, after laughing at him, had asked time to consider the proposals he had made. This was vexing enough to a man whose insufferable vanity had always taught him to expect an easy conquest, and he was fretfully thinking over the matter, when his valet abruptly entered his dressing-room.

"How now, Boulet?" he exclaimed, peevishly. "What news bring you from Madaline? Does she relent? Will she accept the offer I made her?"

"I know nothing about her," replied Boulet; "but here's a letter for you with the English post-mark, and—"

"Ah! let me have it, Boulet," exclaimed the Count, dropping the cup from which he had been indolently sipping his chocolate. "The hand-writing assures me it contains good news; it is from a friend of mine who has undertaken to send me over an Englishwoman ; she is to be young and pretty, and this le tter is to tell me when I am to expect her."

The valet busied himself in picking up the broken fragments of the cup, and the Count de Marceau eagerly ran his eye over the contents of the letter. It was evident to Boulet that his master was highly gratified with the communication, but he ventured not to say a word till he supposed the epistle had been read over three or four times. At length curiosity prevailed, and as the Count raised his eyes from the paper, he enquired whether the intelligence he had received was as good as had been expected.

"It is excellent, Boulet," replied the count ; "a girl has been found that will suit me admirably."

"Is she young ?"

"Humph !—about eighteen."

"And pretty ?"

"Of course."

"And the general description of her person suits you ?"

"I could not have made a better choice had I gone over to England myself," answered the count. "My correspondent is a man of refinement, and perfectly understands the sort of beauty that best pleases me."

"But is the girl willing to come over here on your own terms ?" inquired the valet.

"I suppose so, Boulet ; but if she should disapprove of them, it will be easy to impose upon her by a feigned marriage."

"Very true," replied the submissive valet ; "but her name ? is it very pretty and euphonious ?"

"That is the worst part of the affair," answered the count. "They call her Dolly Pratt, which to my ear sounds harsh and disagreeable."

"It's the case with most of your English names," observed Boulet ; but Dolly I suppose may be softened into Dorothea, which is very pretty."

"True ;—we'll call her Dorothea."

"And now, sir," exclaimed the valet, "may I ask the name of the gentleman who has been at all this trouble to serve you ?"

"Yes, it is Walter Gravestow."

"Ah !" exclaimed Boulet, "I have seen him two or three times when he visited Havre ; the people about here knew him pretty well, too, it seems, for he was detected cheating at cards, and from that time every one has treated him with the contempt he deserves."

"I believe there was an awkward affair of that kind," replied the count, "but I have nothing to do with that you know, and as Mr. Walter Gravestow may be useful to me in more instances than one, it is my desire that it is forgotten. A man may forget himself at times, and yet be a tolerable fellow, take him altogether."

"Very true," answered Boulet, "it is no business of mine, and, therefore, I shall be careful to say nothing to offend you. But I suppose he will bring the girl over in a short time."

"No," replied the count ; "business prevents his coming himself, but he will entrust her to the care of a gentleman who is a mutual friend of ours."

"Humph ! and the gentleman, I suppose, may be depended on ?"

"What mean you, Boulet ?"

"I say, the gentleman, I suppose, may be depended on. A young and pretty companion is a sore temptation to a man's friendship, and I was merely thinking it possible you might in this instance be deceived."

"Boulet, I desire you to hold your tongue, sir," exclaimed the count angrily ; "the honour of my friend is not to be suspected, and yet an insignificant fellow like yourself has dared to give a hint that he will deceive me."

The valet was about to offer a very humble apology for the offence he had given, but ere he could do this the door was thrown open, and Madaline entered the room with all the dignity of an empress. The count was rather startled at her unexpected appearance, but quickly recovering his usual air of easy confidence, he said—

"Ah! my dear Madaline, how kind it is of you to pay me this visit. But you are always so thoughtful and considerate, that I suppose your anxiety would not suffer you to rest till you had inquired how I am this morning."

"I came on no such errand, count," she replied haughtily.

"Indeed! you have some favour to ask me then?"

"You have again mistaken my purpose," she answered; "the truth is, you last night made me certain propositions which I required time to consider. I have done so, and—"

"Oh, my dear, but you are too late," interrupted the count; "you should have thought of all that before we parted."

"Perhaps, my lord, you will condescend to explain yourself."

"To be sure I will; the truth is I have received a letter from a friend in England, who tells me he has found a lovely creature who will exactly suit me. I was always an admirer of English women, Madaline, and, therefore, this offer is too good a one to be rejected."

"I am to understand then, that you no longer entertain the feelings you did towards me."

"You are angry, Madaline, I see," exclaimed the count, with an air of the most provoking coolness. "This rival is not exactly to your liking; but it is all your own fault, my dear, for I made you an offer last night, and you thought proper to keep me in suspense till this morning."

"You are about to leave the chateau then, to visit the native place of my rival?"

"No, she has kindly condescended to save me the trouble; she will be here shortly, accompanied by a friend, and you shall then judge whether I am not a lucky fellow to have obtained so fair a prize."

"And you intend to offer her your hand?"

"To be sure I do."

"And will she accept it, think you?"

"Of course she will. What else do you suppose has induced her to take so long a journey?"

"But you have never met," cried Madaline," and it is likely she believes you to be a young man, instead of one who has already one foot in the grave."

"Ah!" returned the count, "you speak like a woman that is vexed at her own folly. You have lost your chance, Madaline, and now are ready to burst with vexation."

"Your own vanity makes you believe so," answered the girl, with an effort to appear as composed as possible. "I care not for my rival as you are pleased to call her, and it may yet be shown that I have very little reason to dread one whom I have the power to destroy."

"Heavens! what mean you, Madaline?"

"That if ever the Englishwoman you speak of enters this house I'll stab her to the heart!"

"Psha!" cried the count, "you don't mean that, Madaline. You only say it to frighten me from my purpose."

"I warn you," she replied, "not to urge me to the deed. For months past you have promised to make me your wife, and I will hold you to your bargain."

"But you are a coquet, Madaline," he replied. "I made you the offer,

certainly, and you thought proper to put me off, till I have grown weary of
the delay."

"You ought to have known," answered the girl, "that I should not always have refused you; my heart was yours, and I will endure no rival."

"It's your own fault that you have one," replied the Count de Marceau.
"I waited patiently enough, till I supposed there was no more hope left for
me, and now you see the consequences of your own foolish delay. But you
weep, my dear Madaline, and you know I could never bear to see you in
tears."

"And yet you have caused them now!" sobbed the girl.

"Don't say it's my fault," exclaimed the count; "I have always loved
you, and will do so still if you will consent to share my heart with your
rival."

"Share it with her!" cried Madaline indignantly, "I would rather perish
than do that."

"Then how can I hope to moderate your grief?"

"By writing instantly to desire the girl to remain where she is. It will
be better for all of us that she should do so, for you know what I have
threatened; if ever she sets a foot in this house I'll find means to get rid
of her."

"You surely cannot mean to assassinate her?"

"Hear me, count!" she exclaimed vehemently; "you know not to what
fearful extremities revenge may urge a jealous woman. For months past I
have been led to believe that it was your intention to share with me your
rank and fortune; your own lips have sworn it, and I have believed your
words. And now what is the result of my expectations? I am deceived,
and my place is to be taken by a woman whom you have never yet seen!"

No. 10

"But my friend has," replied the count, with the most perfect compo-sure, "and he assures me that my Dorothea is a divine creature."

"Her beauty will not save her from my vengeance," cried Madaline.

"Aye, but her amiable qualities may," answered the count. "She is no doubt a charming creature, and when you see her, I dare say you will be excellent friends."

"I shall meet her as the enemy that has marred the fair prospects I had pictured to myself," replied Madaline. "I can regard her only as the foe that has gained a triumph over me, and heavy shall be the vengeance I take upon her for it. She shall die!"

"Bah! you speak now in the heat of passion," exclaimed the count. "A few hours will serve to change these angry feelings, and you will then confess to me that you have no intention to execute your cruel purpose."

"Do not rely upon such a belief," cried Madaline, "for what I have now uttered has been produced by a feeling that will never alter. The girl may enter your house, perhaps, but it will be to find an early grave."

As she said this, Madaline hastily quitted the room, leaving the Count de Marceau completely astounded at the vehemeut passion that had been called forth. For some few moments he was unable to give utterance to a word, but at length, turning to his valet, he said, with as much composure as if nothing had occurred to disturb him,

"Boulet, that girl absolutely adores me."

"She does," replied the person thus addressed, "but she hates her rival in somewhere about the same proportion."

"We must look closely after her when the charming Dorothea arrives," exclaimed the count;—"she threatens to slay the dear girl, but I dare say they will be good friends enough when they meet. So now help me to dress, Boulet, for we know not how soon my young Englishwoman may arrive."

And with this the Count went through the ceremonies of the toilet, which, on this occasion, were performed with more than ordinary care.

Shifting our quarters, we must take the readers to Paris, where the dili-gence had just put down a couple of travellers—a lady and a gentleman—who had come from Calais. The male traveller was middle aged, and rather shabbily dressed, but his companion was a young and very pretty woman, showily attired, and wearing a garb that was evidently far above her real station in life. Being strangers in Paris they took apartments for the night at a house which had been recommended to them by the conduc-teur, but which, though comfortable enough, did not seem to meet the ap-probation of the gentleman; his companion, however, seemed delighted with everything, for all was new to her, and who was amazed at the vast difference between the styles of living in France and England; she ran through a long list of questions which her friend answered with some little impatience.

"And so," she said, "this is Paris that I've heard so much talk of!"

"It is; are you not delighted with it?"

"Yes, I like it well enough," she replied, "but I don't think it a bit better than London."

"Ah! you have seen nothing of the place, yet," answered her companion. "We are not in the best part of the city; but, however, I shall be able to show you some of the most fashionable places of resort."

"Are you going to remain here any time?"

"I can hardly tell, yet," he replied; "but why do you ask?"

"Because, if we are going to make any stay, I should like to live where the great folks are to be seen."

"That is exactly my intention," answered her companion, "a few days may be passed agreeably enough in Paris, and when we grow tired, it will be time to think of proceeding on our journey to visit the Count de Morceau."

" But don't you think the count will be impatient at the delay?" asked the lady.

" He may," replied the other with indifference, " but, that of course, is nothing to us; Mr. Gravestow has written to him a most flattering description of your person, and I dare say the old count is anxious enough to see you."

" But I have a great inclination to be a countess," replied the female, " and perhaps he may think better of it if we delay our journey for any time."

" Well, we will only stop a few days, then," exclaimed her companion; " Paris was not our nearest road to Havre, but I thought you would like to, see a place that is so much spoken of."

" It's all very well," cried the lady, " but I don't see that it's any better than our own London."

" You can hardly judge from the place we are in," answered the other; " to-morrow I'll take you to a more gay part of it, and then you will be enchanted with it. But you must not forget the name we are to go by."

" No;—you are to be Major Smith."

" Exactly so;—and you are to be Miss Smith;—you are my daughter, and, if any questions should be asked, we are travelling on the continent for pleasure. Smith is an excellent name, for, being rather common, we shall be able to pass along without exciting any particular attention."

Miss Smith had no objection to this arrangement, and having partaken of a slight refreshment, they retired to their separate chambers to ponder over the schemes that had brought them far from their native land.

Next day, Major and Miss Smith left the place to find a lodging in some more agreeable part of Paris. At two or three places where they appeared, they were coldly received, as if the people had an idea that they were not exactly respectable; but nothing daunted by this, they proceeded to the Hotel Montgrand, where they saw a suite of chambers that suited them admirably.

" These will do," said the major, with a patronizing look towards the hostess; " I am perfectly satisfied, and will take immediate possession."

" Monsieur will excuse me, I am sure," replied the landlady, " but we are strangers to each other, and a reference to some person in Paris would ——

" Ah! you want a reference," interrupted the major—" quite right to be particular—always am so myself—great many rogues in the world, and—I think, madam, you said you require a reference?"

" I do, sir."

" Then you have only to apply to my friend, Lord Squander; he'll tell you I'm a respectable man, and of course, when you are satisfied upon that point, I and my daughter can take immediate possession of our apartments."

" I believe it will be unnecessary to make any inquiries," exclaimed the landlady, completely deceived by the high air with which the major spoke, and the reference he had given to a lord; though, had she taken the trouble, she would have found there was no such person in existence. Yet, so convinced was she of the respectability of the persons she was about to take into her house, that she even recommended them to a tailor and a *marchande de modes,* who were to supply them with the most fashionable articles of clothing upon credit. In this way they were enabled on the following morning to appear in the fashionable resorts, where the beauty of Miss Smith was the subject of general admiration.

"Can you tell me," said the Marquis de Noailles, to his friend Count Hautville, "who that lovely girl is, I have been looking at her for the last five minutes, and for the life of me, I cannot recollect ever having seen her till now."

"I was just going to ask you the same question," replied the count; "she is a beautiful creature, but the fellow that's with her, in spite of his fine clothes, is evidently nothing but a low vulgar brute."

"Never mind the man," exclaimed the marquis; "this girl claims all my attention, and by Heavens, I'll speak to her, in spite of the fellow whose arm she has taken."

At this juncture, Miss Smith dropped her handkerchief, upon which the marquis darted forward, picked it up, and returned it with the air of a man of gallantry. Miss Smith blushed, as she found herself the object of universal attention, and twitching the arm of the major, she would have urged him to leave the place had not the nobleman, with another polite bow, requested the name of the persons he had the honour of addressing.

"Smith, sir," replied the major, by no means pleased at the question that had been put to him.

"And this lady?"

"Is my daughter."

"Are you residing in Paris?" asked the marquis.

"For a short time, only," answered the major; "we are at present lodging at the Hotel Montgrand, and in a few days we proceed to Havre, where we have a friend to meet."

"I am obliged to you for your obliging answers," exclaimed the marquis, handing one of his cards, "and perhaps you will increase the obligation, by permitting me to call on you at your hotel?"

"Certainly, my lord," answered Major Smith with a profound bow;—'both my sister and myself will feel much honoured."

Then the Marquis de Noailles, as a matter of course, returned the compliment, and, kissing his hand to Miss Smith, walked off to rejoin the companions he had left.

"Upon my life, that young Englishwoman is a perfect divinity," he exclaimed with the air of a man that flatters himself he has made some progress towards a conquest; "she is very beautiful, and when I have made her mine, I shall be one of the happiest fellows in all Paris."

"But she is not yours, yet," answered Count Hautville, "and perhaps that brother of her's may take care she never shall be."

"He is a vain coxcomb, and can be managed easily enough," returned the marquis, "I observed his surprise when he read my card, and instead of thwarting, I rather expect he will do his best to further my views."

In the meantime, Major Smith had told the young lady the name and title of the illustrious nobleman who had just left them, and her vanity was gratified at the idea of having been honoured with the notice of a marquis, whose youth and good looks had made a favourable impression, and whose fortune she had no doubt was great.

"We have fallen in luck's way, that's certain," exclaimed the Major, as for about the twentieth time his eye glanced at the card; "we have been honoured with the notice of a marquis, and who knows where it will end."

"Aye, who, indeed!" responded the young lady; "and yet," she added, with a sigh, "he may never think of us again."

"Psha! he promised to call," exclaimed the major, "and, as I don't suppose his visit will be made to me, you may make up your mind to expect an offer. There's a bit of luck for you, my dear, and yet you don't seem half so delighted as I should have thought you would."

Miss Smith did not think proper to make any reply to this, and they returned in silence to the Hotel Montgrand, where they had not been any great time, before a servant came to announce that the Marquis de Noailles was below, and requested the honour of an interview. Upon this, the major desired the visitor to be shewn up, and then, either from motives of delicacy or design, he walked out of the room. As he did so, the marquis presented himself, and, apologizing for calling so soon after their introduction, he entered, with all the ease of a Frenchman, into a general conversation.

"What think you of our gay city of Paris?" he asked.

"I think it a very fine place," she replied, "but, after all, I like London better."

"Have you always lived in London."

"No, I was brought up in Summerfield, a village many miles from town."

"And, I dare say,", said the marquis, "have had as many lovers as there are days in the year?"

"I have not had above two or three," said Miss Smith, blushing, and looking prettier than ever.

"And out of the number," observed the marquis, "I suppose one has been lucky enough to gain your heart?"

"At present," she replied, "I have not seen the man upon whom I could place my affections."

"But love and marriage are not necessary companions," answered the libertine. "Many persons marry for expediency, and live as single people afterwards."

"They may do so here in France," answered Miss Smith, "but in England people marry to be faithful to each other."

"I have heard so," replied the marquis, languidly, "but I hardly thought it possible they could be so far behind us in that respect."

"Why do people marry at all then?" asked the young lady.

"Hum!—for the sake of establishment, I believe, and the fortune that generally follows such occurrences."

"And would your lordship marry from such a selfish motive as that?" she asked.

"Why, no," he replied; "I believe I should be vulgar enough to make a very true and faithful husband. But we are growing sadly prosy upon this subject, so suppose we change it for another. Have you seen any of the amusements of Paris since your arrival among us?"

"Very little," she replied.

"Then you have not been to the theatre?"

"I have not."

"Oh! what an enjoyment you have to come! Will you go this evening? Say, yes—and my carriage shall be sent here to convey you."

"What would people say, if I permitted it?"

"Say! why, nothing at all," he replied;—"it's a common thing in Paris, and no one would take the trouble to give the matter a thought."

Upon this subject the marquis grew so eloquent and pressing, that Miss Smith began to see no great harm in accepting the kind offer he had made, and at length she consented to the arrangement. The libertine was satisfied with the progress he was making, and with a few more flattering compliments, he took his departure, reiterating his promise that the carriage should be sent to the hotel at the hour of seven in the evening.

Miss Smith had not been left any long time by her new admirer before the major re-entered the room to learn what had passed during his absence.

"Well, my dear, "he exclaimed, "what luck?—has the marquis made you an offer?"

"An offer!" cried the young lady, "what, in this short time, and after an acquaintance of only a few hours?"

"It don't take long to declare oneself," observed the major, "and I'm certain he already loves you to distraction."

"But it's not the sort of love that pleases me," answered Miss Smith; "he seems to have rather insignificant notions of marriage, and perhaps he saw that our ideas on that subject are quite at variance."

"You have not dismissed him in anger, I hope?"

"Oh, no! on the contrary, we are upon very excellent terms, and he has promised to send the carriage for me to night to take me to his box at the theatre."

"Ah!" exclaimed the major, "that looks somewhat better. In fact, my dear, your fortune is made, if you will but humour the affair a little longer."

"And why should I care about the Marquis de Noailles when I come over on purpose to marry the Count de Marceau? Are we not going to Havre where he has been anxiously waiting my arrival since he received that letter from Mr. Gravestow?"

"That's true enough," replied the major; "but a marquis is a greater man than a count, and if you marry the former, you will live in Paris all the rest of your days instead of being mewed up in a place like Havre.

"But Mr. Gravestow has a purpose to serve," cried Miss Smith, "and, for my own part, I would as soon marry the count as the marquis, since I shall get a title either way."

"And why should Mr. Gravestow influence you in affairs like this?" demanded the major. "Are you not to consult your own interest, and how can your views be so well forwarded as by becoming the wife of the Marquis de Noailles?"

"But I'm not quite certain that he intends to marry me."

"Psha! dismiss such a foolish thought from your mind, girl," exclaimed the major; "is he not going to send his carriage for you, and would he do that unless he was desperately in love?"

With this the major went out of the room, and Miss Smith was left alone to ruminate at her leisure upon the probable chances that would follow her marriage, either with the marquis or the count. The former, it was pretty clear, had rather vague notions upon the subject of matrimony, and the latter, it was equally certain, was an old man, and just entering his dotage. But the principal motive that weighed with her was, that the scheme had been originated by Mr. Gravestow, of whom she was in some little fear; and, therefore, after a good deal of argument *pro* and *con*, she determined, in her own mind, that a little innocent flirting with the marquis, could do her no harm in a country of lax morals like France, and that she could marry the Count de Marceau whenever she got tired of playing the part of a coquet.

At the hour appointed the carriage of the Marquis de Noailles arrived, and Miss Smith stepped into it in all the pride of finery and nodding plumes—articles which had been procured through the scheming of the the major, and for which, of course, he had a soul above paying. Nor was the young lady herself a whit the more anxious upon the subject, for they had come to France for the purpose of carrying out a certain project, nd she saw no reason, as money was by no means plentiful with them, why they should not victimize a few of those easy fools who give credit in the hope of realizing very large and unfair profits. Be this as it may, she entered the box belonging to her noble admirer, and was soon joined by the marquis, who paid her the most flattering attention throughout the evening. In truth, Miss Smith's vanity was gratified in an extraordinary degree, for she saw many a fair one eyeing her with jealousy, and she felt perfectly well satisfied at having made a conquest of the Marquis de Noailles.

CHAPTER X.

A SINGULAR DISCOVERY.

SUSAN HOPLY had not been many days in Piccadilly before her good friend, Mrs. Cheerlie, informed her that she had heard of a situation which, under all circumstances, she thought would suit her young charge till she could find something that would be more eligible. Susan was glad of any-thing rather than live a life of idleness, and depend for support upon the kindness of her friends, and expressing her determination to accept it, if the people were respectable, she enquired of the housekeeper whether she knew anything of them.

" It must be confessed, child, I know very little about the folks I have been speaking of," answered Mrs. Cheerlie ; " but I hear the husband is a clerk in the General Post-office, and that he has lately been advanced to a much higher station than he used to hold. That, at any rate, speaks a good deal in his favour, and as they now intend to keep a female servant, I thought it exactly the thing that would suit you."

" But will they take a stranger into their house that can give no charac-ter from her former place ?"

" Oh, there's no reason to doubt that," replied Mrs. Cheerlie. " I have lived in this situation a great many years, you know, and if they want to know anything about you, I can give them every satisfaction."

" Aye !" sighed our heroine, " but what will they say when you tell them the circumstances that compelled me to leave my native village and come up to London ?"

" There will be no occasion to say anything about it," replied the house keeper ; " I know very well there is nothing against you, and so there can be no harm in omitting to speak about that affair. Besides, if they should ever find it out, a very brief explanation will serve to set all right again."

" Still they would be very apt to think I had deceived them, and the consequence would be, that I must seek another situation without a character."

" Ah, you are a timid, fearful girl, I see," exclaimed Mrs. Cheerlie ; " but never mind, look forward with confidence to the future, and I'll be bound things will turn out much better than you anticipate. Nay, the circum-stance of Mr. Wentford's death is almost forgotten, and no one ever need know that you lived in his service if you choose to keep your own council."

" But I can never cease to remember it," cried Susan, " nor shall anything ever make me forget the vow I have made to discover the murderers of the poor old gentleman. Andrew's name has been covered with obloquy, and it, therefore, becomes my duty to let the world know that he is innocent of the foul crime which has been charged against him."

" All that is very well," observed Mrs. Cheerlie, " but then you must see it has nothing whatever to do with the matter we were talking about.

Here is a situation for you to go to, and it remains with yourself to say whether you think it worthy of acceptance."

"Any home will be better than follow my present idle life," answered Susan. "I will most gladly go to it if they feel satisfied with such a fair statement as you are able to give respecting me."

"In that case, I'll lose no time about it," exclaimed Mrs. Cheerlie, "for these situations are soon filled up, and, therefore, if you like to get ready, I'll go with you to Goswell-street, where the lady lives. It will not take us very long, and I shall think the time has been well bestowed if it should be the means of giving you a comfortable service. Not but what I dare say the wages will be very low and the work tolerably hard; but then you have got to get through the world, and of course it don't do to be too particular on first starting in life."

"I am willing to undertake it under all disadvantages," replied Susan, "and will, therefore, place myself under your hands. If you think it will do, and the lady has no objections to give me a trial, I am ready to enter upon my new situation without delay."

Thus left to do her best, Mrs. Cheerlie lost no time, and in less than half an hour after this conversation, she and her young charge were on their way to the house of Mrs. Graham in Goswell-street. Fortunately, they found the mistress at home, and, as had been expected, she gave Susan fairly to understand that she had no objection to taking her into her service, but that the wages would be low, and she must undertake the entire work of the house. To this Susan offered no objection, and the business being thus far settled, it was further arranged that she was to enter upon her new duties that day week.

It is unnecessary to mention the events that passed during the intervening time, for nothing of any particular importance occurred, though Susan could see well enough that her leaving the house was anything but agreeable to the numerous male admirers who had been so eagerly striving to make themselves agreeable. At length, however, the day arrived, and with a light heart Susan Hoply set forth to enter upon her new situation.

Mr. and Mrs. Graham seemed to be nice, agreeable sort of people enough; rather plodding in their way, perhaps, but tolerably kind to their new domestic, who, it must be admitted, performed her weighty duties with so much zeal and attention that it was impossible they could be dissatisfied. After a time, however, they began to launch out into more expensive habits, for their income had been considerably increased by Mr. Graham's late rise in the Post office, and like many other persons similarly situated, they were unable to resist the temptation of showing off a bit, and most ably were they assisted in this by a lodger of theirs—a Mr. Trump, a fourth-rate actor at one of the minor theatres, but with habits of extravagance, very far beyond the means it was reasonable to suppose he possessed. Yet, somehow, Mr. Trump contrived always to have money at his command; and dinner parties were given three or four times a week, to which the Grahams were always invited. But they could not accept their invitations without having parties in return; and from being quiet, orderly sort of people, they began to dress very gaily, and have new furniture when it was not absolutely required, and to commit many other extravagancies, that even their augmented income could not meet. The consequences of this was, that after a few weeks had passed away, Mr. Graham began to find the various tradespeople disagreeably pressing in their demands for payment, and a great deal of Susan's time was occupied in opening the street-door for people that were unconsionable enough to want their money. But this was not the worst of it, for she was obliged to tell at least fifty false-hoods in a day, through telling the different applicants that neither her

master nor mistress were in the way. Then as matters grew more pressing, Mr. Graham went out at an earlier hour in the morning, and returned later in the evening, to avoid the nuisance of meeting any of his creditors, and he was obliged to find new roads to the post office, for a grumbling butcher lived in one street, an importunate baker in another; in a third lived a tailor that thought his bill had been standing long enough, and in a fourth was a bootmaker who had expressed his determination to commence legal proceedings unless his account was immediately settled; in a fifth,—but why need we particularize all the inconveniences of Mr. Graham was obliged to endure? Suffice it to say, the thoroughfares were no thoroughfares for him, and he was therefore obliged to dodge through all the little courts and turnings that are so peculiarly convenient to gentlemen in difficulties. All this was disagreeable enough, but the worst part of it was that his credit had stopped, and he was unable to cut the dash he had formerly done.

One morning on going into the room where Mr. Graham had been sitting the previous evening, Susan saw a great many scraps of paper lying about on the floor, which she supposed had been torn up and thrown there for the purpose of being burnt. She accordingly began to gather them together, and had put a good deal of it into her apron, when the handwriting on one of the pieces caught her attention, for the characters were perfectly familiar to her, she immediately knew that they were those of Mr. Cornish, the steward of the late Mr. Wentford. How a letter of his should have come into the house was quite inexplicable, but there was even his name and that of her little favourite Edwin, so that however singular the discovery might be, there could be no doubt that the letter was from the party she at first suspected. She next endeavoured to put the

No. 11

pieces together, so as to make out what he could possibly have had to write about, but most of the fragments were unfortunately lost, and she was therefore doomed to remain in ignorance till circumstances should serve to aid her in discovering the truth. A small portion of the address only remained, and as she could distinctly make out part of the word Piccadilly, she imagined that it had been sent from the steward to Mrs. Cheerlie, who was an old fellow servant of his, but how the letter should have arrived at its present destination, was a puzzle that defied all Susan's ingenuity to make out. She, however, carefully put the pieces by, with a determination to see Mrs. Cheerlie on the first opportunity she had, and to obtain from her an explanation of an affair that, though apparently trivial enough, filled her mind with suspicions that she would fain have banished.

But her own time was too much occupied with her household affairs to get leave of absence even for a few hours, and she was therefore compelled to wait with patience till a favourable opportunity arrived. At length, however, Mrs. Cheerlie called upon her one evening, and after the first few greetings were over, the old lady inquired with a good deal of anxiety whether she had received a letter from Mr. Cornish?

"I have not," replied Susan, wondering to herself what was coming next, "and indeed I was just going to make the same enquiry of you."

"Lord, child!—what made you think I had had a letter from him?" demanded the housekeeper.

"Because I found one in this house that I supposed had been directed to you," replied Susan. "It was torn to pieces though, and I thought you had perhaps dropped it one of the times when you came to see me."

"Well," exclaimed Mrs. Cheerlie, "all I can say about it is, that I have had no letter from the steward, and so, of course, if such a thing has been in this house, it was none of my bringing. But are you sure it was from Mr. Cornish, and that it was directed to me?"

"I'm quite certain it was from the steward, ma'am," answered Susan, "and as I could make out part of the word Picadilly, in the address, I thought it most likely it had been sent to you, and that it had been accidentally dropped from your pocket, when you came to see me."

"Have you got the letter?" asked Mrs. Cheerlie.

"Here are all the pieces I could find," replied Susan, taking them from her work-box, and placing them in the hands of the old lady.

The fragments were now disposed in as good order as they could be, considering the great number that had been lost, and after a careful examination of them, Mrs. Cheerlie gave it as her opinion that they formed part of a letter from Mr. Cornish, and that it had been intended for her, though how it could ever have come into the hands of any of Mr. Graham's family, was a mystery that she confessed herself unable to explain. Susan also tried to think of some way or other that it might have come into the house, but try as she would, no satisfactory explanation came of it."

"I declare I would give one of my hands to find it out," at length exclaimed Mrs. Cheerlie, "and yet how to do so, I don't know, unless we put the question point blunt to Mr. Graham, and if I did that, I don't suppose we should get a bit nearer the truth than we are now."

"A thought has just struck me," observed Susan, "that, as there are no signs of the post mark, it is likely enough it may have been sent up to town by private hands."

"Well, returned the housekeeper," and even supposing that to be the case, how are we to account for its being brought to this house, instead of to Picadilly, where it was addressed?"

"That may easily have happened," replied Susan ;—"the bearer, perhaps, knew I was living here, and left it under the idea that it would be immediately sent to you,"

"In that case how was it that you never saw the letter till it was torn up into these fragments?"

"Why, there I must acknowledge lies the principal difficulty," answered Susan. "I suppose, however, it came with other letters and papers into the hands of Mr. Graham, who has accidentally torn it up into these shreds."

"You may think all this very likely to be the case, exclaimed Mrs. Cheerlie, "but for my own part, I cannot think there's any accident about it."

"How otherwise could it have come here?" asked Susan.

"Aye," cried the housekeeper, "that is a question that I cannot answer just at present. Here, however, it is, and I shall not rest satisfied till I have found out the whole affair."

"Which can only be done by asking Mr. Graham, and he, perhaps, may not recollect anything about it," exclaimed Susan, whose wonder had been no less excited than was that of the old lady.

"But on the other hand." returned Mrs, Cheerlie, "he may happen to recollect the circumstance when I bring it to his mind, and most sincerely do I hope he may, for the affair, to say the least of it, has a very ugly appearance."

"Surely," cried our heroine, "you don't suspect him of having done anything wrong?"

"I shall not say what I think about it just now," replied the housekeeper. "One thing, however, is quite certain, a letter has been sent to me, and instead of finding its way into my hands, it somehow or other gets most unaccountably into the possession of your master."

"And have you never heard from Mr. Cornish since?" asked Susan anxiously.

"Yes," she replied; "a young neighbour of yours from Summerfield, called on me a few days since with a message from the steward, saying how much he was surprised at not having received any answer to a communication that he had lately sent. Of course I knew nothing about what he meant, and supposed his messenger had made some mistake."

"Perhaps you may hear from Mr. Cornish soon," observed Susan, "and he, I dare say, will be able to clear up the mystery. At any rate we will not judge anybody too harshly, till we have found out something that may serve as a clue to the discovery of this affair."

"And I'll warrant it will not be very long before I do that," answered Mrs. Cheerlie, "for as there is something very unaccountable about it, there's no telling what mischief may be afloat. It seems pretty certain that your little favourite Edwin is alluded to, and who knows but something may have happened to the poor boy?"

"Heaven forbid!" ejaculated Susan.

"Mind, I don't mean to say, my dear, that anything really has happened, but in cases like this, one don't know what to think."

"I'll write instantly to some of my friends at Summerfield," cried Susan, "and ask them to send me word directly whether anything has happened to Edwin."

"At present," said Mrs. Cheerlie, "I would rather you did not write. I should like to keep this business snug to ourselves at present, for I have thought of a plan, and your taking any notice might spoil it all."

"If that is the case I will take no further steps in it till we have seen each other again," said our heroine. "That the secret will be found out, I have no doubt, but I feel equally certain that Mr. Graham is not at all to blame in the affair."

To this Mrs. Cheerlie thought it prudent to make no reply, and shortly afterwards she took her departure, promising to see Susan again in the course of a few days. Upon being left to herself our heroine thought the matter over a good deal, but all her ingenuity proved vain when she endeavoured to throw light upon an affair that was involved in so much mystery. That the letter had been found in the house was quite certain, and also that it had been torn into a thousand fragments, either by accident or design, was equally evident, but whether there were any bad motives was a question that she found it utterly impossible to discover satisfactorily.

CHAPTER XI.

AN EXPLANATION OF THE FOREGOING CHAPTER.

THE day after the visit of the housekeeper to Susan, it might easily be seen that Mrs. Graham was very fidgetty and uneasy, and when her husband and Mr. Tramp returned to tea, she could hardly restrain her impatience till they had seated themselves at the table; Mr. Graham, as usual, amusing himself with a book during the meal. At length the lady burst forth by saying,—

" Do you know, my dear, Susan has been asking me about a letter that she says was directed to a friend of hers, and somehow or other found its way into this house. I cannot think what the girl means, but I was determined to ask you whether you know anything about it."

" Not I," answered her husband, cramming half a crumpet into his mouth at once, and then resuming his book.

" But the girl speaks so positively about it," continued Mrs. Graham, " and she has even shown me some of the fragments that she says she picked off the floor the other morning when she came in to light the fire."

" What are you talking about, my dear," exclaimed Mr. Graham, by whom not above half of what his wife had been saying was heard.

" I was telling you about this letter that Susan has been talking of," answered Mrs. Graham.

" Well, I know nothing about any letter."

" It seems very strange that it should have come here when it was addressed to another person, who, it seems, lives as far off as Piccadilly," observed the lady.

" Piccadilly ! who was the person it was addressed to ?"

" A Mrs. Cheerlie, I think, was the name."

At this moment the book dropped from the hand of Mr. Graham, and he sunk back upon his seat as if the hand of death was already upon him.

" Good gracious how ill you are looking !" cried Mrs. Graham, jumping up from her seat in alarm.

" A sudden faintness overpowered me," he replied ; " throw open the window, and I shall soon be better."

Mrs. Graham was going to do so, but Tramp, who was almost as much alarmed as herself, saved her the trouble, and the fresh air seemed to revive him.

" I am recovering now," said Graham ; " this hot weather made me feel ill, but it's going off, and my walk down to the office will entirely restore me."

" What shall I tell Susan when she asks me again about that letter ?" asked his wife.

" Tell her !" exclaimed Graham, his voice trembling with emotion ; " tell her I know nothing about it, and that I wonder at her insolence in asking such a question."

" Nay, the poor girl is not to blame," returned his wife, " for it's natural enough, that, under such circumstances, she should have made such an enquiry."

" Why does she trouble either you or me with such questions ?" demanded the husband. " There may have been some mistake about the letter, but am I accountable for its loss ?"

" Certainly not, my dear," replied Mrs. Graham, " but she talks of going to the post office to make enquiries, and I thought that you might be able to save her the trouble."

" There !" exclaimed Tramp, " I declare if he ain't getting as ill as ever !"

" My dear," cried Mrs. Graham, " what is the matter with you to-day ?" you are very ill."

" Psha !—a mere trifle," answered the other ;—" can't people feel a little queer now and then, but there must be all this fuss made about it ?"

" You are much worse that you are willing to acknowledge," cried Mrs. Graham. I know you are very ill, and let me persuade you to send to the office to say you will not be able to attend there to-day."

" Not for the world !" exclaimed the other ;—" I must go, or there will be a stir made about it. Besides, I feel better again now, and shall be able to go through my duties as comfortably as ever I did in my life."

" Well, you do look rather better, certainly," exclaimed Mrs. Graham, " and now, my dear, do give me some explicit answer about that letter Susan has been telling me of."

" Damnation !—haven't I said I know nothing about it."

" Dear ! dear ! how violent you are to-night," cried Mrs. Graham, ready to cry at his severity. " I have said no harm, I'm sure, and as for the poor girl ——"

" Mention her no more to me," interrupted her husband. " The girl is artful and designing, and I shouldn't wonder if she has been set on to do this by the Mrs. Cheerlie you have been speaking about. Yes, yes, there is some rascally plot going on, and I'll find it all out, too, before many hours have passed over her head."

" I see nothing to find out," cried Mrs. Graham ; " the girl has found the remains of the letter in our house, and is naturally anxious to know how it came here, instead of going to Piccadilly where it was directed."

" You are determined to vex me, madam, I see," exclaimed Graham, passionately, " so the sooner I'm off the better."

And snatching up his hat, he hurried away from the house, closely followed by Tramp, whose curiosity had been excited by the conversation he had overheard, and the visible effect had upon his friend. The subject was a difficult one to broach, and though he followed close at the heels of the clerk, it was some little time before he could muster resolution enough to say what he wanted. At last, however, with a desperate effort, he exclaimed :—

" Graham, my dear fellow, what is the cause of all this unusual agitatation ?—The] mention of that missing letter seems to have given rise to much uneasiness, and ——"

" You think I know something about it," interrupted the other fiercely ; " you have heard of dishonest clerks, I suppose, and are charitable enough to regard me as one among the number !"

" Nonsense, man," cried Tramp, " you have entirely mistaken me ; I am a random, haram scaram fellow, I know, but, believe me, I feel for your

your present distress, and would do anything in the world to afford you relief."

"I want none of your kindness, sir," answered Graham, sullenly. "You have thought proper to form a very erroneous opinion to my prejudice, and I'll thank you to leave me, that I may recover myself a little before I go into the office."

"Well, if you are angry with me, I can't help it," exclaimed the other; "but I know a friend is a great comfort to a man when he is in affliction, and I thought if you would only tell me what has been the cause of this sudden alteration, we might contrive between us to set matters right."

"There is no cause but illness," replied Graham, "and yet the worst constructions are to be put upon my conduct, because I don't choose to answer your impertinent questions. Again, sir, I desire you will leave me, and never return to this subject as long as you live."

Tramp found it would be in vain just then to urge the matter any further, and as they were now within sight of the post office, he suddenly stopped, and Graham with a hurried and disordered pace, continued his way. Conscious of guilt, he entered his office with a downcast look, and took his usual place at the table, but he had not been many moments there, before one of the attendants came to his side, and whispered to him that he was wanted immediately in the private room of the secretary. This intelligence came upon him like a thunderbolt, and again a deadly paleness overspread his countenance; there was, however, no way of excusing himself, and rising from his seat, he staggered, rather than walked, towards the room where the much dreaded interview was to take place. The secretary was busily occupied at the moment of his entrance, but looking up, he said, hastily :—

"Oh, Mr. Graham, I wanted to see you about some little irregularity that has taken place in your department."

"An irregularity, sir!" gasped the other.

"Yes, sir,—a complaint has been made to me,—but you are looking very ill, Mr. Graham ;—you had better retire, sir, and I'll speak to you on the subject another time."

"I am better now, sir," answered the clerk, who began to hope the business was not so serious as he had at first imagined. "It was nothing but a momentary faintness that overcame me, and, if you please, I will hear any complaint you may have to make."

"Another time will do for that," replied the secretary, resuming his occupation. "You may leave me now, and, perhaps, you will be here half an hour earlier to-morrow morning, and then we can enter more fully into this affair."

Relieved of half his terrors by those words, Graham left the room, and returned to his own office, under a conviction that the principal offence had not yet been discovered, or the business would have been entered into without delay. Still, however, he was agitated, and it seemed to him his fellow clerks looked at him with suspicion and distrust.

Whilst this was going on, Mrs. Cheerlie paid another visit to Susan, and great was her anger when she informed her young friend that she had written to Mr. Cornish since their last interview, and had received an answer from him announcing the startling fact that the letter which had occasioned so much inquiry, had contained a bank note of five pounds, which had been sent up by Miss Wentford for the use of Susan Hoply. This at once solved the mystery, and it was but too certain that the letter had been destroyed after the money it contained had been abstracted."

"Now, this," continued Mrs. Cheerlie, "is a very serious business, and must be looked into ; so I am going to make enquiries at the post office, and the people there will find it all out, I'll warrant you."

"But if we once make a stir about it," cried Susan, "I'm afraid it will lead to the punishment,—perhaps the death of some unfortunate creature."

"He should have thought of the consequences before he committed the robbery," replied Mrs. Cheerlie. "By the by, have you asked any one here how the letter found its way into this house?"

"I spoke to my mistress about it," replied Susan, "and she has since told me that no one knows anything about it."

"At any rate it couldn't have come here without hands."

"That is true," answered the girl, "and yet it would be cruel to suspect any one in particular, without having good reason for it."

"In my opinion, there's plenty of reason for thinking some one in this place must have had a hand in it," replied the housekeeper. "Of course, I don't say who it is, but the folks down at the post office will make a rare fuss about it, and find out who did it."

"Had we not better let it rest where it is?" asked Susan. "It is but five pounds, you know, and it's never worth while to risk the life of a fellow-creature for such a paltry sum as that."

"I am determined to have the matter set right," exclaimed Mrs. Cheerlie, "for who knows what ruin this dishonest man may bring upon some poor creature, if he is suffered to go on without punishment? So, come with me, girl, and when we see what sort of a dilemma it will get the person into, it will be time to recommend him to mercy."

Susan would have given the world to have got off this disagreeable business, but her arguments failed to make any impression; and, unwilling as she was, she put on her bonnet and shawl, after obtaing permission to get out, and set forth from Goswell-street with a heavy heart. Neither she nor Mrs. Cheerlie spoke much as they went along, for the former felt a reluctance to perform a very painful duty, and it was not till they had entered St. Martin's le Grand that they began to enter into conversation together. It was by this time dark, but, by a shadow that was thrown before them as they passed each succeeding lamp, they knew that they were being closely followed by some one, and they, therefore, hurried onwards to reach the place of their destination with as little delay as possible. Just, however, as they reached the door, the footsteps behind were quickened, and a man, laying his hand on Susan's shoulder, said :—

"Whither are you going, girl, in this hurry?"

"Going, Mr. Tramp?" cried our heroine, with surprise; "my friend has business here, and I am accompanying her, that's all."

"And do you know the consequences of what you are about to do?" he asked.

"You know, then, what has brought us here?"

"I can guess your errand," he replied; "it is about that letter which was found torn in my master's house."

"You are right, sir," answered Susan; "we have since discovered that it contained money, and my friend thinks it ought to be inquired into."

"And who do you suspect has taken it?"

"That I should not wish to answer at present," she replied.

"You suspect some one, of course?"

"I do."

"Then, for the sake of his wife and family, forbear to pursue this inquiry further," cried Tramp, earnestly. "What was the sum of money contained in the letter?"

"Five pounds."

"You shall not lose it," he exclaimed, "if you will but trust to my word. Return home without saying anything more about it, and to-morrow you shall have the money."

"I have no wish," replied Susan, "to carry this unfortunate business any further, and as for the money, I would rather sacrifice fifty times as much, than do aught that might lead Mr. Graham into trouble."

"You are a good girl, Susan," exclaimed the other, "and your kindness in this matter shall not fail to be rewarded; your master has committed a fault, but lenity in this instance, will prevent his ever doing so again."

"But if he should," observed Mrs. Cheerlie, "we should ever afterwards have to blame ourselves for having suffered him to escape, when he justly deserved punishment."

"We must not be too harsh, my dear Madam," cried Tramp, "in the opinions we form of each other. The money that was taken, I dare say, might have been required for some pressing emergency, and, no doubt, would have been replaced when he receives his quarter's salary, which will be in the course of a few days. So he may not have been so bad as we suspect, and a little tender consideration in this instance, will, I have no doubt, be the means of awaking him to a sense of the great peril he has escaped."

"Well," exclaimed Mrs. Cheerlie, "you plead so earnestly for him, that we will return without performing the errand that brought us out. I hope, however, that you will see that this poor girl is not defrauded of her money, and, on that condition, we will say nothing further about it."

"Thanks, my dear madam,—a thousand thanks."

"I want no thanks, sir," cried Mrs. Cheerlie, "for my heart tells me that we have not done our duty in suffering the escape of a man who has not hesitated to commit a robbery. However, my word has been given, and that is quite enough."

Mrs. Cheerlie and her young companion then retraced their steps towards Goswell-street; and Mr. Tramp, wild and thoughtless as he usually was, congratulated himself on having saved his erring friend from ignominy and disgrace.

But Mr. Graham was not safe even now, for danger threatened him, though all peril seemed to have passed away.

CHAPTER XII.

GRAVESTOW APPEARS AGAIN.

PRECISELY at the very moment when Mr. Graham was in the aukward situation described in the last chapter, Mr. Smithson, the confidential clerk of the late Mr. Wentworth, was busily occupied in his counting-house, poring over sundry letters and accounts, and making calculations that seemed to afford him anything but pleasure. At last, he grew fidgetty, frequently looking at his watch, and listening as if he was in momentary expectation of some one's arrival; still nobody came, and he was beginning to believe that the person would not arrive at all, when a hackney-coach was heard to stop at the door, and then the loud ringing of the house-bell announced that the expected visitor had arrived. The slamming of the street-door told plainly that he had gained admittance, and scarcely had Mr. Smithson resumed his seat—which he had left a short time before to pace up and down the room,—when the party expected, habited in his travelling suit, entered the counting-house.

"I am glad you have arrived, sir," exclaimed the old gentleman, "for the time appointed for this meeting has passed so long since, that I began to think you would not come."

"Why, I was sure to come, after the pressing message you sent down

to me at Summerfield," answered Gravestow, for it was he, "and I started off by this morning's coach, but an accident occurred to us on the road, and we were obliged to endure a delay of nearly two hours."

"Did you leave Miss Wentford well, sir?"

"I did,—you have heard, I suppose, that we are to be married this day week?"

"I heard something of the sort," replied Mr. Smithson; "but, to speak my mind freely, I was in hopes there was no truth in the report of the wedding taking place so soon."

"And why, may I ask, were you in hopes of that?"

"I have my reasons, sir," answered the clerk, "but you must excuse my explaining myself any farther at present."

"Well, Mr. Smithson, I'm in no humour to quarrel with you just at present," exclaimed Gravestow, suppressing his rising anger. "We'll let all that pass now, for I have a message for you from Miss Wentford, inviting you, as the confidential friend of her late father, to be present at our wedding."

"Miss Wentford honours me," returned Mr. Smithson, with a stiff bow, "but business of importance requires my presence in London, and, therefore, I must decline the kindness she intended to show me."

"The business can surely go on very well without you for a few days," observed Gravestow; "this is not the busiest time in the year for us, you know——and"

"If you will allow me, sir," interrupted the other, "I will, as briefly as possible, inform you of the reason I had for sending for you so abruptly to town. The truth is, Mr. Gravestow, I have come to the determination of resigning the situation I have held for so many years in this house."

No. 12

"Surely, Mr. Smithson, you cannot be serious!—What!—would you leave the firm, after so long and faithful a discharge of your highly responsible duties?"

"Such is my determination, sir."

"May I ask to know your motive?"

"It is quite unnecessary that I should go into that subject," replied Mr. Smithson; "I have made up my mind to go, and that I hope will be a sufficient answer."

"You are not satisfied with the salary you receive?"

"I have never had any cause for complaint on that score," replied the old gentleman, "for the fact is, my salary has been so liberal that I have been able to lay by sufficient to keep me in comfort for the remainder of my days."

"And being tired of an active life, you wish to pass the remainder of it in privacy and quiet."

"You may take it in that light if you please, sir," answered Mr. Smithson, "but if the truth must be spoken, an active life is the one best suited to me, and I never should have thought of leaving it, had there not been other causes for it."

"Has anything occurred to render the situation less agreeable to you than it was?"

"There has, Mr. Gravestow."

"Name it, and, if possible, the cause shall be removed."

"You are the cause of it," answered the old gentleman.

"I, the cause!" exclaimed Walter Gravestow, "explain yourself, my dear sir, I beg."

"I believe then," answered Smithson, "that on your marriage with the daughter of my late master, the whole of this business will come into your hands."

"You are right there, Smithson, but why should you leave it any the more for that?"

"Because there will not be that good feeling between us that should exist under such circumstances," answered the clerk.

"I know this business, sir, much better than you do, and should not choose to be interfered with, whilst I did my duty as I did, to the satisfaction of my poor murdered master."

"Nay, if that is all, you shall have the entire control and management of it."

"I ask for no favours, Mr. Gravestow," answered the clerk, "nor will I receive any that may be offered. You have heard my decision, and I shall abide by it."

"If money is any object, your salary shall be immediately raised from two to three hundred a-year."

"Three thousand a year would not prevail upon me against my conscience," replied Smithson, resolutely.

"Then, what the devil *do* you mean?" exclaimed Mr. Gravestow, betrayed with more warmth than he intended to exhibit.

"I did not mean to say what reason I had for withdrawing myself from the house," replied the clerk, "but since you grow impetuous, I will at once frankly own that your conduct is the sole cause of my leaving the situation.

"And what, pray, have I done, that deserves this severe rebuke from Mr. Smithson?"

"These letters from our agents abroad will best explain that," answered the clerk. "In fact, sir, they write to demand large sums of money from us, and, which sums, I happen to know, were entrusted to you by Mr. Wentford, for the purpose of being paid into the hands of his agents. It appears they have never received them, and, therefore, it is quite clear you abused the trust that was confided in you."

Walter Gravestow was completely thunderstruck at these words, for he well knew the truth of the charge that had been brought against him ; and now, it appeared, that a full and complete explanation of his villany would take place. Had it happened but a few days after his marriage with Miss Wentford, he would not have cared, for he would have had a large sum of money to discharge the demands, and thus hush up those enquiries and rumours that were sure to take place, and which might lead to revelations in other affairs, that would involve his life, and perhaps send him to meet an ignominious fate upon the scaffold. His heart sank as these reflections rushed through his mind, and he thought over a hundred ways by which he might prevent the ruin that threatened to fall upon and crush him. He knew, however, that Smithson was too honest to be bought with a bribe, and after some little consideration he determined to try the effect of a confession of his faults, and then, by throwing himself upon the mercy of the old gentleman, to obtain from him a promise of secresy. At last, mustering what resolution he could to his aid, he exclaimed :—

" The thoughtlessness and extravagance of youth, my dear sir, frequently hurries them into acts of folly—or crime, if you wishes to use a harsher term—even against their will. I have, unfortunately, been thus situated, and it must be confessed, that sums of money entrusted to my hands, for the purpose of transmitting them to the agents of Mr. Wentford, have never found their way to the channel intended. I have confessed thus much to you sir, and of course you can make what use of it you think proper. It is my intention, however, to repay every farthing of the money that has been thus misapplied, and, therefore, I do trust that you will not seek to injure me by publishing to the world a story that will for ever ruin my character."

" I have no wish to act harshly, Mr. Gravestow," answered the old gentleman, " but there are things to be considered ere I consent to keep secret an affair which involves so much danger to the daughter of my late kind benefactor. You say it will be in your power to refund this money shortly, but as that cannot be done till after your marriage with Miss Wentford, it appears that her fortune is to be sacrificed for the purpose of paying these large sums, which have been squandered away in heartless extravagance. I speak freely, and without disguise, sir ; and, therefore, I trust you will postpone your marriage till some other means have been found for liquidating the heavy demands of our agents on the continent."

" But how am I to do it ?" asked Gravestow.

" That is a question which it is no business of mine to answer," replied Mr. Smithson. " All I have to do or care about in the matter, is to prevent Miss Wentford's property falling a sacrifice to your misconduct. A little delay will serve to shake the credit of the house, and as no other alternative remains, I intend advising her to dispose of the business, which she can readily do at a very short notice.

" But that cannot be done till she is of age."

" I am aware of that, Mr. Gravestow, and also that your marriage must be put off till after that time. Nay, it is no use remonstrating, because I must either be allowed to save the young lady in my own way, or make that discovery of your evil doings that will be sure to plunge you into ruin."

" That," cried Gravestow, " must be prevented at all hazards ; you have refused to remain on condition of receiving a large addition to your salary, but what say you to taking a share in the business ?"

" I ought already to have that," exclaimed Mr. Smithson, " seeing that Mr. Wentford gave me a certain share in the business by the will he made just previous to his murder."

" But that will," cried Walter Gravestow, " strange as it may appear, has never been found."

" There has been some villany at work," said the other, " which time will, no doubt, enable us to discover. Hitherto the assassins have contrived to escape, but I am much mistaken if a very short time will not serve to bring them to the justice their crimes so loudly cry for."

" Is there any suspicion that may be likely to lead to the discovery of the perpetrators ?" asked Gravestow, eagerly.

" At present nothing is known, but we are in hopes they will not escape much longer," answered Smithson. " But we are wandering from the subject, sir ; you were saying just now that I might have a share in the business, as a reward for my past services ; a few months since such an offer would have been too tempting to be refused ; but now I would be out of the concern, lest the money I have saved after long years of toil should be swept away to aid in paying the money you have squandered away in idleness."

" You are too severe upon me, my dear sir," said Gravestow ; " that I have been in fault must be admitted, but you are a man of business, and with a little management this difficulty we have got into may be avoided. Consent to this, and you shall have a half share with me in the concern."

" Your offer is certainly a tempting one, supposing it possible that the affair with our foreign agent can be satisfactorily arranged. That, however, is quite uncertain, and therefore if I consent to this proposition of yours, it can only be on condition that all monies, whether paid or received, shall pass through my hands, and to be accounted for as often as you may think proper to name. Thus we may hope to sustain the tottering credit of our house, and a few months, I dare say, will serve to place everything once more on a fair and secure foundation."

" Let the arrangement be made in any way you please," exclaimed Gravestow, " for since my own folly has been the means of producing this state of things, I must be content to let matters take any course you may think proper to suggest. But it must be understood, mind, that not a word must be breathed about the breach of confidence that I committed in the thoughtlessness of youth !"

" You may rely on me," replied Mr. Smithson ; " the terms I have proposed no doubt seem hard to you, and perhaps my motives may appear selfish, but I have no desire to save more money than I have already got, and that which I am now about to do is for the sake of Miss Wentford, whose fortune has been so recklessly hazarded by the vicious course you have thought proper to adopt."

" But all that is passed now," exclaimed Graveston, " and madly as I may have acted, it is yet possible to make amends by pursuing a totally different career."

" Aye," observed Mr. Smithson, " if you make such a resolution as that, and rigidly adhere to it, much good may indeed be effected. The business, as you are aware, is a very thriving one, and if we only maintain our credit, there is every reason to hope we shall ere long carry it on as prosperously as ever."

" And now that you are to be a partner in the concern," observed Gravestow, " I suppose there is no longer any necessity for deferring my marriage with Miss Wentford ?"

" None whatever, after you have signed the agreement that is to admit me a partner in this business."

"Will not my word be sufficient?"

"Few men's words are sufficient where their interests are opposed," exclaimed Mr. Smithson, cautiously. "You may perhaps intend all you have promised, but there is nothing like having black and white to bind a bargain."

"Write out an agreement, then, at once, and I will sign it directly."

"Nay, it must be done in a business-like way, and by a professional man," answered the other. "Besides, even if you were to sign it as you have promised, there would be no witness to the fact; and, in consequence, I should retain in my possession nothing but a piece of useless paper."

"But the delay is of importance to me," cried Gravestow. "I have promised to return to Summerfield to-morrow night, and my absence will occasion uneasiness."

"There is nothing whatever to prevent your returning by the time you have mentioned," replied Mr. Smithson, "for the agreement may be drawn out the first thing in the morning, and after you have properly executed it, I know of nothing further that need detain you in town."

Walter Gravestow found that he had no alternative, and yielding with the best grace he could, he bade the old gentleman good night, and left the house, cursing him in his heart for the knowledge he possessed of his secret, and the use he had made of it to further his own views. It was in vain, however, to make any attempt towards extricating himself, and he hurried through the street, still meditating further mischief, and neither knowing nor caring in what direction he was pursuing his way.

When Mr. Smithson was left alone, he began to reflect on the interview that had taken place, and the consequences that had arisen out of it. He knew, however, that he had much artifice to contend against, and, as his motive was to serve the interests of Miss Wentford as much as possible, he sat down and wrote a note to his attorney, informing him of the sort of agreement he wanted drawn out, and requesting to have it ready by a certain hour in the morning, when he would be at the office with the other party concerned in it to sign it in the presence of witnesses. This done, he put on his hat and quitted the house for the purpose of leaving the note at the office of his attorney, so as to prevent the possibility of disappointment.

Burning with rage, and maddened with the thought of his own defeat, Walter Gravestow hurried through the streets without any definite object in view; he had been foiled even at the very moment when he thought himself most secure; half the business had been given to the man he would gladly have strangled, and the secret he desired to keep, was known to one, who, in the event of a quarrel between them, would be likely enough to blazon forth his vices to the world. Then he was to be a mere cipher in the concern, for all monies were to pass through Smithson's hands, and if he should ever venture to propose an alteration in this arrangement, it would be at the risk of bringing ruin upon himself. These reflections were like gall and wormwood to his soul; and having unconsciously reached the Strand, he directed his footsteps towards Waterloo-bridge, that he might cool his burning brain with the refreshing breeze that was blowing off the river. It was very dark at the time, and a heavy fog prevented even near objects being distinctly visible, but as he slowly crossed the bridge, his attention was roused by hearing the plaintive voice of a woman and her child, who were seated in one of the recesses. He was, however, in no humour to stop and inquire into the cause of the poor creature's distress; and continuing his way, he was passed by a man, who, at a single glance, he he knew to be Mr. Smithson. It was easy to guess upon what errand he was bent, for Gravestow knew that his solicitor's offices were on the other side of the bridge, and, of course, his visit to him was in connexion with the interview they had had that evening. It would have been easy to have slain him at a moment like that, when the thick fog was so favourable to such a design, and Gravestow, maddened as he was, drew his knife from his pocket, and was about to pursue his victim, when the thought struck him that Smithson would return that way, and it would be better to wait for him till then. With rage gnawing at his heart, the villain paced up and down, unmindful of the mother and her child, who were still seated in the same recess where he had first seen them. Had he listened to the sorrowful outpourings of the poor woman, he would have heard enough to convince him that she meditated suicide, but his thoughts were wrapped up in his meditated crime, and still he continued to pace up and down, feeding his vengeance with thoughts of the conversation that had not long before passed between him and the object of his meditated attack. In the course of a quarter of an hour he heard footsteps again approaching in the direction from whence he expected his victim, and stepping aside into one of the recesses, he waited till Mr. Smithson was passing slowly by, and then, raising his arm, he was about to strike his knife into the heart of his foe, when the latter, uttering a cry of horror, rushed forward with the frantic speed of a madman. It was not, however, that he was aware of the impending blow, but the female we have before mentioned had at that moment climbed upon the parapet with the intention of precipitating herself into the river. Hororstruck at this sight, Mr. Smithson had darted forward to save her from the crime she was about to commit, and thus, as we have seen, preserved his own life from the attempt of an assassin.

CHAPTER XIII.

THE REPENTANT CRIMINAL.

At the very moment of which we are writing, there was another person near the same spot, who had gone there for no other purpose than that he might terminate his life and his woes by self-destruction. This was the unfortunate Mr. Graham, whose extravagance had driven him to the commission of a robbery, the result of which would be, in all probability, a death of shame. As he left the post-office, he, as usual, directed his way towards home, but when he thought of his wife, who was thus far unconscious of the crime he had committed, he suddenly paused to reflect whether death would not be preferable to the exposure that must take place, and the consequent suffering of the heart-broken partner of his cares. Anything, he thought, would be better than to witness the tears which his own misconduct had occasioned, for though she might not hear of his dishonesty for a day or two, yet he dreaded a repetition of the questions she had put to him when they were last together, and the thought of this completely decided him in the resolution we have spoken of.

His feelings as he hurried onwards, may be much more easily imagined than described, but his thoughts were alternately fixed on the wife he was never to see again, and that eternity into whicn he was about to plunge. Then floated imaginations before his mind of the horrors that might await him in another world, for hell itself seemed to be presented to his view, and already did he imagine himself enduring those torments that await the evil-doer in another world. Yet, even this did not deter him from the rash act he meditated, for his life was forfeited by the crime he had committed, and anything was preferable to meeting his doom upon a scaffold, and leaving behind him a name inscribed among the many criminals who had forfeited their lives to the offended laws of their country. With these harrowing reflections, and scarcely knowing whither he had directed his way, he approached Waterloo-bridge, and then hastening his steps, he advanced to about the middle, where the river was deepest, and springing upon the parapet, he was about to make the last, fatal plunge, when the exclamation of Mr. Smithson—spoken of at the end of the last chapter,—startled him, and drawing back, he saw the female on the opposite side of the bridge, in the act of committing the same rash deed he had contemplated not a moment before. In an instant, all thoughts of himself were at an end, and darting across the road, he seized the hapless woman by the clothes, with such suddenness that both she and the child, which she firmly hugged to her bosom, fell back into the arms of their preserver. At that juncture, Mr. Smithson, who had raised the cry of alarm, came running towards them.

"You have saved her, sir," he exclaimed to Mr. Graham; "your promptitude has preserved both the mother and her child."

"She has indeed had a narrow escape," answered the other, "for had I been but a single instant later, it would have been impossible to prevent the plunge; and foggy as the night is, there would have been but little chance of rescuing her, had she been in the water."

"My child!—my child!" cried the woman, recovering from her stupor; "where is it?—have you saved that too, as well as its wretched, heart-broken mother?"

"It is here," cried Mr. Smithson, who had taken it in his arms;—"the poor thing is quite safe, and now, my good woman, tell me what could have induced you to commit such a crime as we have just prevented."

"Hunger, and destitution," she groaned.

"Have you no home?"

"Alas! I have not."

"Nor food?"

"Neither I nor my child have eaten anything this day,"

"Good heavens!" cried Mr. Smithson, "is it possible there can be such misery in a town like this? But be comforted, my poor creature, for you shall have both food and shelter, so take your child, for the poor thing is cold, and sadly needs the care and tenderness of its parent."

The woman eagerly took the child in her arms, and having fondly pressed it to her bosom, burst into a flood of tears.

"There, there," cried Mr. Smithson, "that will relieve you;—you will will feel better now, I dare say, so let us think of some place where you may obtain shelter for the night."

"It's too late to think of getting her a lodging now, sir," observed Mr. Graham, who by this time had so far recovered himself, that he no longer thought of commitiing suicide. "We shall find no respectable place at such an hour as this, where they will take her in, and as for remaining out of doors, that is quite out of the question."

"What is to be done?" exclaimed Mr. Smithson;—"I have no room in my house to offer her, even if I had,—as a single man, though not a very young one,—the world might judge me ill-naturedly."

"She shall go home with me, sir," said Graham, for by this time he had made up his mind to return, and meet the consequences, be what they might. My wife will pity the misfortunes of one of her own sex, and she and her child shall find shelter there, till something better can be done for them."

"Do you live far from here?" asked Smithson.

"In Goswell Street."

"That's a long way, indeed," observed the old gentleman. "But your

offer is a very kind one, and I dare say this poor creature will most gratefully accept it. She must ride there, of course, and if you have no objection, I will accompany you."

Graham felt that he could not object to this suggestion, and leaving the
woman in the care of the old gentleman, he hurried off to engage a coach,
and in a little while afterwards, returned with a vehicle, into which they
lifted the poor woman and her child, and then seating themselves with her,
they were driven off at a sharp pace in the direction of Graham's house; on
arriving at which place, they were met at the door by Mrs. Graham, Mr.
Tramp, and Susan, all of whom were delighted to see the master of the
house return, for his long absence from home, had filled them all with
alarm, lest he had been taken ill, or met with some serious accident. He,
however, made the best excuse he could, and quickly changed the subject,
by briefly explaining the circumstances that had taken place off Waterloo
Bridge; this done, he desired that food should be placed before the famish-
ing woman, but of which, both she and the child partook sparingly for the
present.

"And now, Graham," said his wife, "do tell me what took you from
your office to Waterloo Bridge, when your way homewards lay in a contrary direction?"

"I felt ill," he replied, with some hesitation; "you know I was so
when I left home, and thought the cool air from the river might serve to
revive me."

"It's very late," observed Tramp, looking inquisitively towards him,
"but I suppose there was a good deal of business to do there to-night?"

"There was," replied Graham.

"It seems by what has just passed," said Mr. Smithson, "that you hold
a situation in the post office?"

"I did,—that is to say I *do* sir," stammered the other.

"Perhaps, then," returned the old gentleman, "you may be able to give us
some information respecting rather a singular circumstance that has just
happened there? But I'll not trouble you to-night, by the by, for it's
rather too late to enter into what may turn out to be a very lengthy subject
To-morrow, however, I shall take the liberty of calling to make arrangements
for the future well-doing of this unfortunate woman and her child, and then,
perhaps, I may speak to you further on the affair I was just mentioning.

"Pardon me, sir," interposed Mrs. Graham, "but my husband is out
all day, and till a late hour at night, and as you will want to see him,
perhaps you had better make it about this time before you come."

"I am not sure that I shall be out at all to-morrow," answered Graham,
gloomily. "I have felt very ill, and shall very likely send a note to excuse
my absence."

"I shall take my chance about seeing you when I call," said Mr.
Smithson, "so good bye to you all, and let the poor woman have, at my
expense, any comfort you may think she requires."

Mr. Smithson now bustled away, for it was seldom he kept such late
hours as the present, and as the night air blew rather keenly, he was glad
to get warmth by trotting along at a good smart pace. When he was gone,
Susan lighted the woman and her child to the room up stairs, where they
were to sleep, and no sooner were they there, than our heroine, breaking
through the silence she had hitherto observed, said:—

"You don't seem to remember me, ma'am, quite as well as I do you.
But we have met before, and that too, not very long since."

"Ah!" cried the other, "I recollect now—you are the girl I took home
one night after she had been robbed by some London thieves?"

"I am, indeed, ma'am," answered Susan, "and very grateful I have felt

ever since, for the kindness you showed me that night I was a stranger in this great town, and what I should have done I know not, unless you had taken pity on me."

"I thought it strange," said Amelia, "that I never saw anything of you afterwards."

"Ah!" replied Susan Hoply, "I dare say you thought me a very ungrateful girl for not calling upon you to say how I was getting on in the world; but the truth is, I quite forgot the name of the street where you lived, and though I spent several hours at different times to find you out, yet I was at length obliged to give up my object in despair."

"And who are these people that have been kind enough to open their door to a poor outcast?"

"Their name is Graham, and my master holds a situation in the General Post-office."

"In that case they are little likely to have it in their power to support me and my child, till I can obtain means to do something to keep us from starvation."

"The fact is," replied Susan, "they have been living rather extravagantly, and I am afraid their means are not quite so good as they were a short time ago. At any rate, an affair has just occurred that may lead to a great deal of trouble and uneasiness. But I'll not stand talking here any longer now, for I'm sure both you and the child must need rest; so good night, and may your mind be more at rest when we meet again to-morrow."

With this Susan left the room, and retired to her own chamber, where she thought over the various events of the day, and bitterly did she regret having said anything about the torn letter that she had found, for she saw plainly enough, that it was likely to get her master into trouble, and though

No. 13

she would fain have persuaded herself to the contrary, yet did she feel quite confident that her master, and no one else, was the person that had kept back the letter and stolen the money out of it. His agitation when he left the house, and the anxiety of Mr. Tramp, who had taken the trouble to follow her and Mr. Cherelie down to the post-office, and the few words that then passed between them, all served to confirm more and more the suspicion she had formed. At length, however, fatigue overpowered her, and she sank into a slumber, but it was only to dream of those events that had afflicted her waking moments.

But if Susan was uneasy at these reflections, how much more so was Mr. Graham, who, on retiring to bed, had ample time to think over the peril in which he had involved himself. He felt that it would be impossible to keep the secret any time, and the chances were, that the next morning he would be torn away from his home to become the inmate of a felon's gaol, the exterior of which he would never see again, till the fatal moment when they brought him out to undergo the last and most dreadful penalty of his crime. Not even for so much as a single moment could he obtain the respite of sleep, for his mind was racked with a thousand torments, and it seemed as if an inward fire was consuming his brain. Tortured and afflicted as he was in mind, how bitterly did he regret that he had not thrown himself from the bridge as he had intended, as in that case, his miseries would long ere now have been brought to a termination. Yet such an alternative still remained, and rather than endure such another day or night of wretchedness, he resolved on the following morning to carry into execution the design which had been so unexpectedly interrupted. At length day dawned upon him, and great was his mental agony when he reflected that ere the sun had again finished its diurnal course he would, in all probability, be an inmate of Newgate. At length, however, exhausted nature yielded to fatigue, and he sank into a disturbed sleep, on awaking from which, he found that his wife had risen and, judging from the sounds below stairs, that all the persons in the house had left their beds. Ill as he felt, he could no longer rest in his bed, and hastily dressing himself, he went down stairs, where he ascertained from his wife that Mr. Tramp had good-naturedly gone to the office, to say that he was ill, and would not be able to attend that day. With some difficulty, she prevailed on him to take a cup of strong tea, but all her efforts proved unavailing towards obtaining from him an acknowledgment that he had anything pressing upon his mind. He was less communicative than usual, and occasionally answered her with so much ill nature, that she at length rose from her seat, and bursting into tears left the room.

Two or three hours after this, Mrs. Smithson arrived according to his promise, but his proposal to take Amelia and her child away to another lodging was met by Mrs. Graham with a most decided and determined negative.

"The poor creature is not yet up," she said, "for I thought both she and the child would be all the better for a good long rest, and I have sent Susan up to them with a breakfast, and the woman, poor thing! is so grateful that I would not have her removed just yet on any account."

"It shall be just as you and your husband please, my dear madam," answered the old gentleman, "only you must allow me to say, that all charges for that maintenance will come out of my pocket. Nay, it would be useless to say anything in opposition to my plan, for I am an old man and a bachelor, and have been too long used to have my own way, to be thwarted in it just now. So you will have the kindness to keep an account of all expenses, and when I have arranged some plan by which the poor woman may obtain a decent living, I will fetch her away and pay whatever expenses you have incurred in her behalf. And now, Mr. Graham, I would speak a few words in private with you if it is not inconvenient."

Graham was startled at these words, for how mere a trifle will agitate the soul of a guilty man! But recollecting himself, he rose hastily from his seat, and led the way into another room where they could be to themselves.

"I hinted last night," began the old gentleman, "that there was a singular circumstance connected with the post-office, upon which I wished to consult you. But, in the first place, let all that passes between us be strictly kept as a secret, for it is to be feared that the life of a fellow-creature may be at stake, and a word spoken in thoughtlessness would bring the person I have spoken of to an ignominious end."

"Of whom speak you, sir?" cried Mr. Graham in a voice trembling with emotion.

"It is likely enough you may not know anything of the guilty man I speak of," resumed Mr. Smithson, "but you may assist me with your counsel and advice under the very awkward circumstances I am placed in. The affair is this:—An acquaintance of mine, living at Summerfield, has just written to me, to say that he sent up a letter through the post-office, a few days since, and which letter—containing a five pound note—has never been received by the person to whom it was addressed. Under these circumstances he asks me to go to the principal office in order to make such inquiries as may bring to justice the party who has been guilty of the robbery."

"It would soon be discovered were you to do that," cried Graham, with great emotion.

"I am aware of it, sir," answered the old gentleman, "and knowing the consequences of such a discovery, I have thought it would be better to see if we can get the money restored without entering into any enquiry, the consequences of which I so much dread. I am aware that many thoughtless and inexperienced young men are too frequently placed in situations of great temptation, and that if they err, the law is not slow in bringing them to a terrible punishment. I, therefore, put it to your own feelings, and request your advice as to the best means I can adopt to recover the money that has been stolen, and yet, at the same time to save the unhappy culprit from the consequences of his indiscretion."

Mr. Smithson's eye, at this moment fell upon the countenance of the man he was addressing, and so fearful was the expression he beheld there, that he stood for a moment or two, as if he had been suddenly changed to a statue. He felt convinced that he was in the presence of the guilty man, and the thought rendered him completely tongue-tied. At length, he stammered out something without exactly knowing what, and was proceeding with a great deal of confusion, when a loud knocking was heard at the street-door, the effect of which was still perceptible with Mr. Graham, who, starting violently, made a sudden rush towards the window, and was only prevented throwing himself out by the resolution with which the other held him.

"You are ill and nervous, sir," he said, "and the merest trifle seems to take an effect on you. But you must calm yourself, for the person that knocked, whoever it was, is gone away again, and we may now resume this business. I have told you I believe the chief incidents connected with the affair, and from the agitation it has caused, I begin to fear that the culprit is some friend or relative of your own."

"It is in vain to conceal the truth any longer," cried Graham wildly; "I have heard all you had to say, sir, and now do I freely confess that I am the man that took the money from the letter you have been speaking about. ,Extravagance in my mode of living, rendered my means insufficient, and in a moment of desperation, I opened the first letter, which there was reason to suppose contained money. To my disappointment, I found only five pounds there, but it was too late to retrieve my crime—the deed was done, and my life forfeited in the event of a discovery taking place. From that time I have passed an interval of agony that none can know but those who have committed crime, and now, sir, I am ready to yield myself up, rather than any longer endure the tortures that have lately afflicted me."

" Nay," exclaimed Mr. Smithson, " I can see how bitterly you regret the step you have taken, and pitying you as I do from the very bottom of my heart, I will see whether something may not be done to save you from the fearful consequences. Whose money was it that you took ?"

" Susan Hoply's, our servant maid."

" And of course she is aware of her loss ?"

" She is," answered Graham, " and as the letter, partially torn up, was found in this house, she must, of course, suspect me as being the perpetrator."

ɼ " At any rate, she has no wish to get you into trouble about it, or she would have gone before now to make enquiries at the post-office. Be that as it may, however, I will see the girl, and find means to prevent any danger from that quarter."

" This generous interest in my behalf," cried Mr. Graham, " calls for my warmest gratitude. Yet, I fear sir, your zeal in my cause will be thrown away, for even if I should escape detection about this affair of the letter, yet am I so much involved in debt, that my arrest must speedily take place, and the natural consequences will be the loss of my situation."

" If I may ask the question without appearing to be impertinent, what is the amount of your debts ?"

" Rather under a hundred and fifty pounds."

" Humph ; that is not much, either ;" cried Mr. Smithson, " supposing I lent you the money, would it be in your power to allow me a portion out of your salary ?"

" It could be easily done," replied Graham, " for were I once out of this difficulty, nothing should ever induce me to follow the habit of extravagance again."

" Well," exclaimed the old gentleman, " I have taken a warm interest in your behalf, and I will not suffer you and your wife to suffer for so paltry a sum as a hundred and fifty pounds. I will advance it to you, sir, without delay, and may it have all the good effect I anticipate ; and now, with respect to this servant of yours—I should like to see her, that I may see whether she is likely to mention the subject of the letter, and the money it contained."

Mr. Graham left the room, and in a short time afterwards, Susan Hoply made her appearance.

" You are a servant in this house, I believe ?" said the old gentleman.

" I am, sir."

" Do you know a Mrs. Cheerlie, who lives as housekeeper somewhere in Piccadilly ?"

" Yes, sir."

" And what is that story I have heard about a letter being sent to her from the country, but which never came to hand ?"

" I don't know anything at all about that," replied Susan, who began to fear lest she should say too much.

" Come, come," said Mr. Smithson, with pretended severity, " I shall expect you to answer my questions in a plain, straightforward manner. A letter containing five pounds, intended for yourself, was put into the post-office in some country place or other, but it has never been received by the person to whom it was addressed ?"

"I know nothing at all about it, sir," she replied, though trembling very much at the falsehood she was telling.

"You are not aware, then, that you ought to have received five pounds, which some dishonest persons or other has robbed you of ?"

"I am not," she replied, recovering herself a little; "and even if I did know of such a thing, I should not mention the loss of a paltry five pounds, when I know that the person who took it would lose his life."

"You are a good, faithful girl, at any rate," exclaimed the old gentle-man, "and you shall hereafter be rewarded for your pains. My name is Smithson, and I am a clerk in a mercantile house in London."

"Oh!" cried Susan, with surprise, "you don't come from any of the people in the post-office, then ?"

"I do not," he replied; "but I know your motive for answering me just now with so much caution, and can esteem the person who would re-turn good for evil. You have been wronged of a sum of money, girl; but say nothing about it to any one, and you shall not find yourself poorer at the year's end."

"You may depend upon me, sir."

"I believe I may," answered Mr. Smithson; "but how about the other person that is in this secret ?—I mean Mrs. Cheerlie."

"I must let her know the whole truth of it," exclaimed Susan, "and then I am certain she will be as cautious as myself."

"But she seems to have taken an active part towards discovering the person who took the money from the letter."

"That was in her anxiety to save me from the loss," replied Susan; "she is, however, a kind, considerate woman, and I am sure would rather do anything than bring my master into trouble."

"Well, I'll take your word for it," exclaimed Mr. Smithson; "so now you may leave me, Susan, for I would speak a few words to Mr. Graham before I go."

Susan dropped her very best curtsey, and left the room a much happier girl than she had entered it. She had scarcely gone, when Graham re-appeared before his benefactor.

"You have saved me, sir," he said, with emotion, "from the very lowest depths of despair. An hour ago I feared that all was irrecoverably lost, and now a gleam of sunshine appears that bids me hope the best."

"Say no more about it, my dear sir," exclaimed the old gentleman; "the thoughtlessness of youth has, I trust, been sufficiently punished by the remorse you have felt, and I dare say the future will prove that my confidence in you has not been misplaced. I have spoken to Susan as I promised, and the faithful girl has given me her word never to allude to the subject again."

"I am aware of it all," returned the other. "In fact, I could not re-strain my inclination to listen, and her generous consideration in behalf of the man that has injured her has won my admiration and gratitude. Yet oh, my dear sir, how despicable do I appear in my own sight, now that I know my life has been preserved, when so many have perished miserably, whose crimes were not greater than my own."

"We'll not speak any further about that at present," exclaimed Mr. Smithson. "Things seem to be in a very fair train to be satisfactorily arranged, and we'll talk the subject over the next time I come to see the poor creature that we were so fortunate as to save from the crime of self-destruction."

"I know not how to tell you, sir," cried Graham, "but your conduct to me has been so kind, that there ought to be no secret kept from you. In short, your presence on Waterloo Bridge, last night, was the means of saving another life besides the unfortunate woman and her child."

"Ha! I understand. You went there to seek in death a deliverance from your present miseries?"

"I did, indeed, sir," answered Graham, with a trembling voice. "I saw before me every certainty of my crime being discovered, and knowing, as I did, the consequences to myself, I resolved to end an existence that could not be prolonged with honour. Another moment, and I should have been struggling in the water, had it not been for hearing your voice as the woman sprung upon the parapet of the bridge."

"It was, indeed, a providential circumstance that led me that way," exclaimed Mr. Smithson, and shaking hands with Graham, he hurried away. But the good old man little imagined the narrow escape he had himself had from the knife which Gravestow had raised for his destruction!

CHAPTER XIV.

MATRIMONIAL DIFFERENCES.

It was unfortunate for Miss Wentford that she could never see the baseness of Gravestow's character, as almost everybody else did. That he was somewhat severe and morose in temper she could not help acknowledging, but then she thought he might have had vexations to encounter, and that when matters went on more smoothly he would be a very different man to what he had appeared before. Urged by his repeated solicitations, she consented to their marriage taking place some time previous to her coming of age, but this she did not do till he had promised he would not oppose her intention of bestowing upon Edwin the sum of five thousand pounds as soon as she could legally put her hand to a paper to that effect. In truth, the conduct of Gravestow seemed to be so fair and upright, that she placed the fullest reliance on his honour, and at the appointed time plighted her troth to him at the altar.

By the time, however, that she had been his wife a couple of weeks, she began to see a marked alteration in his conduct towards her. He grew sullen, and found faults where none in reality existed; yet she endured this with resignation, and waited patiently till she came of age, when she naturally enough expected he would keep the promise he had given with respect to securing the future independence of Edwin. But from many hints that had escaped her, he seemed to guess the thoughts that occupied her mind, and resolving to undeceive her, now that she could no longer help herself, he enquired of her one day whether she intended to keep the youth idling about the place all his life time.

"I have been thinking, Walter," she replied, "that we ought now to do for him as we always intended. He is now nearly sixteen, and after settling upon him the sum of money I mentioned to you before, he will be able to make choice of a profession, and thus establish himself for life."

"And do you really believe, madam," exclaimed Gravestow, "that I am going to give five thousand pounds away to this boy?"

"Why, surely," cried his wife, with indignant surprise, "you will not break a promise you solemnly made?"

"Psha!—what care I for promises?" responded the villain. "You annoyed me a good deal upon the subject, and I was glad to give any answer, in order to get rid of your importunities."

"Are you serious," cried Mrs. Gravestow, "or is this only said to try my patience ?"

"I was never more serious in my life," answered her husband, with cold indifference.

"Nay, Walter, that I am sure you cannot be," she cried. "You know it was my father's intention to provide for him, and it is only through the will having been lost in some unaccountable manner that Edwin is now thrown upon our own sense of justice."

"I know nothing about justice, or any of that sort of flummery," answered her brutal husband. "The boy, as you know, was never any very great favourite of mine, and it's hardly likely I should fool away five thousand pounds by giving it to him."

"But he has ever been a favourite of mine, Walter, and surely if you love me, you will not hesitate to perform a promise in which I placed every reliance."

"Don't talk to me, madam, of any such nonsense as love," exclaimed Gravestow, fiercely. "I married you for your fortune, and now that I have got it, the mask of hypocrisy may safely be thrown off."

"Alas !—you acknowledge then that you love me not ?"

"I have no inclination," he replied, "to talk on such a subject as this just now; but once for all, madam, let me tell you that your own future welfare will entirely depend on the conduct you may think proper to pursue. Submit yourself quietly, as a good wife ought to do, and I may perhaps suffer you to remain beneath the same roof with me, but if I see you in tears, or have to endure any of your reproaches, I shall take means to bring the affair to a speedy close."

"Merciful Heaven !" cried the agonized wife, "why am I to endure this cruelty and oppression ?"

"Oh, you are going to reproach me, are you ?"

"Would there was no cause for it !" exclaimed Mrs. Gravestow, mournfully. "Have I not heard from your own lips, that I am no longer loved, and yet you would have me endure all this without complaining."

"You commenced these words yourself, madam, by that ridiculous proposal of yours, to give a large sum of money to a boy that has no claim upon me."

"He has a claim," answered Mrs. Gravestow, "that any honourable man would be prompt to acknowledge."

"Humph !—I am dishonourable, am I ?"

"At least you are unjust," she replied, "for you know as well as I do, that it was my father's intention to provide for the boy to the full amount I have mentioned. Nay, his will even made to that effect, but it has been taken away, or destroyed by the villains that murdered him."

"I have told you before, madam," he exclaimed, "never to mention in my presence the murder of your father. The thought of that dreadful night always fills me with horror, and yet you seem to take a pleasure in racking my soul by recurring to it on every occasion that you can."

"Alas !" she sighed, "how can I ever forget a deed that robbed me of a kind and indulgent parent."

"The old man's time was come," exclaimed Gravestow, "and it was as fit that he should die as anybody else. Besides, all your wailings and lamentations, will never bring him back, so the best way will be for you to forget it as soon as you can."

"I would try to do so," answered his wife, "if your conduct is such that I can love you as well as I did him. But when you tell me that I have no place in your heart, it makes me more bitterly lament the dreadful act that took from me my unfortunate father."

"Will you never cease to annoy me me on this subject?"

F "At present I will say no more about it," she replied, with an effort at submission. "I will remain silent, though my heart burst with its agony, and the only favour I ask in return is, that you will give Edwin the sum of money I have just now named."

"I will give him nothing but my curses!" exclaimed Walter Gravestow, fiercely.

"And why should you curse one who never injured you?"

"Because I suppose you will never cease to annoy me about him," he replied. "The youth is nothing to me, I tell you, and even if he was, I should not be the more likely to do anything for it, through being bored to death by a foolish woman."

"You are cruel, Walter, to speak thus harshly."

"And you are vexing, madam," he exclaimed in reply. "But now, as this is the last time I expect to be worried on the subject, you may tell me what sort of business you would have him put to. I may do something for him in that way, perhaps, but no further."

"Business!" she exclaimed, with surprise; "surely you will not insist upon his following a mechanical pursuit after the education he has received through my father's bounty?"

"I have not yet made up my mind what trade will suit him best," answered Gravestow; "but you, I suppose, have thought a good deal over the affair, and, therefore, I will hear what you have to say about it. There are many excellent trades that I am sure will be good enough for him, and when it has been decided what it is to be, I'll pay the premium to his master, on condition that I am not to be troubled any more with him."

"Nay," cried Mrs. Gravestow, "I am sure he will never consent to such a proposition."

"Then he must starve for an upstart, unfriended beggar, as he is," exclaimed Walter, eagerly. "However, madam, you, perhaps, have thought of something or other, and if it should come any where within the bounds of reason and moderation, I may very likely yield to your suggestion."

"I have heard him speak of the army as a profession that he should much like to follow."

"Indeed!—as a private, of course?"

"Walter, this is cruel of you!" cried Mrs. Gravestow, with evident pain and vexation. "The boy has been well brought up, and a commission would not cost you very much."

"If he never obtains a commission in the service till I buy it for him, he'll have to wait a very long time," exclaimed Walter Gravestow. "A commission in the army, indeed!—pooh! the idea is ridiculous!"

"I only ask for an ensigncy."

"An ensigncy!"—muttered Gravestow;—"you had better behalf make a butcher's apprentice of him."

"This is unkind!—nay, most brutal!"

"It must be confessed you are not very complimentary in your language," answered the ruffian, in a tone of the most provoking indifference. "I can, however, afford to hear all this, for you are no doubt angry with yourself for being such a fool as to fall into my power, and now, like a caged bird, you would beat yourself against the wires that confine you."

"I have sufficient cause to regret that I heeded not the cautions of those friends who saw better than I did the real characrer of the man who now acts the tyrant over me," replied Mrs. Gravestow. "It is now, however,

too late to repair the fatal step I have taken, and, therefore, I must e'en submit myself with resignation to a most unhappy destiny."

"Come, there's some wisdom in that," exclaimed her husband; "and I suppose you will make a beginning by no longer making your unreasonable requests about the youth you take so great an interest in."

"Upon all subjects but that one," she replied, "I will prove my submission. But Edwin has been so long brought up beneath the same roof with me, that I never can cease to importune in his behalf till you have acceded to my request."

"Then I'm afraid you will be taking a great deal of useless pains," he replied, sarcastically.

"Nay, you may not always be as obdurate as you are at the present moment."

"Do not flatter yourself with such a hope as that," exclaimed Walter Gravestow. "I know my own power, madam, and your dependence on me, and the certainty of that will always prevent me from weakly yielding to the tears and entreaties of a woman that I never really loved."

"Then are you most foully foresworn!" cried Mrs. Gravestow.

"Aye, aye, I told you so in our courting days," he replied, with a sneer, "and a most excellent hypocrite I proved, as you, perhaps, will acknowledge. The truth, however, may now be told;—I wanted your fortune, and since I have now got it in my own possession, without any one's control over it, I care not how soon you may take in your head to leave me."

"Man! man!" ejaculated Mrs. Gravestow, "was ever such villany and perfidy known before?"

"Perhaps not," he answered; "because there are few, I believe, that would have the courage to do as I have done, and the honesty to confess it afterwards."

No. 14

" Heaven send you repentance !" groaned his sorrowing wife.

" Repentance and I shall never claim acquaintance," he replied, with his usual apathy. " It may sometimes happen that weak people look back with remorse to their past lives, but I have now plenty of money at my disposal, and should conscience ever grow a little troublesome, I'll drown it in dissipation with companions that will never think the worse of me for anything that may have happened during my life."

" I will ask no favour or consideration for myself," cried Mrs. Grave-stow, her utterance almost choked with grief ; " but Edwin is entirely at your mercy, and for his sake I do most earnestly implore your pity. Re-member, I conjure you, how solemnly you promised ere we were married, that when I came of age I should make a liberal provision for him."

" Aye, aye, I remember all that, and laugh at you for believing me," he replied. " However, I have no time now to waste in foolish arguments like these, so I will leave you, madam, for the present, and may you have more sense in future than to attempt to frustrate my resolutions."

And with this he strode angrily from the room, leaving his unfortunate wife nearly stupified with the heavy griefs that had thus unexpectedly burst upon her. Tears, however, at last, came to her relief, and then, composing herself as well she could, she sat down to the table and wrote to Mr. Harley, the friend and solicitor of her late father, detailing to him her wishes respecting a provision for Edwin, and entreating a speedy reply to inform her whether she had it yet in her power to give him the sum she had proposed. Having folded and sealed the note, she herself put it into the post-office, in order to be certain that it was despatched to its intended destination.

A week after this period, Edwin returned home from school, with an understanding that his education was to be considered to be at an end, and that he was to go to some business with as little delay as possible. Mrs. Gravestow received the youth with the affection of a sister, but her husband regarded him with evident hatred, and whenever he spoke to him, which was but seldom, it was in a tone and manner that showed plainly how little was to be expected from any kindness that he might have it in his power to bestow. Mr. Cornish, the steward, who really loved the youth, wit-nessed his master's brutality with much uneasiness, and at the first oppor-tunity, he drew Edwin aside, to give him what appeared to be very neces-sary advice.

" I do not wish to alarm you," he said, " but I would have you be very careful with a certain person, who, I need hardly say, regards you with a degree of hatred that may some day or other prove fatal."

" You mean Mr. Gravestow," exclaimed Edwin, " but, though I know he hates me, yet, I cannot imagine that he intends any mischief towards a poor unfriended boy."

" You are mistaken in him," answered Mr. Cornish ; " for I have reason to think he would not be very particular if he had but the means of getting rid of you without being found out. You remember falling in the water, don't you, and the reports that people spread about its not being an ac-cident ?"

" I remember all about that, certainly," replied Edwin, " but we have no proof that Mr. Gravestow pushed me in, for I was picked up insensible, and could recollect nothing afterwards, and there was no one else by at the time to say how the affair happened."

" Aye, aye," exclaimed the steward, " he took care to have no witnesses about, and you were lucky enough to escape with nothing worse than a wet jacket. But, mark me,—Mr. Gravestow likes you now no better than he did at that time, and as sure as that I am now telling you so, he is waiting for another opportunity to get rid of you. Aye, and the next time he'll take care to manage matters more to his own satisfaction."

" But what motive can he have for disliking me ?" asked Edwin.

" Motive enough, depend on it," answered the steward ; " had poor Mr. Wentford lived, you would not have been left without a farthing to bless yourself; but he was murdered, you know, and those that did it took care to destroy the will that the old gentleman had made only a short time before."

" Why, surely, Mr. Cornish," cried the youth with alarm, " you do not mean to accuse Mr. Gravestow of—of——"

" I accuse him of nothing, my dear boy," interrupted the steward. " At present, everything connected with that affair is involved in mystery, though, depend on it, Providence will disclose it all in good time. You know Andrew Hoply, poor fellow, was accused of the crime because he was missing, but you may take my word for it, the same hands that murdered Mr. Wentford did the same office for Andrew."

" I always felt certain that he had nothing to do with it," cried Edwin, " yet, for all that, I cannot believe Mr. Gravestow would have had any hand in so foul a crime."

" I've told you before," exclaimed Mr. Cornish, " that I don't accuse him of it, though there's many people that are not quite so particular in what they say. And then, see how ill he treats his wife that's much too good for him."

" Does he ill-use her ?" asked Edwin, with alarm.

" Oh, bless you, yes," returned the old man ; " he tells her plainly that he don't love her a bit, and that he only married her for the sake of her money."

" The villain !"

" Aye, villain indeed," exclaimed the steward ; " but, bad as we know him to be at present, it strikes me he'll prove ever so much worse by and by. So, now that you know what sort of a fellow he is, I should like to persuade you to leave the place before any mischief befalls you."

" You would not have me run away like a coward, Mr. Cornish, would you."

" Why, the truth is, I think it's better to avoid danger than to run into it," replied the old man. " I've had a little more experience in the world than you have, and I can see well enough that if you don't go pretty soon, Mr. Gravestow will find means to rid himself of a person that he don't like."

" I'll see how he behaves to me, at any rate," observed Edwin. " I have not seen much of him lately, you know, because I have been away at school, and, perhaps, in the meantime, he may have forgotten his aversion to me."

" Beware of his smile, Edwin, for I fear it is worse even than his frown," exclaimed the steward. " He may mean you mischief, and in that case, he will appear friendly, that he may the more surely effect his purpose."

" Nay," cried Edwin, " he may not like me very well, but I cannot think he would seek to do me any harm. Perhaps he will allow me to remain here through the holidays, and then do a something towards starting me in life."

" He'll do nothing of the kind," answered Cornish ; " but hark !—there goes the dinner-bell, and perhaps he may be more civil than he will afterwards, for there are two gentlemen from London that dine here to-day, and, I suppose, will sleep here."

" Who are they ?" asked Edwin.

" One of 'em is a Mr. Harley, a solicitor, and an old friend of my late master's," answered the steward; "the other is Mr. Smithson, formerly principal clerk in the house, and now a partner in the concern."

"Have they come on business or as friends?"

"That I can hardly tell you, replied Cornish; "but be it as it may, I hope they'll see how Mrs. Gravestow is treated, and take steps for making an alteration. For my own part, I think a separation would be the best thing that could happen for them; she might have some little chance of being her own mistress. However, you must go to dinner, or perhaps Mr. Gravestow will take it in his head you are sulking with him; so good by and be sure to see me as often as you can while you remain at Summerfield."

Walter Gravestow received the youth with cold civility, and after a few common-place questions, he began to address himself to the other parties without taking any further notice of Edwin. In the course of conversation, however, they began to talk of the choice of a profession, and taking that opportunity, Mr. Harley enquired of Edwin, who sat opposite to him, whether he had yet made up his mind as to the description of life he intended to lead?"

"I have been thinking of the army, sir," replied the youth; "it is an honourable profession, and should I be fortunate enough to obtain my wish, I would take care that my conduct should never bring disgrace upon it."

"Well said, my boy," exclaimed Mr. Smithson.

"Really, Mr. Smithson," cried Gravestow, with warmth, "I hope you will not assist to fill the boy's head with notions that never can be realized. The army is a very honourable profession, no doubt, but how is Edwin to get into it without money, unless, indeed, he enlists and goes as a common soldier."

"Which you, of course, would not suffer him to do?" observed Mr. Harley.

"You have judged rightly, sir," interposed Mrs. Gravestow, "for neither myself nor my husband could withhold from him the means of entering it, so as to bring disgrace upon ourselves."

"You will have the goodness, madam, to speak only for yourself," exclaimed Walter, angrily. "I have said that Edwin has no claims upon my purse, and, therefore, he will now have to shift for himself in the best way he can."

"I have never yet solicited a favour of you," said Edwin, "and there was no occasion to speak so angrily. To Mrs. Gravestow I owe a heavy debt of gratitude, but from some cause or other I have never received from you anything but marks of the most determined hatred."

"I am glad you have understood me so well," exclaimed the other sarcastically; "the truth is now ont, and as soon as convenient you can look for some one else who will be more kind to you."

"Come, come, sir," interposed Mr. Harley, "let there be no ill-feeling of this sort, I request. The poor boy has certainly been much indebted to the late Mr. Wentford for many favours, and, I trust, you will, if only from gratitude, continue to afford him your protection."

"Don't talk to me of gratitude, sir," exclaimed Walter Gravestow; "the boy has already had a great deal more than he had a right to expect, and now he can leave me as soon as he pleases."

"You will give him a sum of money I suppose," said Mr. Smithson, enquiringly. "He has been tenderly brought up, and it would be cruel in the extreme to turn him into the world without a sufficient provision."

"I shall give him nothing, sir," answered the other haughtily, "and to speak my mind plainly, I want no advice either from you or anybody else."

"You mistake me," answered Mr. Smithson; "I merely offered a suggestion, and left it to your gratitude whether it was complied with or not."

"Gratitude, sir !"

"Aye, you are now in possession of nearly all the late Mr. Wentford's property, and surely you cannot suffer his young favourite to go a beggar into the world."

"He came a beggar into the family," retorted Gravestow, "and must be content to leave it in the same way."

▶ "But you are aware that his benefactor made a will, by which he left him a considerable sum of money."

"I am not obliged to know anything of the kind," answered the other, "and even if there were such a will, it is nowhere to be found, and it is therefore to be inferred that he destroyed it."

"I have my doubts about that," said Mr. Harley, "for [that there was such a will I am very certain, having myself been called upon to draw it up. It is now, however, missing, but may be produced at some future time when least expected."

"Is that thrown out as a threat, sir?" demanded Gravestow.

"By no means," answered the solicitor; "I was merely suggesting that it is likely enough Edwin may some day or other receive the five thousand pounds without being obliged to anybody."

"Really it seems to me that this warmth has been carried a great deal too far," interposed Mr. Smithson; "you are both angry, and your violence has already had the effect of driving Mrs. Gravestow from the room."

"Her absence will be of very little consequence," replied Walter with a sneer. "However, I believe, as you say, we have gone a little too far, and so, as the only female that was in the room has deprived us of her company, we will finish the evening in more harmony over a few bottles of wine. What say you, gentlemen, shall we sign articles of peace between us?"

"For my own part I am quite willing to do so," answered Mr. Harley, "and I think I know my friend's pacific disposition well enough to promise as much for him. In fact, I think the business we have been speaking about may be comfortably arranged after you have coolly and calmly turned it over in your mind."

"You can think as you please about that," exclaimed Gravestow, "but I must confess I see very little chance of my seeing the affair in any other light than I do now. However, we will not get into the subject again, so here's a bumper to our better understanding in future."

Edwin had left the dining-room soon after Mrs. Gravestow had taken her departure, and returning to his bed chamber, gave way to those sad reflections that recent circumstances had conjured up in his mind. It was no longer doubtful that he was regarded as being in the way where he was, and as he had too much pride to remain where his presence was considered an intrusion, he determined to bring matters to an immediate close by leaving the house, and seeking his fortune in the world as best he could. Had it been possible, he would have liked to bid farewell to his kind friend, Mrs. Gravestow, but he feared lest she should endeavour to prevail on him to remain, and as his mind was fully made up, he resolved to leave the house without making any one acquainted with his design, and then to proceed with what haste he could to London. Once there, he had no doubt he should succeed even to the utmost of his most sanguine expectations, and in his visions of future greatness, he had looked forward with rapture to the time when he might have it in his power to offer any asylum to Mrs. Gravestow, who he felt assured would be compelled to leave home through the continued brutality of her husband.

When it was quite dark, and no one was heard moving about the house, he tied up a little bundle of such things as he would want on his journey, and then creeping gently down stairs, he passed through the hall door, and crossing the lawn in front of the house, soon found himself in the road that led towards London.   Inspired with youthful ardour, he thought not of the difficulties he would have to encounter, and trudging on with a merry heart, soon left behind him the home he had just abandoned.

Morning came and still he was not missed, for though he appeared not as usual, it was imagined that he had slept longer than usual, and consequently his absence occasioned no alarm.   Mrs. Gravestow, afflicted as she was, strolled into the grounds, where she met the two visitors, with whom she entered into conversation.

" You wrote to me lately, madam," said Mr. Harley, " on an affair of some importance with respect to Edwin, and as I know letters are sometimes wilfully miscarried, I waited till I could come down myself and consult you on the subject.   Mr. Smithson has kindly accompanied me, and I think in spite of the difficulties that oppose us, it may yet be possible to do something for the youth."

" In what way do you advise me to act ?" asked Mrs. Gravestow.

" Consult your husband upon the subject," answered the lawyer; " put it to his honour whether the young fellow ought not to be provided for out of the very liberal fortune that was left by your father, and perhaps his sense of justice may induce him to do something that will establish Edwin in a profitable profession."

" Alas !" sighed Mrs. Gravestow, " I fear it would be useless to urge the subject any further to my husband.   He has taken a prejudice against my young favourite, and absolutely refuses to do anything for him."

" In that case, madam," exclaimed Mr. Harley, " I am afraid the law can be of very little service.   You have no marriage settlements, you know, and Mr. Walter Gravestow cannot be compelled to do anything for Edwin. I was in hopes, however, that you would have taken my advice, and secured your property previous to your marriage."

" Your advice !" cried Mrs. Gravestow, with surprise ; " upon my word, Mr. Harley, I am not aware that you ever spoke to me on the subject."

" No, my dear madam," replied the attorney, " I was too busy at the time, and could not spare a moment to leave London.   But I wrote you several letters about it, and most strongly urged you not to marry on any consideration, till you had had settlements drawn out and signed.   I, however, received no answer, and, therefore, believed you had adopted the suggestion I threw out."

" Indeed, indeed I never received any letter from you," exclaimed Mrs. Gravestow.   " In truth, I myself, wrote to ask your friendly counsel, and was much surprised at not receiving any reply."

" I can only repeat my assertion, that I wrote to you, madam," answered Mr. Harley, " and I must also declare that I never received any letter from you."

" That is most singular !" cried Fanny, " for I do assure you I wrote, and the letter was given to Mr. Gravestow to put into the post."

" Then there is an end of the mystery at once," exclaimed the lawyer ;— " Mr. Gravestow had good reasons of his own for taking care that the letter never reached me, and he also has contrived that you should not receive any of those which were sent by me."

" Good Heavens ! do you think my husband would be guilty of so cruel a deception ?"

" Perhaps it may be as well not to say anything more about it at present," replied Mr. Harley.   " There is a mystery that must be explained, but it will take time to do that, and I, therefore, advise you to take no further notice of this affair till I have spoken to you again about it."

" And what is to become of poor Edwin ?"

" He will be better provided for than you at present imagine," answered Mr. Harley.

" Ah ! explain yourself."

" That I leave to this good gentleman," exclaimed the lawyer, gently thrusting Mr. Smithson forward. " He has been more thoughtful than any of us, and whatever good fortune may fall to the lot of Edwin, he will owe to the kindness of your late father's clerk."

" What do I hear ?" cried Mrs. Gravestow ;—" is it possible, Mr. Smithson, that you have been the means of preserving the poor youth from the destitution to which my husband would have consigned him."

" I have done but my duty, my dear madam," replied Smithson, " and, therefore, no thanks are due to me. The truth is, I know your father's intentions towards Edwin, and having good reason to believe that Mr. Walter Gravestow would leave the poor boy to his fate, I have taken care to provide for him."

" But how," asked Fanny, " have you contrived this ?"

" The salary allowed me by your father," replied Smithson, " was an exceedingly liberal one, and as my expenditure has never been very great, I have contrived to lay by a few thousands, which, at my death, shall go to the favourite of my late honoured master."

" Is it possible that such gratitude can exist in the breast of one who is no relative to our family ?"

" The truth is, madam, that I loved my master," answered Smithson, " and nothing can afford me so much pleasure as to do an act, that had he been living, would have afforded me the satisfaction of his approval."

" Your kindness can never be forgotten," replied Mrs. Gravestow, " and since Edwin will be thus provided for, it shall be my care to support him for the present out of any money that I can save from my own allowance. He shall not want, at least, while I have the means of supporting him."

" I have not yet told you all," exclaimed Mr. Smithson ; " for Edwin will have a share in your late father's business."

" Indeed !" cried Fanny ; " I thought Mr. Gravestow had declared he should not be admitted as a partner ?"

" Aye, aye, he may declare what he pleases," said the old gentleman, " but he cannot help himself if I choose to say Edwin shall enter the concern. But I see you are somewhat surprised, and as I may as well tell you at once, that from motives which I shall not at present explain, Mr. Gravestow was induced to let me have a very considerable share in the business. Heaven knows, I desired it not for myself, but I thought of poor Edwin, and the moment he comes of age he shall take my place. The money that I just now spoke of, he will, of course, wait for till my death."

" Dear, good friend !" cried Fanny, " what a debt of gratitude do we not owe you."

" Not a bit,—not a bit," exclaimed Mr. Smithson ; " everything I possess in the world, I owe to the kindness of your father, and how can I better dispose of it than by giving it to his young favourite ?—Poor lad ! he had nearly been reduced to extremities, but fortunately I have it in my power to rescue him from absolute poverty."

" I cannot thank you for this kindness as I ought," cried Mrs. Gravestow, " but Edwin has a greatful heart, and I will run and fetch him, that he may learn from your own lips the heavy debt of gratitude he owes to his generous benefactor."

And, so saying, she hurried away, before either Mr. Smithson or his friend could urge her to postpone her intention till another opportunity. As may be expected, however, she found his room empty, and as the bed had not been slept in that night, the truth at once flashed upon her mind. The youth, indignant at the treatment he had received from her husband, had secretly taken his departure from the house, and who could say whither he had fled, or whether he would ever return?

In a state of mind bordering on distraction, Mrs. Gravestow hurried back to the two gentlemen she had just left, and told them the discovery she had made, and the suspicion she entertained of his having left home to seek his own fortune in the world. Both Mr. Smithson and the lawyer endeavoured to console her with the assurance that he would return ere long. Advertisements were inserted in the newspapers, hand-bills were circulated, and enquiries instituted in every possible direction; but all was of no avail, and the place to which Edwin had flown, was a mystery which time only could disclose.

CHAPTER XV.

AMELIA RELATES HER ADVENTURES.

WE must now return to the house of Mr. Graham, the post office clerk, to which it will be recollected Amelia and her child were taken after her attempt at self-destruction, by plunging into the river. Every care was taken of the unfortunate creature, and by good management she was soon restored to health, and a tolerable degree of spirits, considering the trials and afflictions she had undergone. She, however, maintained a strict silence in respect to everything that might tend to throw any light upon her history, and it was not till she had been in the house three or four days that she even alluded to any circumstance connected with her previous life. Taking advantage of the few words that had fallen from her lips, Mrs. Graham ventured to enquire whether she had any objection to relate the circumstances that had induced a female to contemplate suicide, whose manners and conversation proved that she had received a liberal education.

"Alas!" sighed Amelia, "how can I, who am under so many obligations, refuse to inform you who it is that has been kindly taken under your roof. Yet I would gladly have been spared the recital, for I fear you will despise me when you know what a weak, frail being you have thus hospitably received."

"Indeed you wrong both my husband and myself," replied Mrs. Graham, "for we are all erring beings, and Heaven forbid that we should censure one who we should rather pity for her misfortunes."

Mrs. Graham spoke feelingly, for her husband had confessed to her the robbery he had committed, a story which, though it afflicted her sorely at the time, afforded subsequent consolation, as she had many reasons to believe that his escape would act as a salutary warning in future. She was therefore the more inclined to think tenderly of the misfortunes of poor Amelia, whose story she was so anxious to hear. Observing that she was still silent, however, she again urged her to proceed.

"I will not hesitate any longer," replied Amelia, "because I believe I among those who, if they cannot excuse, will not condemn too harshly

the errors into which I have fallen. My father, then, was of a good family, and received an education in accordance with the prospects that were before him. But misfortune came upon them in an evil hour, and when his only parent died, he found himself almost penniless, and compelled to seek the means of obtaining a living. He applied for situations, but without success, and seeing that he could not hope to obtain employment in England, he went over to France, where a friend of the family was then residing, and who supported himself by the proceeds of a school. Luckily, his appeal was not made in vain, and he was received into the house as an usher, though upon a salary which was barely sufficient for the purchase of the few necessaries that he required. In fact, the person who thus kindly took him under his roof, was himself very poor, and he received him more out of friendship, than from any real want that he was in of assistance. Be this as it may, the schoolmaster died after my father had been with him about three years, and as the school was then broken up, my father was compelled to undertake a clerk's situation in the office of a lawyer named Fayette. Here he received a more liberal salary, and lived comfortably enough, but for an event that occurred to mar all his prospects."

"He fell in love, I suppose?" observed Mrs. Graham.

"The daughter, and only son of Monsieur Fayette, fell in love with Arnold, (for such was my father's name,)" replied Amelia, " and though under other circumstances, he might have felt flattered by the favour, he felt that it would be ungrateful to return the kindness of his employer, were he to carry on a secret correspondence with a girl who he knew was destined for a wealthy match. Besides, Arnold was already in some degree engaged, for his love had been won by Marie, the daughter of the deceased schoolmaster, whose prospects in life were not much better

No. 15

than his own. It seems, however, that the mother of Marie was by no means pleased with the prospect of her daughter becoming the wife of a man in straightened circumstances, and she forbade her thinking of an union with one who she would not on any consideration admit into her family. Yet, the lovers continued to have stolen interviews, for Marie always contrived to send a note whenever she knew of a favourable opportunity for their meeting, and my father was too deeply in love to miss an assignation with the fair object of his admiration.

"Ma'm'selle Fayette observed Arnold's coldness with surprise, and it was not long before she began to suspect that his heart had been previously engaged, and watching him with an eye of jealousy, she soon had ample proof that her opinions were not without foundation. It happened that she was one day in the office, when a note was brought to Arnold, the reading of which seemed to excite in him unusual pleasure, and directly afterwards he was called out of the office to attend a client, when, in the hurry, he left the epistle upon his desk. The young lady could not resist the temptation to satisfy her curiosity, and snatching up the note, she read as follows.

"'To-night I shall be alone;—when you leave business, hasten to meet me at the usual place of assignation, your ever faithful Marie.'

"The reading of this confirmed all her suspicions; yet, she returned the note to the exact place from when she had taken it, so that, when Arnold returned, he had not the least idea that his secret had been discovered. Indeed, the girl looked so calm and unmoved, that it would have been impossible to imagine that she had made herself acquainted with the nature of the communication he had received.

"Being engaged on very important business on that evening, my father was unwillingly compelled to relinquish the opportunity of seeing Marie, and a note was afterwards despatched, informing her of the disappointment, but making another appointment for the following evening, when he promised to be at the usual place without fail. With this latter circumcumstance, however, Ma'm'selle Fayette was not acquainted, and resolving to break off the match by any means that might come within her power, she made up her mind to get rid of her rival, let the consequences be what they might. At about the hour, therefore, when the business of the day was usually finished, she attired herself in a dress fit for walking out in, and then seated herself in an apartment without a light, in order that Arnold might not be aware of her movements, and that she might watch him and follow in secresy, if he should leave the place. But to her surprise, he kept writing on till an hour far beyond that which was usually devoted to business, and as the time passed on, she wondered more and more what could possibly occupy his attention, when she was thoroughly convinced that he had an assignation to keep with a female, who she would have given the world to find out. It was very provoking to be baulked after all the pains he had taken, but still he kept scribbling on as if he had never received a letter making an appointment to meet the woman who she made sure was a rival. Still, however, Louise Fayette kept watch, and still Arnold seemed to be as far from going away as ever.

"At last a knock was heard at the street-door, and up jumped Arnold to answer it, as if he was afraid anybody else should do so. Louise now listened as though her very existence depended upon what took place; but, in spite of all her efforts, she could make out nothing more than that the person who had just arrived was a man, and out of all that he whispered, Louise could only distinguish the words :—

"'Do not fail to come quickly; follow me without delay, and I will wait for you a short time at the corner of the next street to this.'

" The stranger then departed, and Arnold, returning to the office, extinguished the fire and candles, and then slipped out of the house so stealthily, that Louise was more than ever convinced that he was about to see the female who had so unaccountably excited her jealousy. She then followed him for some distance, keeping on the opposite side of the way, but the street lights served to keep him in view, and though he walked at a brisk pace, she contrived to keep up with him, for her wrath was excited, and she determined to see the end of this adventure, let what might happen. After a little while, she saw that Arnold was joined by a stranger, who she supposed was the person who had called him out, but the darkness of the night prevented her from distinguishing which was which. They then walked more briskly, and it was not without extreme difficulty that she contrived to keep up the pace they were then proceeding at.

"In this way, she followed them completely through the town, and into one part of the suburbs were a great number of very pretty houses were situated. At one of these Arnold and his companion paused, and after knocking, they were speedily admitted, and for a short time they were concealed from her view. It was provoking enough thus to lose sight of them and be left in uncertainty, but she felt quite convinced that Arnold would not pass the night there, and being resolved to find out the mystery, she stood up in a dark recess, where she could observe all, without the probability of being discovered herself. But her patience began at length to flag, and she was just thinking of returning home, when the opposite door opened, and one of the persons left the house, and she could plainly discover that he was one of those who had just before entered it. Whether this was Arnold or his companion, was, however, a question, however, not easily to be solved, but she fancied it must be Arnold, and half maddened with fury, she resolved to follow and see the adventure to a close. She, therefore, kept close behind him, but whether it might happen to be Arnold or a perfect stranger, she found that his pace did not suit her's, and in order to keep up with him at all, she was obliged to run nearly the whole of the way. Still she kept him in sight till he came to an alehouse, at the door of which he stopped, and, having given a signal, was admitted, and once more she lost sight of him. This was very provoking, but she felt pretty well convinced that the person she had been following was not Arnold, for she supposed he would remain with the female from whom he had received the note, and burning with rage and mortification she returned home, without anybody being aware of her absence. But Louise believed she had got a clue to the mystery, and greatly did she exult at the idea of the mischief that was plotting in her brain.

" So much were her thoughts occupied, that she passed a sleepless night, and rose again on the first dawn of daylight, feverish and ill at ease. She was resolved, however, to sift the affair to the very bottom, and left the house for the purpose of putting this design into execution ; she had so carefully noted every step of the way on the preceding night, that she retraced her steps without difficulty, and, at length, found herself within view of the villa where, she had no doubt, Arnold was still to be found. Here she paused to reflect what she should next do, and had not been long there when she saw the door opened with a great deal of apparent caution. Her eyes seemed straining from their sockets as she fixed them on the spot, but instead of seeing the person she expected, a couple of females came out, who, looking around them, as if to see whether they were observed, hurried away, and turning down the first street they came to, were speedily lost to view. Still Louise was was not to be baulked in her plan, for she quite certain the object of her search was there, and creeping forward, she approached to within a few yards of the house she had been watching. There she again paused, for she could hear the creaking of a window that was being slowly raised up, and looking in the direction from whence the sound came, she saw Arnold thrust out his head, and then protrude his whole body, hanging from the window sill till he had got a tolerable balance, and then drop down. Luckily for him, he fell upon his feet, and no sooner had he reached the ground, than Louise rushed forward, taxing him with perfidy, and threatening all sorts of vengeance; but she might as well have spoken to the air, for Arnold heeded her not a bit, and ran off at a speed that rendered hopeless any idea that she might have had of overtaking him.

"This was a source of deep vexation to Louise, for it became more and more evident that he had no regard for her whatever, and the mortification she endured urged her to pursue the adventure to a close, whatever might be the result of it. Recovering herself a little, she returned home, but Arnold was not there, and though she waited for him many hours, yet nothing was seen of him that day.

"It must now be my task," continued Amelia, "to account for the apparently singular conduct of my father. You remember my saying, that on the previous evening, while he was busily engaged in the office, a knock was heard at the door, which he immediately answered. Upon arriving there, he saw a man closely muffled up in a cloak, who, on seeing Arnold, hastily advanced, and in an agitatted voice, inquired whether that was the residence of Monsieur Fayette.

" 'It is,' replied my father.

" 'Is he at home?'

" 'He is not.'

" 'Then you will do as well,' exclaimed the stranger. 'A man is dying, and your presence is required immediately.'

" 'I am a lawyer, not a surgeon,' said my father.

" 'It is as a lawyer that you are wanted,' exclaimed the other; 'a man is dying of a wound, and you are required either to draw out his will, or to take his deposition, in case it should be wanted hereafter.'

"Thus urged, my father hurried back into the office, put on his hat and cloak, and taking with him the necessary implements, returned to the man, who then motioned him to follow him in silence. In this way they proceeded to the house to which Louise watched them, the door of which being a-jar, they entered without difficulty, and proceeded up stairs; my father feeling no distrust, as the story which had been told by the man seemed likely enough, and the urgency of the case rendered secresy and dispatch of importance. Arnold, therefore, followed the stranger into a bed-chamber, which they had no sooner entered, than his conductor said something which he did not clearly comprehend, and then placing a lamp upon the table, he left the room, locked the door after him, and hastened down stairs as fast as he could.

"Up to this time, Arnold had felt no misgivings, but now horrible thoughts entered his head, and he began to think he had been entrapped there for some vile purpose or other, and that he should lose his life through the foolish confidence he had reposed in the stranger. He in vain tried to force open the door, and finding how useless that effort was, he threw up the window and called for assistance, but there were nothing but fields before him, and at that late hour of the night, there was nobody about to answer his cries for help.

"More and more alarmed at his perilous situation, he turned away from the window, and was again going to try the door, and as he passed by the bed, he thought he could observe marks of blood upon it. His terror now knew no bounds, but, with a violent effort to maintain his fortitude, he turned down the bed-clothes, and to his horror, discovered the body of a man weltering in his blood ! Transfixed with horror, even his voice failed him at the ghastly sight which thus met his eyes; the room seemed to turn round, a deadly sickness came over him, and he would have fallen had he not caught hold of the bed-post to support his sinking frame. It was but too evident that a murder had been committed, but for what purpose he had been brought there, was a mystery yet to be explained.

"Whilst his thoughts were thus occupied, he fancied he could observe a slight motion in the body, and overjoyed at this circumstance, he sprang to the bedside, and spoke; but no answer was returned, and after some time, he was again convinced that the person before him was dead. Yet, how to account for the extraordinary circumstance that had befallen him? If the man had been murdered, would his assassin have sent for a stranger, whose evidence would be so likely to bring them to justice? If he had met with an accident, surely there would have been friends in the house to explain the reason he had been sent for, and the cause which had led to so singular an occurrence? Besides, there was nothing about the place to prove that a murder had been committed; the furniture of the room,—which was of a costly description,—had not been disturbed, and it seemed possible that the man was in a swoon from loss of blood, and that he might yet revive to account for the mystery with which the whole affair was enveloped.

"Still, however, Arnold could not help thinking that his own situation was an extremely perillous one, and from the fact of the door having been fastened by the man who had brought him into the room, proved that something more was to be done, whenever an opportunity arrived. This reflection urged him to a renewal of his attempt to escape, and searching her pocket, he found a knife, with which he attempted to force the lock, but in the trepidation with which he did this, the frail implement snapped asunder, and he was thus left to adopt other resources for his escape. His next thought was to try the windows, but by this time the moon, which before had been shining brightly, was enveloped in a heavy mass of clouds, and as he knew not where he should drop should he make his exit that way, he determined to wait till the morning, when with the assistance of light, he might hope to carry this design to a successful termination. Arnold then seated himself in a chair, and in spite of the dangers that environed him, he was just falling off into a doze, when a slight sound startled him, and opening his eyes, he fancied that he could again see a slight motion in the body, which was lying upon the bed. He sprang up, and once more approaching the ghastly object of his terror, demanded the cause of the mystery, which he had not been able to fathom. But no answer was returned, and though he watched with a careful eye, not a motion could be observed that indicated the remains of any life in the bleeding form before him.

"The alarm of my father was now wound up to a higher pitch than ever, for though not given to superstition the singularity of his situation,—his being thrown into the company of a dead man,—and the loneliness in which he found himself, filled his soul with a feeling of dread that he could not for sometime overcome. Again he approached the door, and with a violent effort endeavoured to force it open, but his strength was unequal to his task, and he was compelled to give it up in despair. He then shouted loudly for assistance, but though he listened intently, he could hear only the echo of of his own voice, and finding all attempts ineffectual, he again sat himself down with a determination to wait till daylight, and see what chance that gave him of effecting his escape.

"He watched the body as he sat near the bedside to see if it gave any further indications of life; but it remained motionless, and as my father grew more composed, he thought to himself, that when the matter came to be explained, everything would be quite satisfactory, though there could be little doubt that the unfortunate person before him had received wounds which had caused his death. Perhaps, thought Arnold, he was not quite dead when I entered the room, and the slight movements I have observed, were occasioned by the last struggles of expiring nature.

"Still occupied with these thoughts, my father fell into a profound slumber from which he was roused at daybreak, by a loud knocking at the door of his chamber.

CHAPTER XVI.

AMELIA'S STORY CONTINUED.

"INSTANTLY remembering the desperate situation in which he had been placed, my father thought he was about to fall a sacrifice to the villany of those that had entrapped him; but he was possessed of a fair share of courage, and resolving to put as bold a face upon the matter as possible, he called out for the person, whoever it might be to come in.

"'I can't sir,' replied a female voice; 'the door is locked, and I don't see the key.'

"'It is outside,' exclaimed my father; 'the wretches that lured me, have fastened the door, and I shall be murdered, unless you bring immediate assistance to my aid.'

"By this time, he could hear that another woman had joined one who had spoken to him first, and there was a great deal of whispering among them, and now and then he fancied he could hear them laughing together, as if they enjoyed the desperate plight in which they had forced him. Over and over again he called to them, earnestly entreating them to go for assistance, but they made no reply to him, and at last he heard them go down stairs, probably—as he thought—to inform his enemies that he was safe. At any rate, he could not render his situation more dangerous than it was, and resolving to effect his escape, at all hazards, he threw open the window and leaped down into the garden without venturing to look again at the horrible form which had occasioned him so much alarm.

"So far, all went well enough, but on examination, he found that the garden-gate was fastened, and as no other alternative remained, he clambered up the high wall, and jumped over to the other side; this time, however, he was not so fortunate as he had been on the former occasions, for his feet slipped at the moment he reached the ground, and though he felt no great inconvenience at the moment, he had not got very far before he found that he had sprained one of his ancles, and that it would be impossible to reach home without assistance. Thus situated, he was obliged to sit himself down on a bank, till some one might come that way; but it was a lonely place, and he remained half an hour without seeing even a single being pass that way. At length, however, he was startled, by hearing voices behind him, and looking round, he saw a couple of men running towards him, one of whom, making a sudden spring, seized him by the collar, and called upon his companion to shoot him if he offered any resistance.

"'What means this violence?' exclaimed my father, confounded by the suddenness with which this had been done.

"'Oh, you know well enough what it means,' replied the man that had laid hold of him ; ' you have committed a crime that will cost you your life, but I dare say you will have the hardihood to deny having had anything to do with it."

" ' Good heavens,' cried Arnold, ' what crime do you charge me with ?'

" ' You'll know all about that, presently,' answered the other. ' Our business is to make you a prisoner and not to answer a parcel of questions that you may choose to put to us.'

" ' But I have committed no offence.'

" ' Aye, aye, so you'll say, of course,' growled the fellow, ' but we aint obliged to believe a man that knows the consequences of being found out. You'll be hanged, I tell you, and serve you right too.'

" ' Tell me what I am accused of,' cried my father.

" ' Sharn't do anything of the kind,' exclaimed the man ; ' so come along with you, and the matter will be explained in a way that you can't fail to understand.'

" And with that they dragged him away by the same path he had just before taken, and a little while afterwards, he was conveyed to the house from which he had escaped with so much difficulty. He was then shut up in a room to reflect at leisure on the alarming incident that had befallen him, and was suffered to remain there for the greater part of an hour, without seeing any body of whom he could ask an explanation of the cause of his arrest. At last, footsteps approached the room, the door was thrown open, and the two men raising him in their arms, conveyed him up stairs to the chamber where he had passed so unpleasant a night. To his surprise, however, the supposed corpse was sitting upright in the bed, but the ghastly couutenance showed that this was a last effert of expiring nature, and that a very short time would terminate the wretched creature's existence. On one side of him was a surgeon, who had just given up all hope of saving the life of his patient, and on the other, was a magistrate, who had been sent for to take the dying man's deposition. Other persons were in the room, who it afterwards appeared, attended as witnesses against the prisoner.

" Immediately upon entering the room, my father was placed at the foot of the bed, and as the corpse-like figure caught sight of him, he raised his hand, and pointing to him, denounced him as his murderer.

" ' Are you certain of it ?' demanded the magistrate.

" ' I am.'

" ' Merciful powers !' cried Arnold, horror-struck at these words ; but he was instantly checked by the magistrate, who, after writing down the few words that had passed, demanded of the prisoner his name.

" ' Arnold Robertson.'

' " What occupation do you follow ?'

" ' I am clerk to Monsieur Fayette.'

" ' It is my duty then to inform you that the evidence is conclusive," exclaimed the magistrate ; " and as a denial of the offence can be of no service, I would prevail on you to confess at once, and thus put an end to an affair that has created a great emotion.'

" ' In England,' cried my father, ' no man is ever called upon to criminate himself, however conclusive the evidence of his guilt may appear. Your laws in that respect, differ from ours ; but let me hope that justice will not be withheld from one who is a stranger among you. I have been accused of assassination, but before Heaven, and those who are now assembled around me, I most solemnly declare that I am innocent of the foul crime laid to my charge.'

" He then related all that had happened from the moment of his leaving the office, to the period when he had been followed and arrested as a murderer.

His narrative was listened to with patience, but it was easy to see that no one present believed a word that he had uttered.

"When he had done speaking, the two female domestics were questioned, and most pointingly did they affirm that no one slept in the house but their master and themselves. They further deposed that he had gone to bed in good health, that they had fastened the door, that they had not been disturbed during the night, and that in the morning they knocked at their master's door, and being answered by a stranger, they ran away in a fright to give information to the police. All this was told with a great deal of apparent simplicity, and the evidence was considered as conclusive of the prisoner's guilt.

"The men were next questioned, and they described the scene that had presented itself on breaking into the room. An attempt they said had been made to force the lock, but the knife had broken, and the fragments were laid before the magistrate who ordered the prisoner to be searched, and when they found the corresponding parts in his pocket, it was considered by every person present, that the charge had been most clearly established, and that the prisoner, and no one else, was guilty of the crime that had been committed. Still, however, it was necessary for Monsieur Laroche, the wounded man, to give testimony, and he was, therefore, asked what he had to say upon the subject of their enquiry.

"In reply, he said that he had gone to bed at his usual hour, and that he had been awakened by a violent blow on the head, and that before he could raise a cry for assistance, he was stabbed in the bosom by some sharp instrument. He fainted from loss of blood, and on recovering himself some time afterwards, saw the prisoner trying to make his escape from the window. He saw his face distinctly as he turned round, and could positively swear to him; terror occasioned him to swoon again, and he remembered nothing that happened afterwards till he was found by the officers as they had described.

"'The affair is a very singular one,' said the magistrate, gravely; 'and I believe there are few persons who could for a moment doubt the prisoner's guilt. Hitherto, however, we have seen no motive that could have urged him to so base an act, though you, perhaps, Monsieur Laroche, may be able to throw some additional light on that part of the affair.'

"'I know of no cause,' replied the wounded man, 'unless he came to rob the house.'

"'But nothing has been found on him to warrant that conclusion,' observed the magistrate. 'Perhaps revenge for some fancied injury may have prompted him to the deed.'

"'It is impossible,' answered Monsieur Laroche, 'for I never saw the prisoner before.'

"'He may have been employed by some one,' exclaimed the magistrate, 'so perhaps you will try to recollect who there is that would be likely to have engaged him in this base plot for your destruction.'

"'I am not aware of having such an enemy,' replied the other, 'nor do I see any reason to doubt that this man has been urged by his own evil passions to commit the deed. It is moreover, certain that he struck the blow, and, therefore, I demand justice on him without delay. Let him to prison, and should the law find him guilty, his death will release the world of one of the villains that abound so plentifully in it.'

"The magistrate thought this reasonable enough, and as he had no doubt about the prisoner's guilt, he ordered his clerk to draw out the commitment, and within the space of another hour, my father found himself the inmate

of a felon's gaol, and charged with a crime that, if not disproved, would certainly cost him his life.

"'Leaving him, however, for the present, we must now return to Louise Fayette, whose jealousy had been so strongly excited, and who remained unconscious of Arnold's condition till the arrival of an officer of justice to search the room of the prisoner, in order to see whether any papers might be found by which proof might be obtained to show premeditation in the affair that had created so much consternation. The announcement made by the officer filled Louise with astonishment and dismay, and she eagerly enquired who the person was whose life had been attempted.

"'Monsieur Laroche,' answered the man.

"'Has he a daughter?' asked Louise, whose jealousy had not been diminished.

"'He has not.'

"'A niece?'

"'No.'

"'A young wife?'

"'He is an old batchelor,' answered the man, 'and lives quite alone, with the exception of a couple of women servants.'

"'Ah!' cried the girl, 'Arnold has too much pride and good sense to go and see low bred creatures like them.'

"'It matters not what took him,' exclaimed the officer of justice, 'for he was found in the house, and there is sufficient evidence to prove that he is guilty of stabbing Monsieur Laroche.'

"'It is impossible he can be guilty,' cried Louise, unable any longer to conceal the agitation this news had occasioned.'

"'We shall know all about that when the trial takes place,' answered the

No. 16

other. 'At present we can discover no motive that he had for committing the crime, but I dare say, after all,—it will turn out that he has been employed by some one that wants to get rid of Monsieur Laroche.'

"Louise, however, scarcely heard these words, for hastily putting on her cloak and bonnet, she darted from the house, and made her way towards the prison.

"' Who do you want, young woman ?' said the gaoler, taking her by the arm as she was about to pass him,

"' An Englishman,' she replied,—' one Arnold Robertson.'

"' Ah ! the prisoner that has just been brought in for an attempted murder.'

"' He has been wrongfully charged,' cried Louise ;—' he is as innocent of the crime as either you or I.'

"' And you want to see him ?'

"' I do.'

"' Well,' replied the gaoler, ' it's against rules and regulations ;—but I suppose it's a sweetheart you want to see, so in with you, but mind,—you must not stay with him more than a minute or two.'

"Louise made no reply, but passing through the room pointed out by the gaoler, she entered a passage, at the end of which was a strong iron-bound door, opened by a man who pointed out to her the way to Arnold's cell. My father was at the time occupied in his own gloomy thoughts, but starting up at the sound of her voice, he eagerly enquired the cause of her unlooked for visit.

"' I heard of your hapless situation,' she replied, ' and came to see if I could render any service towards proving your innocence of the charge that has been brought against you.'

"' Alas !' he exclaimed, ' my situation is indeed a hapless one, but if you believe me to be innocent, I can endure my misfortune with tolerable composure.'

"' I feel assured you are,' she replied.

"' And yet,' he continued, ' the evidence against me appears to be so conclusive, that I fear nothing can remove the impression of my being the party that attempted the assassination.'

"He then related to her the adventure that had happened to him on the preceding evening, and having brought it to a conclusion, said :—

"' You will now understand Louise, that my only chance of escaping the dreadful punishment of death, rests in the circumstance of discovering the man that came last night to fetch me. That, however, is an extremely difficult task, for I have no clue to him, nor should I know him even if we were ever to meet together. It is unlikely that he will venture to show himself till this affair is blown over, and I shall thus die with the crime of murder stamped upon my name.'

"' I'm sorry to interrupt you,' exclaimed the gaoler, suddenly presenting herself before them, ' but your time is up, and I shall get into a scrape if any one should happen to come and find you both together.'

"There was something so irressistible in this, that neither my father nor Louise could offer any opposition to it, and having bid each other a hasty adieu, the girl left the cheerless gloom of the prison, and returned home to reflect whether some plan could not be devised for liberating the prisoner, and proving to the world his innocence of the crime that had been laid to his charge. For her own part, she was now quite certain that he had been made the dupe of designing villains, and knowing how impossible it was for him to make any efforts towards clearing up the mystery, she determined to set about the task, and, by zeal in the cause she had taken in hand, to obtain his release from prison. This was no sooner resolved on, than she summoned Blanche, her female attendant, and after some little hesitation, asked if she knew where she could get a youth's suit of clothes to disguise herself, in order that she might carry a little project into execution.

" ' A youth's suit !' cried Blanche, with surprise.

" ' Yes, I must have it immediately,' she replied ; ' so ask me no questions, but assist me in this business, and I will not fail to reward your services.'

" ' A footman's livery, I suppose, would not do ?' said Blanche, after a short deliberation.

" ' It would do admirably,' replied her mistress ; ' but, of course, it must be of a size to suit me.'

" ' It shall,' replied Blanche, and away she hurried out of the room, to fetch the disguise she had spoken of.

" In the meantime Louise began to prepare herself for the task she had undertaken, and so expeditious was her domestic, that scarcely had ten minutes elapsed ere she returned with a bundle, which she quickly opened and displayed a smart livery suit that, having been made for a boy, would fit her as exact as possible. Louise was delighted at the success that had so far attended her, and exchanging her own feminine attire for that which had just been brought in, she looked as dapper a little footboy as might have been found in all Paris. A wig and hat completed the disguise, and she was about to set forth, when Blanche, as a particular favour, asked to be informed where she was going to.

" ' That,' she replied, ' is a secret at present ; but a short time will serve to explain my motives, and in the meantime you may rest assured that I am not doing anything which the world will hereafter censure me for.'

" ' Ah !' cried Blanche, archly, ' I think I can guess what has prompted you to this scheme of yours.'

" ' Indeed ! What do you suspect it is, girl ?'

" ' Love.'

" ' Psha !' interrupted Louise ; ' for whom do you suppose I would take all this trouble ?'

" ' For Mr. Arnold, Miss.'

" ' And why do you think of him ?'

" ' Because he is in trouble,' answered Blanche ; ' and I know you love him in spite of his fancying some one else better than he does you.'

" ' It is false !' exclaimed Louise, indignantly ; ' he loves me, and I did him a foul injustice in supposing that he had given his affections to another.'

" ' And you are now going to try whether you cannot unravel the mystery of last night's affair ?'

" ' That I cannot deny.'

" ' But what excuse shall I make to your father for your absence ?' asked Blanche.

" ' I must leave that to your own wit,' replied her mistress ; ' or, stay— tell him I have gone on a visit to my cousin, Lestelle, and that I may not return for three or four days.'

" ' Three or four days !' cried the girl with astonishment ; ' and where will you be all that time ?'

" ' I know not,' replied Louise ; ' but poor Arnold is in danger of his life, and as he cannot assist himself at present, he shall find there is one friend in the world ready to sacrifice even her fair fame in his service.'

" ' But may you not get into trouble ?'

" ' I may ; yet all must be risked when his life depends upon the exertions I am about to make. So now, Blanche, seek not to throw any further obstacles in my way, for I am determined in the course I have chosen, and no consideration shall ever induce me to abandon it.'

" By this time night had set in, and with it a heavy rain, that would have deterred any one less resolute than Louise from leaving the house. She, however, cared not for storm nor rain, and putting on her hat and great coat, she once more enjoined her attendant to secrecy, and sallied forth unmindful of all difficulties that might present themselves in her way.

"Remembering the direction that had been pursued by the stranger on the preceding evening, she passed along numerous narrow and dirty streets till she reached the low public-house which she had seen him enter, and from the sounds of noisy revelry that issued from it, she ascertained that it was pretty full of company, and for a moment her fears were excited lest she should meet a rougher set of companions than would be desirable. But then she recollected the dangerous situation of Arnold, and forgetting all thoughts of peril that might happen to herself, she roused her sinking courage, and entered the house with as dauntless an air as she could at that moment assume.

"A hasty glance served to assure her that the company was not of a very choice description, for the men evidently belonged to the very lowest grades of society, and the landlady, an old and withered hag, was the only female among them. Her entrance, however, seemed to check the conversation that had been going on among them, and the looks with which they regarded the supposed youth, showed plainly enough that they were anything but pleased at the intrusion of a stranger. Louise, however, affected an air of the most perfect composure, and taking a seat near the fire, she called for a small measure of wine, which she drank off after having pledged all the persons present.

"Shortly after this, a person of more decent appearance entered the room and seated himself opposite to Louise, so that she could obtain a good look at his features without seeming to be too inquisitive. The height of this man exactly corresponded with that of the stranger who had called the night before and taken Arnold out with him; but though she had followed them so far, she had had no opportunity of seeing his features, so that in this respect she was as much mystified as ever. She, however, heard them call him by the name of St. Ange, and this circumstance she thought might hereafter prove of some consequence towards the development of her designs. The company seemed to regard him with much respect, and one of them noticing his wet garb, observed that he supposed it still rained.

"'Aye, heavily,' he replied.

"'And so it did last night,' observed another.

"'You may say that,' exclaimed St. Ange, 'and well I know it, for I was out and got a pretty good soaking.'

"'What time did the rain begin?' asked the hostess.

"'About one o'clock in the morning,' he replied.

"These words, simple as they were, struck Louise, and in her own mind she felt quite certain that was the man she was in quest of. Her sudden surprise, however, was not observed by any one, and recovering herself, she listened with eager attention to all that was going forward. But the conversation took quite another turn, and occasionally glancing at the object of her suspicions, she determined not to lose sight of him till she had ascertained whether her notions were correct or not. At length a dead silence ensued, as if all subject for conversation had been exhausted, and Louise began to fear that she would learn no more, when her attention was arrested by hearing one of the men allude to the murder of Monsieur Laroche. In an instant her eyes were directed towards the object of her suspicions, but his countenance appeared to be so unmoved, that she could not help acknowledging to herself that she had done him an injustice in supposing him to have been concerned in the mysterious affair of the preceding night.

"The subject of the murder was spoken of for some time, and at last

Louise thought she could perceive that both St. Ange and the hostess became more and more interested in what the rest were talking about; and every now and then they exchanged meaning glances with each other. Still this might not prove any guilty knowledge of the transactions, and, indeed, from one circumstance and another, she began to fancy that her own prejudices might have something to do with the suspicions that occupied her mind. Still, however, she continued to watch St. Ange, who evidently grew more and more agitated as the subject proceeded, and at length hastily rising from his seat, he left the house abruptly. This certainly appeared to be rather strange, for it was raining heavily at the time, and consequently the business that took him out must be very urgent.

"But his departure seemed to occasion no surprise whatever among the rest of the company, and they continued chatting and drinking together for some time longer, when, on its being announced that the rain had ceased, they rose from their seats, and paying for what they had been drinking, took their leave of the hostess. Louise, though anxious to remain there for the night, was obliged to make some demonstration of also quitting the house, and rising, she approached the door with so much reluctance, that the old woman could not fail taking notice of it.

"'Now, young man,' she said, 'the company's all gone, and I'm only waiting your departure to close the house.'

"'I was thinking,' said Louise, 'that I should be glad to have a bed here if you can accommodate me.'

"'How is that?' cried the hostess; 'have you no home to go to?'

"'I have not,' she replied.

"'Nor any friends that will give you shelter?'

"'I have friends, certainly,' she replied; 'but the truth is, I have been rather suddenly discharged from my last situation, and I am afraid of letting them know of it.'

"'But they must do so, sooner or later,' replied the woman.

"'I don't know that,' cried Louise, 'for it is likely I may be taken back to my old place, and if I could only remain somewhere till then, no one would hear that I had been foolish enough to offend my master.'

"'Humph!—you want a lodging then?'

"'I do.'

"'Have you any money?'

"'Yes—at least I have enough to last me a few days.'

"'In that case you may have a bed here—that is, if you don't mind sleeping with St. Ange, who will be back again presently.'

"'I must have a bed room to myself,' replied Louise, her face reddening up at the suggestion. 'I am willing to pay for the accommodation, but can, on no consideration, admit of a companion.'

"'You will not sleep with my son, St. Ange, then?'

"'Certainly not.'

"'In that case you must pay well for a separate room.'

"'Most willingly.'

"'Then you shall be accommodated,' exclaimed the hostess, 'though, for the life of me, I can't see why you should object to save half the expense by sleeping with my son.'

"'Monsieur St. Ange, then, is your son?' cried Louise, anxious to obtain all the information she could.

"'He is,' she replied, 'and a very good one he would be if I could only persuade him to work for his living.'

"'Is he indolent?' asked Louise.

"'Rather so,' answered the hostess; 'that is to say, he won't go to any regular labour, but prefers picking up a little money in a way that I don't approve of.'

"'He gambles, I suppose?'

"'I'm afraid he does,' returned the old woman; 'but I never ask him any questions upon that subject now, for he used to get very cross with me if I said anything about it, and so I leave him to follow his own wilful ways.'

"Upon this, the old woman went up stairs to prepare the bed, and Louise was left to the indulgence of her own thought, which still continued to be directed towards St. Ange, who, in spite of her wishes, was still an object of suspicion and distrust. Of the old woman she was inclined to think better, though there were certainly some points she could not help harbouring doubts and fears. Still there seemed to be a little kindness in her nature, and in spite of her feeling some alarm at being among strangers, Louise was inclined to think favourably of her, and she had just made up her mind to place the utmost reliance upon her, when the door opened, and St. Ange once more made his appearance. He seemed to be more agitated than when he left the place, but upon perceiving her, he affected an air of easy indifference, and learning that his mother was up stairs, he followed her thither, and Louise could hear them in earnest coversation, though what the subject of their conversation was she could not make out. It did not, however, last very long, and when they came down again she could observe that both of them were a good deal flurried. But Louise did not wish to be in their way, and having expressed a desire to go to bed, she was lighted by the old woman up stairs, and ushered into an apartment which, though small and meanly furnished, had at least the recommendation of being clean and wholesome.

"'This is to be your chamber,' said the old woman, 'and I have no doubt you will sleep soundly in it.'

"Louise felt an involuntary tremor at these words, for they appeared to have been uttered in a peculiar tone, and her mind was instantly filled with stories that she had heard of persons being murdered in places of this description. At length, mastering her terrors as well as she could, she inquired of the old woman whether her bed-room was far off.

"'No,' she replied. 'I shall sleep in the chamber next to yours, and my son will occupy the one on the other side, so you see there is nothing to fear, young man, though you do sleep in a strange place.'

"'I am not at all alarmed,' answered Louise, mustering up all her courage; 'on the contrary, I feel happy at the idea of having obtained a lodging beneath your roof. So good night dame, and don't fail to call me in the morning in good time.'

"The old woman hobbled down stairs, and Louise instantly began to make an examination of the room, to see that all was right, and in a closet, which she opened to satisfy herself that no one was concealed there, she found a carpet bag, on a brass plate attached to which were engraved the initials S. L. She, however, thought there was nothing very particular in this circumstance, and having again closed the closet, she was going to throw herself on the bed, dressed as she was, when voices were heard below, and curiosity prompted her to listen to what was going forward. Opening the room-door, therefore, she could distinctly hear what was going on between the mother and her son; she could hear the man she had left down stairs mention the name of St. Ange, and thus it appeared there were two persons owning that patronymic, as if to add to her perplexities. Indeed, all their talk was about him, and from what Louise could gather, it seemed that the other St. Ange had a design against the life of an Englishman, and that a plot was in progress for his destruction. Louise immediately imagined that Arnold must be the person they had alluded to, and though she felt alarmed at the dangers that threatened him, there was some consolation in having obtained even this slight clue, and as the conversation between the' mother and her son ceased shortly after this, she crept back into her room, and, having bolted the door, threw herself upon the bed to ponder over the adventure in which she thus found herself involved.

CHAPTER XVII.

AMELIA'S NARRATIVE CONTINUED.

" AFTER a feverish and disturbed slumber, Louise awoke on the following morning, and the first thoughts that entered her head, were those connected with the mysterious affair she was occupied in trying to unravel. She remembered the carpet-bag, and the initials engraved on the brass plate, and now for the first time it struck her that L. might be intended' for Laroche,—the name of the wounded man, and S. for St. Ange.— His name might be St. Ange Laroche, and the person she had seen down stairs might have been his son by the hostess. This was a wild thought, but strange things occur in the course of one's life, and who could tell but her surmises might, after all, be right.

" Be this as it might, she went down stairs, where she found the old woman and two or three of the people she had seen on the previous night, and who welcomed the supposed youth with many inquiries whether he had slept well. To these questions Louise replied with as little constraint as possible, and seating herself at the breakfast-table with them, inquired if they had heard any further news respecting the assassination they had spoken of the night before.

" ' No,' replied one of the men, ' nothing more has been heard since the murderer was sent to prison·'

" ' They are certain then who the murderer was ?' observed Louise, anxiously.

" ' Oh, yes,' replied the hostess, with visible trepidation ; ' they know him well enough ;—he is an Englishman, and lived as clerk with Monsieur Fayette.'

" ' Indeed !' cried Louise, ' and are people certain that he is the man who stabbed Laroche ?'

" " I suppose they are quite satisfied about it,' replied the hostess, ' for they have sent him to prison, and they would not have done that without being pretty well certain of being right.'

" Louise made no further comment, and when the breakfast was over, she made an excuse to go up stairs to her own room, and did not make her appearance till dinner time. This appeared rather strange to the hostess who at length asked why he did not go out to ascertain whether there was any chance of returning to the situation that had been so suddenly left.

" ' I have been thinking of doing so,' she replied, scarcely knowing what answer to make, " but a friend has been kind enough to intercede for me, and I thought it better to wait patiently till I heard how he has succeeded.'

" ' But there's nothing like looking to one's own [affairs,' exclaimed the woman ; " your offence, I dare say has not been so very great one, and by showing yourself at the house, they would see how anxious you are to return.'

" 'I have been thinking of doing so,' replied Louise, 'and am only wait-ing till night, when I shall go and ascertain whether there is any chance of my being restored to favour.'

" These words appeared to satisfy the old woman, and a long silence en-sued, which was suddenly terminated by the door being violently thrown open by St. Ange, who seemed to frown lowering as he perceived the sup-posed youth who he had hoped had left the house before that time.

" 'How is this?' he muttered to the old woman;—'why haven't you sent the young fellow away before this?'

" 'There's no occasion to be afraid of him,' she replied in a low tone; 'he seems a well behaved youth enough, and remaining here a day or two, can do us no harm.'

" 'He may find out more than will be pleasant,' observed the other.

" 'Ah!' cried the woman, 'you mean about the man they attempted to assassinate?—How is he?'

" 'Dead!'

" 'Then we are lost!'

" 'Hush!—the boy may overhear us,' exclaimed St. Ange, 'and in that case, we know what the consequence would be.'

" They then conversed together in lower tones, and Louise could hear nothing more that passed between them. Indeed she found it necessary to appear as little interested as possible in what was going forward, and when night came, she left the house under an excuse that she was going to learn whether it was likely she would be taken back into the family she had left, and promising to return and sleep at her old quarters.

" Upon leaving the house, she directed her steps towards home, that she might see Blanche, and hear what had taken place during her absence. The girl was delighted at seeing her return, and was most urgent for her to venture no more upon an adventure that promised to terminate in no way satisfactory to herself.

" 'I have been miserable,' she said, 'ever since you have been away, and if you had been absent much longer, I should have gone to the commissary of police, who would have given orders for a search to be made after you.'

" 'And had you done so,' replied Louise, 'you know not what mischief might have been the consequence.'

" 'But where have you been?' asked Blanche.

" 'In a lodging where I am perfectly safe and comfortable.'

" 'And did they see through your disguise?'

" 'No, they believe me to be a footman, and entertained no idea of the imposition practised on them.'

" 'But surely,' cried Blanche, 'you will not venture to trust yourself among them again.'

" 'It is unnecessary that I should do so,' replied Louise, 'and if you remain quiet, there is no danger to be apprehended. If, however, you should make any stir in the affair, there is every reason to believe my secret would be discovered, and in that case, it is probable my life would be sacrificed.'

" 'And how are we to know you are safe?" demanded Blanche.

" 'I will come home every evening,' she replied, 'and, thus you may rest satisfied on that point. If, however, I should happen to miss a night, you may believe that some mischance has occurred, and then you will be at liberty to set on foot any enquiries you please.'

" 'I may thus apply to the police, and obtain their assistance to search for you?'

" 'You may.'

" 'And where shall I direct them to go?'

" ' I know not the name of the place,' replied Louise, ' but the people are called St. Ange, and the police would easily be able to find the house when they know who the occupants are.'

" ' I will remember,' said Blanche, ' and now, miss, I must tell you that a young female called here last night to inquire about Mr. Arnold.'

" ' Indeed!—do you know her?'

" ' I do not,' replied the girl.

" ' Was she tall or short?'

" ' Rather tall.'

" ' Fair or dark?'

" ' I think she was fair,' replied the girl, ' but I came to the door without a candle, and could not distinguish her features.'

" ' It is my rival!' cried Louise, with vexation; ' but tell me, girl, did she say why she called?'

" ' Nothing more than that she had heard of Mr. Arnold's misfortune, and was anxious to hear whether there was any chance of his innocence being proved.'

" ' And what did you tell her?'

" ' What could I say?' cried Blanche; ' I know nothing about the affair, and all I could do, was to send her to the prison where he is confined.'

" Louise made no further reply, but taking a key from off a bunch that she found in the table drawer, she took her departure after again cautioning the domestic to act in strict conformity with the directions she had given.

" She now hurried towards the prison, in hopes that she might obtain another interview with my father, in order to inform him of the pains she was taking to prove his innocence, and inspire him with hope that his present

No. 17

misfortunes would soon come to a termination.   The gate-keeper was, however, deaf to her intreaties; and finding that no persuasions were likely to move him in her behalf, she represented herself to be the footman of a distinguished nobleman, who had been sent on a message to the prisoner to inform him that exertions were making in his behalf.

" ' Humph !' exclaimed the man, ' there seems to be a great fuss about this Mr. Alfred, for though he has been guilty of a murder, people are interesting themselves in his favour, as if he was a martyr instead of an assassin.'

" ' Who has been here ?' asked Louise.

" ' Several persons ?'

" ' Were there any females ?'

" ' Yes, one come last night.'

" ' And did she see him ?'

" ' She did,' replied the man, ' for at that time I had not received any orders to prevent it.'

" ' What sort of person was she ?' demanded Louise, eagerly.

" ' Much about your own size, youngster.'

" Louise felt somewhat relieved at this foe ; she had, now, no doubt the female spoken of was herself, and recovering her agitation, she enquired whether any men had been to see the prisoner.

" ' Oh, yes, several,' answered the gaolar ;—' there was one here scarcely half an hour ago, and he made a great many enquiries that I did not consider myself bound to answer.'

" ' Did he wear a dark cloak ?'

" ' He did,' replied the man, ' and, moreover, seemed as if he didn't wish to be known, for he had a large deep brimmed hat on that he took care to keep over his eyes, so as to prevent my seeing much of his countenance.'

" ' It is he !' cried Louise, with alarm.

" ' He ! Who do you mean, boy ?'

" ' An enemy of the prisoner,' answered Louise, recovering a little from her agitation ; ' in fact, I have reason to believe it is the man that really assassinated Monsieur Laroche.'

" ' You don't say so !' exclaimed the gaolor with surprise ; but Louise waited not to make any further reply, and she moved briskly onwards, till she heard some persons following her, and looking round, she perceived to her infinite terror that St. Ange and another person were dogging her steps.   But her terror was soon relieved, for almost directly afterwards, they crossed the road, and turning round the first street they came to, disappeared from her sight.

" Alarmed at this incident, Louise missed her road, and presently found herself near the house which had been occupied by Monsieur Laroche, and anxious to satisfy herself whether he was really dead, as the conversation between St. Ange and his mother would lead her to believe, she knocked at the door, and being answered by an old woman, enquired after the wounded man.

" ' He is no more,' replied the female.

" ' Dead !' cried Louise with terror.

" ' Yes,' answered the other, ' the wounds he received were mortal, and he sank under them about three hours since.   But there is some consolation in knowing that the assassin is in custody, and his own life will answer for the crime he has committed.'

" ' It is a dreadful affair indeed,' said Louise, concealing her agitation as much as she could ; ' but no doubt the son of Mr. Laroche will be able to bring evidence enough for the conviction of the prisoner.'

" ' The poor dear gentleman had no son,' replied the woman, ' but his heir is expected here to-morrow or the next day, and no doubt he will exert himself to punish the guilty wretch that committed the crime.'

" ' Is his heir's name St. Ange ?' asked Louise, trembling with excite-ment.

" ' I believe not,' replied the woman ; ' at least, I have never heard him called by that name.'

" Louise now saw that there was no chance of obtaining any further in-formation, and thanking the woman for her civility, she turned away, and with some little difficulty found the street which she had missed. It seemed clear to her that St. Ange was deeply concerned in the murder of Monsieur Laroche, but in the present defective state of the evidence she had to bring forward, it was quite clear that she must fail were she to make any effort towards bringing the affair forward., She, therefore, determined to watch his actions narrowly, and in spite of the great caution that was used to leave no exertion untried that might bring punishment on the real criminal.

. " On again reaching the public-house, she saw nearly the same persons who were there the night before, and seated near the fire were St. Ange and the person who had followed her during a part of her walk. The former she thought looked scowlingly at her, and scarcely had she taken her seat, when he enquired whether he had not seen her about an hour since at no great distance from the prison. Louise knew not how to reply, but recol-lecting that to acknowledge having been in that direction might betray her, she with some hesitation denied having been near the place he spoke of.

" ' Humph !' he ejaculated, ' and yet I and my friend are positive we followed you some distance.'

" ' You were mistaken then,' she replied.

" And here the conversation was dropped for the present, so that Louise had an opportunity to recover herself from the surprise and consternation into which the question had thrown her. She narrowly observed, too, the old woman, who sat by apparently heedless of what was going forward, and busied herself with some needle-work upon which she was engaged.

" Louise now began to regret the step she had taken, and thought whether it would not be better to give up her project before any further harm came of it. But what excuse to make, or how to get away without exciting sus-picion of her intentions she knew not. At length, as the hour grew later, the company gradually left the house, and at length she found herself left alone with St. Ange and his mother.

" ' How have you got on to night?' asked the old woman ; ' is your late master likely to take you back into his service ?'

" ' I have not been able to learn that,' replied Louise ; ' but the friend who has undertaken to advocate my cause gives me very good hopes of it.'

" ' In that case we shall soon lose you as a lodger ?'

" ' Perhaps so,' replied Louise ; ' but the arrangement may not be so quickly made as that, and it's not at all unlikely that I may continue with you for a week or a fortnight longer.'

" ' At any rate,' exclaimed St. Ange, ' you deny being the person we fol-lowed to-night?'

" ' I have already told you,' she replied, ' that I have not been any where in that direction.'

" Whether he was satisfied with this answer or not, Louise was unable to judge, for he threw himself back in his seat, and giving loose to his thoughts, took no further notice of her or his mother.

" We must now suffer two days and nights to pass away, at the end of which period, as Blanche had seen nothing of her young mistress, she remembered the directions she had given at her last visit, and putting on her bonnet and shawl, hurried down to the chief office of police, in order to inform the commissary of Louise's absence, and to learn whether they had any chance of discovering what had been done with her. The official personage heard her story without making any particular observation, and having written down some of the chief points, desired her to return home, and wait with patience till she heard from him. Blanche departed, and after the commissary had considered the matter a little, he rang a small hand-bell, and was immediately answered by his factotum.

"'David,' he said, 'I have an affair of some importance in hand, which will require the utmost secrecy and caution to carry into effect. Do you know of a public-house in the suburbs of the city kept by a person named St. Ange?'

"'No,' replied David, after some consideration.

"'Prompt inquiries must be made into it,' exclaimed the other; 'and to you I shall trust the management, relying that you will be careful not to let any one know of the affair.'

"'What has happened?' asked David, with all the composure of a man that is thoroughly used to his business.

"'A young lady has most mysteriously disappeared,' replied the other, in a half whisper.

"'Who is she?'

"'Her name is Louise Fayette, and she is the daughter of the old attorney who——'

"'I know him,' interrupted David, 'he is the person with whom the young Englishman lived who stands accused of having assassinated Monsieur Laroche.'

"'You are right, David,' answered the superior. 'His daughter, it appears, left home three days ago, and there is good reason to suppose, has been unfairly dealt with.'

"'Humph!' ejaculated David; 'this, perhaps, is some love affair, and, after all, it may turn out that she has only run away with her lover.'

"'It may be so,' answered the other, 'for she left home disguised in the livery of a footman, and the affair certainly wears something of the complexion you have put on it. But, on the other hand, her female attendant, who has just been here, is in great alarm for the safety of her mistress, and from what she says, there is reason to believe the young lady has fallen into bad hands.'

"'Has nothing been seen of her since she left home?'

"'Yes, she returned on the following evening,' replied the commissary, 'and informed her servant that she was engaged in an attempt to prove the innocence of the young Englishman. The girl, it seems, tried to persuade her against it, but she was resolute, and after telling the domestic the name of the person that keeps the public-house where she was staying, took her departure, and from that time, has never been seen or heard of.'

"'And now the servant has applied to you to assist in the discovery of her mistress?'

"'Precisely so.'

"'Depend on it,' replied David, 'it will turn out to be nothing but a foolish love adventure.'

"'Perhaps so,' answered the commissary, 'for it seems she has formed a romantic passion for her father's clerk,—the foreigner who is suspected of the murder,—and, as she had declared an intention to discover a clue to prove his innocence, we may imagine that the affair will turn out to be a false alarm.'

" ' Has she ever before absented herself from her father's house ?' inquired the other.

" ' Yes,' replied the commissary, ' on the night of the murder, she went out,—it is supposed to watch where they were going to take her lover,—and she did not return home for some hours.'

" ' This is a marvellous story,' observed David ; ' and, as the first step towards solving the mystery, you wish to find out where the public-house is situated ?'

· " ' I do,' replied the other, ' for there is reason to believe the persons belonging to that house are concerned in the robbery.'

" ' And if they should have happened to discover that she went there as a spy, there can be little doubt they have murdered her to make sure of their secret.'

" ' I am afraid so,' answered the commissary, ' and, therefore, it must be your care to discover the house at which Louise Fayette so imprudently took her lodging.'

" ' I rather think there will be no great difficulty about it,' replied David, ' for there is an old woman that keeps a public-house in an obscure quarter of the city, and, if I am not much mistaken, she has a son that they call St. Ange, a wild fellow, and who has long had the eyes of the police upon him.'

" ' You will visit her house then ?'

" ' I will, so give me a little silver, for it may be necessary to spend some money before I come back.'

" This the commissary did, and David, having first disguised himself in plain clothes, took his departure from the place, and was making his way towards the quarter of the city he had alluded to, when he was accosted by a young footman, who told him his clothes had been lent to some one, and from that time he could obtain no information where the person was to be found. David now began to suspect that this might lead to a discovery, as it was known Louise Fayette had left her house disguised in livery, and resolving to make the young fellow his companion in the visit he was about to make, he inquired his name.

" ' Pierre,' answered the other.

" ' Well then, Monsieur Pierre, I believe I shall be able to assist you on one condition.'

" ' What is it ?'

" ' That you accompany me to the place I am going to.'

" ' With all my heart.'

" ' But mind,' said David, ' you must be very cautious in all you say or do when any other persons are present besides ourselves.'

" ' I will,' replied Pierre.

" ' Everything will depend on your acting as I have said,' continued David, ' and, above all things, say nothing that may discover the business you have applied to me about. The clothes shall be restored, but it will be on condition that you proceed with great caution, and take your cue from me whenever you find yourself at a loss what to do.'

" Pierre promised implicit obedience to these directions, and they then pursued their way towards the place of their destination, which David found without any difficulty. Just before arriving there, however, he again cautioned his companion to be very circumspect, and, having pretty well drilled him in the part he was to play, he entered the house, closely followed by the other.

" Madame Junot, the hostess, was at the moment occupied at the fire, and as her back was towards them, she was not aware of any one being near, till David accosted her with the usual salutation of the day.

Upon this, she turned round, and perceiving Pierre in a livery exactly like that which had been worn by her late guest, she became so conscie. ce-stricken, that, uttering a cry of horror, she would have rushed from the room, had not David at the moment seized her by the arm.

" ' Why, how now, Madame Junot !' he exclaimed, justly conjecturing the cause of her terror ; ' am I so ugly that you must run away the moment I make my appearance ?'

" ' It was not that,' cried the old woman, recovering her composure as well as she could ; ' but the youth with you is so much like one that is dead, that at the moment, I mistook him for an apparition.'

" ' Indeed !' exclaimed David, ' but as I can answer for his being flesh and blood, you may as well compose yourself, and remain where you are. You haven't forgotten me, I suppose ?'

" ' I have no recollection of you,' she replied.

" ' Ah !' responded the officer, ' that's one of the failings of old age, and I can readily pardon your forgetfulness. And yet, madame, I have spent many a merry evening in this very room with Monsieur Junot, your husband.'

" ' Poor Justin !' groaned the old woman.

" ' Why, you don't mean to say he's dead !'

" ' He is,' replied Madame Junot.

" ' And your son ?' said the wily David, who all this time was endeavouring to obtain a clue ; ' I suppose he has grown a fine young fellow by this time ?—Can I see him ?'

" ' He is not at home,' replied Madame Junot, uneasily ; —' indeed he is seldom to be found here, as he has nothing at all to do with the business.'

" David now gave a preconcerted signal to his younger companion, and Pierre understanding it, left the house, and hurried back to the commissary, to whom he related all that had passed at Madame Junot's.

" The other remained where he was, in hopes of learning some further particulars ; but the hostess was very cautious in what she said before him, and though several customers came in and out, he could gather nothing from their conversation that could lead to a discovery of the place where St. Ange was likely to be found. He knew, however, that he was a great frequenter of the gaming houses, and having remained where he was as long as there was a chance of hearing anything, the officer took his leave of Madame Junot, and quitting the place, sought three or four of his fraternity, who he stationed near the house, with instructions to observe all who passed into it, and to take any suspicious persons into custody.

" This done, he visited several of the gaming houses in search of the object of his pursuit, but without success, for St. Ange was not to be seen in any of them. By means of cautious enquiries, however, he obtained a pretty good description, and being obliged to be satisfied for the present, he returned to the commissary of police, to whom he related all that had occurred since his departure.

" His own opinion was that Louise Fayette had not been murdered as was at first suspected, but that she had been conveyed to some place of safety till circumstances should permit her to be set at liberty. He also felt certain that St. Ange was either the murderer of Monsieur Laroche, or deeply concerned in the transaction, and as active measures were now in progress, he had no doubt the person they were in quest of would be in custody before many days,—or perhaps hours,—had elapsed. Indeed, the description he had obtained of St. Ange, was so perfect, that he felt assured that he should be able to recognise him, let them meet under what circumstances they might.

CHAPTER XVIII.

AMELIA'S NARRATIVE CONTINUED.

"ON the same evening alluded to in the last chapter, two persons on horseback approached the city, and from the precaution they took, it was very evident that they wished to excite as little attention as possible. They had not yet reached that part where there were many houses, yet they frequently looked round them to see if any persons were observing. These were St. Ange Junot, with whom the reader is already acquainted, and his foster brother, St. Ange Laroche, the heir of the unfortunate man whose murder was just then creating so much noise in the city. They had been riding for some time in silence, but at length St. Ange Laroche said :—

" ' I have been thinking that it would be madness were we to hesitate any longer about an affair in which our own safety or destruction is involved. If a life could have been saved, I should have been glad, but it behoves a man to take care of himself, and as both you and I are in peril, there is no alternative but the one I have proposed. This young Englishman is in prison, and the law will soon remove him out of the way, but the livery servant is in our own custody at present, and the only thing we can do is to prevent the possibility of his escaping from us.'

" ' By cutting his throat !'

" 'Exactly so,' replied the other ' but necessity compels us, and, therefore, hesitation would be madness.'

" ' It must be admitted,' said St. Ange Junot, ' that the boy has brought it all upon himself. He came into our house as a spy, and, no doubt, would have betrayed us before now if I had not conveyed him into the cellar, where he now remains a prisoner.'

" ' But must not remain so much longer,' answered his foster brother, ' for he may find means to escape, and then I shall be utterly ruined. You know my expectations under the will of my uncle, Monsieur Laroche, and if any noise should be made by this stripling, I should be compelled to fly without waiting for any share of the old man's money.'

" ' But if any fuss should be made,' observed St. Ange Junot, ' we can get clear off, and some one else might receive the fortune, and send it to any place where you may think fit to go. Besides, I don't suppose any enquiry will be made about the boy, for he's only a servant out of place, and his friends, if he has any, will not make much enquiry about him, as it will be imagined he has gone to seek a situation in some other part of the kingdom.'

" ' There's nothing like making all things safe,' replied the other, ' and as by killing the boy, we may keep our own necks out of the halter ; I shall stick to my old plan, and so rid myself of the chief object of my fear.'

" ' There can be no danger,' retorted his companion, ' while the boy is kept in safe custody as he is at the present moment. Besides, if there is any cause for fear, I stand quite in as bad a situation as you do."

" ' I know all about that,' replied St. Ange Laroche ; ' for I am your foster brother, and whatever guilt has been committed by one, has been equally shared by the other. The old man complained that I had been extravagant, when I applied to him the other day for money, and refused to supply me with any more till I showed symptoms of retrenchment. I was driven to the verge of desperation by that refusal, and as money must be had by some means or other, we plotted together, and the old man was ————'

" ' Hush!' interrupted his companion, with alarm ; ' you speak too loud, and should a word be overheard, it would not be long before we exchanged places with the young Englishman, who is so snugly housed in prison, through our contrivance.'

" ' Well,' exclaimed the other, ' it seems to me that you are but a chicken-hearted chap after all ; so if you are afraid of getting into any mischief about this affair, the better way will be to part without going any further into the business. If we do so, I must pass the remainder of my days in a foreign country, and may happen to make things tolerably comfortable ; but your fate will not be quite so good a one, for beggarly will be your lot, and lucky may you think yourself, should you chance to escape meeting your doom on a scaffold.'

" ' You have mistaken me,' replied the other, ' for I am not such a coward as to desert a friend at a moment when things look a little black. It is your opinion the boy ought to die, and that being the case, I promise his life shall not be worth half an hour's purchase after I get home.'

" ' Why, that is well said,' exclaimed St. Ange Laroche, ' and as matters have thus been arranged, suppose we part here, lest our being seen to enter the city together should create any suspicion against us.'

" ' As you please,' replied the other, submissively.

" ' Let it be so, then,' exclaimed the one who appeared to be the superior ; ' and if you should happen to want to communicate with me, send a line to the Fleur-de-lis inn, where I intend to remain for the present. But I had forgotten to ask whether your mother may be safely trusted in this affair ?'

" ' She may,' replied St. Ange Junot ; ' for though she approves not of what has taken place, she loves both of us too well to utter a word that might serve to bring us into trouble.'

" The other seemed to be satisfied with this assurance, and they immediately afterwards separated ; one taking the road which led towards the inn he had mentioned, and his companion proceeding by a more obscure direction towards the house of his mother.

" It was about one hour after this period that David enquired of a man whether anything had happened during his watch to lead them to suppose that St. Ange had returned home. The fellow, who was one of those who had been left to keep an eye upon the premises, informed him, in reply, that a person answering the description of the person they were in pursuit of, had returned not half an hour since, and had let himself into the house with a great deal of secresy and caution.

" ' That's him !' exclaimed David, with triumph ; ' the fool has ventured back, but it will not be long before we make him repent the step he has taken.'

" ' He can't escape us,' returned the man, ' for I did not leave the place till I had stationed some of the police all round the house.'

" ' You must return instantly, and see that they do their duty,' exclaimed David. ' Remember, St. Ange is now in our power, and it will be at your own peril should he happen to give us the slip, after having so far succeeded so well.'

" ' Won't you go back with me,' asked the man, ' and assist in capturing the fellow ?'

" ' No,' answered David, ' I must leave that part of the business to your own discretion, and mind I am not disappointed in the result. You will not have to capture him unless he should attempt to escape, but merely keep a strict watch round the place till I come to see what had best be done.'

" The man now took his departure, and David, hurrying off to the

apartment of the commissary, informed him of what had been done, and then suggested a plan by which the capture of the criminal would be rendered certain.

"We must now return to St. Ange, who having, by means of a key, obtained admittance to the house, first of all assured himself that no one was about the place to disturb him, and then lighting a candle, began to make arrangements for the murderous project in which he was engaged. A large sheathed knife, which he took from the mantle-piece, was sharpened till the keenness of the edge seemed to satisfy him, and when this was done, he once more looked round the place to see whether anybody was about, and having set his doubts on this point at rest, he next stealthily crept into an adjoining chamber, and raised a ponderous trap-door, which discovered beneath a dark vault or cellar, to which a ladder gave admittance. St. Ange shuddered as he looked down, and thought of the deed he was about to perpetrate ; but, at length his courage began to revive, and taking in his hand the lamp which he had been obliged to place on the ground whilst he was raising the trap-door, he slowly descended, by means of the ladder, into the darksome vault beneath. Scarcely, however, had he reached the bottom, when a half suppressed cry was heard, and a female form was seen rushing forward as if to interrupt his progress, and prevent the deed he had meditated. Not an instant, therefore, was to be lost, and, believing that the person before him was the supposed footman, he grasped his knife firmly, and raising his hand, struck the weapon to the heart of the hapless victim of his fury. The female sank with a groan that went to his very soul ; for the sound was familiar to him, and holding down the lamp to the form which was now lying at his feet, he beheld, to his inexpressible horror, the well known features of his mother! She was slain, and the murderer, regardless of the object that had taken him there, rushed up the

No. 18

ladder with the frantic speed of a madman, and hastened he knew not whither.

"It is now necessary that we go back to the second night when Louise slept at the public house, and on which occasion she felt rather more uneasy than she had done on the previous evening, for she thought St. Ange seemed to suspect her, and in the event of his doing so, she knew her life would pay the forfeit of her temerity. For some time after she went upstairs she could hear him talking to his mother, but she could not hear what passed between them; and, with an effort to shake off her fears, she laid down on the bed, though, as on the foregoing night, without undressing herself.

"But it was in vain that she endeavoured to obtain any sleep, for her mind was racked with a sense of the danger that threatened her, and she lay for two hours listening to the continual murmur in the room beneath. At length, however, she could hear their chairs move, as if the mother and her son had risen for the purpose of going to rest; but presently afterwards St Ange entered the adjoining chamber, and almost instantly a sliding panel was moved, through which he advanced into her room.

"Terrified at this intrusion, Louise sprang from the bed, and made towards the opening in the partition; but ere she could do this, St. Ange had seized her round the waist, and from thence transferred her to the dark vault where we have just seen so fearful a tragedy enacted. From this time she saw nothing more of her enemy till the night when he descended with the design of taking her life; but in the interval her meals were regularly brought by Madame Junot, who endeavoured to console her with a hope of speedy liberty, and an assurance that she had nothing to fear beyond a temporary confinement in her present dreary abode.

"In this manner three nights passed away, until the arrival of the one on which the event occurred of which I have just been speaking. At that period Madame Junot had visited the prisoner at a much later hour than usual, and remained talking to her up to the period when her son descended into the vault with the design of ending the life of his victim. Madame Junot saw the knife with which he was armed, and at once guessing his purpose, she rushed forward to implore mercy for the captive, and received the weapon in her own body. The wound she had received was instantly fatal, and with one heavy groan she yielded up her breath.

"The terror of Louise may be better imagined than described; a deadly faintness overpowered her, and, on recovering from the stupor into which she had fallen, she found herself surrounded by the police; but, though called upon to give an explanation of what had occurred to her, it was found that excessive terror had taken away all power of speech!

"As for St. Ange Laroche, he proceeded, as he said he would, to the Fleur-de-lis inn, where he slept that night, and on the next morning went to the attorney of his late uncle, to enquire about his disposal of the property, and to desire that the business should be completed as soon as possible, because it was his intention to leave France immediately after the money had been paid over to him. This was, of course, promised on the part of the lawyer, with about as much sincerity as gentlemen of that craft usually practice upon their unfortunate clients; and as St. Ange thought all would be arranged in a day or two, he determined to make himself as comfortable as he could at his inn.

"There was one thing, however, that perplexed him a good deal—he had not heard anything from his foster-brother, and his conduct had appeared to be rather vacillating when they were last together; and he began to fear that he would not carry his murderous purpose into execution, and that, consequently, he would be in continual danger of detection. Unable to endure his suspense any longer, he left the inn at dusk, and pursued his way towards the house where his confederate resided. On arriving at the door, he looked in to see if St. Ange was in, but not seeing him he entered boldly, and was making his way towards the bar, when three men, who were at the fire, suddenly jumped up, and whilst one of them secured the door, the other two sprang towards him, and, seizing him by his arms, effectually prevented all possibility of his escape.

" ' Aha !' exclaimed David, for he was one of the men, ' I thought we should have the happiness of seeing you before long. Monsieur St. Ange is most welcome, for here ends all further trouble on his behalf.'

" ' My name certainly is St. Ange,' replied the other coolly, ' but I have yet to learn why that circumstance is to place me in the hands of a ruffian.'

" ' Ah ! you are impatient to know what the affair is you are wanted about,' exclaimed David. However, it is no part of my duty to explain these things, so you must restrain your curiosity till we take you before a magistrate.'

" ' Take *me* before a magistrate ?' cried young Laroche, with indignant surprise.

" ' Even so,' answered David, and forthwith, they handed him out of the house, and conveyed him to a prison where he was informed he must remain till the time arrived for his examination on the charge upon which he had been arrested. He now suspected that the little footman had been permitted to escape, and that an assassination of a serious nature was about to be brought against him. The thought of this preyed heavily upon his mind during the night, and when he was taken on the following morning before the magistrate, his looks certainly conveyed a pretty good proof of his guilt. But his terrors were soon a good deal softened by the questions that were put to him.

" ' What is your name, prisoner ?' asked the magistrate.

" ' St. Ange Laroche.'

" ' St. Ange Junot, you mean,' observed the clerk, who fancied this was a trick of the prisoner's to set them wrong.

" ' I have told you my name,' replied St. Ange, ' and if it should be necessary, I can bring forward witnesses to prove that I am the person I have stated.'

" ' You are trying to mislead us,' said the magistrate, incredulously.

" ' Indeed I am not.'

" ' Do you deny being the son of Madam Junot, the keeper of a public-house, and who has been stabbed, very probably, by your own hand ?'

" ' I am not the son of Madam Junot,' answered the prisoner, ' she was my foster mother, but I have never seen her for some years past.'

" ' Are you a resident in this city ?'

" ' No, I only arrived here a night or two ago.'

" ' What business brought you here ?'

" ' The death of my uncle, Monsieur Laroche,' replied the prisoner ; " he was murdered by an Englishman, who is now in prison, and as one of his heirs, I have come to claim my part of his estate.'

" ' Can you prove this assertion of yours ?' asked the magistrate.

" ' Certainly I can.'

" ' Who are your witnesses ?'

" ' My cousin, Victor Laroche is one, and the other is my attorney, Monsieur Denoque.'

" ' They shall be sent for,' said the magistrate, and the prisoner was ordered to be taken into a private room, whilst a message was conveyed to the proposed witnesses desiring their immediate attendance at his office. It was not more than half an hour before they both arrived, and the prisoner was again directed to be brought into court.

" ' Do you know the person who has been brought here on a charge that affects his life ?' asked the magistrate.

" Both the persons avowed that they did, and that he had truly stated his name.

" ' This is a most surprising affair,' exclaimed the magistrate, ' and must be thoroughly explained. The prisoner is, it appears, an innocent man, and we owe it to his honour, to sift the matter to the very bottom.'

" ' Perhaps you will inform us why he has been arrested?' said the attorney.

" ' The fact is,' answered the magistrate, ' he has been mistaken for a man named St. Ange Junot, and there is certainly some blame to be attached to himself for not having explained who he was before, by which this inconvenience might have been spared him.

" He then entered into a history of Louise Fayette, the disguise she had adopted, and the cause which had led her to so extraordinary an act.

" ' And she will, of course, be brought forward as a witness,' observed the lawyer.

" ' Unfortunately,' replied the magistrate, ' she is unable to give her testimony, for terror has taken so great an affect upon her, that when discovered in the vault, it was found that the power of speech had been taken from her. Several medical gentlemen have seen her, and they give it as their opinion, she will never again have the power of speech.'

" The attorney paid great attention to all that had been said, and the glances he every now and then directed towards St. Ange Laroche, showed the suspicion that he began to entertain of his being connected with the murder of his uncle.

" This is a most unaccountable circumstance,' he said, ' and one that will require some trouble and attention to bring to a satisfactory conclusion. Monsieur Laroche has been assassinated, and a man named St. Ange Junot is suspected as being the party that committed the deed. But as no robbery was committed, I can see no motive that Junot could have had in shedding the blood of a fellow creature. But perhaps, you, Monsieur St. Ange Laroche, who were nearly related to the deceased, can throw some light upon the mystery ?

" ' I have all along,' answered St. Ange Laroche, with evident agitation, ' believed that Junot was innocent of the crime. In fact, there is every reason to believe it was committed by the young Englishman who is now in prison, and who, it must be remembered, was arrested on the charge whilst in the act of attempting to make his escape across the fields.'

" With this he was about to leave the court, lest his agitation should betray him ; but ere he could do this the door opened, and David, followed by Pierre the footman and another person, entered the place. St. Ange Laroche started back in undisguised terror, for the police-officer carried in his hand a carpet-bag and other articles, which he knew would be likely to afford testimony against himself.

" ' How now !' exclaimed the magistrate ; ' what is the meaning of this interruption ?'

" ' We have just found this carpet-bag in the house of Madame Junot,' replied David ; ' and, as the letters S. L. are engraved on the brass plate, I thought very likely this gentleman might know something about it.'

" ' Does the bag contain anything ?' asked the magistrate.

" ' I don't know.'

" ' Let it be opened,' said the justice.

" The order was instantly obeyed, and some clothes, stained with blood, taken out and laid upon the table. A letter, known to be in the hand-writing of Monsieur Laroche, and addressed to his nephew St. Ange, was also found, the date of which proved it to have been written only a few hours before he was assassinated.

"'Did this carpet-bag ever belong to you?' asked the magistrate, addressing himself to St. Ange Laroche.

"'It does,' he replied, "but I lent it to Junot, which accounts for its being found in his house.'

"'And what have you got to say to the blood-stained garments, and the letter?'

"'Merely that they have been placed there by some one who wishes to fix upon me a crime of which I am innocent," replied the other, in an agitated voice.

"'At any rate,' said the magistrate, 'I rather think we must all come to the conclusion that the Englishman is innocent, though there is certainly some difficulty in accounting for his having been seen in the house where the murder was committed.'

"'He may have been enticed there in order to fix the crime on him,' replied the lawyer, 'and thus prevent suspicion from alighting on the really guilty parties.'

"'It appears,' exclaimed the magistrate, 'that the evidence has taken an important turn against the prisoner, and I shall, therefore, feel it my duty to remand the case for a week, during which time we may be able to collect more proof, by which we may come to a just conclusion.'

"Upon this St. Ange Laroche was carried to prison, in spite of all his remonstrances and protestations of innocence; and now, for the first time, he began to reflect upon the peril in which he was involved, and to form all sorts of schemes for shifting the blame from himself to some one else.

"But there was one at work against him who was determined to come at the truth, and bring to punishment the perpetrator of the murder. Monsieur Denoque, the attorney of the person who had been assassinated, felt quite satisfied in his own mind that the nephew was the murderer: his wild and dissipated habits had always afforded grounds for supposing he would some day or other proceed to acts of violence in order to supply his wasteful extravagance. He knew also that frequent applications had lately been made to his uncle for money, and that those demands having been refused, an angry correspondence had taken place, which ended in the uncle's declaring that he should have no more money from him, and at the same time desiring that he might never see or hear from him again. This last letter was the one that had been found in the carpet-bag, and it afforded reasonable grounds to suppose that the murder had been committed in revenge for having been thus cast off.

"In furtherance of his plans, Monsieur Denoque visited Arnold in the prison where he was still confined, in order to obtain from him a description of the person who had lured him to the house where the assassination had taken place. But my father could afford him no satisfaction on that subject, for it was dark when the man called for him, and on reaching the house the stranger left him, and appeared no more afterwards.

"Thus all hopes of obtaining more conclusive evidence seemed to be at an end, and the day arrived for the prisoner's re-examination without adding in the least to the proofs that would be required to substantiate the charge. On that very day, however, a boy presented himself at the house of Monsieur Denoque, in consequence of an advertisement in the papers, offering a reward to any person who would come forward to prove that St. Ange Laroche was in or near the city about the time of the murder. A few questions put by the lawyer convinced him the boy's evidence would be of importance.   He, therefore, took the lad with him to the magistrate, and the prisoner having been again brought up, the examination was resumed.

" 'Have you anything further to urge against the prisoner ?' asked the magistrate.

" 'This lad,' answered Monsieur Denoque, 'can swear that he saw St. Ange Laroche in his master's house at the outskirts of the town on the very night when the murder was committed.'

" 'What is your name, boy ?' asked the magistrate.

" 'Jacques Renaud.'

" 'Where do you live ?'

" 'With my master.'

" 'What business does he follow ?'

" 'He is a publican, and keeps the 'Black Lion,' just out of the town on the road to Abbeville.'

" 'Did you ever see the prisoner there ?' inquired the magistrate.

" 'Yes,' replied the boy, after a scrutinizing look at St. Ange Laroche.

" 'You positively swear to that fact ?'

" 'I do.'

" 'Was there any reason for taking so much notice of him ?'

" 'He was a good deal flurried when he came in,' replied the witness, 'and I couldn't help thinking he must have done something very bad to make him so agitated.'

" 'Did he say anything ?'

" 'He asked me to tell him where a surgeon was to be found, and I sent him to Monsieur Fayette.'

" 'Foolish boy !' said the magistrate ; 'know you not that Monsieur Fayette is a lawyer ?'

" 'There's two of the name,' replied the witness ; 'one's a lawyer, and the other's a doctor.'

" 'Hah !' exclaimed Monsieur Denoque ; " then here at last we have a clue to the whole mystery.   St. Ange Laroche committed the murder, and being instantly seized with remorse, he hastened to the house kept by this boy's master and enquired for a surgeon, in hopes that he might be able to save the life of the man he had assassinated.   The boy mentioned to him the name of Monsieur Fayette, and in the confusion he went to the house of the lawyer instead of to the doctor's.   The English clerk followed him without knowing the business he was going on, and was introduced into the room under the idea that he was a medical man.   Thus his being in the place is clearly accounted for, and I trust he will be speedily acquitted of a crime which it is evident he did not commit.'

" St. Ange Laroche was observed to be much agitated whilst this speech was being delivered, and on being asked at its conclusion if he had any reply to make, he freely acknowledged that the supposition of the attorney was correct, and admitted that he and the other St. Ange had plotted and committed the murder of his uncle.   He, however, observed the deepest remorse for what he had done, and was conveyed back to prison a repentant criminal.

" Shortly afterwards the trial took place, and on his own confession he was found guilty of the heinous offence charged against him.   But his contrition moved the heart of the king in his favour, and intead of suffering the last penalty of the law, he was sentenced to imprisonment for life.

" Thus, my friend," continued Amelia, " I have related to you the singular adventures that occurred to my parents, and which had so nearly terminated in the ignominious death of my father for a crime of which he was innocent."

CHAPTER XIX.

AMELIA CONCLUDES HER STORY.

" THE narrative is certainly a very extraordinary one," observed Mrs. Gordon, who had been an attentive listener; " but all this time we have not heard anything about yourself."

" I suppose," said the husband of the last speaker, " Arnold and Louise were married, for such constancy and affection as her's surely was not un-rewarded ?"

" They married," replied Amelia, " but my mother never recovered the power of speech that had been taken away from her when she saw the murder committed on the old woman in the vault where she was confined. The union, however, was not a happy one, for my mother continued to be as jealous as ever of her former rival, and no arguments of my father could ever change the unfortunate opinion she had formed that he had married her merely from gratitude, and without feeling any love for her. Soon after their union, her father took Arnold into partnership with him, and about the same time news arrived that the girl my father had formerly loved had given her hand to another. Yet in spite of that, nothing would ever convince my mother that her husband was not with the first mistress of his heart whenever he happened to be out of her sight.

" This was a miserable state of existence, yet it went on for five or six years, till at length the annoyance became so intolerable that my father determined to quit the neighbourhood with his wife and myself—then quite a child; and after a great deal of careful consideration, he resolved to return to his native country, where he would best be able to earn his living, and at the same time he would be far removed from the object of his wife's jealousy.

" The plan was accordingly put into execution, and they settled in one of the most populous towns in England, with every prospect of success. But still my mother's groundless suspicions haunted her fancy like evil spirits. She was jealous of every woman her husband looked at or spoke to, and so notorious did she at length become, that the house was shunned by every one ; and as my father's business fell off in consequence, he was obliged to remove from town to town, in none of which he could remain long in consequence of his wife's infirmity of temper. It is true she could not speak, but she had other ways of showing her violence, more terrible than words would have been. No one, in fact, would venture near his house, and as his professional exertions were thus foiled, he was obliged to sit himself down and contemplate in despair the poverty and ruin that were hurrying on.

" Thus situated, his only solace was in me, who he regarded with true parental love ; and his chief occupation consisted in educating me for the sort of life he thought it most likely I should follow. With grief, however, he saw that I inherited a considerable portion of my mother's violence of temper ; and even now do I recollect the earnest entreaties with which he conjured me to take warning by the example before me, and to check my inclination to passion ere it became too late for control.

" I obeyed him as well as I could ; but the temper was inherited from my mother, and it was not always to be subdued so easily as my father imagined it might. Thus I grew up to womanhood ; and my father and mother came up to London with the idea that I might work at some light business, and thus ward off the penalty which had pressed so long and heavily on us

Of course I was anxious to do all I could towards supporting them, and soon obtained employment as a map-colourer, at which I toiled incessantly from morning till night, receiving but a trifling remuneration for my labour, and sacrificing my health at the sedentary occupation I had chosen to adopt.

"About twelve months had I pursued this wearisome and profitless employment, when one evening I was called by my mistress into the shop to act as an interpreter between herself and a French gentleman, who had called to give an order for a number of maps, which he wanted to have coloured after a peculiar manner. The stranger seemed to be struck with my appearance, but he said nothing just then to occasion my surprise or alarm; and, having given his order, he left the shop with a promise to call again on the following evening.

True to his appointment, he came as he said he would, and brought with him an Englishman, whose attentions to me were even more marked than those of his friend. In fact, from that time the Englishman took every opportunity of calling; and at length I grew so used to seeing him that I felt no alarm at the increasing tenderness of his manner, and as he generally contrived to meet me as I was going home at night from my work, I suffered him to accompany me almost to the door, where we always parted under a promise of seeing him again on the following evening.

"It was imprudent, you will say, to permit this, and still more so that I said nothing of the affair to my father or mother, whose experience in the artful ways of the world would have put me on my guard against the villanous schemes of a libertine. Indeed, I was afraid to mention the subject, for I began to love the stranger, who appeared to be candid and honourable, and I was afraid lest they should forbid me to see him any more.

"At length, however, when he found that my heart had been won, he began to speak of the toilsome business in which I was engaged, and how excellent a thing it would be to get out of it, and to get more money, and thus raise my parents from the wretched state of indigence into which they had fallen. Vice is easily painted in gaudy colours, and so excellent an artist did he prove in that respect, that — though I did not forbid him ever to see me again—I certainly did not take any other measures to show him how much I scorned the sort of life he would have prevailed on me to follow.

"For some months he continued to be the companion of my evening walks homewards; but on one occasion, when he had seen me to the usual place of parting, I left him with a heaviness of heart that I could not account for, and knocked at the door of the house where we lodged. To my surprise, however, no answer was returned, and I had repeated the summons three or four times without effect, when the door was suddenly flounced open, and our landlord, making his appearance, demanded, in angry accents, why I dared to disturb him by knocking at his door.

"'I am the daughter of one of your lodgers,' I replied, 'and expected the door would have been, as usual, opened by my father.'

"'Your father has left,' he replied, gruffly.

"'Left!' I exclaimed, in terror; 'oh, where have they gone?—for they told me not of their intention of removing, when I quitted him this morning.'

"'Ah!' retorted the unfeeling brute, 'that's because they didn't know what was going to happen.'

"'Good heavens!' cried I, 'has any accident befallen them?'

"'No, no, you can't call it an accident,' he replied, 'because they had

every reason to expect that a gaol was what they must come to if they didn't pay the money they owed.'

" 'A gaol!' I exclaimed, with horror; ' have they, indeed, been dragged to one ?'

" 'To be sure,' he answered. 'Your father was arrested soon after you went out this morning, and as your mother went at the same time, I suppose she has followed him.'

" 'Whither have they taken him?' I cried.

" 'That's more than I can tell you,' he said; ' for we have plenty of gaols in and about London, and you may walk about for a day or two before you find the right one.'

" ' Can I not remain for the night,' I asked, 'in the lodgings they occupied?'

" ' No,' he exclaimed fiercely; ' I'm too glad to get rid of the lot of you to let any part of the family in again. They owe me two months' rent, that, I suppose I shall lose, so none of you shall come in now, I can tell you.'

" And so saying, he slammed the door in my face, leaving me to wander about without a roof to shelter me, or a bed in which to rest my weary limbs! Sick with despair, and my heart torn with the thought of the troubles that had befallen my parents, I turned away from the house with an intention of calling upon one of my shopmates to ask her for a night's lodging, intending on the following morning to go forth in search of those whom misfortune had brought to become the inmates of a prison. I had not gone far, however, when I heard a well-known voice behind me, I beheld the person who of late had shown me so much attention. At the moment I would have fled, for I dreaded to let him know the situation to which we had been reduced; but before I could do

No. 19

so, he took me by the arm, and enquired how it was that I had not returned home as usual.

"'Alas!' I exclaimed, bursting into tears, 'I have no longer a home that I can call my own.'

"'Indeed!' he said, with suprise, 'have your friends, then, left so suddenly?'

"'It is in vain to conceal the truth from you,' I cried; 'my father has been taken to prison for a debt that he will never be able to pay, and I am afraid his creditor will keep him there for the remainder of his life.'

"'This is bad news,' said Mr. Willis Gayton—for such was his name— 'very bad, indeed,' he repeated; 'but perhaps something may be done if you will rely upon my exertions.'

"'Heaven bless you, sir!' I exclaimed, 'do but release him, and my gratitude would be for ever won.'

"'I would rather behalf win your love,' he exclaimed, throwing his arm round my waist ere I had time to escape from him. 'Nay,' he continued, 'do not struggle thus to release yourself, for remember, Amelia, I am your friend, and your father's release from prison will depend on my exertions.'

"'Will you, indeed, get him out of that dreary prison?' I asked.

"'I promise it,' he replied; 'and now tell me, my dear, what has become of your mother?'

"'She has followed her husband to prison.'

"'Then you have no friend left in the world but myself.'

"'Heaven will not desert me,' I replied.

"'Perhaps not,' he exclaimed; 'but it seems likely enough you are to pass the night in the streets, unless you think proper to follow my suggestions.'

"'There will be no occasion for it,' I replied, 'for I am about to visit one of my workmates, who, I doubt not, will give me a lodging for the night.'

"'You are determined, then,' he said, 'to reject my offer of friendship and protection?'

"'I am.'

"'Then your parents will perish through the obstinacy of their only child.'

"'Heaven!' I cried, 'will you not assist them on any other condition than the shame and downfall of their daughter?'

"'I love you, Amelia,' he exclaimed, 'and that must be my excuse for the proposition I have made.'

"'Why, then, do you not make me your wife?' I asked.

"'Because by doing so, I should bring ruin upon us both,' he replied. 'My father has great wealth at his disposal and he has threatened to leave it all to some one else if ever I should offend him by marrying a portionless wife.'

"'In that case,' I replied, 'it is time that we part for ever.'

"'Nay, be not rash, Amelia,' he exclaimed; 'but recollect the misery such a determination on your part would bring upon those you love. Without a friend, your father must pass his days and nights in hopeless imprisonment, and what will be your own reflections when you consider that he might be at liberty but for your own obstinacy.'

"'And, on the other hand,' I replied, 'what would be my reflections when I come to consider that my father's liberty was purchased at the expense of my own honour.'

"'But I love you, Amelia,' he cried, 'and will make you my wife the moment I can do so without plunging, ourselves into poverty and the world's contempt. Say, then, that your scruples have given way to filial duty, and your parents shall once more enjoy ease and freedom.'

"It would be in vain,' continued Amelia to her auditors, 'to recount the various arguments he used to remove my sense of duty and virtue. Suffice it to say, he at length persuaded me to accompany him home, and from that moment I became hateful even to myself.

"When my father was arrested, his wife resolved to follow him to prison and share his confinement, for, in spite of all her jealousy and violence of temper, she had an affectionate heart, and would on no account leave him to endure alone the misery that had fallen to his lot. Previously to leaving home she wrote a note to me, explaining what had happened, and informing me of the prison to which my father was going to be conveyed ; that note, however, never reached me, and to the circumstance may I attribute the degradation which ultimately befel me.

"The house to which Mr. Gayton conducted me, was situate a little way out of town ; and though for some time I was not to be reconciled to the course I was leading, his attentions gradually softened my agony of heart, and in his presence I could assume an appearance of cheerfulness. In answer to my repeated questions about my father, he said there were more difficulties in the way than he had expected to encounter ; that his debts were greater than had been anticipated, and that some of the creditors were so harsh, that they were determined not to let him out of prison till their full demands were satisfied. He, however, said there was no doubt they would ultimately come to terms, and that in the meantime he would take care to supply him with all he wanted in prison. This, however, I afterwards heard he never did.

"At length my child was born; and though the sight of it has often brought the blush of shame to my cheek, yet as it advanced in age, I found a solace in its society that I had never known before. When the child was about three months old, her father most unexpectedly informed me that he was going into the country, and that he should be obliged to be out of town for some time ; he, however, requested a friend of his, named Edwards, to see that I was sufficiently supplied with money ; it seemed to me, however, that the friend had made up his mind to supplant Mr. Gayton in my heart, but I always treated him with disdain and reserve, and perhaps fearing an exposure, he never ventured to speak to me upon the subject. At length I requested him to seek out my father, who I heard was in the Marshalsea, and the next day Mr. Edwards visited me, and informed me that he had been as I had requested, and that my father had been released from prison some time previously, and had departed no one knew whither. It was clear to me that he and my mother were gone in search of me, and that all clue to a discovery on either side was lost.

"The absence of Mr. Gayton looked much longer than I expected, but when he did return, I could observe a marked difference in his manner towards me ; he was cold and even repulsive, and frequently spoke to me in a manner that told me plainly enough that he no longer cared for me. I did not reproach him for it, since that would have been useless, but waited patiently till an opportunity should arrive to ask if he ever intended to make me his wife according to the promise he had given me. At length a favourable moment occurred, and I put to him the question upon which so much depended, and never shall I forget the fiendish laugh of derision with which he heard me. It was in vain that I implored him to fulfil the promise he had given ; he was resolute in his refusal, and after telling me that it was his intention to leave town again,

perhaps for a longer period, he advised me to transfer my affections to
his friend, Mr. Edwards, who, he said, was a most warm and ardent admirer. Upon this he left me, with an understanding that he had cast
me off for ever.

"In this situation, what was I to do? I was left absolutely penniless—
my character was blasted—and as no one was likely to receive me in their
house, I was reduced to the alternatives of either accepting the proposition of Mr. Edwards, or of throwing myself upon the town to obtain a
miserable pittance for my unfortunate babe. I, therefore, yielded to
stern necessity, and from that time became the mistress of a man that I
regarded with hatred and contempt. Yet, to do him justice, I must
confess he treated me with great kindness, and as considerable money
was at his command, I was generally well supplied with it.

"Thus we went on for some time tolerably smooth; but at length
Mr. Gayton presented himself among us again, and from that time he
and Mr. Edwards were always out together, the latter never returning till
an early hour in the morning. There was a mystery in this which I
could not understand, nor could I obtain any satisfactory reply, though I
frequently asked for an explanation. By and by Mr. Edwards complained
that money was running very short with him, and I began to be afraid I
should be once more turned out into the world, when all of a sudden he
appeared to be rich again, and from what I could learn, he had been very
successful at the gaming table. This seemed to revive him, and weeks of
thoughtless gaiety succeeded, till the money was nearly spent, and just
when we were reduced to our last half guinea, Mr. Gayton once more
made his appearance.

"He told us he had been entrusted with the care of a young country
girl who was going to France; that she was in a very bad state of health,
and had taken so strong a prejudice against the people who were to have
accompanied her, that she refused to leave England with them. Under
these circumstances I was requested to go and see her, and persuade the
young woman to alter her determination. I accordingly waited upon
Miss Smith, as she was called, and having assured her that she might regard me as a friend, I learnt that she was going over to Havre to be married to an old French Marquis, who she despised for his age, but was
willing to become his wife for the sake of the title and the wealth it would
give her. A few days after this Mr. Edwards was entrusted with the
care of conveying her to the place of destination, and they set out together from London.

"I was now left without money, and as there were considerable ar-
rears of rent, I was ordered to leave the house by my landlord, who,
however, permitted me to take a few things with me. I then took a
more humble lodging, and applied for work at my old trade of map-co-
louring. But it was little that I could earn for myself and child at this
business; and to make up the deficiency I was compelled to pledge article after article, till they became so reduced that starvation or the
workhouse stared me in the face.

"Misfortune never seemed tired of persecuting me, for my child was
taken ill, and I was compelled to give up the little work I had, in order
to nurse and attend upon it. My visits were now made more than ever
frequently to the pawnbroker, to obtain money for the purchase of food
and medicine; and at length I found that nothing was left to me but the
wretched clothing worn by my infant and myself.

"At this discovery despair seized upon my heart, and gladly would
I have died, had there been one soul in the world to take care of my
child. But for her sake I must live to endure all the agonies of re-

morse produced by my past conduct; and another day or two passed away with scarcely any food to support my nearly worn-out frame—my child was dying of hunger, and I had not a morsel of bread to support its life.

"At last I could support my agonies no longer, and, rushing into the street with the child in my arms, I determined to end both our lives at once by throwing myself into the river. How near I was doing so you have already heard from Mr. Smithson, who saved us at the very moment when I was about to make a fatal plunge from the bridge. From that moment I have been among friends, and may Heaven reward those who have thus rescued from destruction the unfortunate Amelia and her child."

CHAPTER XX.

THE JOURNEY TO LONDON.

IT is now time to return to young Edwin, who, it will be remembered, left Mr. Gravestow's house rather than continue under an obligation to a man who evidently wished to get rid of him. Of London he had heard much talk, and, possessing as he did an independent spirit, he thought it very possible he might raise himself to eminence, as many others had done before him. At any rate, anything was better than living in dependance upon a man like Gravestow, and as the metropolis was a large place, there was not much fear but that he should find employment there before long,

He had not much money with him, it was true, but with care it would last him a few days; and as he had no doubt of getting something to do shortly after his arrival in town, he had no apprehension on that score, but trudged forward with a light heart, and hopes that not even his present uncertainty could damp. Every sound, however, made him look round, lest his flight should have been discovered, and a pursuit be commenced after him; but all this alarm gradually wore away, and he was just beginning to fancy that he was out of danger, when a man sprang over a stile just a little in advance, and approached towards him. The youth turned and would have fled, but the person who had caused him so much terror, spoke, and he immediately recognised the voice of William Dain, the young miller, who had so long paid court to Susan Hoply.

"Why, how is this, Master Edwin?" he said, suspecting somewhat of the truth; "you are out late to-night, and might chance to fall into indifferent company."

"It is rather late, certainly," answered the youth, "but as for the company you speak of, I never did harm to any person, and, therefore have nothing to fear."

"But you have enemies for all that."

"I know it," replied Edwin.

"And if I am not much mistaken," continued the young miller, "you are about to leave this neighbourhood, and seek a home somewhere else?"

"What made you think that?" asked the boy, anxiously,

"You have got a bundle in your hand, I see," replied William, "and your being out of the house so late confirms my suspicion. Besides, I happen to know that Mr. Gravestow don't make your home very comfortable, and it's natural that a lad of spirit should seek to rid himself of his dependence on him."

"Well, there's no denying it any longer," exclaimed Edwin, "and so I at once confess that you have guessed rightly. But do not tell any one that we met, or it may afford a clue to my place of destination, and then it's most likely I should be pursued and overtaken."

"You need not fear me," answered the other; "but I should like to persuade you against this project of yours. London is a large place, with many bad persons in it; and you might happen to fall in with some of them, and——"

"I'll take care to fight shy of gentlemen of that sort," interrupted Edwin; "besides, I hope soon to find employment of some kind or other, and then I shall be safe from those fellows who are always looking out for the unwary."

"Have you any friends in London?" asked William.

"Mr. Smithson lives there," replied the youth.

"You will call on him, then," exclaimed the other. "He was the favourite and confidential clerk of poor Mr. Wentford, and, I dare say, will give you a home till a situation of some kind or other has been found for you."

"Mr. Smithson is, at present, on a visit at the house I have just left," replied Edwin; "and, indeed, if I was certain of his being at home, I don't think I should call on him."

"And why not, Edwin?" asked the other.

"Because," replied the youth, he might blame me for what I have done, and send word to Mr. Gravestow where I am to be found, in which case I should have to return, which I am resolved never to do if I can help it."

"Is there no one else you could call on?" asked Dain.

"Why, poor Susan Hoply, who used to be so fond of me, is somewhere in London, I believe," answered Edwin, "but where or how she is to be found, I know not."

"Nor can I help you in that matter," exclaimed William, with a sigh, "for she has not written to say where she is, and I begin to be almost afraid she has forgotten me."

"Nay," cried Edwin, "that I am sure she will never do, for Susan loves you too well for that, and wherever she may be, or however circumstanced, I am quite certain you will never have to reproach her with inconstancy."

"Thank you, Master Edwin, for that," exclaimed William; "you have taken a load off my heart with those words, and I'll never think so badly of Susan again. Poor thing! she has got quite trouble enough upon her mind to drive the remembrance of me out of her head for awhile."

"Ah! you mean that mysterious affair about her brother?"

"I do, Master Edwin," replied the other. "From the moment Andrew Hoply was accused of being the murderer of his master, she has been unceasing in her efforts to discover who was the real perpetrator of the deed."

"And do you think she will succeed?"

"I hope she will," answered the young miller; "at any rate, she is determined about it; and I fancy her suspicions are directed against a person who at present must be nameless."

"I pray Heaven she may find it all out," cried Edwin, "for the assassins of poor Mr. Wentford should be discovered, and I feel quite certain in my own mind that Andrew Hoply would rather have sacrificed his own life than injure a master that he so sincerely loved."

"That Andrew is innocent, I am quite convinced," exclaimed William Dain; "but his mysterious disappearance gives a colour to the charge brought against him, and till we can discover what has become of him, I am afraid there is very little chance of the suspicion being removed."

"The poor fellow has, I dare say, been murdered by the same villains that assassinated Mr. Wentford," cried Edwin.

"Susan has declared that to be her own opinion," answered the young man, "and I must confess it seems but too likely she is correct, Yet, for all that, her assertion will go for nothing unless she can bring forward proof of it."

"Which, I believe, she is at present engaged in collecting," observed Edwin. "She has vowed never to relax her efforts till that object is accomplished; and, depend on it, the day will yet arrive when she will be able to take the stigma from the name of her brother, and to cast it upon those who have thus far contrived to avoid suspicion."

"You will try, I hope, to find her out when you get to London," exclaimed William Dain: "she was always partial to you, and will, perhaps, be a friend when you most need one."

"I may do so," replied Edwin, "but there will be little chance of succeeding in such a great overgrown place as London. Besides, I don't know the name of the family she is with; for though Mr. Cornish, the steward, has written to her, he would never tell me where she is living."

"But if I should happen to hear," said William, "I could send a letter for you to Mr. Smithson, if you think it likely you will call at his house."

"At present, I think it very unlikely I shall," answered Edwin; "but at any rate I shall be a little bit settled when I have been in town a few days, and then I'll write to let you know where I am. But remember, William, you must not let anybody else into the secret."

"What! not even Mrs. Gravestow, who has always been so kind a friend to you?"

"She would be sure to tell her husband, if it was only for the sake of getting me back again," replied Edwin; "and then I cannot forget how much he seems to hate me, and how cruelly he used poor Fanny, merely because she has continued to treat me with kindness."

"Ah!" exclaimed William Dain, "it was an unlucky day for her when she linked herself to a man that married her only for the sake of the money she possessed from her father. They say all her friends tried to persuade her against the match, but she could see no faults in Walter Gravestow till it was too late to complain."

"And bitter cause she now has for it, I am afraid," cried the lad. "However, he may take it into his head one of these days to leave her, and then, perhaps, she may hope to pass the remainder of her days in peace——"

"And poverty," observed William Dain.

"Nay," cried Edwin, "her father died rich, and he left nearly all his property to her."

"I know that," replied the other, "but she unfortunately had so much confidence in Gravestow, that she married him without having any settlement drawn up in her own favour. In fact, people say that he can leave her whenever he likes, and deprive her of all the property."

"And will he be villain enough to do so?" cried Edwin.

"There is no reason to doubt it," replied William; "he don't like her, and the first opportunity that offers will be taken to quit this country and leave her here by herself."

"The villain!" exclaimed Edwin; "but let him beware how he treats her, for every day brings me nearer to manhood, and he may yet have to answer for his conduct in a way that he will not expect."

"Nay, there are others besides yourself that would be glad to punish him according to his deserts, and I dare say the time will come when he may repent the evil he has been committing. So now let me persuade you to give up this design of going to London till you have determined the sort of employment you mean to seek."

"Would you have me return and beg Mr. Gravestow to take me into his house again?"

"No," replied William; "I would not have you do that on any account; but there is a bed in my house that's quite at your service, and——"

"Thank you, William," exclaimed the youth, interrupting him, "you are very kind to make me such an offer, but I have made up my mind to leave the neighbourhood, and, having once left Mr. Gravestow's house, I should not receive very kind treatment were I to return to it."

"There is no occasion for your doing so," replied the young miller;— "in my place you shall be welcome to a home as long as you please. At any rate it will be better than going up to London till you have some house to go to where you may be comfortable."

"It is vain to persuade me, though I am truly grateful for your kind offer," answered Edwin, "but Mr. Gravestow would be sure to hear of my being in the neighbourhood, and I should be taken back again to his house, perhaps to disappear as poor Andrew Hoply did."

"Well, I won't persuade you against your will," said the other, "but if you would only take a bed at our house for the night, you could start in the morning, and have the advantage of daylight to help you on your way."

"Nay," replied Edwin, "the darkness of the night will serve to aid me in avoiding my pursuers. Besides, by to-morrow morning my flight will certainly have been discovered, and it would then be impossible for me to escape, if Mr. Gravestow should take it into his head to prevent me."

"Then, at least, take this money with you," said William, offering him a guinea and a seven-shilling piece. "It's all the money I happen to have in my pocket, but you will want it when you get to London, and I can spare the trifle very well without missing it."

"Thank you, William," cried the youth, pressing the hand that offered the gift; "you have ever been a kind, good friend to me, and go where I will, or be where I may, I never shall forget how like a brother you have been to me. The money, however, I do not want. for I have enough to last me, with care, a few days, and by that time I hope to be doing something that will earn me a comfortable living."

"You won't take it, then?"

"No," replied Edwin. "I can esteem the man whose kindness I have experienced, and, had there been any necessity for it, might have borrowed the money till I was able to repay it. I have, however, money enough for all present purposes, and it shall not be any fault of my own if I should ever be compelled to throw myself on the generosity of my friends."

With this he shook William Dain warmly by the hand, and, dashing away the tear of gratitude that had found its way to his eye, he turned

away, and resumed his journey towards the great metropolis. He, however, soon forgot the momentary agitation that had been produced by his recent interview with William Dain, and ,looking forward with hope to the future, he trudged on as merrily as if fortune had been smiling and beckoning him to proceed.

It was a dark and cheerless looking night when he left home ,but as midnight approached, the clouds become thicker than ever, and the rain which at first descended gently, at length come down in such torrents, that he was compelled to look about him for shelter. At length he saw a barn at the further end of the field, and hastening towards it with all the speed he could, he crept in, and thought himself fortunate in having obtained a roof to cover him from the inclemency of the night.

It was long after day break on the following morning that the clouds slowly broke away, and gave promise of a beautiful day. He then partook of some bread and meat which he had brought away with him, and scarcely had this meal finished, when some men were seen advancing towards the barn, and wishing to avoid observation, lest a clue should afterwards lead to his discovery, he crept away, and once more pursued his way towards London.

He continued to walk unceasingly till mid-day, and then sitting down beneath a hedge, he once more produced his humble fare, and adding to it a draught of pure water from a spring that gushed forth close at hand, he enjoyed the meal with as much relish as if it had been composed of all the delicacies of the season. At any rate, he found himself at liberty, and far away from the man whose presence he most dreaded, which was a source of the highest gratification though he could not help thinking of Fanny

No. 20

and the unhappy destiny that had befallen her. Still, however, he looked forward to the period when he might be able to ameliorate the sufferings she endured through the ill treatment of her husband, and his heart swelled within him as he anticipated the pleasure he should feel in releasing her from the thraldom and persecution which were almost intolerable.

At length when he saw the sun set, Edwin began to think of looking out for a place where he might obtain a more comfortable one than he had had the night before, and quickening his footsteps, he intended to reach the next public-house, and after passing the night there, make the best of his way to London, which he understood would be a distance of about fifteen miles. At length he saw the village at no great distance in advance of him, and he was just congratulating himself on the prospect of a rest after the exertions of the day, when hearing the sound of footsteps behind him, he turned to see who was coming, and observed a couple of men that he had noticed four or five times in the course of the day, as if they were following him for no good purpose. Observing them again, he became somewhat uneasy, but not wishing to shew any sign of fear, he sauntered as slowly as possible in the hope that they would pass on, and leave him behind; but in this he was mistaken; and when at length he came to a dead stand-still, they did the same, evidently not wishing to lose sight of him.

Who or what these men were, he, of course, could form no opinion, but his fears were excited lest they had been sent after him by Walter Gravestow, and if that should be the case, he had very little doubt that they had received orders either to carry him back to the house from whence he had come, or else to convey him to some place from whence there would be no chance of escape. That their designs were against himself, he was certain, else why had they dodged him so long, and why not have passed him when he gave them an opportunity of doing so, by stopping on the road? At all events, be their intentions what they might, it was very clear that he was now in their power, and the only course that remained for him to adopt was to hurry on as fast as possible to the place where he was going to sleep, as he might there be safe from any violence they might meditate offering him. He accordingly stepped out resolutely, though still conscious that the two men were following him at about the same distance as before, and at length reaching the public-house he there saw the landlord, of whom he inquired if he could have a bed.

"Aye, twenty if you can afford to pay for 'em," said them an, eyeing him with a look of suspicion.

"I have money enough to pay for any accommodation or refreshment that I may require while in your house," replied the youth, rather nettled.

"Very good, young gentleman," exclaimed the host; "but we mus be a little particular, you know, about who we take in, and so, as I dare say you don't want to bilk a poor fellow like me, you may stop here to-night, and I'll make you as comfortable as I can."

"Can I have supper?"

"Oh, yes;—what would you like?"

"A couple of mutton-chops."

"Very sorry, sir, but there don't happen to be such a thing in the whole village."

"Well, never mind," replied Edwin, "a rump-steak will suit my appetite quite as well."

"Very sorry, indeed, sir," said the host, "but our butcher—for we have only one in the place,—hasn't killed an ox for the last three weeks."

" Have you a fowl ?"

" No,—it's quite the wrong time of the year for them."

" I thought you said just now I could have anything I liked ?" observed Edwin.

" Aye, but I forgot that we had a party of soldiers billetted in the village yesterday and the day before, and they've cleared everything away like so many locusts."

" Well, never mind," said Edwin, with perfect resignation; " let me have a few poached eggs, and with them I shall contrive to make a very tolerable supper."

" I'm really very sorry," exclaimed the landlord ; but now I recollect myself, my wife told me, not half an hour ago, that she had sent all round the place for some, and there wasn't such a thing to be got for love nor money."

" What the deuce can I have then ?"

"There's some capital cheese in the house," replied the host—" at least it was a good one before they dug all the inside of it out. But if you don't mind putting up with it, we'll see if we can't do something better for you when you sit down to breakfast in the morning."

With that he took his departure from the room, leaving his guest to cogitate at his leisure on the accommodation afforded at a country public house. But Edwin had other matters of more consequence to think about, for no sooner was he left alone than he could hear the voices of two men, who seemed to have just arrived; he at once imagined that they were the persons who had been following him, and that they had made up their minds to pass the night under the same roof with him. Whilst he was thus pondering over the affair, the door of the parlour in which he was sitting, was opened, and a head being thrust forward, he at once recognised one of the persons that had taken so much pains to keep him in sight.

He now felt more convinced than ever that their purpose was hostile to himself, and dreading lest he should fall into their power, he thought over a variety of schemes for eluding them. The only plan, however, for doing this, was to leave the house as soon as he had had his supper, and then to pursue his way towards London by the least frequented road ; but he was tired with the exertions he had already undergone, and anxious as he was to avoid the men, he found it would be impossible to continue his journey till he had had a night's rest in bed.

He was still ruminating upon this affair when the hostess entered the room with a tray, on which was placed the humble fare which was to form his evening meal. Having done this, she was about to depart as silently as she entered the room, but Edwin's curiosity had been excited, and he said—

" You have a couple of strangers, I believe, just arrived ?"

" Yes," said the landlady, who never threw away more words in conversation than were absolutely necessary.

" Are they going to stay here ?"

" Don't know."

" Have you ever seen them before ?"

" No."

" They are travellers like myself, I suppose," continued Edwin, " and are on their way to London ?"

" Haven't asked 'em."

"Perhaps not; but I thought they might have said something that might bring you to that conclusion."

"Ain't at all inquisitive," exclaimed the hostess, and with that she flounced out of the room.

Edwin would have given the world to know what the motive was that had induced these men to follow him. If they had been thieves they had many opportunities of attacking him while upon the road, and as they had not done that, there could be no doubt they had been employed by Mr. Gravestow to follow him wherever he went, in order that some future design might be carried into operation. At one time he thought of mentioning his doubts and suspicions to the landlord, but upon reflection, he feared that whatever he said might be carried back to the men, who would only change their course, and thus leave him more exposed than ever to whatever designs against him they were engaged in.

He then tried to convince himself that all his fears were utterly groundless, and that the fact of the men having followed him was merely the effect of chance. It was possible that they were merely travellers like himself, and that they had not bestowed even so much as a thought upon him. But if that was the case, why did they stop on the road when he paused?—why did they pause at the same house, and why did one of them thrust his head into the room a minute or two before unless it was to assure himself that the person he had been following was there? Look at the question which way he would, there was but too much reason to believe that they had a design against him, and as they were persons that he had never seen before, there was no reason to doubt that they had been employed by Mr. Gravestow for some secret purposes of his own. So certain, indeed, did he feel upon this point, that when the landlord and the two strangers entered the room in the midst of his deliberation, he jumped up, and seizing hold of a chair stood in an attitude of defence.

"Holloa!—what the devil's the matter with you?" exclaimed the host, with surprise. "These gentlemen asked if they couldn't have the pleasure of spending the evening with you, and when I bring 'em you salute 'em as if you meant to knock out their brains with the chair."

"Are they friends?" demanded Edwin.

"I dare say they are," replied the host; "but if you want to satisfy yourself on that point, you had better ask 'em the question."

"Why, in course we're friends," said the man who stood foremost, "what should a nice young fellow like you have to do with enemies I should like to know?"

"I wish to be alone," replied Edwin; "and your intrusion here has annoyed me."

"Intrusion!" cried the fellow in a tone of astonishment, "who ever heard of an intrusion in a public-house?"

"I am willing to pay any reasonable demand the landlord may make for having the entire use of this room," said Edwin.

"Really, young gentleman, I can't do anything of the sort," replied the landlord. "This happens to be the only parlour the house affords, and as these gentlemen don't chose to sit themselves down in the tap-room, you must be content to share this with them."

"Why, in course he must," said the fellow who had spoken; "and so now, young gentleman, if you'll just put down that chair, I dare say we can sit ourselves down together and be very comfortable. I likes sociality, I do, and so does my companion,—don't you, Bill?"

"Yes," grunted Bill, in a ropy voice, that seemed as if he had got a very bad cold.

"There," continued his companion, "you see there ain't no pride about us; we're always agreeable, we are, and if you'll only do as we do, I dare say we sha'n't pass such a werry incomfortable evening together."

"But why am I to be forced to mix myself in company when I wish to be alone?" asked Edwin.

"Because we're good enough to take pity on your loneliness, and to honour you with our company," retorted the other, with a knowing wink at the landlord and his companion.

"An honour that I would rather have declined."

"Werry likely," returned the other, "but it ain't every man as knows what's good for himself. You are young and haven't had no experience; I'm a few years older, and may put you up to a move or two if you've only the wit to take 'em rightly. So, here's to your werry good health, sir, and our better acquaintance."

With this he raised the jug of ale, which had been brought in for Edwin, to his lips, and then handing it to his companion, it was returned empty to the place from whence it had been taken up.

"You see, young gentleman, we're uncommon free chaps in our way," said the foremost of the two; "there's no nonsense about us, and so, as were going to spend the evening together, you may as well make up your mind to it."

"Aye," interposed Bill, "I like to see things upon the square; so, as we've drank the young gentleman's ale, bring in another quart of it, landlord, and a few pipes, and then we may make ourselves what I call comfortable."

The host took the hint, trotted out of the room, and returned in the twinkling of an eye with the articles which had been ordered. This done, he again quitted the room, and Edwin found himself alone with the two strangers. These latter paid their respects to the bread and cheese, and having devoured enough for any four reasonable men, they began to observe that their younger companion was not doing as they were.

"Come, you don't eat, my friend," exclaimed the spokesman, with a mouth as full as it could be crammed.

"I have had quite enough," was the reply.

"Nonsense; you've had a longish walk since last night," observed the other, "and if that won't give a fellow an appetite, I don't know what will; least ways, I know its made me very peckish."

"Have you followed me all the way?" asked Edwin, with anxiety that he could scarcely conceal.

"Don't ask no questions and you won't get no lies," said the fellow, after another good swig at the ale jug.

"Why do you ask them of me then?"

"Because we're friends of your'n," answered the other, "else we shouldn't have been so particular in looking arter you. Bless your soul! we knows all about your stopping to have a chat with the young miller, and your sleeping in the barn when the rain came on."

"You have been near me then all the way?"

"Yes, we've stuck to you like wax."

"What was your motive for doing so?"

"Nothing but our good-natur'," answered the fellow; "we know'd you'd a long walk afore you, and kept you in sight for fear anything might happen."

"There was no necessity for your taking so much trouble," returned Edwin.

"It wasn't no trouble at all," exclaimed the other; "but tell us what put the notion into your head of going up to London?"

"How do you know I'm going there?"

"Where else should you be going to?" retorted the man. "Ain't it the place where all young chaps go to when they want to make a fortin, and why shouldn't you do the same thing?"

"I have not yet made up my mind whether I shall go there or not," said Edwin.

"Oh, yes, you have, though," answered the other; "you know you're a going there;—that is, you meant to do so, if there ain't nothing to prevent it."

"What is to prevent my going where I please?" demanded Edwin, angrily.

"Come, come, don't get into a passion," exclaimed the man, "because there won't be any good done by it, and——"

"I will submit to this insolence no longer," cried Edwin, and starting from his seat, he went to the bar for a candle, and proceeded to his sleeping-chamber, taking care to secure the door, in order to prevent the intrusion of any improper or unwelcome visitors.

CHAPTER XXI.

MORE ADVENTURES.

WHEN the two men were left together, they looked at each other with that cunning expression of countenance that plainly proved they were well satisfied so far with their proceedings, and then they laughed,—not very loudly to be sure, but a suppressed sort of chuckle, such as people of their class usually indulge in when they have been more cunning than usual. They ordered another jug of ale, too, upon the strength of the good luck they had met with, and as the young traveller was now out of hearing, they began to speak about the subject they had in hand.

"If this ain't a prime bit o' good fortin, Bill, I don't know what is," exclaimed Snarley, rubbing his hands in high glee. "The young un's all right, now, and we've only to wait a day or two, and the rowdy will be our'n as safe as need be."

"But are you sure it's the right chap?" asked Bill, after another strong pull at the ale-jug.

"Why, in course I am," replied his worthy comrade; "ain't here the adwertisement,—and can't them as runs read it?"

And as he said this, he took a very dirty scrap of paper from his pocket, headed with the word "Absconded," and briefly describing Edwin, for whom it offered a reward to any one who would take him back to his disconsolate friends. But as reading was an accomplishment in which Snarley was but superficially acquainted with, it took some little time to spell and stumble over the hard words, so that his friend had ample time to consider the affair before the whole of it had been read through.

"I think it is the ticket, Bill," continued the other, as soon as he had brought his task to a conclusion. "The young chap up stairs answers to the description well enough, and now, all we've got to do is to take care he don't slip through our fingers. Shall we go up to him, and——"

"Not by no means whatsomedever," interrupted Bill. "The youngster seems to have a notion that we ain't up to much good, and if he should happen to kick up a noise in the house it would be all over with us."

" Why, you don't think the landlord would care about what we do with him ?"

" May-be not," answered Bill ; " but there may be others in the house that would take part with him, and it wouldn't be worth our while to lose the reward for the sake of being in a hurry in the business. He's ours, safe enough, if we only take care what we're about, and so we'll keep close till we can do the trick snugly."

" Why, he seems to be a little bit wide awake, to be sure," answered Snarley ; " but then there's two to one agen him, and if that ain't enough I don't know what is."

" Well, gen'l'men," said the landlord, who at that moment entered the room ; " the young chap don't seem to like your company much, and as I like to see fair play, perhaps you'll tell me what your'e up to."

" No harm, old fellow," replied Snarley ;—" the boy's run away from his friends, and as a reward has been offered for him, we thought we might as well earn it as any body else."

" Very good," was the laconic reply of the host.

" It will be very good when we get it," said Bill, " and it would be d—d hard times if we miss the chance now that we met the cove, and he's within arm's length of us."

" That's true ;" replied the host, " and as I dare say his poor friends are in a terrible way at his cutting off from 'em, it's a great act of kindness on your part to take so much pains to restore him to 'em."

" So it is," exclaimed Snarley ; " and it's werry good of them to offer a reward that we mean to pocket."

" Are you quite certain this is the youngster ?" asked the landlord.

" Why, to be sure we are," replied both the men at once.

" And what are you going to do next ?"

" Sleep here, to be sure," replied Snarley. " We must share the room with him if it happens to be a double bedded one."

" It is," answered the host. " But won't he take the alarm, think you, if he finds you dodging him too closely ?"

" That's our affair," replied Bill ; " so give no further advice about the business, but draw us another jug of ale, and then, if you think fit you can give us your company to help drink it."

This was a proposition that the landlord was not likely to make any objection to, and having obeyed the instructions he had received, he sat himself down with his guests, and enjoyed himself in their company till a latiesh hour.

As for Edwin, he felt himself anything but comfortable in the chamber to which he had retired, for he saw that it contained two beds, and as their could be little doubt that the men below intended to pass the night in the house, he thought it pretty well certain that they would occupy the other bed. He had fastened the chamber door, to be sure, but if the arrangements had been made, he knew well enough that they would presently afterwards demand admittance, and, of course, his refusal to grant them ingress to the apartment would only serve to insense them still further against him.

Then he thought of the landlord, and what a strange uncouth being he was ; and as he had read in books of fiction that people had sometimes been murdered in houses of this description, he began to fear whether suc a fate might not be his, and most heartily did he now begin to repent that he had ever left the house of Walter Gravestow, where he had at least one friend that would remain faithful to him to the last. But a little reflection

served to convince him that it was useless for him to sink under his misfortunes, and he was begnniing to think of lying down upon the bed with
his clothes on, when voices were heard below, and curiosity prompted him
to listen to what they were saying, as he might then judge of their intentions, and act accordingly.   He, therefore, crept cautiously out of his room,
and descended the stairs so gently, that there was very little fear of being
heard, and having reached the half opened door of the room, in which the
two men and the landlord were seated, and peeping in, heard part of the
conversation we have just now described.   It was but little that reached
his ears, and even that was sufficient to convince him of the danger he was
in, and then softly retreating to the place from whence he had come, he
took up his bundle, and leaving on the table sufficient money to pay for
what he had had, opened the window, which was at no great distance from
the ground, and jumped into the garden.   Once safely landed, he ran towards a gate which he saw just before him, and having passed that, crossed a lane into some fields, and pursued his way along a footpath, leading
he knew not whither, but at all events tolerably safe in case of pursuit.

In this way he continued for about a couple of hours, when the morning
began to dawn, and he saw he was approaching a village, which from
motives of prudence, he thought proper to avoid, by taking a circuitous
route, that at length brought him to the high road, and where he paused for
a few moments to consider whether he should trust to it, er contiuue the
bye paths, which, after all, would lead him he knew not whither.   At
length, however, he resolved upon the former alternative, as he now seemed
to have a pretty good start in advance of his pursuers, and after about
another hour, meeting with a countryman, he ventured to ask where he
was, and to what place the road he was travelling would take him.   Both
these questions were answered to his satisfaction, and the honest rustic,
seeing that he was tired, invited him to go to his cottage, where he should
have a good breakfast, and rest till he was able to continue his journey.

Fatigued as Edwin was with the exertions he had gone through, he was
not inclined to refuse so tempting an offer as this, and as he had money in
his pocket to repay the man for his hospitality, he at once closed with the
proposition, and was conducted to a nice, clean, and comfortable cottage,
where a homely-looking dame was waiting the arrival of her husband, and
who welcomed the young traveller with the greatest kindness, and quickly
placed before him a basin of bread and milk, which proved to be a more
acceptable offer to one who had been out for some time without having
had either rest or refreshment.

Shortly after the meal was over, the countryman took his departure,
though not without having first of all pressed his youthful guest to remain
there a day or two; for Edwin had related to him his adventures since
leaving the house of Mr. Gravestow, and the rustic host thought he had
better remain there in concealment for a few days, when he would be
better enabled to pursue his journey to London, and that, too, without
the fear of being overtaken by his enemies.   This offer, was, however refused, though he hesitated not to ask permission to lie upon the bed for a
short time, after which he could continue his labours with every prospect
of safely reaching his place of destination.

This request was cheerfully assented to by both the man and his wife,
the latter of whom quitted the cottage shortly after her husband, and then
he was left to enjoy in quiet that rest which he so much needed.   It was
three or four hours before the dame returned, and when she did so she
found her guest already risen, and only waiting to see her ere he resumed
his journey.   She would, however, have fain prevailed upon him to remain
there a little longer, but Edwin was anxious to reach the end of his journey

as soon as possible, and after insisting upon her receiving some silver for the kindness he had received, he took leave of his hospitable hostess, and took his road towards Chatham, which was some few miles distant, and where he hoped to find employment either in the army or the navy, without going to London, which, being a much larger place, might present more obstacles than he would know how to encounter.

With all his efforts, however, it was night before he found himself within a mile of the town he was going to, and he was just congratulating himself upon having escaped the danger he had so much dreaded, when he was startled at hearing voices behind a hedge, and almost dreading that they should be his pursuers who were speaking, he suddenly paused, and then drew gently nearer to the place, that he might convince himself whether his fears were too well founded. A little time served to allay his terrors in this respect, for the voices were certainly not those of the persons he had suspected, and yet there seemed to be so much secrecy and caution in the conversation they were carrying on, that he was prompted to ascertain the object they had in view.

"I tell you, you're a fool, Dick," said one of the fellows to the other, " and old sailors like you and I, ought to be ashamed of ourselves to be frightened at what may never happen. No one knows that we left the ship at Dover, and here we are, snug enough to do the business without anybody being the wiser."

" But are you certain," asked the other, "that the captain we're looking after is in the ship?"

"Why, of course I am," replied his comrade. " I made sure of all that before I mentioned the thing to you, and so, if you're afraid to go on with the job after beginning it, say so at once, and I'll do it all by myself."

" You know I aint any more afraid of him than you are yourself," retorted the other, " and as I happen to owe the captain a grudge as much as you do, I'll go' through fire and water but the thing shall be done as we've said it should."

"Why, that's a little more like you, Dick," exclaimed his shipmate, "and if you only stick to that, it shan't be long before he finds out that two to one's too much for him. Mark Larragan is sure to be on watch, and as he's as deep in the business as we are, there aint much chance of the thing going wrong."

"May we trust him?" asked Dick, suspiciously.

"As we may ourselves," replied the other—"he's a prime sort of fellow, is Mark Larragan, and has promised to hang a lighted lantern over the ship's side when it will be safe for us to go on board. So you see, there aint much danger, and, if there was, who wouldn't run it, just to be revenged upon the man that we've sworn to send to Davy Jones's locker."

"And how about the captain's money?" asked Dick. "We must have some of that, you know, or we shall be running a great deal of risk to very little purpose."

"Oh, that's all right," answered his comrade; "everything of the captain's was shipped aboard before they left the dock; and so, you see, we've only got to take courage, and we shall not only revenge ourselves upon the skipper, but his gold will come to pay us for the trouble we are taking to send a brace or two of bullets through his head."

"But suppose he happens to sleep ashore?"

"I never thought of that," replied the other; "but, even supposing he does, I dare say the thing may be managed well enough."

"At any rate," observed Dick, "we may make sure of getting his money and plate."

"What!" retorted his messmate, angrily, "and would you be satisfied with overhauling his money, when both of us have sworn to have his life? No, no, Dick, I never forget an injury, and the money may all go to the devil before I'll ever consent to letting him off like that. So, to-night, the thing must be done whether you like to help me in it or not."

"You only say this to vex me," exclaimed Dick, sullenly; "but never mind, I wont put myself in a passion just now, though, I must say, you ought to know better how to treat a messmate than to call him either a lubber or a coward."

"Why, as for that, I never thought you either one or the other," returned his companion; "but you don't seem to enter into this affair with all your heart; and as you know the whole of the secret, I couldn't help thinking that you might take it into your head to split upon me. But I don't suspect it now, Dick, and as the time's drawing near, we'll go down to the water side, and see whether Mark Larragan has done as he promised he would."

"It's a famous night for us," observed Dick, looking up at the clouds that were quickly spreading themselves over the sky. "We shall hardly be noticed by any one, I dare say; and if once we can put off in a boat to the ship, there'll be very little fear but the job will be done easily enough."

"Aye, aye," replied his friend, "it only wants a little resolution, and we shall manage it well enough. To be sure, some of the fellows on board may be inclined to take the captain's part, when they find out what's going forward, but we shall be well armed, and must not mind the spilling of a little blood in case we should find ourselves in danger of being overpowered."

The fellows were moving away as they uttered these latter words so that Edwin could scarcely hear them; but he had discovered quite enough to convince him that they were a couple of villains, and that they had a design against the life of some one; but who the person was that they intended to kill, or where to follow them, he knew not, for he had lost all trace of them, though he walked as fast as he could, in order to keep close behind them.

At length, he entered the suburbs of Chatham, and from thence proceeding towards the town itself, he stopped at a comfortable-looking public-house, where he engaged a bed for the night, and having partaken of some slight refreshment, he left the place with a vague hope that he might possibly light again upon the ruffians he had lately overheard, and thus prevent the murder they designed to commit. This, and other thoughts more immediately connected with himself, made him unconscious where he was and whither he was going, till he reached the water-side, where he saw a great number of vessels lying off, amongst which, he supposed, was the one he heard the men speak of, and which was to be the scene of this meditated crime. To save the life of a human creature was an object in which he would willingly have risked his own, but it unfortunately happened that he knew neither the name of the captain nor the ship, and as no other chance remained, he was about to return, in order that he might acquaint some of the authorities of the place with what he had overheard, but just as he was going, a voice fell upon his ear with startling distinctness, and he immediately felt assured that he was once more near the villains he had overheard on his journey. Certain of this, he cautiously looked about him, and just behind a fishing boat, that had been hauled up high and dry, he saw the two men, one of whom had a glass in his hands, through which he was looking at one of the vessels that was lying rather apart from the rest.

"Well, what see you, now?" asked Dick, in a low tone, though quite distinct enough for the youth to hear very plainly.

"What do I see?" retorted the other, "why enough to convince me that we're all right. Mark Larragan's on deck."

"Is there any signal made yet?"

"Why, of course not, you fool!" retorted his companion; "he's not going to run himself and all of us into danger by doing anything of that kind just yet, and so we must have a little patience to wait till he sees that the signal can be made without fear of being seen by those that we don't want to know anything about it."

"But it's almost time that he began to think of business," observed Dick; "for the night's growing rather late, and we shall miss the chance if he don't look sharp."

Upon this, they turned away, and left the place followed gently by Edwin: but as he took a parting glance towards the vessel which appeared to have been the object of their attention, he discovered that a lighted lantern had been suspended over her side, which at once reminded him of the signal the ruffians had spoken of as having been connected between them and Mark Larragan. In an instant he resolved to visit the ship in hopes that he might be able to save the life of the captain, who, it was evident, had become an object for these ruffians' vengeance, and running along the shore, he came to a place where a waterman was looking after his boat previous to leaving it for the night.

"I want to be rowed out to yonder ship," he exclaimed, breathless with the haste he had made, "take me to it and it may be the means of making your fortune."

"And what the devil makes you in this hurry?" demanded the man, regarding the youngster with some surprise. "But I suppose I can guess how it is," he continued, "you've had leave to come ashore, and have forgot the time when you was ordered to return."

"I have no time to enter upon any explanation at present;" cried

Edwin impatiently, " for the life of a fellow creature depends upon the haste we make, and even now I almost fear we may be too late to prevent murder."

" Murder !" exclaimed the man, with surprise, " why, surely you don't know of such a crime as that being in the wind !"

" But I do know it," cried Edwin, with increasing impatience, " I overheard the villains plotting the whole foul deed, and the villains have just rowed themselves towards yonder ship."

" Which ship ?" asked the man.

" The one with a light hanging over its side," answered Edwin, pointing towards it. " The captain has given offence to some of his men, and they have plotted together for his murder, which they are going to commit this very night."

" You don't say so !" exclaimed the waterman with surprise, " why yonder vessel is the ' Racehorse,' and its skipper, Captain Gresham, one of the best fellows that ever lived."

" In that case," cried Edwin, " you will, of course, the more readily aid me in saving his life. The villains will be there before us, and our utmost speed alone can save him from the murderous attempts of his enemies."

" It's all very well, young fellow," replied the waterman; " but hasn't it struck you, that in trying to save the life of Captain Gresham we shall be very likely to lose our own ?"

" This is no time to indulge in selfish thoughts," answered the youth, " and let the danger be what it may, I have determined to run the risk rather than let a fellow creature perish when I may have it in my power to save him."

" It may be all very fine for you to go these wild goose errands," replied the other, " but I happen to have sundry reasons against it, in the shape of a wife and five little ones. They depend upon my labour, and must go the workhouse, if so be anything was to happen to me."

" There is no occasion for you to go on board at all," exclaimed Edwin, still more earnestly. " All I require of you is to row me to the ship's side, and if I should, fortunately, be the means of saving Captain Gresham's life, you will have no cause to regret having assisted me in so doing."

" You mean to say then, young gentleman, that I shall be well paid for my services ?"

" As an earnest that you will be no loser through your kindness," replied Edwin, " here is a guinea, which is all the money I can at present spare. From the captain, however, you may expect a much larger sum, for no doubt he will be grateful, and any reward he may offer me shall be yours, since I require no recompense for doing that which, after all, is nothing more than my duty."

" Perhaps you think I ought to act in the same sort of way," observed the waterman.

" Your situation and mine," replied Edwin, " are very different. It is my wish to do my utmost towards saving the life of Captain Gresham from the evil designs of these villains, and if I ask your assistance in so doing, it is with an understanding that your services shall be handsomely rewarded. So now, let us lose no more time, or the horrid deed will be perpetrated before we reach the vessel."

Without making any reply to this, the man assisted Edwin into the boat, and immediately rowed off so silently, that the dip of his oars in the water could scarcely be heard. Of course, their caution made their progress very slow, but at length they reached the " Racehorse," and everything was so silent, that the waterman in a whisper to the youth, gave it as his opinion that he had been mistaken in the supposition that the captain's life was in danger from assassins. Edwin, however, felt but too well convinced that his alarm was not unfounded, and having reached the companion ladder, he crawled up, and favoured by the darkness of the night, succeeded in reaching the deck without being discovered by those who were on the watch. This done, he looked about him, and could barely distinguish the forms of two or three men whose backs were towards him, and who seemed to be occupied in deep and earnest conversation. At all events, it was quite evident, that his presence in the ship was not suspected, and then creeping forward with as stealthy a step as possible, he descended to the cabin, the door of which he found open, and then making his way to the place where Captain Gresham was sleeping, he roughly shook him by the shoulder, and earnestly implored him to rise.

"Holloa!" exclaimed the captain, springing up, and suspecting for the moment that his visitor was there with no friendly intentions towards himself. "Who are you, rascal? Speak, or I'll send a ball through your body in the turning of an hour glass."

"Hush!" whispered Edwin, "and instead of regarding me as an enemy, look upon me as one who has ventured his own life for the preservation of yours."

"Indeed! and how am I to be convinced of that?" asked Captain Gresham, incredulously.

"A few minutes more will convince you that I speak the truth," answered Edwin; "two villains, favoured by another on board, have just entered your ship, and not a minute since, I saw them on deck, whispering and planning among themselves for your destruction."

"Say you so?" exclaimed the captain, "then, in that case, I shall be prepared to give them a warm reception. So do you leave the cabin, and I'll be upon the watch against the scoundrels make their appearance."

"With your leave," answered Edwin, "I shall remain where I am, in order to give any assistance in my power towards frustrating the evil designs of your enemies. You think, perhaps, that I am young, and my aid will be of little service; but I am no coward, Captain Gresham, and you shall presently see that I can cheerfully risk my life when it happens to be in a cause like this."

"Your words and manner would almost convince me that you are an honest fellow," exclaimed the captain, "and yet how am I to know but you will take part against me when the scoundrels come to execute their murderous intentions?"

"Do you suspect me, then?" cried Edwin reproachfully.

"Why, hang it, I can hardly do that either," said the other, after a moment's pause. "But it seems there's foul play going on, and it's enough to make a man suspicious when he hardly knows who may be his enemies or who his foes on board."

"Hush!" cried Edwin, taking up a pistol which the captain had just laid down, "they are coming, and in another moment you will be convinced of the truth of what I have told you."

"I hear the rascals stealing along," returned Captain Gresham; "so stand in a firm and threatening attitude, and of all things, don't fire unless I give the word of command. But they are here, and it now behoves us both to prevent the crime the villains have plotted against me."

A death-like silence now ensued, and presently the door was slowly opened, and the two men entered the cabin with a cautious step, that at once proved the criminality which had prompted their visit. They, however, quickly perceived the sort of reception they were likely to meet with, and judging that to retreat under such circumstances would be useless, they were rushing forward towards the object of their base designs, when Captain Gresham, in a voice of thunder, commanded them to pause. This seemed to awe the fellows, and, stepping back a pace or two, they were about to rush from the cabin, when about half-a-dozen sailors made their appearance and took them into custody.

"And so it's you, Patterson and Crawford, who have been plotting to take away my life," cried the captain, fiercely; "you that I expected were on board the Orion, and by this time on your voyage to China?" ————

"We did go on board," replied Patterson, "but managed to slip away without being missed, and the Orion sailed without us."

"And then," exclaimed Captain Gresham, "you must needs concoct this hellish plot for the murder of a man who is not conscious of ever having injured either of you."

"You know we never liked you, sir," replied Crawford; "and yet, for all that, I don't know that we should have taken away your life if we could have helped ourselves to your money without being discovered."

"You acknowledge, then, that you would have robbed me if it had not been for the timely hint I received from this youth?"

"What youth?" demanded Patterson.

"The one that now stands before you," replied Captain Gresham, glancing his eye towards Edwin. "He has found means to get on board the ship, and to his kindness am I, in all probability, indebted for my life."

"We know nothing of the youngster," cried Patterson, scowling fiercely towards Edwin. "He's a stranger to us both, and must have invented these lies against us in order to creep into your favour."

"I neither have, nor do I intend to ask any favour from Captain Gresham," answered the youth. "Chance gave me an opportunity to overhear your plot against this gentleman, and if I have succeeded in frustrating it, I am more than repaid for any trouble I may have been at in effecting so satisfactory an object."

"Where did you overhear us speaking about the business?" asked Crawford.

"A little way from Chatham," replied Edwin; "you were speaking as I came along the road, and, being unconscious of my presence, spoke without reserve, and thus I became possessed of a secret which has fortunately given me the means of serving Captain Gresham."

"I only wish we had known you was listening," said Patterson, sullenly, "and I'll be bound we hadn't given you an opportunity of serving us this sort of trick. But mark me, young fellow, you had better look after yourself, for though we may happen to get into the bilboes, there's others left that won't fail to remember you for what you've done this night."

"You are alluding to another of your comrades that you called Mark Larragan," exclaimed Edwin.

"Ho, ho!—then let Mark Larragan be instantly arrested," said Captain Gresham. "The fellow has long been suspected as being an enemy of mine, and now we'll see whether he shall have another chance of plotting against his captain. And now, fellow," he said, as the man was brought before him, "it seems you have been in a league with these ruffians to take away my life, and having been discovered in good time to prevent your villany, I shall now take care to prevent any further danger by ordering you into confinement along with your associates in crime."

"What harm have I done?" asked Larragan, sullenly.

"That you have not done any," replied the captain, "is through the vigilance of this youth, who overheard a conversation between your associates, and from what passed, it seems that you were to make a signal when all was ready for your treacherous purpose, and to assist them in getting on board the vessel without noise or discovery. But you have fortunately been found out in time, and have thus been saved the commission of a heinous crime."

"And supposing that to be true," exclaimed Patterson, "are we to be punished as if the thing had been accomplished?"

"That will be a matter for my consideration hereafter," replied the captain. "At present, however, you will all three be placed under restraint, and perhaps, after we get out to sea, if I find you orderly and well behaved, I may restore you to liberty, on condition that you promise never more to plot mischief against me or anybody else that belongs to the ship. So now look to your behaviour, and deserve the mercy I would show by manifesting your sincere repentance."

"Why not set us at liberty now, sir?" demanded Crawford. "It would show your confidence in us, and would be much better than punishing us for nothing."

"At present," replied Captain Gresham, "I can see very little reason for anticipating any amendment in your conduct. I have discovered that you are all three treacherous, and I must make myself quite certain of your repentance before I suffer you to go at large. I will not, however, be very severe at present, and, perhaps, in return, you will prove by your submission that I have not exerted my mercy in vain."

"Depend on it, Captain Gresham," interposed Edwin, "you will yet see cause to repent if these men have any chance given them of setting themselves at liberty. They are all of them desperate characters, and will not fail to revenge themselves for this disappointment on the first occasion that presents itself."

"Very well, young fellow," exclaimed Patterson, furiously, "you have proved yourself to be a bitter enemy of our's, and depend on it we shall not forget you for it. We'll hunt you out, whether it may be on land or ocean, and, take my word for it, the time is not very far distant when you shall be made to repent what you have done for us this day."

"Villains!" cried Captain Gresham, "do you threaten the youth for the share he has had in preserving me from the base crime you meditated against me?"

"All I say is that he had better beware of us," said Patterson, "and if there's any harm in that, why you must send us all three to the bilboes, and I don't suppose there's one among the lot that will ask the favour of his liberty, unless it might be for the sake of being revenged."

"That's quite enough," exclaimed Captain Gresham, wrathfully; "let them be taken away, and after I have given the affair a little cool deliberation, I will give further directions as to what shall be done with them."

Upon this the three fellows were dragged away, though not without some resistance on their part, and in a few minutes Captain Gresham and his youthful preserver were left alone.

CHAPTER XXI.

THE MUTINEERS.

"I suppose, sir," exclaimed Edwin, after they had remained some time in silence, "you do not intend to let these men have their liberty again? They seem to be desperate villains, and you may rely on it they will never be satisfied till they have fulfilled their sanguinary designs."

"Why, as for that," answered Captain Gresham, "the truth is there are too many on board that will keep a watchful look out to give them a chance of executing their evil deeds. Besides, they are safe enough in confinement now, and even if they should contrive to break out, which, by the by, is very unlikely, it would be in vain that they seek to perform thei treacherous designs, since there are quite friends enough on board to take care of my life."

" I suppose," observed Edwin, " you have had reason before now to know that they are your foes ?"

" I have," replied the captain, " and strange as it may appear, my life was, on one occasion, saved by the sagacity of the faithful dog that you see lying yonder."

" Such instances I have heard of," cried Edwin ; " but I have never yet known any persons that have been thus miraculously preserved by one of the brute creation."

" You shall hear the story," said Captain Gresham, " and then you may judge whether I am not deeply indebted to poor Sancho, whose instinct and gratitude together, prompted him to the discovery of a plot, which, if it had succeeded, must have terminated in my death. You see the poor fellow understands well enough that I am talking about him, for he has sprung upon his legs in an instant, and that joyous wag of the tail, tells us plainly enough that he remembers the circumstance, and is well pleased at the important service it was in his power to do me."

" Did the circumstance happen long ago ?" asked Edwin.

" No," answered the captain, " it was about eighteen months since, when I was going a voyage to the West Indies, that these two fellows, Patterson and Crawford, first of all formed a part of our crew. They came to me with very bad characters, but it so happened that men were very scarce just then, and I was obliged to take them on board whether I liked it or not. But the rest of our crew were a very orderly, decent set of fellows, and as they kept a sharp eye upon the two rascals, there was not much fear of their being able to do much mischief."

" But," observed Edwin, " it was not long, I suppose, before they began to show the cloven foot ?"

" You shall hear," replied Captain Gresham. " Our voyage happened to be a very favourable one, and on arriving at a place to take in fresh water and provision, I gave directions to have a few repairs executed in the ship, which, of course, kept us a day or two there. On such occasions it's customary to let the men have leave of absence by turns, and when Patterson and Crawford asked the same favour of me, I could not very well refuse, because, though their manners had been sullen and morose, they had not misbehaved themselves, and were, therefore, entitled to the favour they had asked for. So I granted it, but at the same time, warned them to return to the ship by seven o'clock, which was the utmust limit I ever allowed, except on very particular occasions."

" And they, I suppose," observed Edwin, " thought proper to disregard your commands ?"

" They did," answered the captain ; " for on the following morning, word was brought by the mate that neither Patterson nor Crawford had returned to the ship since they had had leave given them to quit it. Of course I was very angry at this, because on board a vessel it is necessary to keep up a system of the strictest descipline, and if no notice was taken of their conduct, others of the crew would naturally think they might do the same thing without the risk of meeting with punishment. I accordingly gave orders for a search to be made after them all over the place, and that when found, they should be put in irons, and conveyed on board with as little delay as possible"

"I see," exclaimed Edwin, "the fellows regarded you as a tyrant, and from that time they have been resolving to revenge themselves at the earliest opportunity."

"You shall hear all in good time, my young friend," said Captain Gresham, "but I must not be hurried in a narrative that is not yet half finished.—The search I am speaking of was carried into every part of the place, but I suppose they contrived to conceal themselves somewhere, for party after party returned, and still they continued to bring the same news that neither of the men were to be found. I, therefore, began to despair of ever seeing anything more of them, and had determined to set sail without them, when news was brought that several daring robberies had been committed in the place, and I at once judged that the two absent rascals were concerned in them. Men were, therefore, sent out once more to look after them, and I, myself, went ashore to see that they did their duty properly. Nothing, however, was seen or heard of them, and on our return to the ship, it was found that the fellows had sneaked back during our absence, and that they had accounted for their absence, by saying that they had both been seized by a fever, which had almost brought them to the grave, and they had returned as soon afterwards as they possibly could."

"Which, of course," cried Edwin, "turned out to be a fabrication of their own to excuse their conduct?"

"At first we were all inclined to think so," replied the captain; "but in the absence of any proof in favour of our suspicions, we were compelled to take the story as they had related it. In truth they did appear to have been ill, for they were a good deal altered for the worse, and complained of being excessively weak, which might, likely enough, have been assumed to excuse them from their share of the ship's duties. I, however, took every precaution to prevent treachery, and had them searched to see if they had brought back any weapons with them by which they might do us a

No. 22

mischief. But nothing was found upon them, and I began to think that after all we had very likely wronged them by our suspicions. From that time I could observe a marked change in their manners and appearance; they evidently grew more morose, and seemed to go about their work unwillingly; so much so, indeed, that I was obliged to threaten them with punishment if they did not think proper to do their duty as they ought."

"Did that have any effect upon them?" asked Edwin.

"If it had any effect upon them, it was a very different one to what I expected," replied Captain Gresham, "for, from that time, I could see that they were exerting themselves as much as possible to set the rest of the crew against me. They, however, took care not to let me overhear any of their conversation, but I could tell by their looks and actions that they were plotting mischief, and you may be sure I tried as much as possible to get to the bottom of the secret that was evidently between them. I questioned the other men as to any knowledge they might possess relative to the designs of these two dangerous fellows, but all of them professed ignorance, and I dare say truly enough, for both Patterson and Crawford were too cautious to trust any one with a secret till they were quite certain they might be depended on."

"And did then venture on any outbreak?" asked Edwin, who grew more and more interested in the story which he was most anxious to hear to a conclusion.

"No," replied the captain, "they grew rather more quiet and respectful after a time, and I began to hope that as they had seen how useless it would be to risk a mutiny in the vessel, they would now become more faithful in the discharge of their duties; and that, at any rate, I might trust to them for the remainder of the voyage, when I should be able to discharge them and take others in their place, in the event of its appearing that their continuance on board the vessel would be dangerous. At all events, I thought that a strict watch upon them would prevent any mischief happening from them during the time they were to remain with us; and, as I had a thorough command over all the rest of the crew, I had very little fear of their being able to undermine the better principles of their companions. Sometimes, to be sure, I thought of giving them up to the civil authorities of the island where we were lying at anchor, but there was in reality no charge against them except that of their having stayed ashore longer than they ought, and even that had been accounted for in a tolerably reasonable way, if not in one that was altogether satisfactory. And the rascals seemed to know that I only wanted an opportunity to get them more thoroughly in my power, for though they did not do their work cheerfully or in any way that pleased me, yet nothing was neglected that they ought to do, and the work was finished in a manner that defied complaint."

"All which," observed Edwin, "was no doubt done to prevent too speedily a discovery of their plans."

"It was," replied the captain; "yet so clumsily did they attempt to conceal their sullenness, that even their comrades did not fail to perceive the mischief that was lurking in their hearts. Sometimes they would be asked what made them so dull and sullen when everybody else in the ship was happy and contented with his station. But these questions were seldom answered, and even when a reply was deigned, it was to the effect that they were not obliged to reply to impertinent questions, and that those who asked them had much better mind their own business than trouble themselves with that of others. These things occasionally caused high words between them and the rest of the crew, and two or three times on my return on board after going ashore, I heard of fights taking place among them,—and, on one occasion, it was reeportd to me the two fellows had armed themselves with knives, and would have done a serious mischief to their antagonists, had not the mate rushed between them with a brace of pistols in his hand, with which he threatened to shoot the first man that disobeyed his commands. This had the effect of bringing the strife to an end just for the time, but it was evident a great deal of ill blood existed between the two parties, and I was myself obliged to interfere and warn them that a severe punishment would fall upon any one that should venture to renew a quarrel which threatened to terminate in such fatal circumstances This seemed to have some effect upon them, and if there was not more friendship among them, it at least had the beneficial result of keeping more order and decorum on board the ship."

" I almost wonder," said Edwin, " that with two such turbulent fellows your life was not attempted."

" It is rather surprising," answered the captain ; " but, perhaps, it may be accounted for from the fact that they would have no way to escape in the event of their committing such a crime as that, for had they jumped overboard and swam to land, the place was so small that they could not hope to escape the avenging hand of justice for any long time. One night, however, I was awoke by hearing what appeared to be footsteps in my cabin, and as my lamp had expired, I jumped out of bed, and having groped for my sword, felt round the place to ascertain whether my suspicions were founded in truth. At length I struck a light, but no one was seen anywhere near the place, though my dog having been enticed to a distant part of the ship seemed to confirm my ideas that the villains had meditated an attack upon my life, and that they had coaxed the faithful animal away, in order that they might the more certainly succeed in their nefarious designs."

" I am only surprised," observed Edwin, " that they didn't make away with the dog so as to save themselves any further trouble."

" And so they would had they known what was subsequently to take place," answered the captain ; " and that, by the by, brings me to the part of that I alluded to in the beginning. Some few days passed away after I had been disturbed in my cabin, and as Pattison and Crawford had behaved better than for some time previously, I was induced, at their earnest entreaties, to give them leave to go ashore for the last time previous to sailing for our place of destination. I, however, desired the other men to keep a very watchful eye upon them, and not to trust them out of sight on any account whatever. I could see my orders gave them a great deal of anger which, with all their efforts, they were unable to control ; but they appeared to be perfectly civil, and promised that if I would let them go where they pleased, to return at the hour I had named, and to behave better in future. And, really, they pleaded so earnestly, and seemed so sincere in what they said, that I should have granted their request if it had not been for the mate, who, by signs and gestures, implored me not to accede to their proposition. This reminded me that it would be dangerous to do as they had asked me, and, addressing them resolutely, I told the two fellows that they must go on the terms I had offered, or remain on board ship with the few that would be left behind. Thus they found themselves compelled to yield, and most reluctantly they went ashore with the rest of the men that had obtained my permission."

" The rascals," exclaimed Edwin ; " it's plain enough to all that they were after no good."

" So it appeared," answered Captain Graham, " for no sooner had they landed, than they offered all the money they possessed between them to their companions, on condition that they would suffer them to roam about as they pleased, and not to be watched as if they were suspected of entertaining some evil design. But all their entreaties were made in vain, for the others were faithful to the promise they had given; and, at the expiration of the time that had been given them, Patterson and Crawford returned to the ship with their companions, and it was easy enough to see how enraged they were at the disappointment they endured at having been frustrated in the execution of some plot that they had formed. No notice, however, was taken of this, and the next day we put to sea with a fair wind to carry us to our place of destination.

"Ah!" said Edwin, "but I dare say those fellows had not done plotting against you?"

"You shall hear," replied Captain Gresham; "and now I think I shall be able to prove to you what a faithful friend I found in my dog, Sancho, whose watchful care preserved me from the treachery of those who saved my life. To be brief—in the course of the day after we had put to sea, I had occasion to go to my chest, which, by the bye, was never locked, to take out a pair of gloves, which, having found, I threw upon the table, till I had finished a little writing I had to do. Whilst I was doing this, my attention was frequently called towards Sancho, whose whining and fidgetty actions convinced me that he suspected something was going wrong. I could not help remarking this, and spoke several times to him encouragingly, but he grew more and more restless; and, at length, when I rose and was taking the gloves up to put them on, he sprang towards me with a growl, and seizing the gloves between his teeth, tore them from my grasp, and threw them upon the floor. At first angry with the dog, and snatching up a stick, was going to chastise him, but at that moment I remembered how faithful he had always been, and at once supposing there must be some cause for his singular behaviour, I cautiously picked up the gloves, and having turned them inside out, discovered in one of them, to my horror and amazement, a scorpion, which had evidently been placed there designedly, and from whose mortal sting I had been thus providentially saved."

"And you suspected the two men, Patterson and Crawford?" observed Edwin, with astonishment.

"I did."

"And were no means taken to punish them?"

"None whatever," replied the captain; "in fact, I had no positive proof to bring against them, and as, under such circumstances, it was better to say nothing about it, I kept the affair quiet, and contented myself with observing the fellows more narrowly than ever I had done previously. At length we reached the place of our destination, where they contrived to give us the slip, and I have heard nothing of them since till yesterday, when I was informed that they were on board the Orion, which had just sailed from the Downs. It seems, however, that they have somehow or other contrived to get away, and if it had not been for you, my dear lad, I should not now have been alive to relate the adventure you have just heard."

"And most deeply have I been interested," replied Edwin.

"Then so far am I rewarded for my pains," said Captain Gresham; "and now, as one good turn deserves another, perhaps you will tell me who and what you are, and why a youth like you is wandering about the world apparently without either friends or a home to call your own?"

"The truth is, sir," replied Edwin, "I have been unfortunate enough to incur the anger and hatred of a man who ought to have been my friend. At length his treatment of me grew so unbearable, that resolving to endure it no longer, I secretly quitted his house, and was making my way towards the metropolis, when accident brought me to Chatham, which I can scarcely regret, since I believe it has proved the means of saving you from assassination."

"It has, indeed," replied the captain; "and now, perhaps, you will have the kindness to tell me what design you had in going up to London?"

"The truth is, sir," replied Edwin, "I was in hopes of obtaining a commission either in the army or the navy, for it is a matter of indifference which service I adopt."

"My dear boy," exclaimed Captain Gresham; "you have no idea of the difficulty that exists in your way. You must possess powerful interest to succeed in the project you have proposed to yourself, and even then I am not quite certain that you would attain the object of your ambition."

"But suppose I was content to begin at the lowest step of the ladder," said Edwin; "do you think in such a case as that I should never be able to advance any higher?"

"I think you would be disappointed," answered the captain, with a grave shake of the head, "for it so happens that there are many persons waiting for promotion, whose interest is far greater than you possess, and, of course, they would be advanced in preference to those who have not an equal advantage."

"And suppose I particularly distinguished myself in any action against the enemy," cried Edwin, "would they not reward me for it by immediate promotion?"

"If you were to depend upon anything of the kind," replied Captain Gresham, "I fear you would be doomed to endure disappointment and mortification; for merit is very apt to be overlooked in these matters, however deserving the parties may be."

"Then you consider I should have no chance of rising in either of the professions I was so anxious to enter into?"

"Very little, indeed, my young friend," replied the captain. "However, you have done me a very great service, and there seems to be so much frankness and honesty about you, that I have determined to do what I can towards establishing you in some honourable line of life. I think, if I understand rightly, you have neither friends nor home to go to when you reach London?"

"I have not," replied Edwin, "but I have some little energy, and there is no fear but I shall soon be able to do something."

"You don't know what sort of place London is," answered the captain. "It is an overgrown city, where people are too busy to take heed of strangers, and with only a small sum of money in your pocket, I'm afraid you would soon see reason to regret the step you have taken."

"You would persuade me, then," cried Edwin, "to return home, and sue for pardon from the man whose heartless tyranny compelled me to fly from his house?"

"There you are mistaken," returned Captain Gresham; "for I can see you have a bit of spirit of your own, and, of course, such a step as that would be quite impossible. But I'll tell you what you do; I am now going to set sail for a foreign station, and if you think fit to accompany me, you shall do so as a friend, and perhaps an opportunity may offer for you to distinguish yourself. At all events, it will afford you a chance of seeing how you like the sort of life, and if you should not approve of it, I will exert my interest on our return to England, to place you in some situation or other in which you may comfortably establish yourself for life."

This proposition suited the notions of the youth admirably, and with many expressions of gratitude for the offer he eagerly closed with it, and a bargain was made that he should sail with his newly found friend under circumstances that were extremely favourable to himself. Early on the following morning, therefore, he went ashore with Captain Gresham, who fitted him out with all things necessary for the voyage, and with the next tide they weighed anchor, and bidding farewell to old England, our youthful friend soon found himself far away from his native land.

CHAPTER XXIII.

THE ACCUSATION.

LEAVING Edwin to pursue his voyage for the present, we must now return to Susan Hoply, who the reader will recollect was in the service of Mr. and Mrs. Graham. But the embarrassment occasioned to her master and mistress by the culpable indiscretion of the former, compelled them, for a time, to curtail their expenses as much as possible, and Mrs. Graham, willing as she always was to make any sacrifice, proposed that they should do without a servant at present, and, in accordance with that plan, Susan received notice to quit at the end of a month. This announcement was not altogether unexpected by our heroine, because she knew the altered circumstances of Mr. and Mrs. Graham must lead to considerable changes in their mode of living, and at the end of the period above alluded to, she entered the service of a Mrs. Dawson, a young married lady, whose husband being engaged in a large commercial house, was frequently absent for weeks together on his travels. They were, however, a very happy couple; fondly attached to each other, and never anticipating that anything could occur to mar their domestic felicity. The salary of Mr. Dawson was a very liberal one, and, consequently, they were enabled to keep a respectable house with a couple of female domestics, one of whom, as we have seen, was Susan Hoply.

Mr. and Mrs. Dawson had only been married a few months, and as their tempers were somewhat similar, and the match was one of love, they lived together in the strictest harmony. The lady was, perhaps, a little too fond of gaiety, which was a foible that her husband never attempted to check; for though she dressed rather extravagantly, and had a wish to keep a great deal of company, yet he saw that her affection towards him was undiminished, and as the expenses of these things never went beyond his means, he was rather pleased than otherwise to indulge her in a fancy that he knew would wear away when she had a little more experience.

Nor was Mr. Dawson free from faults, though they were not of a very serious nature. Pride was his chief bane, and nothing mortified him so much as the idea that the world should think meanly of him, or that people should blame his wife for that gaiety of heart, which some persons ill-nature might take it into their heads to term levity of conduct. His wife had early detected this weakness, and most earnestly did she set about the task of convincing him that the world had something else to do than to pay attention to his affairs, or to care whether their affairs were extravagant or parsimonious. Her arguments were, however, of no avail, for Mr. Dawson continued to vex himself about those trifles, and his wife was too fond of him to talk very seriously upon the subject.

" My dear," he would say, " you may call it weakness, or whatever you please, but no man can endure ridicule, and perhaps I am more sensitive on that point than other folks. Besides, I hate gossipping and tittle-tattle, for though people may only utter what are intended as harmless jokes they frequently render the subjects of them ridiculous, and that is a thing I could never bear in my life."

" But what can they ever say about us ?" asked his wife, playfully. " Are we not the happiest couple in the world ?—and do you think the envenomed tongue of slander can ever utter a word to the prejudice of people that give no cause for it ?"

" It but too frequently happens, my dear," replied Mr. Dawson, " and, in truth, I have heard it said that there are persons ill-natured enough to throw out insinuations about your partiality for dress and company."

" Indeed !" said the lady, biting her lips with vexation.

" They do, my love," replied her husband, pressing her hand affectionately; " but I scarcely need tell you that such things would never make me think a bit the worse of you. In fact, I know it to be nothing but the offspring of envy and malice, and I should care nothing about it if it was not that it makes one look so very ridiculous in the eyes of the world."

" Aye," cried Mrs. Dawson, " there's your old foible again ; you shrink from the world's opinion as the sensitive leaf does from the touch of human hands. And yet, after all, what need you or I care for the evil sayings of the world ? If, indeed, I was like Mrs. Railton, who, they say, scratches her husband's face, you might have some reason to dread the derision you so much fear."

" That is an extreme case," answered her husband, " and were it ever to be my lot, I should bury myself in some obscure place, and never again mix with my fellow-creatures. Nay, I am not quite certain whether I should not lay violent hands upon myself, and thus escape the ridicule that by nature I am so ill able to endure."

" Heaven forbid that you should ever have cause to commit so rash an act on my account," cried Mrs. Dawson, shuddering at the thought of such an event. " But you seem to be more than usually excited to-day, my dear," she continued, " has anything occurred to move you thus ?"

" The truth is," he replied, " I shall be obliged to leave you for some time."

" Ah !" exclaimed his wife, sorrowfully, " then that fully accounts for your being so dull and melancholy to-day. But it is our duty to bear these things with what resignation we can, and, though I shall deeply regret your absence, you may rely upon it that my every thought will be directed towards you, be in what part of the world you may."

" That, my love, I am quite convinced of," replied Dawson, " but I have been thinking that if the world will say scurrilous things of a woman when her husband is always with her, what may it say when I am absent, and that too, perhaps, for some months ? You see, therefore, how necessary it will be to act with the greatest circumspection ; to keep within doors as much as possible, to be very choice and select in the friends you associate with, and never to give even the slightest cause for the spreading of injurious thoughts against one who I hold far dearer than I do my own life."

" Surely you do not doubt me ?" she said, in a tone of some little reproach.

" Indeed I do not, my dear," he replied; " and what I have said is only to make you as cautious as you can be, during my absence from home."

" That you may rely on," answered Mrs. Dawson, " for I love my husband so well that I would not occasion him a moment's uneasiness by any act of thoughtless levity such as you so much dread to think of. Besides, my own reputation would be at stake, and rather than risk the loss of that

I would keep myself a prisoner in-doors from the time of your departure till your return home again."

" Nay," returned her husband, " there will be no occasion for that ; and I would now have you understand that what I have been saying was actuated by a desire to warn you against falling into a snare which it would be difficult to extricate yourself from. You are neither 'giddy nor thoughtless, and yet might commit some trifling fault that the world would too gladly magnify into some heinous offence."

" Well, then," replied Mrs. Dawson, laughing, " I'll be as like a quakeress as I possibly can ; my face shall never be guilty of a smile, and in dress I'll be so plain that no one shall ever have reason to make remarks on that account."

" There you would be falling into the other extreme," exclaimed her husband ; " and perhaps people would say that you acted so in conformity with my wishes, and thus I should be made a laughing-stock for all those who delight in ridiculing that which they do not thoroughly understand. You can, however, avoid unnecessary gaiety, both in dress and company, and by conducting yourself with that prudence which you so well know how to exercise, we may both of us escape the ridicule of a thoughtless world."

" If I have been rather partial to dress," she replied, " it was because I knew that you liked to see me as other people are ; but, as you are now going to be absent for some time, I shall have no such object in view, and, of course, I shall act with all the prudence that you can desire."

" That promise is quite sufficient for me," exclaimed her husband ; " and, fully relying upon your discretion, I shall quit my house in the full confidence of never finding that you are worse than your word. And now let me once more assure you that throughout this conversation I have intended no unkindness, but what I have said has been dictated by a sincere desire to maintain your happiness as well as my own."

On the day following this interview, Mr. Dawson set out on his journey, and returning home after the lapse of a few weeks, he had every reason to be satisfied with the prudence and admirable conduct of his wife. He was now frequently out for some time together, and never did he have occasion to reproach his wife with breaking her word to him, for slander was silent respecting her, and those who spoke of Mrs. Dawson did so as of one who might well be held up as a pattern for her sex.

In this happy family Susan Hoply remained between two and three years, and it scarcely need be added that her time was passed as comfortable as, under circumstances, could be expected. She was still watching her opportunity to remove the foul stain of murder from the memory of her brother Andrew ; but so far all her efforts were without avail, and all that remained for her to do was to wait with patience till circumstances should render her intentions practicable.

In the meantime Mr. Dawson was frequently absent on his journey, but at length he received orders to go abroad ; and from the extensive route he had to take, it was expected that he would not return home again much under twelve months. This was a source of much grief to his wife, who was unable to conceal the pain she felt at so long a separation.

" I have always regretted your absence, my dear husband," she said to him, " even when it has only been for a few weeks at a time ; but now, when a whole twelvemonth is likely to pass away without seeing you, I must confess that I feel a depression of spirits which I cannot control."

" But as it is necessary," he replied, " I must remind you that it will be your duty to bear the separation with fortitude. The year will come to an end, my love ; and my employers have assured me that I shall remain at home for at least three months after my return to England."

"And in that time," said Mrs. Dawson, "you will find me a mother."
"True," he replied, "and if anything will increase our happiness, it will be the fulfilment of those hopes which have inspired us ever since our union. In the meantime, I shall frequently write to you, and great will be my happiness when I hear that you have added one more link to the joy which it has been my lot to bear."

"And yet," sighed his wife, "I would that you were near me to participate in the rapture that fills a parent's heart on first beholding her offspring. But you will tell me, I know, that it is impossible; and, therefore, will I bow with resignation to an event that cannot be avoided."

Within a few days after this conversation, Mr. Dawson set forth on his journey, and a heavy parting was it between him and his wife, at finding that they must part for so long a period. She, however, took his counsel, and bore up against it with as much fortitude as she could, and even sought to drown her recollection of the circumstance by busily employing herself in making preparations for the infant whose appearance in the world was looked forward to with so much anxiety.

Some little time had elapsed since Mr. Dawson left home, when one day she walked to the linen-draper's where she usually dealt, and looked over a number of things which would be required for the preparations she was making. But, whether she was less easy to please that day, or from whatever other cause it might be, she could not suit herself with the articles she wanted, and, at last, the shopkeeper offered to send a quantity of things to her house, out of which she could make what selection she pleased. This she readily acceded to, and was walking out of the place, when her arm was laid hold of by one of the young men of the establishment, who whispered in her ear that she had taken some property belonging to his master, and in confirmation of his charge, drew from her muff a quantity of lace,

No. 23

which she had taken up with her handkerchief, and, without being aware of the circumstance, had put it into the place where it was discovered.

To describe the confusion of poor Mrs. Dawson at finding herself in this distressing situation would be impossible, but fortunately for her, the man did not suspect that she had done it wilfully, and bowing politely, he took away the lace and returned to his place behind the counter. Mrs. Dawson, however, could not but feel that the affair must give rise to great doubts in the minds of all who had witnessed the transaction, and timidly raising her eyes, she saw that a number of persons were gazing at her, and from their looks she could see but too plainly that they regarded her as a thief who ought to be punished rather than thus be let off to commit her depredations elsewhere. In fact, she went cowering out of the shop, and the one thought which filled her mind was that of thankfulness, that her husband was not present to be a witness of the shame and humiliation she had that day endured.

Soon after reaching home, Mrs. Dawson was called down into the front parlour where the man was waiting with the things which the linen-draper had promised to send for her inspection. It happened, however, that the bearer was going a little further, and leaving the things for her to look over at her leisure, she made the choice of which was wanted, and when the man came back, he measured off what she required, and took his departure with the remainder of the goods.

It was perhaps a couple of hours after this, and while she was congratulating herself on the fortunate turn the affair had taken, that a loud knocking was heard at the street door, and in another minute Mr. Edwards, the master of the shop where she had been dealing, entered the room, and with very little courtesy addressed himself to her :—

"Really, madam," he exclaimed, "this business to day is a very disagreeable one, and I regret the situation it has placed you in; but, the fact is, a considerable quantity of lace is now missing from the parcel my young man brought here, and a remnant of silk, which he positively declares, was among the other goods, is no where to be found."

"Indeed, sir!" cried Mrs. Dawson with astonishment; "you have very much surprised me, for if there is any mistake it must have been made by your young man himself."

"I was first in hopes there might have been some mistake," replied Mr. Edwards; "and I have questioned the young man about it, but he tells me the things were left here while he went a little further; and, therefore, I must say, however unwilling I may feel at doing so, that the affair begins to assume a very bad and suspicious appearance."

"Good Heavens, sir!" cried Mrs. Dawson, with alarm, "you surely cannot suspect me of having been guilty of purloining your goods?"

"What am I to think of it, madam?" asked Edwards; "the fact is, a certain quantity of goods was sent into your house, and after deducting what you purchased and paid for, a considerable deficiency occurs. You, perhaps, may not know anything about it, but there is such a thing as dishonesty among servants, and perhaps one of yours may have had a fancy to obtain the goods under cost price."

"Both my servants are above suspicion in that respect," answered Mrs. Dawson, "and, indeed, now I come to recollect myself, neither of them have been in the room from the time your young man came till now."

"Well," exclaimed the linen-draper, "I don't know anything about that, of course, but I do happen to know that I have been robbed, and as it is necessary to find out how it has been done, I must request you to submit to your being searched, and then of course your guilt or innocence will be manifest."

And with that he went to the door, and beckoned in an officer who was in attendance, and who he immediately brought into the parlour without further ceremony. Mrs. Dawson, conscious as she was of her own innocence, felt highly indignant at this, and ringing the bell violently, was immediately answered by Susan, who, in the greatest alarm, enquired what was the matter.

"Matter enough, young woman," exclaimed Edwards; "your mistress has been doing wrong, and I have taken prompt means to sift the matter to the very bottom."

"My mistress been doing wrong, sir !" cried Susan, with surprise.

"Believe him not," cried Mrs. Dawson, wildly. "He pretends to have lost some goods that were just now sent here by his young man, and declares that I must be searched."

"Impossible !" cried Susan, with indignation ; "my mistress would scorn so base an act as that you accuse her of."

"Aye, aye," answered Edwards, "everybody denies doing anything wrong, and will stick to it to the very last; but it so happens, that we tradesmen suffer very severely by the pilfering habits of many persons that call themselves ladies, and it's a duty I owe to my fellow tradesmen, to prosecute every case that I may happen to be concerned in. So, if you are innocent, ma'am, there can be no reason for objecting to my proposition, and if you are guilty you will deserve punishment for it."

Upon this, he gave a sign to the police officer that had accompanied him, and poor Mrs. Dawson was obliged to go through the degrading ceremony of a search. It was in vain, however, that this was done, for none of Edwards's property was found upon her. Not satisfied with this, they next proceeded to search the room, and from thence they went over every other part of the house, turning everything over, whether they belonged to the mistress or her servants. But, nothing did they find to warrant their suspicions ; and, even Mr. Edwards was compelled to admit that he was somewhat deceived in the result of his labours. Still, however, he persisted in declaring that his goods had been stolen by some one in the house, and as they must have been secretly removed, it was considered nothing more than fair, that Mrs. Dawson should go before a magistrate, who would be better able to judge whether any proof of guilt would be brought against her.

"When people make up their minds to do these sort of things," he said, "they can always find ways and means to get rid of the articles which, if found, must condemn them to infamy !—and in the present instance, I am so thoroughly convinced that they have been stolen in this house, that I am determined not to rest satisfied till the whole affair has been thoroughly investigated before a magistrate."

"I am innocent,—indeed, indeed, I am innocent," cried Mrs. Dawson, in a paroxysm of terror. "And yet, though I am conscious of no crime, I will pay for the goods you say are missing, rather than endure the disgrace that must fall upon me should this charge be made public."

"And why should you wish to pay for the things if you didn't steal them ?" asked Mr. Edwards, insolently. "But I'll tell you what it is, ma'am ;— this ain't the first time you've taken what isn't your own, and it's my duty to punish you as far as ever the law will go. So you must accompany us to the police-office, ma'am, and if his worship believes your story, why, of course, there the matter will end, and you'll be turned into the world again to continue your depredations on honest tradesmen, till some of them happen to fix you with the robbery."

"Will no prayers, no entreaties prevail on you to spare me the shame and disgrace of this public exposure?" cried Mrs. Dawson, almost fainting from excessive terror.

" I shall do my duty, ma'am," replied the other, " and so don't think to get off in that sort of way. But if you don't want all the world to know it, why, I'll go and get a hackney coach, and then we can all ride down to the office, and no one need be anything the wiser, unless you should happen to be remanded or anything of that sort."

"If there is no alternative," groaned Mrs. Dawson, " I must needs accept the offer you have made."

" Well," he said, " I sharn't be gone very long on my errand, and you, he continued, addressing the officer, " will remain here, and of course you'll take care that your prisoner don't escape."

With this he bustled out of the room, as if he was going on a very pleasant errand, and Mrs. Dawson was left to bemoan the hard destiny that had befallen her.

" Is not this horrible, Susan?" she cried, addressing herself to our heroine; " to be accused of such a crime as this, and having nothing but my own bare denial to refute it."

" It is, indeed, shocking, ma'am," answered Susan, weeping bitterly at the misfortunes of her mistress;—" it is a dreadful thing to be accused in this way, and I was thinking whether it would not be as well for me to run to some of our neighbours, who will cheerfully come forward to say how incapable you are of committing such a crime as they have charged you with."

" I would not have such a thing done for the world," exclaimed Mrs. Dawson. " At present no one must know of my disgrace, and on Providence alone will I rely for clearing me from a charge which I shudder even to think of."

" At least, ma'am," said Susan, " you will allow me to go with you?"

" I will, indeed, my good girl," replied her mistress, " and thank you too, for the kindness which has prompted the offer. I shall need a friend to be near me, and upon you I can rely, even though all the world besides may turn their backs on me."

By this time Mr. Edwards returned with the vehicle he had been in quest of ; and all four of them having got in, they were driven off with all speed towards the police office of the district in which the alleged offence had been committed.

CHAPTER XXIV.

THE POLICE OFFICE.

On reaching the place where the examination was to take place, Mrs. Dawson, for the first time in her life, had a glimpse of one of the offices in which criminals undergo their examination previous to being sent before another and a higher tribunal of justice. On the day in question there happened to be a greater number than usual of prisoners, and the officer was going to lock her up, as a matter of course, with the wretched beings who were waiting their turn for examination, had not Susan interposed, and begged that he would at least spare her mistress the indignity of associating with some of the worst and most degraded of human beings. The man, who was not quite so hard-hearted as many of his class, seemed struck by her appeal, and without making any reply, he beckoned for them to follow him; and in a few seconds afterwards they found themselves in the police-office, where a case was just under the consideration of the magistrate. Even here Mrs. Dawson saw quite enough to make her heart sick at the depravity of human nature, and when the examination was over, she scarcely heard her name called by the clerk before she was led to the prisoner's dock, while the evidence was taken against her.

During this time, the attention of Susan Hoply was directed towards a sullen, ferocious looking fellow, who she thought she had seen before; and after some little consideration, she felt quite certain that it was the ruffian she had seen near Mr. Wentford's house on the night the murder was committed. Indeed, she had always suspected that he was one of the villains who had committed the deed; and so thoroughly convinced did she now feel that her suspicions were correct, that she was about to request the officer to detain him, when the fellow opened the door and disappeared from the place like a shot. At her request the man went to look after him, but presently returned, saying that he was out of sight, and, probably being one of a bad sort, would not venture to show himself there again in a hurry.

In answer to her questions, however, he acknowledged having seen him before, and that he was suspected of being an indifferent character. In fact, he had heard that he went by a variety of names, and so numerous were these that he could not undertake to recollect above a twentieth part of them. All this served to convince Susan more and more that she was not wrong in her conjectures, and great was her disappointment at having missed the opportunity of securing a ruffian who, in all probability, could clear her brother Andrew from the foul crime of murder which had been charged against him. As it was, however, there was no help for it; but the circumstance reminded her still more forcibly of the duty she had undertaken, and as one of the villains was still lurking in the neighbourhood of London, she hoped that ere long she might have an opportunity of bringing him to justice.

In the mean time the magistrate had been engaged in a long conversation with a gentleman who had entered the office on business, and seemed altogether to have forgotten that he had any further duty to perform. This was a period of anxious suspense to Mrs. Dawson, who knew that all eyes were directed towards her, and feared lest there might be any one in the office to whom she was known. She, therefore, covered her face with her hands, and having been accommodated with a seat, threw herself forward upon the rail, and wept bitterly for the misfortunes with which she had been so unexpectedly overwhelmed.

From this state of wretchedness and despair, however, she was at length aroused by the officer, who, touching her on the arm, nodded his head significantly towards the magistrate, as much as to say that his worship had finished his conversation, and was now ready to commence upon the next case. Upon this hint Mrs. Dawson rose, and, arranging her veil so as to conceal her countenance as much as possible from the gazing and inquisitive multitude, stood in trembling anxiety to await the result of the examination.

" What is the charge against the prisoner, Tomkins ?" said the magistrate, glancing towards Mrs. Dawson as if he wished to ascertain whether she had ever been brought before him on any former occasion.

" Robbery, your worship," answered the man.

" Is the prosecutor in court ?"

" He is, your worship."

" Let him stand forward, then."

Upon this Mr. Edwards advanced, and having taken the usual oath, was about to proceed with a long rambling story, when the magistrate interrupted him by asking his name.

"Josiah Edwards, your worship."

"Has the prisoner robbed you, sir?"

"She has."

"What evidence have you of it?" asked the magistrate.

"My own, and that of my shopman."

"I suppose, then, you saw her steal the goods in question?"

"No, your worship, I didn't see her steal them," replied Edwards, "but I measured off every article before they were sent to her house, and when my young man came back, I found that, after deducting for what she had bought and paid for, a quantity of lace and a remnant of silk were missing from the package."

"Is it usual," asked the magistrate, "to measure goods before you send them to a customer's house?"

"Not always, your worship," replied the linendraper; "but the truth is, I rather suspected the prisoner of dishonesty, and on this occasion I did it for my own satisfaction."

"You suspected her?" observed the magistrate; "pray, sir, had you any reason for so doing?"

"I had, your worship'" answered the prosecutor; "in fact, it was only this morning that she came into my shop to look at some goods, and after giving a good deal of trouble, she desired some to be sent to her house in the afternoon. Upon that she was going away, when one of my shopmen saw a piece of lace hanging from her muff, and having stopped her, he took several yards, which I have no doubt she meant to purloin."

"Did you immediately give her into custody?"

"I did not," replied Edwards, "for she had been a customer of mine on several previous occasions, and I was inclined to believe her assertion that she had accidentally taken it up with her handkerchief, and put it into her muff."

"And in that belief, you suffered her to depart from you premises, did you?"

"Yes, your worship," answered the prosecutor; "but I could not help feeling some suspicions, and so, as I observed before, I measured the goods that were sent to her, and on my young man's return, I found that the articles mentioned had been stolen."

"Is your shopman here?"

"He is."

"Let him take your place, then," said the magistrate, "and I'll hear what evidence he has to give."

Upon this a very curly-pated and dandified fellow stepped forward, and with a bow, announced himself as the next witness in the case.

"Your name, sir?" demanded the justice.

"Richard Joblins."

"You were sent to the prisoner's house, I believe, with some goods belonging to your master?"

"I was, sir."

"And some of them, it seems, are missing;—did you see her steal any of the missing articles?"

"No, your worship."

"Then how do you know that she is the party who stole them from your parcel?"

"There is good reason to suspect her, sir," replied Joblins; "for I had a little further to go, and when I went away, I left her looking over the things."

"To say the least of it," observed the magistrate, "it was imprudent to leave your master's property in the care of another person. However, I suppose, on your return, you discovered the loss, and at once accused her of the theft?"

"No, sir," replied Joblins, "I didn't make the discovery at all, but went back to my employer——"

"Your *master* you mean, I suppose?" interrupted his worship, with marked emphasis. "However, go on, sir, and let me hear what followed."

"On my return," replied the abashed counter-jumper, "Mr. Edwards measured the goods, and having taking an account of what I had sold, he discovered that the articles mentioned were not in the parcel."

"And both he and you at once suspected that the prisoner must have been the thief?"

"There could have been no doubt of it, your worship."

"And upon that suspicion an officer was called in, and the party given into custody?"

"Yes, your worship," cried Tomkins; "I went with Mr. Edwards to the prisoner's house, to see what could be made out of the case."

"Was the prisoner searched?"

"Yes, your worship."

"Was anything belonging to the prosecutor found on her?"

"No, your worship."

"Did you search the house?"

"Every corner of it from kitchens to attics."

"Did you find any of the missing goods there?"

"Not an article."

"In that case how can we expect to bring forward any proof that will convict the prisoner?" asked the magistrate.

"Begging your pardon, sir," interrupted Mr. Edwards, "but I was about to ask a remand in this case, for though our evidence is certainly defective at present, I have every reason to believe we shall be able to prove the charge to the satisfaction of a jury. In fact, between the period of the young man leaving her house, and my visiting it with the officer, there was quite sufficient time to have sent the things clear away from the premises. Such, I have no doubt, was the case, and if your worship will grant me the remand, I have no doubt, we shall be able to make a case in the course of a day or two."

"And what about your shopman," asked the magistrate; "are you quite convinced that he is honest and trustworthy?"

"I am certain of it," replied Edwards. "He has lived with me now going on two years, and I received a most excellent character with him from his last situation."

"And during the time he has been with you, there has been no reason to doubt his honesty?"

"None whatever, your worship."

"Well, well," said the magistrate, "I merely asked the question, because I know there are many young men in London who live beyond their means, and finding themselves involved in debt, they will sometimes pilfer things from their employers. Not, however, that I have any reason to suppose that your shopman has done anything of the kind, but as it is my duty to look in some degree after the interests of a prisoner, I thought it nothing more than right to ask a question relative to his character while in your service."

"Your worship is perfectly right," said Edwards; "and I am most happy at having it in my power to say that the young man has never committed any act to forfeit the high opinion I have always entertained of him."

"That is a very high character, indeed," said his worship, and he was about to order a remand, when another magistrate entered the office, and after a good deal of whispered conversation had taken place between them, it was announced that as strong circumstantial proof had been brought forward, there was quite enough to warrant the prisoner's committal for trial, and the witnesses were ordered to be bound over to prosecute.

Previously to this being done, however, she was asked whether she had any answer to make to the charge, and then summoning what little fortitude remained, she advanced to the front of the bar, and said emphatically :—

"As heaven is my witness, gentlemen, I know nothing whatever of the things said to be missing; as the person brought them to me, so were they taken away again, and the only answer I can make to the charge is, that some mistake must have occurred on the part of Mr. Edwards, and which has led to the accusation he has thus preferred."

"We are sorry, madam," returned the magistrate, "to see a female of your respectability in so degrading a situation; but the fact is Mr. Edwards has supported his evidence by an oath, and I and my brother magistrate are bound to receive it. But perhaps you may suspect who the person is that has committed the theft, and if so, we will make every effort to ascertain the truth of it."

"I suspect no one," she said.

"You keep servants, I believe?" observed the justice.

"I do."

"Have you ever had any reason to doubt their honesty?"

"Never, sir."

"Well, to say the least of it," resumed the magistrate, "the case is an extremely suspicious one, though, at present, there is no direct proof that you are the person who committed the theft. But we have the evidence of Mr. Edwards, who swears most positively that he sent the things to your house, and his shopman says he left them there whilst he went a little further on some business of his master's; and then we have the testimony of the police officer, who says that he searched the house, and though he found nothing in the place, there was sufficient time for them to have been removed for concealment. The case, it must be admitted is not a very strong one, but there are circumstances of suspicion about it, and I should not be doing my duty were I to omit sending it before a jury."

"Alas!" cried Mrs. Dawson, "and must I be sent to a felon's gaol though innocent of this crime?"

"I must confess my unwillingness to do so," replied the magistrate; "and I believe my friend here will not object to take bail for your appearance at the next Old Bailey Sessions. You have friends, I suppose, who will come forward in an emergency like this, to save you from going to prison?"

"I have friends," she replied, desponding, "but I would rather submit to anything, than publish my own shame, by letting them know of my present unfortunate situation."

"And yet they must know it," returned the magistrate, "for an affair like this is sure to be talked about, and you may as well avail yourself of the opportunity I have offered."

"No," answered Mrs. Dawson, "I will endure anything rather than ask such a favour as has been proposed. The terrors of a prison are, indeed, great, but even that shall not induce me to reveal the situation I am in."

"If your worship will allow me," said a gentleman, who had been an anxious listener to these proceedings, "I will become bail for the prisoner to any amount that may be required."

"Do you know anything of her?" asked the justice.

"I have never seen her till to-day," was the reply; "but I can feel for her misfortunes, and perfectly understanding, as I do, the delicacy which prompts her to keep this matter a secret from her friends, I, as a stranger, am ready to become responsible for her appearance at the sessions."

"This is certainly an act of great kindness," said the magistrate, "and for my own part, I am inclined to accept you as bail for the prisoner; so, if you will favour me with your name and address, I'll desire the clerk to prepare the bond."

The gentleman hereupon gave his name, and place of residence, but in so low a tone, that no one could hear it except the person to whom he addressed himself. The magistrate, however, seemed to be perfectly satisfied, and the clerk was immediately set to work with all possible despatch.

"You have been fortunate, madam," said the magistrate, addressing himself to Mrs. Dawson, "in having found a friend under the very peculiar situation in which you are placed. This gentleman has consented to answer for your appearance at the ensuing sessions, and it may, therefore, be necessary to say that he will forfeit the amount of his bond, in case you should fail to surrender yourself for trial. This I mention for your information, though, I dare say, you will not suffer him to lose so large a sum of money through any neglect of your own."

"I am deeply obliged to the gentleman for the kindness he has shown me," replied Mrs. Dawson, "and it may, perhaps, appear ungrateful of me to declare that I would rather be sent to prison than be thus indebted to a person who, till this moment, I never saw in my life."

No. 24

"Aye, aye," said the magistrate, good-naturedly, "you feel some little delicacy about accepting this offer from a stranger; but the fact is, anything will be better than going to a prison, and since the gentleman has been so kind as to make the proposition, I should most strongly urge you not to throw away the only chance of regaining your freedom."

"The truth is," interposed Edwards, bluntly, "the prisoner is married, and as her husband happens to be absent just now, I suppose she is afraid of exciting his jealousy when he comes to hear how much interest this gentleman has taken in her behalf."

To the great disappointment of Edwards, no notice was taken of this little bit of sarcasm; and as by this time the bond had been filled up and signed, Mrs. Dawson was informed that she could quit the court as soon as she pleased, an intimation which she readily followed; but scarcely had she reached the outside of the office, when the strange gentleman was by her side, and congratulating her upon having so easily obtained her release. Under any other circumstances she would have passed on without taking any heed of him, but gratitude demanded civility, and having thanked him for the favour he had done her, she was about to resume her way, when he hailed a hackney coach, and requested that she would permit him to see her home. This was done in so respectful a manner, that, being accompanied by Susan, she assented, and on reaching her own house, the stranger took his leave, with a request that he might be permitted to call and see how she was.

CHAPTER XXV.

GOSSIPPING NEIGHBOURS.

NEVER had Mrs. Dawson returned home with such feelings of shame and distress as those which harassed her after the distressing events of this day. She felt that she was eternally disgraced, for, however careful she and her servants might be to keep the matter a secret, there could be no doubt that the affair would soon be spread about, and that she would thus become the scorn of those by whom she had once been respected and caressed. The thought was madness to her, and yielding to despair. she indulged in tears of bitterness and grief. The faithful Susan, however, sought by every means in her power to allay the sorrow of her mistress by assuring her that the result would prove less disastrous than she anticipated; but all her efforts were in vain, for the hapless woman could see no ray of hope, and again bursting into a flood of tears, she said—

"It is useless to speak to me now, Susan, for the die of my destiny is cast, and I feel that the remainder of my wretched life will be covered with shame and disgrace. My husband must hear of this, and sensitive as he is of the world's opinion, he will cast me off as no longer worthy of his love and protection."

"Nay," answered Susan, "I am sure you wrong him, ma'am."

"I do not say that he would act with injustice towards me," replied Mrs. Dawson; "but every circumstance connected with this horrible charge is so much against me, that, much as he has ever loved me, he cannot do otherwise than give credit to the assertions of my accusers. And in that case, Susan, what must he think of a wife who could so far forget herself as to be guilty of such a crime as that laid to my charge?"

"But he will not believe it," answered Susan; "and though at first the news may startle and distress him, he will soon see through the falsehood, and institute so strict an enquiry into it, that your innocence will be made plain, whilst confusion and punishment will fall upon those who have really been guilty of this base act."

"That he loves me I well know," replied Mrs. Dawson ; "but even such regard as his may be turned to hate when he hears that he has been married to a thief."

"But you are no thief, ma'am."

"Thank Heaven I am not!" replied her mistress ; "but the world wil regard me as one, and happy would it have been for me had I died ere this report had been raised against me."

"Perhaps," observed Susan, " if you were to write to master, and be the first to tell him of what has happened, it would be better than to let him find it out when he comes home."

"How can I do so ?" cried Mrs. Dawson, despairingly ; "how can I find words to tell him that I have been accused of robbery ? Would he not execrate my name as he read the fatal announcement, and swear never more to see one who had brought disgrace upon his name ? No, Susan, the secret must remain undisclosed till he returns home, and then Heaven knows how I shall support the scorn of him whose esteem is more valuable to me than anything else the world contains."

"I'm sure, ma'am, he'll not take it in the light you are afraid of," said our heroine. " He has always loved you, and when he hears the foul slander, will treat it exactly in the light that it deserves. Besides, your trial may bring the whole truth to light, and in case your innocence should be proved, he will love you the more fondly for the persecutions and dangers you have escaped."

"Alas !" cried Mrs. Dawson, " I fear there is no chance of my being acquitted ; the same witnesses will appear against me that gave evidence to day, and, though innocent of the robbery, I have no one to bring forward who can say that I have been wrongfully accused of this crime."

" But Heaven will ever protect the innocent," replied Susan, " and bad as matters appear at present, I still hope that something will yet turn up in your favour."

" I will trust to the goodness of Heaven !" exclaimed Mrs. Dawson ; " but if this man Edwards persists in the story he has told, the jury will have no alternative but to pronounce a verdict of guilty against me."

" Aye," answered Susan, "but he is evidently labouring under some mistake, and he may recollect himself between now and the day of trial, and in that event he will surely not be so unjust as to withhold his testimony in your favour."

Mrs. Dawson, however, was not to be comforted by anything Susan could say, and when the faithful girl saw that she was only adding to the distress of her mistress, she left the room, in the hope that her solitary reflections would tend towards relieving her mind of the dreadful load that oppressed it. But it was in vain that the unfortunate woman sought to find comfort in looking forward to the future ; she could see nothing but horror and despair in her onward path, and at length wearied out with her thoughts, she retired at an early hour to bed, in hopes that a little sleep and rest might banish for a time thoughts which were too heavy for endurance. It was in vain, however, that she sought to find forgetfulness in sleep, for trouble and anxiety were lying heavily upon her soul, and when she rose again in the morning, her pale and care-worn countenance betrayed but too plainly the agony she had endured.

This did not pass unnoticed by Susan, who, however, carefully avoided making any allusion to a subject that she knew was painful in the extreme, and having brought in the breakfast, she was about to retire in silence, when a loud knocking was heard at the street door. The sound, accustomed as she was to it, startled Mrs. Dawson, who expected that it announced another messenger of evil, but, in a few moments Susan returned to inform her that Mrs. Mortram and Mrs. Robson, a couple of her near neighbours, had called to pay her a morning visit. Now, both these ladies were notorious gossips, and were well known to be spiteful ones, so that Mrs. Dawson was about to send out a message begging to be excused seeing them on account of indisposition; but ere she could do this, the two visitors bounced very unceremoniously into the room.

"Ah! my dear Mrs. Dawson," said Mrs. Mortram, "how glad I am to see you so well after the fright you have had. It was a shocking thing, wasn't it? But, never mind, the best people are liable to suspicion sometimes, and——"

"I really don't know to what you allude," said Mrs. Dawson, endeavouring to assume an appearance of as much composure as possible.

"Dear me, how very strange!" exclaimed Mrs. Robson. "To think now that such reports should be spread about and *you* know nothing about them."

"And how very strange it is," chimed in Mrs. Mortram, "that people should say things that there's no foundation for!"

"It is not at all strange," answered Mrs. Dawson, "for I have seen that there are always a parcel of inquisitive people in the world, who, having no business of their own, either interfere with other persons, or invent falsehoods for their own gratification."

"Really, my dear, I don't understand you," exclaimed Mrs. Mortram. "We came quite in a friendly way, I assure you, and both Mrs. Robson and myself thought it would be only kind to give you a call to see if we could be of any service under these distressing circumstances."

"I have no need of any services that you can do me," replied Mrs. Dawson; "in fact, privacy and retirement are at present all that I require, and could I but be permitted to be alone, I should feel much obliged to those who make professions under the mask of friendship."

"I hope, my dear, you don't suspect that *we* came out of any motives of impertinent prying curiosity?" said Mrs. Mortram.

"Or that we wish to annoy you under these very peculiarly distressing circumstances," added her friend.

"I would fain hope you have done all in kindness to me," replied Mrs. Dawson, calmly. "I have been rather agitated by a trifling event that has occurred, but a day or two will serve to restore me, and then I shall be happy to see you both at your earliest convenience."

"Aye, that's spoken something more like yourself, my dear," said Mrs. Robson, "and I'm sure both my friend here and myself would rather do anything than annoy you. By the by, Mrs. Dawson, how very badly that dress of yours becomes you; don't you think a silk one would be much better?"

"Especially if it was trimmed with lace," added Mrs. Mortram, spitefully.

"I have no fancy for any thing of the kind," replied Mrs. Dawson, without appearing to heed their ill-natured sarcasm; "and even if I had, I scarcely think it would be prudent just now to indulge myself with expensive luxuries."

"But, my dear," exclaimed Mrs. Mortram, "both silk and lace are sometimes to be got so very *cheap*,—absolutely for *nothing*, as one may say."

"Perhaps so," continued Mrs. Dawson, who felt ready to sink at the certainty which these words implied of her much dreaded secret having got abroad.

"However," resumed Mrs. Mortram, "of course we have no right to dictate to you what to wear; only, if you should happen to want any of the articles we have mentioned, I can tell you they are to be had on very reasonable terms at Edwards's shop,—where, I believe, you sometimes deal."

"I have dealt there," faltered out Mrs. Dawson.

"We are going there on our way home," said Mrs. Robson, "and, perhaps, you will accompany us?"

"Not to-day," replied the trembling victim of their persecution. "I have particular business that will keep me at home, and must decline going out."

At this moment another knock was heard at the street door, and presently afterwards Susan entered the room to say that Mr. Cavendish had called and requested an interview with her mistress. A sign intimated that he might be admitted, and the next moment the stranger, who had been Mrs. Dawson's bail on the previous day, entered the room. He was approaching the lady of the house to inquire how she was after the painful situation she had been placed in, but, perceiving that strangers were present, he drew back, and bowed with stiff formality to all around.

"Come, my dear Mrs. Robson," exclaimed her friend, "we will bid Mrs. Dawson good morning. She is engaged, you see, and it would be a thousand pities for us to remain and interfere with the business they have to talk over."

"There is no occasion for you to leave the room," said Mrs. Dawson, "for the gentleman is a perfect stranger, and has merely called to inquire how I am after a very distressing situation that he saw me placed in."

"We have no wish, my dear, to pry into your secrets," said Mrs. Mortram, with another of her sneers. "Our visit here was quite a friendly one, I assure you, and you must think how delighted we should have been to have had your company with us to Edwards's; he's a nice man, isn't he, and so very civil to his customers,—that is, when they don't attempt to steal any of his goods?"

With this the two gossips left the room, and Mr. Cavendish, placing a chair near Mrs. Dawson, inquired who those disagreeable women were that had just retired. But scarcely were these words out of his mouth when Mrs. Mortram again presented herself, and by the angry flashing of her eyes, it was quite evident that she had heard what he uttered. She, however, endeavoured to conceal her anger as much as possible, and putting on a forced smile, said :—

"I beg your pardon, dear, for returning so abruptly when you are so *particularly* engaged; but you said something just now about being glad to see us in a day or two, and so Mrs. Robson and myself have arranged to come and have a quiet cup of tea with you next Thursday. And now good morning, once more, and pray, whatever you do, keep up your spirits, and don't be frightened at what Edwards says."

"Thank Heaven! she's gone at last," said Mr. Cavendish, as the door once more closed upon her; "and now, madam, tell me how you find yourself after what took place? But your countenance tells me that the affair has cost you much uneasiness and alarm."

"It has, indeed," replied Mrs. Dawson, "not so much, however, on my own account as for the agony that I know it will cause my husband, when he hears that I have been accused of so heinous an offence as this. It seems to be already known to the two persons who have just left me, and through them the story will be circulated in every direction."

"It shall be my care to see them, and urge the necessity of silence," replied Mr. Cavendish. "Flattery, well applied, will keep them quiet, and as there was but one reporter in the police-office, I have prevailed on him to keep the article out of the newspapers. To be sure, Edwards, the shop-keeper, seems to be disagreeably busy in the affair; but I dare say a sum of money will keep him quiet, and it shall be my care to sift him upon the subject directly."

"There's no chance of his hearing anything about it," cried Mrs. Dawson, in despair; "for I have myself offered him the full value of the things he has lost, and instead of accepting my proposition, he chooses to say that it is a further proof of my guilt."

"I will see him myself," exclaimed Mr. Cavendish, "and I promise you, if zeal in your cause will effect the good I anticipate, you may make up your mind to hear nothing more of this disagreeable business. Nay, to relieve your mind at once, it may be as well to inform you that I intend to offer him a large sum of money, on condition that he takes no further steps in the prosecution."

"Alas!" cried Mrs. Dawson, "he will reject your terms, and the circumstance will be brought forward at the trial to prove that I really stole his property."

"Not if it is well managed," replied Mr. Cavendish. "In fact, you must not appear in it at all, but, by your silent and apparent unconcern, must appear to be quite indifferent to the situation in which you are placed. I will be the party to offer the money, and it shall be done in such a way, that he shall not be able to make any use of it against you."

Mrs. Dawson saw the impropriety of this, and would have urged him to take no further interest in her behalf; but he probably guessed what she would have said, and wishing her good morning, hurried away ere she had time to make her request. In short, from that time Mr. Cavendish became a very frequent visitor at Mrs. Dawson's house; so much so, indeed, that she began to grow uneasy at what the world might say, at her permitting the visits of a stranger during the absence of her husband. And, in truth, people were ill-natured enough to whisper all sorts of strange things which fortunately never reached her ears; yet, so conscious was she of what might be said, that she very seldom left home; partly because she had no wish to be seen at present, and partly because when she had, at first, gone out, Mr. Cavendish—quite accidentally, of course—had met her, and politely insisted upon seeing her home.

She now began to see that his visits were those of a libertine endeavouring to undermine the principles of a virtuous woman, and fearing that even the most prudent conduct on her part would not be sufficient to guard her against the sneers and evil reports of the world, she consulted with her confidant, Susan Hoply, as to the best means she could adopt under such circumstances. But the affair was not to be decided on with too much haste, and it was two or three days before Susan gave it as her opinion that the better way would be to leave the house for the present, and take a retired cottage a little way from town, where they might live quietly by themselves, and thus avoid the future visits of Mr. Cavendish, who might thus soon forget an unfortunate attachment which could only terminate in the foulest calumnies and suspicions.

Circumstanced as she was, Mrs. Dawson yielded her assent to this proposition, and a house, desirously retired, being found at Peckham, she and Susan shortly afterwards removed to it, leaving the place in town to the care of the other female domestic who was purposely left in the dark as to their present residence, so as to avoid the effect of any bribe that Mr. Cavendish might offer for a discovery of their present place of retreat.

CHAPTER XXVI.

PAINFUL SUSPICIONS.

It happened, however, with Mr. Cavendish as it does to a great many other people, that difficulties only served to make him the more determined to accomplish his object, and when, after repeated calls at Mrs. Dawson's house, he found that the servant knew nothing of her present abode, he began to think of a thousand wild schemes by which he might obtain the much-desired clue. At first he thought of putting an advertisement into the papers, with the initials of her name, and requesting an interview immediately on the subject of certain recent disagreeable transactions. But, upon reflection, this would not do, as Mrs. Dawson was certain not to take any notice of it, and, therefore, after a great deal of useless consideration, he resolved to ride round about among the suburban villages, as he had no doubt she was not far off, and thus endeavour to see, once more, the fair object who had thus enslaved his heart. But he might just as well have stayed at home for any good results that this brought about, for Mrs. Dawson never left her house, and, after wasting a great deal of time in this manner, he was obliged to give up his daily rides in despair, and content himself with making frequent calls at her house in town, in the hope that she would either return very shortly, or the servant would learn where her mistress was residing.

On the other hand, Mrs. Dawson, from over excitement and agitation, had been taken very ill directly after her arrival at the new residence, and the consequence was the premature birth of a child, which thus fortunately escaped the troubles and anxieties which its hapless mother had been doomed to endure. On recovering, however, Susan was sent to town to ascertain how matters were going on there, and, returning again in the course of a few hours, brought the intelligence that Mr. Cavendish had frequently called and left word that it was necessary he should see Mrs. Dawson as soon as possible, in order that he might inform her of what had been going on during her absence.

"And so, ma'am," continued Susan, "I really think you had better see him at once, and then the affair will be over, and, if he is an honourable man, he will never trouble you again, after telling him how much pain and uneasiness his visits at your house have given you."

"It is a sad alternative, Susan," replied her mistress; "and yet, under all circumstances, there is, perhaps, no way of avoiding it. But where can I see him, for, should he find out this place, it will be as difficult to get rid of him as it was before I fled from town."

"That's quite certain, ma'am," cried Susan; "and so I was thinking you had better go to London for a day, and when you have heard the business he wishes to see you about, it will be easy to return here, and you will be safe again for some time to come."

"I was thinking of that myself," answered Mrs. Dawson; "but you know what busy, prying neighbours we have, and should they happen to see him come to the house, it will at once be said that we met there by appointment."

"You will not go up to London, then?"

" Certainly not, at present, Susan ; but, perhaps you may think of some other place that will be less objectionable ?"

" It's hard to think of anything that would be what the world might call prudent, ma'am," replied Susan, " and perhaps you would object to meet him at some place where no one would be any the wiser for your interview ?"

" Even that would be better than running the risk of meeting Mr. Cavendish at my own house," replied Mrs. Dawson, after a pause. " In fact, after the service he has been to me by becoming my bail, I know not that it would be exactly right to refuse to see him, and I certainly will do so if a meeting could be arranged that might be strictly private, and wherein I might entreat him to seek no more intercourse with one whose character must suffer should it become known she has encouraged the visits of a stranger during the absence of her husband."

" What think you, ma'am," said Susan, " of meeting him at Forest Hill ? It is a lonely place, to be sure—but, I will accompany you, and that —even if the circumstances should become known —would disarm the evil sayings of even your very worst enemies."

" Very true, Susan," replied her mistress ; " you, of course, must go with me, and yet, after all, I feel that, in gratifying this interview, I am doing that which may hereafter occasion a great deal of trouble and sorrow."

" I should not like to advise you, if I thought any harm could come of it," returned Susan ; " but as it seems you cannot very well get off seeing Mr. Cavendish, I thought the more privately you did so the better it would be. And as Forest Hill is no very great way off, it would be convenient in your present weak state, and it will be quite impossible for him to find you out in this cottage if we only take care to watch him away before we return here."

This plan, though not highly approved off, was, at length, acceded to by Mrs. Dawson, and within an hour afterwards, Susan was sent up to town with a note for Mr. Cavendish, appointing a meeting for the next day, and earnestly requesting that her rather troublesome friend would no more seek to obtain an interview with her.

We must now return to Mr. Dawson, whose anxiety to see his wife again, had urged him to complete his commercial travels a good deal sooner than he had expected, and who happened to reach his own home on the very day when the meeting was to take place between his wife and Mr. Cavendish. Never did a man feel happier than Dawson on reaching London, and without waiting to call upon the firm by whom he was employed, he hurried off to his own house under the joyful anticipation of again seeing his beloved wife. But a trifling incident gave him uneasiness ere he had reached his home, for scarcely had he turned into the street when he saw a gentlemanly-looking person quit the house, and put into his pocket a piece of paper, which, to the jealous husband, had a great resemblance to a letter. At any rate, the circumstance was sufficient to occasion him no little uneasiness, and he determined to mark well the features of the person who had raised this strange tumult in his heart, but ere he could do this, the object of his suspicion turned down another street, and ere he could follow, was out of sight. All this, to be sure, might be a foolish surmise on his part, but Mr. Dawson loved his wife, and the very circumstance of a strange man leaving the house gave rise to unpleasant thoughts, that he would gladly have banished from his mind had it been possible to have done so.

At length, with forced composure, he reached his own door, which was opened by the servant who had been left to take care of the house, and who

expressed the utmost astonishment at seeing her master so much before his expected arrival in England.

"Mercy on me, sir!" she exclaimed with surprise; "I'm so glad you've come back, for the place is so dull since mistress and Susan have been away, that—"

"Your mistress is not at home then?" cried Mr. Dawson, with a feeling of astonishment as great as that which had been expressed by his servant.

"At home!" cried Hannah, "lor' bless you no,—mistress aint been very well, and so she's taken a small place a little way out of town for the benefit of the air."

"Where is she?" he demanded in a tone of impatience.

"Oh, not very far," replied Hannah; "she's got a snug little house at Peckham, and Susan has gone to attend on her and keep her company."

"Humph!—and who was the gentleman I just now saw leave the house?"

"The gentleman, sir?"

"Yes,—no equivocation, girl, but tell me at once who and what he is."

"Lor', sir!" cried Hannah, "that's just what has puzzled me to find out. But he's something great, I believe, for I've heard him speaking of his friend Lord *this*, and the Duke of *that*, and so I suppose he must belong to some great family or other."

"His name?" demanded her master impatiently.

"His name, sir?"

"Yes,—he has one I suppose?"

"Oh yes,—they call him Mr. Cavendish."

"Humph!—Cavendish!—and pray what makes him a visitor at my house?"

"I don't know, sir," replied Hannah; "but I suppose he comes to see my mistress."

No. 25

"And does she encourage his visits?" asked Mr. Dawson, trembling with emotion.

"Oh dear no, sir," she replied; "she don't like it at all, and indeed I rather think that was one reason why she left home. Indeed, she has been denied to him over and over again, but at last he has called so often that I believe she has at length agreed to see him."

"Curses light upon him!" muttered the enraged husband between his teeth.

"Dear! dear!" cried Hannah, in alarm; "I declare if I hav'n't said something to make you angry."

"You have done right in telling me of this," he replied with forced calmness; "and so you say you have seen him frequently here since I have been away from home?"

"Y—e—e—s, sir," stammered the servant.

"What was his object in coming here to-day?"

"For a letter from my mistress."

"Doubtless, appointing a meeting!" exclaimed Mr. Dawson, and maddened with the thought he rushed out of the house, with the intention of making immediate enquiries into the circumstance that had filled him with so much uneasiness and dread. Scarcely, however, had he left his own house than he was hailed by Mrs. Carver, an opposite neighbour, who had been watching ever since she had seen him return home, and who seemed to be bursting with the news she had to tell him. Now, though Mrs. Carver had never been a favourite of his, he thought it likely enough she might know something that had been going on during his absence, and, accordingly, crossing the road, he entered the door which had been opened for his admittance. On entering the room he found Mrs. Mortram and Mrs. Robson setting in conclave with their hostess, and he would gladly have escaped could it have been possible to do so without absolute rudeness.

"And so you've returned at last, Mr. Dawson," said the gossip who had called him over; "and a very nice journey you've had I dare say; but there's nothing like home after all, for as the old proverb says, you know, 'when the cat's away, the mice will play,' and, between ourselves—"

"I know not, madam, whether your allusions apply to myself," interrupted Mr. Dawson; "but if they do, I must tell you, once for all, that I have no wish to hear the petty scandal that may be so amusing to a parcel of people who have nothing else to do than to interfere in the business of their neighbours."

"Oh, you needn't suppose we do such things," exclaimed Mrs. Carver, as mildly as she could under the circumstances; "we are merely met together for a little friendly chat, and I was saying just now to Mrs. Mortram, what a pity it is that your wife should go away and leave her home so long as she has done."

"How long has she been absent?" asked Dawson, in spite of the determination not to hear anything they had to say.

"About three months," replied Mrs. Carver.

"Three months and a fortnight would be nearer the mark," said the precise Mrs. Mortram; "indeed, I'm not quite sure whether it is not a day or two more than that, for I remember being here at the time, and it was on the very day when I first put on my lavender-coloured silk dress that you all admired so much, and said it was the sweetest thing you had ever seen in your lives."

"I suppose Mrs. Dawson had her reasons for going," exclaimed Dawson, impatiently; "she was ill, I dare say, and has been recommended, perhaps, to try change of air."

"Can't say, indeed," replied Mrs. Carver; "never heard she was ill, but might be so, you know, for all that."

"Did you ever hear of any other reason, madam?"

"Never."

"Have you any suspicions of your own upon the subject?" enquired Dawson.

"Humph," drawled out the mischief-making Mrs. Carver, "may be you would be jealous if I was to say too much upon the subject."

"Jealous, madam!" stammered the alarmed husband.

"Aye, sir," she replied, "for it hasn't a good look for a wife to have a strange man visiting at the house when her husband happens to be out."

"Has Mrs. Dawson done so?" enquired the other.

"Dear, dear! I declare if I haven't been doing mischief," cried Mrs. Carver, with much apparent concern; "but never mind what I have been saying, sir, for I dare say it was all a mistake of mine, and—"

"I must have no equivocation, madam," exclaimed Dawson; "you have said a strange gentleman visited my house during my absence, and I insist upon knowing the whole truth?"

"Hey day! here's a pretty rumpus I've got myself into," cried Mrs. Carver; "and so, sir, you insist upon my telling you what will make you an unhappy man for life?"

"It matters not, for anything is better than the torture of suspicion," exclaimed Dawson; "I am perhaps rude, madam, upon the present occasion, but some excuse may be made for a husband under such circumstances as these, and therefore I must again demand an explanation of the words you just now uttered."

"Well, if you will have it you must," answered Mrs. Carver, glancing triumphantly at her female guests; "you know, Mr. Dawson, my house commands a very good view of yours, and though I am never given to pry into other people's affairs, I sometimes can't help seeing things that I am very sorry for. For instance, who could have thought when I stood at my own window, no very long time ago, that I should see your wife and Susan getting into a hackney coach that was almost filled with the things they were taking away with them."

"There was nothing very extraordinary in that," observed Mr. Dawson, with as much composure as he could assume; "she was going to her cottage at Peckham, and surely she was at liberty to do that without giving rise to the ill-natured reports of her neighbours."

"But may be the gentleman sees her at Peckham," observed Mrs. Carver, with another look at her female friends.

It was evident that Mr. Dawson thought 'so too, for an ashy paleness spread itself over his countenance, and snatching up his hat, he hurried away without bidding farewell to those who were enjoying his tortures. On regaining the street, however, the fresh air somewhat revived him, and after having paused a few moments to consider what it would be better for him to do next, he hailed a hackney coachman, and jumping into his vehicle, desired to be driven, with all expedition, to Peckham.

Occupied with the harassing thoughts that filled his mind, he was unconscious that the man had taken him through the village he was going to, till the coach suddenly stopped, and the driver enquired to what house he was going.

"To Ivy Cottage," was the reply.

"We passed that some time ago," said the man.

"Then hurry back to it with all the speed you can," exclaimed Mr. Dawson, and the coachman was about to do as he was ordered, when two females passed, one dressed in a white bonnet and black shawl, and the other attired in the more homely garb of a servant. Dawson could almost have sworn that these were his wife and Susan Hoply. So strong indeed was this impression, that he ordered the man to stop, and leaping out of the vehicle, he paid the fare and hurried after the persons who had thus attracted his notice.

But he had not gone far before he began to reflect that he was acting rather a foolish part in the affair, and resolving rather to watch than accost the females, he crossed the road and kept at a sufficient distance to observe them well. This he did for some little time, and then a gentleman came up, as if he was there by appointment, and addressed the superior of the two females, and they walked on arm-in-arm, apparently engaged in very important conversation, for they paid no attention whatever to the girl who still continued to follow them at a respectful distance.

Now all this might appear ridiculous enough, and so thought Mr. Dawson, for after he had been watching them some time, he reflected that it might not be his wife who was upon such familiar terms with the gentleman, and the more he thought about it, the more thoroughly was he convinced that his wife could never act in the manner this lady had done. And so, having argued himself into a complete conviction that he had been hunting a shadow, he hurried back to Ivy Cottage, where he had no doubt he should be convinced of his mistake.

But a fresh source of uneasiness awaited him on his arrival there, for the person who opened the door, informed him that Mrs. Dawson and her servant had gone to take a walk up the hill, but that she believed they would return soon, if the gentleman would please to walk in. Upon this he immediately entered the house, and was conducted into a neat parlour, where he saw many articles belonging to his wife, and, therefore, he was perfectly convinced that he had made no mistake with respect to her place of residence. But he was in no very enviable state of mind during his loneliness there, for he could not help thinking of what Mrs. Carver had said, and though he knew she was a censorious, gossip-loving woman, he felt mortified that his neighbours should have it in their power to make such remarks on the conduct of his wife, and he determined to remonstrate rather sharply with Mrs. Dawson upon her return, and to point out to her the weakness of her conduct in permitting a stranger to visit the house during the absence of her husband. He was, in fact, framing in his own mind the very words in which to express this admonition, when a loud double knock was heard at the street-door, and in another minute Mrs. Dawson entered the room, in the identical white bonnet and black shawl that he had seen under such suspicious circumstances scarcely half an hour before.

This sight so startled Dawson, that he stood rivetted to the spot with surprise, whilst his wife equally astonished at seeing him, and mortified at the evident coldness of his manner, uttered an exclamation of surprise, and sunk into a chair completely overpowered by her emotion. At length he spoke to her with as much composure as he could assume; enquired where she had been to, and whether she had met anybody in her walk, and being convinced by the hesitation of her replies, that the reports to her prejudice were but too well founded, he told her that business of an important nature required his immediate return to town, and promising to visit her in the course of a day or two, took his departure much to the surprise and mortification of his wife, who, naturally enough, imagined that all this unusual coldness was occasioned by his having heard of the affair at the linendrapers.

The husband had not been gone more than two or three hours, when Mrs. Dawson received a letter from Cavendish, informing her that he had seen her prosecutor, and from what had passed between them, he had every reason to hope a satisfactory arrangement would be the consequence. Indeed he felt quite certain that such would be the result, and, therefore, requested another meeting on the following evening, at the same place, in order that he might have the pleasure of congratulating her on the termination of their very disagreeable affair. The request was one which she felt well assured ought to be refused, and yet it was so important that she should know exactly how she was situated with respect to the alleged robbery, that after a careful consideration of the subject, she wrote back an answer, informing Cavendish of her husband's return, and agreeing to meet him at the time and place appointed, on condition that it should positively be their last interview.

That night was a sleepless one to Mrs. Dawson, for though her intentions were dictated by the strictest nature, yet she could not but feel that her conduct would be liable to suspicion, and after pondering over the unfortunate situation in which she was placed, she rose on the following morning pale and agitated. It was in vain that Susan endeavoured to console her with an assurance that matters would turn out better than had been anticipated; and after suffering all the tortures of regret for the situation she was placed in, she set off at the appointed time, accompanied by Susan, whose presence on the occasion might serve in some degree to disarm suspicion.

On reaching the spot, Mr. Cavendish was already waiting for her, and after the first compliments had passed, he described his recent interview with the linendraper, and informed her that all further ground for alarm on his account was at an end, for that the matter had been amicably arranged, and that, therefore, she had nothing more to dread from an exposure which would for ever have alienated the affections of her husband. He, however, did not inform her that this change had been brought about by the offer of a large sum of money, and as Mrs. Dawson really thought that all this had been effected by the personal exertions of Mr. Cavendish, she could do no less than express her gratitude for the inestimable favour he had done her.

Upon this Mrs. Dawson would have returned home, but ere she could leave the place, her husband rushed from his concealment, and struck Cavendish a blow in the face that knocked him upon the earth, whilst the wife, terrified at the dreadful suspicion that the meeting would give rise to, sank fainting into the arms of Susan.

In an instant Mr. Cavendish started upon his feet, and heaping the bitterest invectives on his assailant for the cowardly attack he had made, demanded satisfaction for the blow he had received, and having presented his card to Dawson, he desired him to write where he would meet him at an early hour on the following morning, and then strode off in a rage that he found it impossible to control.

Nor was Dawson's fury less violent than his antagonist, and no sooner was he out of sight, than casting a withering glance of scorn towards his still unconscious wife, he hastily took his departure in a state of mind bordering on distraction.

Poor Susan, with all the efforts she used, was unable to restore her unfortunate mistress. At length, however, a labouring man who happened to be passing by the spot, offered her assistance, and with the aid of her faithful servant, Mrs. Dawson was conveyed to her home.

CHAPTER XXVII.

AN AFFAIR OF HONOUR.

IN about an hour after Mrs. Dawson had been taken back to Ivy Cottage, she began to revive, and as she did so, the horrible recollection of the late scene rushed upon her mind with overwhelming force. A flood of bitter tears followed, and somewhat relieved, she exclaimed :—

"Tell me the worst, Susan :—where is my husband?—Is he in this house, or has he indeed left me for ever?"

"He is not here, ma'am," she replied, "but pray don't take on in this way, for he'll grow more cool by and by, and when his passion is over, he will listen to reason."

"It is in vain to tell me so," cried the distracted wife, "for he believes me unfaithful to him, and will cast me off as one that is no longer worthy his regard. But tell me all what passed between them, for I became insensible when my husband's form appeared before us, and I know nothing of what occurred, though I have but too much reason to fear that the blow received by Mr. Cavendish will not pass unresented."

"I am afraid so, too, ma'am," replied Susan, who judged that it would be wrong to disguise anything under present circumstances."

"Were there any angry words between them?"

"Not many," answered Susan, "but Mr. Cavendish gave his card to Mr. Dawson, and I think from that it is likely there will be a duel between them."

"There will!—there will!" cried Mrs. Dawson, wildly springing from her couch ;—"there will be bloodshed between them, and upon me will rest the crime that rises out of this night's madness. But tell me, girl, did you hear when they were to meet?"

"To-morrow morning, I believe."

"And where?"

"That was not said," replied Susan, "for the gentleman only gave his card and desired master to write and inform him where they were to meet."

"Do you know where Mr. Cavendish lives?"

"I do not, ma'am," answered Susan, "for the letters you have written to him were sent to your own house, and he has called for them there, because, I suppose, he did not wish you to know where he was to be found. But surely, ma'am, you would not see him again after what has just passed?"

"I would," cried Mrs. Dawson, "but only that I might entreat him on my knees not to raise his arm against the life of my husband. I have been weak and foolish, Susan, in having permitted his visits at my house, and it is only proper that I should thus humble myself to him, when he, who I love, is in peril from his vengeance. So run, Susan,—procure a conveyance to town, for there is not a moment to be lost now that my husband's life is in danger."

This order was promptly obeyed; a carriage was procured from a neighbouring inn, and within a hour afterwards, they reached their house in town, the door of which was opened by Mary, the other servant, who in reply to Mrs. Dawson's enquiry, informed her that her husband was not at home.

"When did you see him?" asked her mistress, in sorrow.

"Not since yesterday," replied Mary ;—"he called here as soon as he come to London from abroad, and I thought he had gone down to Peckham to see you."

"Did he not return here last night ?"

"No, ma'am."

"Alas !" cried Mrs. Dawson, "it is but too evident that he must have heard some slanders against me."

"That's very likely ma'am," replied Mary, "for I saw him go over to Mrs. Carver's when he went away from this door, and there's no knowing what an ill-natured woman like that may think proper to say about her neighbours."

"But surely," exclaimed her mistress, "he would not believe the words of a woman who is notorious for talking scandal about her neighbours ?"

"I dare say he might not think much of her gossipping reports, ma'am," answered Mary; "but he happened to see Mr. Cavendish just as he was leaving the house, and you have no notion how angry he seemed at finding that a stranger had been visiting you during his absence."

"Ah! then I am lost !" cried Mrs. Dawson, in accents of despair; and sending Susan out for a coach, she almost immediately afterwards drove off in the direction of the mercantile house belonging to her husband's employers. Here she saw one of the partners, of whom she inquired, in frenzied accents whether Mr. Dawson was there.

"He is not, madam," replied the person she had addressed, and who knew her perfectly well; "indeed, we are rather surprised at not having seen him, as we are aware he has returned to England, and, of course, we are anxious to meet him, in order that he may acquaint us with the result of his journey abroad. But *you*, of course, have seen him, Mrs. Dawson, for he is a man devoted both to yourself and his home, and would naturally hasten to meet you immediately on his coming to London."

"I have seen him, sir," stammered Mrs. Dawson, "but he left me again almost directly, and fearing some accident has befallen him, I—I—"

"Nay, madam, there is no cause for any alarm of that sort," interrupted the other; "Mr. Dawson is a very punctual man, and, I dare say, some business or other has required his absence for a short time."

Poor Mrs. Dawson was obliged to acknowledge that it might be so, and thanking the gentleman for his politeness, she once more entered the coach, and desired to be driven to Montague-street, in the neighbourhood of which place she had heard Mr. Cavendish say he resided. This effort was, however, quite as unsuccessful as the other, and after making a great many useless inquiries, she was about to return home in despair, when Susan suggested that it was likely enough he might live in some hotel thereabouts. This hint was quite enough for her mistress, and forthwith they began to drive about from one hotel to another, but the answer at every one of them was the same, till, at length, they heard from a surly porter in the hall, that a person of that name had apartments in the house.

"Is he in ?" asked Mrs. Dawson, eagerly.

"He is not," replied the man, "and even if he was, I don't think you'd have much chance of seeing him at such an hour of the night as this."

"He would see me, even though it were later," replied Mrs. Dawson; "he is a friend of mine, and will favour me with a few moments interview if you will only say my name is Dawson."

"Dawson ! and is there any magic in that name, ma'am, that he should see you, however particularly he might be engaged at the time ?"

"If he is at home," she replied, "I am convinced he will see me without an instant's delay."

"But he aint at home I tell you."

"What time do you expect him in ?" asked Mrs. Dawson.

"Can't say," replied the porter; "sometimes he don't come here for a week together, and we never expect him till we see him."

"Did he say whether he would return to-night?"

"I didn't ask him," answered the other, gruffly; "and, in my opinion, you, ma'am, would be acting more like a modest woman if you wasn't to run after the gentleman in this sort of fashion."

"I know—I know appearances are against me," she cried, despondingly, "but the lives of two persons depend upon my finding him, and I will not give up my search till I have either met Mr. Cavandish, or I see that all hope of meeting with him is at an end."

"Phew!" whistled the porter, "why you don't mean to say the gentleman is engaged in a duel?"

"He is,—he is!" she cried, wildly, "and it is to save his life, as well as that of his antagonist, that I have thus ventured to follow him to this place."

"But he aint at home, ma'am," replied the other, "and, of course, you can't see him."

"Do you know where to find him?"

"Not I," replied the man; "he's here, there, and everywhere; but, if he should happen to come in, I'll tell him you have called, if you like."

"That would be useless," exclaimed Mrs. Dawson, and thanking him for the little information he had afforded her, she quitted the place, and once more returned to the coach.

"Where would you like to go now, marm?" asked the driver, who began to think he had got a very strange sort of fare.

"Back to the house where you first took me up," replied Mrs. Dawson, and then fixing an earnest gaze upon a figure that was passing, she sprang from the coach, and darted after the retreating form that had just caught her view. In another instant Susan also jumped from the coach to follow her mistress, but the driver, suspecting that she intended to cheat him out of his money, seized her by the arm, and expressed his determination of giving her in charge unless she instantly paid his demand. She had not, however, money enough to do this, and giving him the few shillings she possessed, she desired him to call at her master's house in the morning, when the remainder, with a handsome present for himself, should be given him. This satisfied him, and pocketing the money he had received, he suffered Susan to go, and in an instant afterwards she was pursuing her mistress with all the speed she could.

In her way she ran against a man whose savage expressions of anger were uttered in a well remembered voice, and looking in his face, she at once recognized the dark, scowling features of the ruffian she had seen in the grounds of Mr. Wentford on the night of his murder. Horrified at the sight, she looked round to see if there was any person near to whom she could give him into custody, but the fellow, as if anticipating her design, darted off, and was out of sight in a minute. As all further pursuit after either the ruffian or her mistress was now in vain, she returned home in hopes that by this time Mrs. Dawson might be there; but on reaching the house, she found, to her alarm, that nothing had been seen of her since they both went out together in the coach.

Throughout the whole of that night, Susan and her fellow-servant sat up watching for the return of their mistress; but their care was all in vain; for the dawn came, and nothing was yet heard of either Mr. or Mrs. Dawson. The terror of the two girls now became greater than ever, and having waited till eight o'clock to see if either of them returned, Susan began to prepare herself for going out again, when a messenger arrived with news that Mrs. Dawson had been found wandering about Peckham in

a state of madness, and that she had been taken to her own house there, where a keeper had been sent to watch over the unfortunate woman, lest she should attempt to lay violent hands upon herself.

This news was enough for Susan, who immediately started off for Peckham, where she found her mistress suffering under the dreadful malady alluded to by the man, and having procured immediate medical advice, she had the satisfaction of hearing that, with strict attention and quiet, there was every reason to hope Mrs. Dawson would recover the use of her senses in the course of a short time.

But it is now necessary that we should return to Mr. Dawson, who, by this time, was in safe custody in Newgate, on a charge of having murdered Mr. Cavandish. It appeared that a conviction had seized the mind of the unfortunate man that his wife had formed a guilty attachment for Cavendish, and being goaded to madness at the imaginary dishonour he had sustained, he immediately wrote to his antagonist, demanding immediate satisfaction for the injury he had sustained, and appointing to meet him at seven o'clock at a place which he named, in the vicinity of London. This challenge, which had been anticipated, was accepted by Cavendish, and at the hour named, he went to the place, accompanied by his second. Here he found Dawson, who refused to hear any explanation that was offered, and, in reply to the remonstrances of the friend of Mr. Cavendish, he said that he had received an irreparable injury, and that he had come there with a determination either to lose his own life, or take that of his antagonist.

After this declaration, all further argument would have been vain ; the ground was therefore measured out, and the two combatants took their places, though not before Cavandish had again offered such an explanation of his conduct towards Mrs. Dawson as would have cleared her character from the imputations that had been cast upon it. But her husband refused

No. 26

to hear anything he had to say, and the word being given, they both fired without effect.

Again the seconds interfered to prevent any further proceedings in this affair, declaring that sufficient had already been done to satisfy both parties, and recommending Dawson to seek any further remedy he might desire in a court of justice, where his antagonist would have an opportunity of explaining his conduct, which, at present, it was admitted, appeared rather doubtful.

This proposition was, however, rejected, and fresh pistols having been handed to them, they again fired; but this time the effect was more fatal, for Cavandish received the ball of his antagonist in his heart, and in a few words, exonerating the other from all blame in the transaction, he expired in the arms of his second. Upon this melancholy termination of the affair, those present would have urged Dawson to fly, but he doggedly refused all intercession in his behalf, and, in a few minutes afterwards, he was arrested by a couple of officers, who arrived on the spot, and was immediately conveyed back to London, and carried before a magistrate on a charge of murder.

The evidence brought against him was so clear and conclusive, that there was no occasion for a remand, and within an hour afterwards he was conveyed as a prisoner to Newgate.

CHAPTER XXVIII.

THE PRISON.

FOR nearly a month after this melancholy event, Mrs. Dawson continued under the influence of madness, during which time she was constantly attended by Susan, who, with untiring zeal continued to watch over her mistress. At length, however, the disorder took a turn, so that she had occasional lucid intervals, but at these moments, the recollection of what had passed, recurred to her mind, and again she sank into the same state as before.

At length, however, a marked improvement began to manifest itself, and she began to inquire about her husband, and whether he had been to see her during her illness; but Susan evaded these questions as well as she could, till, being pressed for a reply, she acknowledged that Mr. Dawson had not been to the house, and then begged that no further questions might be asked at present, as the doctor had ordered her not to explain past occurrences till he gave her permission.

Thus several days passed away, till, at length, Mrs. Dawson began to get so much better, that Susan was allowed to speak to her upon the subject she had so much at heart, though, even then, it was on condition that no explanation should take place respecting the present situation of Mr. Dawson. This the young woman promised, and when next her mistress inquired after her husband, she replied that she believed he was very well, and that pressing business had compelled him to omit calling upon her.

"Do you know when I am likely to see him?" asked Mrs. Dawson.

"I do not, ma'am," replied Susan, "and, indeed, you are forbidden by the doctor to see him for some time to come."

"Is he in London, Susan?" asked her mistress.

"He is," she replied, "and I have been thinking that, as I dare say he feels uneasy about you, perhaps, if I could be spared for a few hours, it might be as well to let me go and tell him that you are getting better."

"Do you know where to find him?"

"Not exactly," replied Susan, with hesitation; "but I dare say I should soon be able to find out where he's living, and it will be some consolation to let him know that you are recovering from your illness."

"I'm afraid he's still so angry with me that he would not listen to you," sighed the hapless wife. "He believes me guilty of encouraging the visits of Mr. Cavendish, and, in that case, how can I ever hope for his forgiveness? I was wrong, Susan, very wrong, ever to have permitted him to see me, but the error has been repented, though, perhaps, alas! too late for my own happiness. Mr. Dawson still resents my conduct;—his coolness proves that he does, and loathing me as one that has dishonoured him, he has kept away, though he knew how ill I have been."

"Well, well, we won't blame him for what's gone by, till we see what the future promises," replied Susan; "and so, ma'am, if you will please to let me go and see master, I'll try whether he cannot be convinced that you are not the guilty being he takes you for."

"You are a kind, faithful girl, Susan," cried Mrs. Dawson, affected by the earnestness she had displayed; "and have my permission to go whenever you please. See him, and, if you can, convince him that I deserve not the cruel coldness with which he has treated me ever since his return to England. It is a painful alternative, Susan, yet, since it must be done, tell him of the charge that was brought against me by the linendraper, and perhaps, when he hears that Mr. Cavendish generously came forward to release me from that foul charge, he will learn to regard him rather as a friend than as an enemy."

It was then too late to go up to town that evening, but on the following morning Susan took the stage, and having reached the end of her journey, proceeded to Newgate, where she saw one of the turnkeys, to whom she related the errand that had brought her. The man seemed to hesitate how to act, but after a few moments, he said:—

"The prisoner you speak of, young woman, has taken it into his head to be rather sullen, and though several people have been here to see him, he won't let any of 'em enter his cell, and I dare say he would refuse to see you as he has done all the rest."

"Would he refuse it, think you," asked Susan, "if you told him I came from his wife?"

"I dare say he would," replied the turnkey; "but if you like, I'll go and try him."

"Is there no way that I could see him," inquired Susan, "without his being aware of my coming?"

"Oh, yes," replied the man, "you can follow me direct to his cell if you like; but he'll be in a rage about it, I dare say, and if so, you must take the consequences upon yourself."

"That I am quite willing to do," she cried; "only take me to him, and, angry as he may be, I dare say I shall tell him that which will soon soften his wrath."

The turnkey eyed her for a second or two, as if doubtful whether to accede or not, but at length, turning upon his heel, he desired her to follow him, and then led her through numerous passages, till he reached the cell he was going to, and in another minute Susan found herself alone with the man who she so much wished and yet dreaded to see.

Dawson was reading at the moment of her entrance, but when he raised his eyes from the book he was perusing, he started up from his seat, and furiously demanded whether she had come to triumph in his downfall.

"Indeed, sir," said Susan, meekly, "I came here with no such intention;—my mistress——"

"Mourns the death of her paramour," interrupted Dawson, furiously, "and has sent you here to heap curses and reproaches upon the man who has slain him."

"You wrong my poor mistress, sir," answered Susan, "for she knows not of Mr. Cavendish's death, nor—"

"Of my imprisonment?"

"She does not."

"How, then, came she to send you to me *here*?"

"It was at my own request that I came on this errand," replied Susan; "but she believes that you are still at home, and that I should see you there."

"Humph! and you say she knows nothing of my having slain her worthless lover?"

"She does not."

"She has been ill, then?"

"Mad, sir."

"Hah! and so have I," cried Dawson, through his teeth; "I, too, have been mad; but there is yet one consolation in knowing that I have killed the villain who who so recklessly brought my dishonour."

"You wrong both my mistress and Mr. Cavendish by your suspicions," cried Susan, earnestly. "She is innocent, and you have been fatally deceived by appearances."

"Indeed!" cried Dawson, incredulously; "then, perhaps, you will have the goodness to convince me that I have erred in believing that she has proved unfaithful to her marriage vows, and that Cavendish was the villain I take him to be."

"With your permission, I will endeavour to do so."

"Proceed," exclaimed Dawson, "for it requires only proof of my wife's innocence to make me even more loathsome to myself than I am at present. Go on, girl, and let me know how her acquaintance with this man commenced."

Susan then related in her own artless manner, the whole affair between the linendraper and her mistress; her being dragged before a magistrate on a charge of theft, and having described the sort of evidence that had been produced, concluded by mentioning the conduct of Mr. Cavendish in coming forward to be her bail. To all this Dawson listened with much attention, and after a few moments' consideration, enquired how it was that the gentleman happened to be in the office at the moment when his services were so much required.

"That question," she replied, "I am unable to answer."

"I thought so," exclaimed Dawson; "and I dare say you are also unable to say whether he met her there by chance, or whether they had been acquainted previously?"

"I am sure they were not," replied Susan.

"How came he in the police-office then?"

"I know nothing about that," answered the girl; "except that it afterwards appeared he was acquainted with one of the magistrates, and I suppose he was there on that day to see him. Besides, my mistress did not know his name for some days afterwards, and then she heard it by a mere accident."

"But he visited her, I believe?"

"He did," replied Susan, "but it was much against the wish of my mistress, though she knew not how to forbid him the house."

"And it never occurred to her then, that she had friends who, if consulted upon the subject, would have found means to let him know that his presence in my house could be dispensed with in future?"

"Aye, there was the fatal mistake," replied Susan; "but my mistress, probably, thought he would soon discontinue his visits, and it was also certain that it was necessary to make him a friend till it should be proved who was the thief that robbed Mr. Edwards."

"And has it never been found out?" asked Dawson.

"Never, sir; but I have my own suspicions about it, though I have not liked to mention them for fear of bringing another innocent person into trouble. Besides, it's never been proved that the missing goods ever actually came out of the linendraper's house."

"Surely you don't suspect your fellow-servant?"

"No more than I would myself," replied Susan, "for she never went into the parlour while the things were there."

"And what think you of your mistress's conduct in permitting a stranger to visit her home?" asked Dawson. "Was she foolish enough, think you, to imagine that all was done out of pure friendship, and that he did not entertain an idea of undermining her honour?"

"I am quite certain," replied Susan, "that his visits occasioned her a very great deal of uneasiness; in fact, she often mentioned her alarm to me, and at length she went to live at Peckham, for no other purpose than to avoid him and to get rid of his company for the future."

"Then a falsehood has been told," exclaimed Dawson, "for the only time I have seen her since my return, she said she went out of town for the benefit of her health."

"Aye, sir," answered Susan, "but she was flurried at your unexpected return, and knowing how much suspicion was attached to the affair, she hesitated to tell you the real fact till a better opportunity offered itself for an explanation. And, indeed, she was very ill for some time after we went to live at Peckham, and no wonder at it, considering how much she gave way to her grief for that disagreeable affair with Mr. Edwards."

"Did any medical gentleman attend her during the illness you speak of?"

"Yes, sir," replied Susan, "the same gentleman who is attending her at this very time."

"She is ill, then?" exclaimed Dawson.

"I told you so just now, sir," answered the girl, "and, indeed, I may say, with truth, she has been almost dead."

"Am I to believe you, girl?"

"You may, sir, for I have spoken nothing but the truth; and I am sure you believe me, for your manner is so different to what it was when I first came in."

"And even if you have spoken truly," replied Dawson; "it goes but a very little way towards exculpating your mistress for the conduct she has pursued. I, myself, saw her with Mr. Cavendish, who she had met by assignation, and none but a guilty motive could have induced her to forget herself so far, as to encourage a libertine, whom it was her duty to have shunned as she would the appearance of a fearful pestilence."

"There's no denying that, sir," answered Susan, "but so far you have blamed my mistress without knowing how powerful a motive she might have had for doing as she did. The truth is, however, she was driven to desperation by the terror of exposure about that business of Edwards's, and as Mr. Cavendish had promised to get her over it, there is nothing very singular in her having met him, to know how he had succeeded in his attempts to arrange the affair without its coming to a trial."

"And thus," observed Dawson, "she was willing to put herself under an obligation to a man who was ready to take every villanous advantage of her weakness."

"But I dare say she didn't think of that in the terrible situation she was placed in," cried Susan; "at least I'm sure I should not, and it is not everybody that have got their wits about them when they are in danger of exposure and disgrace."

"And what, pray," asked Dawson, "was the cause of your coming here to see me ?—Was it to add to my bitterness of soul, by confessing that you have no reasonable answer to make to the suspicions I entertained of my dishonour ?"

"I came," replied Susan, "to explain this business in the best way I could, and, if possible, to convince you of your wife's innocence."

"And neither of which you have done," exclaimed Dawson; "you have not yet proved that Cavendish was guiltless in thoughts and actions, nor am I convinced that I have taken away his life without just and weighty cause."

"Why, to say the least of it, sir," cried Susan, "you have only acted in this matter upon suspicion. You have had no proof whatever that my mistress was unfaithful, and yet she has been treated with a degree of harshness that could only have been deserved by the most guilty and abandoned."

"Did I not see with what a welcome she received him," answered her master; "and when I first of all met her at Ivy Cottage after my return from abroad, did she not seem to be confused as if my presence were as unwelcome as it was unlooked for ?"

"And that's not much to be wondered at," replied Susan; "since she knew well enough that there was a secret which, if it should be known to you, would forfeit your esteem and regard for ever. That alone was quite enough to terrify her. Besides, you looked as I never saw you look before, and then she thought you had heard all about that affair of Edwards losing some of his goods, and of course the idea of it was quite enough to make her flurried and perplexed."

"Susan!" exclaimed Dawson, after an interval that had been given to the most painful emotion; "your words have given rise to thoughts that have not visited me before. It is possible my wife is not the guilty, abandoned creature I have believed her, and in that case I have murdered the man who would have shielded her from injury during my absence."

"You have, indeed, carried punishment where it is not due," answered Susan; "my mistress, I again say, is innocent, and hard as it may be to bear, I must accuse you of having most foully wronged an affectionate and loving wife."

"Where—where have you left her ?" exclaimed Dawson, in an agony of of remorse.

"At Ivy Cottage," replied Susan, "where she had been suffering under a most dreadful malady ever since the day when you met and killed Mr. Cavendish."

She then, at the request of her master, narrated all that had occurred from the fatal morning when he had slain his antagonist; described the dreadful anxiety of Mrs. Dawson to discover them, and prevent the meeting which she but too surely predicted would take place; she described their driving through the streets of London, till at length she imagined that she saw her husband, and the wildness with which she had rushed in pursuit of the imaginary phantom that had thus cheated her. She then proceeded to relate the fact of her having wandered about all night, and being found in the morning in a state of madness—the terrible malady that ensued was then mentioned, and every expression of tenderness and uneasiness for her husband was related in detail, till Dawson writhed and groaned under the infliction which was thus heaped upon him. At length, unable to endure any more, he abruptly started from his seat, and in a voice trembling with emotion, said :—

" Away girl, and torture me no more with words that consume my soul, and drive me on to madness. Return to her who sent you to me—to my wife, whose innocence you have almost convinced me of, and say, that I sincerely repent the violence of temper that has reduced her to the verge of despair, and will bring me to an ignominious death. Ask her to forgive me the wrongs I have inflicted, and, as my last request, say, that I beseech her to give no further thought to one who has proved himself to be totally unworthy of her regard."

" Will you not see her, sir ?" asked Susan, moved to tears by the pathos with which these words were spoken.

" Not at present," he replied ; " I have now to devote all my time in endeavouring to procure pardon for the heavy sins I have committed. When I have had time for reflection, I will see her, and in the meantime, you must comfort her as you best can ; and say, that grievous as my crime has been, it was occasioned by my love for her, and the fear that my honour had been destroyed by a man who, under suspicious circumstances, I imagined to be a villain !"

As he said this, he sank exhausted upon his seat, and at the same moment, the turnkey entered the cell, and led her from it towards the entrance hall of the prison, from whence she immediately afterwards stepped into the street, crowded as it was with thousands of persons, who little thought of the misery and woe that are endured by some among their less fortunate fellow creatures.

CHAPTER XXIX.

THE WIFE'S MISSION.

It was impossible to conceal the truth much longer from Mrs. Dawson, and at length in reply to her oft repeated questions, Susan, with as much gentleness and caution as possible, related the duel which had taken place between her husband and Mr. Cavendish, and the fatal termination to which it had been brought. She also related the situation in which Mr. Dawson was placed, and the fears that were entertained of his being found guilty of murder.

To the unhappy wife all this had come like a thunderbolt, for she little suspected the fatal truth, and thinking that her husband merely stayed away from the house, because he had not yet forgiven the apparent levity of her own conduct, she endeavoured to console herself with the idea that by and by he would be convinced of her innocence, and then happiness and peace would once more be restored to them. But now, when she heard that he was lying in a felon's cell, under the fearful accusation of murder, her spirits sank, and for some time Susan was alarmed, lest a relapse of her late dreadful malady should take place. But the urgency of her present situation roused Mrs. Dawson to greater exertions than she had used before, and resolving to make every effort to save the life of her husband, she began to consider in her own mind how she might best accomplish the one great and sole object of her thoughts.

It was, however, determined to make the effort whatever difficulties might be in the way, for though innocent of all intention to commit wrong, she could not help feeling that there had been some imprudence on her own

part in not having at first discouraged the visits of Mr. Cavendish, and
the thought seemed to nerve her for the task she had then taken upon
herself.

Her first care was to procure the best legal assistance she could, to guide
and advise her in the course she was to adopt, and in this instance it so
happened that she proved particular fortunately, for the gentleman she engaged to conduct her husband's case was both industrious and humane, and
after a careful consideration of the whole affair, he admitted that the charge
brought against Dawson was a most serious one as affecting his life,
but at the same time, he expressed some little hope that by cautious management, the accused party might yet avoid the terrible fate that threatened him.

His first object was to visit the house of Mr. Eversfield, the brother-in-law
of the person who had unfortunately lost his life in the duel, and endeavour
by every argument in his power, to prevail on him not to prosecute the person who was now awaiting his trial on the charge of murder. But Mr.
Eversfield, though really a humane man, conceived that he had a solemn
duty to perform in bringing the full vengeance of the laws against the culprit, and though he listened with the kindest attention to all the arguments of the lawyer, he was still determined to follow the affair to the very
fullest extent.

It was in vain too, that the other represented how heavily the affliction
would fall upon the innocent wife of the prisoner, and the hardship of
making her suffer for the crime which had been committed by Dawson
under very aggravating circumstances ; for he failed not to represent in
vivid colours what must have been the feelings of the husband on his return after a long absence, to find, as he imagined, the affections of her he
loved, transferred to another who had insinuated himself into her favour by
the most artful means. Mr. Eversfield was willing to admit that there was
great provocation, but the person whose life had been sacrificed, was the
brother of his wife, and as the nearest relative, he felt that he was in duty
bound to see the fullest justice brought upon the malefactor. In fact, after
using every argument he could think of, Mrs. Dawson's friend was obliged
to take his leave with permission to call again in a couple of days, when
Mr. Eversfield would have considered the subject of his application with
more attention.

But when he went according to his appointment, he found the prosecutor still entertaining the same opinion that he did on his previous visit.
Mr. Eversfield regretted the severe suffering, which must be endured by the
wife of the unfortunate man, and declared that he had no vindictive feel-
ngs against the culprit himself; but his relative had fallen by the hands of
his antagonist, and the world, he said, would not be very gentle in their remarks upon his conduct, were he to omit a prosecution in such an instance
as this. The lawyer pleaded hard for his hapless client, but all his entreaties were in vain, and at length he was obliged to leave the house with the
melancholy consciousness that every hope of avoiding the prosecution
against the prisoner was at an end.

It was with an aching heart that he returned to Mrs. Dawson to inform
her of the unfortunate result of his application. She had, however, nerved
herself to hear the worst, and though, certainly much affected at the dreary
prospect before her, she was still resolved to persevere in her efforts to procure the release of her husband. Again she consulted with her legal adviser as to the best means that could now be adopted, and the result was,
that she determined to go herself to Mr. Eversfield, and by her own earnest entreaties endeavour to move his heart to pity towards him whose
life depended upon the exertions she might make. She had heard from the

lawyer that he was a humane and conscientious man, and though she dreaded the task she had then voluntarily imposed upon herself, yet no other alternative remained, and she, therefore, resolved to hazard all in behalf of her husband.

Early on the following morning, she left her own cheerless home, and proceeded with trembling footsteps to the house of the person she was so anxious to see. Fortunately Mr. Eversfield was at home, and on being shown into the room, she found him and his wife sitting at breakfast. He rose as she entered, but as Mrs. Dawson announced her name, she observed a marked ominous change in his countenance, which argued fearfully against the cause she came to advocate. He, however, quickly resumed his usual placidity, and desiring her to be seated, said :—

" I presume, madam, your business is already known to me,—you come, in fact, to plead for your husband, who is now in gaol on a charge of murder !''

Mrs. Dawson was too much agitated to reply, and as she bowed her head in token of an affirmative, he continued :—

" I am sorry, madam, that my duty imperatively demands the course I am now pursuing towards your husband ; but you are aware that a relative of mine has fallen by his hands, and, much as I pity your unfortunate situation, I cannot forget the duty I owe both to the public and to him who perished by so untimely a fate.''

" The public, sir, would applaud, rather than condemn you for an act of mercy like this," replied Mrs. Dawson, " and as for Mr. Cavendish, I see no good that can possibly arise from punishing with death the man who, in a fit of madness, sent him to an untimely grave.''

" Madness, such as Dawson's, offers no plea for the crime he has committed," answered Mr. Eversfield ; " indeed, from all I have heard, jealousy was the cause of the quarrel between your husband and my re-

No. 27

lative, and as that was probably groundless, it rather serves to aggravate than to soften the crime that has been committed."

"There certainly was jealousy on the part of my husband," cried Mrs. Dawson, with agitation that she could not suppress, "but I hope you, sir, and this lady, will acquit me of having given any occasion for it."

"I do," he replied, "for Mr. Cavendish informed me of the whole affair only the evening before his death, and on speaking of you, he declared your virtue was beyond impeachment, and described your conduct in such terms of respectful admiration, that I cannot harbour a thought to your disadvantage."

"But, for all that," answered Mrs. Dawson, "there were apparent grounds for the jealousy my husband felt. Mr. Cavendish had proved a friend to me in an hour of shame and distress such as seldom occurs to the innocent. In fact, he saved me from the disgrace of a public proceeding, and from that time became a frequent visitor at my house during the absence of my husband on business abroad. It is true, I ought to have pointed out to him the impropriety of his coming to see me under such circumstances, but I was weak enough to shrink from that duty, and the consequences have led to the misery and ruin which have thus fallen upon two families."

"Perhaps pity, madam," exclaimed Mr. Eversfield, "would be an insult to one situated as you are, and yet I cannot but express how much I feel for the misfortunes under which you at present labour."

"In that case, sir," cried Mrs. Dawson, "you will render me the only service it is in your power to bestow, by engaging to guarantee my husband."

"Nay, you ask that which is impossible," continued Mr. Eversfield; "for I have already appeared against him as a witness before the police magistrates, and there is now no way left but to carry the case before the highest earthly tribunal."

"Then am I indeed lost!" cried Mrs. Dawson, bursting into an agony of tears.

"Is there no way, Edward," interposed Mrs. Eversfield, "by which you may spare the sufferings of this most unfortunate female? I plead for her as one of my own sex, and though it was my brother that fell by her husband's hand, I cannot endure the thought of letting the innocent suffer as well as the guilty. Besides, all vindictive feelings should now cease, since the utmost vengeance of the laws cannot restore to life him who has unfortunately fallen in this disastrous transaction."

"I have no vindictive feelings to serve, my dear," answered Mr. Eversfield, "for it is nothing but a sense of justice that prompts me to seek vengeance against the shedder of your brother's blood. The laws have declared that the murderer shall die, and surely in that case I should not be further urged to spare a man who has committed the greatest crime that is known."

"True," replied the wife, "but this is what the world calls an affair of honour, and I need not tell you how many have not only escaped punishment, but have been regarded afterwards with the greatest esteem, even though their adversaries may have met the same fate as that which befel my poor brother."

"It is strange," said Mr. Eversfield, "that you who have most cause to complain of the fatal result of this duel, should be among the first to urge me into pity for a man who has deprived you of a beloved relative."

"You are wrong there, Edward," cried Mrs. Eversfield, "for it is not so much pity for the man who slew my brother as compassion for his unfortunate wife that impels me to plead thus hard in his cause. That you have no vindictive feelings I am well aware, and, therefore, do I again solemnly implore you to reflect well ere you send an affectionate wife to mourn the hardness of heart that deprives her of the object of her warmest love."

"I must be urged no further upon this subject at present," exclaimed Mr. Eversfield, with evident emotion. "It is, in fact, a matter that requires much consideration, and since I know your feelings upon it, I will promise to give the subject a careful and attentive consideration."

"And what need is there for consideration when the life and happiness of two persons depend upon your choosing the most merciful course? The blood of this victim will not restore my brother to us, and, therefore, do I entreat you to make Mrs. Dawson happy by an assurance that you will proceed no further against her husband."

"I tell you, my love, I must have time for reflection," said Mr. Eversfield, impatiently; "I am not yet convinced that the culprit deserves the lenity you would have me show him, and till I have made enquiries respecting his former conduct, I must insist upon following the course you so much deprecate."

"Then," cried Mrs. Dawson, "you will consign a fellow-creature to death, rather than exercise the power you have of suffering him to live, that he may repent an act that was committed in the height of frenzy."

"I seek nothing more than justice," replied Mr. Eversfield, "and as a proof that I have no ill-feeling against the prisoner, you may call upon me to-morrow morning, and I will then tell you the result of my deliberation."

"And why not decide upon it at once, Edward?" exclaimed Mrs. Eversfield, earnestly; "remember the agony of suspense you will cause this poor lady, and if you are really determined to send her husband to the gallows, say so at once, that she may know the worst she has to expect."

"But my dear—"

"Nay," interrupted his wife, "let us have no further delay, but if the prisoner must perish say so now, and let us learn how little mercy lodges in that heart which I once thought harboured nothing but goodness. Oh, stay, Edward, I have another proposition to make! you remember that to-morrow will be our wedding-day, and you promised me a diamond ring in token of the happiness we have enjoyed for seven years in each other's society; I have no occasion for the ring since I am well satisfied with the affection you have regarded me with, and in lieu of that present, I ask you to make me happy by restoring to Mrs. Dawson the husband for whom she has this day come to plead."

"Well, well, my love, I can hold out no longer," exclaimed Mr. Eversfield, "and so, for this time, I suppose you must have your own way. And now, Mrs. Dawson," he added, addressing himself to the person he had named, "you understand to whom it is that you are indebted for your husband's life, and at the same time I must candidly admit that, had I been left to my own judgment in this affair, I should most certainly have suffered this case to take its own course."

"Then I must caution Mrs. Dawson to beware how she gives too much credit to your assertions," cried his wife; "for I know your heart, Edward, and am well assured that it would have prompted you to this act of mercy even if I had not been present to urge my request. However, I see Mrs. Dawson is about to pour forth her gratitude, and therefore I will leave the room, for I would rather avoid hearing those expressions of thankfulness, which are scarcely needed since, after all you have only done that which, in mercy and kindness to a fellow-creature, you were bound to do."

"In that case, madam," replied Mrs. Dawon, "I will reserve what I have to say till another opportunity, and will merely express the deep sense of obligation that I feel towards both yourself and Mr. Eversfield, for the kindness you have this day done me."

"I want no thanks," replied Mr. Eversfield, "for I can well understand the feelings you experience at having thus rescued your husband from an ignominious doom. To your affection and perseverance he owes his life, and I most sincerely trust he will henceforth acknowledge how little cause he had for the jealousy that urged him to the deed for which he had so nearly suffered. He has now had time for serious reflection, and perhaps the escape he has had may prove a lesson for his conduct in future."

"Are you going to see him in prison?" asked Mrs. Eversfield.

"Not at present," replied Mrs. Dawson; "indeed, he has expressed a wish that I would not go to him till he is better able to endure a meeting which must occasion so much pain and affliction on both sides."

"It is better that it should be so," observed Mr. Eversfield; "for under all circumstances, it would be advisable not to let him know of his safety just at present."

"Ah, sir," cried the now happy wife, "but think of the torture of suspense he must now endure."

"Nay," he replied, "his torture is, perhaps, not so great as you may imagine. His mind, I dare say, is made up for the worst, and perhaps the sudden news of this change in his prospects would prove so violent as to unsettle his reason. The trial will take place in a few days, and he will then be better able to support this unexpected reverse from probable death to preservation from the gallows."

Thanking them again and again for the confidence with which they had inspired her, Mrs. Dawson promised to follow the advice she had just received, and taking her farewell of Mr. Eversfield and his kind-hearted wife, she returned home lightened of nearly all the sorrows with which she had left it.

At length the day of trial arrived, and Dawson was arraigned at the bar on a charge of having murdered Mr. Cavendish; but when the names of the prosecutor and witnesses were called over, none of them answered, and the consequence was, that the prisoner was immediately acquitted to the great joy of a number of his friends who were in the court. The surprise, however, was too much for him, and he fell upon the floor of the dock in a fainting fit, in which state he was carried out of the court, and immediate assistance procured.

CHAPTER XXX.

THE SURPRISE.

THE employers of Mr. Dawson had so good an opinion of him, that they readily took him back into their service a day or two after he had returned home to his wife, and thinking that change of scene would do much towards restoring him to his former buoyancy of spirits, they sent him on their commercial business to Germany, on his return from which place, they hoped to find that the painful affair in which he had been engaged would be forgotten.

This arrangement was readily acceded to by the clerk, and within a fortnight afterwards, he took leave of his wife, who it was agreed, as her health was not yet perfectly restored, should go to Ramsgate for change of air, and that she should remain there for a month or six weeks with Susan, whose fidelity and zeal caused her to be regarded, both by her master and mistress, more in the light of a friend than as a menial servant.

They had not, however, been in their lodgings at Ramsgate more than a day, when an event occurred, which seemed likely enough to prove of some consequence. In fact, Susan had been much struck with a remarkably pretty child that she had seen playing several times in the hall, and being very fond of children, she tried several times to coax it to come to her. But the little girl was shy, and would run away on her approach, till at last Susan offered it a cake, upon which they became the best friends imaginable. She then took the child in her arms to caress it, but scarcely had she done so, when her attention was attracted by some lace in the little girl's cap, which, the more she looked at it, the more did she feel convinced that it was exactly of the same pattern as that which had been missed by the linendraper, and which Mr. Edwards had sworn was stolen by Mrs. Dawson. This discovery filled Susan with amazement, and she scarcely knew what to do or think about the matter, but at length resolving to satisfy her doubts, she began to praise the beauty of the lace, and then the child, who began to grow more communicative, said that her mamma had trimmed her cap with it on purpose to go down to Ramsgate with. Now in all this there was nothing very remarkable, because, of course, the same pattern might be seen on many persons besides this child, but it carried Susan's memory back to past events, and she sighed as she thought of the many troubles and disasters that had followed the accusation that had been brought against her mistress.

She was then going to ask the child a few further questions, but scarcely had she commenced, when the parlour door was quickly opened, and the mother bouncing out abruptly, snatched the child from her arms and retreated to her own room in the same hurried way that she had left it. Susan was vexed at this, because she was just going to enquire of the little girl what her name was, which would at once either have fixed or removed her suspicions. As it was, however, she determined to watch another opportunity of speaking to the child; but throughout the remainder of that day nothing more was seen of it.

This Susan thought was rather vexatious, but the circumstance of seeing the little girl with the lace, and the evident desire of the mother to conceal her from her view, made a strong impression on the mind of our heroine, and she determined to speak to the landlady of the house, that she might learn the name of her other lodgers, by which she would be better able to judge whether there was any foundation for the strange thoughts that had taken possession of her mind. But it so happened that the landlady was out of the way all the remainder of that day, and though Susan was bursting with impatience, she was obliged to restrain her curiosity till a future occasion.

Early on the following morning, she had to attend her mistress in a walk down to the sea side, and as they passed the door of the other lodgers, she could see that they were packing up a trunk, as if making ready for an immediate departure; but she had hardly time to observe this, for the door was instantly slammed to, and she was again left to form her own conclusions respecting these mysterious people, and the motives that could have induced them to observe so much secrecy and caution.

She was still pondering upon this when her mistress and herself left the house, but, upon returning, she saw a porter go into the lodgers' apartment, and this at once confirmed her in the notion that they were going to take their immediate departure, and though not much given to prying curiosity, she went to her mistress's window and watched till the strange people and the porter left the place. Still, however, she could not see the man's face, though his wife frequently looked round to see if they were watched, and when she observed Susan looking after them, she nudged her husband's elbow, and they moved on at a quicker pace. In fact, their conduct altogether had been so odd, that Susan began to think more and more about the lace she had seen in the child's cap, and being determined to sift the matter to the bottom if possible, she made an excuse to her mistress, and hurried out of the house to follow them.

In a little time she saw the porter with his load, and supposing they had stopped at a shop to buy something, she continued her way to the coach-office, where the man put down his trunk and bandages, which were quickly transferred to the boot of the vehicle ; she, therefore, mixed among the crowd of idlers that were congregated about the place, and presently the people she had been looking after arrived, and took their seat on the roof. Still, however, she could not catch a glimpse of the man's countenance, and she was almost despairing of attaining this object, when, just as the coach was starting, he turned round, and she recognized the well-remembered countenance of Mr. Richard Jobbins, the shopman of Mr. Edwards, who had brought the goods to the house of her mistress on the very day when she was accused of having stolen them. The same glance also told her he was the same person she had run against when she was pursuing her mistress after they had left the hackney-coach, and that again brought it to her recollection that she had seen him at Newgate whilst she was going backwards and forwards to visit her master, and that she had been told he went there every day to see a friend who was a prisoner there for a robbery that he had committed. In fact, the suspicion flashed upon her mind at once that Richard Jobbins was the person that had stolen the goods from his employer, and most deeply was she vexed at the idea that she had suffered him to go off by the coach without making an effort to have him arrested on a charge that would at once have cleared her mistress from the foul imputation that had been brought against her character.

It was, however, no use to regret the circumstance now, for the coach was a mile or two on its journey, and, of course, by the time it reached London, he would take care to conceal himself so as to prevent all possibility of her being able to find him. She, therefore, returned home undecided whether to inform her mistress of the discovery or not, and on entering the house, she inquired of Mrs. Dingle, the landlady, the name of the strange people that had just left her apartments.

"Ah, my dear, you may well call 'em strange people," answered the landlady, "for though they've been in my house above a week, I've not been able to make 'em out yet. They took my lodging for two months certain, and yet, last night, all of a sudden, they sent for me, and said that particular business called 'em unexpectedly to Dover, and that they must leave this place by the first coach that started."

"Do you know who or what they are?" asked Susan.

"No ; they were always very mysterious about their own concerns," replied the landlady ; "for, to tell you the truth, I've made three or four attempts to learn something about them, but whenever I have done so, they turned the conversation to something else, and left me to find the matter out as well as I could. However, I think he's nothing more than a shopman, in spite of their being so fond of cutting a dash, and, between you and me, I shouldn't wonder if he has robbed his master for the sake of coming pleasuring down here."

At this moment Susan was summoned to attend her mistress, and the subject was dropped for the present ; but our heroine could not help thinking the matter over, and the more she reflected upon it, the more convinced did she feel that there was an important secret to discover, and she determined, however difficult it might be, to ascertain whether her suspicions were correct.

The remainder of their stay was not marked by any adventure worth recording, at the end of a month, Mrs. Dawson and Susan returned to town, when the latter began to form various plans for ascertaining the truth or falsehood of her suspicions. But the task she had set herself was by no means an easy one, and she could not help despairing of the success she desired, when accident threw in her way a newspaper, in which she found a paragraph that mentioned the recent committal for trial of a young man for robbing his employer, Mr. Edwards, the well-known linendraper. The delinquent she at once believed could be no other than Richard Jobbins, and obtaining permission to go out in the afternoon, she made the best of her way to Newgate, in order to satisfy herself whether the prisoner was indeed the person she believed. In this she had very little difficulty, for the turnkey remembered her from having seen her so often when she used to go there to visit Mr. Dawson; and, in answer to her questions, he replied that the prisoner was a young man, and that the name under which he had been committed was Jenkins.

"However," he continued, "it's hardly likely that he has given his real name, for they tell me he has got half-a-dozen other aliases, and, if that's the case, he may be the person you suspect."

"Can I see him?" asked Susan.

"Oh, yes," replied the man; "if you like to follow me into the yard, you can have a look at him. But mind, you mustn't say a word if it should turn out to be the chap, because I'm acting against orders in taking you."

I This injunction Susan promised to obey, and then she inquired whether the prisoner had ever been in custody before.

"I've never seen him that I know of," replied the turnkey, "but, it seems, his master has suspected him for some time of pocketing his money. However, come along with me, and you shall presently satisfy yourself by seeing him."

With this Susan followed him through two or three long, dismal-looking passages towards a place that commanded a view of the airing ground, where he pointed out the person of whom they had been speaking. But a single glance served to convince Susan that the prisoner was not Richard Jobbins, and thanking her conductor for the trouble he had taken, she returned once more to the lobby, from whence she emerged once more into the street.

It now remained to be considered what she should do next, and as it was not necessary that she should return home immediately, she made the best of her way towards the shop of Mr. Edwards, where, under the pretence of making a few trifling purchases, she had an opportunity of looking round the place to see whether Mr. Richard Jobbins was still in the same employment. But though she looked round the place with a scrutinizing glance, the person of whom she was in quest was nowhere to be seen, and believing that he had been turned away for his misdeeds, she quitted the shop, wondering whether it would ever be her good fortune to meet with the man who she felt thoroughly convinced was the thief, whose dishonesty had occasioned her mistress so much obloquy and disgrace.

For some days after this, Susan was almost constantly occupied in forming plans for the discovery she had so much at heart; but, on the following Sunday, being at church, her attention was drawn towards a crowd of persons in the opposite aisle, and there, to her utter astonishment, she saw Mr. Richard Jobbins standing among them, and, apparently paying the most devout attention to the preacher. Her first impulse was to make her way towards him, and give him into the custody of the beadle; but then she recollected that there was no direct evidence against him, and as such an act would only serve to put him upon his guard with respect to her suspicions, she determined to remain quiet, and at the end of the service to watch him home, in order that she might afterwards reflect upon the best method of proceeding.

She, therefore, kept her eyes almost constantly fixed upon him, and it was not long before she discovered that he had three or four friends about him; for though they did not whisper together, she could observe an interchange of glances among them, and that which struck her as being more singular than anything else, was the fact of their shifting about from place to place, and jostling against people, apparently by accident, but, as she thought, by design. Sometimes they apologised for the annoyance they caused, but, in most instances, they rudely pushed their way onwards, and looked about them as if they expected to see some friends of whom they were in quest.

All this seemed strange enough to Susan, and she continued to watch them from place to place with a determination not to lose sight of Jobbins, with whose place of residence she was determined to become acquainted. At one time it seemed as if he was making his way towards the aisle in which she was standing, but a great crowd of persons that stood near the pulpit effectually barred his progress that way, and retreating by the way he had come, he got back to near the place where she had first seen him, and where he stood during the remainder of the service, apparently deeply engaged in listening to the discourse of the preacher.

At length, when the service was concluded, the throng of persons began slowly to retire, and at that moment our heroine could see Jobbins making vigorous efforts to force his way towards the door; a task in which he succeeded to his heart's content, for there were few who felt disposed to resist his violence, and in a few minutes afterwards she saw him approach the door, which he had no sooner reached, than darting out, he was immediately lost to view. This was vexatious enough to Susan, who had resolved to follow him, but as the crowd still continued to be very great, she was obliged to remove from where she was, and whilst she was yet thinking how unfortunate the affair had turned out, a buz went round the place that several persons had been robbed of their watches and purses, and though many suspected who the thieves were, it was now too late, since the thieves had quitted the church some few minutes before. Susan, too, had her own opinions upon the subject, and she returned home with a stronger determination than ever, to discover whether Jobbins was really the villain that she took him for.

But she still found herself as far as ever from the object upon which her whole soul was set, and deeply mortified did she feel at the prospect that, in spite of all her efforts the villain must escape, unless by some means or other, she could contrive to fix him with any one crime which might have the effect of bringing his others to light. Still, however, she was not to be easily deterred, and on the following day she once more took her way to the shop of Mr. Edwards, in order that she might, if possible, convince herself whether he had left that person's service.

Here she again glanced her eyes round the place, and for some little time her search was fruitless; but at length she saw him standing behind a counter at the further end of the shop, and making her way towards the spot, she observed his countenance change as he perceived her approach. At first he turned round, as if for the purpose of concealing himself from her view, but he at length, however, recovered his composure, and then darting round to the opposite side of the shop, began to busy himself in

rolling up and putting away a quantity of goods that had just been taken **down for** the inspection of a customer.

At first, Susan was inclined to charge him with being the thief who had brought so much disgrace upon her mistress, but a moment's reflection convinced her that such a course would be foolish till she had more proof of her assertion, and she returned home, pondering in her own mind how she should next proceed. She was, however, determined not to say anything to her mistress, just yet, and having reflected upon what course she had better pursue, she determined to go to Mr. Derwent, the attorney usually employed by her master ; and after relating all the particulars of the case to hear what advice he would give her upon the subject of her anxiety.

When she went to him, Mr. Derwent heard her simple statement with a great deal of attention, for he was already acquainted with the charge that had been brought against Mrs. Dawson, by the linen draper, and from the first, he had suspected that there was a plot at the bottom, which time and patience alone could unravel. He remembered having heard too, that Mrs. Robson was in the house at the very time of the alleged robbery, and as subsequent enquiries had convinced him that the lady in question did not bear a very good character, he had a notion that she might very likely be the thief. But at present, there was no sort of proof to fix her with the crime, and as it would not be prudent at present, to give even the slightest hint of his suspicions, he kept his thoughts to himself, resolving to watch an opportunity when he might take from Mrs. Dawson the foul imputation that had been cast upon her character. At length, when Susan had finished her statement, he said :—

"You have taken a very proper course in this affair, young woman, and your zeal in behalf of this oppressed lady reflects the highest honour upon you. At the same time, I must inform you, that we have no substantial

No. 28

ground to go upon at present, since the most we can say is, that we believe your mistress to be innocent, and that she has been made the victim of artful and designing people. This Jobbins, for instance, has been playing so artful a game, that we can bring no proof against him ;—the lace which you saw upon the child's cap may have been of the same pattern as that which was stolen, but we can bring no evidence to bear upon it, and as for the robbery, which was committed in the church, we may certainly suspect Jobbins of having been engaged in it, but I am quite certain that if we had him taken up it would only be to endure the mortification of seeing him come off with flying colours."

"You think then, sir," said Susan, "that there is very little chance of our succeeding in this business ?"

"Nay, I don't go so far as to say that," replied Mr. Derwent, "but the law is never very certain, and fortunately, for the innocent, juries are never found to convict except upon the clearest evidence, and were we to proceed against him upon mere suspicion, he could not only get off, but we should have no further chance of finding out whether he is really the culprit."

"Then he will escape," cried Susan, "and my poor mistress must still bear the blame of committing an act that no poverty could ever have drawn her to."

"It shall be my care," answered the lawyer, "to prevent as much as possible, her suffering any inconvenience from the course you mention. I have some idea upon this subject, and will endeavour to bring the offender to justice : but it must be done cautiously, or we shall defeat our own purposes. So now return home, young woman, and I will communicate with you as soon as I have seen a little further into the business."

Susan felt somewhat relieved at this, and thanking Mr. Derwent for the promises he had made, she returned home with a lighter heart than she had had for some time before.

CHAPTER XXXI.

THE TABLES TURNED.

On the very day of Susan's visit to him, Mr. Derwent paid a visit to Newgate, and obtained an interview with George Jenkins, the young man who had lately been committed for a recent robbery of Mr. Edwards. He, however, went there as the legal adviser of the prisoner, and having explained the motive that had induced him to call upon him, he said :—

"You will now understand, young man, that I do not ask you to make me your confidant unless you place the fullest reliance on the integrity of my purpose. It, however, appears that a robbery had been committed on Mr. Edwards, and of course, sufficient evidence has been brought against you, or the magistrates would not have sent you here to await your trial."

"What is it you want me to do ?" asked the prisoner.

"I ask you to do nothing against your own free will," replied Mr. Derwent, "but of course you are aware that the sessions will commence in a very few days, and it is necessary for you to decide immediately upon what course you mean to adopt."

"I shall plead not guilty, to be sure," answered Jenkins.

"So I expected," exclaimed the lawyer, "but that plan will do very little service, unless you act under good advice, and have a careful advocate to watch your case. Now, I do not mean to take any great credit to myself in this matter, but if you choose to confide to me, I will, at least, use diligence in your cause, and expect neither fee nor reward for any service I may happen to do you."

"But," asked Jenkins, " do you think you can get me off?"

"That I shall know better when I have heard from your own lips, what share you have had in this robbery, and whether any other persons were concerned in it with you."

"And how do I know that you will not turn round and make use of what I say against me?"

"There is certainly no way of proving the sincerity of my intentions," replied Mr. Derwent, " but I can assure you that all prisoners confide such secrets to their legal advisers, and the confidence reposed in them is never abused. In fact it is necessary that accused persons should do so, or it would be impossible for persons to undertake their defence."

"But there must be some reason," said the prisoner, suspiciously, " for you taking this interest in the fate of a person that I believe you never saw in your life till now."

"I admit that I have a purpose of my own to serve," replied Mr. Derwent, " and as you can in no way suffer through it, I trust you will repose that confidence in me which I expected. I will be your friend as far as lies in my power, and when I know how far you are culpable, I shall be able to judge what probability there is of your being acquitted."

"Will it serve yourself, sir," asked Jenkins, " if I make the disclosures you ask of me?"

"Not in the least," he replied, " but I have a friend who may be materially served by any confession you may think proper to make to me, and in return for that service, I will do all in my power for you."

"Well, sir," exclaimed the prisoner, " what is it that you so much want to know?"

"Whether you are really guilty the crime for which you have been committed for trial."

"I am not guilty of it," answered Jenkins.

"Do you solemnly declare that to be a fact?"

"I do," replied the prisoner ;—" in fact, I thought to have proved that before the magistrates, but unfortunately my witnesses were persons of bad character and their evidence served rather to do me harm than good."

"Indeed!" observed Mr. Derwent ;—" according to your own shewing then, you have associated with persons of indifferent habits."

"That I don't deny, sir."

"Then, perhaps," resumed the lawyer, " you will not object to let me know who these witnesses were?"

"Will it do them any harm if I tell you?" asked the prisoner.

"None in the least," replied Mr. Derwent; " so now tell me candidly where you were on the night of the robbery?"

"At the house of a Jew, named Moses Lazarus."

"Humph!" ejaculated the lawyer; " I have heard of that man's name as a reputed receiver of stolen goods. Surely that was no place for a person of respectability to be in?"

"That's true enough, sir," replied Jenkins, " but I have told you nothing but a fact for all that. I was in the house of Lazarus all the evening, and heard nothing about it till the Jew mentioned it just as I was leaving him."

"And from what passed between you," said Mr. Derwent, " have you any ground to suspect that Lazarus knows who the parties were that committed the robbery?"

"I don't much think he does."

"That is to say," returned the other, " he was cunning enough not to say anything that might involve him in difficulty."

"It might be so," answered the prisoner, "for he made me very drunk that night, so that I can recollect very little that passed, and when the morning came, and I had recovered myself a little, I was glad enough to get away from the place as fast as I could."

"That man is more or less implicated in the robbery," said Mr. Derwent, half aside. "He can throw all the light that we want upon it, and it shall be my business to see him with as little delay as possible." Then addressing himself more particularly to the prisoner, he enquired if the Jew was acquainted with any of the shopmen belonging to Mr. Edwards' establishment.

"That's more than I can answer for," returned the other.

"At any rate," exclaimed Mr. Derwent, "we must some how or other find that out, so I'll make it my business to see the Jew, and try whether he feels inclined to assist me in this business."

"You must make up your mind to bleed pretty freely if you expect to get anything out of him," returned Jenkins. "The old fellow's a shy bird, I can tell you, and wouldn't do a service for the best friend he had in the world, unless he is handsomely paid for it."

"It shall be tried, at any rate," said the lawyer; "so now tell me, young man, whether you can throw any light on this affair, that may serve to bring the guilty parties to justice?"

"You mean to ask me, I suppose, whether I know the person that did it?"

"That was exactly my meaning."

"Then I cannot give you my assistance," replied the prisoner; "for I've been kept in the dark, and, I suppose, the reason of that is, that they make me the victim. All I can say is, that I had no hand in it, but I dare say the jury won't believe me when the day of trial comes."

"Had you ever reason to suspect any of your fellow shopmen of pilfering from their employer?"

"Not any one in particular," replied Jenkins, "but I know some one must have been doing it, for I've been sent here for stealing upwards of two pounds out of the till, and all that I really took was seven shillings, so that it's pretty clear that somebody must have been there before me."

"That must be enquired into," said Mr. Derwent, "for if you are telling the truth, there must indeed be some miscreant on the premises whose supposed honesty shields him from the suspicion that would otherwise bring him to justice. And yet it seems, that you, who having been living for some time in the house, have no idea who it is?"

"How can you find a man out if he's determined to be sly and artful?" asked the culprit. "However, you may as well see Lazarus, for he most likely knows all about it, and, if you don't stand something handsome, it's pretty certain he'll peach, if it would bring his own brother to the gallows."

"Well, I'll lose no time about trying what can be done with him," exclaimed Mr. Derwent, "for it appears quite certain there must be a thief in Mr. Edwards' house, and if my conjectures are right, I'll drag the scoundrel out into the open light of day, even if it costs me five hundred pounds out of my own pocket. And so now, young man, I shall take my leave of you for the present, and you may rest satisfied that I will do all in my power for you against your trial comes on. My first business on leaving this place shall be to visit the Jew, and let the result of that turn out as it may, I will see you again before the present week is ended."

With this he left the prisoner, and quitting the gaol, directed his footsteps towards that quarter of the town in which he knew Lazarus resided. He had no great difficulty in finding the house, and entering the shop, which was kept as a sort of blind to the real business that was being carried on in the place, he encountered a Jewish-looking personage, who he at once guessed was the very man he wanted to see.

"Is your name Moses Lazarus?" said the lawyer, in a tone as little calculated as possible to avoid giving suspicion.

"It is, sir," replied the Hebrew, eyeing him askance, and wondering enough whether the stranger belonged to the class of persons with whom he usually transacted business.

"In that case," resumed Mr. Derwent, "I wish to speak to you in private;—I shall not detain you long, and ——"

"I'll attend to you in a moment," interrupted the Jew, and motioning to a boy that was assisting to take care of the shop, he led him into a room behind, fully anticipating that his visitor came to negociate for the sale of some goods that had lately been stolen. There was a window looking into the shop, and opposite to this Mr. Derwent seated himself, so as to command a full view of all that was going on in the front part of the premises. The Jew evidently felt restless and uneasy at his not coming to the point at once, and at length he enquired the nature of the business that had brought him there.

"I came to ask you a favour, Mr. Lazarus," replied the other;—"nay, you need not put on so black a look, for it is not the loan of a sum of money that I want, but a little information, which it may be in your power to give, and for which I shall be able to pay you handsomely."

"To the point, sir,—to the point," exclaimed the Jew impatiently.

"I will be as brief as possible," answered Mr. Derwent; "the fact is a young man that you know something about is at present in Newgate, under an awkward charge of robbery, that may be the means of sending him for some years out of the country. It is sufficient for me to say that I feel a deep interest in the prisoner's fate, and;—but of course I needn't ask whether you know the person to whom I am at present alluding?"

"Upon my word, sir," exclaimed the Jew, "I must beg you to explain yourself a little more clearly if you expect me to understand your meaning. What is the name of the young man you are speaking of?"

"George Jenkins is the person I am interesting myself for," replied Mr. Derwent, "and as I know you are well aware of his innocence, I am anxious to procure your testimony in his behalf. So now you know my business, and it only remains for you to say whether you will do anything towards clearing him from this charge?"

"I would do anything in my power to serve a fellow-creature," replied Lazarus, with assumed humility, "but what can a man like me do in such a case as this?"

"Why," exclaimed Mr. Derwent, "I don't suppose you'll attempt to deny that the young man was here on the night of Mr. Edwards's robbery. At all events, I have it on pretty good authority, and it is equally certain that he was made very drunk for certain purposes which I need not at present mention."

"Really, sir," stammered the Jew, "you are telling me a great deal that I was not before acquainted with."

"Come, come, Mr. Lazarus," said the lawyer, "you know better, and I should be sorry to be obliged to bring this matter to your recollection by more disagreeable means. The young man, I tell you, was in this house on the night when the theft was committed, and as I am determined to do all in my power to get him off from this affair, it would be better for you to rub up your memory a little before you answer me too positively on this particular point."

"Really I know nothing about it," answered the Jew, with evident agitation; "he might have been here, certainly, but I could not have been at home at the time, or, of course, I must have remembered the circumstance."

"Well, you may take my word for it he was here," replied the lawyer significantly; "and if necessary I shall be able to prove it all in good time."

"I hope you don't suspect me of any wish to injure the young man?" exclaimed Lazarus.

"That remains to be seen," answered Mr. Derwent; "for, if necessary, a way may be found to discover a great deal more than certain persons think for. However, I dare say your memory is not so bad but you will, by and by, be able to throw some light upon this affair."

"One can't help one's memory, sir," exclaimed Lazarus, "and mine unfortunately happens to be a very bad one. Besides, it must be three or four months ago since this happened, and I'm sure I couldn't tell you positively what took place yesterday, let alone such a long time as that. It's a sad thing to be so forgetful, sir,—a very sad thing, indeed, and for a man in business, like me, there's no saying what I may lose in the course of a year."

"But perhaps you are not quite so forgetful in matters that concern your own interest?"

"Oh, yes, sir, it's just the same with everything," answered the Jew, with a melancholy shake of the head; "it's quite an infirmity, I assure you, and one that, as I said before, has proved terribly against my wellbeing in the world."

"Aye, aye," said Mr. Derwent, "your memory is so bad, I suppose, that among the vast number of customers you have, you scarcely remember who among them owes you money?"

"I dare say," replied the Jew, "I should forget even that, if it were not for my books."

"Really, my dear sir," cried Mr. Derwent, "we are wandering very far from the point I came to see you about. I came to ask a few questions about George Jenkins, who was here on the night of the robbery, and who was made so drunk that he was unable to leave the house till the following morning."

"Who says so besides yourself?" enquired the Jew.

"That is a question that I cannot answer just at present," replied Mr. Derwent. "However, I have proof that he was in the house, and much intoxicated on the night in question, and I would now ask whether you recollect speaking to him in the morning about the robbery at Mr. Edwards's, which he had never heard of till you told him?"

"I might have done so if he was in the house as you say," answered Lazarus.

"And if you told him that which he knew nothing about before," exclaimed the lawyer, "how could he possibly have been engaged in the crime for which he now lies in Newgate, with every prospect of being sent abroad for the remainder of his life?"

"I'm not quite sure that I did tell him about the robbery," replied the crafty Israelite; "and even if I did, it's most likely I told a great many persons the same thing."

"Indeed!—are there many persons that visit you to whom such a piece of intelligence would prove interesting?"

"Merely as a matter of general conversation," answered Lazarus; "one can't talk to every person on business, you know, and when customers have finished making their purchases, they sometimes sit down with me for a little time, and then the conversation turns upon a variety of subjects."

" We are leaving the main point, Mr. Lazarus," said the lawyer, " and now let me assure you that I am not come here to pry into your affairs further than concerns this young man, George Jenkins; I am engaged to conduct his defence, and as I think it quite possible to prove that he is not the most culpable party that has robbed Mr. Edwards, I wish to know whether you are willing—on certain considerations, mind—to guide us to the real perpetrator of the robbery?"

" Is there any money to be given for the information?" inquired the Jew, in an eager tone.

" There is."

" How much?"

" That will depend upon the value of the disclosures," replied Mr. Derwent; " but I think it is in your power to assist us in this matter, and in that case, I promise you that the amount shall be perfectly satisfactory."

" I'm afraid my memory won't serve me," said Lazarus, trying, by delay, to make a good bargain for himself. " It's a bad thing to forget oneself so, but—"

" And a great loss too," interrupted Mr. Derwent, rising as if to go away, " for I was just going to say that I should not mind giving a hundred pounds to any man that can afford a clue to the real perpetrators of Edwards's robbery."

" A hundred pounds did you say?" exclaimed the Jew.

" I did."

" And when would you pay it?"

" Directly after receiving the information."

" But perhaps, you mayn't happen to have so much about you at this moment?" quoth Lazarus.

" Well, well," returned the other, " it must be confessed I do not carry such large sums about with me, for fear of finding myself in suspicious company at any time." And as he said this he directed a meaning glance towards the Israelite, whose fingers seemed to be itching to grasp the promised reward; " however," he continued, a minute afterwards, " it matters very little whether I have the sum in my pocket or not, as I can procure it by only stepping home, which is not very far off."

" And supposing," said the other, " anybody was to give you the information you want, it would not be told, I suppose, who it was that gave you the hint?"

" Certainly not," replied the lawyer; " my business is to clear this young man, who is suspected of the robbery, and if I can only do that, I promise not to say a word that may serve to let anybody know who it was that gave me the information."

" If that's the case," said Lazarus, after another pause, " perhaps I may be able to —"

At this moment the boy called him to a customer that had just entered the shop, and Mr. Derwent could observe through the glass window, a young man of rather smart appearance, who was making his way towards the parlour, when the Jew, anxious to prevent his doing so, darted out of the room, and seizing him by the arm, led him back to the counter, and whispered something in his ear, not one word of which Mr. Derwent could catch. But the young man was not so tractable as the other wished, and after uttering three or four exclamations of impatience, he broke forth with :—

" What's the use of making all this fuss, old fellow?—Aint I come on business with you, and—"

" Hush!—there's a stranger in the parlour," exclaimed Lazarus, " and if you don't keep dark it may be all up with you."

"A stranger !" retorted the other; "aint he one of our sort then, my tulip?"

"No,—he's a lawyer."

"A lawyer, eh?—then I'm sure he can't be after any good here, so let's get rid of him, and prevent any mischief that he may try to do us."

"Why, you wouldn't kill him, would you, Thompson?"

"No, I wouldn't do that," replied the other; "but I would like to put him down in your cellar, and keep him on bread and water for a month or two."

"Don't speak so loud, or he'll hear you," said the Jew. "I'm half afraid of him already, and if he should happen to know what we're talking about, it would be all up with us."

"Well then, come a little further off, and we shall be quite safe," replied the other; and they then proceeded nearer to the shop-door, where they were engaged for about ten minutes in a conversation, not one word of which the lawyer could overhear. He, had, however, gathered quite enough to convince him that he was not very safe there, and glad would he have been to have effected his escape, but he knew that the least demonstration of alarm on his part would have convinced them that he was aware of what they had been saying about him, and when, at last, the young man took his leave of the Jew, he collected all the courage he possessed, and as Lazarus entered the room, began humming a tune, with as much indifference as if he was perfectly at his ease.

"Well, Mr. Lazarus," he said, abruptly bringing the air to a close; "you know what I was saying just as you left me?—A hundred pounds shall be the reward of him who gives me the information I require."

"Aye, aye, I remember, now, what we were talking about. But, really, my good friend, I know nothing about who it was that committed the robbery at the linendraper's, and, even if I did, it is hardly to be expected that I should earn a hundred pounds by selling a fellow-creature."

"Nay, but my good sir," replied Mr. Derwent, "you were just coming to my terms when that person came into the shop."

"Was I?" said the Jew, not knowing exactly what to say.

"Why, of course you were, and—"

"Ah!—but one can't help a bad memory, you know," interrupted the Jew; "I dare say I was thinking of something else at the time, but about this affair at Mr. Edwards's, I know no more than the person that has just gone away."

"Does he know anything about it, then?"

"He know anything about it!" exclaimed Lazarus; "why, he's a respectable man, and would scorn to do such an act as we are speaking about."

"Then, you mean to tell me that you can throw no light whatever on this business?"

"Not the least."

"And that the young man in Newgate," continued the lawyer, "must suffer for a crime that was committed by another?"

"I dare say he did it, or he wouldn't be there," answered the Jew, coldly. "It's a dreadful thing, sir, when people can't be honest, and if they will pilfer and steal things that don't belong to them, we ought to be thankful that we've got such good laws to punish them for their crimes."

Mr. Derwent saw that it would be useless to urge the matter any further at present, and pretending to be quite satisfied with the answer he had received, he took his leave, determined to exert himself to the utmost to see whether something could not yet be done to bring Lazarus to his recollection. The more he thought over the affair, however, the more convinced

was he that the Jew was well acquainted with the whole transaction, and it also seemed pretty clear to him that the person who had come into the shop while he was there, was George Jobbins, the very man of all otheres whom he most suspected of being the thief that had robbed his employer. Still he was uncertain whether Jobbins was really the guilty party, and in the absence of direct proof, he was obliged to controul himself with the hope that something would turn up by which he might, by and by, fix the guilt upon the real criminal, and thus clear Mrs. Dawson from the foul charge that had been brought against her.

According to the promise he had given, Mr. Derwent shortly afterwards visited Jenkins in Newgate, and communicated to him the result of his interview with the Jew, and at the same time giving it as his opinion that no sort of information would be got from him relative to the business in hand.

"Ah, sir!" replied the prisoner, "that's no more than I expected to hear, for Lazarus is a cunning rascal, and I dare say all the money you could offer him would not be equal to the loss he would meet with in case he should offend any of the chaps he has dealings with. Nay, I don't know that his life would be safe if he was to split upon any of them, and if he was to get one of them punished, the others would expect that their turn was not far off, and depend upon it, they'd take care to prevent his doing any more mischief."

"I have been thinking of that, myself," replied Mr. Derwent, "and yet at one time I fancied he was tempted by the offer of a hundred pounds; and I don't know but he would have accepted my offer, only some person came into the shop just at the moment, and when he came back to me after speaking to him, he pretended not to remember anything about the business."

"Perhaps the chap had been putting him up to it," said Jenkins.

No. 29

"Most likely he did," replied the lawyer; "but I found he was obstinate, so I left him with a determination to give him another call in the course of a few days."

"I think you had better not, sir," answered Jenkins, "for he'll begin to think there's something more in this than he at present knows of; and if he once takes such a notion as that into his head, it won't be very easy to make him say a word about who it was that committed the robbery."

"Well then," said the lawyer, "if that's the case, I shall let the matter take its own course, and as your trial comes on the day after to-morrow, we must trust to the ability of the counsellor that I have retained for your defence. He will, no doubt, do his best, and I, for my own part, shall keep a careful watch upon the proceedings to take any advantage that may happen to present itself in your favour."

Upon this Mr. Derwent again left the prisoner, and most indefatigably did he set himself to work to arrange matters so as to lead to a satisfactory result. Nearly the whole of that night he sat up to get everything in readiness for the defence of the accused, and when the moment of trial came on, he was seated within the bar in earnest conversation with the prisoner's counsel, informing him of some particulars that had transpired since they had last met, and urging him to try whether he could not, by a right cross-examination of the witnesses, obtain some clue that would lead to a discovery of the culprit who had been so extensively engaged in robbing Mr. Edwards.

The linendraper himself was the first person put into the witness box, but his evidence was not of any very great importance, except that he proved the fact of having been plundered for a long time past by some unknown person in his employ, and said that, in order to discover who the thief was, he had placed seven marked shillings in the till, all of which were afterwards found upon the prisoner. He could not swear, however, that Jenkins had ever robbed him before, and, indeed, expressed an opinion that the prisoner had previously been honest, but that he had fallen among bad company, and had been tempted to commit the act for which he now stood at the bar.

The next witness called, was Richard Jobbins; and no sooner did he stand up to be sworn, than Mr. Derwent recognized him as the young man that had visited the Jew's shop whilst he was there, and who, on that occasion, passed by the name of Thomson. The lawyer, however, said nothing at the time, and it was not without some little difficulty that he could prevent an exclamation of surprise from Susan, when she beheld the person who she had seen before under such very extraordinary circumstances.

Richard Jobbins, however, gave his evidence with an air of perfect fairness, and spoke of the robberies that had been committed upon his master with so much concern, that no one would ever have thought that he could be guilty of such a heinous offence. On mentioning the discovery of the money on his fellow-shopman, the prisoner, he seemed very much affected, and declared he had always entertained so high an opinion of him, that he never should have suspected him, or have believed that he was guilty, if he had not been present at the time when the marked shillings were found upon him. All this seemed perfectly fair, when all of a sudden the prisoner's counsel rose, and stated that the last witness was known under other names besides that which he had been sworn by, and that he had a witness in court, who could swear to having seen him, within the last few days, at the house of a notorious receiver of stolen goods, and that he, there and then, was addressed as Mr. Thomson. In conclusion, he called upon Mr. Derwent, who gave a brief narrative of his visit to the Jew's house, and all that he had seen and heard while he was there.

This evidence was so decisive against Richard Jobbins, that the court immediately ordered him into custody, and the trial proceeded against Jenkins, who was found guilty, but in consideration of its having been made evident that he had been made the dupe of others, he received only a slight punishment, with a sharp admonition to be more careful of his conduct in future.

On the same day a search warrant was sent to the house of Richard Jobbins, where an immense quantity of his master's goods were found, and among them part of the lace and other articles which it had been alleged were stolen by Mrs. Dawson. Upon this, finding that the game was up, he confessed the evil practices he had been carrying on so long, and pleading guilty on the day of trial, was ordered to be transported for life.

Thus was the character of Mrs. Dawson cleared, chiefly through the perseverance of her faithful domestic, Susan Hoply.

CHAPTER XXXII.

JEALOUSY.

WE must now return to the Count de Morceau, who having married Madalene, had left Havre with his young wife to enjoy the gaieties and frivolities that are to be found in Paris. And, to say the truth, the newly made countess soon proved that, though her birth was rather low, her notions were extremely high: for no sooner did she find herself in the metropolis of fashion, than she plunged herself into a round of pleasures that surprised even her husband, whose exalted rank had many years before introduced him to scenes, such as can be indulged in only by men who are favoured with the smiles of fortune.

It was about a week after their arrival in Paris that, being one evening with his countess at the theatre, he was struck with the excessive beauty of a female in an opposite box, and so much was his admiration excited that his constant gaze in one direction attracted the notice of the countess, who, presently, took care to give him pretty plain hints that it would be much more becoming of him to pay more attention to herself, and less to the lady who sat opposite. To this suggestion the Count de Morceau replied with all the politeness of a Frenchman, and having assured the indignant lady that her jealousy had been excited without any foundation, he began to pay a little more attention to the play, and only stole sly glances at the fair stranger at those moments when he thought the countess was not looking at him. He had, however, seen quite enough of her to make him wish for a more particular acquaintance; and when the comedy was over he left the theatre with his countess, resolving, in his own mind, to find out who the lady was, and then, if possible, to obtain an introduction to one whose beauty had so greatly excited his admiration.

The next morning, as he was taking his chocolate, he addressed himself to his favourite valet, Boulet, and enquired if he had observed the lady who had sat opposite to him on the previous night at the theatre.

"I did, my lord," was the reply.

"And did you not think her beautiful?"

"A divine creature, my lord."

"You are right, Boulet," exclaimed the count, throwing down the newspaper he had been reading; "she is, indeed, a paragon of beauty, and what is more, I must be introduced to her."

"My lord!"

"Ah!—you wou ld say it is impossible," exclaimed his master; "but in love, Boulet, there are no difficulties which are insurmountable, and once more I tell you, the lady's name and place of residence must be discovered, and when that is done I will find means to obtain the required introduction."

"Your lordship," observed the valet, "requires the assistance of a faithful and discreet agent;—may I hope that your confidence in myself will procure for me the honour of being employed in this service?"

"It's the very thing I was about to propose," answered his master. "Upon you, Boulet, I can confidently rely, and I need hardly say, that if the task is well performed, I shall not forget that a handsome reward will have been fairly earned."

"And the countess?"

"Must at present remain ignorant of my designs," quickly replied the other. "She is a little apt to be jealous, you know, and should this affair come to her knowledge, she would take good care to deprive me of the pleasure of her rival's acquaintance."

"But the lady herself may object to receive you among the number of her friends," said Boulet.

"I rather think she will be flattered by my attentions," returned the count, in a tone of confidence; "my high rank will prove a passport to her favour; and if I may judge from the glances she now and then directed towards me there is very little fear but I have already made a conquest in that quarter."

"That is likely enough," answered the valet, "and I think, with a little care, it will be no difficult task to obtain for you an interview with the lady."

"We must, first of all, be satisfied by discovering who she is," exclaimed the count; "and when that has been ascertained, I shall form my own plans for obtaining the interview I am so anxiously looking forward to. At any rate, I should suppose that my rank will secure for me the honour of an interview."

"Perhaps so," observed Boulet; "but it may so happen that the lady is virtuous, and in that case—"

"Well, sirrah," exclaimed the Count de Morceau impatiently; "why do you hesitate?"

"I was merely going to say," resumed the valet, "that if she should be very strict in her notions of propriety it is likely enough that she will avoid forming an acquaintance with a nobleman, whose affairs of gallantry have rendered him so well known from one end of France to the other."

"Ha! ha! ha!" chuckled the count, "there is some truth in what you have said, Boulet. It must be acknowledged that I have obtained some notoriety in that respect; but the ladies, deprived of it, will think none the worse of me for being an admirer of their sex, and as for the men, I shall care very little for what they may say, since their evil reports will have their origin in envy at the better fortune that attends my love affairs."

"But the countess?" observed Boulet.

"Must be content to put up with my acts of gallantry," replied the count. "She was much beneath me before I married her, and since I have raised her to this station it will be her duty to submit quietly to my general love for the fair sex. Besides, have I not brought her to Paris at her own particular request, and shall she afterwards reproach me for joining in the gaieties of this city?"

"Undoubtedly, my lord, you have a right to do as you please," answered the subservient valet, " and I dare say the countess will soon see the folly of interfering with you."

"To be sure she will," exclaimed his master languidly; " so now set about your business cheerfully, Boulet, and let me know as quickly as possible who this charming female is, and it will then be my own fault if I do not throw myself at her feet before she is many hours older."

Boulet required no further bidding, and immediately afterwards, quitting the room, he left his master once more to the enjoyment of his own thought. He was, however, not allowed to remain long in this peaceful state of contentment, for, all of a sudden, the door was thrown open, and the countess, with a flushed and angry brow, presented herself before him."

" My lord," she said, " I come to desire that Boulet may be instantly dismissed from your service; he is insolent, and I can no longer endure his presence in the house."

" What has he done, my lady?" asked her husband carelessly.

" I met him just now, as he was leaving the place," replied the countess, " and he positively refused to tell me where he was going to."

" Did you particularly wish to know, my dear?" enquired the count.

" I did," she replied,—" in fact, my lord, I have reason to believe he is going on some business of yours that I ought to be made acquainted with."

"There you and I differ, my love," answered the count, " for it would be very inconvenient to let one's wife know too much, and I question, also, whether they would be any the happier for prying too much into their husband's secrets."

" I can guess pretty well the errand he has now gone upon," said the Countess de Morceau. " Your attention last night was occupied by the lady in the opposite box to ours, and I have but too much reason to know that Boulet has been despatched on a message to her."

" Psha! how can that be, my love?" exclaimed the count. " The lady you speak of is a perfect stranger to me, and how, let me ask you, is it possible to send messages to persons when you don't happen to know where they live?"

" But Boulet can soon discover that for you, my lord."

" Boulet is much obliged to you for your good opinion, my lady," exclaimed her husband. " It must be admitted he is a clever sort of fellow in his way, but you wrong both him and me by supposing that he has gone on such an errand as you have mentioned."

" Then you positively assert that the strange lady has never occupied your thoughts since we saw her last night at the theatre?"

" Most certainly I do."

" And yet," observed the countess, " she was extremely beautiful."

" Ah!—beautiful as an angel."

" You really think so, my lord?"

" How can I do otherwise?" asked the Count de Morceau. " Have you not said yourself that she was beautiful, and—and—is there any more harm in my saying it, my love, than that you should have given such an opinion?"

" You have no right, sir," cried the countess, " to see beauty in any other woman than your own lawful wife. I only said it to hear what sort of reply you would make; but, to speak the truth, the charming woman you think so much about, has a snub nose, and, in my opinion that is a defect that is anything but favourable to beauty."

" A snub nose, my lady!"

" Yes, my lord, I particularly noticed it," replied the countess, spitefully; " and I am not quite certain whether she has not the agreeable accompaniment of a decided squint."

"A squint!" ejaculated her husband.

"Yes," cried the countess, "and, as if nature was determined to make her as frightful as possible, she has red hair."

"Nay, my love, you are prejudiced against the lady," exclaimed the Count de Morceau; "this is the mere effect of jealousy, because you happen to have taken it into your head that I took more notice of her than I ought."

"I am not quite so jealous as you imagine, my lord," answered the indignant lady. "I may, perhaps, feel angry at being treated with coldness and indifference; but, as for feeling jealous of a creature like that, I flatter myself you will never have to reproach me with caring for a man who can so soon forget his vows and protestations of love."

And with this she flung out of the room in a manner that was quite sufficient to convince the count how angry she was at the rivalry that had sprung up so suddenly against her. As for her husband, he was too much a man of the world to feel any uneasiness at this little display of his wife's temper; for he knew that she would by and by see how useless it was to interfere with his whims, and again snatching up the newspaper, which had been laid down when his wife entered the room, he continued to read over the politics of the day, till Boulet returned with news respecting the mission on which he had been sent.

"Now, sir," cried the count, eagerly, "have you been able to learn anything of the lovely woman I saw last night at the theatre?"

"I have, my lord."

"That's well,—and who is she?"

"An Englishwoman, my lord."

"Indeed!—and what, pray, is her name?"

"Smith, my lord."

"And is she married?" asked the count.

"She is not," replied Boulet.

"Then I suppose she has friends with her in Paris?"

"There was a Major Smith that came over with her," replied the valet, "but he is now gone, and the lady, I believe, is, at present, in—"

"Well, sir, why do you hesitate?"

"Because I'm afraid you'll be angry, my lord."

"Psha!—go on, sirrah;—what can I be angry about?"

"Why, the fact is, I have made a discovery that I think will very much surprise you."

"What does the dolt mean?" exclaimed the count, impatiently.

"That the lady you saw last night at the theatre, is no other than the Miss Smith that you expected over from England some few months ago," replied the valet.

"The devil she is!" exclaimed his master, with surprise. "You mean the girl that Walter Gravestow was to send, and of whom he spoke in such glowing colours?"

"There can be no doubt of it, my lord," said the other.

"Confusion!" muttered the count; "then the beautiful creature I saw last night is the girl that was to have been my wife, and whom I had given up in despair when I promised to share my rank and fortune with my present lady?"

"It is so, indeed, my lord," replied Boulet. "It seems she came over with a person that called himself Major Smith, and that, stopping a day or two in Paris, she chanced to be seen by the Marquis de Noailles, who instantly fell over head and ears in love with her."

"And is she now living with him as his mistress?" asked the disappointed count.

" She is, my lord," replied Boulet ; " the marquis, it seems, met her by accident, and introduced himself to her in the same way you were just now proposing to do. The lady, I suppose, was struck with his title and handsome person, and in less than a week after her arrival in Paris, she eloped with her lover, and from that time, they have never parted."

" And what became of Major Smith ?" asked the count.

" That is more than I can tell you," replied Boulet, " and I believe that there are many persons in Paris who would be be very glad to learn where he is to be found."

" Ah! he got in debt, I suppose, and having lost the young lady he had in charge, has decamped, rather than run the chance of being put into prison by his creditors ?"

" Exactly so, my lord," replied Boulet ; " in fact, they say he swindled everybody that had anything to do with him—jewellers, tailors, lodging-house-keepers, and all have fared alike. He showed neither favour nor affection to anybody, and when credit was no longer to be got, and people began to grow importunate for their money, he suddenly left the place, and has never been heard of since. As to the lady, she returned some time afterwards, and it was then pretty well understood that the beautiful English woman had become the mistress of the Marquis de Noailles."

" It seems, then," said the count, " that I have had a lucky escape, for her character must have been extremely light, or she would not so soon have fallen into the snares of my more fortunate rival."

" There I believe you do her an injustice," replied Boulet ; " for she was deceived by a false marriage, and from what I understand, the priest that performed the ceremony was represented by Morley, the favourite servant of the marquis."

" Good Heavens ! was ever such villany heard of ?" ejaculated the Count de Morceau, with an affectation of horror.

" It was a dreadful thing, to be sure, my lord," replied Boulet ; " and yet, as the young lady seems to be happy enough with her lot, I don't see that there's much reason for regret."

" And are you quite certain that she still lives with him ?" asked his master.

" Quite sure, my lord," was the reply. " Indeed, what else could the poor girl do ? Her character was gone, and so, I suppose, when she found that the marquis really loved her, she thought it advisable to remain under his protection, rather than endure the coldness of the world, that never makes any allowances for faults, even though they may happen to have been produced by unavoidable misfortune."

" I really begin to feel quite interested in behalf of this young English woman," exclaimed the count. " She may need a friend in these troubles that have come upon her, and I will see her with as little delay as possible."

" Has your lordship forgotten the countess ?" asked Boulet. " Won't she be jealous if she should happen to discover that you take an interest in the lady ?"

" Her ladyship must learn to repose the utmost confidence in my actions, however suspicious they may appear," replied the count. " I feel that it will be my duty to see this Miss Smith, and I will immediately do so, let the consequences be what they may."

" But how are you to get an introduction to her ?" asked the valet, cautiously.

" By writing her a note," replied the count. " I will explain to her who I am, and the heavy disappointment I have endured, through not meeting her as I had anticipated. This will raise an interest for me in her heart, and she will then welcome me as a friend, and, perhaps, honour me with that love which she has so unworthily bestowed upon the Marquis de Noailles."

He accordingly sat himself down at his desk, and after some little consideration, penned such an epistle as he thought best calculated to excite the tender sensibilities of the female he was addressing. He, however, carefully avoided saying anything that might serve to give her an idea that they had met in the theatre, lest his designs should be suspected, and his plans thus thwarted ere he had well begun to put them into operation.

"You will take this note," he said to his valet, "and deliver it into no hands but her own. It will, at least, serve to convince her she has one friend in Paris, and gratitude may, perhaps, induce her to give me a speedy answer. She will, no doubt, give me credit for good intentions, and, of course, will send a reply, requesting a speedy interview."

Boulet took the note without making any further observation, and seeing that his absence was more required than his company, he left the room, and made instant preparations for going on his errand.

CHAPTER XXXIII.

A PROSPECT OF CLEARING UP CERTAIN DOUBTS.

BOULET so far succeeded in his mission, that he obtained an interview with Miss Smith, to whom he delivered his master's letter, and, in return, was desired to inform the Count de Morceau that she would see him on the following morning. This intelligence was exceedingly gratifying to the nobleman, who, having well rewarded his servant for the zeal he had manifested in his behalf, retired to his own apartment, in order that he might see no more of the countess that day, and thus avoid those outpourings of jealousy with which, of late, she had been very apt to assail him.

At the hour appointed on the following day he set out, accompanied by his valet, for the splendid mansion occupied by Miss Smith, and having reached the place of destination, he was speedily introduced to the lady, who, however, he could not fail to observe received him with marked coldness. But the count would not appear to observe this, and having briefly alluded to the letter he had sent on the preceding day, he continued,—

"With the explanation that has thus taken place, you may now conceive, madam, the despair that has taken possession of my soul from the moment that I learnt the sad fact of your being the lady that I had once expected to make the sharer of my wealth and titles."

"Perhaps, my lord," she replied, "it would have been as well if this interview had been spared us; but since you have been pleased to honour me with this visit, I will take the opportunity to say, that whatever disappointment may have taken place, I cannot in any way blame myself for it. In fact, I have been deceived by a villain, and—"

"I see, madam," interrupted the count; "you are now alluding, of course, to the treatment you have received from the marquis."

"Indeed, you have mistaken my meaning altogether," she replied. "The villain I mention, is the person who brought me over from England, and who, instead of taking me to Havre, where I was to have met you, conducted me to Paris, and after betraying me to the Marquis de Noailles, made his escape with what precipitation he could."

"Something of this I understood before," exclaimed the count, "and execrating, as I do, the villain who thus basely betrayed you, I am now here to offer my poor services in your behalf. The scoundrel shall be sought out, even though he may have fled for refuge in the furthest corner of the world, and thus I may, at least, prove to you, madam, the devoted love which has been blighted through the machinations of the fellows who brought you here."

"There is no necessity for taking any further trouble in behalf of one whose destiny is now fixed," replied Miss Smith, coldly. "You are, of course, aware, my lord, of my present situation, and to accept the offers you have been pleased to make, would make it appear to the marquis that I am ungrateful for the kindness and indulgence with which he treats me."

"But he has deceived you, madam," said the count, "and, therefore, merits not the gratitude you feel towards him."

"If I have been deceived," she replied firmly, "the fault has been entirely my own. I was ambitious to fill a station far higher than my humble birth gave me any right to expect. At first, I believed myself to be the wife of the Marquis de Noailles, and great was my disappointment and shame when I discovered the imposition that had been practised on me. But reflection brought its own antidote, and instead of repining at the fate that had befallen me, I saw that I had suffered the just punishment of my ambition, and resigning myself to my fate, determined to endure with patience that which there was no possibility of avoiding."

"And does the marquis still love you?" asked her visitor.

"He does," she replied, "and every day convinces me more and more, that though he cannot raise me to his own level, yet does he still continue to treat me with that kindness which my dependence upon him so much requires."

No. 30

"May I ask you, madam," said the count, "whether it is your intention to visit England?"

"I believe I shall never do so," she replied, "for there are none there that I ever wish to see. I would, however, ask whether you ever open to hear from Mr. Walter Gravestow since he communicated with you respecting myself?"

"He is a villain!" exclaimed the count; "would you believe it, madam, he tried to bargain with me for your ruin, and your falling into the hands of the Marquis de Noailles has alone saved you from becoming the victim of the man who professed to be your friend."

"I have lately began to suspect as much," she replied; "and now, pray sir, can you inform me what has become of this Gravestow?"

"I know but little of him, except that he is married," replied the Count de Morceau.

"And to whom is he married?" asked Miss Smith.

"To the daughter of his late employer and benefactor, who, I suppose, you have heard, was basely murdered."

"Good Heavens!" she exclaimed, "was Mr. Wentford murdered?"

"He was."

"By whom?"

"It was reported that he fell by the hand of a male servant in his employ," answered the count.

"And how long is it," said the female, anxiously, "since this dreadful occurrence took place?"

"Why, I can't tell you that very well," replied the count, "but it was some time ago, at any rate. However, if you wish to know any further particulars, my valet is in your house, and he, perhaps, remembers more of the affair than I do myself. Shall I call him in?"

"By all means, my lord."

Boulet was accordingly summoned, and in reply to the questions that were put to him he began a long rambling narrative, which was at length checked by his master, who demanded if he recollected by whom the murder was reported to have been committed.

"Oh, yes," he replied, "by his man-servant, to be sure."

"Did you ever hear his name?" enquired the female.

"I heard it at the time," replied Boulet, "but I have quite forgotten it now."

"How long ago was it that the murder was committed?" she asked.

"Somewhere about the time of your expected arrival at Havre," answered the valet.

"And did they ever take the man who was suspected of the murder?" inquired Miss Smith.

"No, he escaped."

"What motive had he for doing it?"

"That would be difficult to say," replied Boulet; "but I believe he ran away directly afterwards with the dairy-maid, and so, perhaps, they both had a hand in it."

"Good Heavens!" cried Miss Smith, "is it possible the female could have been suspected of any share in the cruel deed that robbed an old man of his life?"

"Why, it's hard to believe such a thing," replied Boulet, "and I dare say, after all, there's no truth in the report."

"As far as the girl is concerned," observed the count, "I dare say, rumour was mistaken. But that the old gentleman was murdered there can be no doubt, because we heard it through Mr. Smithson, whose word, I believe, is worthy of credit."

"And what says the world of Mr. Gravestow?" asked the female in a tone of anxiety.

"Why, I believe, there are very few who have a good opinion of him," replied the count; "but he is an artful villain, and whenever he practices evil he always contrives to place himself beyond suspicion. As I told you just now, he made a bargain to deliver you into my hands, and it was only by an accident that you were betrayed to the marquis."

"I remember," said the female, "that he told me you were a wealthy nobleman, who was anxious to unite yourself with an English female, and that I was the fortunate person who had been selected to become your wife."

"And what motive could he have for proposing a pretended marriage?" asked the count.

"That, I believe, I can explain," she replied, "for the truth is, he thought I should be anxious to visit England as soon as I come to be possessed of a title, and as that was a thing but ill united to his plans, he proposed that I should become your mistress in order that shame might prevent my ever wishing to return to my native country."

"Well," exclaimed the count, "that he is a black-hearted villain has, I think, been pretty clearly proved. But, perhaps, as he is now married he may have reformed, and turned from the evil of his ways."

"Are you certain that it was Miss Wentford that he married?" asked the female.

"I am quite sure that he married the daughter of the unfortunate gentleman that was murdered," answered the Count de Morceau."

"And, I suppose, has since succeeded him in his business?"

"He has a large share in it, I believe," replied the nobleman, "but he is either too indolent or too proud to take any active part in it, and I rather think the management of it is entrusted to Mr. Smithson, who has long been engaged in the firm as principal clerk."

"And Mr. Gravestow, I suppose," she observed, "lives at his ease, and squanders away the money which poor Mr. Wentford was at so much trouble to save?"

"I rather think you are right enough there, madam," replied the count; "for he is reckless of every thing, and is shunned by every one that is not as base and abandoned as himself."

"And his wife, perhaps, lives unhappily with him," cried the female.

"There is but too much reason to fear she does," replied the nobleman; "for a man like Walter Gravestow is hardly likely to make a happy home for his wife. He married her, I believe, for the sake of her money, and once having that in his possession, he will care very little for her afterwards."

"Then bitterly must she repent that she heeded not to the advice of those friends who would have persuaded her to place her affections upon a more worthy lover," cried Miss Smith;—"but she always thought better of him than any one else did, and now she has, no doubt, seen cause to repent the partiality she showed him."

"You knew her, it seems?" observed the count.

"Slightly," replied the female, with hesitation;—"I lived in the village near where Mr. Wentford resided, and what little I knew respecting the family, was picked up from the rumours that went about the neighbourhood."

"And did you happen to hear," asked the count, "whether any disagreement ever took place between Walter Gravestow and Mr. Wentford?"

"I never heard anything of the kind," she replied; "but perhaps you had some motive in asking me the question?"

"No," replied the count, "it was merely a passing thought, and popped out quite unawares. But I dare say they were very good friends, for Gravestow is too artful a dissembler to quarrel with the man whose daughter he was courting, and whose property he expected at some future time to enjoy."

"It is most likely, my lord," she replied; "and, indeed, if any disagreement had taken place between them, it would surely have been talked about in the neighbourhood among persons who always interfere with the business of other persons. However, I should like to know the address of Mr. Smithson, as it is not at all unlikely I may have to write to him before long."

"I can get it for you, madam," said the count, "and with your permission, I will call upon you again, as soon as I have ascertained the direction of the person you have just named."

This request was instantly complied with, and the count took his leave, well pleased at having an excuse to call again upon a lady with whom he was so well pleased.

CHAPTER XXXIV.

A VISIT TO OLD ACQUAINTANCES.

AGAIN returning to England, we must now briefly inform the reader that in consequence of Mrs. Dawson's bad state of health, she was recommended to try a change of climate, and as her husband was about to take another journey to the continent, for the firm he was employed by, it was arranged that she should accompany him in the hope of recovering from the effects of those serious disasters which had so much underminded her constitution. The consequence of this was, that they let their house furnished for the period it was expected they would be absent, and thus our heroine and her fellow servant were compelled to look out for new situations.

With Susan this proved to be a task of very little difficulty, for she shortly afterwards engaged herself in the family of a Mr. Plumley, once an eminent drysalter in the city, but now a wealthy man, retired from the turmoils of a mercantile life, and dwelling at this time in the neighbourhood of Dalston, where, with his wife, and a couple of grown up daughters, he determined to pass the remainder of his days in that peace and quiet for which he had long been toiling.

In this situation Susan had reasonable grounds for supposing she should live comfortably enough; and as two or three days intervened previous to entering upon her new service, she determined to visit a few friends she had in London, in order that they might know where she was, in case they should at any time want to find her.

The first visit she paid was to Mrs. Cheerlie, of whose kindness and good intentions she had had so many proofs, and to do the worthy old lady justice, she received her young acquaintance with all the affection of a mother; congratulating her upon the good luck she had experienced in meeting with a situation that promised to be so comfortable, and over and over again assuring her that she was still disposed to be her friend and counsellor, and desiring that should she ever want advice, to come to her, and she would always do the utmost in her power to relieve her from any difficulties that might rise in her way.

"You have so far been tolerably lucky," she said; "but none of us can foresee troubles, and though you have hitherto acted with great prudence for one so young, it may yet happen that you will want my experience to guide and direct you. And now, my dear, having said thus much, I must ask whether you have heard anything of Edwin since he left Mr. Gravestow's house so mysteriously?"

"I have not," replied Susan; "for I never receive any news from Summerfield, and one of my objects in paying this visit was, to enquire whether you had any intelligence to give of my little favourite?"

"Nothing," answered the housekeeper, "except that he went to sea, but whether he ever returned to England afterwards, I have been unable to find out."

"Is it certain he went to sea?" asked Susan, anxiously.

"Why, there can be no doubt about that," replied Mrs. Cheerlie, "because he wrote from on board ship to poor Mrs. Gravestow, and the letter was brought in a vessel that they fell in with on their outward passage. But where he was going to, or what he intended doing nobody knows, for he was quite silent upon both those subjects."

"And why, I wonder," cried Susan, "did he leave us in doubt, when he knew how anxious his friends would be to learn his future destination?"

"Why, the truth is," said Mrs. Cheerlie, "he had enemies to think about as well as friends. He knew very well that Mr. Gravestow would never cease to prosecute him as long as he knew where to find him, and, for my own part, I think Edwin has acted very prudently in keeping out of his reach till he is old enough to take care of himself. By and by, I dare say, he will return home a rich man, and then Mr. Gravestow will have the additional satisfaction of knowing that it was his own base conduct towards the boy that drew him from a course of inactivity, to one that has ended in raising him to independence."

"But I am afraid," sighed Susan Hoply, "we shall never see anything more of the poor boy."

"Depend upon it we shall, though," replied Mrs. Cheerlie, "and that, too, before long. Edwin has friends in England that he will be glad to see again, and he will take the first opportunity that offers to come back again."

"And if he should return," exclaimed Susan, "he'll find Mrs. Gravestow a more unhappy woman than he even left her."

"That's likely enough," observed Mrs. Cheerlie, "but, at any rate, he'll find her released from the society of her good-for-nothing brute of a husband."

"Indeed!" cried Susan; "have they separated, then?"

"Oh, yes, some time ago," answered the housekeeper. "She put up with her husband's savage cruelty as long as she was able, and at length, finding that his treatment was no longer to be endured, she made up her mind to leave him. And, I dare say, he was not sorry to part with his poor wife, for he had secured all her property to himself, and as there was no chance of any more money coming from that quarter, he agreed to allow her a small pittance to subsist upon, and from that time they have been living separate. Alas! she deserved a better fate; for Mrs. Gravestow is not like some wives who bring their troubles upon themselves by giving way to their own violent tempers."

"Do you happen to know where she is living now?" asked Susan, in a tone of anxiety.

"I do not," replied Mrs. Cheerlie, "and I believe she wishes to remain in obscurity so as to avoid the man who has so cruelly blighted her prospects. I have, however, reason to believe she is residing with a female relative somewhere on the sea coast, and in which place she intends to remain till circumstances shall happen to turn more in her favour."

"And what," asked Susan, "has become of Mr. Cornish, who used to live with them as steward?"

"He has left the family altogether," replied the housekeeper, "but I believe is living somewhere in the neighbourhood of Summerfield. It seems his master's temper was so bad that the old gentleman could not bear it, and as Mrs. Gravestow is no longer able to support an establishment, he is now living upon the interest of the money he has been able to save while he has been in service."

"And his wife," observed Susan, "has, I suppose, also left the family where she lived so long?"

"Oh, yes," replied Mrs. Cheerlie, "but the poor creature's health has declined so much of late, that her husband wrote to me a short time ago, to say that he believed there was no chance of her surviving many weeks. Indeed, Mr. Cornish seems bitterly to regret the prospect of being left alone, and in a postcript to his letter he throws out pretty broad hints that, as I am a lone widow, it might be as well to consider in good time whether it would not be worth while to leave my situation, and to enter with him once more into the holy state of matrimony."

"Which, it must be confessed," cried Susan, with surprise, "is rather a premature proposal, to say the least of it."

"Very true, my dear," replied Mrs. Cheerlie, "and so I shall tell him the next time I write. However, he is not a young man, you know, and, perhaps, he thinks if ever he should marry again, there will be very little time left for courting, and all that sort of thing that is so agreeable to younger folks than himself. Besides, after all, you know, my dear, it was only said to try me on the subject, and you may be sure that a steady, middle-aged widow like myself, could never think of taking a husband again, unless the offer was such a one as prudence would not suffer me to refuse."

"You are not inclined, then, to marry again, Mrs. Cheerlie?" observed Susan.

"Oh, bless your heart, no," replied the housekeeper; "I have had one very good husband in my time, and that ought to be quite sufficient for any woman,—unless, indeed, she happens to be left a widow at a very early age. However, talking upon this subject, reminds me of your own little love affairs before you left Summerfield; there was William Dain, you know, the young miller, that everybody supposed was going to be your husband; and yet, after all, it seems that he has forgotten you in your absence, and——"

"You wrong him, Mrs. Cheerlie," interrupted our heroine; "William Dain will never forget me, though it must needs be confessed that my long silence, after the many letters he has written to me, is enough to make him think that I have altogether ceased to think of him."

"Ah!" cried the housekeeper, "then that accounts for what I heard about him the other day."

"What have you heard?" demanded Susan, eagerly.

"That he is courting another girl."

"Nay, then, believe me, 'tis a false and wicked report," cried our heroine, "for William Dain loved me too well ever to transfer his affections to another."

"And yet," answered Mrs. Cheerlie, "I think you will find the report too true; and if you wish it, I can name the person that is likely to be his wife."

"Do so;" exclaimed Susan; "yet, even then I shall continue to believe that you have been imposed upon by persons who delight in slandering those of whose goodness they are envious."

"What think you of Martha Pratt, for a rival?" asked the housekeeper.

"You mean the sister of Dolly Pratt, the dairy-maid, who ran away from the service of Mr. Wentford on the very night of the poor old gentleman's murder?"

"I do," replied Mrs. Cheerlie; "and as your brother Andrew disappeared on the very same night, there was a report among the neighbours that——"

"I remember it but too well," sighed our heroine; "it was said that he murdered his master and ran away with Dolly Pratt, from which time, alas! nothing has ever been heard of either of them."

"Be that as it may," said Mrs. Cheerlie, "your lover, William Dain, is now paying his addresses to her sister Martha, and if all that I hear is true, it seems likely enough that they will be married before very long."

"And if so," replied Susan, wiping away a tear, "I can hardly blame him. I have, myself, treated him with coldness and neglect, and it was, therefore, hardly to be expected that he would continue to regard one who had given him every reason to believe no longer remembered him with kindness. Indeed, when last we met, I told him that I would never marry till I had cleared my brother's name from the foul crime he had been charged with, and at the same time, conjured him to think no more of me, as I feared it would only be the means of blighting his own future prospects."

"Then, in my opinion, my dear, you acted rather foolishly," exclaimed Mrs. Cheerlie, "for husbands are not to be found every day, and William's was too good an offer to be rejected by a girl in your situation. Besides, though Martha is considered to be a tolerably pretty girl, I believe it is not so much for her beauty that he is courting her as for a good sum of money that he expects to have with her."

"Martha Pratt," observed our heroine, "never had any expectation of money, that I am aware of."

"Aye, aye," replied the housekeeper, "but circumstances have changed for the better with her. She is continually receiving handsome presents of money from some quarter, that she couldn't make out; but at length she received a letter from her sister Dolly that cleared up the mystery, and now it seems that the runaway dairy maid is living in great splendour and magnificence."

"Is it possible," cried Susan, "that Dolly Pratt has thus raised herself above the lowly situation in which she was born?"

"You may depend on it, as I've told you nothing but the truth," replied Mrs. Cheerlie, "though I'm sorry to add there can be very little doubt that the poor girl has been made the victim of some wealthy libertine, who keeps her in some retired place where she may never be seen or heard of."

"Then, of course, we have proof," cried Susan, "that the story told of her having eloped with my brother Andrew is false!"

"That's clear enough," answered Mrs. Cheerlie; "and, in fact, from what I have gathered, it appears that Dolly, in the letter to her sister, speaks of only just having heard of Mr. Wentford's murder, and alludes, with astonishment, to the rumour which had reached her of your brother being suspected of the cruel deed; she then goes on to express her own decided opinion to the contrary, and earnestly requests her sister Martha to send a full account of all that took place after the old gentleman's death, in order that she may ascertain whether it is in her power to throw any light upon the subject. This, I believe, Martha has done, and we may, therefore, soon expect an answer that will satisfy us whether or not it is in her power to clear up the mystery that has so long clouded the affair."

"Then, at any rate," cried Susan, "she declares that Andrew did not leave the house with her on the night of the murder."

"To be sure she does," replied the housekeeper; "but that's no more than I always thought myself, and so, I believe, did every body else, but those that wanted to throw the blame upon his shoulders."

"But ere I rest, all must be equally well satisfied," exclaimed Susan, firmly. "Tell me, then, where I can find Martha Pratt's sister, and though I might have to walk to the farthest extremity of the world I would willingly undertake the task to clear up my brother's character."

"Bless your heart," exclaimed the housekeeper, "neither you nor I are ever likely to know where she is to be found; even Martha herself is kept in the dark upon that subject, and in my opinion, Dolly is so thoroughly ashamed of her conduct, that she will never let any body know where she is, for fear of meeting the reproach she deserves."

"And why do you think she is ashamed?" asked Susan.

"Because she particularly cautions her sister against ambition," replied Mrs. Cheerlie, "and hints that vanity has been the cause of her own downfall from virtue."

"But from that," observed Susan, "we might also argue that she has married some wealthy man, who treats her with harshness and neglect."

"I'm afraid it's worse than that," said Mrs. Cheerlie, shaking her head gravely.

"But I suppose Martha has answered her letter," observed our heroine.

"Oh, yes, that I know she has done."

"And where does she address her communications?"

"Not direct to her sister," replied Mrs. Cheerlie, "but sends through an agent, who undertakes that any letters shall be safely conveyed to her."

"That agent then," exclaimed Susan, "can surely give me the information I require."

"Indeed, but you are mistaken," answered the housekeeper, "for Martha has applied to the agent on the subject, and he professes to know nothing more of the affair than that he sends to another person, who is the immediate channel through whom Dolly receives any communications that her friends have to make."

"It is strange, too," cried Susan, "that so much mystery should be observed even with her friends."

"Why, the fact is, she is ashamed of being seen," answered Mrs. Cheerlie, "and I suppose she's afraid of her own bad example being followed by her sister, who is quite pretty and simple enough to be led away by flattery."

"But from what you said just now," observed Susan, with some little hesitation, "Martha Pratt is likely, ere long, to become the wife of William Dain."

"That's true enough," answered the housekeeper; "he has been courting the wench for some little time, and it's natural enough to suppose that it will end in their marriage. I've heard say, however, that William was rather cautious at first, but now that he sees her sister is so well off, he begins to think differently I suppose, and no doubt he will be glad to get a wife that can bring him some money."

"You wrong him, Mrs. Cheerlie," cried our heroine; "William Dain has a soul too independent for avarice, or he would not have sued for one as humble as myself even against the express commands of his more worldly-minded father."

"Well, well," exclaimed Mrs. Cheerlie, "I see it would be in vain to

say anything to the prejudice of so great a favourite, and as that's the case
I can only advise you to make up your mind to see him the husband of your
rival, who, after all, ought not to suffer from any suspicions we may happen
to entertain against her sister Dolly."

"Perhaps he could not have made a more suitable match," returned
our heroine; "for whatever people may say to the contrary, I believe Martha
Pratt to be a very discreet and prudent girl."

"But," said Mrs. Cheerlie, "for all that, I don't see but you might as
well have had him yourself, my dear."

"And so I might if it had not been for what I told him when we last
parted," answered Susan; "he offered to marry me, even at a time when
most people were regarding me with coldness, because they chose to suspect that my brother Andrew was concerned in the murder of his master.
But I loved William too well to bring disgrace upon him and his family,
and for that reason I determined never to marry him nor anybody else till
I had fixed the crime upon those who really committed it."

"Which I'm afraid you will never be able to do," observed the housekeeper.

"I have sometimes thought so myself," replied Susan; "but just at this
moment I despair less than ever I did; and, in spite of the length of time
that has elapsed, I have yet hopes of being able to denounce the villains
that robbed a helpless old man of his life. At any rate we have now proof
that Andrew did not elope with Dolly Pratt on the night in question, and
if we can only discover where she is to be found, it is likely she may be
able to throw some light on the affair that will guide me to a successful
termination of my labours."

"But I believe," observed the housekeeper, "that Mr. Gravestow has
spread it abroad that Dolly Pratt and your brother Andrew were lovers."

"He has stated that which he knows to be false then," cried Susan, "for

No. 31

every one was aware that, though my brother had confessed his love to
Dolly, her pride had induced her to reject him, in the hope that a better
offer would be made from some other quarter. In fact, I remember very
well seeing a stranger prowling about Mr. Wentford's gardens on the night
of the murder, and I have since had my suspicions that he was the person
that eloped with Dolly Pratt."

"And have you any idea who the person was?" asked Mrs. Cheerlie
with deep anxiety.

"I never knew his name," replied Susan; "but dark as it was at the
time, I had a notion that it was a man that I had seen two or three times
engaged in secret conversation with Mr. Gravestow."

"Why, bless my heart!" cried Mrs. Cheerlie; "who knows but that
may have been the very ruffian that murdered your poor master? And
yet," she continued after a pause, "one would hardly think—bad as Mr.
Gravestow is—that he would associate with a villain like that."

"I have had my suspicions about it," answered Susan; "but like yourself, I have been unwilling to believe that Mr. Gravestow could have made
such a companion as I have been speaking off."

"What sort of man was he?" asked the housekeeper.

"One of the very lowest description that you can possibly imagine,"
replied our heroine; "his appearance denoted him to be a ruffian, and I
have often, since that time, wondered how Mr. Gravestow could hold communication with a person whose character was so evident."

"And did it ever strike you," asked Mrs. Cheerlie, "that the man
you are speaking about might have been the person that murdered your
master?"

"I have thought so," answered our heroine; "but from that time I have
never seen him, and for that reason I have kept my suspicions to myself."

"Well, patience and time may perhaps bring matters to light," said Mrs.
Cheerlie; "and meanwhile we must content ourselves with waiting for the
result. Mr. Gravestow, I must, however, tell you, is now a magistrate
of the county in which he lives, and, of course, will afford us any information or assistance that we may happen to require."

Here the conversation ended, and Susan returned home to ruminate on
all she had heard, and to devise fresh schemes for making the discovery she
had so much at heart.

On the following day she again left home and went to visit Amelia, who,
by the assistance of her friends, had been enabled to open a small millinery
shop for the support of herself and child. She was much pleased to see our
heroine again, and after the first greetings were over, began to relate all that
happened to her since they had last seen each other.

"Thanks to my generous benefactors," she said; "I am now placed in
a situation that gives me an opportunity of supporting myself and poor
little Amelia, without asking the aid of those who, in my distress, would have
left us both to starve. Indeed, I have began to think that all my troubles
were at an end, and so they would have been, I believe, but the other day
who should pass, as I was standing at the door, but Mr. Edwards—"

"Mr. Edwards!" interrupted Susan, hastily; "what, the great linendraper in Dover-street?"

"No, not him," replied Amelia; "but the libertine friend of Mr. Willis
Gayton, who I several times mentioned to you in the course of my narra-
tion."

"I remember," said our heroine; "he was a worthless fellow, and it is
indeed, most unfortunate that he should have discovered where you are
living. But, of course, if he should have the impertinence to thrust himself again into your society, you will know how to treat him."

"In that case," replied Amelia, "I should desire him to leave me, and at the same time express my wish that he honours me no more with his visits. However, I am not quite sure that he wishes to renew the acquaintance, for he was rather cool in his manner, and after telling me that he had been abroad nearly ever since we had last seen each other, he spoke of a will, or paper of some kind or other that was left in our lodgings, and which, it seems, he now wants very particularly."

"And do you recollect ever having seen such a document as he spoke of?" enquired Susan.

"Oh yes, there was such a paper lying about I know," replied Amelia; "but what became of it is more than I can undertake to say; for troubles came fast upon me after he went away, and whether the papers were burnt among others that I considered as being of no use, or was taken with the rest of my goods by my rapacious landlord, I know not."

"And does he say it was of any particular consequence to him?" asked our heroine.

"He does," replied Amelia, "and if I may judge from the agitation of his manner, he would give almost everything that he is worth to have it restored."

"Did it immediately concern himself?" inquired Susan.

"I should rather imagine not," answered the other; "and as he is not a man of very strict honour, it strikes me that he only wants it for the purpose of doing some one else an injury."

"In that case," observed Susan, "it is better that it should be lost than fall into such hands. Indeed, I never hear a will mentioned, but I think of the one that was made by poor Mr. Wentford, and which never could be found after the old gentleman's murder, though the house was thoroughly searched from the very top to the bottom. That it was there a very short time before, everybody about the place was quite certain, and so, as if Mr. Walter Gravestow had not already injured my brother Andrew quite enough by accusing him of the murder, he must needs throw out hints that he had no doubt he had taken it with him when he so mysteriously disappeared."

"But it could have been of no use to him even if he had taken it away," returned Amelia.

"That's just what I said myself," answered our heroine; "but you know when people once take a prejudice into their head, it's no easy thing to argue them out of it. So the story still went against Andrew, and I dare say, even to the present time, the people in that neighbourhood would tell you that he first murdered his master, and then ran away with all he could lay his hands upon."

"It is hard that the innocent should have to bear such a cruel accusation," said Amelia; "and yet there is a consolation in knowing that some day or other the truth will come out, and that those who did the deed, will have to bear the punishment they so justly merit."

"I try to console myself with that thought," replied Susan; "but it's not easy to get rid of the weight of one's cares, while the guilty are triumphing over the misery that has been inflicted on my unfortunate brother. However, it's useless to talk of that now, so tell me what this Mr. Edwards said when you told him the will was not in your possession?"

"Why, of course, he could not say much," answered Amelia; "but his looks were quite enough to convince me that he felt the disappointment greatly, and no doubt he would have been very angry with me for losing sight of the will, only that perhaps he thought mildness would be more likely to make me assist him in the discovery."

"Did he ask you to exert yourself for that purpose?" enquired Susan.

"Oh yes," replied the other; "but he was very cautious how he spoke to me about it at first. He said the thing was not of so much consequence to himself as it was to others, and that though its loss would be trifling to him, there were parties who were so deeply interested, that its loss might terminate in their utter ruin. But I am convinced that he was only trying to deceive me in that respect, for I have been acquainted with him some time, and never do I remember him caring for anybody so long as he was himself secure."

"He has some deep scheme to play, I have no doubt," answered our heroine, "and it will be your own fault if you do not discover what it is before you have done with him. Not that I would advise you to keep up any acquaintance with him, for he seems to be a very worthless man, and the less you have to say to him the better."

"I have made up my mind to get rid of him as soon as possible," replied Amelia; "but if he will come to my house, I know not how I can very turn him away. Besides, he is still on intimate terms with Mr. Gayton, and in spite of my dislike to the man, I am willing to sacrifice my own personal feelings in favour of my poor child."

"And do you think then Mr. Gayton will ever care anything for your little Amelia?"

"I am in hopes he may, though, perhaps, I am wrong," replied Amelia, with a deep sigh. "I have already told you that he married after he left me, and from what this Mr. Edwards has told me, none of the children that have been born to him are now living. That circumstance may make him remember Amelia, and if he would but do something towards raising her from her present lowly condition, I could, without a murmur, drag out my own life in penury and want."

"I am afraid you are placing your reliance upon a broken reed," exclaimed Susan, "and though I would not say anything to make your spirits lower than they are, I cannot help advising you to think nothing more either of Mr. Godfrey or his friend, for they are both bad alike, and would not see you at all unless it was to serve some selfish purposes of their own."

Susan now took leave of her friend, and once more turned her footsteps towards home, upon reaching which she thought over all that she had heard from Amelia, and the more she reflected upon the subject, the more did she wonder what could have made Edwards so anxious about the will.

CHAPTER XXXV.

THE CITIZEN AND HIS FAMILY.

At the time appointed Susan Hoply went to her new situation, and though the family was not all that might have been wished, yet it seemed to be composed of kind-hearted people, who would do their best towards rendering her stay among them comfortable.

Mr. Plumley himself was a man that had passed the whole of his life in the bustle of business, and so intent had he been upon the one object that guided him,—that of making money,—that he had troubled himself very little with observing the usages of society, and consequently when he retired, he found himself utterly at a loss what to do with himself. Nor was Mrs. Plumley in any way superior to her worthy lord and master, for he had married her from his kitchen, and though in every respect a most prudent wife, yet being totally without education, she was anything but fitted for the society which their wealth and respectability might otherwise have introduced them to.

Thus profoundly ignorant themselves, they saw no use in spending a great deal of money in the education of their two daughters, who, it must be confessed, had no great liking for the drudgery of school exercises, and the consequence was that they left off their studies nearly as they had commenced them, and felt perfectly satisfied that ignorance would not stand in their way of contracting favourable marriage alliances, when it should become known that they were each the heiress of a tempting fortune, of about thirty thousand pounds. At any rate, they took very good care that the after piece of intelligence should be pretty generally spread abroad, and their father, instead of reproaching them for such an act of folly, added a clencher to it, by hinting to a few select friends that half as much again might come to them in the event of their marrying men of whom he could entirely approve.

Yet even this bait seems to have made very little impression, except a few fortune hunters, who had no sooner made known their pretensions, and explained their own circumstances, than Mr. Plumley sent them to the right about, with an assurance that his daughters must have husbands with fortunes nearly equal to their own, or in the event of their allying themselves with men of desperate means, there must be something in the shape of a title,—not lower than that of a lord, to compensate for the deficiency in pecuniary means.

This was quite sufficient to prevent any offers being made, for there are few wealthy men that would seek to ally themselves with ignorance, such as was to be found in the two Miss Plumley's, and there seemed to be a very tolerable chance of their dying old maids, when a lucky circumstance threw them in the way of a man of title, who seemed quite disposed to marry one of them, though which one,—as their fortunes were equal, was a matter of perfect indifference to him. Be this as it may, however, they were determined that he should be the husband of one or the other, and after a good deal of coquetting, it was perceived that his chief attentions were directed towards Miss Emma Plumley, the elder of the two ladies.

This introduction had taken place whilst they were visiting one of the watering places, and when it was imagined they had sufficiently interested the Marquis Valliere in their behalf, they announced their intention of immediately returning home, in the expectation that by so doing the marquis would at once declare himself, and thus bring the affair to a climax. But in this they were doomed to be disappointed, for the aristocratic lover received the announcement with perfect composure; expressing himself, however, as rather sorry that he should be for a time deprived of their society, and requesting permission to visit them at Dalston as soon as certain important business would allow him to do so. This, of course, was acceded to with much willingness by the young ladies and their mother, and they returned home a few days before our heroine entered their service.

Susan had not been in the house many hours before she heard the whole history from Lucy, the attendant on the two young ladies, who related the affair with a great deal of satisfaction as it so happened that she had been let into the whole secret by the ladies themselves, on the express condition that she was not to mention it to anybody else, for the world. It was in vain that Susan endeavoured to check a narrative in which she took so little interest, for Lucy could keep the secret no longer, and as the new servant was quite a stranger in the place, she was determined to prove her confidence in her, by making her a sharer in a secret which she considered of so much importance.

"It isn't everybody I'd tell such things to," she said, "but somehow or other I've taken a mighty fancy to you, my dear, and I'm sure you wouldn't on any account get a poor girl like me into a scrape, by saying who it was that told you how lucky young missis has been to pick up a noblemanf or a lover."

"But are you sure he is what he represents himself to be ?" asked our heroine.

"Of course he is," replied Lucy ;—"you don't suppose such a fine gentleman as he is would condescend to impose upon either of my young ladies."

"I hope your confidence in him is well founded," answered Susan ;—"but there are adventurers in the world who are ever upon the look out for dupes, and as I never heard of this Marquis Valliere, as he calls himself, I feel some doubts as to his being the nobleman he represents."

"Ah !" cried Lucy, "you haven't heard of him because he's a foreigner. Bless your heart, he's got immense estates abroad, and from what his footman, John, told me, there's no end of his wealth."

"And so," said Susan, laughing, "you have contrived to pick up an acquaintance with his servant ?"

"It wasn't me that began it," answered the other, "for I don't like putting myself forward in any such way. No, no, Mr. John introduced himself to me, and of course I couldn't be so rude as to refuse exchanging a few words with so civil-spoken a young man."

"But did it never strike you," asked Susan, "that the servant may be in league with his master, and that he only paid you a few unmeaning compliments in order to try what information he could pump out of you ?"

"I never thought of that," replied the girl ; "but even if such was his intention, it has done him no good, for I was very cautious what I said, and only told him that Miss Emma would be very willing to marry such a nice nobleman as his master seemed to be, and that she would have thirty thousand pounds of her own on the day of her marriage."

"Which I dare say was all the man wanted to know," observed our heroine. "However, the mischief, if there is any, has been done, and I should now like to know how this supposed servant contrived to scrape an acquaintance with you."

"Oh, that all happened quite by accident," replied Lucy. "The truth is I was going to the milliner's one day for my youngest mistress, when up comes a smart footman in full livery, and having said a great many polite things, he began to ask about my young ladies, and hoped they were both in good health. So I told him they were both pretty well only that I thought one of 'em was in love, and then all of a sudden he asked if I thought it was with his master.

"'Who is your master ?' says I.

"'The Marquis Valliere,' says he.

"Then I up and told him the marquis was the very man, and that if he cared anything about Miss Emma, he'd relieve her mind at once by declaring his intentions, and that I could answer for it he wouldn't find her hard-hearted."

"That was imprudent at any rate," observed Susan.

"So it might be " replied the other, "but I'm a plain spoken girl, and hang me if I could help saying what I did. However, John didn't seem to take any advantage of what I'd said, for he remained silent a moment or so as if considering the matter over in his mind, and then, after telling me what a great man his master was, he enquired very particularly whether the Plumley's were respectable people.

"'Why, of course they are,' said I, 'or you may depend on it I should not be long in their service.' Then he asked whether they kept a carriage, and when I said three, he replied that was nothing, for his master had twenty-seven, and I don't know how many horses besides."

"His exaggeration," observed Susan, "convinces me more and more that this marquis is neither more nor less than a rank impostor."

"I can't think it," replied the other, "because John was such a well-spoken young man, that I'm sure he'd be above doing a dirty action. He confessed, however, that he had heard my master was nothing but a retired drysalter, and that, says he, would put a stop to the marriage at once, because the marquis belongs to such a noble family, that if Miss Emma possessed twenty times thirty thousand pounds, he could never introduce her as his wife, if she was nothing more than the daughter of a tradesman. Well, thinks I, that's uncommon proud of him to be sure; but then great folks have queer notions, and perhaps it wouldn't be right to offend his friends by marrying beneath himself."

"And did you tell your young lady of this conversation with the footman?"

"Oh, yes, I told her of it directly."

"And I suppose she was so disgusted that she resolved never to think any more of the marquis."

"There you are wrong," replied Lucy, "for she is so desperately in love with him, that she declares if he won't have her, she'll never marry at all, but live and die an old maid. There's a horrid thing, Susan, only think of a young girl of twenty making such a vow as that."

"Did the marquis know where they lived?" asked Susan.

"Not till I told John," replied the other; "and, of course, it was not long before he let his master know all about it. I said we had got a nice place here at Dalston, and then John laughed, and said he had no doubt the marquis would honour us with a call, and that if ever it should come to be a match, that it would be a glorious thing for my young lady, as it was something worth looking after to get a title and a handsome husband such as those she had in view.

"'Why, as for that,' says I, 'I don't know that it will be better for her than for him, for, I dare say he ain't so rich but her thirty thousand pounds will be worth adding to his own fortune.'

"'Why, as for that,' says John, 'it's a mere flea-bite that my master won't think about; for, the truth is, he's so fond of Miss Emma, that I shouldn't wonder if he was to give up her thirty thousand pounds to make her sister's portion all the better.'

"'That,' said I, 'would be uncommon generous of him.'

"'It would,' replied John, 'but generosity ain't a novelty to my master, and so you'll find out, my dear,' says he, 'if you'll only help him to get the girl.'

"So then I told him again that I was sure Miss Emma wouldn't have any objection, and that her father and mother would jump at an offer that was likely to make their daughter the wife of the Marquis Valliere."

"That was imprudent of you, Lucy," cried our heroine; "for if this man is—as I suspect,—an impostor, it will serve to encourage him in the prosecution of the base schemes he has been forming."

"But we don't know that he is an impostor," replied Lucy; "and what's more, I feel quite satisfied in my own mind that he's what he seems to be. I only wish I'd such an offer, that's all, and see if I wouldn't accept it. To be sure, it's likely enough that John may make me his wife, but there's a vast difference between marrying a real marquis and a footman."

"And yet, mark my words," said Susan, "they will turn out to be one no better than the other."

"Ah!" cried Lucy, "that's because you've taken it into your head that the marquis ain't what he says he is. But never mind, we differ on that point, for I still think Mr. John a very nice sort of young man. But I haven't finished what I had to say yet, for I was going to tell you that the footman threw out a hint that his master would only have one more opportunity to see my lady, as he was going up to London on a visit· to the French Ambassador's, and that it might be a matter of a week before he should see her again; and that, you know, Susan, is a long while for lovers to be away from each other."

"And has he called here since your return home from the sea-side?" asked Susan.

"No, he ain't called yet," answered the other, "but master and mistress, and the two young ladies are anxiously looking for him every hour. He hasn't finished his visit at the the ambassabor's yet, but I dare say it won't be long before he comes to see Miss Emma, and settle with her father and mother when the happy day's to be."

"It's to be hoped Mr. Plumley will have his eyes opened to the artifices of this false marquis," replied Susan; " or who knows the misery and ruin that may follow the introduction of that man into the house. I have, indeed, a great mind to tell Miss Emma of my suspicions; it may serve to put her upon her guard against the schemes of a villain, and thus rescue her from the snare which he has artfully laid for her destruction."

"I'd advise you not to do anything of the kind," exclaimed Lucy, " for my young missis don't think so badly of him as you do, and there'd be the deuce to pay if you said a word against the man that she loves. However, that's her bell that's just rung, so I must leave you now, and, whatever you do, don't whisper a word to any one that you think the marquis an impostor."

And so saying, she bustled away, leaving Susan to ponder over the long narrative she had related to her. But the more our heroine considered the matter in her own mind, the more thoroughly did she become convinced that villany was at work, and though it might not be prudent just then to mention her suspicions to the parties most concerned, she determined to keep a sharp watch upon the marquis, should he visit the young lady as he had promised, and, in case her doubts were verified, to expose him to the well-merited obloquy of those he would have imposed upon.

On the following day, Susan observed a great bustle throughout the house, and running to the window, she saw the Marquis Valliere dismounting his horse, with all the airs of a finished coxcomb. Unfortunately, however, she could not catch a glimpse of his face, but from what she did see, she was more convinced than ever that he was the impostor she had at first imagined him to be. The would-be great man was then ushered into the drawing-room, where Mr. and Mrs. Plumley, and their two daughters, were assembled in state to receive their illustrious guest, who approached them with many bows and grimaces; having given utterance to the usual common-place nothings of fashionable life, he seated himself next to Miss Emma, who he ogled with the insolent familiarity that is fortunately known only to what are called the upper classes.

"My lord marquis, we're uncommonly obleeged to you for this visit," said the cringing Mr. Plumley; " we've been looking for you these three or four days; that is, my daughter Emma has, for all she looks just now as if butter wouldn't melt in her mouth. But, lord love you, she's young and innocent, and isn't up to the ways of the world just yet."

"Lawks, pa, how you talk!" said Emma, burying her face in her pocket-handkerchief to conceal the blushes that these remarks had called up. "I'm sure I haven't been looking for his lordship, though he did promise to call upon us as soon as he could after he came to town."

"I have taken the first opportunity of coming to see you, my dear, dear Miss," drawled the marquis; "though 'pon my honour I scarcely knew how to get away from my friends, who are pressing me on all sides to visit them, now that they know how short a time I've got to remain in England."

"Your lordship ain't going to leave us, I hope?" said Mrs. Plumley, in alarm.

"Family reasons compel me most reluctantly to do so," replied the marquis; "and, though I don't wish it to go any further than your-selves, I'm afraid my return home will prove anything but conducive to my happiness."

"Your lordship has met with no loss, I hope?" exclaimed Mr. Plumley, anxiously.

"Oh dear no," he replied, "no loss, my good sir; but the fact is, I happen to have rather an obstinate father, who is never satisfied unless he has his own way; and, would you believe it, he has actually written to me desiring my immediate return home, as he had made arrangements for my speedy marriage with one of the wealthiest heiresses in all France."

"Your marriage, my lord!" murmured all present, and poor Miss Emma was observed to grow so dreadfully pale, that her mother instantly rushed to her assistance with a huge smelling-bottle, which she thrust most unmercifully to her nose. Nor was Mr. Plumley less agitated, for his visions of title and honour were instantly put to flight, and in his de-spair, he already saw his daughter doomed to bestow her hand and fortune

No. 32

upon some unworthy plebeian. He, however, presently recovered himself, and, in a doleful tone, inquired whether he was compelled to obey the commands of his father, when they were thus arbitrarily laid upon him.

"I'm afraid there's no help for it, sir," replied the marquis. "In fact, I have considerable expectations from the duke, my father, and if I disobey him, it will be at the risk of forfeiting a very considerable fortune."

"But, if I am not misinformed, you are very rich, my lord?" observed Mr. Plumley.

"True, sir," answered the other, "but there are few of us that can afford to sacrifice a birthright, whilst there is a possibility of obliging those who are, perhaps, authorised to command our obedience. I have ever considered it my duty to obey my respected parent, and, much as I regret the course he has adopted, I must do violence to my own feelings, and give up the idol of my affections, rather than offend the author of my being."

And as he said this, he looked languishingly towards Emma, who had just sufficiently recovered herself to raise herself in her mother's arms, and gaze wildly about her.

"You see, my lord," said Mrs. Plumley, "how much my poor daughter takes on at hearing your determination. Poor thing!—she feels for you the affection of a sister, and nobody knows what will become of her when you leave us to go and live in that horrid country, where they say the men and women live upon nothing but nasty frogs."

"Does the gentle Emma indeed grieve for one so worthless as myself?" drawled his lordship.

"You may see with your own eyes that she does," replied Mrs. Plumley. "I'm sure she's done nothing but talk about you ever since your first meeting, and now to part never to meet again, is more than her nerves can bear."

"Upon my life I'm very sorry for it," said the marquis; "but one can't help being fascinating, you know, and as it ain't my fault that she fell so desperately in love with me, I hope she'll resign herself to the disappointment; and if it should ever happen that I am left a disconsolate widower, she shall be my second wife, in case she thinks it worth while to live single for the chance of having me."

"Your lordship is pleased to be joking with us," exclaimed Mr. Plumley, rather warmly.

"Upon my life I was never more serious in my life," returned the Marquis Valliere. "Unfortunately, the laws only allow us to take one wife at a time; and as, on the present occasion, I must marry to please my father, I will at the next opportunity—if one should ever offer itself—please myself."

"You will really leave us then?" cried Mrs. Plumley.

"Most positively I must," replied the marquis.

"And this," said the drysalter, "you are obliged to do in obedience to your father?"

"Yes, sir, I am compelled by filial duty, and my prospects of succeeding to my father's estates."

"And what," asked Mr. Plumley, "are they supposed to be worth per annum?"

"In English money," replied the marquis, "I should estimate them at about thirty thousand pounds and their annual proceeds I leave to the calculation of your own brain."

"Thirty thousand pounds!" exclaimed Plumley, "why, that's exactly the sum I intended to give to the man that marries either of my daughters."

"Is it possible?" vociferated the marquis, with as much apparent surprise as if he was not already aware of the fact. "And is it indeed a fact that you can give each of your daughters the sum of thirty thousand pounds ?"

" It is, my lord," replied the old man ; " and hard enough I've worked for it in my time, I can assure you."

" Would that I could marry them both !" muttered the marquis, but, luckily for himself, in so low a tone as not to be overheard by any one in the room.

" Hark'ye, my lord," exclaimed Mr. Plumley, " do you mean to tell me that in your country a man at your time of life is obliged to marry just according as his father pleases ?"

" Unfortunately, my dear sir, it is so," replied the marquis ; " or in case of disobedience, we are disinherited from what we should otherwise possess."

" My goodness !" sighed Miss Emma, clasping her hands together, and looking the very picture of woe. " And you are doomed, then, my lord, to become the husband of some woman that you may never love."

" Love !" exclaimed the marquis ; " how can I ever love any one but my adorable Emma ?"

" In that case why don't you have her ?" was the plain question of the honest citizen.

" I have told you my reason," replied the marquis.

" True," exclaimed Mr. Plumley ; " you have said that you will lose estates to the value of thirty thousand pounds. Now I mean to give just that sum to my daughter, and if you think fit to have her you can, and that, too, without being a loser by the bargain. Now that's a bit of logic that I rather think would puzzle any one to deny."

" I'll not attempt to deny it," exclaimed the marquis ; " and as we seem to understand one another so well, I'll accept your offer, and Miss Emma shall be the Marchioness Valliere, even though twenty fathers were to rise up and forbid the banns. What say you, my charming Emma—are you satisfied with the agreement we have just made ?"

" Quite so, my lord," stammered Emma, and blushing deeply as she gave the important assent.

" And do you approve of it, my dear madam ?" said the marquis, addressing himself to Mrs. Plumley.

" Oh, my lord," cried the mother, " how can I do otherwise when you have been pleased to honour us so greatly ?"

" And you, Miss Betsy," said the marquis—" do you feel no jealousy at the high rank and honour to which I am about to raise your adorable sister ?"

" I can feel no envy," replied Betsy, " and for a very good reason, too ; for as a marquis has thought fit to marry my sister Emma, who knows but a duke may take it in his head to fall in love with me ?"

" Very well argued, indeed," said the Marquis Valliere. " And now, as matters are thus far arranged, suppose we name three months hence as the period when our nuptials shall take place."

" In my opinion one month is better than three," interposed Mr. Plumley ; " at least, we always used to think so in bill transactions in the city, and I don't see why the argument shouldn't hold as good in love as in business."

" A month, my dear sir," said the marquis, " is rather a short time for courtship."

" And why shouldn't courtships be short ?" asked Plumley ; " why spend a long while in talking soft nonsense to each other, when it's known to yourselves and everybody else that you are going to be married ? For my part, I popped the question to Mrs. P. one morning, and exactly at the same hour, that day three weeks, we stood at the altar, all the happier for having cut the matter short."

"Lawk, papa, what a hurry you are in, to be sure," cried Miss Emma, who had surprisingly recovered herself on finding that she was not to be disappointed of being made a marchioness; "I declare his lordship must think we are strange people, and that it's my fault we are hurrying him into this sudden marriage."

"Oh, by no means, my dear," replied the marquis, languidly; "I am perfectly indifferent to these sort of things, and if the arrangement could be made in so short a time, I should positively have no objection to our marriage taking place to-morrow, or even earlier, if it should be the wish of your friends."

The worthy and unsuspecting Mr. Plumley and his family were delighted at the honour which was about to befall them; and when the marquis talked of leaving them to return to town, they were loud in their entreaties that he would pass the remainder of the day with them, and most condescendingly did he yield to their earnest solicitations. He, however, particularly requested them not to let the affair get abroad, lest it should chance to reach the ears of his father, who would be so enraged at his undutiful conduct, that there was no doubt he would take instant measures, not only to prevent the marriage taking place, but also to recal him home, in order to marry the lady he had himself chosen as his future daughter-in-law. This hint was quite enough for those to whom it was expressed, and the required promise was not only given, but a resolution was formed among themselves not to let any of the domestics about the place know of what was going forward, lest they should tittle-tattle about it in the neighbourhood, and thus cause to be brought about a catastrophe that was so little to be desired.

After dinner the conversation turned upon different subjects, and at length Mr. Plumley, in the most off-hand way that can possibly be conceived, said—

"By the by, my lord marquis, I quite forgot to ask you before in what part of France your estates lie?"

"Oh—ah—in what part of France?" said the marquis, a little bit confounded by the suddenness of the question; "why, the fact is, my dear sir, it is almost impossible to name them all, unless I had a whole day before me to do it in. Some lie here, and some there, and some——"

"Aye, aye, I perfectly understand you, my lord," interrupted the old gentleman—"they are scattered about over the entire kingdom; and as you entrust your business affairs to a steward, I dare say you hardly know where your estates are to be found."

"Exactly so," replied the marquis, well pleased at getting so well out of his dilemma; "I trouble myself very little about these things, I assure you, but when I am married to your daughter I shall take her to see them all, and I dare say she will be astonished and delighted at their number and magnitude. Besides, I shall wish her to make her choice as to which of my seats she will prefer as a residence."

"That's very kind of you," said Mr. Plumley; "but Emma is rather of a romantic turn, and I think she'll choose the oldest castle that happens to belong to you."

"Aye, that I shall," said Emma, who was quite delighted at the prospect of so grand a marriage.

"Then I can exactly suit you," exclaimed the marquis, "for I have a fine old castle on one of my estates that was erected some hundreds of years ago by King William Rufus."

"Rufus," cried Emma, "and who was he?"

"One of the kings of France, my dear."

" Nay, there I think you are mistaken, my lord," interposed Betsy, "for though I was never very fond of reading, yet somehow or other I think William Rufus was a king of England."

"Very likely, child," said the marquis, with perfect coolness ; " I don't at all doubt that there might have been a king of England of that name, but France also had one ; and—and——"

" Ah, I dare say you are quite correct, my lord," said the old gentleman, "and really it's not worth troubling our heads about whether his name was ;Rufus or not. The castle is an old one, it seems, and that's quite enough for any reasonable person."

The marquis was very glad to get over his blunder so easily, but he made many others in the course of the day, all of which he managed to flounder through by means of sheer coolness and assurance. At length, however, the time came for parting, and, with many expressions of unmeaning flattery, the Marquis Valliere took his leave, but not until he had promised to visit the hospitable family again on the following day.

CHAPTER XXXVI.

A STARTLING DISCOVERY.

THE intimacy which had thus commenced was taken every advantage of by the marquis, and not caring to show much pride on the present occasion, he soon became a daily visitor at Mr. Plumley's house ; and the affability which he exhibited made him a general favourite except with Susan, who was now more than ever convinced that he was not what he represented himself. She, however, was too prudent to give utterance to suspicions that she knew would only be laughed at, and, keeping her thoughts to herself, she determined to watch him closely, and, if possible, prove him to be an impostor ere it was too late.

At length the marquis became so great a favourite that Mr. Plumley, after a consultation with his wife upon the subject, proposed that their illustrious visitor should sleep there, as the house was sufficiently large to accommodate him with two or three rooms ; and as he at present required the assistance of his valet, the apartments selected for his use were quite sufficient. At all events the marquis made no scruples upon the subject, and, thanking his future father-in-law for the kindness he had manifested towards him, he wrote for his servant to come down immediately, and bring a portmanteau, filled with such things as he imagined would be required.

Accordingly, on that very afternoon John arrived with the luggage, as he had been desired, and no sooner had he swaggered into the house than Susan was struck with astonishment at his appearance, for he bore a remarkable likeness to a person she had seen before ; and so agitated was she that, in spite of all her efforts to appear calm and collected, she found it impossible to give utterance to a single word. She, however, led him to the place where the portmanteau was to be deposited, but still looking round upon him every now and then, as if to be certain whether she was not mistaken.

" Now, young woman," he said at length, "is this the place where my master is to sleep? is this his chamber key?"

" It is," she stammered, almost unconscious of what she said.

" Humph ! and do you know who I am ?"

" I believe you are the servant of the Marquis Valliere," she replied.

" Right," exclaimed the other ; " I have the honour to serve that great man. And now, my pretty lass, you'll be kind enough to explain why you have been staring at me ever since I came into the place ?"

" I was not aware that I did ;" replied Susan ; " and yet I was rather struck at first by the likeness you have to a person that I have seen before."

" Indeed ! and who may that be ?"

" That's what I want to recollect," she replied, " your face seems quite familiar to me ; and yet, though I've been trying to think where we have met, I cannot call it to mind."

" It's quite impossible that you can have seen me before," returned the other, with cool assurance ; " for it so happens, that I have been abroad with my master ; and unless you have been on the continent also, it seems pretty clear you must have made a confounded mistake."

Susan, however, was quite certain there was no mistake about it, and stealing another sly glance towards him when he was looking another way, she all on a sudden recollected where it was that she had seen him. She was, in fact, just going to mention the subject, when John, who was not very anxious to continue that conversation, quickly changed it into another channel, by observing that he had no doubt the family of Mr. Plumley was very respectable, and that she had a snug berth enough with people that seemed to be in such easy circumstances.

" Why yes," she replied, " the place is a very nice one, and I like my master and mistress, and the young ladies, for they are all very kind to me. But I feel very sorry for poor Miss Emma, who it seems is going to marry your master, and, somehow or other, I can't help thinking she won't be so happy as I could wish."

" And why not, my pretty dear ?" asked the other.

" Because I think he is not what he represents himself to be," she replied.

" Not what he represents himself to be ?" returned John ; " don't you think he is a marquis, then ?"

" That is best known to himself," answered Susan ; " but there are impostors in the world, and I should have liked Mr. Plumley to have made some enquiries before he allowed a perfect stranger to pay his addresses to his daughter."

" And have you ever given such a hint as that to your master ?" demanded John.

" Never."

" Then let me advise you to keep your tongue quiet upon that subject," exclaimed the other, " for though the marquis is one of the best tempered fellows in the world, he's a terrible spiteful one if people show anything like a prying disposition towards him."

" You mean to say, then," observed Susan, " that he has all the mansions and castles abroad that he's been talking so much about ?"

" Why, there's no end to them," replied the other , " bless your heart they are palaces of places, and you could put the whole of this house into even the smallest of the rooms that he's got on the continent. Talk about pitying Miss Emma, indeed, why she's one of the luckiest girl's that ever lived, and so she'll acknowledge when she sees the splendour that's in preparation for her."

" Well," replied our heroine ; " she ought to find something very grand, for your master is to have thirty thousand pounds with her on the day of their marriage, and that would secure her a wealthy English husband without going abroad for one."

" And what do you suppose the marquis cares about her paltry thirty thousand pounds ?" asked John in a tone of supreme contempt. " Ain't he rich enough himself; and is it likely he could marry your young mistress if he wasn't over head and ears in love with her ?"

"That remains to be proved," answered Susan, "for I have a notion that he cares more about her marriage portion than he does about herself."

"There you are quite mistaken," replied the other, "for I tell you he's uncommonly fond of the young lady; and as a proof of it, ain't he going to stay here night and day because he can't bear to be far away from her ?"

"There may be other reasons for his staying here," answered Susan, " and all I wish is that I may be mistaken."

"Well then, don't you drop a word to any one of what you have been saying to me," exclaimed John. "The marquis wouldn't like anybody to throw out hints that might touch his character; and, between ourselves, I've heard him speak so highly of you, that I shouldn't be at all surprised if he was to give you a hundred pounds on the day of his marriage as a reward for your uncommon prudence and discretion."

Here the conversation ended for the present, but Susan, whose suspicions had been previously excited, was now more than ever convinced that the supposed marquis was an impostor, and that he was playing a deep game to impose upon the easy credulity of Mr. Plumley, whose thirty thousand pounds was the bait that had induced him to practise a deception upon him. In her own mind, she felt quite certain that she had seen him in the police-office on the day when Mrs. Dawson's examination had taken place, and though no charge was at that time brought against him, he was in conversation with a man that had been taken up for a robbery, and that circumstance alone was enough to convince her that the marquis, as he called himself, was anything but what he had represented. Still, however, she was not quite certain on this point, for it was easy enough, she thought, to be mistaken in the likeness after the interval that had taken place, and as it would be better to go upon sure grounds, she determined to wait a little longer, and, by carefully observing all that transpired, to satisfy her own mind as to whether he really was the person she had seen in the police-office.

As for the man that represented himself to be his servant, she was quite certain that she had seen him down at Summerfield only a few days before the murder of Mr. Wentford, and though there was nothing very remarkable in that circumstance, she could not exactly reconcile it with the man's assertion that he had passed so many years abroad in the service of the Marquis Valliere. There was, in fact, quite enough to convince her that it would be very necessary to watch both the parties with a jealous eye, and though it was possible she might be mistaken in some particulars, it was equally certain that an artful scheme was in progress, which was likely to bring misery into a too-confiding family.

From this time matters seemed to go on smoothly enough, for the marquis became a prodigious favourite with those he was so artfully imposing upon, and the stories that he told of his great wealth and the exalted connections he had abroad, told admirably with Mr. Plumley and his family, all of whom were so delighted at the high alliance that was in view, that a suspicion never entered their minds to the prejudice of their visitor, who was thus honouring them with his company, and eating and drinking at their expense when, as the old gentleman observed, there could be no doubt that some of the first people in the land were jealous at the marks of respect he paid to those into whose family he was about to enter. At all events, both he and Mrs. Plumley were completely dazzled by the brilliancy of their daughter's prospects, and as for the two young ladies themselves, they never harboured a single thought in any way prejudicial to the aristo cratic Marquis Valliere.

Thus time passed on till it only wanted two days to that which had been named as the one on which the nuptials were to be celebrated, and in accordance with the earnestly expressed wish of the marquis, not a word was suffered to transpire out of the house relative to the marriage that was about to take place. This caution, he said, was absolutely necessary to prevent the news reaching her father's ears, as in such an event as that, the marriage might be formally forbidden, and thus the happiness of all parties be destroyed through the want of a little caution.

But there was one who never ceased to watch the marquis narrowly, and as the time approached that was to give her young lady to an adventurer, she became more and more vigilant in the self-imposed task that she had undertaken. And at length her care was in some respects rewarded, for two days previous to that on which the nuptial rites were to be celebrated, she happened to be passing the room usually occupied by the marquis, and as the door was a little way open, she could hear him talking to his servant in a tone sufficiently loud to reach her ears. At first she was rather inclined to pass on without taking any notice of the circumstance, but hearing the name of Miss Emma mentioned, she paused, and soon gathered enough to convince her that all her previous suspicions were but too well founded, and that a villanous scheme was in progress to destroy the peace and happiness of those who had been imposed upon by the artifices of a designing scoundrel.

" The people of this house are certainly a set of infernal fools," were the first words she heard the marquis utter ; " they believe anything I tell them, and I don't know that it would be such a very difficult task to persuade them to let the other sister go with us to France."

" It would be easy enough if you only like to try," answered the other ; " the old man and woman have a high opinion of you, and if the proposal is once made, they'd let the girl go with you and her sister, if it was only for the notion that she might make a good match over the other side of the water."

" It shall be tried at any rate," said the marquis ; " but mind you, it's on condition that you keep everything close and snug. Two more days will make all right for me, and if once we get safely out of this cursed country and its laws, I don't care what follows. I shall have thirty thousand pounds in hard cash as soon as the ceremony is over, and that will do to cut a dash with for some little time to come. By the by, the old gentleman must be rather a soft one, not to have made a few enquiries before he took all I've been telling him for granted."

" Why, the truth is," answered the other, " old Plumley has a mighty great fancy for marrying his daughters to people of consequence, and the title of marquis, was a capital bait to catch the old gudgeon with. We have fairly hooked him, and all the floundering about in the world won't get him out of the dilemma he has been blind enough to fall into. There's a clear thirty thousand for you, and—"

" Another similar sum for yourself," interrupted the marquis ; " if we can only persuade the old folks to let their other daughter go abroad with us. Once out of the way of the old man, and we can do as we please, for if Miss Betsy Plumley don't think proper to accept your offer, we can make her that's all I know about it."

" Villains !" exclaimed Susan, who could not repress the indignation with which these words inspired her, and she was hastening away to tell her master and mistress of all she had heard, when she was overtaken by John,

who, seizing her by the arm, led her back to the room, threatening her with all sorts of vengeance if she dared utter a word above her breath.

"So, young woman," said the marquis; "you must be listening and prying about, must you? to overhear what people are saying in order to carry favour with your master and mistress. But I was all along aware that you were listening at the door, so I gave my valet a hint to say something that should surprise you, and, no doubt, you believe every word of what we have been saying."

"I don't deny that I heard you talking together," replied Susan, "but I had no intention of listening, nor should I have done so if I had not heard my master's name mentioned, and then I stopped a moment to ascertain whether you were plotting mischief against him."

"Oh, indeed!" said the marquis with a sneer; "and so, because we said a few words in a joke, you must be running off to give information to your master and mistress."

"I certainly was a going to tell them," replied Susan; "and, in my opinion, it was nothing more than my duty, when I found out that you have been trying to deceive them and their two daughters."

"Humph!—and do you really believe we were in earnest?"

"I do indeed."

"And it is still your intention to tell them that I am not what they take me for?"

"I shall," replied our heroine; "and if you were really only joking just now, it will be easy to explain your meaning to my master. He is a fool, you say, but whether he is or not, it shall be my task to let him know what sort of a man he has encouraged to sue for his daughter's hand."

"Oh, oh! if that's the case, we must look to our own safety," exclaimed John; "so now, my girl, down upon your marrow-bones this instant, and swear never to say a word to any one of them what just now passed between

No. 33

my lord and me, or you shall have this knife in your heart before you are two minutes older."

"Would you murder me?" said Susan, falling upon her knees and clasping her hands imploringly.

"Why, as for murder," interposed the marquis, taking a pistol from his pocket, which he cocked, and then presented at her head, "we have no wish to shed your blood, my girl, but you have placed us in danger, and you must either give the pledge that has been demanded, or death will be the forfeit of your folly and temerity."

"I would have you beware how you discharge your weapons," cried Susan, collecting all the fortitude she possessed; "for the report of fire-arms will bring assistance, and though my own life will be sacrificed, there will at least be the consolation of knowing that villany will be defeated."

"They cannot take me or my companion," replied the assumed marquis, "for yonder window is but a few feet from the ground, and our escape will have been effected long ere any one can reach this room. You, however, will have perished through your own folly, and, long ere search can be made after us, we shall be out of reach of danger."

"You hear how it is, young woman," said the other, "and so now, as we don't want to hurt you, all you have got to do is to swear that you will not say a word to anybody of what you heard, and then you have got nothing to fear from us."

"I will not swear to that," answered Susan, "which I know I shall not be able to perform."

"Then you shall die," muttered the fellow, and raising his knife, he was about to strike it at her heart, when his arm was caught by the other.

"Come, come, this will never do," he exclaimed, "for if once we commit an act of violence, the game will be up with us for ever." Then addressing himself to Susan, he continued—"young woman, you have been deceived in our intentions I can assure you, for the few words you overheard just now were merely spoken in jest, because we happened to know that you were listening to us. You may, therefore, take my word for it, that no harm is intended against any part of this family, and all I now ask of you is, that nothing may be said of a foolish freak that would go very much against me if it should happen to be mentioned."

"If it was only a joke, as you say," returned Susan; "what occasion is there for your being afraid of my mentioning it?"

"Because your master and mistress might happen to think I am not what I represent myself to be," replied the self-styled marquis. "Suspicions, you know, are very easily excited, and if once Mr. Plumley should take it into his head that I have been practising upon his credulity, I should be forbidden the house, and then my brilliant prospects would be destroyed for ever."

"What is it you require of me?" asked Susan.

"I will take your bare promise not to mention what has taken place to any one," said the marquis. "Give me that assurance, and you shall now take your departure without further parley."

"Well, I will promise thus much," replied Susan; "but, remember, I shall keep a strict watch upon both of you, and, should anything else occur to arouse my suspicions, I shall then consider the promise at an end, and will at once put my master and his family on their guard."

"You must be careful how you do that," replied the marquis; "for, in such a case as that, your own life would certainly pay the forfeit of your folly."

"You would murder me, then?" cried Susan.

"I make no threats of what I will do," replied the marquis, "but when a man is driven to desperation, he hardly knows how to command himself. You are aware that I am in two days more to marry Miss Emma Plumley, and I certainly do not feel inclined to see an advantageous match broken off merely because I happened to say a few words in joke to my servant, which, having been overheard by yourself are construed into something which, if reported, might go very much against me."

" Well, I give the promise you have asked for," said Susan, " but, at the same time, I cannot help telling you that I suspected something was wrong before I overheard what you were just now talking about. There is mischief brewing between you, and though I have given my word not to say anything about the past, I shall take good care to keep a good look out for the future."

" Hang her, but we've caught a Tartar at last!" exclaimed John, as our heroine hurried away ; " that girl knows a great deal too much for us, and it's my opinion we ought to think of some way of getting rid of her."

" Why, that's all very true," replied the marquis, " but if we think upon any plan at all, we must make up our minds to go quietly about it. But hush !—don't let us utter what we've got to say too loud, for we have once been overheard, and there's no knowing but other listeners may be about."

" Likely enough," whispered the other, " but it's necessary we should be prepared in case any mischief should come of this. I've seen the wench before, and if she only knew half as much as I do myself, a very little time would serve to bring me into a mess that it wouldn't be very easy to get out of again."

" Have you ever seen her before we came here ?" asked the marquis.

" I have."

" Where ?"

" Down at Summerfield, just before the affair of the old man's."

" You mean the murder ?"

" I do ; the girl saw me, I believe, and it would be rather awkward if she should happen to recollect the circumstance."

" True," answered the marquis, " but it is certain she has not recognized you, or she would have told about it long before this time."

" I don't think she remembers where or how we met," replied the other ; " but the girl told me the other day that she was quite certain my face was familiar to her, and at one time I was half afraid her memory would serve her too well. However, the thing passed off better than I expected, and as we have met several times since without anything being said upon that subject, I began to hope it would all pass off without any further danger."

" And so it will," answered the marquis, " for two days more will see me the husband of Emma Plumley, and as it is my intention to set off with her immediately to the continent, I think there can be very little fear of an explosion taking place in that short interval. The other girl, I dare say, will be glad enough to accompany us, and when once we get her on the other side of the water, it will be no very difficult task to persuade her to bestow upon yourself her hand and fortune. However, the less that's said about that, at present, the better, so keep your own counsel, and, from this time, let you and I be seen together as little as possible."

" But do you think the girl will hold her tongue after what she heard us talking about just now ?"

" I expect she will," replied the other. " At all events, I shall not let her be out of my sight much, and if anything should happen to escape her lips that might do us a mischief, I will be prepared with an excuse to make it appear that she is mistaken. So now, leave me, and remember what I just now said about being seen together as little as possible."

Upon this the two worthies parted, the marquis going to the drawing-room, and the other betaking himself to the servants' hall, where he watched Susan with so much jealousy, that, even if she had been inclined to break the promise she had given, there was no opportunity of her mentioning to any one the startling discovery she had just made.

The next morning, soon after breakfast, Susan was sent for by Mrs. Plumley, who, after alluding to the near approaching marriage of her daughter with the marquis, began to regret that on her arrival in a foreign country, she would be surrounded by strange servants, as all who had been spoken to on the subject, declined accompanying her, in consequence of the distance from home, and the probability of their never again seeing England.

" In fact, Susan," she continued, " I have seen so much reason to be satisfied with you since you have been in my service, that I at length made up my mind to ask whether you will go with her, as, of course, it will be a very fine thing to get into the establishment of the Marquis Valliere, where you will have everything your own way, and perhaps, before long, will be made housekeeper in one of the numerous castles that he possesses."

But Susan, who knew that the marquis possessed no more castles than those which were built in the air, did not see things in so favourable a light as her mistress seemed to do, and after some little hesitation, she said :—

" I'm obliged to you, ma'am, for the kindness that I know you intend, but, the truth is, I have particular reasons for wishing to remain in England, and nothing, I believe, will ever induce me to leave it till I have succeeded in a task that I imposed upon myself some time since."

" And may I ask what that task may be ?" asked Mrs. Plumley.

" Why, there are particular reasons why I cannot answer the question at present," replied Susan. " I may, however, tell you that my brother's name has suffered foul wrong from the unjust accusations of some secret enemies, and I have vowed never to relax my efforts till I have proved his innocence to the world, and brought well-merited odium upon those who have so cruelly heaped injuries upon one, who, I fear, is not alive to justify himself."

" Well," said Mrs. Plumley, " I shall not attempt to inquire further into your family affairs ; but, I cannot help saying that you have set yourself a difficult task, if any considerable time has passed away since the injury you complain of."

" It is a long while," sighed our heroine, " and sometimes I have almost despaired of succeeding ; but, lately, events have occurred that revive my hopes, and I believe a very little more patience will serve to expose the whole villany that has been practised by those who have thus long sheltered themselves beneath the secresy with which they have concealed their evil deeds. For that reason I wish to remain in England, though my respect for yourself would otherwise have induced me to accompany your daughter to a foreign country."

" Ah, poor dear ! I shall soon lose her," exclaimed Mrs. Plumley ; " but the marriage is an excellent one for her, Susan, and, therefore, it is my duty to submit with patience when the advantage of my daughter is so nearly concerned. She will be a lady of title, Susan ; and, with the immense wealth she will be mistress of, it is impossible that she can be unhappy."

" I hope so, ma'am, with all my heart," said Susan.

" And yet the tone you speak in," observed her mistress, " seems to say that you don't expect much happiness from this match."

" I should be sorry to say anything that would make you uneasy," replied our heroine ; " but there are times when we ought to speak out boldly, and I would, therefore, venture to say that the marquis is a perfect stranger, and even you and my master know nothing more of him than that the young ladies met him at a watering-place, and that he has since been a tolerably frequent visitor at your house."

"The fact is, Susan, you are ignorant of the ways of the world," replied Mrs. Plumley, rather sharply, "and of course know nothing of high life. The marquis, it is true, was a stranger when we first saw him, but we have seen a great deal of him since then, and the more we know of him, the more both Mr. Plumley and myself like him. Then Emma, as you are aware, adores him, and I believe there is no reason to suppose but that he is equally attached to her, and that, consequently, there is nothing but a life of happiness before them."

"I wish it may be so, with all my heart," exclaimed Susan.

"Your words make me suspect that you think there's something wrong," cried Mrs. Plumley, whose fears were naturally excited on such a subject as this. "Perhaps you know something, Susan, that I ought to be acquainted with; and if so, I desire you to tell me without hesitation whether you are aware of anything that the poor girl's father and I ought to be acquainted with. Nay, don't hesitate, girl, for though I am rather partial to the marquis, I am ready to hear anything you say against him, if you have but proof of what you say."

"I have only my bare word for it," answered Susan; "and perhaps that will not be enough against a person that it seems you so much respect."

"Let me hear it," said her mistress; "and even though I may believe you wrong, you may take my word for it I will not be angry at anything you may say."

"Well, then, ma'am," began Susan, "last night, as I happened to pass the marquis's room, I overheard him and the valet talking about——"

"And pray what was I talking about?" said the marquis, who at that moment presented himself so suddenly before them that Susan started back aghast, and would have run out of the room, if he had not taken hold of her arm and forcibly detained her.

"You are trying to make mischief here, young woman," he said, sternly, "and no doubt a very pretty story would have been related to my prejudice, if I had not happened, most fortunately, to come into the room in time."

"I was merely going to tell my mistress," stammered Susan, "that I heard a conversation between you and your valet that I thought she ought to be made acquainted with."

"And you know very well what I told you would happen in the event of your blabbing," muttered the marquis in her ear; and then, addressing himself to Mrs. Plumley, he continued—"The fact is, my dear madam, I and my man were speaking about an affair that was in no way connected with your family, when this girl thought proper to listen, and from the few words she gathered, I have no doubt she intends to trump up an artful tale to my prejudice. You, however, will, of course, have more sense than to listen to the idle chattering of an ignorant girl like her, who, from some cause or other, has taken a most unaccountable prejudice against me, and would, if such a thing were possible, persuade you that I am an impostor, undeserving the confidence and kindness that I have received, both from yourself and your excellent husband."

"You quite astonish me, my lord," cried Mrs. Plumley; "why what, in the name of fortune, can Susan Hoply have to say against a person like you?"

"She is at liberty to tell you if she pleases," replied the marquis; and then, directing a fierce look towards Susan, he continued—"but if she says anything that should be the means of causing a rupture between me and your family, I will take care to retaliate in a way that will teach her to be less inquisitive and more circumspect in future."

And having uttered these words he bounced out of the room, in a way that filled Mrs. Plumley with serious apprehensions that her intended son-in-law might take it into his head to leave the house, and break off an engagement, the fulfilment of which had been looked forward to with so much anxiety. Her fears on this head, however, were quickly dissipated by his almost immediate return, and so changed was his manner from what it had been only a minute or two before, that it was scarcely possible to believe him to be the same person.

"I believe I was a little too warm just now, my dear madam," he said, in the mildest tone possible; "but a man in my station of life cannot bear to have his motives doubted, even for a moment; and fearing lest anything your servant had said might operate to my prejudice, I gave way to a burst of anger for which I now beg leave to apologize."

"There is no need for apology, my lord," replied Mrs. Plumley, "for I have the highest confidence in your honour; and, therefore, anything that might be said, would not make me think the worse of you till I had reasons of my own for so doing. And as for poor Susan, I know she is very sorry for what has passed, and if you will only pardon her this time, I am quite sure she will not repeat the offence."

"At your request, my dear madam, I can overlook it," said the marquis, "but I must caution the young woman to be more discreet in future, and not to take in earnest words that were intended merely in jest. You are forgiven, Susan," he continued in a patronizing tone, "and if I find you better disposed towards me, henceforth, I may, perhaps, be induced to do something towards raising you from your present lowly situation. And now, my dear madam, I again take my leave, with an earnest hope that nothing which has passed this day, may disturb the harmony and good feeling that has existed between me and your excellent family."

Mrs. Plumley would have poured forth a profusion of assurances of the kindest feelings towards him, but he disappeared ere she could command a sufficient flow of words, and then turning towards Susan, she continued :—

"You see what an angel of a creature he is—how forgiving, how kind, even towards those he believes would have injured him. So now think better of him in future, and, as you would preserve my good opinion, never utter another word to show that you think ill of such a man."

"I will not, ma'am," replied Susan, "and at the same time, wish you to believe that I had no paltry malice to serve in taking the course that just now gave so much offence. You and my master are, however, satisfied with the marquis, and as you have had a better opportunity of judging of him than I have myself, it is likely I may have been mistaken in the zeal with which I have wished to serve you."

"Why, that's well said, Susan," exclaimed her mistress, "and now, as you begin to see your fault, let me hope that you will accompany the bride and bridegroom to their new home abroad. My youngest daughter, at the particular request of the marquis, is to go home with them, and as she will want a companion on her return back to England, there is no one I would so soon trust her with as yourself."

"Is Miss Betsy to go with them?" asked Susan, in a tone of surprise, as she remembered the conversation she had overheard the day before between the marquis and his man.

"She is," replied Mrs. Plumley, "for both the marquis and her sister pressed me so earnestly upon the subject, that I could not refuse; though, to confess the truth, I find it a very hard trial to part with both my daughters at once."

" And does the young lady wish to go abroad ?" asked Susan.

" She does," replied her mistress, " and perhaps it's only natural that she should do so, for the marquis does nothing but talk of the magnificence of the country where they are first of all going to, and having, besides, hinted that she may, with her wealth, marry some prince, or other great man, it is hardly to be wondered at if her head is a little bit turned with the idea of the splendid alliance she may form. So promise me, Susan, that you will go with them, and I shall feel all the more comfortable in knowing that my daughters will have one person to speak to that they have been used to at home."

" Well," exclaimed Susan, " if I thought it was only for a month or two, I should not object, because I dare say, it will take more time than that to bring about what I so much desire."

" You will go with them, then ?" said Mrs. Plumley.

" I will, ma'am."

" In that case, I will be at the expense of fitting you out so as to appear more like the friend than the servant of my daughter," said Mrs. Plumley, " you shall have all your wants, and on your return to England, I will give you a hundred pounds for having relieved my mind of at least one of the causes of uneasiness that perplexed me."

" And when do they set out for the continent ?" asked Susan.

" Immediately after the marriage ceremony has been performed," replied Mrs. Plumley. " My daughter Emma has a new carriage provided for the occasion, which will convey them to Brighton, from whence they will go by one of the Dieppe vessels on the following morning. So now prepare yourself for the journey, Susan, and I will undertake that everything I have provided shall be ready by the appointed time."

Susan then left the room, but her mind was full of doubt, for she still suspected the marquis to be an impostor, though, at present, she knew it would be in vain to say anything to people who were so thoroughly prejudiced in his favour.

CHAPTER XXXVII.

AN EXTRAORDINARY CHANGE.

At the time appointed, the marriage was celebrated between the Marquis Valliere and Miss Emma Plumley, and having partaken of the refreshment provided by the father of the bride, the happy couple set out in their carriage, accompanied by Miss Betsy, and having John and Susan as outside passengers. With their journey we have nothing to do, except to observe that they stopped a night at Brighton, as had been previous arranged, and the next morning crossed over to Dieppe, where they put up at one of the principal hotels.

So far, all went well enough, for the marquis, his bride, and her sister, were most excellent company among themselves, but no sooner had they reached a foreign shore than Susan could observe a marked change in John, who, instead of being the humble servant of the Marquis Valliere, now began to throw off the previous humility of his manners, and to address Miss Betsy more as an equal than as the mere servant of her sister. Nor was the curiosity of our heroine lessened, when, after having disappeared for some little time, he again made his appearance, not as the valet which he had represented before, but as a smart military officer, swaggering and strolling about with all the consequence of a man that had a right to play the part he had assumed.

This, of course, could not fail to attract the particular observation of Susan, who began to suspect that some singular discovery was about to take place, and that the notion she had formed of the marquis and his friend was not without foundation. She, however, said nothing at the time, but when at length the transformed valet left the hotel to take a walk, as she supposed, she sought out Miss Betsy, to whom she mentioned the singular change that had taken place, and certain misgivings that she had upon the subject. But the young lady seemed to think nothing at all about it, for she smiled as Susan related what had taken place, and having heard her to an end, replied carelessly, that the disguise had been assumed merely to serve some particular purposes of his own, and that having got back to France, there was no longer any occasion for him to appear in a false character.

" But isn't it rather strange that he should have disguised himself as a valet if he is really a military officer ?" asked Susan.

"Not at all," replied her mistress, who was too simple-minded to have any suspicions. " It may have been done for a wager, or for any other motive that neither you nor I have any right to question or enquire into."

" Very true, Miss," answered our heroine ; " but people can't help their thoughts you know, and I have noticed a great change in his manners ever since we first landed in this country. But he's a friend of the marquis's, I suppose, and I dare say the affair is perfectly understood between them."

" That I know nothing about," replied Miss Betsy, " but I understand we shall not see him again in this town, for he's gone on to Paris where we are to join him."

" Indeed !" exclaimed Susan with surprise ; " I understood when we left England that we are not going to Paris at all, but that the marquis intended to take your sister immediately to one of his old castles in the country, where we were to remain till the honeymoon is over."

" I believe that was their intention at first," answered Miss Betsy, " but it seems they have changed their mind, and very likely the other gentleman has gone on to secure them comfortable accommodation. Besides, Paris is very gay just at present, and it would be a shame to pass it for the sake of visiting a dingy old castle, that we can see another time quite as well as now."

" But there must be some other motive for so sudden a change," observed Susan. " In fact, I have thought all along that the marquis had no intention of going to the castle he talked about, at least, for the present."

" I dare say there is a motive," answered Miss Betsy, who was too indolent to trouble herself much upon the subject ; " indeed, now I come to think of it, the marquis said just now, that he was going to meet a Major Smith there, a very particular acquaintance, who he is anxious to see previous to shutting himself up in the country.'

" And so," exclaimed Susan, " for the sake of a friend he is going to drag us nobody knows where, though his castle, I believe, lies in quite a contrary direction. But I am convinced, there is some mystery in this, and all I hope is, that it may turn out better than my fears lead me to anticipate "

" Psha !" returned the young lady, " what is there to be afraid of, and why should you think there is anything strange in our going to Paris ? Besides, the marquis is extremely kind to us all, and in my opinion it's done to oblige us that he has taken this sudden whim of changing the direction of his journey."

" But that don't account for the strange alteration we have seen in his

valet," replied Susan; "the man has always passed himself off as a servant, and no sooner does he get over here than he appears as the friend of the marquis, and away he goes all of a sudden without any body knowing why or wherefore."

"Nor have we any business to know," answered Miss Betsy, "for I dare say he could give a very good reason if he was called upon to do so, and whether or not, I feel no inclination to trouble myself at all about it."

Here the conversation ended, and after a couple of days had been spent in Dieppe, they started once more in their own carriage, with the intention of reaching the French metropolis by easy stages. But poor Susan was now more bewildered than ever, for the mysteries were continually increasing, and the circumstance of the valet proving to be an impostor, served but to convince her more than ever that the marquis was not what he had represented himself to be. She, however, knew that it would be in vain to make any enquiries into the subject, but as she was to remain with them some little time longer she determined to keep a vigilant eye upon the marquis, and, if possible, unmask his hypocrisy, ere the period arrived for her return to England with Miss Betsy.

On reaching their place of destination, they found some splendid apartments already engaged for their reception, and no sooner had they recovered from the fatigue of travelling, than they began a round of pleasure such as is to be found only at Paris. Balls, plays, and parties occupied the whole of their time, and for some days, at least, Susan could observe nothing to confirm the suspicion she entertained against the Marquis Valliere.

At last, however, when they had been in Paris about a week, Susan was one day surprised at hearing the name of Major Smith announced to the marchioness and her sister, and looking up to see who the stranger was, her surprise may be imagined at discovering that the major was no other than the late valet, John, who had so suddenly quitted them on their first arrival in France.   She looked at the ladies expecting to see them as much astonished as herself, but they were quite unmoved at what had occasioned her so much wonder, and knowing of no other way to account for it, she supposed the secret had been revealed to them, and that consequently they were quite prepared for his visit under this new character.   At that moment the marquis entered the room, and taking his visitor by the hand he welcomed him with as much warmth of friendship, as if one had never been the master and the other the servant.

"Ah! my dear major," he exclaimed; "we have been anxiously expecting your arrival, and here, at length, you are, just as we had began to give you up."

"Am I as welcome to the ladies as I am to yourself?" asked the major, with an affectation of gentility that Susan could not help thinking was rather constrained.

"Why, to be sure you are, my dear fellow," replied the other, squeezing his hand with all the ardour of friendship; "at least I can answer for the marchioness, and as for Miss Betsy, I shall leave her to answer for herself."

"You hear that," said the major, taking the hand of the young lady and pressing it to his lips; "the marquis has left you to answer my question, and it now only remains for you to declare whether I shall be a happy or a miserable dog."

"Upon my word, major, I hardly know what to say," replied Betsy, blushing as she heard the titter that was going on about her; "I will, however, confess that I am not sorry to see you again, and that we all thought to have seen you at least three or four days ago."

"And so you would have seen me," answered the major, "but the fact is, I have been so urged to stay on a visit to the Prince Ferdinand, that I found it quite impossible to get away without appearing to be absolutely rude.   This detained me two days beyond the time I had intended to start for Paris, and at last I was obliged to leave a note for his royal highness, thanking him for his condescension, and excusing my abrupt departure in the best way I could."

"And did you leave our friends well?" asked the marquis.

"Perfectly so," replied the major, "but I can assure you they were sadly disappointed at not seeing you and your lovely bride on your way to this city.   However, I promised them you would pay them an early visit with the marchioness, and hearing that Miss Betsy had accompanied you from England, they made me promise to bring her at the same time, so that we shall make quite a snug family party when we go to see his royal highness."

"The palace, I suppose, is very full of company just now?" observed the marquis, carelessly.

"Very full," replied the major; "the Marquis de Noailles was there, as well as Count Hautville; but if I was to name all that I met there, I should mention most of the principal families in France.   The prince, indeed, as you know, is justly celebrated for his hospitality and the elegance with which he plays the host, so that it is hardly to be wondered at that he is visited by the whole fashionable world.   However, you must positively take the ladies there as soon as possible, or it will be regarded as a slight, which I am sure is the last thing you would wish to show towards so illustrious a friend as the prince."

"Most assuredly I will," replied the other; "the marchioness will be quite delighted with the easy affability of that excellent family, and, as for her sister, I am sure she will be quite charmed with the attention they manifest towards every one of their guests.   We must, however, make the best use of our time now we are in Paris, and as there are several sights to be seen, you will perhaps accompany us in a walk that we were just about to take?"

"With the greatest pleasure," said the major, and as the ladies were both already attired for walking, they left the place, the marquis and his bride leading the way, and the major and Miss Betsy bringing up the rear. The last named young lady, indeed, seemed to think it not at all strange that she should now be escorted by a man that she had lately known only as a menial, and as they walked along, she laughed and chatted with him as familiarly as if they had been old acquaintances. As for Susan, she could not help expressing her astonishment, and as she watched them to the further end of the street, she said to herself—

"This is the strangest business I ever saw in my life, and all I hope is, that matters may end no worse than they have begun. But what can all this mean, I wonder? for here is the valet received as Major Smith, the particular friend of the marquis, and yet nobody seems to be surprised at the disguise he assumed over in England, and both the young ladies seem as willing to accept him as a friend as if they had known him to be a respectable gentleman all the days of their life. But it is a strange world we live in, and every hour shows us something new, and all I can say about it is, I hope my suspicions may not prove correct, and that there will be no reason to repent these doings."

As they walked along, the major gave utterance to a great many sighs, and whispered innumerable soft nothings, such as many young ladies are apt to construe into compliments. Such, in fact, was the case with Miss Betsy, who began to think the major a very nice man, and wondered how it was that she was so simple as not to see through his disguise when he was acting the part of a servant to the marquis over in England. She supposed too that he had taken that singular step for the purpose of being near her at a time when he fancied that his addresses would not be permitted by her father and mother, and she was just wondering in her own mind how parents can ever be so cruel as to check the course of true love, when a heavy sigh from the major woke her from the sentimental dream she had fallen into.

"I am afraid you will think me a very foolish fellow, Miss Betsy," he said; "but positively I have been so deeply in love, that I know not how many acts of folly I have committed since you and I were first acquainted."

"Are you in love, major?" she asked with affected surprise.

"I am, indeed," sighed the major in reply,

"With whom? may I be so bold as to ask?"

"There was, indeed, no occasion to ask," he replied; "for with whom could I have been so desperately in love as with yourself, most incomparable girl? However, before I declare myself any further, let me hear from your sweet lips that I am pardoned for the disguise I assumed in England."

"Oh, to be sure you are," she replied with a smile; "but for the life of me, major, I cannot imagine why you made such a fright of yourself, when the uniform you now wear is so much more becoming."

"I thought my friend, the marquis, had already satisfied you on that point," he said.

"He has never once mentioned the subject to me," replied Miss Betsy; "indeed, now you speak of it, he must have been aware of the trick you played on us, and it does indeed seem strange that he has been so silent about it."

"This is most extraordinary," exclaimed the major, part to himself, and yet loud enough to be heard; "he should have mentioned it to you," he continued in a more direct manner, " and then we should both have been spared the agitation of this moment."

‑ " I think I can understand what you mean, sir," said the young lady, who had no wish to affect any disguise upon the subject; " and now, as you have gone so far, major, allow me to ask why you came as the servant of the marquis, when, had your real name and rank been known, you might have been welcomed to my father's house as a friend?"

" Oh, my dear Miss," replied the other; " my reply to that question must be sad and brief. The fact is, poverty has ever been my greatest curse, and understanding that your father had it in his power to bestow a princely fortune upon his daughters, my modesty for some time forbade me making any advances. But love cannot be long repressed you know, and at last I hit upon the expedient that was so happily the means of bringing me into your society."

" Lor, major!" cried Miss Plumley; " and so it was all through love that you come to our house in disguise?"

" To be sure, my dear."

" Well,—did I ever!" she exclaimed; " and yet, after all, Major Smith I cannot remember having seen you at any time till you came with the marquis as his valet."

" Ah! that's another proof of my modesty," sighed the major; " I had seen you often, my dear girl, when you and your sister were at the sea-side with your mamma in the beginning of the summer. I remember the first time I saw you, how much I was struck with your beauty, and had you been alone, I verily believe nothing could have restrained me from declaring my passion at that very moment. But your mamma and sister were most provokingly present, and I was obliged to tear myself away to sigh and lament over the mischance that had prevented me from having you declare whether I might ever hope to obtain your hand."

" Dear me, how very romantic!" cried Miss Plumley; " and so I suppose, if the truth were known, you and the marquis used to follow us about wherever we went?"

" We did, indeed," answered the major; " and little is it to be wondered at, for the first time I ever had the happiness of seeing you I uttered aloud, 'That's the girl for me if I have to follow her all over the world.' 'What do you mean?' asked the marquis, surprised at my exclamation. 'Exactly what I have said,' I replied; 'you see yonder females that we have just passed?' 'I do,' said he; 'and what of that?' 'Nothing more,' replied I, 'than that one of those girls must be my wife, or I'll live and die a bachelor for her sake.' 'Which is the one you mean?' he asked. 'The one in white,' I replied, and then he seemed to be satisfied, for as it afterwards appeared he had already determined in his own mind to make a conquest of your sister's heart."

" And did you think much about me afterwards?" asked Miss Plumley.

" Your divine image was never out of my sight," answered the major, " and from that moment I could not be said to have a heart of my own. At length the marquis became the declared and accepted lover of your sister, and from that moment I felt the curse of poverty with tenfold bitterness."

" What a pity it is, major," said Miss Plumley, " that such men as you should not all be rich."

" It is, indeed, a pity," he replied; " because there are certain hard-hearted parents in the world that will not suffer their daughters to marry unless they can get a fortune equal to their own, I don't mean to say that such was the case in the present instance, but I was afraid of it, and had not the courage to pop the question for fear of meeting with' a direct refusal."

"That was a pity," said the young lady; "for my father is by no means a severe man, and had he known how respectable your connexions are, I dare say he would have given his consent."

"Will he do so now, think you, if I was to write?" demanded Major Smith.

"I don't know, I'm sure," replied Miss Plumley, "but if you like to try him you can. However, we'll talk about that another time, and now, perhaps, you will be kind enough to inform me what put it in your head to come to our house in disguise?"

"Love," replied the major, "urged me to a desperate deed, and the marquis suggested the plan. He knew your passion for me, and seeing that I was drooping and in despair, he at length hinted that he thought there was a very fair chance of succeeding in my suit, if I thought proper to follow his advice."

"And he told you to disguise yourself as his valet?"

"He did."

"Well, it was an excellent thought," observed Miss Plumley, "and I must give you the credit of having performed your part admirably, for no one in this world could ever have taken you for anything better than a gentleman's servant."

"I believe I acted it pretty well," said the major, hardly knowing whether to take it as a compliment or not. "At any rate, I tried as much as possible to forget that I was a gentleman, and I don't think anybody in your father's house ever suspected for a moment that I was otherwise than what I represented myself to be."

"But how was it," asked Miss Betsy, "that you never gave me a hint of who you were?"

"My natural timidity prevented me," replied the major, "or I should have taken one of the many opportunities that offered for so doing. However, I don't regret that now, for in consequence of the good generalship of my friend, the marquis, you were permitted to accompany him and your sister to the continent, and now I can speak freely to you upon a subject on which all my happiness depends."

"Why that's all very well, to be sure," said the young lady; "but I'm quite certain my father and mother would have welcomed you to their house had they known that you were a major in the army, and, besides that, a particular friend of the Marquis Valliere's."

"Of that I was not quite certain," replied the other, "and as a discovery of name and intentions might have been the means of separating me from you for ever, I chose the other alternative, and thus had the supreme happiness of being constantly near you."

"Well," exclaimed Miss Plumley, "you must have been uncommonly deep in love to have submitted to such a step as that. However, as you have been thus far candid, Major Smith, perhaps you will now now tell me what your intentions are?"

"In the first place," he replied, "I would know whether my attention to yourself are acceptable?"

"They certainly are not disagreeable," answered the young lady, candidly. "That is to say I should not object to them, provided you apply on the subject to my father and mother."

"I have thought of doing so," he replied, "but am almost afraid of meeting with a refusal in that quarter."

"Then what do you propose, sir?" she asked.

"Merely that you will consent to a clandestine marriage," he exclaimed "and thus you know it will be of very little use for the old folks to raise any objections. In fact, my dear girl, it is the only way that I can see to secure our happiness, and if you throw any impediment in the way I'm afraid we must both pine away the remainder of our days in wretchedness and woe."

"But," observed Miss Plumley, "if I marry against my father's will, he'll never give me a farthing, and as you are not very rich yourself, we should have but a very sad prospect before us of poverty for the rest of our lives."

"Humph!" ejaculated the major, "the money is rather an object to be thought of, to be sure.—But then perhaps your father is not a vindictive man, and when he sees that all further opposition would be useless he may take it into his head to forgive us both, and bestow upon us his blessing and thirty thousand pounds."

"I hope it's not for the sake of my money only that you would marry me though," exclaimed the young lady.

"The money, my dear Miss Plumley, is quite a secondary consideration, I do assure you," answered the major, placing his hand upon his heart, and taking care to speak in a very tremulous accent. "I am not a mercinary man, nor one that cares anything about fortune, for I declare I would marry you without a shilling in the world, But it is for your own sake that I look forward to obtaining your money, for you have been brought up to great expectations, and it would be base in the extreme on my part were I to make you my wife, with only the pay of a major for our mutual support."

"And yet you just now proposed a clandestine marriage," said Miss Plumley, with surprise.

"I did so," he replied, "but it was only conditionally that you gave me reasonable grounds for hope that your father's forgiveness would immediately follow."

"Then you would not marry me for love?"

"Love is a very essential ingredient in matrimony," answered the major; "but unfortunately it does nothing towards the support of its votaries. Indeed I should be undeserving of your regard were I to plunge you into comparative poverty by persuading you to a union that would for ever shut the doors of your father's house upon you."

"Well, that's very kind and thoughtful of you indeed," said Miss Plumley, who was unable to penetrate the craft and subtlety of the fortune-hunting major. "It is not everybody that would have considered such a matter, I'm sure when I tell my father how prudently you have acted, he will see that he ought no longer to oppose the happiness of his daughter."

"You acknowledge then, that your happiness depends upon our union?" said Major Smith.

"Perhaps I ought not to have said quite so much," answered the young lady, blushing at what she had uttered. "You, however, are, I am sure, too honourable a man to take notice of what has escaped by mere chance?"

"I will trust only to your love for me," exclaimed the major, "and since it seems that I am not disagreeable in your eyes, I would now suggest that you write immediately to your father, and gently break the subject to him."

"I will not fail to do so," she replied, and ere anything more could be said, they found themselves close to the marquis and his bride, who had been waiting till they came up.

According to promise, Miss Plumley wrote off that very day to her father, and, quite incidentally, of course, mentioned the major and the very kind attentions he had paid her. This was followed at frequent intervals by other letters, each of which spoke more and more warmly of the person who had gained her heart. But though she received regular answers to these epistles, not one word was said about the major, till at length one came full of anger, and peremptorily desiring that she would give no encouragement to the lover till her father arrived in Paris, which he assured her he should do in the course of a few days.

When this was announced to the marquis and his friend, a consultation took place between them, and half an hour afterwards the carriage was ordered, and the whole party, accompanied by Susan, left the French metropolis, with the avowed purpose of proceeding without delay to the castle of the Marquis Valliere.

CHAPTER XXXVIII.

VILLANY DISCOVERED.

Our travellers proceeded all that night and the next day, stopping only to partake of slight refreshments at obscure houses on the road side, and then hurrying on at a rate that would have set all pursuit at defiance. This rather surprised the marchioness and her sister, who repeatedly enquired of the gentlemen why they were travelling so fast, when there appeared to be no occasion for it; but the marquis informed them that particular, and very urgent business required his immediate presence at his castle at Valliere, and as this was the only reply they could get, they were obliged to appear satisfied. They observed too that they were passing through a very thinly inhabited country; a house only now and then to be seen, and a human being very rarely meeting their sight, except when they stopped at some dingy-looking inn to refresh the horses, and obtain a brief rest for themselves.

This again occasioned some enquiries from the marchioness, who wondered to what strange out of the way place they were going, but her husband laughed at her idle fears, as he called them, and admitting that their present road was dreary enough, he assured them that the country they were going to was a most delightful one, and that they would be amply rewarded when they reached the rich domains of Valliere.

"We could have gone by a more cheerful road," he said, "but the urgency of my business is so great that I have been induced to take the nearest way, in order that we may reach the end of our journey all the sooner."

"Is the castle much further, my lord?" asked Miss Betsy, who, like her sister, began to grow weary of the dull road they were travelling.

"No very great distance," replied the marquis.

"Perhaps we shall reach it to-night," added his bride.

"Not quite so soon as that," he replied;—"to-night we must sleep at an inn that we shall by and by come to, and to-morrow evening I hope we shall come in sight of the castle which is to be your future home."

"I wish we were there now, said Miss Plumley, "for, to confess the truth, I begin to be heartily sick of travelling so long without having any time allowed us for rest or refreshment."

"Never fear, my dear Betsy," exclaimed the major, "for the longest road has an end you know, and *when we do* reach your brother-in-law's castle, you will scarcely regret the little temporory inconvenience you have suffered."

"But I can't see any reason why my sister and myself should have suffered inconvenience at all," cried the young lady. "In England we were never used to it, and I'm sure travelling along such roads as these is anything but pleasant to any one that writes marchioness before her name."

"Do you begin to grow dissatisfied?" asked the marquis, in a tone of greater severity than he had ever used before.

"Why, I can't say that I exactly like it," she replied; "but, as it's no use saying anything about it now, I suppose the only way is to put up with it quietly."

"Wisely argued," said the marquis, with returning good humour; "and since you begin to see the necessity for resignation, I'll tell you that all the reward for this disagreeable travelling is to be found when we reach the end of our journey. There you will find everything the heart can possibly desire, and the good humour that was so nearly destroyed, will be quickly restored."

"But what will my father think of it," said Miss Plumley, "when he reaches Paris, and finds that we have left it so suddenly without giving him any clue by which he may be able to follow us?"

"I'll write to him as soon as we reach the castle," replied the marquis, "and then he can follow us there as soon as ever he thinks proper."

"Ah!" exclaimed the marchioness, overjoyed at hearing this; "then we shall soon see him, and I shall be able to show him over one of the castles that has come by marriage to his daughter. The good old man will be delighted when he sees the place, and perhaps he and my mother will make up their minds to leave England for the sake of coming to live near us."

"Perhaps he may," said her husband, "and you may depend on it, Emma, I shall urge him to do so as much as possible. It will be delightful to have him near us, and even if we had no other companions at the castle, he and I and the major would be able to pass our time happily enough."

"And you promise to write to him as soon as we get there?" exclaimed the marchioness.

"To be sure I shall, my love," he replied. "In fact, I should not have left Paris till after his arrival there, only that very particular business required my presence at Valliere, and, of course, he knows as well as I do that such things must be attended to, even at the hazard of sometimes appearing to act from mere caprice."

The marchioness could not but tacitly agree him with in this suggestion, they all proceeded some leagues further with few observations from any party, except such as were occasionally drawn forth by any remarkable objects that met their sight on the road. At length the shades of evening began to draw in, and about an hour after sunset they arrived before the door of a miserable-looking roadside-inn, where the marquis and the major alighted, and, having assisted the ladies out of the carriage, informed them they were to sleep there that night. This intimation was anything but agreeable to the marchioness and her sister, for they could see plainly enough that the house would afford them but scanty accommodation. But they were well aware that it would be in vain to utter any remonstrances upon the subject, and having desired Susan to look to their luggage, they slowly directed their steps towards the interior of this most uninviting house of entertainment.

"Hark'ye, young woman," said the marquis, addressing himself to Susan, who was busily engaged in obeying the directions she had received from her mistress; "there's no occasion for dragging all that luggage into the house. It will be quite safe where it is, and as we shall start again at

a very early hour to—morrow morning, it's not worth while disturbing anything just now."

"But my lord," replied our heroine; "the marchioness and her sister
will require their night-clothes, and——"

"Well, I suppose you will find all you want in that small trunk," he
said; "so take that in to them, and I dare say, if anything more should
be wanting, they'll put up with the inconvenience, as it's only for one
night."

And so saying he pulled out the little trunk he had spoke of from among
a good deal of other luggage, and giving it into her hands, desired her to go
immediately to the marchioness, and say he would follow directly.

This done, he ordered the carriage to be backed into a shed, which was
dignified with the name of " the coach-house," and having seen the horses
led away to the stable, he entered the house, where he found the marchioness rather warmly remonstrating with the major, on the subject of
the scanty accommodation they were likely to find in that out-of-the-way
place.

"Really, my dear marchioness," the major was saying, "it is no fault
of ours, I can assure you; for this road is so little frequented, that there is
no other place for leagues onwards, in which you could have found a
night's shelter. Nay, here, I see, is the marquis himself, and he will tell
you that however disagreeable your situation may be, there was, in fact, no
help for it."

"There was really no help for it, my dear," said the marquis, upon
being thus appealed to. "We must either have travelled all night, or rest
here, and of the two alternatives, I, of course, took what I conceived to be
the least."

"And Susan tells me," answered her ladyship, "that you have ordered
her not to remove anything out of the carriage."

No. 35

"Nothing but the trunk, which I believe she has brought into the house," replied her husband. "And as that, I suppose, contains all that you and your sister will want to-night, it would be useless to drag the luggage about, when we must start again on our journey at so early an hour on the following morning."

"And how many bed-rooms can be spared us?" asked the marchioness; "we shall want four, and the whole house don't seem to contain more than that number."

"I believe there is but one bed-room," replied the marquis, with great indifference; "but that contains two beds, which will do for yourself, your sister, and Susan."

"And what is to become of yourself and the major?"

"Oh, we can put up with anything," answered her husband; "and he and I have agreed to set up before a good fire, which will be no great hardship, seeing that we must resume our journey the first thing in the morning."

Upon this he and the major quitted the room, and the marchioness, who really began to feel rather uneasy at so unexpected an adventure, now directed her attention towards the hostess, who had been bustling about the room to prepare supper, and who every now and then seemed to regard them with a look in which pity might be plainly observed. She, however, spoke not, and even if she had, neither the ladies nor Susan would have understood a word she uttered, for none of them knew the French language, which was a circumstance that added no little to their embarrassment. A little further observation served to convince the females that the hostess was dumb, for she conversed even with those about her by signs, as she did also with her husband, who sat by the fire, and stared upon the glowing embers with all the stupid vacancy of confirmed idiotcy.

At length, the marquis and his friend, Major Smith, returned, and the wife of the former inquired whether there was no better room in the house to which they could retire to partake of supper, but the person she had addressed heard her with a smile, and assured her that she must be content where she was for that night, and console herself with the reflection that on the following evening she would be rewarded for her patience with all the elegance and splendour that she would find on her arrival at the castle.

"These little incidents on the road are mere trifles, my love," he said, "to those who are prepared to take life as they find it. For my own part, I always feel thankful for whatever I can get when I am travelling, and you will do well to follow an example that is deserving your most serious attention."

"My lord," exclaimed the marchioness, bitterly, "you seem to exult in the inconveniences I am put to. You make no effort to get more accommodation for me, and after sitting me down in a damp stone kitchen, you coolly preach to me about the virtue of resignation."

"Well, then, joking apart," said the marquis, "let me prevail on you to put up with the inconvenience as well as you can. A few hours will relieve you from it, and after a night's refreshing sleep, you will rise in the morning and laugh at the impatience you are now showing."

"But did you ever hear of a marchioness being obliged to put up with inconveniencies such as these, my lord?" asked Miss Betsy Plumley.

"Not very frequently, it must be confessed," he replied; "but when such things do happen, it is our duty to make as light of them as we possibly can. I and the major, for instance, shall be obliged to sit up all night, instead of having the comfort of a good warm feather bed; but we shall not grumble at it, though we have not been used to put up with inconveniences any more than you or your sister."

"Aye," replied the marchioness, "but if we had gone the other road, we should have found plenty of inns where they could have accommodated us according to our rank."

"And by so doing," answered the Marquis Valliere, "we should have been one day more on our journey. That was more time than I could spare, and, for that reason, I chose this shorter but less comfortable way."

"It's very unfortunate," said his wife, "that we could not remain in Paris till my father arrived. There we were happy enough, and surrounded by every luxury that the heart could desire; but who can look round upon this miserable hovel, which they call an inn, and not feel the sad contrast which the sight brings to one's mind?"

"I'm sorry you feel it so severely, my dear," replied the marquis; "but it's now too late to find a remedy, and, therefore, I can only advise you to make the best of it, by submitting with resignation."

At this moment the conversation was broken off by the announcement that supper was ready, and seating themselves round the table, they were rather agreeably surprised at finding a meal spread before them far better than, under circumstances, they had expected. This served to restore some of the good humour of the party, and the marquis and his friend, Major Smith, having indulged in a hearty laugh at the disappointment experienced by the ladies, began to chat over sundry affairs, in the course of which they took care to speak in high terms of the magnificence of the castle they were going to, and the illustrious company that was to visit the marquis and his bride, shortly after their arrival there.

This acted, as was intended, as a great palliative to the marchioness and her sister, who now began to reason with themselves on the folly of giving way to trifles, and, by the time the ladies rose to go to bed, the good humour which had been disturbed, was completely restored; and they took leave of the gentlemen with an understanding that they were to set off on the following morning immediately after an early breakfast.

The bed-room they found furnished in the same homely style that marked the rest of the house, but no dissatisfaction was uttered on this subject, for they were heartily tired of the long journey they had had; and, under those circumstances, almost any accommodation was a luxury that they felt was not to be despised. Neither the marchioness nor her sister could forget the strange sort of people that lived in the house, and from Susan, who it seems had been making inquiries, they learnt that the landlady was dumb, and her husband nearly, if not quite an idiot. However, the two ladies at length talked themselves to sleep, and Susan would gladly have obtained some rest too, but her mind was occupied with a good many thoughts, and though she tried to forget them all, she lay for some hours without being able to obtain the repose she so much desired. At last, however, she fell into a disturbed slumber, in the course of which all sorts of horrible visions haunted her imagination, and from which she was aroused by hearing a great deal of talking under the window, and among the voices she thought she could recognize those of the marquis and Major Smith. This, however, seemed so improbable, that she again sunk into a short slumber, but only to be once more awakened by the noise of what appeared to her to be coach-wheels. She listened anxiously to this, and still she heard the same voices talking loudly, but not with sufficient distinctness for her to hear a word that was said. Then succeeded the heavy sounds of footsteps, as they tramped across the freshly-gravelled road, and she began to wonder what all this could mean, till she recollected that she was now at an inn, and that most likely other travellers had arrived, who, not being able to find accommodation there, were obliged to go further.

This, for a time, satisfied her, and she was insensibly falling into another nap, when she heard the sharp smack of the postilion's whip, and immediately afterwards the rattling of carriage-wheels assured her that the persons, whoever they might be, had proceeded on their journey. Upon this she jumped out of bed and ran to the window, to see which direction they had taken, but in this respect, she was disappointed, for, owing to the darkness of the night, she could not distinguish objects at any distance from her, and as she saw the ostler with his lantern, returning towards the house, she again stepped into her own bed, without disturbing either the marchioness or her sister, who, overpowered with fatigue, had heard nothing of what was going forward.

After this, she fell asleep and woke not again till seven o'clock in the morning, when her mind once more reverted to what had taken place during the night. She thought, however, that there was nothing very remarkable in an occurrence of that kind at an inn, where the inmates were liable to be disturbed at all hours of the night by travellers, and as neither of the ladies had been disturbed by the noise and clatter that had been made, she said nothing about it, expecting that if anything particular had happened, the subject would be mentioned by the marquis and his friend, whose voices she was almost certain were to be distinguished among others, whilst the carriage was waiting at the door.

By this time the marchioness and Miss Betsy had quite recovered their good humour, for they were in high spirits at the idea of so soon setting forward again on their journey towards the castle of Valliere. On proceeding down stairs, however, neither the marquis nor his friend were to be seen anywhere about the place, and as neither of the females could speak a word of French, they were obliged to rest satisfied with the supposition that they had gone to see the horses and carriages got ready for their immediate departure. To satisfy themselves, therefore, upon this point, Susan was sent out to see if she could find them in the stable or coach-house, but what was their consternation and alarm when she returned a short time afterwards with the intelligence that neither the marquis nor the major were to be seen anywhere about the place, and that the carriage and horses were no longer in the same situation where they had been left of the previous night.

Startled at this news, the marchioness put a number of questions to the hostess; but the woman could make no reply except by signs, and when she immediately afterwards addressed herself to the man who was setting by the fire exactly in the same position that she had seen him occupy on the preceding night, she found that he understood not a word that she had been speaking to him, and that, therefore, all hopes of receiving any information from that quarter were equally vain.

In this dilemma, however, she exerted herself to maintain all the firmness she could command, and endeavouring to exhibit as little alarm as possible, she declared it to be her opinion that the marquis and Major Smith had gone out for a short ride, and that they would return again in the course of an hour or two. But they waited many weary hours, and saw the evening advancing towards them, yet not one word had they heard respecting those for whose appearance they were waiting with such breathless anxiety!

"Well!" exclaimed Miss Betsy on one occasion when Susan, for about the fiftieth time returned with the usual answer that she could neither see nor hear anything of the absentees; "if this ain't a strange adventure, I don't know what is. Here are we, left in a barbarous and scarcely inhabited country, whilst your husband and Major Smith are rambling about, nobody knows where, as if one had not a wife and the other a sweetheart, that expected a little of their attention."

" Psha ! they will be back by and bye," said the marchioness, " and I dare say come when they will, we shall hear a very satisfactory reason, for the absence which at present fills us with so much uneasiness. Some unexpected business, I dare say, has compelled them to leave us for a few hours, or perhaps, which is still more likely, they intend to give us a sudden surprise, which will more than make up for the temporary alarm they have occasioned."

" I wish I could think upon the matter with as much philosophical coolness as you do, sister," exclaimed Miss Betsy, who began to wear a very long face upon the matter; " but, for the life of me, I cannot help thinking it very queer that they should have gone away and left us in this abrupt manner."

" Why, what strange notion have you formed now ?" asked the marchioness, unable to conceal the uneasiness which these words had occasioned. " They have never left us till now, even for a moment, and we have, therefore, no reason to suppose that they have brought us here with the base design of leaving us to find our way as well as we can."

" You may think as favourably as you like about it," replied Miss Plumley ; " but to say the least of them, their conduct is very unaccountable, and even should they return, as you expect they will, I shall not fail to let Major Smith know that I, for one, am not inclined to endure this sort of treatment without showing my resentment."

" What is your opinion of it, Susan ?" asked the marchioness, " for you have seen nearly about as much of the Marquis Valliere as either of us, and, therefore, may have formed some notion as to what may be the cause of this most extraordinary conduct."

" Perhaps, your ladyship," answered Susan, " the reply I should give, may not be uttered without offence."

" You have been asked the question," exclaimed her mistress, " and, therefore, need not fear exciting any of my anger."

" Well, then," replied Susan, " if the truth must be told, I have a notion that we shall never see anything more either of the marquis or his friend."

" Indeed ! you believe then, that they have absconded, and left us here to our fate ?"

" I do, indeed, my lady."

" But there must have been some cause for doing so," replied the marchioness, " and I declare, most solemnly, that I am not acquainted with any reason that could possibly excuse such base and heartless conduct."

" Perhaps they have gone on to the castle of Valliere," observed Miss Betsy Plumley.

" I rather think that's not very likely," replied Susan, " for, between ourselves, I rather think there is not such a place to be found in all France."

" Psha !" exclaimed the marchioness, " that is but an assumption of your own, without any foundation to warrant it."

" I was afraid your ladyship might be offended if I spoke my mind too freely," said our heroine, " and yet, I am sorry to say, I think there is but too much reason for thinking the affair stands exactly as I have said. At any rate, from the little I have been able to gather, it seems quite certain that when they went away from here, they took an exactly contrary direction from that which they have all along said, led towards the castle of Valliere."

" And if that don't look suspicious, I don't know what does," said Miss Plumley. " Indeed, sister, I no longer feel any doubt upon the subject, and if you will only take my advice, we shall return to Paris with all possible despatch, where we shall meet our father, who will not only afford us the protection we so much require, but will also take speedy measures to hunt out this precious marquis of yours, and if he proves to be an impostor, it will not be long before he meets his deserts."

" Do you believe it possible he can be an impostor?" exclaimed the marchioness, in a tone of terror.

" I am afraid it is very possible," replied her sister; " and, consequently, that you have married a mere fortune hunter, who had not a farthing in the world to save himself from gaol."

" But he has not yet got any fortune," said the marchioness; " for, luckily, our father would not pay it to him till we had been three months married, so that, if your suspicions are correct, we shall have escaped his snares better than might have been expected."

" And you may depend upon it I am not far from right," exclaimed her sister.

" Yet still I can hardly think it possible," said the marchioness; " for even if he should be the villain you have pictured him, he would hardly have committed so glaring an act of folly as this; for had he waited a short time longer, he would have received from my father's hand the marriage portion that was promised with me, and which would have been so well worth his having."

" There's no doubt it was for that he married you, my lady," interposed Susan; " but, at the same time, I must suggest that there's no telling exactly what may have been his reason for disappearing so suddenly. He may have done something that has set the police in search after him, or a thousand other causes might be thought of as the reason for disappearing so suddenly with the major."

" And now I think of it," said Miss Plumley, " it seems very strange that they should have left Paris almost directly after we had received my father's letter, announcing his direct refusal of the major for a son-in-law, and declaring his intention of joining us without delay. I remember thinking it very odd that the two gentlemen should hold a consultation together immediately afterwards; but as I knew Major Smith was greatly disappointed at the refusal he had met with, I thought most likely they were conferring together to arrange how they might best bring my father to consent to his wish of becoming my husband. Now, however, I can see through their schemes, and I have no doubt it was then decided between them that it would be better to decamp before they found themselves in a dilemma."

" Especially," said Susan, " as your father said he should go on a visit to the marquis's castle, and as that, perhaps, was not very conveniently to be found, it was very certain that an immediate explosion of the whole villany must follow."

" And after all," cried Miss Plumley, " I should not wonder if the stories told by the major about his visits to the prince and other great personages were all falsehoods."

" There's no doubt about it, Miss," exclaimed Susan; " for I have no great opinion of people that go about in all sorts of disguises. First of all you knew the major as a valet; then when we got to Dieppe, he was something else, and at last, upon reaching Paris, he again introduced himself to you as Major Smith. But I rather think I have known him longer than you, and if my suspicions are correct, it's likely enough that he was concerned in an affair that may cost him his life on a gibbet."

" Good Heavens!—what mean you, Susan?" exclaimed both the ladies, in breathless astonishment.

" Why, I am not quite certain that he committed the crime, or was even concerned in it," replied Susan; "but you have heard me mention the circumstance of Mr. Wentford's murder, and I am positive that on the very night that was done, I saw Major Smith, as he calls himself, prowling about the garden, and a very ragged, miserable object he was then, in spite of the fine clothes he now wears."

"Are you quite sure it was him?" asked the marchioness.

"As sure as one can well feel," replied Susan; "and what's more than all, think I am right, is, that he has never looked me straight forward in the face, and always tried to avoid me as much as possible whenever we chanced to meet."

"But there may have been other reasons for his doing so," answered Miss Plumley; "for he knew you to be a faithful and attached servant of our's, and, perhaps, felt afraid that you would say something to us to his prejudice."

"And he had very good reason to be afraid of me," exclaimed Susan; "for even before your sister's marriage, I found him and the marquis at their dirty tricks."

"And yet you told us nothing about it till this moment," said the marchioness.

"That was because I was threatened with death if I ever dared utter a word that I had overheard," replied Susan. "However, I took an early opportunity of mentioning it to your mother, but scarcely had I begun what I had to say, when the marquis entered the room, and turned all that I had been relating into a jest. In fact, he told Mrs. Plumley that both he and the major were aware that I was listening, and that they afterwards said things in joke to see what mischief I would make of it."

"And my mother believed him?" said the marchioness.

"She did," answered Susan, "and I got lectured for my pains, and was desired never to speak again upon a subject that had no foundation in truth."

At this point the conversation ended, and the remainder of the day was spent in anxious expectation; but no news arrived of the fugitives, and at a late hour of the night they all three retired to bed—not, however, to sleep, but to think over the villany that had been practised on them, and, if possible, to devise some scheme or other by which they might find means to reach Paris, where it was expected Mr. Plumley would arrive before long.

CHAPTER XXXIX.

SUSAN'S DIFFICULTIES INCREASE.

Two days of intense anxiety and suspense passed away without bringing even the slightest improvement in the situation of those who had been left thus helpless among strangers and in a foreign country. The marchioness and her sister were in terrible alarm at the misfortune to which they had been reduced by the villany of the men they had placed so much reliance in, and had it not been for the coolness and better judgment of Susan, they would have given way to the despair which their forsaken condition was so likely to give rise to. She, however, consoled them with the hope that succour would arrive in spite of the present unfavourable aspect of affairs; and having in some degree succeeded in restoring the young ladies to a confidence in the future, she began to consider how she might best aid them in the perplexing dilemma into which they had fallen.

But it was in vain that she addressed herself to the hostess, for it became more and more evident that she was dumb, and equally useless was it that she spoke to the man, for he was an idiot, and not one word could she get from him that would serve in any way to clear up the mystery in which the whole affair was involved. Thus situated, she next applied to a boy that occasionally gave assistance in the house, but her language was not understood by him, and staring at her with surprise, he walked away muttering something or other, but what it was, she was altogether unable to make out. So, finding that she could do nothing towards releasing themselves from their difficulties, she hurried off to her young ladies and told them all she had been doing, and how unsuccessful she had been.

"Alas!" cried the marchioness, in despair, "then, it is even as bad as my worst fears anticipated. We have been left here by those in whom we relied, and, no doubt, measures have been taken to prevent our returning to Paris, or having any communication with those who, if they knew the situation we are placed in, would gladly hasten to our rescue."

"We have been cruelly deceived," exclaimed Miss Plumley, "and, doubtless, they have gone to our father with some false tidings of us, and when your husband receives the portion he was to have with you, he and the pretended major will go somewhere abroad, and thus escape the punishment they so richly deserve."

"I dare say they will do their best to get the money from your father," said Susan; "but it must be our task to prevent their succeeding in that design before it is too late."

"And how are we to do that?" asked the marchioness.

"Not very easily, it must be admitted," replied Susan; "but sitting down quietly here will do no good, and so, if my advice is taken, we will begin our task at once."

"What task do you propose?" asked Miss Plumley.

"I would have you write a couple of letters to your father," answered our heroine—"one of them to be addressed to him at his house at Dalston, and the other to be sent to the hotel in Paris, where we lodged previous to setting out on this unfortunate journey. He will, of course, go there to make enquiries after you, and should the first letter happen to miss him, the other will be sure to be put into his hands immediately upon his stating who he is, and the object that brought him to Paris."

"Alas!" sighed the unhappy marchioness; "it is easier to suggest such a scheme than to carry it into execution. The letters, I grant you, may be written, but in this out of the way place where are we to find a person that will put them into the post-office?"

"I dare say that may be managed much better than you expect," replied Susan; "the boy that I have seen about the place will, I dare say, be glad to earn a trifle by performing the service, and in case of his refusal, I will myself walk to the next town, however far it may be off from hence, and put the letters into the post-office; so that your father will soon learn the scandalous trick that has been played upon you, and in the course of a few days he will hasten to relieve you both from this place."

"At all events it will be worth trying," observed Miss Plumley; "and if it should indeed prove the means of our deliverance, I know not how we can be grateful enough to you, Susan, for the faithful zeal with which you have served us throughout the trial that has so unexpectedly befallen us."

"But surely," cried the marchioness; "you would not have Susan leave us, merely that she may convey a letter there, which, after all, may never reach our father?"

"Why, the truth is, I see no other way," replied Miss Plumley; "for it seems to be pretty clear that no one about this house is likely to be our

messenger, and as Susan has offered her services on the occasion, I see not how we can very well refuse to accept them."

" Are you afraid of being left here whilst I go ?" asked our heroine.

" I must confess I am," answered the marchioness.

" And so am I," answered her sister ; "but of two evils I think we had better choose the least, and as Susan will not be very long gone, we must keep up our courage as well as we can, and if she only succeeds in getting the letters into the post, we may expect assistance in the course of a few days."

" But the next town," observed the marchioness ; "may chance to be at some distance from this place."

" I have no doubt it is," replied Susan ; "for yesterday the boy was sent there on an errand, and it was nearly eight hours before he came back again."

" And would you leave me for so long a time as that ?" asked the marchioness, in alarm.

" I would not do so if it could be helped," answered the other ; "but what else can be done under our present circumstances ?"

" That's true enough," exclaimed Miss Plumley ; "for the little money we have will not last us long, and when that is gone the people here will, perhaps, turn us adrift, without so much as a farthing to take the three of us back to Paris."

" Well," exclaimed the marchioness ; "let it be as you please then ; but before you go, Susan, let me again beg of you to come back as soon as possible. We have much need of your services, and to lose them under our present circumstances, would, indeed, be one of the heaviest misfortunes that could befall us."

" There is very little doubt but what I shall succeed," answered Susan ; " but I would just hint to you not to be alarmed in the event of my being

No. 36

longer away than we at present anticipate. The distance may be greater than I expect, and as I don't understand one word of their language, I may be put to some trouble before I am able to find the post-office."

"It is, indeed, most unfortunate that none of us should understand the language of this country," cried the marchioness; "in fact, had we known ever so little, we might have obtained some information from the people here, who, it is likely enough, know something of the marquis and his friend, and whether either of them have a right to the rank and title they have assumed."

"There's no doubt whatever in my mind, about that subject," observed her sister.

"You believe, then, I have been imposed upon?"

"Aye, most cruelly."

"And that I have been married to a mere adventurer, whose only aim was to secure the large fortune that everybody was aware my father intended to give me?"

"What else can we think?" asked Miss Plumley; "have they not brought us away from all those who would have protected us from their villany; and having drawn us to this out of the way place, have they not both decamped, leaving us with scarcely money enough to support us for a fortnight?"

"And there's no doubt," interposed Susan; "that they would have had even that little money, had there been any way of getting possession of it without exciting your suspicion as to their honourable intentions. And in my opinion they ought to be satisfied with what they have got, for if chance should throw them in your father's way, he will not fail to punish them as far as ever the law will go."

"And serve them right too," exclaimed Miss Plumley; "I declare I cannot think with patience of my own folly in believing the falsehoods of the self-styled Major Smith, whose coarse vulgarity ought to have been quite sufficient to assure me, that he held no rank whatever in the army."

"That's very true," said Susan; "and for my own part I had no opinion of him after we discovered that he was no other than the servant that had waited upon the marquis at your father's house. To be sure he said that it was love for you that had prompted him to assume the disguise, but you may rest assured no honourable man would have taken such a step, seeing that he had no reason to suppose that your father would reject him in the event of his having fairly stated his love for you, and proved that he belonged to a respectable family."

"Aye, there was his difficulty," exclaimed the young lady. "He knew how impossible it would be to satisfy my father in that respect, and, detecting my weakness, he had recourse to a stratagem that had but too nearly proved successful. In fact, to confess my own folly, he proposed an elopement, and so little did I then suspect his villany, that I verily believe, had he spoken again upon the subject, I should have been romantic enough to have run away with him."

"Your escape, Miss," cried Susan; "has indeed been a most miraculous one."

"So much so," replied the young lady; "that I think I shall hardly be inclined to place my reliance on the word of man in future. However, I feel rejoiced at the lucky escape I have had, and as for our detention at this place, I should think nothing of it, if it was not for the trouble that has befallen my sister, and the mortification she must endure at the reflection of having been married to a swindler instead of being the Marchioness Valliere, as, of course, she naturally enough expected. But I see she has finished the two letters for our father, and as her mortification is quite enough without reminding her of the past, you will now merely receive her instructions respecting the method you are to adopt in your visit to the next town; and remember, Susan, above all other things, not to be absent from us one moment longer than you can help."

"That you may be sure of, Miss," replied Susan; "for depend on it, I shall be quite as anxious to come back as you and your sister will be to see me."

"I have every confidence both in your desire to serve us, and your ability to undertake this task," said the marchioness, placing in the hands of Susan the two letters which she had been writing. "The task, however," she continued; "is by no means an easy one, and therefore if you feel any disinclination to go on this errand, you have but to say so, and we will all three remain as we are till fortune once more smiles upon us, and guides my father to the place where we have been so shamefully abandoned and forsaken."

"I shall take the letters, let what may come of it," exclaimed Susan; "and though I may not succeed to the extent of my wishes, I can, at all events, promise to do my best towards the fulfilment of the task I have taken upon myself. Besides, I have got all the day before me, and by the time evening begins to close in, I hope to return with news that I have succeeded to the utmost of your hopes."

Having attired herself for walking, our heroine now took leave of the young ladies, and was about to quit the house on her errand, when it occurred to her that she might as well go into the kitchen and make one more effort to render herself intelligible to those who had been unable to understand a word that she had addressed to them. Still, however, she was doomed to disappointment in this respect, for the hostess remained just as silent as she had been all along, and her husband, who listened to her words with an air of idiotic surprise, started all on a sudden from his seat, and walked out of the house as if he had understood what she had said, and was offended at the bribe that had been offered in the event of his taking the letters to their intended destination. Under these circumstances, Susan left the place, and having first looked carefully about to see if anybody was watching her, she took the first road that presented itself before her, leaving it to chance to direct her in the right course.

And soon she regretted more and more her inability to speak the language of the country, for occasionally she met persons who would have been able and, no doubt, willing enough to give her the information she required, but having made two or three unsuccessful attempts, she gave the matter up in despair, resolving to trust entirely to her own unwearying patience, and to walk on until she reached a town, even though she might have to travel a dozen miles ere she accomplished a task that would be so important in its results.

At length she came to a dreary part of the road, where, for a long time she saw no signs of a human habitation, and then believing that she must have chosen a road that did not lead to a town, she paused for a few moments to consider what she had better do under the doubtful circumstances in which she was placed. In fact, she made up her mind to retrace the steps she had taken, and pursue some other route, when a figure was seen at no great distance, and hoping to obtain some intelligence that might be of service, she resolved to wait where she was till the stranger came up, and then to ask those questions which had been so uselessly put on every previous occasion. As the man approached nearer, she recognized him as a person that she had occasionally seen at the house where she and the young ladies had been left, and having formed no very favourable opinion of him from the mystery that he seemed to observe, she was on the point of turning her footsteps in another direction, when he held up a letter in his hand, and shouted something to her that she did not understand. She, however, thought a brief interview might terminate in her favour, and in that hope remained where she was till the stranger had reached the spot where she was standing.

He then asked her a question which she was unable to answer, but quickly changing his tactics, he by signs enquired whether she did not come from the road-side inn a few miles off. To this she nodded an assent, upon which he put the letter into her hands, and requested that she would give it to the people of the house immediately upon her return. This, by another sign, she assured him she would do, and the man bowing civily, turned away, and left her to pursue her journey without further molestation.

This, to Susan, appeared rather odd, but the man's conduct was not marked by the lest rudeness, and though she could not imagine why he should have made her his messenger, she thought there was probably some mistake originating in their being ignorant of each others' language, and thinking there could be no harm in delivering the letter, she put it in her pocket, and once more set forward in the hope of being able to find a town, as she had at first anticipated. But she walked on three or four miles further, without any better result, and was at length almost despairing of success, when, on reaching the summit of the hill, she saw just at the foot of it, a large populous-looking town, where she doubted not she should be able to execute the errand which had cost her so much toil and weariness. This sight served to give her fresh courage, and exerting herself to the utmost, she was increasing her speed, when a couple of men came down suddenly upon her, from a cross road, and briefly addressed her in words that she did not understand. She, however, answered, by earnestly imploring them not to delay her journey, and making a sudden spring forward, endeavoured to avoid a longer interview by flight.

But in this she was doomed to disappointment, for her alarm was soon increased by hearing them in rapid pursuit, and scarcely had she proceeded twenty paces, when she was seized hold by the two men, one of whom placing a pistol at her head, growled something, that she was but too conscious was a threat of instant death, unless she quietly submitted herself to their custody. This conduct, together with their surly manner of addressing her, convinced Susan that she had fallen into the hands of robbers, and in the terror with which this thought filled her, she fell upon her knees, and earnestly besought them not to delay her journey, but to take what little money she had in her possession, and then permit her to depart without further molestation.

But she might as well have addressed herself to the winds, for the men knew not a syllable of what she had been uttering, and roughly lifting her upon her feet, they pointed to a house just at the entrance of the town, and by signs, intimated that she must go with them to the place they had indicated. This, at any rate, was some consolation to Susan, for she thought that had they indeed been robbers, they would not have lived so near the place she saw before her, and then recollecting that she had heard when in England, that on the continent every town was guarded by barriers, through which people could not pass till they had gone through certain forms, she began to grow more easy upon the subject of her adventure, and intimated that she was quite willing to accompany them without force to the place they had pointed out.

Upon this they once more set forward, and Susan could perceive that though the fellows no longer laid their hands upon her, yet was she watched by them with a jealous eye, and any attempt to escape, would not only have been frustrated, but the consequence would have been anything but favourable to herself. Still, however, she experienced less fear then she did at their first meeting, and believing they would allow her to proceed after certain forms had been complied with, she felt perfectly easy as to the result of this unexpected adventure.

But in this she was bitterly disappointed, for no sooner had they entered the house, than a surly-looking old woman was summoned, to whose care they committed our heroine, and the next moment she was led to an inner apartment, where she was strictly searched, to ascertain whether she had any smuggled goods about her. All that her pockets contained, were then taken possession of, and the old woman was about to lock her up in an adjoining chamber till further orders, when Susan, unable any longer to endure the delay which this subjected her to, burst into tears, and earnestly implored to be released.

"Oh, ha!" exclaimed the woman; "you are an Englishwoman, are you? and that accounts for our men not being able to understand anything you said."

"I am," said Susan, delighted at having at length found some one to converse with; "I am a stranger in this country, and you, perhaps, will be the friend of one who has much need of kindness."

"Kindness is a thing that can't be thought of here," replied the other, shaking her head. "We are put in this place to keep people honest, and if we happen to find any one breaking the laws, we are obliged to detain them till they are carried before a magistrate for examination."

"But I am not aware that I have broken any of your laws," answered Susan, "and even if I have, it has been in consequence of my not knowing the customs peculiar to the country in which I have only just arrived."

"Humph!" exclaimed the woman, "here are three letters, I see, and they, I suppose, will pretty well explain your business in France, and whether or not, you are connected with the smugglers."

"I am not connected with any such persons," replied Susan; "and as for the letters you have found upon me, two of them I was going to put into the post for my young ladies, and the other one I received from a man as I came along, who asked me to give it to the people where we are at present staying."

"And what is the name of the people?" asked the other.

"Deleroix," replied Susan.

"And how long have you lived with them?"

"Only a few days."

"You have lived there a few days," exclaimed the old woman, "and yet know not that they have the reputation of being the most desperate smugglers in all the province!"

"It is as I have told you," replied Susan;—"we went to their house by mere accident, and my young ladies are now staying there sorely against their own will."

"Indeed!—is there any restraint placed upon them?"

"That I cannot answer," returned Susan, "for no intimation has yet been given of their wish to leave the place, though I have reason to suspect that if they attempted to quit the house, they would be prevented doing so."

"They are kept there as prisoners, then?"

"I cannot say they are exactly prisoners," answered our heroine; "but our adventures, if once entered upon, would take so long to relate, that I can only inform you my mistresses have been deceived by villains, who have now abandoned them at the house I have mentioned, and where they must remain till the arrival of their father, which, I expect, will take place in the course of a few days."

"Does the old gentleman know where to find his daughters?" asked the other, inquisitively.

"At present he does not," replied Susan; "but two of the letters you have taken from me, are intended for him, and, therefore, I trust you will throw no obstacle in the way, when speed is of so much importance."

"But there are two letters addressed to one person;—surely that was unnecessary?"

"That," replied Susan, "was to make sure that he receives an intimation of the misfortunes that have befallen his daughters. One of the letters, as you may convince yourself, is addressed to my master's house in England, and the other to an hotel, where it is expected he will go immediately on his arrival in Paris. So you see he will be certain to receive intelligence of the young ladies from one source or the other."

"And do they know where to direct him in search of them?"

"No," answered Susan; "but when he hears the situation they are placed in, he will apply to the police, and through their means, I dare say he will soon be able to discover the place they have been taken to."

"Humph!" ejaculated the other, after a short pause; "this is a very marvellous story you have been telling me, young woman, and there may be some truth in it, though, I must confess, I don't give credit to all I hear."

"In this instance you are not deceived," exclaimed Susan, anxious that her story should not be discredited. "We have been taken to the place I told you of, and then deserted,—a fact which you may readily convince yourself of by enquiring at the house where the young ladies are waiting my return."

"It's no business of mine to make any questions about it," replied the woman; "and as for the anxiety of the ladies you speak of, they must console themselves in the best way they can, for if even you get out of this affair tolerably easy, they'll have to wait till to-morrow afternoon before they see you."

"Good Heavens!" cried Susan, in alarm; "am I a prisoner?"

"You are."

"On what charge?"

"Come, come," exclaimed the woman, "you mustn't pretend quite so much ignorance as that. Wasn't you going to pass the barriers on the sly?—And haven't we found letters on you, one of which is directed to a person that has long since been suspected of being engaged in smuggling?"

"That I know nothing about," cried the alarmed girl;—"the letter was given to me by a stranger to give to the people it's addressed to, and not suspecting there was any harm in doing a good-natured action, I readily undertook to perform the little service."

"And a very awkward dilemma it's likely to get you into," exclaimed the old woman.

"Not, I should imagine," returned Susan, "when I come fairly to explain the affair. The magistrate will see that a stranger has been led into an unvoluntary error, and surely he will then order me to be discharged from custody."

"That's more than I can answer for," said the other. "In short, I rather think you will have to give a more satisfactory explanation of this affair before you find yourself at liberty to return from where you came."

"They can enquire into the truth of my assertions," said Susan.

"No doubt they will do so," replied the woman; "but they may not hurry themselves about it, and in that case you will have to remain in custody three or four days."

"Three or four days," cried our heroine, in despair; "and must my young ladies remain in suspense all that time, uncertain of my fate, or perhaps believing that I have forsaken them, to secure my own safety in flight?"

"There's no help for it," said the old woman, coolly.

"Can I send a message to them?"

"Not very easily," replied the other; "for if matters should take a serious turn, those that go on your errands will stand a chance of being suspected to belong to the smugglers. So the only way is to let things take their course, and, perhaps, the worst that will happen, may be a few days loss of liberty."

"It is not my liberty that I care about," answered Susan, "but those I have left behind, will be terrified at my absence, and cruelly forsaken as they have been in a foreign country, there is not one friend left to comfort or console them."

"Aye, aye, it's a very bad case, I dare say," exclaimed the old woman, "but it can't be helped, you know; and, therefore, the only way is to put up with it as quietly as you can."

"I could do so," replied Susan, "if I was only certain that any one would go for me and inform the marchioness and her sister of the accident that has befallen me."

"What!" exclaimed the woman, "and do you mean seriously to tell me that a marchioness is lodging among a parcel of smugglers, and people of bad character?"

"I know nothing about their being smugglers," answered Susan, "but I have already told you that the young ladies were taken to the house under false pretences, and in the course of the night the two *gentlemen* that were with us, found means to leave the house in the carriage, and from that moment nothing has been seen or heard of them."

"And were they the husbands of the ladies?"

"One of them was married to my eldest mistress," replied Susan, "and the other was courted by the major, who, for some reason, which yet remains to be explained, decamped at the very moment when he might have secured the thirty thousand pounds, which will be her marriage portion."

"Upon my word, young woman, this is a very romantic story you have been telling me," said the other, shaking her head. "One of the men was a marquis, you say, and the other a major; yet they run away from a couple of ladies, and leave them in an obscure place without any cause being given for their doing so."

"I believe them both to be swindlers," answered Susan, "and that the rank they assumed, was as false as they themselves have proved. Nay, I am quite certain that they are impostors, and when once Mr. Plumley arrives, steps will be taken to prove their villany, and procure a divorce for the unfortunate lady, who has been so cruelly deceived."

"And, pray," asked the other, "what was the name the marquis thought proper to go by?"

But before Susan could reply to this, the two men who had taken her into custody entered the room, and in a surly tone, addressed the old woman. But the conversation that ensued, was not understood by the prisoner, who saw the female give them the letters she had taken from her, with which they left the room, after muttering something else, which she construed into a command to keep strict watch, and not to suffer her to escape on any account."

"I told you how it would be, young woman," said the other, as soon as the men were fairly out of hearing. "The letter addressed to Deleroix is considered of great importance against you, and they have gone before their principal to hear from him whether you are to be kept a prisoner here."

" I expected as much," exclaimed Susan, " and, therefore, am not surprised at the information you have given me.   In fact, I submit myself to my fate, and all I request is, that I may be taken before a magistrate with as little delay as possible."

" Most likely it won't be long before they do that," answered the woman; " and I only hope you may be able to convince your hearers that you know nothing more of the Deleroix family than from the circumstance of having been taken to the house, and there deserted by the two men you have been speaking about."

" I am afraid," observed our heroine, " that there will be little chance of my doing so, since I know not one word of the language, and, therefore, any assertions that may be made, will remain uncontradicted, and thus my silence will be construed into an admission of guilt."

" Perhaps so," replied the other, " and yet if many persons happen to be in the court, there may be some among them that will understand English."

" But as that is a poor chance to rely on," exclaimed Susan, " it has just this moment struck me that you will perhaps go with me and explain this affair exactly as I have related it to you."

" That would not be allowed," she replied, " for it is my duty to be constantly in this place, and were I to leave it for such a purpose you have mentioned, I should be turned out upon the world to suffer beggary and starvation.   So now, as you know the worst, I will leave you for the present, and all I can say further is, that I hope you will find matters not quite so serious as you seem to expect."

Upon being left alone, Susan had more leisure and opportunity to think over the strange vicissitudes that had befallen her, and never did she yield so much to despair as she did on finding herself in this situation, far from her friends, and in a strange country, where she could look for neither pity or compassion.   The letter found upon her, would, she was convinced, prove important evidence against her, for even if it had been in her power to speak the French language, there was little chance of anybody giving any credit to her assertions that she had received the letter from a stranger whom she had met in her way, and had been induced to promise that it should be delivered into the hands of the party to whom it was addressed.

She, therefore, saw little probability of regaining her liberty for some time to come, and her principal aim now was to convey intelligence of her situation to the marchioness and her sister ;—cautioning them to leave the Deleroix family as soon as possible, and to make no enquiries about herself, lest they should fall into the same dilemma, and endure the terror of imprisonment, through a kind, but useless effort, to release her from bondage. But she could find no opportunity of conveying the message upon which so much depended, and she reflected with pain upon the anxiety and uneasiness that must afflict those, who, uncertain of the cause which had led to her long absence, would suffer a degree of painful suspense that she could but too well imagine.

Tortured by a thousand conflicting thoughts, she was left three hours to herself, at the end of which period the men she had seen before again made their appearance, and by signs intimated that she was to follow them without delay.   This command, of course, she had neither the power nor inclination to resist, and rising from the seat on which she had thrown herself she gave them to understand that she was quite willing to accompany them as soon as they thought proper to lead the way.   Hereupon a brief consultation took place between them, and when that was concluded to their satisfaction, one of the men advanced towards the door, and Susan stepping immediately after him, was closely followed by the other officer, and thus

she was guarded before and behind, so as to leave no chance for her escape, even should she happen to attempt it.

It was a sore disgrace to poor Susan to be thus publicly paraded through the town, for she could observe the surprise with which people stared at her, and the words which they uttered, though not absolutely understood were judged to be of such a nature, as would have been deeply mortifying had she really known what they meant. But she was among strangers, and that circumstance served in some degree to soften the shame and humiliation that she would have endured, had there been any likelihood of being seen by persons with whom she was acquainted.

At length they reached a large building, handsomely decorated on the exterior, where a crowd of persons were assembled, and from the eager conversation that was being carried on among them, it was pretty evident that something had occurred in the town which had occasioned more than usual excitement. Susan at once conceived that the building before her was the Town Hall, and having seen crowds in front of the police offices in London, she at once imagined that a case of particular interest was going on within, and that the people were waiting to catch a glimpse of the parties as they were conveyed from thence to the prison, where they were to await their trial. All this, however, was nothing more than a guess on her part, and as her conductors paused at the entrance of the Town Hall, she kept her eye steadfastly fixed upon the door, in anxious expectation of seeing the persons whose evil doings had created so deep a sensation among the inhabitants of the place.

At length, a buz was heard among the assembled multitude, and a great bustle took place among the foremost of the crowd, indicating that the examination was over, and that the persons in custody were about to make their appearance. This served still further to increase the anxiety

No. 37

of our heroine, who immediately rushed forward to catch a glimpse of the parties that had occasioned so much curiosity, but as she did so, the two men who had conducted her there sprang after her, and she was dragged back, but not before she had seen the two prisoners, and recognized in them no other persons than the Marquis Valliere and Major Smith.

Again she would have darted forward to address them, and demand an explanation of their conduct, but the men who had her in custody imagined that she intended to give them the slip, and, in spite of her earnest entreaties, they dragged her a little way from the crowd, and in another moment the two persons she so much desired to speak to, had disappeared with the guards by whom they were accompanied. This was mortifying enough, and at that moment she regretted more than ever her inability to ask questions of the people about her, for she could see plainly enough that the pretended marquis and his friend had in some way or other committed themselves, and were now in a fair way of receiving the punishment which their crimes against others so justly merited. Her thoughts, however, were again interrupted by the buz and general curiosity that she could observe among those about her, and once more directing her eyes towards the door, she saw an elegantly-attired female step forward, and who should this be but the very Dolly Pratt who had eloped from Mr. Wentford's house on the night of the old gentleman's murder.

Again did Susan make a vigorous attempt to break from those who were guarding her, but her efforts were as useless as before, and, to her deep mortification, she saw the female pass onwards and disappear through the gates that gave admittance to the street. It was in vain that she called out, for the confusion was so great that the person she addressed was unconscious of her presence, and Susan found that the hope of making the inquiries she desired were at an end, perhaps for ever.

Here was food for conjecture, and poor Susan was, for a time, completely at a loss to form any reasonable ground for clearing up the mystery in which she found herself involved. That the female she had seen was Dolly Pratt, she felt quite convinced, and that her condition in life was far above the commonalty, was certain from the elegance of her attire, and the profound respect that was paid her as she passed through the multitude that thronged each side of her path. Perhaps, thought Susan, she has married well, as people have several times hinted, though no one was able to give a very clear explanation of the assertions they thought proper to make. Or she might be under the protection of some great man, who, fascinated by her beauty, had raised her to this present state of eminence, without thinking himself bound to make her his wife. That she had not visited the Town Hall as a criminal, was certain for more reasons than one, and the fact of the marquis and Major Smith being in custody on some charge or other, rendered it extremely probable that she had gone there either as a witness, or to prosecute them for some crime they had committted. Be that as it might, however, Susan determined to make every effort to see her on some future occasion, and she had just come to this determination, when a crowd of persons began to pour out of the hall, and it became evident that the business of the day had been concluded.

In fact, all doubt upon this subject was immediately afterwards at an end, for the two men once more gruffly addressed themselves to her, and by a sign, she was directed to follow them, which she did, and in a short time found herself in the place from whence they had taken her.

CHAPTER XL.

THE FRENCH POLICE COURT.

THE ensuing night was a weary and restless one to Susan, who could get no rest through thinking of the fresh troubles that had befallen herself, and the uneasiness which her absence would occasion the young ladies, when they found her absence protracted beyond the night. It was in vain that she looked forward to a speedy termination of the imprisonment she was at present compelled to endure; for even if she found herself released on the following morning, there was Dolly Pratt to be searched out, and as it was hardly likely she went by that name at present, there was every reason to anticipate a great deal of difficulty ere she could hope to find any clue that might obtain for her the much-desired interview.

Then she had observed—though the glance she obtained was a very brief one,—that Dolly was in great trouble, for she had a handkerchief at her eyes, and seemed to be weeping as if something had occurred which gave her a great deal of pain. What it all meant, however, Susan could not tell, for though she had asked the old woman whether anything particular had occurred in the town, she could obtain no information that served in any way to clear up the mystery she was so anxious to penetrate. Then her own troubles served to keep her awake during the remainder of the night, and at an early hour on the following morning she rose unrefreshed from her straw mattrass, and looked out of the grated window to watch the rising of the sun, which was just then appearing above a mass of golden clouds in the east. This served in some respects to make her forget the troubles that pressed so heavily upon her, and, as the old woman entered the room shortly afterwards, she felt more composed than she had been for some time past.

"Here is your breakfast, young woman," said the other, throwing a cloth over the table, and placing upon it the humble fare which the place afforded. "Our folks haven't forgot to provide for you, you see, but there's not much time to lose, for yours is the first case to come on, and if you should happen to get over this affair easily, there will be time for you to return to your young ladies before the night sets in."

"And I see no reason why they should detain me," replied Susan; "for I have committed no harm, and I could convince them of it if I only knew a little of your language."

"It's a pity you can't speak it, certainly," observed the old woman; "but you will find our magistrate a very worthy, humane man, and if he sees reason to believe your innocence, he'll be sure to let you off, for they say pretty women have seldom cause to accuse him of harshness."

"I ask for nothing but justice," answered Susan, offended at this latter remark. "That I am innocent is known only to myself, and he will not be doing his duty unless he institutes so rigid an inquiry into this affair as will satisfy him whether I ought to be committed to prison, or acquitted the charge."

"You will have nothing to find fault with, I dare say," returned the other; "so take my advice and prepare yourself for any sort of defence that you may be inclined to make."

"I shall state the truth," replied Susan; "and if that is not sufficient to procure my release, I must submit with patience to the fate that I cannot avert."

"You forget," exclaimed the other; "that he understands no more of the English language than you do of the French. You will both be at a loss what to do, and as he will not like to show his ignorance, the chances are, that you may be sent to prison unless you think proper to act very discreetly in the affair."

"My trust will be placed in Heaven," answered Susan; "and come what may, I shall submit, without a murmur, to the fate I may have to endure."

"Well, of course everybody has a right to do as they please," observed the other; "and you are not obliged to take my advice, though I may happen to give it with the best and kindest feelings towards yourself. The truth is, my dear girl, I am sorry to see you in this dilemma, and all I shall say further about it is, that I hope you will take warning from the past, and have nothing to do in future with people that can't get their living in a more honest way than by smuggling."

"I have never been in any way connected with such a class of people as you have mentioned," answered Susan, indignant at the suspicion that had been uttered; "chance alone led me and my young ladies to the inn where I have left them, and if those who keep the place are engaged in unlawful traffic, I have neither seen nor heard anything of it, during the time we have been there."

"And how long is that?" asked the woman.

"Rather more than a week."

"Well, in that case, indeed, you may not know what has been going on there," said the other; "but I can tell you that the woman of that house, dumb as she is, is pretty deeply engaged in smuggling affairs, and as a letter from certain well-known parties, addressed to Madame Deleroix, was found in your possession, it was natural enough to suppose that you knew something about it. However, that's no business of mine, and as I hear the two men coming this way, perhaps you will put on your bonnet and shawl, for they are roughish fellows in their way, and will not have patience to wait very long, knowing as they do, that the time is almost up, and that you must be down at the Court House within half an hour."

Susan wanted no second bidding, and hastily obeying the suggestions of the old woman, she was ready for walking by the time the two men entered the room. After a few words had passed between them and the dame, they muttered something to Susan, which she, of course, did not understand, though she supposed it was an intimation that she was to follow them. She therefore accompanied them out of the place, and in the course of a short time, she entered the court where the magistrate and a great crowd of persons were already assembled.

"Which is the prisoner?" asked the president.

"This woman," answered one of the men.

"A woman, eh?" said the magistrate, eyeing her keenly through his spectacles; "and pray what is the charge you have to bring against her?"

"Smuggling, sir."

"Have you any proof of it?"

"We think so," replied the man; "at any rate we have good reason to suppose that her name is Deleroix, and that person, your worship will recollect, has long been known as one of the most dexterous smugglers in these parts."

"What reason have you to suppose that this is Madame Deleroix?" inquired the magistrate.

"Madame Deleroix is supposed to be dumb," answered the other, "and so I suppose is this woman, for though we have asked her a great many questions, she has not been able to answer any one of them,"

"Perhaps she has her reasons for remaining silent," said the magistrate.

" I don't know how that may be," replied the officer; " but as the prisoner has not replied to a question since we first apprehended her, I think there can be no doubt that she is the Madame Deleroix."

" I suppose she is deaf as well as dumb?" observed the magistrate.

" No, I don't think she's deaf," replied the other; " for she seems to hear us very well, though what she says in reply, no one has yet been able to understand."

" You have heard what this man has said," exclaimed the magistrate; " and therefore, if you are not able to answer with your tongue, you may do so by writing what you have to say on paper, and we shall thus be able to judge of your innocence or guilt. You can write, I suppose, sufficiently well to give me some idea who you are, and what means you have of obtaining a living?"

But all this was as little understood by Susan as if it had been spoken in Greek or Hebrew, and when the person who addressed her had done speaking, she shook her head in token that she knew nothing whatever of what he had been saying. Like many other persons, however, who exercise the magisterial functions, he was not endowed with any very large share of sense, and mistaking the meaning she intended to convey, he said :—

" You see she denies that she is able even to answer my questions in writing, and that being the case, I know not how we can very well proceed in the affair."

" But there's no doubt," said the officer; " that she is engaged with the smugglers, and if she is permitted to escape, we shall have all the rest of her people shamming in the same way to escape punishment."

" How do you know she is engaged in smuggling?"

" Because we have long had our eye upon her house," replied the man; " and for some months past we have known that the place was a regular resort for a great many persons that follow the same pursuit."

" Have you got any evidence against the woman?" enquired the administrator of the laws.

" I have your worship."

" What is it?"

" Upon searching her these things were found upon her," replied the man, producing the articles and handing them to the magistrate; " there are three letters, as you see, a golden locket with some initials on it, and an English half guinea, containing a mark that is likely enough to be the means of restoring it to the rightful owner."

" You think then," observed the magistrate; " that the last named articles have been stolen?"

" It's likely enough your worship," replied the officer; " but I've no proof of it at present, and therefore I shall content myself at this time with merely proving that she is connected with the smugglers that government has ordered us to route out."

" Did she make any objection to being searched?"

" Not that I am aware of," replied the other; " but she tried desperately hard to pass through the barriers without being seen, and ran away as fast as her legs would carry her when she saw us in pursuit."

" That looks rather bad," exclaimed the magistrate; " for people seldom run away unless there is good reason for wishing to avoid enquiries. However, we have no evidence she is Madame Deleroix, and as it would be hard to punish an innocent person, I think the better way will be to let her go this time, and if ever she should fall into our hands again, we shall know how to deal with her."

" If your worship will excuse me," said the officer; " I would suggest that she had better be remanded for another examination, and by that time,

I dare say, I shall be able to bring forward proof of her being the person I have named : and perhaps you will oblige me by reading those letters, which I have no doubt will serve to throw some little light upon the subject."

"Certainly I will," said the magistrate, and forthwith he took up the epistles and began to examine the addresses, and then broke them open in order that he might satisfy himself with their contents. But in this he was defeated, for after looking over the two first that came to hand, he threw them down in despair, exclaiming—

"These letters are both written in the English language, and as I know nothing about it, we must postpone the reading of them till she is brought before me again. But this," he continued, taking up the other one, "is in our own language, and perhaps we shall be able to learn something of its contents."

"And then, with spectacles on nose, he began to peruse the contents as follows :—

"MADAME DELEROIX,—According to your desire we have lost no time in seeking the persons you wish to see, and having succeeded in finding them, we have taken measures for an immediate interview between you and them. They will be at your house to-morrow, and I leave it for yourself to judge whether they will be of the service you expected. Both of them are expert in a certain line, and I dare say would answer the purpose exceedingly well if they can only be trusted. That, however, is a subject that must remain for your own consideration, as I can only speak of them as being expert fellows in their way, and men that will hazard much when the prospect of remuneration is good. But you will yourself see and judge of them for yourself, and should you be convinced that they are trustworthy, you will, of course, employ them in the manner that has been proposed. In a few days I shall see you, and in the meantime believe me to be,

"Yours, &c.,
"HENRI DUBOURG."

"This begins to make the affair assume a more serious character," exclaimed the magistrate, as he finished reading the epistle; "here is evidence of Madame Deleroix being engaged in a correspondence with a man who, there can be no doubt, is a freetrader, and that being the case, I think there is every reason why we should detain her for another examination."

"There can be no doubt now, your worship," said the officer, who was glad to see that his charge was likely to be made good; "the men that are spoken of in the letter are, of course, smugglers; and we shall have an excellent opportunity to capture them and break up the band that has been carrying on such an extensive trade."

"They will not carry it on much longer though, it is to be hoped," said the magistrate, rubbing his hands gleefully; "they have had their day no doubt, and now it will be for us to let them see that the law is too strong for them. They shall all be taken up, and I promise them there is not a man belonging to the band but shall meet his deserts for daring to carry on illicit traffic in the neighbourhood over which it is my duty to watch with a vigilant eye."

"But are you quite certain," exclaimed a bystander, "that the woman at the bar is the person you take her to be ?"

"Of course I am, sir," replied the magistrate; "has she not got the letter in her own possession, that was addressed to her, and is not that fact alone quite sufficient to prove her identity without anything else ? Besides, the woman before us is dumb, and that is another proof that she can be no other than the notorious Madame Deleroix."

"I don't mean to say that this person is not Madame Deleroix," exclaimed the gentleman; "but 1 certainly have reason to believe that she is not dumb as you have just now asserted."

"Not dumb!" shouted his worship.

"Such, sir, is my opinion, though I do not mean to make any positive assertion on the subject."

"Oh, this is absolute madness!" exclaimed the magistrate, growing extrumely figetty in his chair. "You must take me for a fool, sir, or you would never make such an assertion as that. Haven't I asked her questions, and don't she shake her head in token that she has not the power to answer me?"

"That may not be because she is dumb, sir," replied the stranger; "and, in fact, I am rather inclined to think she is a foreigner, who, not understanding our language, was, of course, unable to reply when she was not even aware of the nature of the questions put to her."

"Then she ought to be aware of it, sir," said the enraged magistrate; "and you, sir, whoever you are, might have known yourself better than to come here and insult one of his majesty's officers learned in the law, and who, of course, is perfectly well aware of his duty, without being instructed by a man like yourself."

"I had no intention of insulting you, sir," answered the other; "but as I thought the prisoner might have been unjustly suspected, I thought it nothing more than my duty to observe that it was extremely probable she is not the person she has been taken for."

"Indeed, sir," said the magistrate, with a sneer; "then, as you think she is not dumb, perhaps you will have the kindness to put a few questions to the young woman, in order that we may be satisfied."

"I know nothing of her language, which, if I am not mistaken, is English," replied the gentleman. "Perhaps, however, there may be some one in the court who can speak to her in her own tongue, and in that case I can answer for it she will prove to possess the faculty of speech as well as anybody present."

"Perhaps if some persons present had not quite so good a faculty as you speak of, it would be all the better for themselves and every one else," retorted his worship. "At all events, sir, I don't require any instruction in the duty I have to perform, and you will, therefore, do well to let the affair drop where it is."

"Does your worship intend to remand her for another examination?" asked the officer.

"To be sure I do," replied the person addressed, "and she will remain in your custody till we have been able to procure further evidence against her."

"And what about the two men that are mentioned in the letter as are about to visit her?"

"We must lay a snare for them," answered his worship. "The two rascals must be taken, and when once they are secured, we may find means to rout the whole band. Egad! they have had it their own way long enough, and now we'll see whether it is not possible to get rid of them by one well-directed blow. As for the woman you have brought before me, I have no doubt she is a rank impostor, and, perhaps, even her dumbness is feigned. But we'll find all that out in time, and if she does prove a cheat, it shall be the last time she shall ever practice her deceptions, for I'll have her locked up for the remainder of her life, so as to teach her that, though women often talk a great deal too much, it don't follow that they should impose upon people by pretending that they have altogether lost the power of speech."

"And what's to be done with the two English letters?" asked the officer.

"I have not made up my mind about them yet," replied his worship; "but in a day or two, perhaps, I may be able to decide what had better be done with them. I'll get them translated if I can, for I dare say they are written to some English smuggler, and in that case we shall discover a very pretty system of robbery going on against our own countrymen."

"And the men spoken of in the other letter you would have arrested immediately?"

"Aye," answered the magistrate, "let no time be lost, for they are cunning rascals, I dare say, and will be for making their escape as soon as possible after they find that Madame Deleroix is already in our custody. But they must not be suffered to get away on any account, and remember, sir, there is a large reward offered by the government for the capture of all smugglers, and if you take these two fellows it will be the making of your fortune—do you hear, sir? it will be the making of your fortune, I say."

"And may I take as many persons with me as I shall consider necessary for the purpose?"

"To be sure you may," answered the magistrate, "for I dare say these two fellows will make a desperate resistance, and the greatest caution must be used to prevent any mischief to our men. However, I needn't repeat that the two smugglers named in the letter must be taken, at all hazards, and when they have been well secured, by binding their arms to prevent any danger to myself, you may bring them before me, and I will immediately enter into the examination."

"And I suppose," said the officer, "this woman is to be removed to a place of safe custody?"

"Aye, away with her," said the magistrate, "take her out of the court, and as you would receive future favour, see that she escapes not."

Upon this, his worship rose from his seat with great dignity, and Susan was conveyed back to her former lodging to pass another night of anxiety for the result of an adventure that promised to turn out so unfortunate.

CHAPTER XLI.

MYSTERIOUS VISITORS.

WE must now lead the reader back to the house where both the marchioness and her sister were waiting in trembling hope for the return of their faithful attendant. But hour after hour passed away without bringing her who they were so anxious to see; and when at length the night closed in, and no Susan returned, they began to give way to a thousand fears which her greatly prolonged absence naturally gave rise to. Neither of them, however, would express to the other the alarm she felt till bed-time arrived, and then, no longer able to restrain their terrors, they gave utterance to the painful doubts that agitated their minds.

During that night sleep was out of the question, for they still clung to a vague hope that their messenger would return, and with the most intense anxiety they listened to every sound they heard, believing that she had been benighted, and that having lost her way, she would return ere the arrival of morning. But day broke, and still they were doomed to endure the bit-

terness of disappointment to such an excess that they imagined she had been way-laid and murdered, and that they were now left alone amongst those strangers whose motives they could not at present fathom, but who they could not regard otherwise than as the associates of the marquis and his worthless friend, and, consequently, as enemies of their own. At least, they could see no reason to regard them in any other light, for though no rudeness had hitherto been displayed towards them, there was an apparent sullenness in their manners which seemed to assure the two young ladies that any attempt on their part to escape would not only be frustrated, but might lead to their being more closely and rigorously confined in the house. Such were their fears, and there was nothing certainly in the conduct of the host and his dumb wife to lead them to a more favourable conclusion.

It was at an early hour on the following morning that they rose and stationed themselves at the window to watch for the long expected return of Susan; but when the usual hour for breakfast arrived, and still nothing was seen of their attendant, the marchioness seemed to call fresh courage to her aid, and having given it as her opinion that the absentee would return no more, she enquired of her sister whether they ought not to make some effort for releasing themselves from the painful situation in which they were involved.

"To remain here inactive," she said, "would be a folly which I doubt not we should hereafter see bitter cause to regret, and, therefore, I was about to propose that we take an opportunity to escape from this place as soon as possible."

"And most willingly should I be to agree to your proposal," said Miss Plumley; "but I think if we were to attempt such a thing, they would commence an immediate pursuit, and if we should happen again to fall into their hands, Heaven only knows what would become of us."

No. 38

" Yet, on the other hand, we might have the good fortune to get clear away from the neighbourhood," answered the marchioness, "and in that case, we should be able to make enquiries about Susan, who, if she has not lost her way, is, no doubt, in some terrible difficulty from which the assistance of friends only may release her."

" And do you really think," asked her sister, " that the poor creature will not return in the course of the day ?"

" I am afraid not," returned the other, " especially as it is but too likely that she has been followed by the people of this house, and if such should be the case, they will take care that we see no more of her."

" And yet, after all," exclaimed Miss Plumley, " I see no reason to believe that these people are so bad as you appear to imagine them. It is true we have received but little civility from them ; but, on the other hand, they have not offered to do us any harm, and that ought to give us some hopes of their future good intentions."

" But," said the other, " if they are not people of bad character, why should the marquis have left us with them, since it is but too evident that we have been trapanned to the place for the purpose of being forsaken ? It seems strange, too, that Susan should have been absent so long, and I cannot help thinking she must have fallen into bad hands, and that the people here must know something about it."

" And yet they may be perfectly innocent of any such knowledge as that you suspect them of," answered Miss Plumley. " Besides, it may be some distance to the town where the post-office is, and as it was probably dark when she set out to return here, she may have lost her way and found a refuge in the house of some person on the road."

" Such may certainly be the case," replied the marchioness ; " but you must recollect that she does not understand one word of the language of this country, and, consequently, she would find it impossible to make known the difficulties she might have to encounter."

" That may be the very reason of her being gone so long," observed the other ; " and as I do not yet quite despair of seeing her return, I think we ought to remain contented here for a time, as it would be most unfair to leave the house during the absence of her who left us for no other purpose than to endeavour to serve us."

" You forget, then, that we may be risking ourselves without having a chance of serving her ?"

" I have not forgotten that," replied Miss Plumley ; " but, at the same time, I think we ought to remain while there's a chance of poor Susan's return to us."

" Which I fear will never be," sighed the marchioness ; " and really I have formed so strange an opinion of the people here, that, under all circumstances, it is impossible to remain among them any longer."

" Luckily I have not so bad a notion as you seem to have," said Miss Plumley, " and we may be sure that Susan thought pretty well of them, or she would never have gone away and left us in their power."

" It was the only chance we had of escape," replied her sister, " and if she had only succeeded in getting the letters conveyed away, we might have been rescued by our father in a very short time. As it is, however, I am afraid we are utterly lost unless we make a desperate effort for our own release."

" You think, then, Susan is not likely to return ?"

" I am afraid so."

" And I, on the other hand," replied Miss Plumley, " am quite satisfied that if she is alive, we shall either see her or hear something of her before we are many hours older. Susan is a shrewd, quick-thoughted girl, re-

member, and somehow or other she will contrive to let us know the reason
of this most unaccountable absence at the very earliest opportunity that
offers."

"But even if she should find anybody to bring us a message," answered
the marchioness, "I am afraid the people down stairs will take care to prevent our knowing anything about it."

"Your opinion of them is certainly anything but favourable," returned
her sister; "yet for all that you have said, it must be confessed I am not
so prejudiced as you are, for we have now been here some little time, and
though they are not very courteous in their behaviour, we have no incivility
to complain of at present."

"That," said the marchioness, "may be because they are waiting to hear
from the persons that left us in their charge."

"Ah! the villanous marquis and his friend," cried Miss Plumley. "To
them we owe all this trouble and anxiety, and all I hope is, that we shall
hear from them, that our father may have it in his power to retaliate on
them as they deserve. And depend on it they will not get off quite so
easily as they expect, for they will be traced out yet, and then let them beware of what is to follow."

"It was our own fault that we were so easily imposed upon by
the pretended marquis," answered her sister with a sigh. "But we
were all too anxious for what appeared to be a high alliance, and the idea
of a coronet so dazzled our eyes that we were unable to see through
the shallow artifices that were practised for our deception. Yet now
that I can reflect more coolly upon the past, I cannot but wonder that
we were so foolish as not to detect the imposition of these heartless adventurers."

"The truth is, and there is no disguising it," said Miss Plumley, "we
have all been to blame for not having made enquiries before the marquis,
or whatever he is, was admitted to become a visitor at our house. But
it's too late now, to give way to these regrets; and as we have got into
this dilemma, it only remains for us to get out of it in the best way
we can."

"And so you propose that we should both run away, though there is
almost a certainty of our being pursued and overtaken."

"It may be so," answered her sister, "but we shall at least be as well
off as if we quietly remain here in uncertainty as to what sort of doom
awaits us."

"That is to say," replied Miss Plumley, "if they don't take it in their
heads to ill-treat us for trying to escape."

"I see how it is," exclaimed the marchioness in a tone of vexation,
"you are determined to stay in this fearful place without making any effort
to get away."

"You mistake me, sister," answered the other, "I am as anxious as you
can be, to find myself clear of this house and its inhabitants, but at present
I can see no chance of doing so, since, if we really are prisoners, they will,
no doubt, keep such a watchful eye upon us, that we shall be foiled in the
attempt."

"And yet," replied the marchioness, "we have seen that Susan found
means to get off undiscovered."

"Nay, that remains to be proved," exclaimed Miss Plumley, "for at
present we know not whether she has succeeded in getting away or fallen
into the hands of these people."

"But we may guess that she has escaped," answered the other, "or
there is every reason to believe she would have been brought back before
this time."

"That depends upon circumstances," replied Miss Plumley; "however, I would rather put you into good spirits than discourage you, and really, in my own mind, I believe this affair will turn out better than either of us expected."

"You have forgotten, then, the circumstances under which I have been fraudently brought to this place ?"

"My memory must be a very treacherous one if I did," replied Miss Plumley, "for it is hardly possible to forget either the false marquis or his equally villanous friend, the major, as he calls himself. I have, however, hopes, that we shall never see either of these again, and that is some consolation hard as the case is."

"And I have also the consolation," said the marchioness, reproachfully, "of knowing that I am married to a man who is likely enough to pay the forfeit of his crimes on a public scaffold."

"In which case you will get rid of a husband who deserves neither pity nor commiseration," said her sister.

"But you forget the disgrace that will fall upon me as the wife of such a man."

"Nay," answered the other, "you forget that a divorce will easily prevent all that, besides setting you at liberty to marry some more deserving man."

"And what chance have we at present of doing so ?" asked the marchioness. "Are we not confined in a place where I fear no one will have a chance of finding us; and are not our misfortunes aggravated by the fact of being unable to comprehend a word we utter ?"

"That is, indeed, a misfortune, that I must confess, perplexes me more than anything else besides," replied her sister. "We are unable to ask a question of these strange people, though perhaps, as far as that goes, they would not satisfy us, even if they understood us ever so well."

"Which," replied the marchioness, "is one argument in my favour, that we ought to make our escape from hence with as little delay as possible."

"If we could do so to a certainty, I should not attempt to throw any obstacle in the way," answered her sister; "but when I come to consider that neither of us, unfortunately for ourselves, understand a word of the language, it seems to be absolute folly that we should leave this place to throw ourselves upon the humanity of strangers, who, for ought we know, may be worse than the people from whom you are so very anxious to fly."

"You are afraid then ?"

"To confess the truth, I am."

"And would prefer risking yourself among these mysterious people to making an effort that might happily be the means of restoring us to our father ?"

"Why, as for the risk, I am not very anxious upon that score," replied Miss Plumley, " for between ourselves, I think our host and hostess entertain no ill-feeling towards us, and that they have perhaps been as much imposed upon as ourselves by the pretended Marquis Valliere and his friend, the major."

"And having this confidence in them, you would rather remain here than take the chance of escaping ?"

"If the chance was a good one, I might perhaps think as you do," answered her sister; " but believing that we should only be making a useless attempt that would only end in our own discomfiture, I really think we had better remain as we are, a few days longer, and see whether the letters that have been sent by Susan may have the effect of bringing our father."

"I cannot, indeed, I cannot stay here any longer," exclaimed the marchioness, rising from her seat and pacing the room uneasily; "I last night endured tortures of suspense, such as I never felt before, and I then made up my mind to leave the house in the course of this day."

" And you intend to keep that resolution ?"

" I do."

" And will no persuasion that I can urge prevail on you to remain a little longer ?"

" No," replied the marchioness, " I am resólved, and if any harm befalls, the consequences must rest upon my head. I do not, however, wish to persuade you to accompany me in my flight; you seem to have some confidence in these people, and probably you are right, but, for my own part, I will not stay here one moment longer than I can help."

" Then, of course, right or wrong, I must go with you."

" I was going to tell you that there is no occasion for anything of the kind," replied the marchioness ; " there will, perhaps, be more chance for one of us to escape, and if you do not mind remaining behind, I will exert myself to the utmost to reach Paris, and if once I succeed in getting there, I shall soon be able to get assistance to aid me in your rescue."

" Psha !" cried Miss Plumley, " this is really a most wild and romantic notion of yours."

" Not so wild or romantic as you may imagine," answered her sister; " I see danger, but whether it is imaginary or not, remains to be proved, and as I have some hopes of being able to avert it by a little timely exertion, I shall cheerfully undertake the task even were Paris further off than it is."

" But I fear," said Miss Plumley, " our little remaining money will not suffice to take you there."

" Even if I had to beg my way every step to Paris, it should not deter me from my design," replied the marchioness firmly; " I, however, can make half the money we have do for the purpose, and the remainder I will leave with you to pay these people what we owe them."

" You are resolved to go then and leave me here to my fate ?" cried the other reproachfully.

" On the contrary," answered her sister, " I would much rather you accompanied me, provided you went with a resolution to overcome all difficulties. But, as I see you have no desire to quit this house immediately, I will go alone, and, rely on it, in a few days I will send those who will convey you in safety to Paris."

" Yet it seems cowardly of me too," cried Miss Plumley, " to let you take such a long journey alone, when you have so much need of a companion."

" Depend on it I shall not reproach you on that account," replied the marchioness, " for it is my own voluntary act, and I have no right to expect that you will enter into a scheme that seems to be so visionary. Besides, you have no fear of these people, and it's likely enough they may not be so bad as I suspect, and if Susan should return, which I hope she may, you will have a companion to share the brief imprisonment you may have to endure."

" You are determined upon going, then ?"

" I am."

" And when do you leave me ?"

" This very day, nay, there is not one hour to be lost, and I shall take the first opportunity that offers, to slip away without giving rise to any suspicion as to my intentions."

" And should any accident befall you on your way," cried her sister, " I shall for ever reproach myself with the cowardice that induced me to let you go alone."

" I have no fears on that subject," replied the marchioness ; " and all I require of you is to appear ignorant of my intentions when these people miss me."

"There is little need for caution," answered Miss Plumley, " since I cannot speak a word of their language ; and even if I could, you may be sure I would not say a word that might give them an opportunity of following in pursuit. You may, therefore, rest quite satisfied on that point, and the only favour I ask is, that you will send here immediately on your safe arrival there."

" I will not waste a moment, you may depend," replied the other, " for my first care shall be to go in search of my father, and if he should not yet have arrived in this country, I will then go to the police, and relate the adventures that have terminated so unfortunately for us both. They will then send here for you, and I shall have the satisfaction of knowing that a little resolution on my own part will have rescued us from the snares of those worthless men."

At this point the conversation was broken off by a message that breakfast was waiting for them, and on descending to the lower room they found the host and hostess seated at the table in the same silence that had been observed between them throughout. It was in vain, that the marchioness and her sister looked round for the faithful Susan, who, till this morning, had never been absent from them since their arrival at the inn. She, however, as may be expected, was not there, and after exchanging significant glances with each other, the two ladies sat down to the meal, of which neither felt the least desire to participate in.

On this occasion they thought Madame Deleroix seemed to be more than usually gloomy in her appearance ; but that, perhaps, might only have been the effect of their own imagination ; or she might have her suspicions about Susan's absence, which probably occasioned some uneasy reflections, which she was unable to conceal. But be this as it might, the marchioness was more determined than ever to put her project into execution, and as soon as breakfast was over, she and her sister again retired to their own chamber, where, attiring themselves for walking, they came down and passed the hostess and her husband with as much apparent unconcern as if they were merely going for a short stroll.

Upon leaving the house, they took care not to walk beyond their ordinary pace, lest any suspicion of what was going on should take place, and they even proceeded across some fields, the more completely to deceive those who they feared would pursue them in the event of their purpose being guessed at. On getting some distance from the house, however, they turned towards the road, by which the carriage had arrived at the inn, and taking a sorrowful leave of each other, the marchioness set forth on her long toilsome journey, whilst her sister slowly turned her steps towards the house she had just left, and gave herself up to the sad reflections that forced themselves upon her mind.

On entering the inn she observed that Madame Deleroix appeared very much surprised at seeing her return alone, but she immediately hurried to her own room, where she remained the rest of the day, refusing to go down to dinner, on the plea of indisposition. But when night closed in, she could no longer bear the loneliness of her situation, and going down stairs, she seated herself by the fire, and gave way to the gloomy thoughts that her sister's absence gave rise to.

Yet, some relief was afforded her by the fact of Madame Deleroix not appearing to take any notice of her sister's absence, and the more than usual kindnesss with which she seemed to regard her. What the reason of this was, Miss Plumley could not imagine, and she was puzzling herself to find out a satisfactory cause, when a loud knocking was heard at the door, and her thoughts were instantly put to flight by the wonder which succeeded, and the anxiety she felt as to whether the sound denoted the return either of her sister or Susan Hoply.

But her uncertainty was of no very long duration, for on a signal being given by the mistress, the servant girl hastened to the door, and opening it, gave admittance to a couple of strangers, who walked in with as little ceremony as if they had been intimate friends of the hostess and her husband. Yet, Miss Plumley, though rather startled at seeing such unexpected visitors, could not help remarking that there was something mysterious in their deportment, and, moving her seat to a corner where she might be as little seen as possible, she determined to watch all that was going on, though she might not be able to understand a word of what was said.

Their first request seemed to be for refreshment, for the cloth was quickly spread upon the table, and all the meat produced that the house afforded. And well satisfied they appeared to be with what had been produced, if the execution they performed might be taken as an evidence of that fact; and when, at length they had finished their meal, they drew their chairs closer to the fire, and began a conversation with Madame Deleroix, which was, of course, wholly unintelligible to the anxious observer of their actions. We will, however, give it for the benefit of our readers.

"Your name," said one of the men, " is Madame Deleroix, I believe ?"

A nod answered him in the affirmative.

"Why don't you say so at once then?" exclaimed the first speaker. "Can't you speak out, and tell us we're right, without all that dumb show ?"

Madame Deleroix looked earnestly at them, and replied with a shake of the head.

"Humph!—you're dumb, then ?"

"Yes, sir, my mistress is dumb," replied the servant girl, "but I can talk to her with my fingers, and any reply she she has to make, I'll tell you."

" So, she can hear what I say, then ?"

"Oh, yes, every word."

" That's strange, too," exclaimed the man, " for most people are deaf as well as dumb."

"That's true," answered the girl, " but my mistress could once talk as well as you or I, only that she lost the power of speech through a fright, or something of that kind."

"The devil she did!" exclaimed the man, and he whispered something to his companion, upon which Madame Deleroix looked very hard at them, till their eyes were once more turned towards her, and then she partly turned her head away, as if to avoid their gaze.

"This is a very singular circumstance," said the man who had previously spoken, "for I never knew but of one person that lost her speech through fright, and that was Louise Fayette, a young girl that used to live in Paris when I was there."

"I remember it well," exclaimed the other, "she married one Arnold Robertson, if I'm not mistaken, and went with her husband to England, where, it was said, she recovered her speech."

Miss Plumley could perceive that the hostess started, and turned very pale at this part of the conversation, but, as she knew nothing of what they were saying, she thought it might be a sudden and momentary illness. The two men, however, did not seem to have taken any notice of it, for, after a little whispering between themselves, one of them said :—

" It's no use talking about that now, old boy, for we came here on bu-

siness, so the sooner we get to it the better." Then addressing himself to
Madame Deleroix, he exclaimed bluntly : "You have been looking for our
arrival here to-night, of course."

"I had no reason for expecting you to-night," replied the hostess,
through her servant's interpretation; "but, from your conversation, I believe you are from the seaside?"

"Exactly so, madam," answered the principal spokesman; "our name
is Laroche, and we are here upon a little business that you, of course, perfectly well understand."

"I am quite aware of the object of your visit," was the reply.

"Well, and do you want our services?"

"Indeed we do," she answered; "our business has been sadly falling
off of late, and unless something is done, we must find some more profitable employment."

"I see," exclaimed the man; "the revenue officers are growing very
sharp, and you want a few active chaps to put you upon a new plan of
cheating them?"

"We do."

"Well," replied the other, "I flatter myself you have found just the
sort of chaps that will set business stirring a bit. We are old hands at
the work, and it shall be no fault of ours if affairs don't soon make a change
for the better."

"You will assist me, then?" said Madame Deleroix, through the signs
which she made to her servant girl.

"Aye, that we will;—and now tell us when we are to begin the glorious
work."

"Almost directly," replied the hostess; "but before we do that, there
is another affair I wish to speak to you about."

"Well," returned the other, "you have but to name it, and I dare say
we shall not be long before we understand each other. So out with it
at once, and let us know what you mean, without any more of this
mystery."

"It is not the time for it yet," she replied; "but you shall know more
by and bye. But you don't drink your wine, gentlemen, and I should
be sorry to know that you are not comfortable beneath my roof."

But the gentlemen needed very little pressing upon this particular subject, and, accordingly, three or four glasses were emptied in a very brief
space of time, just by way of assuring the hostess that they were a
couple of as happy fellows as need to be. Then a good deal of whispering
took place between them, and at length, the man who had spoken most
said :—

"You have heard, I suppose, madam, of what has taken place at no
great distance from you?"

"I have not indeed," she replied.

"Can it be possible?" exclaimed the other, with surprise; "why the
whole country rings with it, and it has made the police so confoundedly
sharp, that, I assure you, we have had the hardest matter in the world
to get here."

"What has happened?" exclaimed madam, as much by her looks of
alarm, as by the signs she gave her interpreter.

"A very serious affair, I assure you," replied the man. "I say a serious
affair, because it is a sad interruption to our business, and anything that
sets those confounded fellows, the police on the alert, is to be deplored as
the most unfortunate event that can happen to the like of us. In fact,
Madame Deleroix, I don't know but we shall be obliged to give up smuggling altogether, and take to some honest employment."

"What can have happened," she asked, "that has so greatly alarmed men like you and your friend ?"

"A calamity, madame," he replied, "that may lead to the most serious consequences. There have been two strangers sneaking about this neighbourhood ;—chaps that follow our line of business, and yet don't belong to any of us. In fact, they have been trying on very thick ;—travelling in a carriage and four, and making a splash that has brought the eyes of people upon them and their actions."

"Who are they ?" enquired Madame Deleroix by her interpreter.

"Ah! you may well ask that question, but it ain't so easy to answer, I can tell you," returned the other. "It seems, however, they are Englishmen, and having plenty of brass in their countenances, they have contrived to carry on a very pretty business in spite of a sharp look out that has been kept by the officers."

"And you say they have been in this neighbourhood?" said the landlady, speaking by deputy.

"Yes, they crosssed the frontiers not many days ago, and came back with a cargo in their carriage, that might well make you and I envious of them. The style they travelled in was enough to throw dust in the eyes of those who make it their business to look after these sort of things, and there's no doubt they would have made a profitable speculation of it, if it hadn't been for an accident, that was the means of exposing the whole affair. And now they're in for it nicely, I can tell you, for I wouldn't be in their place for all the gold you could count from now to a twelvemonth."

The hostess looked eagerly at her visitor, and desired the girl to enquire what had happened.

"Why, the story is rather a long one," replied the man, "but I'll tell you the principal facts in as few words as I can.—It seems these two

No. 39

Englishmen were returning, as I just told you in their carriage, with plenty of laces and silks, that would have served to set up half the haberdashers' shops in Paris. Well, all went on right enough, till just as they were approaching the other side of the next town, when they met a lady and gentleman, with a servant or two riding on horseback. Now, that you may think was nothing very particular, but it turned out badly in the long run, for the gentleman was no other than the Marquis de Noailles, who, it happened curious enough, was perfectly well acquainted with both the Englishmen ;—not, I believe, as friends, but he happened to know something of them that was not much to their advantage. What the transaction between them was, however, I don't pretend to know, but it seems both parties knew each other when they met, and to the Englishmen this circumstance was anything but agreeable."

"And was that all?" asked Madame Deleroix.

"All!" responded the other, with surprise; "no, there's a good deal to come after that, I can tell you. The Marquis de Noailles, it is said, wished to speak to the men about some business or other, and just after they had passed, he spurred his horse, and desiring one of his attendants to accompany them, galloped after the vehicle to see in what part of the the town the travellers intended to put up."

"And the others," said the hostess, "I suppose suspected that he was following them to give information to the police?"

"That's just what they did think," replied the man, "and so as they had no inclination to visit the town gaol, one of them popped his head out of the carriage window, and without a word of warning, shot the unfortunate attendant like a dog. The poor fellow was dead in an instant, and the marquis no sooner saw what had happened, than he quickened his pace after the fellows, and just as he had reached the carriage, another shot was discharged, that served him in a manner similar to his unfortunate servant."

"And was the marquis slain?" asked Madame Deleroix, whose manner betrayed the deep interest and horror she felt in the appalling narrative she had been listening to.

"Yes," replied the other, "he died before any assistance could be got, and when the lady arrived at the place, and saw the horrible scene, she fainted, and was carried home by the other servants in a state of insensibility."

"But what of the murderers?—Have they escaped?"

"Why, as soon as the mischief was done," replied the man, "they drove off as if all the country had been at their heels. Some of the servants, however, followed as hard as they could make their horses gallop, and came up with them just as they had reached the barriers. They then shouted out that the two men in the carriage were murderers, the vehicle was stopt, a party of gensd'armes sent for, and the two gentlemen handed over to the police. They were to be examined before the magistrates yesterday, but as I and my friend here didn't think it safe to enter the town, we, of course, know nothing as to what has been done. But it's quite certain they'll be committed, and as the evidence is strong against them, they'll meet with their deserts."

"And serve them right, too," said Madame Deleroix, "for two more cold-blooded villains I never saw."

"Hey!—you know 'em, then?"

"I do,—they came here a few days ago, in the carriage, and went off in the night, leaving two ladies behind them. One of them you see in yonder corner, and the other has gone I know not whither."

"Did they leave anything else behind them?" he asked.

"Yes, a good deal of property that I want you to dispose of for me, and which we'll speak more about by and by."

"We are snug and all right here, I suppose?" and the other, looking round towards the door and windows.

"Oh yes, there is no fear of a visit from the officers here," replied the hostess. "I believe our house is not suspected;—at least we have never had a hint of anything of the sort."

"And the girl yonder;—the stranger, I mean;—is she to be depended upon?"

"She is, and for a very good reason," answered Madame Deleroix;—"in fact she don't understand a word of our language, so the very thing we have been speaking about, is quite a mystery to her."

And so indeed it was, for Miss Plumley could find no amusement in listening to a conversation that she knew nothing about, and taking a light from the table, she withdrew to her chamber, leaving the hostess and her guests to chat among themselves as long as they thought proper.

CHAPTER XLII.

THE SEARCH.

THE young English lady passed a very restless night, for she could not help thinking of her sister and the difficulties she would have to encounter; and favourable as her opinion had hitherto been of Madame Deleroix, the visit of the two men on the previous evening, and their very doubtful appearance gave rise to many notions that had never previously entered her head. Indeed, she began to think over all the dismal stories she had heard of bandit hosts, and guests mysteriously murdered in their beds, till she could not sleep for the horrible visions that were continually passing through her imagination.

At the usual hour of rising, therefore, she felt feverish and ill, yet resolving not to show any mistrust of those who had hitherto behaved with perfect civility to her, she descended to the room she had left the night before, and seated herself with as much unconcern as if not a single suspicious thought had entered her head during the preceding night. As usual, the meal passed in silence, and she was wondering how it happened that the men who had arrived the evening before, did not make their appearance among them, when the door was abruptly pushed open, and in walked half a dozen men, whose dress was quite different from any that she had previously seen during her stay in France. They seemed, however, to make themselves perfectly free, and directed their gaze towards every part of the room, as if expecting to see something, or somebody, that was not there. In fact, it was a party of police from the neighbouring town, though Miss Plumley, fortunately for her comfort, was not aware of the particular position they held in society. She heard them talking, too, a great deal, and sometimes rather loudly, but their language was not understood, and, therefore, she kept her seat at the table with as much unconsciousness as if nothing at all was the matter.

But it was not so with Madame Deleroix, who had reasons of her own for guessing the object of this unexpected visit, and having beckoned for her servant girl to approach, she by signs, desired her to ask the gentlemen what they wanted.

"We have come in search of a couple of men that arrived here last night," replied the sergeant.

"The men you speak of have left the house," was the reply of the hostess.

"Indeed !—what time did they go away ?"

"As soon as it was light."

"Come, come, we must have no falsehoods about it," exclaimed the sergeant. "They came here last night,—slept in your house, and are here at this very moment."

"Really, sir, I have told you nothing but the truth," answered Madame Deleroix. "They were mere casual visitors, and having had a night's rest, left us as soon as they could see to pursue their journey along these rough roads."

"And you mean to tell us they are not here ?"

"I have told you so already."

"Aye, aye, but we don't believe you," exclaimed the sergeant. "It's not convenient for fellows of that sort to travel by daylight, and they have been stowed away in some snug place about the premises."

"If you think so, it is easy to search the place," replied Madame Deleroix ;—"we are poor, honest, hard-working people, and never till now has anything been said or thought against the character of either myself or my husband."

"That's because you've been cunning enough to keep all snug," answered the other. "But we're not asleep, you know, and as we are quite aware that the fellows passed the night here, there's very little doubt but we shall find them somewhere about the place."

"Hadn't we better look after them, sergeant, before they've time to sneak away ?" suggested one of the men.

"To be sure we must, and that's just what I was going to do," replied his superior, rather indignant at being dictated to by a man under his command. "I was just about ordering a search to be made, and let it be your business to remain here to watch the family, and mark me, sirrah, let no one leave the house till our return, on pain of my severe displeasure."

Having delivered these orders, the sergeant and four of his subordinates proceeded to pay a visit to every part of the place, and when they had searched every part of the house, without any success attending their labours, they went to the stables and coach-house, as they were termed, but though every place was opened, and everything turned over and over, nothing whatever could be seen of the men of whom they were in search. They, however, were still convinced that they were somewhere about the premises, and full of this conviction, they returned once more to the room they had left.

The sergeant, whose temper was by no means improved by the result of their search, now began to question the servant girl, but not a word in the shape of a satisfactory reply could they get from her. Then they asked a great many things of Miss Plumley, which, as she understood nothing of what they were talking, she was unable to make any reply to. Finding her obstinate, as they imagined, they applied themselves to Monsieur Deleroix, but he, poor fellow, was in his second childhood, and his replies were anything but satisfactory. In fact, he stared at them with such a stupid expression of idiotcy, that despairing of being able to make anything of him, they once more applied themselves to questioning the maid servant, who they threatened with all sorts of punishment if she aided and abetted in the escape of men who were the particular objects of their present enquiry.

"Really, gentlemen," she said, "I know nothing more of them than that they came here last night as travellers, and that they left the house this morning, as you have heard."

"And were you in the room whilst they were here?" demanded the sergeant, impatiently.

"I was, sir."

"And there was a great deal of conversation, I suppose, between them and your mistress?"

"Nay, that was impossible," she replied, "for you may have observed my mistress is dumb."

"True," answered the other, "but I have also observed that you act the part of interpreter to her, and perhaps you did so on that occasion?"

"Indeed sir, you ——"

"It's in vain to talk to me, girl," interrupted the sergeant. "The truth is you have all conspired together to let these men escape, and that being the case, I shall take every one of you back with me to the town, except the unfortunate host, who, being an idiot, is, of course, not answerable for the misdeeds of those about him."

"My mistress bids me say, sir," exclaimed the girl, "that it would be cruel to part her and her husband. He will not know much about the difference of this place and a gaol, and if she has him with her, she will be able to attend upon him better than anybody else would."

"Psha!" he replied, "how can we de that? we can't convey him on our backs, can we?"

"It is not necessary to do so," returned the hostess, through her usual interpreter. "There is a horse and cart in the stable, which will serve to take us all."

"Well, I don't want to be hard about that," said the sergeant, "so she may have her way, and the old man may go with us. But who is this young lady here, and how comes she to be in the house?"

"She is a native of England," answered Madame Deleroix, "and has been left here by some persons who came here some days ago."

"Is she to remain with you?"

"Oh, no ;—I am expecting them to fetch her immediately."

"Well, at any rate she must go with us before the magistrate," said the sergeant. "What you have said about her may be all very true, but as we are not quite certain about that, we must take her with us, and hear what our superiors say about it."

Upon this orders were given to get the horse and cart ready, and whilst the sergeant was making other arrangements for some of them to remain and take care of the house, Madame Deleroix began to prepare her husband for their unexpected journey, and by means of signs to Miss Plumley, intimated that they were going a little way, and that it would be necessary for her to accompany them. This was no disagreeable news to the young lady, who was heartily tired of the monotony of her life, and running to her own chamber, she was quickly attired for the journey, though wondering in her own mind what all the bustle she had witnessed could be about.

Whilst Madame Deleroix was absent, one of the men, who was perhaps a little more shrewd than the rest, fancied he could discover something like a sliding panel near the fireplace, and thinking it might lead to the place where the two men were concealed, he, with the assistance of his sword, forced it back, and revealed a cupboard well stowed with bottles, which, upon drawing the corks, were found to contain contraband liquor, which even a revenue officer could not but pronounce of the finest quality. At any rate it was tried by them all, and having been well approved of, without a dissentient voice, the man who had made the discovery, began to prosecute a further search, in hopes that the men might be found there.

"It's no use looking in that place," said the sergeant, "for it ain't big enough for a dog to sleep in, much less a couple of strapping fellows like them."

"But it's worth looking after, for all that," exclaimed the other; "and particular when such things as these are stowed away in it, that can't have any business to be put into a cupboard at all."

"What things are they?" enquired the sergeant.

"Why, a couple of portmanteaus," answered the other, lugging them out of their hiding place, and throwing them on the floor.

"These things belonged to the fellows, sure enough," said the superior, examining them minutely; "and here are brass plates on 'em, too,—one of 'em marked with A. L., and the other V. L." Then turning towards the servant girl, who was anxiously watching their movements, he added:—"These things belonged to the men that slept in this house last night."

"That's likely enough," she replied.

"Of course they did, huzzy, and you know it."

"Well," she answered, "I don't deny it."

"You admit it, then?"

"I admit nothing," she replied, with her usual *sang froid*, "but what would be the use of denying anything when once you have asserted it as a fact? But here comes my mistress, who, I dare say, will desire me to answer any question you may think proper to put."

"You hear what I have said," exclaimed the sergeant, addressing himself to Madame Deleroix;—"we have found these portmanteaus in yonder cupboard, and, I believe, you cannot deny that they belong to the men of whom we are now in search."

"You are quite right, sir," she replied, through her interpreter. "They do indeed belong to the persons you mention, and I believe they will return here in a few days, when they will, of course, take them away with them."

"Well, I can make nothing of any of you," said the sergeant; "but I suppose the magistrate will be able to gather some particulars when I come to tell him all about it. So now jump into the cart all of you, and let's be off, or we sha'n't reach the town before the office hours are over."

Upon this they were all handed into the vehicle, and driven off at a smart pace by the man who undertook the task of driving an old, and not very active horse.

On being placed before the magistrate, a great deal of astonishment was expressed at the production of another dumb woman, as one had been placed before them only the day before;—at least Susan was supposed to be so afflicted, from the fact of her being unable to speak a word in the language of the country.

"What is this woman's name?" asked his worship, impatiently, and at the same time pointing to the hostess.

"Madame Deleroix," answered the sergeant.

"And what was the name of the dumb woman examined here yesterday?"

"Madame Deleroix."

"What!" exclaimed the indignant magistrate, "do you mean to tell me these two prisoners are both named Madame Deleroix, and that both of them are charged with exactly similar crimes?"

"It's very strange, your worship," answered the sergeant of police, "but I begin to suspect there must be some most unaccountable mistake in this business."

"Mistake indeed!" exclaimed the justice, "and how dare you, sir, stand before me, and confess that a mistake has been made in so serious an affair as this?"

"I'm very sorry for it, your worship, but ———"

"I want none of your buts, sir," vociferated the magistrate. "The fact is a very awkward mistake has been made, and the sooner it is rectified the better it will be for all the parties concerned. And now, sir, can you tell me in your wisdom which is the right Madame Deleroix?"

"The one that now stands before you, sir," replied the other, not exactly knowing what answer to make.

"In that case, sir, let the other woman be released immediately after the business of the office is closed," said the magistrate; "and now, as we have got so far, what charge have you against all these prisoners?"

"Madame Deleroix," answered the officer, "is accused of being concerned in smuggling, and with having last night opened her doors to a couple of men who are well known to be concerned in smuggling transactions; her servant is accused of aiding her in the business; the husband, who is weak in intellect, has been brought here because there is nobody left at home that can take care of him—and the other female—who, I understand, is a young English lady, I thought proper to bring here, that she may explain how it was that we found her dwelling with persons that are so notorious as belonging to the tribe of smugglers."

"How am I to question the dumb woman?" asked the justice.

"She has her hearing perfectly," replied the other, "and will answer any question you put through her servant."

"Perhaps you will tell me, Madame Deleroix," said the magistrate; "how it was that you harboured the men of whom the police are in search?"

"They came to me as travellers," replied the hostess, "and I gave them shelter as I would any one else."

"And what became of them in the morning?"

"That I know not; they rose before I was up, aud left the house without saying anything to me."

"And this you solemnly affirm?"

"I do, your worship."

"Have you any reply to make to this?" asked the justice.

"I deny her assertions, altogether," answered the officer of police;—"I set men to watch the house after the men were seen to enter it, and they positively swear that no one left it previous to our all entering to search the premises."

"Now, girl," cried the magistrate, addressing himself to the servant, "what have you got to say about this affair?"

"I have nothing to say about it," replied the girl, "except that I saw the men enter the house; but how or when they left it I can say nothing."

"You mean to say then that they went away before you were up in the morning."

"And now what says this English female?" asked the magistrate, glancing towards Miss Plumley. "I suppose she is able to give us some account of the people and the means they have of getting a living?"

"I don't know anything about that, your worship," answered the other; "all I can say about it is, that I asked her a great many questions; but what she said in reply, I couldn't understand for the life of me."

"Is there anybody in the office," asked the magistrate, "that understands enough of the English language to put a few questions to the female?"

"Yes, I can," said a little man elbowing his way through the crowd, and bowing most obsequiously to the bench. "What does your worship want me to ask?"

"Enquire of her," said the justice, "how she came to be in the house where our officers found her."

"She says, your worship," returned the little man after he had put the question to Miss Plumley, "that she and her sister were taken there by two gentlemen, who ran away in the night and left them among strangers."

"Where is the sister she speaks of?"

"The other young lady," replied the interpreter, "became alarmed at their situation, and secretly left the house to try and make her way to Paris in the best way she could."

"And what was she going to do when she got there?"

"She expected to find her father in Paris," answered the little man, when he had made Miss Plumley understand the question, "and when he was found, she had no doubt instant measures would be taken to release the sister from the disagreeable situation she was placed in."

"Humph!" ejaculated his worship, "a very romantic story indeed! But how are we to know there's any truth in it."

"The lady says," replied the interpreter, "that the people of the house can answer for her having been taken to it in the way she has described."

"Do you recollect," asked the magistrate of the servant girl, "the arrival of this young English female at your master's house?"

"I do."

"Did she go there alone?"

"No, her sister and herself were brought there by two gentlemen, and they came in a carriage."

"What became of the gentlemen you speak of?"

"That nobody can tell," replied the girl;—"they disappeared in the course of the night, and my mistress, rather than turn them out in a strange place, thought she would keep them till their friends came to their release."

"There's something very mysterious in this affair," said the justice, "and if the story I have heard is true, the young lady deserves our pity. However, I cannot set her at liberty just at present, so let her be taken to some private lodging, where she may be kept in safe custody, till something further has been discovered to confirm the truth of her story. The other prisoners will be conveyed to prison till search has been made after the two men that slept there last night, and if it should appear that the strangers were not known as smugglers, I shall order their discharge after the next examination."

"Please your worship," said the sergeant of police, "there can be no doubt that the men were well known, and were invited to go there to assist in removing some contraband goods."

"Did they leave anything behind them?"

"Yes, your worship, two portmanteaus were found concealed in a secret closet."

"Are they known to belong to the men?"

"There can be no doubt of it," replied the officer, "for the fact of their being hid is a proof that they were afraid of our finding them, and if there was any doubt remaining in your worship's mind, the initials that are engraved upon the lid may perhaps not only convince you that I am right, but also lead to the detection of the men."

"Let the strictest search be made after them," said the justice, "and a handsome reward shall be given to those that have the good fortune to apprehend the knaves. And now take your prisoners away, and I'll give further instructions when they are to be brought up again."

This order was promptly obeyed, the host, hostess, and their servant, being conveyed to prison, and Miss Plumley to a private lodging as had been previously commanded.

The police required very little urging to be vigilant on this occasion, for the smugglers had been very successful of late, and angry communications had been received from head quarters, complaining of a want of attention to their business, and threatening them with high displeasure if any further instances of suspicion should occur. Then there was the murder of the Marquis de Noailles and his servant, which had been committed in this district by men who were proved to have been engaged in contraband traffic. These circumstances together, put them all upon the *qui vive*, and as a reward had been offered for the apprehension of the two men who had slept on the previous evening at the house of Monsieur Deleroix, there was every inducement to make the utmost exertion for their capture.

All this time Susan Hoply had endured her captivity with a degree of coolness and resignation that was hardly to have been expected from one placed in her peculiar situation. But she knew her own innocence, and perhaps relied upon that circumstances for an acquittal from the charges that had been brought against her. The only source of uneasiness was when she thought of her young ladies, and the alarm they would endure through her absence from them; but even in this, she consoled herself with the hope that they might perhaps hear of the situation she was placed in, and then take steps for releasing her from so awkward a predicament. A few days she thought would be sufficient to do all this, and as she was not harshly treated, it required no very great stretch of patience to endure a little longer the confinement in which she had been so unexpectedly placed.

At last, within an hour after the examination we have just described, the old woman, under whose care she had been placed, entered the room, and said abruptly :—

"Now, young woman, you are free to go from here whenever and
No. 40

wherever you please. You are no longer a prisoner, and orders have just been sent to tell you that there is no longer any charge against you."

"How is that?" asked Susan; "what proof can they have had of my innocence?"

"I was not told to give any explanation upon the subject," said the woman; "and perhaps if I was to say anything, it might get me into trouble."

"You can at least tell me," said Susan, "whether it is through my young ladies that I am thus unexpectedly discharged from imprisonment."

"I don't much think they have had anything to do with it," answered the other. "All I know is, that I was told to set you free, and that ought to satisfy you, since it's a lucky chance to get out of trouble so easily."

"There's no particular luck in it that I knows of," said our heroine, "for I have not committed any crime, and, therefore, all that I have endured has been undeserved."

"Why, as for your being innocent," exclaimed the old woman, "that's nothing to do with it, if people happen to take it into their heads that you are guilty."

"Perhaps," observed Susan, "they have discovered that I am not Madame Deleroix, as they suspected."

"I know nothing about it," replied the woman, determined not to be surprised into making any admission that might afterwards be to her own disadvantage.

"Nor will you tell me, I suppose," asked Susan, "whether my two young ladies have yet been taken away from the place where I left them?"

"I can't answer your question," replied the other. "The young ladies you speak of are nothing to me, and whether they have left the place or not, makes so little difference that I haven't asked any questions about them."

"But do you think they are safe under the care of Madame Deleroix?" asked Susan, anxiously.

"That's more than I can tell," replied the other. "Madame Deleroix is well knnown to be connected with smugglers, and though in other respects, she may be a very good sort of woman, I should be very sorry to let a daughter of mine be under her protection."

"Good Heavens! you think they are in danger then?"

"I don't think anything about it," returned the other; "you asked me a question, and I have answered it candidly, but whether there's any cause for your being alarmed about the young ladies is more than I can undertake to say."

"But what of the men that left them behind in so scandalous a manner?" asked Susan. "Has anything yet been heard of them?"

"Something, I believe," answered the other.

"Have they escaped out of the country?"

"That's more than I mean to tell you," replied the woman; "you are asking me a great many questions, and I told you before hand, that I should not answer anything."

"Are you forbidden to speak?"

"No; we are only cautioned against saying too much; and we know very well what to expect if we are foolish enough to talk about affairs that don't concern us. The last woman that held my situation, chattered to a prisoner, without meaning to do any harm, and when it came to the ears of the chief commissioner of police, he sent down an order for her discharge, and she was sent away at a moment's notice."

"That," observed Susan, "was indeed a severe punishment for so trivial a fault."

"It may appear a trifle to you," answered the old woman; "but everything in this country is done upon a system of secrecy, and if people will disobey the orders of those above them, they must take the consequences of their own folly."

"But what harm," asked our heroine, "could possibly follow a reply to such questions as I have put to you?"

"It's not my business to enquire what harm may follow it," replied the old woman. "All I know is, that orders have been given not to indulge the idle curiosity of prisoners, and that being the case, I should deserve punishment if I disobeyed them."

"That may be all very true," answered the other; "but you must remember I have your own words for it that I am no longer a prisoner."

"You have been though," answered the old woman, "and as I'm not inclined to let my tongue do me a mischief, I tell you once for all, that it's no use asking me any further questions. There are others that have not the same reasons that I have for being silent, and they I dare say, will give all the information you require."

"Nay, you forget that I am an Englishwoman, and I may ask a thousand persons the question before one of them will be found that can give me an answer."

"You, being a foreigner is no fault of mine," said the old woman sharply, "nor is it any reason why I should risk a good situation by speaking of things that don't concern me. Besides, there's plenty of people in the town that, if you can only find them, that understand your language, and having got your liberty, you've nothing to do, but to go about and make enquiries about the place for them."

"Which would be a waste of time that I can ill afford at present," answered Susan; "and so, with many thanks for some little acts of kindness you have done me, I shall now take leave of you, most likely, for ever."

"And where are you going to, may I ask?"

"Back to the house of Madame Deleroix," answered our heroine; "There I shall find my young ladies, and as the letters I brought with me have been sent off to their father, there's little doubt the old gentleman will come immediately to release them from their present unpleasant situation."

"Well, I hope you won't be deceived, that's all I have to say about it," exclaimed the old woman, who knew well enough all that had happened at the house of Madame Deleroix, yet had not the kindness to save Susan a long and profitless journey.

Our heroine now took leave of the old woman, and having left the place of her confinement she began to retrace her steps by the same road which had led her to the town, and though she was not in very high spirits, yet did she feel some gratification at the idea of returning to her mistresses who she imagined must be in great alarm at her long and most unaccountable absence.

CHAPTER XLIII.

AN IMPORTANT DISCOVERY.

QUITTING France for a time we must now return to the offices of Mr. Derwent, the lawyer, who it will be remembered had taken so warm an interest in Mr. Dawson's affairs, and to whom Susan had applied when she was making such rigid inquiries after the delinquent shopman of Edwards the linendraper.

At the period we speak of the worthy old gentleman was comfortably seated at his breakfast table, and reading the contents of a newspaper, when his housekeeper entered the room and informed him that a person wanted to see him as soon as he could make it convenient to give him an interview.

"Who is it, Mrs. Markham?" asked her master, raising his eyes for a moment from the huge folio which he was perusing.

"I don't know, indeed, sir," she replied; "but he seems very fidgetty and anxious to see you."

"Did you ask him his name?"

"I did, but he said that didn't matter, as it was most likely you would not remember him."

"Is he an elderly man, did you say, Mrs. Markham?"

"Rather so, sir."

"And I suppose you have never seen him before?"

"Never."

"Did my clerks seem to know him?"

"Neither of them are there, sir," replied the housekeeper; "Mr. Red-tape has stepped out to the judge's chambers, and the junior has gone to serve a copy of a writ."

"Humph!—who can it possibly be?" said Mr. Derwent, musingly, and without appearing to take any heed of the latter words.

"I should say he is a Jew by the look of him," exclaimed Mrs. Markham; "but I didn't stop a minute in the office, for he told me to make all the haste I could."

"Ah!" cried her master; "I think I know who it is. Send him up, Mrs. Markham, for I'll see him in this room instead of going down to him."

The old lady departed, and Mr. Derwent throwing down the paper, began to wonder in his own mind what business could have brought the Jew on this visit. He knew, however, that he had an artful customer to deal with, and assuming an air of indifference, he waited till the door opened, and the next moment Moses Lazarus stood before him.

"Ah! Mr. Lazarus, is that you?" exclaimed the lawyer, as if quite surprised at seeing him. "It is some little time now since you and I met each other, but I can assure you I feel most proud to see you again."

"You are very kind, sir," said the Jew, seating himself in a chair towards which the lawyer pointed; "I knew you would not be sorry to see me, especially as I have a little business of importance to communicate."

"You are not engaged in law, I hope, Mr. Lazarus?"

"No, sir, I am not," replied the other; "but the truth is, I am in possession of a very important document that would be of importance to its legal owners."

"Then why not give them at once, Mr. Lazarus?"

"Because, you see, it don't belong to myself," said the cunning Israelite. "It belongs to a friend of mine, and he came to ask me what he ought to do with it."

"Tell him then," said Mr. Derwent; "that as the document is not his own, and may be of great importance to other parties, he should, as an honest man, give it to those who have the greatest right to it."

"My friend is a very honest man," answered the Jew; "but he thinks if the thing is of any value at all, the people that would be glad to possess themselves of it, should reward him handsomely for the trouble he has had in the business."

"And I dare say they would do so, Mr. Lazarus," replied the lawyer. "Tell your friend, from me, that common justice demands the restitution of the papers, and that it would be an act of great dishonesty to withhold them when he believes them to be of such value."

" Ah, my very good sir," exclaimed Lazarus; " you forget how Christian folks scoff and deride us poor Jews. Yet you must know that such is the case, and therefore it is not to be wondered at if my friend resolves to make a good bargain out of this affair before he parts with the papers."

" Well," said Mr. Derwent, impatiently; " what do the papers you mention consist of ?"

" There is a will, and—"

" The will may be valueless," exclaimed the lawyer, interrupting the other.

" Ah ! but this is not so," answered the other.

" How do you know that ?"

" Because a great stir has been made about it. It has been enquired for and advertized."

" Then really, sir, I can give you but one piece of advice upon the subject," answered Mr. Derwent; " your friend, of course, knows very well who it belongs to, and it is his duty to restore it."

" What ! without being paid for his trouble ?"

" He would, no doubt, be handsomely rewarded," said Mr. Derwent: " and there would be the further gratification of knowing that he had done an honest action."

" But honest actions don't very often put money in the pocket," said the Jew; " and as my friend thinks he might only get empty thanks for his pains, he came to ask my advice upon the subject, and I thought the better way would be to come and mention the subject to you, who understand the sort of business."

" How did it come into his possession ?" asked Mr. Derwent.

" Quite by accident," replied Lazarus; " it was found in the pocket of an old coat some time ago, and thrown aside as useless, till this stir of late came to be made about it."

" Does he know who the coat was purchased of ?"

" He remembers something about it," answered the Jew : " but at present his memory is not very clear, I believe."

" That is to say, I suppose," said Mr. Derwent; " a little gold might act as an excellent refresher in the case ?"

" I believe it would not be badly applied."

" How much would his conscience prompt him to require ?"

" That, I believe, he would trust to your cwn opinion upon the subject," answered the Jew; " the property mentioned in the will is, however, very large, and as a matter of course, the man that is the means of putting it in the possession of the right owner ought to be well rewarded."

" And he will be well rewarded I have no doubt," replied Mr. Derwent. " But at present, Mr. Lazarus, I am quite in the dark as to the whole affair, and therefore am unable to give my advice upon the subject. Perhaps, however, you will be good enough to be a little more explanatory, and when I have heard all the particulars, I will candidly give my opinion about it."

" And you won't take advantage of the poor man that has been lucky enough to find it ?"

" I see how it is, Mr. Lazarus," said the other; " you have, like the rest of the world, no very favourable opinion of us lawyers, and think we shall take you in as Jews do when they sell their old clothes. However, I can assure you that I will act honourably towards all parties, and if the will you speak of is really worth anything at all, your friend shall have the benefit of his discovery."

" I have told you," said Lazarus, " that I—that is, my friend bought it in the coat in the way of business."

" That is to say he bought the coat, Mr. Lazarus," replied the lawyer ; " but I rather think if the affair was to go before a jury, it would be decided that the will formed no part of the bargain."

" Then perhaps my friend had better burn it," observed the Jew, " and say nothing more about it."

" There's no occasion for him to do anything of the kind," replied Mr. Derwent ; " for the fact is, I have no doubt, when the heirs come to hear that the will they are seeking for is in safe hands, they will be most happy to make a fair compensation to the finder for any trouble he may have had in the business."

" Well, sir," exclaimed the Jew ; " as I've a notion you are an honest man for a lawyer, will you undertake to negotiate the affair for me—that is for my friend ?"

" Certainly I will," answered Mr. Derwent ; " but I need not tell you, sir, that I must know all the particulars, without the least reservation, before I can move in it."

" Ah ! you want to see the will, I suppose ?"

" I do, indeed. Do you happen to have it with you ?"

" I have," replied Lazarus, cautiously ; " but you must remember, sir, it is not mine, and if it should happen to be lost or mislaid, there'll be terrible work about it, and I shall have to pay for it."

" You may depend upon its being safe," answered Mr. Derwent ; " and, further, I give you my word that no time shall be lost in bringing the affair to a settlement."

" Well, this is it, Mr. Derwent," said the cautious Israelite, taking from his pocket a very ragged handkerchief, and unfolding it, he, with trembling hands, placed it on the table before the lawyer.

" How is this ?" said Mr. Derwent, looking at it with surprise ; " here are stains of blood on it !"

" True," replied Lazarus, with a shudder ; " the man that made that will was murdered, and there are marks of the assassin's blood-stained hands as plainly visible as on the day when the act was committed."

" In Heaven's name whose will is it ?" exclaimed Mr. Derwent in alarm.

" It was made by the late Mr. Wentford," answered the Jew ; " who, I dare say, you remember was cruelly murdered a few years ago in the country."

" I remember it," replied the lawyer ; " and I believe to this day the assassins have never been discovered."

" They have not," answered the other ; " but I recollect it was said the deed was committed by a dairy-maid and one of the men servants belonging to the old gentleman. At any rate they both of them disappeared on that very night, and from that time nothing has ever been seen or heard of either of them. People said that they had escaped and gone abroad, and so I suppose they did, or they never would have been so long undiscovered."

" I recollect some such persons as you have mentioned were suspected," said Mr. Derwent ; " but on the other hand, I must do them the justice to say, that the report was strongly contradicted at the same time, by persons who knew both the parties well. Even Miss Wentford, the daughter of the deceased, declared that she was convinced the murder was committed by other hands, and the principal ground of suspicion rested upon the facts of their having disappeared on the very night when Mr. Wentford was assassinated in his bed."

" If you remember so much as that, sir," exclaimed the Jew, " you must also recollect that it was said the old gentleman made his will only a day or two before the murder ; the will, to this time, has never been found, and it was owing to a fortunate chance that it came into the hands of my friend."

" It may, indeed, turn out so," answered Mr. Derwent; " but a man may make as many wills as he chooses, and this may be one that was made previous to that which was executed within a few hours of Mr. Wentford's death."

" If you look at the date, sir," said Lazarus, " you will soon be convinced that it is the one that has been so anxiously inquired after. Besides, the blood-stains prove it to be the one that was taken away on the night of the murder, and, I have no doubt, when you come to read it through, you will be convinced that it is the right one."

" Well, I shall give it a most careful perusal," exclaimed Mr. Derwent, " though there are things connected with the mysterious affair that require some explanation ; for instance, how came it that the murderer should let it pass out of his hands, when its possession was of so much importance to himself ?"

" That," answered Lazarus, " is a question that I can't undertake to answer. But I dare say it was lost by accident, and that whoever it belonged to would give something pretty handsome to have it returned."

" Did you discover it in the pocket of the coat at the time you made the purchase ?" asked the lawyer.

" No," replied the other, " nor for a long while afterwards."

" And did the man that sold it you ever apply at a subsequent period for the purpose of ascertaining whether you had found such a thing ?"

" The same person that I bought it of never showed his face in my shop again," answered Lazarus. " However, some time afterwards, a young woman—very likely it might have been the dairy-maid herself,—came into the place, and inquired if something had not been left in the pocket which was of no use to anybody but the owner. I told her no, for, the truth is, I had not found it then, and I believed I was telling her the fact."

" Was anybody with her when she called ?"

" Only a child."

" And nothing more passed that is likely to throw light upon this mysterious business ?"

" No, sir," replied Lazarus ; " she seemed to be very much disappointed when I gave her the answer, and then she left the shop without saying anything further."

" And how long after that event was it that you found the will ?" inquired Mr. Derwent. " I am speaking, now, Lazarus, as if this business were your own, because you have entirely ceased from making any allusions to your friend ; and, therefore, I can perfectly well understand the motive that induced you to say the will had been found by another person. How long, I repeat, was it after the young woman applied at your shop, that you found the will now produced ?"

" Oh, a long while," replied the Jew, " for the coat was a very old one, and I had put it away in a closet, because I thought it was only fit to cut up to mend others with. One day, however, a poor man came into my shop, and after trying a good many on, he said he couldn't afford the price I asked, and observed that anything would do for him, if it was but a little better than the one he was then wearing. Upon that, I recollected the coat I had put away in the cupboard, and off I ran to fetch it for my customer to look at."

" And then," said Mr. Derwent, " I suppose you made the discovery that is likely to prove of so much importance ?"

" " You shall hear, sir," said Lazarus; " I fetched the coat, as I have already told you, but it was so very old and worn, that he began to find a thousand faults, and I began to be afraid I should not be able to make a customer of him, after all the trouble I had had. So I persuaded him to try it on, that I might tell him how beautiful it fitted, and whilst I was passing my hand over it, to hide the bad places as much as I could, I felt something hard in the pocket, and then I began to think that perhaps I was going to sell him too good a bargain for his money."

"And upon searching the pocket," said the lawyer, " you found the will?"

"When I made this discovery," continued the Jew, " I began to tell him that I was afraid the coat would not fit him, and making an excuse that I would find him another, I took it off and threw it on one side till I had got rid of him. Well, sir, as you may suppose, I was anxious enough to see what my prize was, but upon drawing it forth, you may judge what my disappointment was when I found that it was nothing but an old piece of parchment. I could have bit off the ends of my fingers with vexation, for not selling the man the coat, for he would have given me a very fair price for it, and I even sent my daughter to run out and bring him back, but he was out of sight, and I was obliged to put up with my disappointment as well as I could."

"And how came you to keep the will after you thought it so valueless?" asked Mr. Derwent.

" Why, sir," replied the other, " whilst I was blaming myself for losing a customer, the thought came across me about the young woman that had called to inquire whether I had found anything in the pocket of a coat that I had bought some time before. Then, thinks I to myself, this must be of some consequence, or she would not have taken so much trouble about it ; so I put the will in a place where it has been ever since, till I heard that some of the late Mr. Wentford's family were making a great stir about a will that was missing, and an idea struck me that the one I had might be it. And away I ran to have a look at it, and there, sure enough, I saw the name of Wentford, and I knew that all was right."

"And this happened very lately?"

"Yes, sir, only a very few days ago. At first, I hardly knew what to do, for the thing was of no use to me ; and yet, I thought I ought to receive something for taking care of a document of such importance. At length, I thought it would be better to call upon you, and, for fear of losing my chance, I said it belonged to a friend of mine."

"And you have never seen the man since that you bought the coat of?" said Mr. Derwent.

"Never."

"Nor the woman?"

"No, the poor creature got an answer, and I suppose she thought it would be useless to call again."

"Have you any notion where we might find her?" inquired the lawyer.

"Not the slightest," replied Lazarus. "Indeed, it's hardly likely that she's to be found in London, sir, for, if she happened to have had any hand in the murder of Mr. Wentford, she would not make a parcel of inquiries that would be sure to end in her detection."

"But," answered the other, "we are by no means certain that she had anything to do with it. The coat may have come into her possession in more ways than one, and I'm half inclined to try an advertisement in the newspapers, offering a reward if she will apply at my office, where she may hear of something to her advantage. Such things have been done before, Mr. Lazarus, and with very excellent effect, I can assure you."

"But if you do that," replied the Jew, " it will give the guilty parties a hint of what's going forward ; and, in that case, they would no more mind cutting her throat, by way of keeping their secret safe, than they did murdering Mr. Wentford, for the sake of that dirty bit of parchment."

"That's very true," exclaimed Mr. Derwent, " and, on that considera- tion alone, I will try all other expedients before I have recourse to an ad- vertisement. The villains, I dare say, may yet be discovered, and they may depend on it, be who they may, I will use every exertion in my power to bring them to punishment."

"But of course, sir," said the Jew," whether they are found out or not, that will I have just given you, will be the means of giving Mr. Wentford's property to the persons he intended should share it."

"Certainly it will," replied the lawyer, "and I shall make it my busi- ness to set about arranging the affair with as little loss of time as possible."

"And you will also make it your business to secure for me such a re- ward as my services in this instance justly deserve."

"That you may depend upon," answered Mr. Derwent, "for, though the document was of no service to yourself, the course you have adopted will prove most beneficial to those who would otherwise have been robbed of their rights. I shall state your conduct to the parties concerned, and I have no doubt they will make you a remuneration that will perfectly satisfy your expectations."

"You may tell 'em at the same time," added Lazarus, "that I'm a very poor man with a large family, and that the sooner they let me hear from them the better it will be."

"As for your poverty, my friend," said Mr. Derwent, "I am, of course, unable to give any opinion upon that subject, though I believe you have nothing to complain of on that score. Your large family, however, I have my doubts about, for, to my belief, you have but one child, and she is an assistance to you in your business.''

"But there's no occasion to tell 'em that," exclaimed the Jew. "Make my condition out as badly as you can, and perhaps they may be inclined to add a hundred or two out of charity to the man that has done 'em such good service.''

"In my opinion, it will be better to let matters take their own chance," said Mr. Derwent, smiling at the avarice of the old man. "You will find them both liberal and grateful, I am convinced; and, take my word for it, they will be more inclined to be generous where they see straight-for-ward conduct, than they would be were they to find that there was any shuffling in the transaction. So leave the matter in my hands, and I'll answer for it I'll give you reason to be satisfied with my management of your business."

"Well, well," said the Jew, "do anything you like, only mind and make as good a bargain as you can. Tell 'em what an honest man I am, and perhaps they'll reward me well for it."

"Nay, I shall leave you to sound your own praise, Lazarus," answered Mr. Derwent; "for I should be sorry to answer for that which I know nothing about. I will tell the parties all the affair exactly as it stands be-tween you and them, and when that is done, I shall leave you to conclude your bargain according to your liking."

"When shall you see' em, sir?"

"Immediately;—that is to say, as soon as possible after I have written to inform them of the discovery that has been made in their favour."

"Do they live far off?"

"I believe so; but what is the reason for your asking that question, Mr. Lazarus?"

"I was merely going to say that coach-hire is expensive," replied the Jew; "and that it would be as well to mention to them, if they should happen to want me to go down, they had better send money to pay for it."

"Ah! you have ever a sharp eye to business I see, Mr. Lazarus," said the lawyer.

"Obliged to have, my dear sir," answered the other. "I'm a poor man, you know, and if I didn't look after these things, what would become of me and my daughter, Rachel?"

"By the bye, talking of your daughter," said Mr. Derwent, "reminds me that she may be useful to us. Perhaps she saw the man that brought the coat to your shop for sale, and could recognize him in the event of sus-picion falling upon any one."

"Perhaps she might," replied the Jew; "but if she would be of any use in the business, what would you give her for the trouble she'd have?"

"That remains for future consideration," answered Mr. Derwent. "But do you happen to know whether she saw the man when he was in your shop?"

"I don't know."

"You can ask her the question, then, and let me know the result as soon as possible. And now, perhaps, you can tell me whether she saw the wo-man that came afterwards to make enquiries whether you had found any-thing?"

"I don't know, my good sir," returned Lazarus; "but to the best of my recollection she was in the little back parlour at the time, and as you may remember, there's a glass window that gives a full view of the shop."

"I recollect the glass window very well," said the lawyer, whose thoughts were immediately directed to his visit to the Jew's house, when, from the very window in question, he saw a man enter the shop, who afterwards turned out to be the dishonest shopman that had robbed Mr. Edwards. "Yes, yes," he continued, "I remember the place you speak of, and if your daughter was there at the time we are speaking of, it is likely she may have observed the woman sufficiently to be able to identify her. So make enquiries about it, sir, and let me know the result at our next meeting."

"But the will, my good sir," exclaimed Lazarus, rising to take his departure, and at the same time holding out his hand for the document he spoke of. "I must have the will, or I shall lose my chance of the money."

"I'll take care that you shall be properly rewarded," said Mr. Derwent; "but the will must for the present remain in my possession. Nay, you need not be under any apprehension on that account, for, upon the word of a man, you shall have all justice done you."

"Must I go without it?" cried Lazarus, in a tone of mortified disappointment.

"You must, indeed," answered the lawyer, "for it will be necessary that I produce it before any steps can be taken in the business. And now let me caution you to keep this matter very secret, for should anything be rumoured abroad, our plans will be defeated, and you will lose all hope of receiving the reward you are looking forward to."

Lazarus could plainly see that all remonstrance would be in vain, and having once more requested that the affair might be brought to as speedy a termination as possible, he took his departure to indulge his imagination in the prospect of the reward that awaited him.

CHAPTER XLIV.

WALTER GRAVESTOW BETRAYS SYMPTOMS OF UNEASINESS.

Mr. Derwent was more overjoyed at the recovery of the long lost will than he thought proper to confess to the wily Jew. It had been the object of his unceasing enquiries ever since the murder of Mr. Wentford, for he had himself drawn it up, and was, therefore, well aware of the importance it would be to Mrs. Gravestow and Edwin, both of whom had been amply provided for by the testator. Besides, the husband of the former had exercised a great deal of cruelty towards his wife when he found that she had no control over the property, and so unhappy had his conduct rendered her, that she had been compelled to leave him, and support herself on the paltry sum he thought proper to allow for her separate maintenance. In fact, Mr. Derwent was not without his doubts that some unfair practices had been going on with respect to the missing will, and anxious as he was to assist the daughter of his old friend, he had set himself secretly to work, in order to discover whether the important document was really in existence. But as time wore on, and no trace of it could be discovered, he began to give it up as a hopeless case, since there was every probability of its having fallen into the hands of Gravestow, who was likely enough to have destroyed that which would at once strip him of his power, and place his wife in that situation which was intended by her father.

It was, therefore, with no little satisfaction that he received the will from Lazarus, and perceiving that it only required caution to bring matters to a satisfactory conclusion, he began to consider within himself how it would be best to proceed in a business where he had so artful an adversary as Mr. Walter Gravestow to contend against. Not that there could be the least doubt in any man's mind as to the authenticity of the document he had become so unexpectedly possessed of, but he knew the quirks and quibbles of law, and could see well enough that Gravestow might throw difficulties in the way which would thus have the effect of throwing the whole affair into Chancery. This he knew the other would not hesitate to do, for though he would thus debar himself from possessing the property, there was sufficient cause to know that he would exult in keeping his wife out of it, and that it would at the same time give him an excuse for withholding even the trifling sum he allowed for her support.

Under these circumstances, therefore, it was absolutely necessary that the utmost secrecy should be observed till matters were in a fair way for settlement, and as he wished not to take the whole responsibility of it upon his own hands, he set out shortly after Lazarus had left him, and hastened to the house of Mr. Smithson, who was one of the executors under the will, and who, as a man of business, was well able to offer advice under the peculiar situation in which they were placed.

The satisfaction experienced by Mr. Smithson was fully equal to his own when he heard of the discovery that had taken place; but in some points he differed from the opinions entertained by Mr. Derwent, and after some argument had been used on both sides, it was agreed that they should both set off without delay for Summerfield on a visit to Gravestow, and that they should first sound matters, and then either tell him about the recovery of the will, or keep the secret a little longer, as circumstances might render it prudent.

"We both of us know what sort of a man Gravestow is," said Mr. Smithson, "and there's very little doubt he will be alarmed when he finds that we are a match for him in spite of his cunning and duplicity. Perhaps he will see the prudence of a surrender before it's too late, and, in that case, we shall be able to bring this affair to a satisfactory conclusion without having recourse to any disagreeable conclusion."

"He will be rather surprised," said the lawyer, rubbing his hands gleefully, "when he finds that the only foundation upon which he holds this property is crumbling beneath him."

"We shall see how he receives our communication," answered Mr. Smithson, "though, as you say, there's no doubt he will be terribly enraged on finding that he can no longer keep the property from falling into the hands of those for whom it was intended by the testator. He has become a person of some importance now in his neighbourhood, and it will mortify him exceedingly to be obliged to sink down into his former insignificance."

"Well," replied the lawyer, "there are few, I believe, that will pity him, for his conduct has been arrogant in the extreme towards all who are beneath him, and I dare say the satisfaction will be pretty general when it becomes known that he has no longer the means to hold his head as high as he does at present."

"Have you seen him lately?" enquired the other.

"Not for some time," replied Mr. Derwent; "but I understand he is much altered in his manners from what he was."

"He is, indeed, altered," exclaimed the old gentleman. "When first I knew him he was a wild, racketty fellow that could never live within his means. Horse-racing and gambling occupied the greater part of his time, though he always took care to conceal that fact from the knowledge of Mr. Wentford. Now, however, he is quite the reverse; money has become his idol, and though he has no children, it is said he is laying by money, in order that he may by and by boast of being the richest man in the county."

"Which he might, perhaps, have been able to accomplish but for this discovery of the will," observed Mr. Derwent. "However, in spite of the wealth he would have amassed, I can answer for it he would not have been the most respected man in the county."

"You are right, sir," replied Mr. Smithson; for his overbearing conduct on the bench has rendered him very much disliked by his brother magistrates, who can remember when he was only a clerk to his late benefactor, and, therefore, far beneath the humblest of those he now takes every opportunity of insulting."

"You have heard something of him lately, I suppose?" said the lawyer.

"Yes," answered the other, "Mr. Cornish, his steward, was up in town a few weeks ago, and though the old man was careful not to say a great deal about his master's concerns, yet he could not help throwing out a few hints as to how things were going on at home. It appears that Gravestow has taken a great deal of interest in the formation of a new road which is making in that direction, and which, according to the original plan, will render it necessary to pull down the old manor-house, which I dare say you recollect is in a very dilapidated condition. Mr. Gravestow, however, strongly objects to this, and having no better reason to allege for the course he is pursuing, he says it is a fine, ancient building, and that it would be a pity to pull it down."

"I remember the house very well," returned Mr. Derwent. "It belongs, I believe, to a person named George Ramsden, who, having squandered away his inheritance, is now living somewhere abroad in obscurity and poverty."

"That is it," said the other; "and why Gravestow is so anxious that the place should not be pulled down is more than I can satisfactorily account for. In fact, if the road is to be rendered serviceable, the house must be razed to the ground, or it will make a difference of more than half a mile."

"And has he succeeded in carrying his opposition into effect?" asked Mr. Derwent.

"Oh, yes," replied Smithson; "for though he stood alone in his opposition, he, in the end, came off victorious. The worst of it, however, is, that it will cause the road to cut through the property of a neighbour, who would have done anything rather than have his land injured, as it must be by the proposed alteration. But Mr. Gravestow has always entertained a decided dislike towards the person, and as no better reason can be given for his obstinacy in the affair, it is whispered about the neighbourhood that it was done to spite the man whom he could not otherwise injure."

"Upon my word, this Gravestow seems to have turned out to be a very pretty sort of fellow," said the lawyer; "and between ourselves, my friend, I am not sorry that we have so good an opportunity of clipping his wings for him a bit. He richly deserves the mortification he will have to endure, and I, for one, shall not spare him when once I find that we can proceed with certainty in the business. And yet it seems strange how a man of the world, like poor Mr. Wentford, could ever have been deceived by such a fellow."

"There's no accounting for it, certainly," returned Mr. Smithson; "but we know pretty well what a double-faced fellow this Mr. Gravestow is, and when he found that the old gentleman entertained a great regard for him, he commenced a system of deceit that would have imposed upon any one else besides his generous patron. Indeed, there was no reason for thinking that Walter was a hypocrite, except among a few that were in the secret, and they pretty well judged how matters would turn out. But Gravestow cares for nothing now, you see, for he has married the daughter of his too-confiding friend, and no sooner does he get possession of the money, than he begins to ill-use his poor wife, and turns out of doors the orphan boy that had been so handsomely provided for in the missing will."

"I always understood," observed the lawyer, "that the boy ran away from the house."

"So he did," answered the other, "but it was the constant ill-usage he received that caused him to do so. The boy had a spirit above his years, and rather than endure the insults that were hourly heaped upon him, he took the first opportunity that offered, and disappeared from the place."

"And has nothing been heard of him since?"

"Oh, yes," replied Mr. Smithson, "one letter was received by Mrs. Gravestow shortly after his departure, informing her that he was going a voyage with a captain with whom he had somehow or other picked up an acquaintance at Chatham. But what part of the world he has gone to, or whether he has yet returned is at present doubtful."

"I should hardly think he has returned," observed the lawyer, "or he would have gone to see Mrs. Gravestow, who he loved as a sister. Perhaps the young dog has got into good quarters, and will not return to England till he can bring with him a handsome fortune."

"Poor fellow! I hope he may do so," exclaimed Mr. Smithson; "and yet that's hardly necessary now that we have found the will which puts him in possession of a handsome independence. And besides that, I have secured him the principal share in the late Mr. Wentford's business, which was done in consequence of Gravestow's throwing himself into my power."

"Hang Gravestow! I've no patience with him," exclaimed the lawyer. "His whole life seems to be made up of scheming and chicanery, and I can never forget him for his conduct towards his unfortunate wife; indeed, it often surprises me how she ever could have thought of marrying him, especially as she must have had such good opportunities of judging of his disposition long before they married."

"Ah!" returned Mr. Smithson; "but he was artful enough to assume a very different sort of demeanour before he married her to what he did afterwards. Besides, they had known each other a great many years, and wild as Gravestow could be when he was out of her sight, he was steady and serious enough, I can tell you, when in her presence. Even I, who knew so much of him, was deceived for a time, for I really began to think he had sown his wild oats, and that he was going to turn out a steady man of business. As for Mr. Wentford, he, poor man, was completely prejudiced in his favour, and I fancy it was principally at his request that the young lady received the hypocrite as her lover. But now he shows himself in his true colours, and it is to be hoped, before long, he will be brought down to his own proper level."

"Aye, aye," replied Mr. Derwent; "with the assistance of this will, we shall be able to do it, little as he at present anticipates such an event. The tables shall be turned upon him, and we shall then see how much commiseration the world will bestow upon a man who has so greatly abused the good fortune which chance bestowed on him. However, we have not much time to lose, and as I intend going down to see him immediately perhaps you would like to accompany me."

"Most willingly," replied Mr. Smithson, and as they had very little preparation to make, they were soon ready to start, and within an hour afterwards they were seated in the coach and on their way to Summerfield. As no one else was with them, they had an opportunity of arranging proceedings before they had reached the end of their journey, and no sooner had they got down at the inn, than they set off for the house of the person they had come to visit. Mr. Gravestow was at home, but engaged with a gentleman on business, and as the travellers were in no hurry to see him, they were ushered into a room adjoining that in which the master of the house was sitting with his visitor. As it happened, too, the door which communicated with the next apartment stood ajar, so that every word which passed could be overheard, and as the conversation related to a subject upon which they had themselves been speaking not very long before, they listened with some little curiosity to what passed between them.

"Curse the road!" were the first words they heard Gravestow utter; "haven't I carried my point about it, and am I now to be told that it is necessary it should run in a direction contrary to that which I wished?"

"It is as near what you wish as possible," replied the other; "but since the work has been commenced, we have discovered that the old manor-house must come down so as to prevent a very awkward turn that might, perhaps, hereafter be the cause of many serious accidents."

"And what have I to do with any accidents that may happen, sir?" demanded Gravestow. If coaches overturn it's nothing to me, and as for the few lives it may be the means of losing, it's a matter of so little concern to me, that I am not going to have my plans changed merely to avoid such chances as you have mentioned."

"I'm afraid it can't be helped now, Mr. Gravestow," said the other; "for the trustees have decided upon the point, and I have positive orders to pull down the manor-house with as much despatch as possible."

"And you have my orders to do nothing of the kind," vociferated Gravestow very loudly.

"I am sorry I can't oblige you in this matter, sir," said the surveyor; "but there's a majority of the trustees against you, and you are, of course, aware I am but a servant, and compelled to give way."

"Refuse to pull down the old house," exclaimed Gravestow; "and I'll undertake to exonerate you from blame."

"Really, sir, I dare not," replied the surveyor; "for there is a determination that the place shall come down, and were I to leave it standing, there would at once be an end of my contract."

"And I am to be defeated, then, by these men that will exult in, for once, getting the better of me."

"Pardon me, sir," replied the other; "but it is entirely your own fault; you would insist upon the road being cut through Mr. Handley's land, and the consequence is, that it brings the old house more in our way than it would if we had taken another direction. I pointed it out to you, sir, at the time, if you recollect, but you were so determined to take the road through Handley's farm, that you wouldn't hear a word I had to say."

"Then why didn't you explain yourself more clearly?" exclaimed Gravestow; "if you had told me that the effect of the alteration I suggested would be the means of pulling down that house, I would have given up the point, much as I wished to annoy Handley, who once offended me, and who I have never since forgiven. You might have explained it then, sir, as well as now, and yet at the eleventh hour you come to tell me that orders have been given for the demolition of the house."

"You would not hear me, Mr. Gravestow."

"But I hear you now, sir," said Gravestow, angrily; "and you will please to understand that you have my positive commands not to move a stone belonging to the manor-house."

"What am I to do, Mr. Gravestow?"

"Why, make a bend in the road to be sure, and let it pass round by the orchard wall."

"But the work is in progress just there about," replied the surveyor;

" and besides the expense that has already been incurred thereabouts, we should have to purchase more land, and the commissioners already think too much money has been spent in consequence of your determination to cut through Handley's property."

" I care nothing about what they say," exclaimed Gravestow; " my word is as good as their's, and once for all, I tell you the manor-house shall not be pulled down."

" You will excuse me, Mr. Gravestow," said the surveyor; " but upon my word I cannot see any reason why it should be suffered to stand. It has been going to decay a great many years, and as the owner of it is abroad, it seems likely to fall down of its own accord, unless something is done for its support. So as that's the case, sir, the better way is to pull it down at once, and when the owner returns he will be paid the value of it."

" But it's an ancient edifice, sir," replied Gravestow; " and as I have a particular fancy for old buildings, I should like it to stand as it does now."

" I'm sorry to tell you it's too late to think of that now," answered the surveyor; " Mr. George Ramsden's solicitors have been applied to upon the subject, and as the price offered was a very good one, they have agreed to take it, and I believe the purchase money has already been paid into their hands. However, that I'm not quite certain about, and as I have nothing to do with it, why ——"

" But I have something to do with it," interrupted Gravestow; " and that I shall take care to let my fellow commissioners know. They are going to squander away money that is merely entrusted to them for a particular purpose, and as an honest man, it is my duty, sir, to check any abuses of the kind. I'll not sit down quietly and see such a robbery committed on the public purse. I'll not indeed, sir, and if the commissioners think proper to persist in such a course, I shall take such measures as will most speedily bring them to their senses. Besides, sir, I never heard of this arrangement before, and I should like to know why I was not spoken to upon the subject before it was determined to pull down the old house?"

" I don't know anything about your being spoken to about it, Mr. Gravestow," answered the surveyor; " but you were at the meeting of trustees when the subject was introduced, and that, of course, would have been your time for making an objection. But I remember all your thoughts were occupied in trying to get the road carried through Mr. Handley's farm, and——"

" Damn Mr. Handley's farm!" vociferated the other; " and so, because I was engaged in another important subject of our meeting, they were to carry this resolution without even so much as asking my consent."

" It was done by a show of hands," answered the surveyor; " and as your's was not held up at all, I suppose they took it for granted that you agreed with them. Indeed, you were talking to some one at the moment about Handley's affair, and very likely was not aware of the business that was going on at the moment."

" Curse that affair of Handley's!" muttered Gravestow; " it seems to rise up against me at every turn, and now it appears to lead to more mischief than I had reckoned on."

" Really, Mr. Gravestow," observed the other; " I can see no great mischief likely to arise from pulling down an old house."

" You know nothing at all about it, sir," exclaimed the other snappishly. " There may be much mischief in it; the house has always been a great favourite of mine, and I would rather lose my right hand than live to see it pulled down."

"Well, there's no accounting for taste, certainly," replied the surveyor; "but for my own part, I can see no beauty in it, and even the bats and owls have forsaken it, fearful, I suppose, that it will fall down about their ears."

Mr. Gravestow did not immediately reply to this, for he was just then engaged in thinking how he might best avert the demolition of the building about which he had expressed so much interest. He was not a man to suffer obstacles to stand in his way, whenever he had determined to carry a point; but in the present instance, it was clear that he had defeated himself in his anxiety to do an ill turn towards his neighbour Handley, and the reflection which this circumstance brought to his mind, caused him more anger than anything else that had occurred for a long time past. He cursed Handley and his farm too, in his heart, but do or think as he would, he could think of no plan by which he might save the manor-house from its threatened demolition. All he could, therefore, do, was to delay the event as much as possible, and having turned the matter a little over in his mind, he said :—

"Is there any one, think you, that would be likely to second any objection that I might make? Any one, I mean, whose interest will be injured in consequence of the road taking that particular direction?'

"I have not heard of any one objecting to it, sir," replied the surveyor; "Mr. Handley, you know, was not satisfied with it, and I believe would have carried his point, only that you insisted upon it, and the other trustees gave in rather than interrupt the business by being obstinate. Poor fellow! it was a terrible cut up for him, for his farm was not a very large one, and people do say that it's likely enough to be the ruin of him and his family."

"Why do you perpetually bring up that man's name?" asked Gravestow, sullenly.

No 42

"Only because I pity him, sir."

"Well, then, don't let me hear it mentioned again," exclaimed the other; "he's nothing to you or me, and I am heartily sorry I interfered in the business. So now, to go back to the old manor-house; you say the place has been purchased, but suppose the proprietor himself should refuse to part with a mansion that has been in his family so many years."

"Why, that would be very inconvenient, certainly," replied the surveyor, "and would delay us a good deal, besides spoiling a road, that will be excellent if it cuts directly through the site on which the house stands."

"But supposing that the person it belongs to should declare that he will not sell the property, you could change the direction, I suppose, with little trouble?"

"It could be done, certainly," exclaimed the other, "but the expense would be very considerable, for the road has been commenced in a good many different places, and some of the work would have to be done over again if any alteration was made now."

"Well, sir," exclaimed Gravestow, "and perhaps I may feel disposed to lay down a handsome sum rather than suffer the house to be pulled down."

"Ah! that would make all the difference, certainly," exclaimed the surveyor; "but, between you and me, Mr. Gravestow, there's no time to lose, for the thing is going on very rapidly, and I shall want to begin pulling down in the course of a day or two, at furthest. Indeed, we ought to have commenced before now, but the men were engaged in another part of the line, and so there it stands at present just as it did."

"Has the owner of the house been consulted upon the subject we are speaking about?" asked Gravestow.

"Oh, dear, no," answered the other; "he's in rather queer circumstances, I believe, and perhaps it's not convenient to be where people are likely to find him. At any rate, I know there was a great deal of trouble before anything could be heard of him, and when they went, expecting to have a meeting, it was found that he had just started for some place abroad, but what place that is, nobody knows."

"Who are the persons," asked Gravestow, "who have the management of his affairs?"

"You mean who was it that the trustees negociated the sale with?"

"I do."

"Laboon and Gregory I think were the lawyers," replied the other; "they live somewhere in London, but where their offices are, I never happened to hear. There's another person that has to do with Mr. Ramsden's affairs, however, and he perhaps knows more about him than the others do."

"Who is he?" demanded Gravestow.

"His name is Dunlop, and his chambers I know are somewhere in Lincoln's-inn. He's the man you ought to see about this affair, because he happens to know most about it."

"But with respect to this Mr. George Ramsden, himself," said Gravestow; "you say he's gone abroad?"

"So I have heard, sir."

"And do you think it possible to get any information that may lead to a clue that would find him?"

"I don't know, sir, I'm sure," answered the surveyor.

"Will you undertake to try whether his present place of abode is to be discovered? I'll undertake to pay you well for any trouble or expense you may be at, and——"

"I understand you perfectly well, sir," interrupted the other; "you wish to communicate with him respecting the old manor-house, and perhaps feel inclined to give a better price for it than the commissioners, so that it may not be pulled down. Well, sir, I don't mind doing my best for you."

"Be speedy then, or it will be of no use," said Gravestow, "and if you should happen to get any information, let me know it upon the instant."

"By all means, sir."

"And cause as much delay as you can in pulling the place down," continued Gravestow; "a week or two, you know, can make very little difference, and it may give me an opportunity of purchasing the property."

"I'll do all I can for you, Mr. Gravestow," said the surveyor, rising from his seat, and moving towards the door. "So good day to you, sir, and you may depend upon seeing me again as soon as I hear anything about Mr. Ramsden."

The surveyor then left the room, and Gravestow taking a few hasty strides up and down the room, threw himself into a chair to indulge in certain uneasy reflections which the recent interview had given rise to.

CHAPTER XLV.

INDICATIONS OF DANGER.

WALTER GRAVESTOW was too much vexed and irritated to rest for any long time in one position, and in a few minutes he jumped up from his seat, and was making his way through the next room, when he encountered the two men, who, of all others in the world, he would most carefully have avoided, for he knew they were no friends of his, and the moment his eyes encountered them, he at once felt an instinctive conviction that their present visit to him boded no good. That his proud, overbearing conduct had made enemies in all directions he was perfectly well aware, but he paid very little heed to the opinions entertained of him by the generality of the world, for he was reckless of what might be said or thought of him so long as certain events in his life were not too freely canvassed.

It was, however, different with Mr. Smithson and the lawyer who had paid him this unexpected and most unwelcome visit, for he was well aware that he had very little mercy to expect from them if once they had any ground to work upon, and as he could never feel perfectly safe, it is not to be wondered at that he should be startled at seeing them so suddenly presented before his sight. They had both been upon the most intimate terms of friendship with the late Mr. Wentford, whose mysterious death they were determined to unravel, and the interest they took in the affairs of both Fanny and Edwin, afforded him but too much reason to believe they would do all in their power to release them both from the power he possessed over them.

They had often spoken to him of the murder of Mr. Wentford, and expressed a conviction that, in spite of suspicious appearances, they were convinced neither Andrew Hoply nor Dolly Pratt had had anything to do with the crime. It was in vain that he asserted his own opinion that no one else was likely to have been guilty of the foul deed, for they were still positive in their own notions upon the subject, and frequently hinted that the mystery would some time or other be cleared up, and punishment overtake the guilty wretches who had so long eluded the vigilant search of justice. These observations alarmed him greatly, for he knew they only wanted a clue, and in the event of their finding out any circumstance that might set

them on the right scent, the result would be such as he trembled to
think of.

Against Mr. Smithson he entertained a dislike which nothing could ever
serve to remove, for the old gentleman had succeeded in forcing him to yield
up a large share in the business, which it afterwards appeared he had done,
not for his own profit, but for the benefit of Fanny and Edwin, both
of whom would thus be rendered independent of him. This latter fact
alone would have been quite sufficient to excite the anger of Walter Gravestow, for he had formed plans which would be entirely overturned by
what he was pleased to term the meddling interference of his foolish old
dotard. It is, therefore, not to be wondered at that he felt startled at
perceiving in his house the two men, who of all others, be most hated and
feared, whose visit proved that they came on business that would prove anything but agreeable. Besides, he entertained no doubt that they had ever-
heard the conversation between him and the surveyor, and though no expression had been dropped of which any use could be made, yet important
results often spring out of trifling circumstances, and who could tell but
his anxiety for the preservation of the old manor-house might give occasion for suspicions that he had every reason to dread? But all these
thoughts which have taken us some time to describe, passed through his
mind in one instant, and almost as quickly did he recover the appearance of
composure, so as to affect great pleasure at seeing them, though somewhat
surprised at the suddenness of their visit.

"Really, gentlemen, this is an unexpected pleasure," he said, "for I
was not aware, till this moment, that you were in the house; have you
been long here?"

"Oh, yes," replied Mr. Smithson, "some time, sir; but, hearing that
you were engaged with a friend in the next room, we sat ourselves down
contentedly enough, till you had leisure to see us."

"Ah, I have been talking to the surveyor about that confounded road,"
exclaimed Gravestow, impatiently. "No one can tell the trouble I've had
in that affair; for, though I wish to do my duty fairly and honourably,
there are some of my colleagues that would fain make a job of it. The
thing has already cost a great deal of money; and yet, would you believe
it, gentlemen, they have been squandering away some thousands of pounds
in the purchase of an old house that they want to pull down, because
they've taken it into their heads that it stands in the way of the line."

"And does it do so?" asked the lawyer.

"Why, I believe it is rather in the way," replied Gravestow; "but
what difference need that make, when all they've got to do is to make a
slight turn, which would skirt along the orchard fence. The direction
would not be quite so straight, to be sure, but it would be quite sufficient to answer all the purposes for which it is intended."

"And yet, in my opinion," said Mr. Derwent, "if the road you speak of
is really required at all, it would be a pity to spoil it for the sake of the
additional sum of money you mentioned."

"Ah, sir!" exclaimed Mr. Gravestow, with one of his most insinuating
smiles; "but, if we suffer one expense to pass without opposition, who
can say where the mischief would end? Besides, the old manor-house
is a favourite object of mine, and I would not have it pulled down for the
world."

"That's very strange, too," observed Mr. Smithson, "for the last time
I was down here, I could not help thinking what an unsightly old building
it was. Besides, it is in a shocking state of dilapidation; and I dare say
the owner thinks it better to part with it in this way, than lay out a large
sum of money in useless repairs. If it was mine I should not hesitate

about pulling it down, and should think myself very fortunate in having got rid of a useless encumbrance."

"Well, for my own part, I never like to see old buildings destroyed," answered Gravestow. "And I am not singular in my regard for the place, for poor Mr. Wentford was also very partial to it, and if it was only for his sake, I should wish to preserve it from destruction."

"By the by," said the lawyer, "talking about Mr. Wentford,—have you ever found any clue that may lead the detection of the villains that murdered him?"

"No," replied Gravestow, turning deadly pale, and averting his head from the steady gaze of the querist; "I have made every inquiry that was possible; but it is most likely the guilty parties have escaped out of the country, and, in that case, we shall never hear anything more of them."

"There I don't agree with you," said Mr. Derwent, pointedly; "for I rather think some of them are in England, and not very far from us at this moment."

"Did you come down to made any inquiries upon the subject?" inquired Gravestow, endeavouring, but in vain, to conceal his agitation.

"No," replied Mr. Smithson, "our visit was very suddenly resolved upon, I can assure you. In fact, we have both of us been rather closely occupied by business, lately, and, knowing you would be glad to see us, we came down just for the sake of a little change of air."

"Really, I feel much honoured by your company, gentlemen," said Gravestow, somewhat relieved by these words. "My doors are always open for the reception of my friends, and——"

"Aye, aye, we are quite aware of that," interrupted the lawyer; "but, in spite of what Mr. Smithson says about our coming down merely for a little change, I always like to combine business with pleasure, and, if you please, we'll speak of an affair in which you are somewhat unpleasantly concerned."

"Indeed!" faltered Gravestow; "I was not aware of being concerned in any business that could prove unpleasant."

"Well, you shall hear, and judge for yourself," said the lawyer, glancing a look of satisfaction towards his companion. "You are aware, I believe, Mr. Gravestow, that your late friend and benefactor, had made a will just before his death, and that the document was never found, though a strict search has been made after it in every direction?"

"There was none in the house at the time," replied Gravestow, "for I myself, took great pains to look for it, and nothing of the kind could be discovered."

"Yet, that there was one I am quite certain," answered the lawyer.

"It may be so," replied the other, with as much composure as he could assume, "but whether there was one or not, I can only say it was not found after the murder of Mr. Wentford."

"There was the will and a copy of it," exclaimed the lawyer, "and that renders it still more singular that neither of them should have been discovered."

"What think you has become of them then?" asked Gravestow, with impatience.

"That they were both stolen at the time of the murder of the old gentleman," replied Mr. Derwent.

"Indeed!"

"Such has always been my opinion," answered the lawyer; "and, to tell you the truth, sir, I had given up all hope of ever finding them, as there was every reason to imagine that the robbers would destroy documents that could be of no use to them, but might at a future time be brought as evidence against them."

"If they were stolen, as you have suggested," observed Gravestow, "there is little doubt but they have been destroyed."

"Yet, strange as it may appear," continued the lawyer, observing the changing countenance of Gravestow, "the will still has not been made away with, for it has come into my possession in a most singular manner, and I have at this moment got it in my pocket."

"Indeed!" exclaimed Gravestow, absolutely gasping for breath; "and are you certain that it is no forgery?"

"Forgery!" returned the other, with a smile of triumph; "oh no, there can be no doubt of its being the last will and testament of poor Mr. Wentford."

"What proof have you of that, sir?"

"A very melancholy one, Mr. Gravestow," answered the lawyer, taking the will from his pocket, and presenting it to the view of the tortured man before him. "You see, sir, here are the marks upon it of the bloody hands that stole it immediately after the murder was perpetrated."

"Let me look at it, sir," exclaimed Gravestow, who, pale and trembling, advanced with outstretched hand to grasp the damning evidence before him. The lawyer, however, kept safe possession of it, for he knew Gravestow to be a desperate man, and, fearing lest it might be destroyed, he was determined not to let it go out of his own safe keeping.

"You will excuse me, sir," he said, "but there is no occasion for you to see more of it, since you are already acquainted with the contents. I myself read the draught to you after all search for the will had been fruitless; and, therefore, you are of course aware that Mr. Wentford disposed of his property in a manner very different from the arrangement that took place after the testamentary document was supposed to be lost."

"Really, gentlemen," said Gravestow, recovering his self-possession as well as he could, "this is a most singular affair, and you must excuse me if I express my doubts about the validity of the will, till I have seen good proof of it. The sudden announcement has agitated me, as you see, but I am not disposed to throw any impediments in your way, and all I wish to know is, whether you are quite satisfied upon the point yourselves?"

"We are, Mr. Gravestow," answered the lawyer; "in fact, it is our intention to proceed immediately for the recovery of the property, which now, of course, must be disposed of according to the instructions of the testator."

"I hope, sir, you don't suppose I would attempt to do anything dishonourable in the affair," said Gravestow, who saw that he was in a dilemma, and that he must get out of it in the best way he could. "I am certain I am in honourable hands, and shall cheerfully accede to any arrangement that may be made."

"That is all we want," said the lawyer, who was surprised at the submission of a man from whom he expected to receive the most violent opposition. "We want nothing but justice, sir, and it gratifies me very much to see that you take so honourable a view of the affair, which will bring the whole, I hope, to a satisfactory conclusion."

"But you have forgotten to tell me," said Gravestow, "how the will came into your possession."

"I was going to tell you about that," answered Mr. Derwent, "and perhaps the recovery of the document is not the least singular part of the affair. The truth is there lives in London a Jew named Moses Lazarus, a strange fellow enough in his way, but in this instance he has performed a service that deserves to be well rewarded. However, to make short of my story, it seems that a woman called upon him some time since, to enquire if a parchment had been left by accident in the pocket of a coat that she had sold him at some former period. He said he had not seen anything of the kind, and she went away greatly disappointed at the result of her mission."

"What has this to do with the discovery of the will?" asked Gravestow, impatiently.

"It has everything to do with it, as you will presently hear," answered Mr. Derwent. "About a week or two ago, Lazarus happened to stumble upon this very old coat, as he was trying to please rather a difficult customer, and by the nicest accident in the world, he discovered the treasure it contained. At first he felt rather disappointed at only finding what he thought to be a piece of old parchment, but upon looking it over, he fancied something might be made of it, and brought it to me with a view of seeing whether I could find out the parties that had been named in the will, and who he rightly thought would be very glad to give him a handsome sum for the discovery he had made."

Gravestow could not conceal his agitation as he listened to these words, and it was not without difficulty that he faintly inquired what had become of the woman.

"Why that's more than I can tell you," replied the lawyer; "for though I questioned Lazarus, he seems to know nothing more about her than that she had been in his shop on previous occasions. He, however, suggests that it's likely enough she was no other than Dolly Pratt, the long missing dairy-maid, but whether it was so or not, we have at present had no opportunity of ascertaining."

"Was she young?" asked Gravestow, eagerly.

"The Jew says she was, and tolerably pretty in the bargain," answered the other. "She had a child with her, too, it seems, and as he remembers her countenance perfectly well, I have given him the task of discovering where she lives, which, I have no doubt, he will do, because I have offered him a liberal reward if he is successful. So you see, Mr. Gravestow, I have not been idle in the business, and if we have any luck, we shall get to the bottom of this mysterious affair before a great while passes over our heads."

"You think so, do you?" exclaimed Gravestow.

"I have no doubt of it, sir."

"Well, we shall see about that," said the other, gloomily. "However, Mr. Derwent," he continued, "I have no wish to throw any obstruction in the way of a fair and proper settlement. Satisfy me at any time you please that the will is genuine, and I shall at once bow to any decision that may be pronounced."

"I am very happy to hear you say so," replied the lawyer, "for I was afraid you might take it into your head to be obstinate, and then the consequence would have been that my clients must have gone to law with you for the restitution of their rights."

"It is my wish to avoid all controversy," exclaimed Gravestow, "for I have naturally an aversion to entering a court of justice, and when once I am convinced that the will is as you describe it, I shall make no further scruple about giving up all that has been bequeathed to other persons. That, sir, is my answer, and I trust that you will now admit that I am not the unprincipled man you took me for."

Both the gentlemen were indeed surprised when they heard him speak in this apparently candid manner, but they knew not the subtle artifice of the man they had to deal with, and indeed the forced civility with which he spoke, might well have deceived men of more suspicious natures than those to whom he had addressed himself. Mr. Smithson, in particular, began to think he had reformed since last they had met together, and the lawyer was taken off his guard by the artful words he had heard ;—but he was determined not to be defeated by any chicanery of the man he had to deal with, but rather to keep a careful watch upon him, and thus prevent his gaining any advantage that might subsequently defeat the ends he had in view.

Gravestow remained silent for a minute or two, but recollecting that it would not do to let his guests reflect too much, he proposed a walk before dinner, observing that he had made great improvements lately in his property, and offering to show them over the estate, if they felt inclined to accompany him. This was a proposition that the others could not very well object to, though Mr. Derwent knew well enough that it was only made to gain time and consider how he should act in the serious dilemma which had so suddenly befallen him. They, therefore, acceded to the suggestion with apparent willingness, and left the house in company, though never did three people feel more uncomfortable in each other's society, than did these when they set off for their walk.

Yet it was plainly to be seen that Gravestow was a prey to the most intense mental agony, for the perspiration stood upon his brow, and whilst a livid paleness overspread his countenance, there was a violent trembling in his limbs, that he in vain endeavoured to conceal. Mr. Derwent observed it, and was determined to let the other know that it was so.

"You appear to be ill, Mr. Gravestow," he said, "have you been suffering long from indisposition ?"

"No, not very long," he replied, with hesitation ;—"the truth is I am just recovering from a fever, with which I was attacked, and the subject of my conversation with the surveyer, has rather excited me, that's all."

"Ah !" exclaimed the other, "this road, I see, is a subject of more importance to you than it really seems to deserve."

"It is of so much importance," answered Gravestow, hastily, "that I would rather sacrifice all I possess in the world than be defeated by a parcel of men that seem determined to oppose me. But they only do it because they see I have an objection to the demolition of the manor-house, and let the trouble and expense to me be what it may, I will yet carry my point."

"You had better by half let them have their own way," observed Mr. Smithson ; "for, in my opinion, the suggestion they are acting upon is a great improvement upon the original plan, and for my own part, I can see no reason why a crazy old tumble-down place like that should be suffered to stand in the way of public convenience."

",Perhaps," suggested the lawyer, slily, "Mr. Gravestow has his own reason for wishing the house to remain as it is."

"I have my reasons for it, sir," replied the other, affecting not to understand the allusion. "The house has always been a favourite object of mine, and if it should be pulled down, I am convinced it would cause my death."

"Dear me," said Mr. Smithson, "your's must be a remarkably strong attachment indeed."

"It is so, sir," replied Gravestow ; "but men have their whims, and the indulgence of mine, in this respect, could not injure anybody."

"But, perhaps, your opponents in this case think there is some reason for your singular partiality besides a veneration for an old building that, if left alone for a year or two longer, would tumble down of its own accord," observed the lawyer.

"They have no right to think anything of the kind," exclaimed Gravestow, sharply. "I have wished to live upon friendly terms with my neigh-

bours, but they seem to shun me, and I don't see why I should give way to them in the present instance."

"And on the other hand," answered Mr. Derwent, "I suppose they see just as little reason why they should give way to yours."

"The house," said Mr. Smithson, wishing to change the conversation, "belongs, I believe, to a young scapegrace, named George Ramsden."

"It does, sir," replied Gravestow, "but after squandering away a fortune, he has gone abroad, and nobody knows at present where he is to be found."

"I wonder he has not sold the manor house to supply his extravagance," observed Mr. Smithson.

"He would have done so if he could," replied the other; "but nobody felt inclined to purchase a place that had been so long going to ruin and decay. Had I known where to seek for him, I should have made an offer for the house myself for the mere purpose of letting it stand as long as it would."

"And a very odd fancy it is," exclaimed the lawyer; "but I suppose you have some other reason for wishing to prevent it being pulled down?"

"What reason do you suppose I can have?" demanded Gravestow, with a momentary look of alarm.

"I can't tell you the reason, sir," replied the other, "but it's natural to suppose there is one from your great anxiety on the subject. Look at it," he said, pointing towards the manor house, which at this time was within sight; "is there anything about such a crazy heap of bricks and mortar that any man could feel a reverence for? If, indeed, it was the place of your birth, or it had ever belonged to any part of your family, I could perfectly understand why so great a regard is entertained for it. But you have no such reason to allege, and as its demolition appears to be abso-

No. 43

lutely necessary for the completeness of the road, I should really advise you to think no more about it, nor care whether it comes down or not."

"What!" exclaimed Gravestow, "and suffer myself to be defeated by a parcel of men that would glory in such a result?"

"I don't suppose they would think about it an hour after they found your opposition had ceased. Besides, I think I heard the surveyor say it had been already purchased of this George Ramsden, and if that's the case, I don't see what you can do further in the business."

"The bargain may not have been finally closed," exclaimed Gravestow, "and if that should prove to be the case, I'll offer them a larger sum, and thus secure it from the fate they would doom it to."

"But you will pardon me, sir, I hope," said Mr. Derwent, "for I have no wish to remind you of disagreeable affairs, and yet it may be necessary to state, that when we come to pay the different bequests according to the will of Mr. Wentford, you will find a vast difference in your resources."

"I know it, sir, I know it," exclaimed Gravestow, impatiently; "I shall lose a good deal, I dare say, but I have not been an extravagant man, Mr. Derwent, and though it took every farthing of my ready money, I would cheerfully part with it rather than suffer this defeat."

"I suppose then," observed the lawyer, "that in the event of your becoming its purchaser, you would take up your residence in it?"

"Heaven forbid!" exclaimed Gravestow, with a shudder.

"How strange," said Mr. Derwent, who had noticed his agitation; "that you should confess so great a partiality for a place that you would not like to live in."

"Why, the fact is," replied Gravestow, "the expense of putting it in repair would be so great, that I should hardly feel inclined to lay out any money upon it. Besides, a man may feel a liking for an antique building, and yet feel no inclination to make it his home. Indeed, there is an air of gloomy loneliness about it that quite unfits the house for a place of residence."

"I perfectly agree with you there," said Mr. Smithson, "for if any one would give me the house and a large fortune to boot, I would not be bound to pass even so much as a single week in it."

"Nor I," exclaimed the lawyer.

"Then why," asked Gravestow, "should you wonder that I also have an objection to residing there?"

"Only because you seem to be so extremely partial to it in other respects," answered Mr. Derwent. "For my own part, I can see neither beauty nor ornament about it; it don't add anything to the picturesque character of the scenery, and in my opinion, appears rather to be an ugly excrescence than anything else."

"That is a difference in taste," observed Gravestow.

"And so great is the difference," returned the lawyer, "that I can see no reason for the partiality you have expressed in favour of a clumsy building that can scarcely stand upon its foundation."

"Yet, as I have taken a liking to it," said the other, sharply, "I may of course be indulged in it without being called to account for it."

"My dear sir—I have no wish to call you to account for it," exclaimed Mr. Derwent, who had no wish to offend Gravestow till the business between them was brought to a conclusion; "I have merely expressed an opinion in opposition to yours, and I rather think you would find ninety-nine men out of a hundred that would say exactly as I do in this matter."

"Very likely," answered the other, "but, in spite of the majority against me, I should still entertain the same notion that I do now. The house may be old, ruinous, and unsightly; but with all its faults, it is a favourite of mine, and I will never rest satisfied till I have made it my own, even though I shall have to pay three times its value for it."

"Well, there's no accounting for taste, that's certain," said Mr. Derwent; "and as you seem to be so much in earnest, I shall say no more about it. You have your own private reasons, I dare say, and I have no wish to enquire into them with impertinent curiosity."

From this time, the conversation took another turn, and they returned home immediately, upon which Mr. Derwent went to his own room, where he remained so long that his friend at length went to see whether he was coming down to dinner.

"Gravestow is waiting for us," he said, "and I almost think he begins to grow tired of our company, for he seems restless and fidgetty, and just now threw out a hint that he should be obliged to visit London without delay on some very important business."

"I am inclined to think he meditates some design against us," observed the lawyer, "and for that reason I shall decline dining with him to-day."

"What design can he possibly form against us?" asked the other with surprise.

"That's more than I can undertake to tell you," replied Mr. Derwent; "but I have noticed the malignant expression of his countenance, ever since he heard the will is in our possession; and though he strives to conceal it as much as possible, there is something in his manner that assures me he will not let us leave this house if he can find means to prevent it."

"Do you think he would make prisoners of us, then?" asked Mr. Smithson.

"I believe he would do more than that," replied the other, "if he could contrive to put us out of the way without fear of discovery."

"What!" exclaimed Mr. Smithson, startled by these words, "is it possible you think our lives are in danger here?"

"I have my suspicions," answered the lawyer; "and I have no doubt of his base intentions towards us if he can only provide for his own safety. At any rate, I am sure he would not mind coolly putting me out of the way, because he knows I have the will in my possession, and by an act of villany like this, he could easily prevent the consequences that he knows must follow the claims we are about to make."

"But any violence he might commit," answered Mr. Smithson, "would certainly be discovered, and he knows what his fate would be then."

"Very true," returned the lawyer, "and his knowledge of that fact will only serve to make him the more cautious. He may not cut our throats, perhaps, as we sleep, but there is such a thing as poison, my friend, and should anything happen it would be easy to invent a falsehood to cover his crime."

"Nay," said his friend, "I really believe in this instance, your suspicions wrong him. He may have no very friendly feeling towards us, but he well knows that should both of us die whilst under his roof, it would give rise to inquiry into the affair, and thus lead to his own punishment."

"And for that reason he may satisfy himself with getting rid of one of us," said Mr. Derwent.

"And which would that be?"

"Me, of course," answered the lawyer; "he knows I have the will, and that I should be a most important witness against him in a court of law. You he has less to fear from, and therefore he may be disposed to spare your life lest too great a stir should be made in consequence of the sudden death of two of his guests."

"Surely," exclaimed Mr. Smithson, "reckless as he is, he will never commit such an act as this."

"Don't make too certain of that, my good friend," returned Derwent, "for I am much mistaken if he has not been concerned in something of the kind before, and if such should be the fact, I see no reason why you and I should not look a little to our own safety."

"What do you mean?" demanded the other with surprise.

"I mean," replied the lawyer, "that I begin to entertain a suspicion that Gravestow had a share in the murder of poor Mr. Wentford."

"Good God! you never mentioned such a suspicion to me, before."

"Because I never thought of it till since we have been down here," answered Mr. Derwent.

"And what has put it into your head now?"

"His strange conduct, to be sure," replied the other; "did you not observe his dreadful agitation when I showed him the marks of blood upon the will, and the wild, incoherent expressions that he muttered till he was able to recover himself a little?"

"I certainly noticed a wildness in his manner," answered Mr. Smithson; "but that I attributed to the horror he felt at recollecting the events of that dreadful night."

"And what think you of it now?"

"That you may be mistaken," replied the old gentleman: "nay, I feel assured in my own mind, that bad as Gravestow may be, he never could have been guilty of a crime that, if proved against him, would at once stamp the perpetrator as one of the most heartless and cold-blooded villains that ever lived."

"Well, we shall know all about it by and by," said the lawyer; "for I shall begin to make secret enquiries into the affair, and if I should see any reason for thinking my suspicions are well founded, I shall not hesitate to take such steps as will bring the guilty parties to justice."

"But if there had been any evidence of the fact, we should have got hold of it before now," observed Mr. Smithson; "we have left no steps untried, that might lead to a discovery, and you are aware, as well as myself, that we have no clue at present."

"Aye, aye, I know all about that," exclaimed the lawyer; "but we don't know what may be done till we try. Besides, I have great hopes that we shall be able to trace the woman that made enquiries at the Jew's house respecting the will which had been left in the pocket of the coat which she had sold him. She can, no doubt, afford important evidence, and it shall be my business to find her out if she is still living."

"Which it is likely she is not," observed Mr. Smithson, "for in the event of there being any fear of her saying anything upon the subject, those who were guilty of the deed will take care to secure her silence."

"Aye, by putting her quietly out of the way," said Mr. Derwent. "However, I intend to go very quietly about the business, and as I have secured the services of Moses Lazarus, there is very little doubt but we shall be able to succeed in the task we are engaged on."

"But after all," exclaimed the elder gentleman, "it is to be hoped you have suspected Mr. Gravestow without any just cause. That he is a man of violent and wayward temper I am well aware, but it seems hardly possible that he could have had the base ingratitude to assist in the murder of a generous friend."

"It would give me great pleasure to discover that I have been in error," said Mr. Derwent; " but the more I think of this man's agitation whilst we were speaking upon this subject the more do I feel convinced that he was in some way or other connected with the horrible transaction. And there is another thing that goes far to confirm my notion—he is particularly anxious about the preservation of the old manor house, which, in reality, he cares no more about than either you or I do, and you may take my word for it, there is some mystery connected either with the place or its neighbourhood which we shall soon find out."

" Why, it must be admitted there is something curious in that circumstance," replied Mr. Smithson, " because I happen to have heard him very frequently laugh at what he called the folly of some people in their regard for ancient buildings."

" And yet you have now heard him declare that his only reason for wishing to preserve the manor house from destruction was its antiquity. But there's something more at the bottom of this than we at present know of, though a very brief time may serve to put us in possession of those facts he has been so careful to conceal."

" You really think, then," said Mr. Smithson, " that this man was connected with the crime that robbed his patron of life?"

" I do, indeed," answered Mr. Derwent, " and so serious am I in my belief, that I can hardly restrain myself even now from giving him in custody on the charge of murder."

" That would be an imprudent step at present," said the old gentleman, " and I would, therefore, advise you to keep your thoughts very quiet till all necessary inquiries have been made. And since, with such suspicions upon our mind, it would be madness to remain here any longer, I would now propose that we return to town without delay, lest we should suffer for our confidence."

" It is impossible that we can leave till to-morrow, as there are no coaches to London till the morning," replied Mr. Derwent. " We will, therefore, conceal our doubts as well as we can, and at as early an hour as possible will take our departure from hence, when I will lose no time in instituting inquiries into the truth of my suspicions."

" And you will not dine with Gravestow to-day?"

" I would rather not," replied the lawyer; " say I am ill, or make any other excuse for me that you please. I will remain here till our departure, and rely on it, I shall devote all my thoughts to the best means for bringing this mysterious affair to light."

Mr. Derwent kept his word, for he saw no more of Gravestow that day, and on going to bed he took care to fasten the door securely, and placed the will in such a situation that no one should be able to take it away without disturbing him. Nothing, however, occurred during the night, and rising at an early hour he took leave of his host, and, in company with Mr. Smithson, returned to London, well satisfied at the result of his visit to Summerfield, and congratulated himself at having escaped with his life from the house of a man who he knew bore the utmost ill-will towards him.

CHAPTER XLVI.

THE STINGS OF CONSCIENCE.

NEVER had Walter Gravestow felt the agony of terror as he did after the interview he had had with Mr. Smithson and the lawyer, for it seemed that an end of his guilty career was approaching, and unless some desperate means could be thought of, he felt but too well assured that he must fall into the snare which was ready to receive him. A thousand horrible schemes of counteracting the dreaded mischief passed through his burning brain, but he could not yet make up his mind to a further perpetration of crimes such as had already been committed, and after rejecting each thought as it rose to his mind, he determined to pay an immediate visit to London, and see if something might not yet be done to avert the blow he so much dreaded to encounter.

As soon, therefore, as his visitors had taken their departure, he ordered his horse to be saddled, and informing his housekeeper that he might not return for some days, he set forth on his journey to London with a mind harrowed and perplexed by the dangers and difficulties which had thus suddenly beset his path. At length, however, his meditations were disturbed by hearing his name pronounced by some one close at hand, and looking round him terror, he was somewhat relieved at perceiving that it was only Mr. Snell, the surveyor, who had thus accosted him. At first he felt indignant at being interrupted on his journey, but feeling anxious to know whether he had any important communication to make, he reined in his horse, and in an authoritative voice demanded what he wanted with him.

"I beg your pardon, sir," said Mr. Snell, "for interrupting you in this way, and perhaps you would rather see me down at your house some other time."

"You had better say what you've got to tell me now," returned Gravestow, "for I am called up to London suddenly, and may not return for some days. By the bye, if you can give me George Ramsden's address, I shall be glad, for I wish to see him on a little business."

"Really, sir," answered Snell, "as I told you yesterday, I have no idea where he is to be found at present. He finds it convenient to stop away from his creditors, I suppose, and if that's the case, he will take care not to let anybody know where he is to be found. Besides, I have heard that he goes by half-a-dozen different names, so that we may look a long time before we find him."

"Well, if I can't find Ramsden," said the other, "I can at least see his attorney. What was his name did you say?"

"Dunlop, sir."

"Where does he live?"

"Somewhere in Lincoln's Inn," replied the surveyor; "I don't know exactly in what part, but I dare say you won't have much difficulty in finding him."

"That will do," exclaimed Gravestow; "the attorney, of course, knows where to communicate with his client, and I shall be able to get the address from him."

"No doubt of it, sir," answered the surveyor. "At any rate, it's pretty certain Mr. Dunlop knows where to find him, but, perhaps, he may not be very willing to give the information."

"At all events, I will try him," exclaimed Gravestow, with as much placidity as he could assume. "And now, Mr. Snell, let me request that you will send any particulars you may happen to get to my usual lodgings in town. You know where I always go to; and remember, sir, that any trouble you may be at in this business, shall be handsomely rewarded."

"And how about this road, Mr. Gravestow?"

"Why, I told you yesterday how to manage in that affair," replied the other. "There's no occasion to hurry the work, and it will be easy for you to throw a few delays in the way, so as to give me time to complete my arrangements about the purchase of the old manor house. So, now good morning to you, sir, for I have some distance to travel, and my business in London is very urgent."

"And how about the little farm that you said I was to have?" asked Mr. Snell.

"Oh, that you may do as you like about," answered the other. "I have told you what I mean, and you needn't be afraid of my forgetting a promise to an old friend like you."

"Very true, Mr. Gravestow," exclaimed the surveyor; "but there's many a slip between the cup and the lip, you know, and as I always like business to be done in an off hand way, perhaps you'll sign a little bit of parchment for me, and then I shall know the conveyance has been properly made."

"Well, do it in your own way, sir," said Gravestow, impatiently; "let the deed be sent up for my signature, and it shall be immediately returned. But remember, I do this on condition that you occasion as much delay as possible in the formation of this road, and if you fail in keeping your promise, I shall know how to make you repent it as long as you live. And now, good morning, Mr. Snell, for I have no more time to waste in this conversation."

And off he galloped at a rapid pace, leaving the surveyor surprised at the impatience his latter words had occasioned, and wondering what in the name of fortune could have made Gravestow so touchy with him all of a sudden.

"There's something very mysterious in all this," he said, as he turned his steps homewards. "This new road of ours seems to have turned his brain; for, though he was always a roughish customer to deal with, yet, with a little management, I have never found so much to complain of as many other people have done. To be sure, it seems rather strange that he should think so much about pulling down that rubbishing old manor house, which, after all, is rather a disfigurement than an ornament to the neighbourhood; but some people take strange fancies into their heads, and if he don't mind paying a good round sum of money for it, I don't see that anybody else has anything to do with it. And now with respect to that little bit of land that he has promised I shall have;—it's just the very thing I've been wanting for years, and luckily enough I have found him in the humour to gratify my whim. And yet, to be sure, people do sometimes repent of a good-natured action, and perhaps, when he comes to reflect coolly about it, he may take it into his head to throw an obstacle in the way. Ah! that would indeed be awkward, so I'll hurry home, prepare the necessary deeds, and get his signature before he thinks better of his promise."

With this resolution, Mr. Snell entered his own house, and repairing immediately to the small room, that he dignified with the name of his study, he was soon occupied in preparing a draft of the deed that was to put him in possession of the long-coveted prize.

As for Walter Gravestow, he proceeded on his journey with so much haste that his horse began to tire before he had accomplished half the distance to London, and as the jaded animal would not move with half the speed he required, he stopped at an inn on the road side, and leaving his horse to be taken care of in the stable, took his place in the next stage coach that passed, and reached London some time after the night had set in.

It was not, however, so late but he could see a person he was most anxious to meet with, and having hurried through innumerable bye lanes and streets, he at last stopped at a house, the shop of which was closed for the night. But he was not to be baulked by this, and knocking at the door, was shortly answered by a female domestic, by whom he was immediately recognized, and conducted into the back parlour, where her mistress was seated.

"Mrs. Mansel," he said, "I am rather a late visitor this time, but I hope none the less welcome on that account?"

"Good heavens!" cried the female, "as I live if it ain't Mr. Willis Gayton."

"The same, at your service, my dear madam," answered Gravestow, acknowledging the name he had previously assumed for purposes of his own.

"And what in the name of fortune has brought you here, sir, at this time of night?"

"Oh, I had a little business in London, that's all," he replied, "and of course I couldn't think of going back again without giving you a call for old acquaintance sake. And how have you been, madam, since we last met?"

"Oh, much as usual," answered the lady, in a tone of familiarity; "but I needn't ask the same question of you, for you are looking stouter than you were, and altogether better, except being rather pale in the face."

"Aye, I have had my share of troubles, Mrs. Mansel, I can assure you," he replied. "However, I have a question to ask, which you can perhaps answer. Pray do you know anything of Amelia Robertson, the young female that I used to be acquainted with, and who, I am sorry to say, I have lost sight of some time past?"

"Amelia Robertson?—do you want to see her?"

"I do," he replied; "in fact, Mrs. Mansel, I'm afraid she is in great distress, and having seriously reflected upon the affair for some time past, I have now made up my mind to seek her out and do something for her in a little business that may support her in comfort. Do you happen to know anything about her?"

"Not much," answered Mrs. Mansel; "for she has not been to see me I don't know how long. However, some time ago I met with her by mere accident, as I was going down to Tooting."

"Does she live that way?" asked Gravestow.

"Yes" replied Mrs. Mansel, "she is in a little shop at Clapham, and is making a very comfortable living for herself and the child."

"Indeed!" exclaimed Gravestow, with surprise, "and what good-fortune has enabled her to take a shop? She was in a wretched state of destitution when last I saw her, and must have found some friend to do this for her."

"Ah! she was in a miserable state, sure enough," said Mansel, "for the poor creature was glad to take any odd jobs of plain work that I could give her, and if it hadn't been for that, she must have been starved outright. Between ourselves, Mr. Gayton, I wonder how she managed to live at all, but somehow or other a lucky turn took place, and things began to grow better with her."

"What lucky chance was it?" he asked.

"Why, she jumped over one of the bridges with her child," answered Mrs. Mansel. "That is to say she was going to do so, but was prevented by some gentleman who happened to be passing that way at the time."

"Humph!" ejaculated Gravestow, "and I suppose she was so grateful to him for the service he had rendered, that she went to live with him as his kept mistress?"

"No, no, hang it, she was not quite so bad as that," replied Mrs. Mansel. "It seems, however, that he was a kind-hearted creature, and having heard her story, and ascertained its truth, he took the shop for her that I've

been telling you about, and there she's been living ever since as comfortable as anybody need wish to be."

"You are sure she's there still ?" said Mr. Gravestow, not best pleased that his victim was in circumstances that might place her beyond the schemes he was forming.

"She was at the time I'm speaking of," replied Mrs. Mansel ; "and I dare say she's there now. She spoke to me as if she was very happy, and mentioned Mr. Smithson as being one of the best creatures that ever lived."

"Mr. Smithson !" cried Gravestow, with breathless haste ; "and who the devil, madam, is he ?"

"Why the person, to be sure, that prevented her jumping over the bridge."

"Do you know him ?" demanded the other in a voice so hoarse that Mrs. Mansel started with alarm.

"Lor' bless you, no sir," she replied ; "I never saw the gentleman in my life ; but I hear he's a very respectable merchant, and lives somewhere in the city."

"It is enough," exclaimed Gravestow ; "I must see her immediately, or it may be too late."

"Dear sir, what a hurry you are in to be off," exclaimed Mrs. Mansel, with surprise, as she saw her visitor snatch up his hat and make towards the door. "Poor Amelia, I tell you, is doing very well, and, if you must see her, to-morrow will be a much better time to go than now."

"I don't know that I shall visit her to-night," he replied, "and yet there is not an hour to be lost in idle delay. She may be in the hands of some villain who is only doing this kindness as a snare for her."

"Well, that's very thoughtful of you to be sure," observed Mrs. Mansel. "There may be some trick in all this pretended friendship, and I'm sure it's very kind of you to take so much pains about Amelia and her child.

No. 44

But I hope you'll stay a little longer, sir, for we don't meet very often, and I've a great many questions to ask you about——"

" I must request you to defer them till another opportunity," exclaimed Gravestow ; " it is now growing late, and I have not yet been to my lodgings to say that I am in town. But stay, you have not yet told me in what part of Clapham Amelia lives ?"

" It's on the right hand side, a little before you get to the Common," she replied. " It's a smart little milliner's shop, and you can hardly help seeing it as you go along the road. Besides, everybody knows Amelia Robertson in that neighbourhood, and any one can tell you where she lives."

" And you are quite certain the name of the person that set her up in business was Smithson ?"

" I am quite certain about that, sir," answered Mrs. Mansel, " for Amelia mentioned him so many times, that it's impossible I could have made any mistake about it."

" But don't you know what particular line of business he follows ?"

" I didn't ask her that question," replied Mrs. Mansel ; " but I believe I told you before, he's a merchant."

" You say he lives in the city," continued Gravestow ; " do you chance to know the name of the street ?"

" No," she replied ; " it was no business of mine, and so, of course, there was no reason why I should ask a parcel of questions that did not concern me. However, Amelia seems to be very comfortably situated just now, and as the old gentleman has been so kind to her she has every reason to be grateful."

" He is an elderly man, then ?" exclaimed Gravestow.

" So Amelia tells me."

" It *must* be him !" cried Gravestow, striking his clenched fist upon the table.

" Lord, sir ! what do you mean ?"

" Nothing—nothing—" he replied with more composure. " I was thinking of something else just then, Mrs. Mansel ; in fact, an affair has recently occurred that causes me a great deal of trouble and uneasiness, and I was vexed at the moment, and certainly forgot that I was in the presence of a lady."

" Oh, don't mention that, Mr. Gayton," exclaimed Mr. Mansel ; " for I know people can't always command their tempers, and it does one a deal of good to let a little of the steam off, when one's ready to burst. I know, even in my own case, though I'm as quiet and peaceful a woman as you'll find, that there are times when I can't help flying out as you have done, and Heaven knows, I always feel a great deal better for it afterwards."

" You are quite right, madam," replied Gravestow, calmly ; " these outbursts of passion do a great deal of good, and I feel all the better for having given vent to the momentary indignation I felt. And as for this Mr. Smithson, I may perhaps call upon him after I have seen Amelia, and if I find he has been playing a villain's part towards her, I'll make him remember it the longest day he has to live."

" Well, really it's very kind of you to take so much interest in her behalf," observed Mrs. Mansel. " It's acting the part of a Christian, and I hope, sir, you may live to meet your deserts."

" It's more than I hope myself, ma'am," said Gravestow, thoughtfully ; " for if we all got what we deserve, some of us would rather be out of the way when the rewards are given."

" Ah ! that's only your modesty," cried Mrs. Mansel ; " however, we won't talk any more upon the subject, so just sit yourself down and we'll speak of old times when you used to know more of Amelia, and—"

"I have no time to talk of anything now," exclaimed Gravestow, and shaking the hand she had extended towards him, he hurried through the shop, and was half down the street ere she could reach the door.

CHAPTER XLVII.

WALTER GRAVESTOW VISITS AMELIA.

HURRYING on like a madman, Gravestow passed through the streets without knowing where he was, and unconscious of all things save the one dread object that occupied his mind. The past now rose before him in all its hideous deformity, for he knew that guilt had stained his soul, and though he would have given worlds to have retraced the steps he had taken, it was now too late for repentance, and he saw in the future nothing but despair, ruin, and disgrace.

The only hope he had, and a very faint one it appeared to be, was in the regard in which he had once been held by Amelia. That she had once loved him he was certain, but her affection had been returned with the basest ingratitude, and at the first opportunity that offered, he had left her in a state of abject destitution and misery. Yet circumstanced as he now was, what else could he do but visit her and try the effect of persuasion in preventing her from taking part in any proceedings that might be commenced against him. At any rate he knew the kindness of her disposition, and trusting to the effects of hypocrisy and a smooth tongue, he thought it possible that she might yet be prevailed on to forget the past, and even render some assistance to help him out of his dilemma.

Faint as this hope was, it had served somewhat to allay his irritation, and by the time he had reached the house occupied by Amelia, he had formed a plan by which he hoped to gain the object of his visit. He knew it would be necessary to exhibit some of his former kindness, and, in addition to that, he felt assured that a show of affected repentance for former misdeeds, would secure for him that pity which he was so anxious to obtain.

On knocking at the door it was opened by a little girl, who he passed in the passage, and making his way towards the parlour, presented himself abruptly before the astonished and terrified Amelia.

"Merciful Heaven!" she cried, almost sinking with fright, "do my eyes deceive me, or is it indeed Mr. Gayton that stands before me?"

"It is me, Amelia," he replied, taking her hand. "It is some time since we met together, but let me hope that absence has not lessened the respect you once bore me. But you appear to be faint and ill; my presence has startled you, and—"

"I was indeed taken by surprise," she answered in a voice scarcely audible. "Indeed I had expected never to have seen you more, Mr. Gayton, and much better would it have been for both of us had you spared me this unlooked-for visit."

"Nay," he said with affected earnestness, "you have no doubt thought me cruel to neglect you so long, Amelia; but there have been causes for it over which I had no controul, and when you hear my explanation, I am sure you will pardon my apparent unkindness. So compose yourself, I entreat, and when you are able to attend to me, I will relate the occasion that has brought me here at this hour of the night."

"If your desertion of me was the result of necessity, I have nothing further to complain of," she replied. "I, however, had reason to believe that you had grown weary of me, and that you took the first opportunity that offered to rid yourself of one whom you had ceased to love."

" And very natural it was that you should think so, my dear Amelia," answered the hypocrite. "There was indeed a mystery about the affair that required explanation, and now that we have again met, I can assure you that my thoughts have never ceased to wander towards you. I have seen many changes since the time we were happy together, and fortune has smiled upon my endeavours to become rich; but what is wealth without peace of mind, and how can I expect happiness unless I know that Amelia has pardoned my former neglect?"

" I never harboured a feeling of resentment towards you," she answered, " though I must own it appeared hard that I and my helpless child should have been deserted and left to the coldness and neglect of a heartless world. Yet, even in the midst of my despair, I thought we should yet hear from you, and that the guilty mother and her infant would not be suffered to perish through want and deprivation. I had been betrayed from the path of virtue by a libertine, but though he had apparently deserted me, it yet remained to be proved that he was the villain his actions would lead me to imagine.

" You must, indeed, have thought badly of me," he replied, with a smoothness of tone that he knew so well how to assume if he had a motive for so doing. " My conduct was such as I cannot attempt to palliate, though, believe me, when you have heard my history, you will see that I have been the creature of circumstances, and that my leaving you as I did, was the result of unforeseen misfortunes."

" I require no explanation," answered Amelia, " for that which is past should be forgotten, and since I am no longer the victim of poverty, such as I once endured, it would be better to let oblivion conceal all that which would but again open the fountains of sorrow."

" And our child," he asked, " does she still live?"

" She does."

" Can I see her?"

" Not at present; she is away from home, and even had it been otherwise, I never wish her to see you, nor to learn the sad story of her mother's shame and disgrace."

" Where is she?" asked Gravestow.

" At school."

" And are your means sufficiently good to enable you to support her there?"

" That expense has been spared me," replied Amelia, " for a friend has taken the charge upon himself, and you know not how heavy a load of uneasiness it has removed from my heart to feel assured that she will be brought up in the path of innocence and virtue."

" And is it a male friend that you are so deeply indebted to?" asked Gravestow.

" It is."

" A lover, perhaps?"

" There you are mistaken," she answered, " for he is a man many years older than myself, and would scorn to take advantage of the generosity he has been kind enough to bestow upon a poor wretched outcast."

" How did you become acquainted with him?" he asked.

" By an accident which I cannot at present relate," she replied. " I will, however, tell you that he saved my life and that of my child, and from that time to the present I have never known the want of a warm and generous friend. My poor little Amelia, too, is an especial favourite of his, and as he has promised to provide for her, I have the cheering consolation of knowing, that at my death, she will not be thrown upon the world forlorn and friendless."

" And did you believe then, Amelia," he said, " that I would ever suffer the poor child to want a friend or guardian should she have been deprived of your protection ?"

" I didn't know what to think," answered Amelia, " for you had been absent from me so long that it seemed hardly likely we should ever see each other again. However, I don't wish to return to that subject again, since it brings to my mind painful reflections which are much better forgotten."

" Well, then," said Gravestow, " let us speak of something else—of your generous friend, for instance—who and what is he, Amelia ?"

" His name," she replied, " is Smithson, and he is one of the most eminent merchants in the city."

" Humph! has he been here of late ?"

" No," answered Amelia; " it is some weeks since he was here, and when you knocked at the door just now, I thought it must have been him."

" I should like to see him," exclaimed Gravestow.

" Would you ?" she said; " then call upon me again to-morrow, for I dare say he will be here, and you will then have an opportunity of seeing that I have not formed an improper acquaintance with my generous preserver. He has been like a father to me, Mr. Gayton, and I'm sure if you were to see him, you would form as favourable an opinion of him as I have already done."

" It is hardly likely I shall see him to-morrow," exclaimed Gravestow; " for important business calls me from town immediately, and I shall be far away from here by the time you see this Mr. Smithson."

" And shall you be absent long ?" she enquired.

" It is most likely I shall," answered Gravestow. " In fact, I am going on the Continent, and my present object in visiting you, was to enquire whether you have any objection to go with me ?"

" Not for worlds, Mr. Gayton."

" And why not ?" he asked. " Is the love you once bore me so completely obliterated, that you can never pardon the apparent neglect with which I treated you ?"

" I have pardoned you for that long ago," answered Amelia, " but there are other considerations that must for ever put an end to all further acquaintance between us."

" What considerations do you speak of ?"

" Why, first and foremost," she replied; " you are now married, Mr. Gayton, and therefore you could not take me abroad with you as your wife."

" Psha! what of that ?" he exclaimed, pettishly. " But who told you I was married ?"

" Your friend, Edwards."

" Ah! and when did you last see him ?"

" It's some time ago now," she replied; " he was passing by here when I was standing at the door, and stopped to speak to me. He said he had just come home from France, where he left Miss Smith."

" And he told you I was married ?"

" He did."

" Did he tell you anything else ?"

" No," replied Amelia; " but as he had mentioned Miss Smith's name, I asked how she was getting on over there."

" And what said he to that ?"

"Why, that she had made a fortunate trip of it," answered Amelia. "I think he said she was married to a marquis, or an earl, or something of that sort."

"So, so!" exclaimed Gravestow; "she has married a marquis or an earl, has she?"

"So Mr. Edwards told me," replied Amelia; "but I wonder you didn't know it, as you seemed at the time to take so deep an interest in getting her over to France."

"I felt no particular interest in it," returned Gravestow, "and yet I wonder the news of her marriage has not reached me before this."

"I wonder at it too," observed Amelia; "but perhaps Mr. Edwards did not know where to find you."

"That may be the reason, certainly," answered the other. "I have often thought I should like to know how Miss Smith got on abroad, for Edwards, you know, is not a man of very strict honour, and I fancied that he had persuaded her to become his mistress. However, the mystery is now cleared up, so perhaps you will have the kindness to relate any further conversation that passed between you and Edwards."

"Let me see," said Amelia, trying to recollect herself; "he spoke about old times, and—and—yes, he mentioned something about a will that was missing, and which he said he had no doubt had been left in the pocket of an old coat that he had sold to a Jew at a time when he was very hard pressed for a shilling or two."

"And did he ever take any steps to recover the lost will?" demanded Gravestow, with breathless anxiety.

"He asked me, as a particular favour, to make enquiries about it for him," she replied. "I did so, but on applying to the Jew, he said he knew nothing about any such document as I spoke of, and that if it had been left in the pocket at all, he had most likely sold the will and coat together to the first customer that it happened to fit."

"That was unfortunate," observed Gravestow.

"It was," replied Amelia, "and so Mr. Edwards seemed to think, for I never saw a man so much disappointed in my life as he was, when I told him the result of my errand. I, however, told him I would make all the enquiries I could about it, and he was to call again in a few days, but from that time to the present, I have never set eyes upon him."

"Do you know what has become of him?"

"I believe," she replied, "he is now in France again. At least he said something about going there the last time I saw him, and told me that in case he should not have an opportunity of calling again, I was to communicate, by letter, any information that I might get hold of, and that I was to address to Major Smith, at the Post Office, Paris."

"But, I suppose," said Gravestow, "as you have not heard anything about the will, no letter has been sent to him?"

"I have not written," she answered.

"Did Edwards say anything else?"

"No," replied Amelia; "except that I was to call again on the Jew, and inform him that if he could, by any means, find the will he should receive a very handsome reward."

"And I suppose you have seen the Jew?"

"No, I have not," she replied. "I am, in fact, so tied here that it's impossible to leave the place even for an instant. But some day or other, perhaps, I may be able to get a friend to mind the shop, and I'll call once more on Lazarus to tell him what Mr. Edwards says."

"I should not be in any hurry to do that," observed Gravestow. "There may be more mischief in it than you think for, and it's hardly worth while getting yourself into trouble merely for the sake of Mr. Edwards, who seems to be playing a very selfish game in this affair."

"What trouble could I get into through merely asking a question?" asked Amelia.

"It's impossible to say what danger there might be in it," replied Gravestow. "For instance, the will may not have been obtained in a very honourable manner, and in that case the persons most interested in it would take active means for its recovery, and should this Jew find out that a reward is offered for its production, he would most assuredly give you into custody the moment you enter his shop."

"So he might, indeed!" said Amelia, "and I was foolish enough not to think of the danger, though, if I had given it a thought I must have been well convinced the will had not been honestly come by. I have often fancied there was something very mysterious in the conduct of Mr. Edwards, and now I begin to entertain a strong opinion that some foul work has been going on."

"Indeed!—and do you suppose he had any accomplices?"

"That's more than I can say, Mr. Gayton," she replied; "but if I knew anything for certain, either against him or his accomplices, I should not hesitate to give them into the hands of justice as men that deserve their fate for attempting to rob the rightful heirs by stealing a will."

"Let me caution you to beware how you say too much on that subject," exclaimed Gravestow; "for the man that would steal the will would have very little hesitation in murdering any witnesses that might appear against him. However, to quit this subject, let me ask whether you happened to hear the name of the marquis—that Dolly—that is, Miss Smith, I mean, that was so fortunate as to marry?"

"I didn't hear his name mentioned," said Amelia; "but did you say her name was Dolly?"

"No, no, that was a mistake of mine," replied Gravestow; "I was thinking of somebody else at the time, and the name of Dolly slipped out quite by accident."

Amelia made no further observation for some little time, and Gravestow took the opportunity it afforded him of thinking over, in his own mind, what he had better do under all the circumstances of the case. That his case was growing more and more desperate every moment that he lived was now quite evident, and as a crisis seemed to be rapidly approaching, he felt that it was very necessary to think of some scheme by which he might avert the consequences he so much dreaded.

Yet look at his situation in what light he would, he could not but feel convinced that Amelia knew quite sufficient to place his life in constant peril, and as he was rendered desperate by the danger with which he was threatened, he scrupled not to make up his mind that she must die, and as he might not have a more favourable opportunity than the present, he determined to get rid of her that night, and as he was upon the point of leaving the country, he was in hopes the murder would be attributed to somebody else, and that he might thus escape without even the shadow of suspicion. Her acquaintance with Mr. Smith, the Jew, Edwards, and Dolly Pratt, under her assumed name, all threatened him with danger when he might, perhaps, be least prepared for it, and as self-preservation was his chief thought, he felt very little scruple in making up his mind as to what course he should pursue.

Had it been safe to confide to her the secret of his crimes he would have done so; but Amelia was not likely to hear such a confession without shuddering at the depravity of the perpetrator, and it was quite certain she would, without loss of time, make a statement of what she had heard to a magistrate, and thus he would find himself a victim to his own want of caution. Neither could he hope to ensure her silence, by pretending friendship for her and the child, for she had already experienced the coldness with which he could turn away and leave her to the scorn and contempt of her heartless fellow-creatures.

Nor was he without his fears, lest she might at any time be recognized by Moses Lazarus, to whom a reward had been offered for her discovery, and he entertained no doubt that the Jew would be too well pleased at the chance of adding to his stores of gold, to let so favourable an opportunity as that pass by without making use of it. He, therefore, saw that Amelia must immediately be got rid of, and having made up his mind upon that subject he suddenly roused himself from his horrible reverie, and in as calm a tone as he could command, he enquired whether she lived in that house entirely by herself.

"At present, I do," she replied, "because my late lodgers are gone away; but, in a few days, I believe I shall have another family to live with me."

"You are quite alone, then?" he said.

"Yes," she answered, "there's not a soul in the house besides you and myself. Poor little Amelia was a companion for me when she was at home, and I miss her sadly now that she's gone away from me."

"I dare say you do," said Gravestow, looking wildly towards her, which, however, she did not perceive. "It is dull being in a house alone, and sometimes rather dangerous."

"Oh, I never think about danger," replied Amelia; "for I don't know that I have any enemies in the world, and why, therefore, should I be afraid of coming to harm?"

"True," he exclaimed; "but are you sure there's no one in the house but you and myself?"

"Quite sure," she replied, with surprise at his anxious enquiries on this subject. "But why do you ask me if we are alone?"

"Merely because I am going to speak upon business that I should not very well like to be overheard," he answered. "There are few persons that have not secrets of some kind or other, and the object of my present visit must remain unknown to everybody except ourselves."

"But, perhaps," cried Amelia, "it would be better not to say anything about it to me. For my own part I never liked hearing people's secrets, for I might be tempted to speak of them, and I should be sorry to do that after you had showed so much confidence in my prudence."

"I can trust you for that," he said in a hollow tone; "you will not tell the secret, I can answer for it, or I might be more distrustful in making the communication. All I want to be satisfied in is, that no one is likely to hear us,' and as I have your assurance to that effect I can now say what I have got to tell you."

"Again I tell you we are quite alone," she replied, though not without some anxiety at the tone and manner he had latterly assumed.

Upon a sudden Walter Gravestow now started from his seat, and closed the door which communicated with the shop, and when that was done, he paced up and down the room, meditating upon the deed he was about to commit, and wondering how it should be accomplished so as to involve him in as little danger as possible. Still, however, hardened as his heart was, it sickened as he thought of the crime, and willingly would he have spared himself the one evil deed, had it been possible to make himself secure. But it was necessary that he should leave England without delay, and if she was left behind, it was likely he would never dare return to his home, est something might have been whispered to his prejudice during his ab-

sence. His present purpose in visiting France, was to seek out George
Ramsden, of whom he was so anxious to purchase the manor house at
Summerfield, as there were circumstances connected with it which rendered
it of the highest importance to himself that the house should not be pulled
down. At any rate, he was determined to offer a sum for it which would
be sure to be accepted, and when once that was secure in his own possession,
he felt assured that all other dangers would sink into insignificance.

Irresolute as he felt at this moment, he had scarcely the heart to accomplish the black crime he meditated, and gladly would he have rushed from
the presence of his intended victim, had he been quite certain that he would
not have been placed in peril by it. To be sure he might prevail on her to
accompany him to France, and when once she was there he would not
have much to fear from her meeting with friends, as it would be easy to
take her to some obscure place where she would never afterwards be
heard of.

The only two persons, besides her, that he had any reason to be afraid
of, were Dolly Pratt and Edwards, though, when he came to consider of it,
there was very little to apprehend from persons who were now abroad, and
who were very unlikely ever to return to England. The murder which he
now contemplated might very easily be accomplished without any great
hazard to himself, for no one knew of his visit to the house, and as there
was not a person within call, his victim might be slain, and his own escape
ensured long before pursuit could take place after the unknown perpetrator
of the crime. Besides, he was known only by most people in the town, by
the name of Willis Gayton, and this circumstance served considerably to
strengthen his determination to secure his own safety by killing the unconscious object of his diabolical vengeance.

As for sparing the life of Amelia, and taking her with him to France, he
No. 45

would gladly have done so if his own safety could have been ensured at the same time. But it was too dangerous an experiment to be tried by a man circumstanced as he was, for it was scarcely likely that she would ever thoroughly forgive his desertion of her, and even were it possible for her to do that, he was quite certain no argument he could use would ever make her forget the duty and affection she owed her child. Then her gratitude to Mr. Smithson was another barrier to such a plan as this, for his kindness had made a deep impression upon her heart, and Gravestow felt assured that any proposition he made would first of all be submitted to the judgment and consideration of her generous friend. Besides, she had just before acknowledged that she had heard of his marriage, and whatever might have been her former indiscretion, he was perfectly well assured that she would now reject any dishonourable proposition with scorn.

And in this notion he was perfectly right, for at the very time he was occupied in these harassing thoughts, Amelia was pondering over the conversation that had passed between them, and wondering whether he was really serious in wishing her to accompany him abroad. At any rate, she resolved to give him a blank refusal, and scarcely knowing how to break the silence, she sat musing and trembling, though she could scarcely have told why.

Every moment of delay served to increase the difficulties in which Gravestow found himself, and he gazed upon his victim, who sat with her back to him, and as he paced still more uneasy up and down the room, he became thoroughly convinced that his fatal mission must be performed, and that speedily too, for even a brief delay might be the means of delivering him into the hands of justice. Yet he could not help thinking of past times, when he had really loved the unfortunate creature he had now doomed to destruction, and of the misery she had endured through his cruel desertion. Had it been possible, he would have rushed from the house, and thus saved himself from the commission of the crime he contemplated, but the certainty of his own danger, should she ever be called upon to give evidence against him, armed him with renewed determination, and in spite of all else, he resolved to accomplish the deed, which would stain his soul with another crime, and rob his unsuspecting victim of that life which his own base conduct had rendered so heavy and full of woe.

At last, urged on by desperation and the malignity of his own heart, he grasped a knife which had been left upon the table, unperceived by Amelia, felt the edge, to assure himself that it was sufficiently keen for its intended purpose. Again he ventured to gaze upon her,—for she was still sitting with her back towards him,—and as he did so, his heart sank within him, and the wretched man would have fallen to the ground had he not leaned for support on the back of a chair. In a few seconds, however, he again recovered, and stealing towards her on tip-toe, he raised the knife for her destruction, when the street door was suddenly opened, and footsteps were heard coming along the passage. In an instant the knife was concealed, and as he and Amelia turned round to see who was approaching, a neighbour made his appearance, and with many apologies, begged to be excused for entering the house so abruptly.

"I should not have taken this liberty, Mrs. Robertson," he said, "but as I was passing your door just now, I saw that it was not quite closed, and fearing something was wrong, I stepped in to put you upon your guard in case any villain should have entered your house to murder you."

"Mrs. Robertson was quite safe, sir," answered Gravestow, who by this time had somewhat recovered himself. "The door was left open by an accident, and I am sure she is much obliged to you for the care and thought you displayed in her behalf."

"Of course I didn't know Mrs. Robertson, had a gentleman with her," said the neighbour, glancing significantly towards Gravestow.

" He is an old acquaintance of mine, that I have not seen for some years," cried Mrs. Robertson, unwilling that any evil report should be spread against her through this circumstance. " The gentleman is going to leave England, and he merely called upon me to say good bye—most likely for ever !"

" Well, I wish you good night, ma'am," said the neighbour, moving towards the door, " but as there's a good many bad people about, I'd advise you to take care that the house is fastened of a night. There's been two or three murders lately, and it behoves us all to be careful, for we none of us know whose turn it may next be to fall into bad hands."

Hereupon the neighbour bowed himself out, and Gravestow fancied he directed a look of peculiar meaning towards himself as he left the room. Be this as it might, however, it had evidently given his thoughts a new turn, and he paced uneasily up and down the room, undetermined whether to commit the horrible crime he had contemplated, or at once fly from the scene of temptation, and by hastening over to the Continent, remove far from her whose life but a few moments before had been so nearly sacrificed by his own hands.

The whole of the next day it was observed that Amelia's house remained close, but this circumstance attracted but little attention, as two or three times before the shutters had not been taken down in consequence of her having to go to town on business. But when on the next day it remained in the same situation, people began to think it very strange, and the constable being sent for, the door was broke open, and a search made all over the house. No trace of Amelia was, however, to be found, and when the neighbour mentioned the circumstance of finding the place open, and a stranger in company with Mrs. Robertson, a very general belief began to be entertained that she had been murdered, and the body afterwards concealed to prevent discovery of the crime. Yet in contradiction to this, no traces of blood were to be found anywhere about the house, and at last a person who knew her very well, said, he had seen her with a strange gentleman on the road to London at an early hour of the morning, and that he was certain he had not been deceived in her identity. This gave rise to fresh rumours, and at length it was currently reported that she was deeply in debt, and had recourse to flight, in order to elude her creditors.

CHAPTER XLVIII.

SUSPICIOUS CIRCUMSTANCES.

Mr. Plumley, good, easy man that he was, felt so satisfied with the marriage of one of his daughters to a marquis, that he began to think the other would be sure to get either a duke or a prince. He was in fact congratulating himself upon the rank and honours which his fortune would procure for his two girls, when he received a letter from Miss Plumley, describing in glowing colours the happiness her sister enjoyed with the Marquis Valliere, and at the same time hinting that there was a certain Major Smith who had been paying her great attention, and who she should not object to for a husband, if her father would permit him to pay his addresses.

This was anything but agreeable to the views formed by the worthy drysalter, for his ambition had looked higher for a son-in-law than a mere major in the army, and having consulted with his wife upon the subject, it was agreed between them that they should consider the affair at their leisure, and return no answer to the letter till they had made up their minds whether they could admit so humble a person into their family. To be sure he was the very particular friend of the marquis, which seemed to afford a convincing proof of his respectability, and as it was likely enough the Marquis Valliere would be able to procure titles and honours for his friend, it was considered advisable to consult their lawyer upon the subject, and take his opinion as to whether Miss Betsy should marry the major, or wait for a more splendid offer.

Accordingly, on the first opportunity, Mr. Plumley called on Mr. Dunlop, his solicitor, and having read to that gentleman such portions of his daughter's letter as related to the questions he had to ask, he expatiated largely upon the high alliance that had lately been formed, and then enquired whether he should lower the dignity of his family by admitting a less aristocratic personage to become his son-in-law. Mr. Dunlop listened with the air of a man whose suspicions had been awakened, and having suffered his client to go on with his explanations, he inquired if the lover of his daughter was a friend of the Marquis Valliere.

"Oh, yes, a most intimate one, I understand," replied the old gentleman. "They all live together at the same hotel in Paris, and, as that's the case, though I wish he was something better than a major, there can be very little doubt but he belongs to a noble family. Perhaps, at the very least, he's an honourable."

"Or," suggested Mr. Dunlop, "which is quite as likely, a dishonourable scamp, that is tempted by your daughter's fortune, to prevail on you to consent to a marriage that would terminate in misery to herself."

"But do you think," asked Mr. Plumley, "the marquis would allow a man of indifferent family to visit him?"

"Why, the truth is, my dear sir," replied the lawyer, "I know nothing at all about this marquis. You kept the affair secret from me, and I knew nothing at all about the marriage of your eldest daughter, till it reached my ears by a mere accident."

"Ah!" returned Mr. Plumley, "that was because the marquis was particularly anxious that the thing should be kept as snug as possible. He thought his father might object to his marriage into a family without a title, and as I thought it too good an opportunity to be thrown away, I yielded to his suggestion, and now, you see, my dear friend, she is the Marchioness Valliere."

"Do you happen to know where his estates are situated?" asked the lawyer.

"Oh, yes, I took good care to ask him all about that," replied Mr. Plumley.

"And pray where are they?"

"Everywhere, my dear sir," answered the old gentleman; "he mentioned about fifty in different parts of the world, but my memory is so bad that I can't remember a quarter of them."

"Can you recollect any one of these estates?"

"To be sure I can;—there was one he spoke of in Switzerland, and he described it as being so beautifully situated, that at my daughter's request, he settled it upon her for life."

"I wish you had consulted me before this matter had gone so far," exclaimed Mr. Dunlop, "for though I cannot say anything positively against these two persons, yet there is a great deal of doubt in my mind about them; though, for the sake of the young ladies and yourself, I most sincerely hope you have not been victimized by swindlers."

" Swindlers !" cried the old gentleman, with indignant surprise ; " why, surely, sir, you don't think I have been foolish enough to permit this marriage till I was thoroughly convinced of his being a man of rank ?"

" Well, I don't wish to offend you, my dear sir," said the lawyer, " but pray what evidence had you that your daughter's suitor was what he represented himself to be ?"

" I had his own word, to be sure," answered Mr. Plumley, " and that, I think, ought to be quite enough."

" His own word would not have been enough for me, though, had I been consulted in the affair," said Mr. Dunlop. " I must have had more substantial proof than that ; and you, no doubt, as a prudent man, took care to make further inquiries ?"

" Why, to tell you the truth," replied the old gentleman, " I didn't like to seem suspicious ; but, from what his servant told my servants, the thing is as right and comfortable as we could wish it to be."

" And think you his servant's word might be safely taken ?" asked Mr. Dunlop.

" I should hope so," answered the other ; " and then the lawyer that drew up the marriage-settlements,—a very nice fellow, I assure you, and he spoke of the marquis as one of the highest noblemen in all France."

" Did he give you any proof of it ?"

" I didn't ask him for any," replied Mr. Plumley, " for if one can't take a man's word, you know, it would be a very hard case, indeed."

" And what was done about your daughter's fortune ?" asked the lawyer. " Did you pay it down on the day of the marriage ?"

" No, I wouldn't do that," replied the other, " though both the marquis and his attorney were very pressing that I should do so ;—however, I gave my daughter a few hundreds just to start them off to Paris, and in a few days I shall give the young couple the remainder."

" Let me advise you to keep the money in your pocket till we know a little more about the man you are going to bestow it on," exclaimed Mr. Dunlop. " At present, I am not satisfied with the truth of what the marquis has told you, and I have a notion that a little inquiry will prove him to be nothing better than a swindler."

" Lord, sir, you don't say so !" cried the astonished drysalter.

" I don't positively assert it, my good friend," replied the other ; " but, at present, there are suspicious circumstances which require explanation. By the by, what is the name of the gentleman that has made an offer to your other daughter ?"

" Smith, sir ;—Major Smith."

" Humph !" returned the lawyer, " a very common name indeed. Do you happen to know what regiment he belongs to ?"

" No, my daughter has not mentioned that in her letter."

" Have you ever happened to see him ?"

" Oh, dear, no," replied Mr. Plumley, " that is to say, I don't remember him ; though Betsy says I shall be surprised when I meet the major, at recognizing a person that I have frequently seen at my house. However, the marquis knows him, and I should think that is sufficient to prove he is somebody of distinction."

" It may be a plot between them," said Mr. Dunlop. " In fact, I happen to know that there is a worthless vagabond in Paris, assuming that name ; and if your daughter should unfortunately have formed an acquaintance with him, the sooner she is undeceived with respect to such a scoundrel, the better it will be for her and her family."

" What sort of man was he that you are speaking of ?" asked Mr Plumley.

"A tall, sallow, ill-looking fellow," replied the lawyer; "his counte-nance denotes that he has lived a dissipated life; and one thing which renders him very remarkable, is a large scar over the right eye, from a wound which he received in a night frolic, which had nearly terminated in his death."

"A scar over the right eye!" exclaimed the old gentleman, with sur-prise.

"Yes, does the description I have given answer the appearance of any one you have ever seen?"

"It does," replied Mr. Plumley; "the servant of the marquis was exactly such a man as you have mentioned."

"Well, then, you may depend upon it," exclaimed the lawyer, "that it is he who has assumed the name of Major Smith, for the sake of getting possession of your daughter's fortune."

"And you really think he is no major, after all?"

"I feel convinced he is an impostor," answered Mr. Dunlop; "and if you wish to know more about him, I dare say it would be in my power to afford a very great deal of important information."

"Who is he?" asked the old man.

"If it is the same party that I mean," replied Mr. Dunlop, "his name is George Ramsden, as great a scoundrel as is at this moment unhanged, though born of a good family, and once in possession of a large fortune."

"The rascal!" exclaimed Mr. Plumley; "and pray sir, where does he come from?"

"His father lived and died at a place called Summerfield," answered the lawyer, "and a very excellent character he bore in the neighbourhood. But the son no sooner became possessed of the property, than he fell into extravagant habits, and was ruined in a very short time."

"And did you ever hear what became of him?" asked the other.

"Occasionally I heard a little about him," replied the lawyer; "but never that he had amended his conduct, or forgot the evil of his former days."

"Do you know how he contrives to keep up so good an appearance?" asked Mr. Plumley.

"That, I believe, is best known to himself," answered the other. "He however, lives upon his wits, and swindles all those that he can impose upon by a smooth tongue."

"And this," cried Plumley, "is the fellow that is making love to my daughter!"

"I have no doubt it's the same person," replied the other, "for my de-scription of him appears to tally with the fellow that passed as the servant of the Marquis Valliere."

"But do you really believe he is a marquis after all?" exclaimed the drysalter.

"Ah! there, I must confess, you puzzle me," said Mr. Dunlop; "for, though I feel no doubt that he is another swindler, yet I have no clue at present to pronounce, with any certainty, who he is. That he is a friend of George Ramsden's is, however, pretty clear, and that circumstance is quite sufficient to convince me that you have been most cruelly imposed upon."

"I begin to be afraid of it myself," exclaimed Plumley; "and, if your suspicions should prove to be well-founded, it shall not be long before I make him remember the hour when he came to my house with his false-hoods about being a marquis. I'll hunt the rascal through the world but what I'll find him; and, when he does fall in my way, I'll take good care he shall never have an opportunity to cheat anybody else as he has me.

And now, sir, supposing you have guessed correctly in saying that he is a swindler,—what course had I better pursue to get my daughter away from him?"

"Their marriage, I suppose, was a strictly legal one?" observed Mr. Dunlop,

"Oh, yes, I took care to see to that," he replied. "The ceremony was performed at our parish church,—and she is his wife as safe as the laws of the country can make her."

"Well, so far there's some consolation in knowing that she has not been deceived in that," said the lawyer. "She is a wife, though unfortunately united to a worthless husband. But troubles are seldom so great but they can be amended by pursuing a proper course ; and, as you have plenty of money to spare for such a purpose, we must set about getting a divorce, the expence of which is a mere trifle, in comparison with the disgrace of having your daughter married to a man that may come to the gallows."

"And yet, after all, said Mr. Plumley, "he may not be so bad as you think."

"I believe there can be very little doubt upon that point," answered the lawyer, "for if he was not a worthless scoundrel, he would not have associated with George Ramsden, whose character is so notorious that he has been compelled to change his name for another."

"Then what course would you advise me to adopt?" asked the old gentleman.

"Why, caution must be your principal guide," returned Mr. Dunlop, "and perhaps you will be the best judge of what ought to be done under circumstances so disagreeable as this. If, however, I was in your place, I should go over to France without delay, and pay a visit to the pretended marquis, under the plea that you are about to pay him the large sum of money promised with your daughter as her marriage portion. That will serve to blind him as to the real motives of your visit to Paris ; and, whilst he is thus deceived, you will have an excellent opportunity to make what observations you please relative to his conduct in Paris. He will be off his guard, and will be more likely to show his real disposition, than if he thought you knew anything of the swindling transactions that have been going on between him and his friend George Ramsden."

"Well, if you think I'd better go, I'll do so," answered the old gentleman ; "but the truth is, neither I nor Mrs. Plumley were ever further away from London than Margate and Ramsgate, and such places as those ; and I don't know whether I could find courage enough to cross over from Dover to Calais, for I have heard it's a dangerous passage, and people at my time of life don't like risking themselves if there's any way of avoiding it."

"There is no way of avoiding it, if you would save your daughter from destruction," said the lawyer. "One of them is already married to a fellow that we have every reason to believe is a rascally swindler, and the other is courted by a man who I know to be as arrant a scoundrel as was ever suffered to victimize society. You must, however, not think of taking Mrs. Plumley with you, for it's likely enough there will be a great deal of trouble in the affair ; and, if they have any notion that you have discovered their tricks, they will remove from Paris to some other place, and you may have to travel half over France before you succeed in pouncing upon them."

"A very pretty prospect, indeed, for a man that has worked hard all his life to gain a fortune," cried Mr. Plumley ; "and then, when he ought to set himself comfortably down for the remainder of his days, he finds that he's got more trouble to go through than ever he had to encounter before."

"It's the only course I can at present advise you take," said Mr. Dunlop. "The young ladies, it seems, are in rather a dangerous predicament; and, if you do not see after them shortly, I'm afraid you will repent when it may be too late."

"And wouldn't it do as well if I was to send over some confidential friend?" asked Mr. Plumley, who felt a great horror at the idea of so long a journey.

"Why, there is no one that would enter into the business with so much earnestness as yourself," replied Mr. Dunlop; "and, for aught I know, the French authorities may require your presence before they take any steps against these two fellows. So let me prevail on you to go yourself; and, above all things, let there be no delay about it."

"If it must be so, it must," said the old gentleman, with a look of despair; "but what a pretty figure I shall cut there, through not understanding a word of the language; I shall get laughed at for my pains, and do no more good than if I remain where I am."

"You are mistaken, my dear sir," answered Mr. Dunlop, "for there are few hotels in Paris where the English language is not spoken by some of the persons connected with it; and, as you will go immediately to the place where your daughters are lodging, the affair will be settled in a very short time."

"At any rate, I see there's no way left but to go," said Plumley; "and so, if I can muster up resolution enough, I'll start to-morrow morning, and if I find these fellows have been playing any tricks upon me, they'll see that, for once in their lives, they have gone a little too far."

Upon this the old gentleman took leave of his solicitor, and returned home; but, upon talking the matter over with Mrs. Plumley, he found more opposition to his plan than he had expected; for, instead of meeting with her concurrence in it, she expressed the greatest alarm at the idea of his going so far away from her, and invented a thousand perils that never yet occurred to anybody, and gave it as her decided opinion that, if he was foolish enough to trust himself among a parcel of foreigners, he could never expect to see his own home again.

Mr. Plumley listened to all this with profound attention; for, not having many thoughts of his own to spare, he usually bowed with submission to the opinions of his wife, and, in this instance, he certainly had more reasons than one for doing so. He, therefore, promised to give the subject three or four day's careful consideration; and, as Mrs. Plumley took care to talk to him about it on every occasion that offered, he at last came to the opinion that there was a great deal too much danger in it to suit his notions of parental duty; and, having decided upon this point, he at last betook himself to the offices of Mr. Dunlop, in Lincoln's Inn, and explained, in the best way he could, his reasons for declining so long a journey. The lawyer heard him with attention; and then, expressing some surprise at his not having started for the Continent, he said:—

"It appears to me, my dear sir, that you have imagined danger that cannot possibly exist. Your errand to Paris is quite a necessary one, and I can assure you that every assistance will be afforded by the French police, when they are made acquainted with the object of your visit."

"Ah!—but my wife thinks otherwise," he replied; "we have talked the matter over between ourselves,—and, though she is naturally anxious to save our daughters from those fellows, yet she has no inclination to lose her husband, and I have half promised not to go."

"Really, sir, it is absolutely necessary that you should undertake this journey, even if there was as much danger in it as you imagine. The young ladies will need the protection of a friend, and who is so proper to take upon himself the duty as their own father?"

"Very true, sir," replied Mr. Dunlop; "but what good can I do them, if I get into a confounded scrape among these strange people?"

"There is no fear of anything of the kind," answered the other; "and, if that is the only obstacle in the way, I have a friend who starts for Paris to-morrow morning, and you can go with him if you think proper."

"Why, that alters the case very considerably," exclaimed Mr. Plumley; "and, as I dare say my wife will have no objection to my going under those circumstances, I think I may promise to start with him at the time you have mentioned."

"That's right," said Mr. Dunlop, well pleased at finding that he had succeeded at last. "And now, let me advise you to go immediately, on your arrival in Paris, to the place where your daughters are lodging; and, if it happens that they have not been removed, you will hear from them what sort of persons the marquis and his friend are. They will have discovered some of their tricks, I dare say, by this time; and my friend, who accompanies you, will advise the course it will be best to adopt. It may happen that you will be obliged to apply for the assistance of the police, and very civil, obliging fellows they are, I can assure you."

"And will they put me in the way for punishing these men if they should prove to be impostors?"

"Aye," replied the lawyer, "and with so much despatch will they perform their duty, that before you have related your story two hours to them, they will know every particular connected with these two men, and take measures for giving you the justice you demand."

"Upon my life I begin to believe there's less danger in this journey than I thought for," exclaimed Mr. Plumley.

"You have fully made up your mind, then, this time to go?" said the lawyer.

"Oh, yes," he replied, "I'll go since you tell me the thing is to be

No. 46

done so easily. Indeed, I have all along wanted to ascertain how my daughters are getting on there, and it was only because I fancied I could do no good that I hesitated about starting on the journey."

"Then to-morrow at six o'clock you will be ready to accompany my friend?"

"Certainly I will," said Mr. Plumley; and after arranging a few other matters with his legal adviser, he returned home and told Mrs. Plumley the determination he had come to. This time she made but little opposition, because she found he was to have a companion, and forthwith she commenced preparations for his journey, so that by the appointed hour he met his fellow-traveller, and off they started on their way to the Continent by the way of Dovor.

We will not follow them on their way, but merely observe that when they reached Paris, the first thing Mr. Plumley did was to go to the place where he understood the marquis had taken up his temporary abode. To his disappointment, however, he found, upon enquiry, that they had all left there some few days previously, and it was supposed they were going towards the Spanish frontier. This was terrible news to Mr. Plumley, who, besides the suspense he felt as to the fate of her daughters, saw the probability of another long journey before him, and that, too, in all likelihood without a companion, as the friend who had come thus far with him had no business to take him any further, and it was not by any means certain that business would permit him to go beyond Paris. Under these circumstances, he resolved to return to England without delay, and there is no doubt he would have done so had not his companion concluded his business sooner than had been expected, and induced him to go on, under a promise of travelling with him in the event of any clue being obtained relative to the direction taken by those they were in search of. This decided Mr. Plumley, and on this condition he determined to go in pursuit of his daughters.

The next step to be taken was to make enquiries as to the road they had taken, and with little difficulty they succeeded in ascertaining that they had indeed gone towards the Spanish frontier, and upon that a letter was addressed to the chief magistrate of a town through which it was supposed they would pass, requesting to be informed whether such persons as were described in the letter had, within the last few days, been seen travelling that way. The reply to this was prompt, but unsatisfactory, for it was stated that a carriage had passed through the town within the period named, but the writer was quite certain that no females accompanied them, Where the travellers were going to was, however, uncertain; but it was supposed they were still in France, as they had suddenly turned back on hearing some intelligence that seemed to have completely altered their views.

"This is very singular," said Mr. Plumley's friend; "for there can be no doubt as to the gentlemen being the very parties of whom we are in search, and it now remains for us to discover what they have done with your daughters."

"Good Heavens, sir! do you think they are in danger?" cried the alarmed father.

"Why, I'll not go so far as to say that," replied the other; "but it certainly appears but too probable that they have deserted the ladies, in order to make off with what cash and jewels they could lay their hands on. I am unwilling to alarm you, Mr. Plumley, with these suspicions of mine, but it is necessary to speak plainly, and, therefore, I think the sooner we set about discovering your daughters, the better it will be."

To this suggestion Mr. Plumley gave his instant assent, and after once more visiting the police-office and handing over to the principal officer the letter they had received, the two gentlemen engaged a carriage, and set off on the route which they were pretty well satisfied the fugitives had taken. The journey, with all its unpleasant accompaniments, was anything but agreeable to the drysalter; but it was pretty clear that his daughters had fallen into bad hands, and for once, therefore, he was disposed to put up with the personal inconvenience, and to hazard the difficulties in the discharge of so imperative a duty.

CHAPTER XLIX.

MATTERS BEGIN TO CLEAR UP.

WITHIN a few days after Mr. Smithson had returned home from his brief visit to Summerfield, he was surprised at receiving a note from one of the fashionable hotels at the west end of town, requesting him to go there as soon as possible after the letter came to hand, and ask for Monsieur Lemare, the writer of the present communication.

The old gentleman scarcely knew what to make of this, for he had lived a little too long in the world to be imposed upon very easily, and he thought whether it might not be a trick of Gravestow to get him in his clutches, and thus prevent the possibility of his being a witness against him, should the validity of the recently discovered will be tried in a court of law. At all events he thought there were good reasons for being cautious in the affair; and throwing the note into his desk, he was going to reach down his ledger, when the thought struck him that Monsieur Lemare might want to see him on business, and, as the interview was to take place at a public hotel, he thought there could be no danger to himself so long as he took care not to agree to any subsequent appointment elsewhere.

Thus prudently resolved, he set off for the place that had been named, and on enquiring for Monsieur Lemare, he was introduced to a very respectable-looking elderly foreigner, who no sooner learnt who the visitor was than he led him up stairs, threw open the door of an elegantly-furnished apartment, and introduced him to an exceedingly beautiful female, who was writing at a table near the window. She rose and received him with much courtesy, and, begging him to be seated, enquired if she had the honour of addressing herself to Mr. Smithson, the partner of the late Mr. Wentford.

"Yes, ma'am," said the old gentleman, stammering and wondering what all this could mean, "my name is Smithson, and I was the partner of poor Mr. Wentford."

"Who, I believe, was murdered?"

"He was, ma'am."

"Will you have the goodness, sir," she said, "to inform me of the particulars connected with that melancholy event?"

Mr. Smithson could see no objection to this, and in as brief a manner as he could, he narrated all the circumstances connected with the mysterious affair, and in concluding, observed that, as so long a time had elapsed, he was afraid a discovery of the perpetrators would never take place.

"You have no clue, then, to assist you," said the lady; "and in consequence of the disappearance of Andrew Hoply and the dairymaid, you have some reason to suspect that they were concerned in the murder?"

"Many people have suspected them," answered Mr. Smithson; "but for my own part, I rather think they are as innocent of the crime as I am myself. Andrew, they say, was a very honest, industrious young man, and much attached to his master; and as for the dairymaid, the worst I ever heard of her was, that she gave herself a great many fine airs, which, after all, only proves that she possessed some of the weakness of her sex."

"You have judged her quite correctly, sir," cried the lady; "for I have the means of satisfying you that she had no knowledge of Mr. Wentford's murder till a short time since. Perhaps you understand me, sir, and it will be almost unnecessary to inform you that I am the female who lived as dairymaid at Summerfield, and whose mysterious absence has caused so many rumours to her prejudice."

"You the dairymaid!" ejaculated Mr. Smithson, in a tone of amazement.

"I am, indeed," she replied, "and if you will listen to me with a little patience, I'll inform you of some few particulars of my life. I was born near Summerfield, of humble parents, though both my father and mother were descended from families of some consideration. This circumstance, aided by the pride of my mother, instilled into my mind certain high-flown notions that made me look down upon my neighbours with scorn, and, ultimately led to the sorrow and disgrace which it has been my unfortunate lot to bear. I never associated with people of my own class of life, but shunned them as if they were unworthy of my consideration, and thus I grew up without one friend or confidant in the world.

"At length, however, when my parents found that they could no longer afford to keep me in idleness, I was compelled to look out for a situation, and as Mr. Wentford at that time wanted a dairymaid, I entered his service, though not without a feeling of mortification at being reduced to this necessity. But I never associated with any of my fellow-servants, and for that reason, I suppose, a general feeling of dislike was entertained against me, and in the course of time, they began to shun me quite as much as I avoided them.

"I had not been long in my new situation when Mr. Gravestow came down on a visit to my master, and from his very first appearance there, I could not help observing that he took more notice of me than of any other of the servants, and as it was my duty to be up in the morning before the rest of the servants, he used to rise at an early hour for the pleasure, as he said, of talking to a girl who had made a conquest of his heart.

"To a young and thoughtless girl like me this was very welcome flattery, and I began to think my mother was right when she said I was born to a high destiny. But when, at length, I found that he was courting Miss Wentford, I saw that his intentions towards me could not be honourable, and so I took the first opportunity that offered to tell him that he must not speak to me any more upon the subject of love, or I should be under the necessity of leaving my situation, in order to throw myself on the protection of my parents. This seemed to take him by surprise, but he assured me that he did not care for Miss Wentford, and that if I would only consent to run away with him, he would make me his wife. But it was in vain he talked to me, for I could begin to see that he had not a particle of honour about him, and I told him plainly, that if he spoke to me any more upon the subject, I should acquaint Mr. Wentford, and hear what he had to say of it.

"This seemed to have the desired effect, for he sought no more private interviews, till he came down the next time to visit Summerfield, when accosting me one morning before any one else in the house was up, he said—

"'After the last interview between us Dolly, you have seen how carefully I have guarded against giving you offence by recurring to the forbidden subject. I, however, still feel the strongest interest in your welfare, and it is now my pleasing task to inform you that it is in my power to assist you in rising to that eminence in life that shall make you the envy of half your sex.'

" ' Indeed, sir,' I replied ; ' but perhaps the means I may take to raise myself so high are not honourable.'

" ' You may rely upon my word that everything is strictly honourable,' said Mr. Gravestow. ' To be brief, I am acquainted with a French count, who resides at Havre, and as he has not met with one of his own country-women to please him, he has commissioned me to look out for a pretty English girl who, upon my recommendation, he will immediately make his wife. I at once thought of you, Dolly, and it now only remains for you to decide whether you will become a countess or remain a dairy-maid all the rest of your life.'

" ' But is he really a count ?' I asked.

" ' He is,' replied Mr. Gravestow, ' and belongs to one of the oldest and most respectable families in France.'

" ' Is he young or old ?' I enquired.

" ' Why, not very young, it must be admitted,' he replied, ' but there is an advantage even in that, for he will the sooner die, and leave you in possession of an immense fortune, which will afterwards be the means of bringing half the unmarried nobility of France at your feet. You will then have an opportunity of making your own choice, and it will be your own fault if you are not a duchess before you are five years older.'

" ' A duchess !' I exclaimed ; ' why surely, sir, you don't think a poor girl like me can ever have such a chance as that ?'

" ' I know it is quite possible,' he said ; " and if you think proper to follow my advice, you shall be the count's wife before another fortnight has passed away.'

" ' Well,' I said, ' if that's the case, I'll just mention what you've been saying to my father and mother, and if they think well of it, I'll be ready to go with you as soon as you please.'

" ' Psha ! you'll spoil everything if you say anything about it to them,' exclaimed Mr. Gravestow. ' They are old-fashioned folks, you know, and perhaps would spoil your chance out of some foolish whim of their own. No, no, my good girl, this affair must be kept snug between ourselves, and so, if you chance to follow my advice, you've only got to say the word, and I'll take care that you get over to France safely without there being any occasion for your father or mother to know anything about it. Of course they will be delighted enough when they find that you are a countess, and only think how delightful it will be to have it in your power to make them happy and comfortable for the remainder of their lives.'

" Well, Mr. Smithson," continued the narrator, " I began to think so well of this project, that Mr. Gravestow could see easily enough that I should not offer much opposition to it. But he tried to appear very careless about it, and after giving me a few minutes for consideration, he said :—

" ' Well, young woman—have you made up your mind yet whether it will be better to be a lady or a drudge all the rest of your life ?'

" ' Why, Mr. Gravestow,' I replied, ' the difference between the two is so great, that you may pretty well guess which I should like best. But there is one thing that strikes me as being very awkward, and that is, how am I to get over without money or a friend to take care of me ?'

" ' Oh, that shall all be arranged satisfactorily enough,' he answered ; ' for I have a friend that will undertake the task of seeing you safely over, and as for money, you shall have that, and plenty of fine clothes to make you appear respectable to your intended husband.'

" ' I'm half afraid of accepting your offer,' I said, ' but if I might be allowed to mention it to some one, perhaps I should not think so badly of it.'

" ' And what occasion have you to think badly of it ?' he asked; ' counts are not to be picked up every day, you know, and if this opportunity is allowed to pass, you may very likely marry a ploughman or a chimney-sweep, or some such delicate husband as that. So take my advice, Dolly, and accept the good that is offered to you ; but mind, girl, it must be on condition that you promise not to say a word about it to any one.'

" ' And who is to go with me ?' I asked.

" ' Why, a very respectable friend of mine,' he replied ; ' it is very kind of him to undertake the trouble, but he does it, I can assure you, entirely to gratify me.'

" ' And when are we to start ?' I enquired.

" ' Two nights hence,' he said. ' My friend will find means to get into the garden without being discovered, and if you are in readiness, you will start away from the place long before anybody can be aware of your absence. So now tell me, shall he come to fetch you, or must I look after some other female who will have fewer scruples about being made a countess of ?"

" ' I'll accept your offer, Mr. Gravestow,' I replied reluctantly, ' but though I do so, I cannot help taking shame to myself for acting in this underhanded way towards my poor father and mother. It will break their hearts sir, if you are only doing this to deceive me.'

" ' Psha ! what deception can there possibly be in it ?' he exclaimed. ' However, we won't say anything more about that now, so remember the caution I have given you as to keeping the matter secret, and at the time appointed, my friend will be here to conduct you safely to London.'

" And upon that," continued the female to Mr. Smithson " he left me to reflect alone upon the singularity of the proposition he had made, and it must be confessed, that much as I was pleased at the idea of becoming a countess, I could not help reproaching myself for keeping the affair from my poor father and mother.

" At length, on the appointed night, when all the people in the house were in bed, I heard a gentle tap at the window-shutters, and instantly opening the door, a man presented himself before me, and in a whisper, said, that he had come from Mr. Gravestow, who was waiting close by, and that I was to accompany him with as little delay as possible. The appearance of the man was anything but prepossessing, but as he brought a note from Mr. Gravestow, assuring me that the person was the one he had spoken to me about, I consented to go with him.

" Scarcely, however, had I done this, when Mr. Gravestow came bustling in, and saying that any further delay would entirely mar our plans, he desired me to get ready as quickly as possible, and as I was leaving the room to go and put on my things, he said there would be no occasion to trouble myself about carrying a change of clothes as everything that was necessary would be provided for me in London. So away I went, and scrambled on my things as fast as I could, but when I returned to the room where I had left them, I found, to my surprise, that they were no longer there. I then began to think they had been playing me some trick, and after waiting about ten minutes or a quarter of an hour, I was beginning to despair of seeing anything more of them, whan they both came from an inner room, and told me they thought it as well to hide themselves till I was quite ready, lest anybody should be about and guess what was going on. There was no time for any further explanation, and leaving the house with them, we passed through the large iron gates that lead from the garden into the high road, where we found a chaise waiting for us, into which we all stepped, and Mr. Gravestow's friend drove off as fast as the horse could go.

"Well, sir, it must be confessed, I now began to repent the folly I had been guilty off, and we had not gone far before I begged of them to let me get down, as I was already heartily sick of the adventure, and would rather remain a dairy-maid all my life, then take the chance of being a countess, without knowing where I was going to, or who the person was to whom they said I was to be married. But they only laughed at my fears, and bidding me to be quite comfortable upon that point, we were driven on at a greater speed than ever. At length the chaise was stopped all of a sudden, and Mr. Gravestow jumping up, said :—

" ' I am now about to leave you, young woman, for a little time, but my friend understands what is to be done, and when you get to London, I shall see you, to make what further arrangements are necessary.'

" ' Indeed, indeed, sir, I would rather go back,' I cried ; ' I have done wrong in taking this step, but I see my fault, and would amend it by returning to my master's house.'

"Why, what nonsense you are talking about," exclaimed Mr. Gravestow, pettishly ; ' here have I been taking a great deal of pains to get you married to a count, and now you would spoil all by an act of folly.'

" ' I have no longer a desire to marry above my station,' I exclaimed ; ' and now the only favour I have to ask is, that you will let me go back to Mr. Wentford's."

" ' Why, what madness is this ?' retorted Mr. Gravestow ; ' your absence will have been discovered before you can return, and what sort of a story could you make that would not get both yourself and me into disgrace ? No, no ; be advised by me, and pursue your adventure to a close, for I can answer for it you will have no occasion to regret the step which, for your own sake, I advised you to take. So drive on, old fellow,' he said, addressing himself to his friend, ' and mind you take her safely to the house I told you of, where I'll meet you at the time appointed.'

"With this we again set forward, and though I felt a good deal alarmed at the situation I had so thoughtlessly placed myself in, I knew it would be in vain to plead any more, and we passed through two or three towns and villages before we stopped either for rest or refreshment. At length, just before we reached the inn where the horse was to put up, my companion soothed me with assurances that Mr. Gravestow's intentions were strictly honourable, and cautioned me against letting any one suppose either from word or gesture of mine, that I was accompanying him against my will. This injunction I promised to observe, because I began to be afraid of my companion, and entering the inn shortly afterwards, we had refreshments, and remained there nearly four hours. At the end of that time, we set forward again, and travelled some miles in silence, but at last my companion seemed to think it necessary te say something, and then he broke forth in praise of Mr. Gravestow's honour ; speaking of him as the best friend he had in the world, and expressing his own willingness to go through fire and water to serve him at any time.

" ' But I needn't tell you, miss,' he continued, ' what a good creature he is, for his conduct towards you has proved what kind feelings he possesses, and I can assure you this project of marrying the count is certainly his own, because he had such a high respect for you.'

" ' I wish he had never mentioned it to me,' I replied, ' for it has filled my mind with all sorts of folly, and now, when it is too late, I would give the world to return back to my master, where I live so happily and contented.'

" ' Ah !' replied he, ' but you will think differently when you come to be a fine lady, and keep horses and carriages, and servants of your own, besides having mansions, that even the King of England might envy you the possession of.'

" ' All that may be very good,' said I, ' but what certainty have I that this may not be a plot to get me up to London for the worst of purposes ? Mr. Gravestow knows I have no friends there, and I begin t fear both he and you have been deceiving me.'

" ' Nonsense ! how can you think that ?' he exclaimed. ' Haven't I told you he is one of the most honourable men in existence ? And do you think he would stoop to do a dirty act when he has so many great friends that would never acknowledge him if he was found out in a dishonourable transaction ?"

" ' It may be so,' I said, ' but at present I have only your word for it that I have not been deceived by artful representations. Mr. Gravestow professed great love for me himself, not very long since, and then I was obliged to remind him that it was out of his power to make me his wife, as he was already engaged to Miss Wentford, whose fortune, I know, was the chief object he sought after.'

" ' But if he hadn't loved you, he would not have made the offer,' returned my companion. ' Besides, you are much mistaken if you think he cares anything about Miss Wentford's money, for he has got quite sufficient to live on as a gentleman, and would spurn the idea of marrying for the sake of a little paltry gold. And as for yourself, I'm sure his intentions towards you are strictly honourable, or he would not have made a confidant of me, who, he well knows, would be the first to condemn him for it, and the very last to render him the assistance I am now giving him.'

" ' And where are we going to, now ?' I asked.

" ' To the house of a lady, who is an old and very particular friend of his,' he replied. ' Under her care, you will perhaps remain a day or two, and then I shall have the pleasure of escorting you over to France, where the count is anxiously expecting the moment that is to make you his wife.'

" ' But does he really intend to make me his wife ?' I asked.

" ' To be sure he does,' replied my companion. ' Mr. Gravestow is quite convinced of his honourable intentions, or he never would have suffered you to go over. Besides, he has got letters from him, expressing the highest satisfaction at the description he has heard of you, and declaring that immedietely after your arrival at Havre, he will make you his countess.'

" ' Well,' said I, somewhat assured by these words ; ' at any rate, there's some consolation for me in the prospect of so high an alliance, and if all should turn out as you have said, I shall feel myself deeply indebted both to you and Mr. Gravestow as long as I live. At present, however, all is uncertain, and my suspicions have been chiefly aroused by the positive injunctions that were given me not to speak of the affair to any one."

" You may make yourself quite easy about that," answered the other, " for depend upon it Mr. Gravestow had none but good motives for wishing you to be silent till the affair was completely settled. However, you will find everything right enough, I can promise you, so think only of your good fortune, and before a month has passed over your head, you will have reason to be thankful for the confidence you placed in me and my friend Gravestow."

" From this time no more was said by either of us till we reached Lon-

don, when putting up the horse and chaise at a livery-stable, he desired me to take his arm, and we walked through a good many streets till we reached the one where he said the lady lived, and with whom I was to remain till the period arrived for going abroad. Upon knocking, the door was opened, and we were immediately led into the parlour, where we found an elderly lady seated at tea, who was introduced to me as Mrs. Evans. There was an expression of good-nature in her countenance, that served to allay some of the doubts that had risen in my mind, and from the manner in which she received me, I had every reason to believe that I was not an unexpected guest.

"'This is the young person,' said my companion, 'that you were told was coming up to town, and I dare say you will do all you can to make her comfortable while she remains here, which will not be long, however, I must tell you, because it is necessary that we lose no time about the business we are upon. And you," he continued, addressing himself to me, "will find Mrs. Evans a very nice, comfortable, motherly kind of woman, that will be willing to do all she can to make your visit here an agreeable one. At any rate your patience will not be tried for any long time, for we shall soon set off again on our journey, and when we reach the end of it, you will acknowledge that your confidence in my friend has not been misplaced.'

"With this he hurried out of the house, and I was left alone with Mrs. Evans, who—"

Here the narrative was broken off by the entrance of Monsieur Lemare, who having whispered something in the lady's ear, retired again to give some orders about which she had been directing him."

CHAPTER L.

CONTINUATION OF THE NARRATIVE.

" ' I was telling you,' continued the female, addressing herself once more to Mr. Smithson, 'that when my companion left the house, I found myself alone with Mrs. Evans, who, assisting me to take off my cloak and bonnet, made a few common-place observations about the long journey I had had, and the beautiful weather it was for travelling. She then made me sit down and take tea with her, and when that was over, observed that she had no doubt I should be glad to go to bed early and rest myself after the fatigue I had endured.

" ' As you are tired,' she said, ' there will be no occasion for you to rise very early in the morning, so lie just as long as you please, my dear, and I'll bring your breakfast up as soon as it is ready. And as for clothes, I shall be able to provide you with what is necessary for the present, and the rest of them you will have either before you start on your next journey, or immediately after you have got to the end of it.'

" I expressed my obligation to her for the kindness she had manifested towards a stranger, and retired to bed quite satisfied that so far I had fallen into very good hands. The next morning my breakfast was brought up according to promise, and when that was over, a silk gown and other articles of dress were given me, upon which I got up, and was going down stairs, when Mrs. Evans took me by the arm and led me into a little dark back room where she told me I must remain till Mr. Gayton arrived, for that it seemed was the only name by which Gravestow was known at that place. I would have remonstrated against this, but Mrs. Evans said it was done at the particular request of Mr. Gayton, who did not wish any person to see me just yet, and under those circumstances I yielded, though much against my own inclination.

" Fatigued as I was, the confinement I was subjected to was an affair of very little consequence, but when two or three days passed away, and I saw no chance of a change for the better taking place, I began to grow uneasy, and when next I saw Mrs. Evans, begged she would provide some better accommodation for me. She, however, only laughed at this, saying, ' that in London, houses were not so comfortable as in the country,' and assuring me that it would not be long before Mr. Gayton arrived, she advised me, with a cold and constrained air, to reconcile myself to that, for which there was at present no remedy.

" This was the first time I had observed any incivility in the woman, and in all other instances she was perfectly good-tempered, occasionally visiting me in my little uncomfortable back room, and endeavouring to divert my mind from unpleasant reflections by cheerful conversation. Yet, in spite of all this attention, I felt very uneasy at the position in which my own folly had placed me, and bitterly enough did I repent the step I had so inconsiderately taken. At length, when I had almost despaired of seeing Mr. Gravestow, he suddenly presented himself before me, and I thought I could detect a lurking expression of triumph as he then saw me secluded from the world totally without the means of communicating my situation to any one. I remonstrated with him upon the harshness of being shut up like a prisoner, and earnestly entreated that he would desire Mrs. Evans to let me go out when and where I pleased. But he said that it would be madness to do so, for a great deal of stir had been made about my mysterious disappearance from Summerfield, and that, should I happen to be discovered, it was not at all unlikely I should be taken up on suspicion of having robbed my master. This news frightened me terribly, and answered all the purposes he intended, for after that time I asked no more to leave the house, and only wished for a front room, that I might be able to see something that was going on. He, however, resisted even this moderate request, and said it was likely I might be seen and recognized by some passing passenger, and once more desiring me to make myself as comfortable as I could, and promised, that as soon as it was practicable, he would either come or send some one to fetch me away, and that I should then go over to France and marry the count, according to the promise that had been given me.

" He then left me, and it was about three weeks before I saw anything more of him. I was very ill when he came, for the confinement and close air had had a serious effect upon my health, and I was so much indisposed that he became alarmed, and two or three times took me out for a walk after the darkness of night set in. But all this served the more to convince me that I was a prisoner under the care of Mrs. Evans, and so great an effect had this upon me, that my illness assumed a more alarming complexion, and at last I became so weak that I was unable to leave my bed. During this time the landlady paid me as much attention as I could expect, but though I repeatedly requested it, no doctor was sent for, and Mrs. Evans gave it as her reason for not doing so, that Mr. Gayton had desired that no stranger was to see me, as in that case it might lead to a discovery which would be extremely unpleasant to all parties. So there I lay, getting more feverish every day, and no doubt I should have died, if the servant girl had not noticed how much worse I was getting, and fetched a doctor one morning when her mistress happened to be out shopping. Mrs. Evans was exceeding angry when she found what had been done, but as there was no remedy for the mischief then, the doctor was permitted to continue his visits, and under his care I began rapidly to recover.

"Just as I was able to sit up again, Mr. Gravestow came once more and brought with him a young female who he introduced to me as Amelia Robertson —"

" Amelia Robertson!" exclaimed Mr. Smithson, interrupting the narrative at this point; " did I understand you rightly, that the female's name was Amelia Robertson ?"

"That was the name he called her by," replied the female; "but by your surprise, sir, I suppose you know something of her."

" I certainly know a person of that name," answered Mr. Smithson. " But proceed, madam, I beg, for I feel exceedingly interested in your story."

" I was going to tell you, sir," she continued, " that I found much relief from the frequent visits of Amelia, and to her friendship during the short time we were acquainted together, I owe much of that peace of mind which my own folly had so nearly destroyed. Mr. Gravestow, too, was very often a visitor, and as soon as I was strong enough to endure the fatigue of a journey, he told me that everything was prepared for my departure to France, and that his friend, Mr. Edwards,—the person who had brought me in the chaise from Summerfield—would accompany me as he himself was unable to leave London at present, through some very particular business in which he was engaged. This arrangement was quite satisfactory, for it at once removed from my mind a suspicion that Mr. Gravestow had drawn me away from home for some guilty motive, which he was ashamed to acknowledge.

" Within three days afterwards I left Mrs. Evans's house and proceeded with my companion to Southampton, where we embarked for France, but instead of proceeding to Havre, as I expected, my fellow traveller thought proper to go to Paris, where he took fashionable apartments, and passed himself off as Major Smith. I was introduced as his sister, and by some means or other, he contrived to obtain credit enough to clothe us both in a superb style, though I need scarcely tell you, he never intended to pay a single franc of the debt he had contracted.

"We had not been long in Paris, before I became accidentally introduced to the Marquis De Noailles, a nobleman of very high family, whose attentions to me were of so marked a character, that I could not help seeing he was smitten with me, and from that moment my head became turned with the great conquest I had made. He used to call frequently at our lodgings, and several times he invited me to take a share in his box at the opera, and so strictly honourable did he appear to be in his professions, that I had every reason to believe it was his intention to make me his marchioness. Indeed, so much did I think so, that I gave up all thoughts of the old Count at Havre, and congratulated myself on the prospects of marrying a man of even higher rank than I anticipated. At length I was prevailed upon to accompany him to one of his country mansions, where a mock private marriage ceremony was performed, and I became the victim of my own thoughtless folly. Indeed, sir, from what I have since heard, I was betrayed into his hands by the companion of my journey, who, in consideration of a bribe, had thus sold me to the man who sought my ruin.

"It was some time, however, before I was aware of the cruel deception that had been practised upon me, for every means were taken to keep me from the knowledge of that fact, but at length the truth broke upon me by a mere accident. At the time of my feigned marriage, I knew no language but my own, and as the marquis could speak English fluently, I felt no difficulty arising from my ignorance. But supposing I had a right to the title I had assumed, and of course expecting to mix a great deal with my lord's country-people, I made up my mind to study the French language in order that I might not feel ashamed of myself when the time came for visiting Paris. In consequence of this determination, I engaged a person to instruct me, and by great application to my studies, got on so well, that in the course of a few weeks, I was able to understand, and even converse with, my master, in the language I was so anxious to attain.

"This circumstance was the means of disclosing a secret that had hitherto been withheld from me, for as I was one morning sitting in my boudoir, my attention was arrested by hearing the Marquis de Noailles in conversation with some of his acquaintances, and the slight knowledge I had obtained of the language, was sufficient to convince me that I had been imposed upon by a fictitious marriage, and that instead of enjoying rank and station in society, I had sunk down to a state of shame and degradation, that I shuddered to think of. They were speaking of a projected union between the marquis and a young lady of high family, and the conversation turned upon the amount of fortune that would be given by the bride, and the settlement which the marquis intended to make on his intended wife. A condition was then made that he must part from me, which he replied to, by saying, that he felt well assured, when I found the deception that had been practised, I should quit his house in anger, never again to see him.

"It would be impossible to describe, sir, the mingled feelings of rage and indignation which this discovery raised in my heart. I was humbled to the very dust at finding that I was merely the mistress, when I had believed myself to be his lawful wife, and for some few moments I could scarcely refrain from going into his presence, and reproaching him for the perfidy of which he had been guilty. I, however, had sufficient mastery over myself to abandon this course till he was rid of his company. But when next we met, which was within an hour afterwards, I endeavoured to acquaint him with the fearful discovery I had made, and then leave his house for ever, and without delaying my departure even for a single instant. A faintness, however, overcame me, and I should have fallen had he not supported me in his arms. But my looks were sufficient to convince him that I had found out his deception, and then expressing the greatest contrition for the duplicity he had practised towards me, he declared that love alone had prompted him to an act of which he was thoroughly ashamed, and that the difference in our stations had been the only obstacle to our lawful union. He had perceived from the first, he said, that Major Smith was nothing but an impostor, and as I happened to be in his company, and passed as his sister, there was every reason to believe that my design in visiting France was to get married to some wealthy husband, and then ruin him with my extravagance. He informed me too, of the bargain which had been made between himself and the pretended major, who was base enough to abandon me to my fate for a sum of gold which he lost the same night at a gaming table.

"'You will, therefore, see,' he went on to say, ' that under any circumstances you would have been disposed of by that designing villain, for all he wanted was money, and if he had not accepted the sum I offered him, he would have sold you to some one else who would perhaps have treated you with less kindness and consideration than I have. That I love you still, I pledge my most sacred honour, and nothing would afford me so much grief as to know that we must separate for ever.'

"In this latter respect I was thoroughly convinced that he had not deceived me. I felt that in some degree I had deserved the downfall I had sustained, for ambition had been my only thought when he addressed me, and through that error had I failed to see that it was scarcely probable so great a man would pay honourable addresses to a girl who was a perfect stranger in the country. Be that as it might, however, I could not easily forget the affection with which the marquis had ever regarded me, nor could I cease to love him, though I owed my degradation to him, and I felt that, part with him when I might, or go wherever I would, I should never feel the same degree of regard for any one else that I did for him. He had never shown me the least unkindness either by word or action, but had treated me throughout with as much respect and affection as if I had indeed been his wife.

"The consequence of this was that I continued with him, though he candidly admitted that owing to the circumstances he had mentioned, it would never be possible to make those amends which he frankly acknowledged my conduct towards him deserved. He, however, provided for me in case of his death or our separation from any other cause, by a most liberal settlement, and I thus found myself placed far above the reach of want. From that time he seemed to love me more than ever, and on no occasion, till the hour of his death, did he give me cause to remember the frail terms that united us. It is even likely that he would have privately married me had the subject been urged ever so little, but I forbore to mention the subject to him, because I knew in case of a discovery, it would expose him to the ill-nature and ridicule of those who could not have appreciated the honourable motives that had induced him to consent to such a sacrifice. Besides, I could not help being aware that I was chiefly to blame for throwing myself in his way, when I ought rather to have shunned, and though I had deeply felt the disgrace which had fallen upon me, I could not but confess that I might still have been innocent if it had not been for my ambitious wish to become a marchioness.

"The result of my culpable folly was that I should be condemned to pass the remainder of my life as an outcast from the virtuous of my own sex. But then his kindness would make up for other species of annoyance, and so long as he loved me, I cared very little for all that the rest of the world might choose to say against my. Thus situated, I felt less unhappy than might have been expected after the discovery I had made, and being anxious to forget as much as possible the past scene of my life, I once more commenced my studies, not only of the French language, but in the polite accomplishments of the day, in order that my defects of education might be less apparent, and that I might thus secure the constant society of the marquis, who would thus have no inducement to pass any of his time away from me. In these studies I advanced rapidly, for I took great pleasure in them, and anticipated with pleasure the surprise of De Noailles when he discovered that I was not the ignorant peasant he had found me on our first acquaintance together.

"Thus situated, I had little time for reflections on the past events of my life, and all went on smoothly enough till a few months since, when I was surprised at receiving an unexpected visit from the Count de Morceau, the nobleman to marry whom was the express visit to France. He had seen me, I believe, at the opera, and visited me from sheer impertinent curiosity ; but let that be as it may, the circumstance led to various explanations, and the disclosures that followed were highly important, not only to myself, but to other parties, who I am anxious to serve.

"In the conversation that ensued, I first heard the news of poor Mr. Wentford's death, and though he could not explain everything to my satisfaction, I could find that my secret flight from Summerfield on the very night of the murder, had given rise to rumours in which my own name was connected. I was also shown a letter from Mr. Gravestow, in which the writer suggested it to the count to practice towards me the same species of villany to which I had become a victim, through his agent Edwards, or Major Smith, as he thought proper to call himself. Thus I found that the false marriage was thought of and proposed by Mr. Gravestow, who all along had professed so much friendship and esteem for me. It further appeared that Count de Morceau had no notion of my having been a servant ; he knew me only as Miss Smith. The Marquis de Noailles was equally ignorant upon that point, for I could not bear that he should know how humbly I had been brought up, and had it not been for the fear of a discovery taking place, I should have communicated with you, sir, and thus perhaps the fatal event I now mourn for might never have occurred.

"But perhaps I weary you, Mr. Smithson," she continued, "for my story has been a very long one, and is uninteresting to you. except the portion I am presently coming to, and which is more immediately connected with your friend Mr. Wentford, whose murder has never yet been traced to the real perpetrators."

"I feel so much interested in it," said Mr. Smithson, "that I am most anxious you should relate everything without the least abridgement. But you spoke just now of some fatal event ; may I enquire what it was?"

"Some short time ago," she resumed, "the marquis's regiment was quartered at a town some few leagues from Paris, towards the Spanish frontier, and as duty demanded his presence there, I followed him at his own request as soon as possible. Whilst there we frequently rode out together to see the beautiful country, for which that part of France is celebrated, and one day as we were returning homewards, attended by a couple of servants, we saw a carriage approaching at a pace which threatened us with danger. We accordingly drew up on one side, and as they passed, obtained a glance at the travellers. In an instant we recognized the two men that was inside, one of whom was the pretended Major Smith, and the other a person named Morley, who had been a servant of the marquis. At the instant of recognition, I thought of Mr. Wentford's murder, and wishing to hear some particulars about it, I asked the marquis if he had any objection to my speaking to the pretended major.

" ' Not in the least,' he replied, and addressing a few words to his attendant, he desired him to ride after the carriage, and request an interview with the two gentlemen. The poor fellow promptly obeyed, but just as he had nearly overtaken the vehicle, one of the men thrust his body out of the window, and shot our servant through the heart.

" In an instant the marquis set off in pursuit of the ruffians, but, alas! only to meet the same fate that had been dealt out to his groom. Suspecting, I suppose, that his object was to arrest them, one of the villains again fired, and shot him with so deadly an aim, that he fell, and had expired ere I could reach him. The ruffians then set forth at full gallop, but were stopped, and immediately carried off to prison. My feelings at being thus deprived of the man I loved best upon earth, may be more easily imagined than described, nor will I dwell longer upon an event that has caused me more sorrow than anything else that ever befell me during the whole course of my life.

" Within a day or two afterwards I appeared as principal witness against the prisoners ; they were asked whether they had anything to say for themselves, but they maintained an obstinate silence, neither admitting nor confessing anything, though from the quantity of contraband goods contained in thecarriage, there could be no doubt entertained of the object of their journey. They were then committed for trial,' andas I found that I should not be wanted to attend at the criminal court for some time, I determined to visit my native country, and see if anything could be done towards clearing up the mystery in which Mr. Wentford's murder was involved. This was in fact highly necessary, as my own character had been blackened, and I felt that it was due to myself to clear it in the best way I could. Besides, I am not without my suspicions that these two men, Major Smith and Morley, or one of them at least, had some share in the murder of the old gentleman, I wished to discover whether my notion is correct, before they suffer for the other crime on a public scaffold.

" It was with this object that I set off on my journey, and had not travelled many miles, when I discovered another act of heartless perfidy of which they had been guilty. As we rode through a hamlet, I saw a crowd of persons at no great distance off, gathered round a miserable hovel ; as we approached, I could discover a female nearly fainting from fatigue, and who was the object that had caused the assemblage of persons that had first attracted my attention. I then left the carriage, and advancing nearer, could see the female was a young Englishwoman. I then desired Lemare to go forward and enquire whether any accident had occurred in which I could be of any service, and he shortly returned with news that the young female had arrived at the place not long before in a very exhausted state, and sinking from want of food, and the exertion she had made to proceed on her journey. It further appeared that she was a foreigner, and that in spite of all the questions they had put to her, she could neither inform them where she came from or whither she was going. I then approached, and addressed her in my native language, upon which she seemed to revive, and never did I see so much delight manifested as when she at last found some one with whom she could speak. I then learnt that she had lately made her escape from some place where she believed evil designs had been entertained against her by the people of the house, and that she was on her way to Paris, where she hoped to find her father, who she expected would be there by that time.

"Finding that I was on my way to the capital, she requested permission to accompany me, which being willingly acceded to, she was assisted to get into the carriage, for such a dreadful weakness had overpowered her limbs that she was scarcely able to move without our aid.   She, however, revived sufficiently to acquaint me with the occurrences that had reduced her to this destitute condition, and I learnt that she was the daughter óf a very wealthy Englishman, and that she had been married to Morley, under the supposition of his being the Marquis of Valliere.   She came to France with him, accompanied by her sister, and were met by the pretended Major Smith, who had nearly succeeded in prevailing on the unmarried sister to elope with him when some unexpected news from England put them to the route.   They then left Paris all on a sudden, and when night came on, stopped at a miserable inn that was far removed from any other human habitation.   Here the two villains deserted them in the course of the night, and thus were a couple of females abandoned to the care of strangers, without knowing one word of the language, or being able in any other way to explain the sad condition to which they had been reduced.   I shall not, however, detail (all the adventures she related to me, but for the present will merely content myself with saying that the elder sister, seeing no other chance of relief, contrived to leave the inn secretly, and was making her way to Paris, when hunger and fatigue compelled her to stop at the place where I was so fortunate as to find her.

"It was night when we reached the French capital, and my first care on the following morning was to inquire at the hotel where they had lodged, whether her father had yet arrived.   But to this question I could obtain no satisfactory answer, for all that the people of the place knew about it was, that two persons had been there a day or two before inquiring about the Marquis Valliere and his friend Major Smith, and the moment it was announced that they had gone away with the two ladies that were with them, the two strangers turned from the place, and nothing more had since been seen or heard of them.

"We then thought that in all likelihood they had gone off in quest of the fugitives, and, as we could do no good by remaining in Paris, we set off on the following morning for Calais, and getting on board one of the packets, soon found ourselves once more on English ground.   By this time my companion had somewhat recovered from the exhaustion and debility in which I had found her, and as she was as anxious as myself to continue the journey, we set off from Dovor within an hour after our arrival there, and reaching London, took a lodging for the time I might remain in town, at this hotel.

"The next morning,—which was yesterday,—I took the young lady home to her parents' house at Dalston, and never shall I forget the gratitude of the poor mother, at once more beholding a daughter whom she had almost given up as lost.   Mr. Plumley, too, it appeared, had set off some few days before in search of the villains that had duped him; and, as he was accompanied by a friend who would be well able to advise him how to act, there was good ground to hope that the object of their journey would not prove fruitless, and that they would find the other daughter who had been left behind at the inn.   Having thus far fulfilled my mission, I returned to this place, and wrote off to you, requesting this interview, which you have been kind enough to grant.   My next care will be to make inquiries about Mr. Wentford's murder, and, if you will give me your assistance in it, I believe it will be no difficult task to prove the innocence not only of myself, but also of Andrew Hoply, who, I suspect, was assassinated at the same time with his master."

Having heard her narrative to an end, Mr. Smithson made a few neces-

sary inquiries relative to the affair he had taken in hand, and having satisfied himself in every particular, he took his leave, with a promise never
to relax in his exertions till he had brought the whole affair to light, and
cleared the innocent from the foul imputations that had been cast upon
them.

CHAPTER LI.

FURTHER DISCOVERIES.

MR. SMITHSON was too much the man of business to waste time that
was so valuable, and no sooner had he left the hotel, than jumping into a
hackney coach, he drove off to the house of Mr. Derwent, the lawyer, with
whom he obtained an immediate interview. The narrative he had just
heard was then briefly given, and, commenting on various parts of it as he
went on, he at length expressed it as his opinion that certain long-con-
cealed mysteries were upon the eve of being unveiled. Mr. Derwent was
of the same opinion, and entered heart and soul into the cause; but, as it
was necessary to make a few more inquiries, he hastened back to the hotel
with his friend, and having satisfied himself in these particulars, again left
the place with Mr. Smithson, and proposed that they should next go
to Clapham, and see Amelia Robertson, who, it was expected, would be
able to supply a few deficiences in the evidence, and thus make the road
smooth and clear before them.

To their surprise, however, the house was closed, and on making inquiries about the neighbourhood, they ascertained that nothing had been

seen of her since three nights before, when a strange gentleman called at her house, and it was supposed she had gone away with him. The next object of Mr. Smithson and the lawyer was to call upon the neighbour who had entered Amelia's house on the night in question, and from the description he gave of the stranger that he saw, there could be very little doubt that it was Walter Gravestow, and the motives that must have induced him to pay this visit were so manifest, that the greatest consternation was created, lest Amelia had fallen by his hands, in order to prevent her giving that evidence against him which he had so much reason to dread. It appeared, however, that she had been seen alive with him on the London road; and, from the statement given by the latter witness, there was nothing to prove that she had not accompanied him voluntarily. In fact, it did not appear that they were quarrelling, for though they were talking very earnestly, there was nothing in the conduct of either of them to prove that they were on bad terms with each other.

That the person who had taken her away, however, was Walter Gravestow, there was no doubt, for the account given by the man who had seen him in the parlour, exactly answered his description; and when his worthless character came to be considered, there could be no hesitation in suspecting that his visit had been prompted by the worst of motives. It was also certain that Gravestow and Gayton were one and the same person, and that Amelia Robertson was the female spoken of by the Jew, as the person who had made such anxious inquiries at his shop about the will which had been left in the coat pocket. In that case, she must have been employed by the fellow Edwards, or Major Smith, as he sometimes chose to call himself; who, if such proved to be the fact, was no other than one of the villains that had been concerned in the murder of poor Mr. Wentford. Thus a clue began to be formed, that would bring the inquiries to a satisfactory termination; and the two gentlemen congratulated themselves on the hope that at length began to dawn upon their exertions in the pursuit of justice.

The conduct of Gravestow at their recent visit to Summerfield, was another link in the chain of evidence; for it was very evident to Mr. Smithson and his friend, that he had been aware of Amelia being the female who had gone to the Jew's shop, and as any statement she might make against him would be followed by the most disastrous consequences, it was to be feared that his object in visiting her was to prevent any mischief she might do him, and from the circumstance of their leaving the house together, it was imagined that he had induced her to do so by some excuse or other, and that he would take care to put her out out of the way as soon as he could effect that object without fear of discovery.

"The scoundrel," exclaimed Mr. Smithson, "will yet add another crime to the many he has already committed, and I fear no exertions of ours will succeed in preventing it. We must, however, lose no time in hunting him out, for, depend upon it, he will take the first opportunity to leave England, and thus we should lose sight of him for ever."

"There is not a moment to lose," answered Mr. Derwent, "and my proposition is that we instantly make inquiries to satisfy ourselves whether he came up to London after the unpleasant interview we had with him at Summerfield. I will, therefore, write down to some one in the neighbourhood of that place, and ask the question, so that by return of post, we shall know something of his movements; and if he has left his home so suddenly we may pretty well guess the reasons that have prompted him to do so."

"But I'm afraid the loss of time will be altogether against us," suggested Mr. Smithson, "and, as we are out, we may as well go round to

Jermyn street, and inquire at his usual lodgings, when in town, whether he has been seen there lately."

To this reasonable suggestion no objection was offered, and they immediately proceeded to the street above-named, and on inquiring of the landlady, they ascertained that Gravestow had called there three nights previously, to tell her to take in any letters that might be addressed to him, and keep them till his return, which he expected would be in a few weeks.

"Have you received any letters, ma'am?" asked the lawyer.

"Only one," she replied, "and that came this morning."

"Perhaps you will have the kindness to give it me," said Mr. Derwent; "we are well known to Mr. Gravestow, and will take care that he shall receive it in a parcel we are going to send off to him."

"I don't know what to do about it," exclaimed the landlady, "for he told me to keep his letters in my own possession, and he would be angry, perhaps, if I gave them to anybody else."

"You need not think anything at all about that," replied Mr. Derwent, "for I will undertake to say you will not offend Mr. Gravestow by doing as I have proposed. The fact is, he has been obliged to leave England very suddenly, and he desired me to call for his letters, and forward them to him as fast as I received them. You will, therefore, be pleased to give me the one you have, and I will send it as I have promised."

The landlady muttered her dislike to doing this, but she happened at the time to be in a great hurry, and wishing to get rid of her visitors as soon possible, she stepped into the parlour, and fetching the letter, placed it in the hands of Mr. Derwent, who put it into his pocket, and walked off with his friend Smithson.

"And now," asked the latter gentleman, after they had turned into the next street, "may I inquire what you intend to do with the letter?"

"Open it, to be sure," answered the other; "it may serve to direct us where he is to be found; and in that case, will be an invaluable acquisition."

"But it will hardly be fair," observed Mr. Derwent, "since we have not obtained possession of it in the most honourable manner."

"Why, the truth is," answered the lawyer, "we have got a rogue to deal with, and must not be too particular as to the method we adopt to discover him. Walter Gravestow is cunning and wary, but it shall go hard if I do not find means to drag his villany to light. This letter is doubtless from some friend of his, and I'll be bound we shall get some insight into the present whereabouts of our slippery customer. So, here goes to read his correspondence, whether Mr. Gravestow likes it or not."

In an instant the seal was broken, and the lawyer glancing his eye down the page, quickly made himself acquainted with the contents of the letter.

"Who is it from?" asked Mr. Smithson, as he saw his friend had finished it.

"From Mr. Snell, the surveyor, that we saw down at Summerfield the other day," answered the other.

"Indeed!" exclaimed Mr. Smithson, "then of course, it contains nothing that concerns our present inquiry. Something more, I suppose, about this new road that Gravestow is making so much fuss about?"

"There you are mistaken," said the lawyer, "for the information is more important than that, since it fully confirms our suspicions about his having taken his departure for Paris. Mr. Snell, it seems, has had instructions to ascertain where George Ramsden is to be found, and having learnt that he is now in the French capital, he has sent up to inform his patron about it. No doubt, Gravestow has ascertained that fact from other parties before now, and, of course, we shall either see or hear something of him, if we find it necessary to go to Paris."

"And who is this George Ramsden, that you are talking about?" asked Mr. Smithson.

"The person that the old manor house down at Summerfield belongs to," answered the lawyer.

"Aye, aye, a wild, scapegrace sort of fellow."

"He is, indeed," replied Mr. Derwent. "From what I have heard, his father possessed a very handsome estate adjoining to that which belonged to Mr. Wentford. Things, however, I believe, went rather crossly with the elder Ramsden, for he was obliged to sell a considerable part of his landed property through the extravagance of his son, and perhaps he would have been ruined altogether, had not death interposed to save him from the horrors of beggary. When the son, this George Ramsden, succeeded to the property, he found it very much diminished, but instead of taking care of what remained, he plunged deeper into extravagance than ever, and having sold everything but the manor house, he found himself so heavily involved in debt, that he has been obliged to live abroad ever since, only occasionally venturing to come to England, and then disguised, and under an assumed name. However, it is said there was a sort of friendship existing between Gravestow and him, which is likely enough, seeing that they were both confounded rascals, and birds of a feather, you know, flock together."

"And how was it," asked Mr. Smithson, "that he never sold the manor house, as it would have done something towards raising money to support his extravagance?"

"Why, the truth is," replied the lawyer, "the house had fallen into so dilapidated a state, that no one would lay out money to purchase it. Besides, Ramsden was not very anxious that people should know where he was hiding himself, and so the place has gone more and more to decay, till you see they are about to pull it down, and sell the site for the new road that is making in the neighbourhood."

"Then Ramsden, I suppose, is never seen in England, now?" said Mr. Smithson.

"I rather think he is in this country a great deal more frequently than is suspected," replied the lawyer. "Indeed, to let you into a bit of a secret, I have reasons to believe that Edwards, Major Smith, and George Ramsden, is one and the same person."

"Why, you don't say so!" exclaimed Mr. Smithson, with the utmost astonishment.

"I feel almost certain about it," replied his friend; "and so much am I convinced that there is no mistake, I intend to set about an investigation into the circumstance without delay."

"Do you know where he is now?"

"This letter says he is in Paris," answered Mr. Derwent; "and as I do not mean to let him escape me, I shall immediately go over to the Continent to prosecute my enquiries; and if you think proper to accompany me there, I rather think you will not hereafter have to regret the little inconvenience it may put you too. So what say you? Shall I have the pleasure of your companionship in this journey?"

"Willingly," replied Mr. Smithson; "for though I am almost too old now to care anything about travelling, yet there will be some satisfaction in pursuing this enquiry to an end, and I would travel barefoot to the furthest extremity of the earth could I but succeed in bringing the murderers of Mr. Wentford to justice. But at present we are not quite certain who were the perpetrators of the deed, and, therefore, we must be cautious in our enquiries, or the villains may, after all, find means to escape from us."

"Why, I can't say that we have any direct evidence against them at present," said the lawyer; "but we know enough to lead to a great deal more, and, perhaps, when Ramsden sees us, and finds that the game is up, he will confess the deed, in hopes of escaping at the expense of the accomplices in the crime. At all events, the experiment is well worth trying, and if it fails, we shall have done nothing more than our duty, and must then look out for further evidence that shall have a more satisfactory conclusion."

"And when do you think of starting for the Continent?" asked Mr. Smithson.

"To-morrow morning," replied the other, "unless your engagements will prevent you going with me so soon."

"I know of nothing to hinder me," answered Mr. Smithson. "Besides, I am most anxious to see Walter Gravestow, that I may learn from him what's become of Amelia Robertson, who, there is but too much reason to believe, has been basely murdered. At any rate, her sudden absence from home is most unaccountable, and I will never rest satisfied till I have learnt what has been done with her."

"Perhaps we may find her in Paris," observed the lawyer; "for one would imagine that Gravestow will not kill her if he can make himself safe by any other means. He will, perhaps, keep her in confinement, which he will have many facilities for doing over there, and thus prevent a discovery taking place of those events which he has but too much reason to conceal."

"But do you know anything about Paris?" asked Mr. Smithson, who was not without his apprehensions at leaving his own native land for one which he had never seen. "I have heard," he continued, "that it is a very different place to London, and, therefore, we ought to be very careful how we trust ourselves so far from home."

"Oh, you need be under no apprehension on that account," replied the lawyer, smiling at the caution of his friend. "I have been over there two or three times, and can assure you the people neither eat one another, nor show worse instances of a depraved nature than we do in this country. Nay, I am not quite sure whether you will not be delighted with Paris; though, perhaps, if our mission there proves unsuccessful, we shall have very little time to see much of it. And now, my dear sir, I have another proposition to make, which I believe you will not object to, as it will secure us a companion for our journey to the French metropolis."

"That," answered Mr. Smithson, "that will depend upon who the companion is."

"Well, what say you to Dolly Pratt, then?" asked Mr. Derwent. "Confound the name, say I, for pretty as she is, that spoils all."

"Do you think she will return to France so soon?" enquired Mr. Smithson.

"I am certain she will," replied the other. "In fact, she has got the trial of these men to attend, and the affairs of the late marquis are just now in the course of settlement, so that she is obliged to return without loss of time. Poor creature, I cannot help pitying her from my soul, for though she has been a weak, foolish girl, there is an interesting simplicity in her manners that makes one almost forget her faults."

"The truth is," said Mr. Smithson, "she is more sinned against than sinning, and what faults she possesses are those consequent upon the manner in which she was brought up. Pride, when very young, seems to have been her chief fault, and basely did Gravestow take advantage of that weakness when he proposed her marriage with the French count."

" Do you think the Count de Marceau ever had any serious thoughts of marrying her ?" asked Mr. Derwent.

" I should imagine not," replied the other; " not that I know anything of the count, but judging from Gravestow's usual cool villany, I am inclined to think that he was negociating the affair for the sake of the money he might get by it. The letter which the count afterwards showed the girl when she was the Marquis de Noailles' mistress, proves that Walter Gravestow had proposed a sham marriage, and the affair was only broken off through her happening to meet the marquis in Paris."

" And, of course," said Mr. Derwent, " she has never seen Gravestow since her discovery of his villany ?"

" Never," replied his friend; " the scoundrel could not face the woman he has wronged, and, it seems, took good care to avoid her from that period. It strikes me, however, that he will at last find her to much for him, for she has a clue, as you are aware, to connect him with the murder of the old gentleman, and if he should come to the gallows for his crimes, he will owe his punishment to the very woman that he betrayed to ruin."

" And serve him right," exclaimed the lawyer; " he seems one of those scoundrels that act as a scourge against their fellow-creatures, and the sooner the world is rid of him the better it will be for mankind. By Jove! I could almost turn hangman myself, for the sake of doing justice to such a villain as he is. However, we will see this young female again, if you please, and if she has no objection to be our fellow-traveller, it will be company for her back to France, and we shall have the further satisfaction of not losing sight of her while there is a chance of discovering the mystery connected with Mr. Wentford's murder."

" And neither of us being very young men," observed Mr. Smithson, with a smile, " she will not run much hazard of provoking the scandal of those who are ever ready to create mischief out of trifles. She is very pretty, it is true, but what care you or I for beauty, when the only object of our journey is to seek for that justice which has been too long suffered to sleep. We can rather pity her errors and the consequences that have arisen from them, than condemn her for faults which she was led into through the artful representations of a villain. In fact, ambition has been her curse, and the desire of becoming a countess has plunged her into an ocean of misfortunes from which she can never extricate herself."

" Yet, strange to say," observed the lawyer, " the very circumstance, grievous as it is to herself, will, perhaps, be the means of bringing punishment upon the scoundrel that sold her for a paltry sum of gold. The retribution will be a just one, and though the affliction to the poor girl is very heavy, yet, from what I hear, she has conducted herself with so much propriety under these degrading circumstances, that, though she has not found friendship from her fellow-creatures, yet she has their commiseration, which is, perhaps, as much as she can expect."

" And she deserves it," answered Mr. Smithson; " for we have good evidence that her fall was none of her own seeking. She was deceived by a false marriage with the Marquis de Noailles, and when the discovery was made, I know not that she could have acted otherwise than she did. He was a libertine, but not a heartless one, as his subsequent conduct proved, and though he made her not his wife, I have a notion that had he lived a little longer, he might have risked the sneers of the world and raised her to that eminence which her faithfulness to him deserved. As it is, he has left her a very considerable settlement, and she may yet live happily enough in some quiet, secluded place, where she may remain unknown to those who, if they knew her misfortunes, would, perhaps, follow the heartless example that is usually set by the rest of the world. For people are rarely just in their condemnations of each other ; it is enough that a certain person commits a fault, for all the excellence they may show in other respects will never obtain oblivion for the past, or even the respect of those who, though unknown to the world, are more criminal than the person they condemn. However, we are now at the hotel where she lodges, so we'll just enquire if she will accompany us, and in the event of her not having any objection to do so, we will set off to-morrow morning and go with her to Paris."

The female they had been speaking about had no hesitation in accepting the offer of their company on the journey, and at the appointed hour they all set off for Dover, and in due time reached the gay metropolis of France.

CHAPTER LII.

THE PICTURE.

LEAVING them to pursue their way, we must now follow Walter Gravestow and Amelia in their rapid flight towards Paris ; the former, indeed, had sufficient reason to use all the despatch he could, for in the first place, it was necessary to see George Ramsden, with as little delay as possible, in order that he might make a bargain for the manor house, and thus prevent its demolition, which he looked forward to with so much alarm ; and, in the second place, he was anxious to put Amelia out of England before she had time or opportunity to say anything that might lead to a discovery of the crimes he had committed. Once safe in France, he fancied all danger would be at an end, for he would take care that Amelia should find few friends over there, and if he saw any cause to apprehend danger from anything she might say, it would be easy for him to make away with her, and nobody would be the wiser, or think of making enquiries about a stranger of whom they know nothing. On this account, he travelled with the utmost speed, and having arrived at Paris, took a wretched lodging for Amelia, in one of the most obscure streets in the city ; promising that he would marry her in the course of a very short time, and hinting that, as a matter of prudence, it would be necessary they should reside in different houses till he could make the necessary arrangements. Amelia then alluded to his already having a wife, but he spoke of the unhappiness that existed between them, and said it was his intention to sue immediately for a divorce.

This served to quiet the apprehensions she had begun to form as to his motives for bringing her to Paris, and with her usual submission, she waited patiently the result of the proceedings he was then engaged upon. But his designs were still of the same dark tendency that they had ever been, and he was only waiting an opportunity when he might either drown her in the river Seine, or rid himself of her by means of poison ; either of which plans would suit his purpose, as it would be easy to satisfy the public that she had made away with herself.

Gravestow had been nearly a week in Paris, when happening to take up a newspaper his attention was attracted by the name of Major Smith, and eagerly perusing the article, he discovered that it related to the forthcoming trial of that person and his associate for the murder of the Marquis de Noailles and his groom. This intelligence afforded him the utmost satisfaction, for the two persons who had him most in their power were thus in

a fair way of being disposed of for ever, and if he could but obtain an interview with the pseudo Major, he felt satisfied that his future life might be
passed without those racking fears that had hitherto tormented him.   Dolly
Pratt, it was true, still lived, but as he had been informed by Amelia that
she had formed a high alliance in France, it was most likely she would
not trouble herself to speak upon a subject that might give rise to awkward enquiries with respect to her own former situation in life.

But Gravestow could not feel quite easy whilst affairs remained in this
unsettled state, and throwing down the newspaper which had afforded this
information, he leaned back in his chair, and gave way to the thousand
thoughts that hurried through his ever plotting brain.   At length, starting
suddenly up, he hurried towards the closet, and drinking off two glasses
of brandy in rapid succession, he left the house, determined to bring matters to a crisis without further delay.

"It shall be done," he muttered himself, "for she is a stranger in this
place, and even if she was missed no one would ever take the trouble of
making any enquiries about her.   The people where she lodges neither
know from whence she come, nor who she is, and if I take care to pay the
trifling rent that is due, they will not care whether they ever see her or not.
I'll do it at any rate, and to-morrow will set off to see the prisoners, and
if I can but get a private interview with George Ramsden, the thing may
easily be settled about the old manor house at Summerfield, and then another source of my uneasiness will be removed.   As he must be hanged, I
suppose, and if he will only act according to my suggestions, I shall be
home again so soon that my absence will not occasion any surprise, and I
shall be able to prevent the pulling down of the house."

With these reflections, and caring nothing for the new crimes he was
meditating, he walked on, determined that no obstacle should prevent the
execution of a project upon which his own safety depended.   He was
not, however, without some few misgivings, but dangers threatened him on
every hand, and he resolved to perish at once, if need be, rather than risk a
fate which he trembled to think of.

It happened that in the same place where Amelia lived, there resided also a
young painter, whose poverty and obscurity compelled him to live in this
out of the way part of Paris till some lucky chance should occur to make his
talents known and appreciated.   His room was immediately joining hers,
and it so occurred that he had frequently opportunities of seeing her as
she passed in and out.   Gravestow, too, he had seen on several occasions,
and there was something so marked and peculiar in his countenance, that
the young artist had been induced, in secret, to make portraits of them
both, for the purpose of introducing into a large picture that he was then
painting, the subject of which was a murderer slaying a woman, who was
upon her knees before him.

It appears that some short time previous to the Marquis de Noailles' last
departure from Paris, this young artist had been introduced to him as a
painter, of very promising genius, who was likely to attain great eminence
in his profession.   The marquis, who was a liberal patron of the fine arts,
had promised to exert himself in his behalf, and at the earnest solicitation
of Dolly—or Dorothea, as she was now called—he had allowed the young
man permission to take his portrait.   This task had been commenced, and
was considerably advanced in progress, when the marquis was suddenly
called away upon the unfortunate journey from which he was doomed
never to return.   The first thought, therefore, which occurred to Dolly
when she came back to Paris, was to send for the painter to inquire whether
he thought he could remember enough of the countenance to finish the portrait, which would now become doubly valuable to her in consequence of

the disastrous event that had robbed the nobleman of life. He sent word back that he had no doubt he should be able to do it, and promised to make the attempt out of respect for a nobleman whose memory he had so much reason to venerate.

As every portrait of the marquis had been taken possession of by the next heir, she had this likeness of him, and this one would be doubly valuable from the circumstances under which it had been taken. She, therefore, immediately sent Lamare with a message to the young man, conveying her wishes in this respect, and desiring him to bring the picture with him in order that she might see it before he proceeded any further, and point out whatever alterations it might appear necessary to make. This was good news to the artist, for his affairs were at that time in a very deplorable state, and he was just beginning to despair of realizing his hopes of future eminence when this event occurred, to cheer him with renewed prospects of becoming a painter of distinction.

He therefore eagerly embraced the opportunity which was thus offered him, and gathering together all the sketches that he happened to have by him, he put them into a portfolio, and with that and the pictures under his arm, set out for the place to which he had been directed. He thought the sketches rough and unfinished as they were, would afford some testimony of his abilities, and full of hope for the future, he imagined that this first stepping stone would lead on to fortune, and, in imagination, he could already fancy himself climbing up to the highest pinnacle of fame. Never before did he feel so happy as upon the present occasion, for he looked upon the past as a painful dream that was over, and the future was so full of brighter prospects that he could think of nothing else but of the glorious chance which Fortune had at last thrown in his way.

The portrait of the marquis, unfinished as it was, gave the greatest satis-

No. 49

faction to Dolly, and so much was her admiration excited, that she immediately sent for Mr. Smithson and the lawyer, that they might join in their
opinion upon the work of the young artist. It was, in truth, well worthy
the admiration that had been bestowed upon it, and as no fault could with
any justice be found with it, the two Englishmen joined most cordially in
the praise which had been bestowed upon it. This, as may be expected,
was most grateful to the ears of the young painter, for he had seldom obtained much credit for his labours, though he had toiled incessantly to
obtain it, and when he found how kind the people were who had thus pa-
tronised his efforts, he declared his willingness to undertake the completion
of the portrait, and even promised that it should be nearly as good a
likeness as if the marquis had sat to him the necessary number of times.

The visit was so pleasant to all parties that the artist remained some
time longer than he had intended, and he would perhaps have stayed another hour had he not chanced to recollect that he had an appointment
with some one also about a trifling job he expected to get, and putting the
portrait under his arm, he took his leave, promising to get on with his
work as quickly as possible, and bring it home as soon as it was finished.

In the excitement of the moment, however, he quite forgot the portfolio
in which he had put the sketches which he had intended to show as an
evidence of his skill in the art he professed. It was some time afterwards
before they were seen by any one, for they had been left on a table in the
further part of the room, and it was not till Mr. Smithson and the lawyer
were going out, that the former saw them lying in the place where they
had been left, and hastily untying the strings of the portfolio, the first
thing which presented itself was the sketch which we have before alluded
to as having been made by the artist in his leisure moments.

"Why, I declare," exclaimed Mr. Derwent, "if we might not almost
swear that this figure, though only a rough sketch, was intended for
Gravestow. How like him to be sure! And yet it is impossible that it can
be so, for it is not very likely he should have sat to the obscure artist that
has just left us."

"Why bless me! It is indeed an astonishing likeness," said Mr. Smithson,
who was instantly attracted to his side by these observations. "It is the
very man himself, and we might swear by the dark scowl he wears
upon his features, that it can be intended for no one else. And the
woman——"

"Ah! I know nothing about her," interrupted the lawyer; "though, I
suppose, like the other, it is the first rough sketch of a portrait the young
man is going to take."

"It is Amelia Robertson," exclaimed Mr. Smithson.

"Amelia Robertson!" shouted his friend.

"Aye, as sure as that you and I are now looking at it," answered Mr.
Smithson. "I could swear to her among a thousand, and as sure as fate it
could have been painted from no other face."

"Psha!" observed Mr. Derwent, "it can be nothing but a mere acci-
dental likeness."

"I would have granted that such might have been the case, had there
been but one likeness," returned Mr. Smithson; "but when we see
two in the same picture that bear such striking resemblances, we can no
longer believe it to be the effect of chance."

Mr. Derwent was unable to give any opinion about the likeness of the
female, because he had never happened to see Amelia; but Dolly was well
able to coincide in the notion that had been expressed by Mr. Smithson,
and she spoke positively as to the impossibility of its being intended for
any other person. The position of the two figures next attracted their at-

tention, for the composition possessed a good deal of interest, and though parts of it were sketched in a very slight manner, there was quite enough to show that the man was raising a knife with the design of plunging it into the heart of the kneeling female.

"I would give the world to know what all this means," cried Mr. Smithson, "for something assures me that this circumstance, trifling as it is, will afford another link in the chain of evidence we are so anxious to complete."

"In that case," said the lawyer, "our better way will be to see the artist again with as little delay as possible. At any rate he will be able to tell us whether they are sketched from living subjects, and if it should turn out to be so, we can very easily find out all the rest."

"Suppose I send Lamare to say I wish to speak with him immediately," said Dolly; and without waiting for an answer, she rang the bell to summon the man to her presence.

"I don't know but what it will be better to go ourselves and make the inquiry," exclaimed Mr. Derwent. "It may be necessary to act with a great deal of caution in this affair, and if too much bustle is made in it, we shall lose all chance of sifting this matter to the bottom."

"I perfectly agree with you in that respect," observed his friend, "for we pretty well know what a slippery fellow Gravestow is, and if he gets but the slightest notion that we are so close upon his heels, he will be off from Paris before we can get a sight of him."

"And if he is the original of this sketch," said Mr. Smithson, "there can be no doubt that Amelia is with him, and in that event it will be necessary to take very active and cautious steps, for we know him to be a villain, and Heaven only can tell what his intentions may be with respect to the poor woman that he has brought with him."

"Perhaps," exclaimed the lawyer, with a shudder, "he will murder her, if he thinks such a step necessary for ensuring his own safety."

By this time Lamare had entered the room, and though the evening had by that time drawn in, they followed the valet from the house, and began their journey through the city towards the obscure part where the artist resided. At length, however, they reached the place of destination, and proceeding up stairs, they found the young man at home, and diligently employed upon the portrait of the Marquis de Noailles, which he had promised to complete within a certain time. He seemed to be surprised at seeing them, but when he observed the portfolio in the hands of Lamare, he at once saw what had been the purpose of their visit.

"We should have sent these sketches home without troubling you with this visit," said Mr. Derwent, who was the most proficient of the two in the French language; "but the fact is two of the heads are very much like persons of our acquaintance, and we wished to enquire whether they were done from the life?"

"They were," replied the artist.

"Are you acquainted with them?"

"I don't know much of them," answered the artist. "The female lodges in this house, but keeps herself very private, and it is only occasionally that I see her."

"She lodges here, does she?" exclaimed Mr. Derwent;—"and the gentleman; does he also live in the house?"

"Oh, no," replied the painter; "he lives somewhere else, I suppose. He, however, calls here occasionally, but I have never had any opportunity of speaking to him."

"May I ask what object you had in taking these likenesses?" asked the lawyer.

"It was done out of mere idleness, I believe;—in fact, sir, I had nothing to do, and the sketches were made just to keep my hand in practice. However. I must confess that I was a good deal struck with the contrast between them, and as I have occasionally employed myself in painting a large picture, I intended introducing them into it in the attitude you see them there."

"And the female, you say, has taken apartments in this house?" said Mr. Derwent.

"She has."

"Has she been here long?"

"About a week, I should think."

"Is she likely to remain here long?"

"I should imagine not," answered the painter; "for as our chambers join each other, I overheard what passed when the place was taken. The gentleman that came with her told the landlady that he should only take it for a week at a time, because he knew not how soon or how suddenly he might be obliged to leave Paris."

"And if I understand you rightly," observed the lawyer, "you have not seen much of them?"

"Very little indeed," answered the other. "In fact all I have seen of either has been when they have been going in or out of the room. They seem to keep themselves very quiet, and from that circumstance together with the downcast looks of the female, I have sometimes thought there might be a reason for their wishing to avoid meeting with other people."

"Does she ever go out in the daytime?" asked Mr. Derwent.

"Never," replied the artist; "night is the period she chooses for that purpose, and even then she is absent as short a time as possible."

"Pray, sir, do you happen to know the name of either of the persons?" asked Mr. Derwent.

"I do not; nor I believe do the people belonging to the house know anything of them."

"What time does the gentleman come to visit her?" inquired the lawyer.

"Mostly of an evening."

"And this is all you know about them?"

"It is all I know with any certainty," replied the artist, "but from what our landlord, down stairs, told me yesterday, it seems she is to be married very shortly to the gentleman, and then I suppose they mean to return back to England."

"The villain!" exclaimed Mr. Derwent; "why he is already married to a most excellent woman, who he has cruelly deserted."

"Ah!—you know him then?"

"Most assuredly I do, if it's the person I mean," said Mr. Derwent. "The sketch I have seen is extremely like him, and most fortunate will it be for all parties if I can but trace him out."

"Well," observed the painter, "you can remain in this room as long as you please, and when he comes back, which will be by and by, you will have an opportunity of satisfying yourself whether your suspicions are correct."

"I would rather see the female first," answered the lawyer, "because, if it is the person I mean, I should like to speak with her, in order to learn the motives that had induced her to accompany this man to France. Do you think she is now in her own room?"

"That's more than I can answer for," said the artist, "because, as you are aware, I have not very long returned home. However, if you think proper to satisfy yourself upon that point, I will show you to her door."

Mr. Derwent and his friend accompanied the young man as he left the room, and after knocking at the door several times without receiving any answer, it was concluded that she was gone out.

" She can hardly be at home," whispered Mr. Smithson, " or she would have shown herself, I should imagine, before this time."

" No, she is not here, sure enough," returned the lawyer, " and that's plaguily vexing too, for if we could see her only for a minute or two, it might be the means of guiding us in the next course we are to take."

" Perhaps," observed Mr. Smithson, " the landlord may be able to afford us some information. We will see him, at any rate, for now I have taken this matter in hand, I shall not give it up till some clue has been obtained for the discovery of that villain, Gravestow."

They accordingly went down stairs, and were soon introduced to the owner of the house, who, having ascertained their errand, seemed ready enough to afford them every facility that it might be in his power to give.

" I understand, sir, that you have a couple of English persons living in your house," said Mr. Derwent.

" It is only the female that lives here," replied the party that had been addressed. " The gentleman only visits the house once or twice in the course of the day, and at night returns to his own lodgings in some other part of Paris."

" Do you know where he is living ?" asked the lawyer.

" I do not," replied the man ; " in fact, it is no business of mine, for he has promised to pay a week always in advance, so that there was no occa-sion for me to make any enquiries about who or what they are."

" Humph !—I suppose you are not acquainted with their names, then ?"

" No,—it was no business of mine, and as they have not thought proper to tell me, I had no excuse for asking a question that might appear im-pertinent."

" Do you know whether they come direct from England, or if they have been living in any other part of the city before they took the lodging in your house ?"

"'I am almost certain," replied the landlord, " that they have just come from England."

" And do they seem to have any business in France ?"

" I rather think not," replied the other. " My wife fancies they are going to be married, and I dare say she may have heard the young woman say something about it, or else such a thought would not have occurred."

" Perhaps," said the lawyer, " she has been still more communicative with your wife."

" She has never dropped a hint about her affairs, I know," answered the landlord, " for it is not half an hour since that my wife was saying to me what mysterious people they were in their ways. But then, what is that to us ? we get our money from them, and that's quite enough for folks like us that often lose by lodgers that appear to be much more pleasant in their manners."

" Then, it seems you know nothing more of them than that they took your lodgings, and are English people ?"

" Yes, sir, that's all I know, or care about knowing of them," returned the other.

" Will you allow me to step into your room to write a note to the young woman ?" asked Mr. Derwent.

" Certainly, sir," answered the landlord, showing them into his own apartment, and placing pens, ink, and paper before him. Mr. Smithson, therefore, wrote the note, which was very brief, and asking her to be at home on the following day, as it was his intention to call upon her. This the young artist promised to give her, and as nothing further was to be learnt that night, the two gentlemen left the house, followed by Lamare.

CHAPTER LIII.

A RESCUE FROM DEATH.

IT was a beautiful night when they left the house, and as they were in no great hurry to return home, their guide led them through different parts of the city, pointing out objects of curiosity, and explaining as well as he could, the history and uses of the various buildings they passed. At length they reached one of the bridges that cross the river Seine, and pausing here for a few minutes, they gazed down upon the waters that were silently gliding beneath. They were thus engaged, when a shout was heard at some distance, and almost at the same moment, a little boy running up to them, said, that a female was in the water, and implored them to go and help to get her out.

"Good Heavens!" cried Mr. Derwent, in accents of horror; "in which direction shall we fly to her rescue?"

"Follow me," said the boy, "and I'll lead you to the place."

And as he said this, the boy scampered off as fast as he could with Mr. Smithson, the lawyer, and Lamare close at his heels. The little guide turned abruptly immediately after leaving the bridge, and running down a narrow street, soon led them to the water-side, where a crowd of people were chattering and making a great noise, but not one of whom made any effort to save the unfortunate creature from the fate that was staring her in the face.

"Where is she?" cried Mr. Derwent, when he had elbowed his way down to the water-side.

"Yonder she is," answered the boy; "don't you see her, sir, clinging to the boat out there?"

The lawyer looked in the direction towards which the boy pointed, but though he could dimly discern a boat, he could see nothing of the woman. He, however, heard her screams, and the splashing of the water, and being thus convinced that the report they had circulated was but too true, he turned towards the person that was near him, and implored him to lose no time in rescuing the woman from death.

"Ah, sir!" exclaimed the man, "it's all very fine to talk about saving her, but what's to become of my wife and family if I should happen to lose my life in doing so?"

"Why surely you wouldn't suffer a fellow-creature to perish without making an effort to snatch her from this horrible fate?"

"I suppose she has chosen it," said the man coolly, and shrugging his shoulders.

"Chosen it!" exclaimed the lawyer.

"Aye, sir," answered the man; "a great many people put an end to their miseries in the river Seine; and I dare say she, like the rest of them, has some reason or other for being tired of life."

"It is not the case in the present instance," exclaimed Mr. Derwent; "for don't you hear how piteously she is calling for assistance?"

"They generally do that when they find they're sinking," replied the man. "It makes them reflect, and they would give anything to get out again when it's too late."

"It is not too late to save this woman, at any rate," exclaimed Mr. Derwent, "and I'll give five louis d'ors to any one that will make the attempt to save her."

The offer had an instantaneous effect upon the crowd, and those who had been previously looking on with the utmost apathy and unconcern, were now eagerly pressing forward to see what could be done. A boat was then loosened from the post to which it had been fastened, and in an instant half a dozen men had leaped into it, all anxious to share in the reward that had been offered. Mr. Derwent and his friend would have accompanied them, but ere they could reach the place, the little vessel had been pushed off and was rapidly gliding towards the spot from whence the cries of distress proceeded. In a few minutes they could see something dragged from the water into the boat, which quickly returned to the shore, and the body of the woman was laid upon the beach. It was too dark to distinguish her features, and by this time she had fainted from exhaustion, so that no question could be asked as to how she came into the water. Fortunately, however, a surgeon happened to have arrived at the spot, who attended to her with the greatest promptitude.

The boy who had been the first to give the alarm, seeing that all was right, now threw his bag over his shoulders, and bidding the two gentlemen good night, was going away, when Mr. Derwent called him back.

"Stay, my lad," he said, "you have done us a good service, and must be rewarded for it."

"Thank you, sir," answered the youngster, "but I didn't think of getting anything for doing my duty in raising the alarm when I saw the poor creature in the water."

"You are a good boy and deserve encouragement," exclaimed the lawyer. "But tell me how was it you were first aware of what had taken place?"

"Why, you see, sir," replied the youngster; "I was passing this way towards home, when I heard the cry for help, and as the moon was just then shining very brightly, I could see her struggling in the water quite plainly. Presently she caught hold of the side of a boat, and then I ran off to get assistance. You were the first person I saw, and as she has been saved, I'm quite satisfied."

"You are a brave lad, and here are twenty francs for your pains," said Mr. Derwent, taking out his purse, and presenting the boy with the sum we have named. "You are poor, I can see, and if you think proper to call at the place mentioned on this card, I will see to-morrow if something better can be done for you."

"But I can't read what's on the card," said the boy.

"Well, never mind, somebody else can do it for you," said Mr. Derwent. "But be sure you come, for I am so well pleased with your conduct this night, that I interest myself in your behalf."

"Well, sir, if you wish it, I'll come," said the boy; "but you have already given me more money than I ever had in my life before; and with this sum I can make my poor old mother happy. But you are an English gentleman, I think, ain't you, sir?"

"I am."

"Then yonder poor creature that has just been saved, is a countrywoman of yours."

"Indeed!"

"Yes, sir; when she first began to cry for help, she made use of words that I was not able to understand."

"Were you near her when she fell in?" asked the lawyer.

"I don't know, sir," he replied, "because the first that I knew about it was, when she was screaming in the water; I had been out at work all day, and was returning home, when I heard a terrible cry, that I was sure came from the river, and I stopped to see what was the matter, and, as I told you before, the moon was shining very brightly at the time, and I was just able to see that there was somebody drowning in the middle of the stream."

"And was there nobody else near the place at the time?" asked Mr. Derwent.

"Only one person," answered the boy, "and instead of stopping to do any service, he ran away as fast as his legs could carry him."

"What sort of person was he?"

"He looked like a gentleman," replied the boy, "but I thought he must be a shocking brute to run away just when he might have been of service."

"Did you notice his face or figure?"

"There was not time to do that, sir," he replied; "for he was off like a shot."

"Should you know him again if he was ever to come before you?" inquired Mr. Derwent.

"I'm not quite sure about that," answered the boy; "but I rather think I should, though he was not in my sight any long time."

"My reason for asking the question," said the lawyer, "is, that I think it very likely there has been some foul play in this affair; and if so, your evidence may be required to bring the guilty party to justice."

"I'll be willing enough to do anything you want of me," answered the youth; "but mind, I don't say I should know him again, for it was hardly an instant that I saw him, and that's too short a time to swear a man's life away, unless one's quite certain of being in the right about it."

"Did you speak to him at all?"

"Oh, yes, I called after him."

"And he paid no heed to your words?"

"Not the least," replied the boy, "he seemed to run all the faster for hearing my voice, but whether it was that he was frightened, or was afraid of being seen here, I don't know."

"Well, at any rate I shall make every enquiry into this affair," exclaimed Mr. Derwent; "and it is likely enough that your evidence will be of the highest importance. So don't fail to call upon me to-morrow morning and any trouble you have shall be well rewarded."

The boy made his best bow and retired, when the lawyer, turning to his friend, Smithson, said :—

"There is a something in this so mysterious, that I am determined to sift the matter to the very bottom. The woman has not sought self-destruction, or she would have perished without calling for assistance."

"I am exactly of your opinion," answered Mr. Smithson, "and was just now trying to make my way through the crowd to ask her a few questions; but the surgeon has desired that she shall not be disturbed just yet, and so I thought we would ascertain where she lives, and to-morrow we will call upon the poor creature, and make the necessary questions."

"You have not seen her then?"

"I have not."

"And have not heard, I suppose, whether she is young?" continued the lawyer.

"Why they say she is rather young; and from what I have been able to gather among the crowd, it seems that she is an Englishwoman."

"I have heard so too," said Mr. Derwent; "and in that case it is our duty to make every enquiry into the cause of her being found in the water."

"Is there any doubt upon that point?" asked Mr. Smithson.

"In my own mind I entertain a good deal," replied the lawyer, "for I

have just now heard that a man was seen hurrying away from the spot at
the time when his assistance was required. That circumstance, at least,
looks very suspicious, and as the unfortunate creature is a countrywoman
of our own, it behoves us to make every exertion towards ascertaining the
truth or otherwise of my suspicions."

"It certainly has a very ugly look, my dear sir," answered Mr. Smithson, "and, as far as possible, I shall be most happy to render all the assistance in my power. But what think you will be the best thing we can
do for her for the present?"

"Why, I should say, we ought to have her taken home as quickly as
possible."

"But we have got to find out where her home is," exclaimed a man that
had just pushed his way out of the crowd.

"Which, of course, she can tell us," observed Mr. Smithson.

"I don't know when that will be though," answered the stranger, "for
she has just gone off into another fainting fit, and no one about the place
remembers ever having seen her before."

"Perhaps she'll recover herself presently," said another person who had
been listening to their conversation. "She'll soon be out of the fit, and if
once we know in what part of Paris she lives, there's plenty here that will
help to get her home."

"If I recollect rightly," exclaimed Mr. Derwent, "you are one of the
men that helped to save her?"

"I am sir," replied the man, "and perhaps you haven't forgot promising
five louis d'ors to those that went out for her preservation."

"I have neither forgotten the bargain, nor have I any wish to evade it,"
answered the lawyer, handing the man the sum he had promised. "You
will divide this among the companions that assisted you, and perhaps, in

No. 50

future, if you should happen to see a poor creature drowning, you will attempt a rescue without waiting till a reward is offered."

"Why, the truth is, sir," replied the man, "that there's already too many people throwing themselves into the river, and if it was known that there were people ready to jump in and save them, there's no knowing where the evil would stop. So the best way is to let them take their chance, and if they will leap into cold water, why the best way is to let 'em find their way to the bottom."

"Did this woman say anything when you first dragged her out of the water?" asked Mr. Derwent.

"She was almost gone when we reached her," answered the man; "but she certainly did mutter something that no one could understand."

"Should you think she threw herself into the water, or is it likely the act may have been that of some villain that wished to get rid of her?" enquired Mr. Derwent.

"Why, that's more than I can answer for," replied the man; "but from her being so anxious to be saved, I shouldn't at all wonder if she was thrown in. Such things have happened before now, and they may again. However, be that as it may, she seems likely enough to recover, and of course she will be able to tell you all about it when you see her to-morrow."

"But it seems," observed Mr. Smithson, "that the unfortunate woman is unable to say where she resides."

"Why, she is insensible at present," answered the other; "but she'll recover herself by and by, and then I dare say she will tell where they are to take her."

"And in the mean time what are they going to do with her?" asked Mr. Derwent.

"She must remain where she is, I suppose," answered the man. "It won't be for long, and as they have thrown some cloaks and great coats over her, she won't take much harm for an hour or so."

"This must not be," exclaimed the lawyer, taking the arm of his friend and moving towards the crowd. "We will take her home with us to our lodgings, where she shall be attended to, and to-morrow, if she is well enough, she may return to her own place."

They now urged their way through the mob, but though they saw the poor creature lying before them, she was so covered over with the clothes that it was impossible to catch even a glimpse of her countenance. This, however, was a matter of very little consequence to them just then, and desiring a man to fetch a coach, Mr. Derwent expressed his determination to take care of her that night, and then addressing himself to the surgeon, he inquired whether she might now be removed to some place where she would be sheltered from the chilly night air. To this there was no objection, and a vehicle shortly afterwards arrived near the place, the poor creature was lifted into it, and Mr. Smithson and his friend entered the coach to take care of her, while Lamare rode on the box along with the driver. On arriving at the hotel where they lodged, she was taken out and given into the care of the landlady, who, under a promise of being well rewarded for any trouble she might be at, undertook that every care should be bestowed upon her that her necessaries required.

"Why, what in the name of fortune ails her?" exclaimed the hostess, as she helped to carry her to the nearest room. "I declare the poor creature is soaked through with water."

"That's likely enough, my good madam," answered Mr. Smithson, "for she has just been taken out of the river."

"Ah!" cried the landlady, "she has been attempting to make away with herself, I suppose."

"It may have been an accident for aught we know," replied the lawyer; "however, you will be kind enough to attend upon her, and when she recovers, we shall come down and speak to her."

Upon this he and Mr. Smithson hurried up stairs to Dolly Pratt, who had been for some time anxiously looking for their return.

"You are late, gentlemen," she said, "and I was just thinking of going to bed, only that I was anxious to hear what you did at the artist's."

"Very little, indeed," answered the lawyer, "except that we have ascertained the parties from whom the sketches were made, live in the house."

"That is to say, the female lives there," interposed Mr. Smithson, "and the gentleman is frequently there as a visitor."

"And are they the parties you suspected?" inquired Dolly.

"That we have yet to find out," answered the lawyer. "We have, however, discovered that they are both from England, and my friend here is more convinced than ever, that the female will turn out to be no other than the Amelia Robertson, whose late sudden disappearance from her house caused so much astonishment."

"And if our surmises in that respect are true," added Mr. Smithson, "there can be very little doubt, I should imagine, that the gentleman is Walter Gravestow, of whom we are at present in search."

"And in that case," observed Dolly, "he will soon take alarm at the inquiries you have been making at the house, and by to-morrow morning he will most likely be far enough from Paris."

"I am afraid we shall lose him," replied Mr. Smithson, "but what more could we do under present circumstances? He may, as you have observed, leave this city, but at any rate, we are upon the right track, and we only want a favourable opportunity to bring our charges home against him, and I'll warrant he never has another chance of playing off his scurvy tricks."

"And have you any hopes of seeing the female, in order to ascertain whether she is the person you suspect?" asked Dolly.

"Oh, yes, there's very little doubt about that, I believe," replied Mr. Smithson. "We have left a note at the house, informing her of our intention to call there to-morrow morning, and requesting that she will be in the way to see us."

"But do you think she will do so?"

"I see no reason to doubt it," he replied.

"Well," exclaimed the female, "I hope you may not be disappointed; but, for my own part, I think it very extraordinary that she should have left her house in company with Walter Gravestow, and her doing so argues, in my mind, that she must be almost as bad as himself."

"Then pray do not think so any longer," exclaimed Mr. Smithson, "for I have now been acquainted with her some time, and, whatever faults she may formerly have been guilty of, I can assure you that a more worthy creature does not exist."

"How, then, do you account for her leaving home with this man?" asked Dolly.

"I must candidly confess that I am unable to account for it," answered Mr. Smithson. "The affair, like everything else connected with Gravestow, is involved in the deepest mystery; but I have no doubt in my own mind that he has imposed upon her by means of some artfully-contrived scheme, and has thus prevailed on her to quit England with him."

"At all events," continued the lawyer, "it seems to be pretty certain that she knows a great deal too much for him, and, as a natural conse-

quence, he would be most anxious to get her out of the way. What his
ultimate object may be, Heaven only knows; but I must confess I am
much alarmed lest he should resolve to make away with her."

"Why, surely," cried Dolly, "you don't think he would murder the
poor creature?"

"Walter Gravestow is a desperate man, and there is no saying what act
of villany he would not do to screen himself from justice," answered Mr.
Derwent. "At present we have nothing but suspicions against him, but
matters are gradually clearing up, and before long, ruin must fall upon him.
This he is himself well aware of, and I am only afraid he will commit further crimes if he thinks it necessary to shield him from those which have
lready stained his soul."

"In that case," cried Dolly, "there ought not to be a minute lost in
getting the poor woman away from him."

"We are well aware of it," replied Mr. Smithson; "and to-morrow
morning it will be our task to take her from the place where she is, and
thus preserve her from the danger which threatens."

At this moment the hostess entered the apartment, and informed the two
gentlemen that the female they had saved from drowning had revived and
asked to see them. This request was promptly acceded to, and no sooner
did he enter the room than, to his astonishment, he discovered that the woman he had rescued from a watery grave was no other than Amelia Robertson.

CHAPTER LIV.

A PERPLEXING SITUATION.

By the time Susan Hoply had been released from the custody of the revenue officers it was growing late; but so anxious was she to return to the
road-side inn and allay the terrors of her young ladies, that she thought
nothing of the length and dreariness of the road before her, but set forward with a good heart towards the place she had determined to reach. It
must, however, be confessed that the solitude and gloom of the road, at
length, began to make her regret that she hadnot postponed her object till
the next morning, but having proceeded some distance on her way, she
thought it would be better to go on than return, and calling what courage
she possessed to her aid, she increased her speed, and at last had the satisfaction of finding herself once more standing within a short distance from
the inn of Madame Deleroix. Joyfully stepping forward, she was about to
enter the house, when strange voices within met her ear, and looking
through the window, she could see three or four strangers sitting round the
fire, among whom she recognized two of the men that had detained her as
she was entering the town, and who she had good reason to suppose were
revenue officers.

What they could possibly want there she was unable to imagine, and beginning to suspect that something must be going wrong, she tried to get a
glimpse at two other persons who were also sitting there, but who evidently did not belong to the other party. It was in vain, however, that
she sought to satisfy her curiosity in this respect, for both the latter mentioned persons had their backs towards her, and all that she could make out
was, that one appeared to be an elderly gentleman, and the other a very
young one. She thought to herself they must be travellers that had put up
there for the night, but though that was probable enough the absence of

Madame Deleroix and her husband was most unacountable, and the presence of revenue officers in the house gave rise to fears and suspicions that she in vain tried to lull. Nothing was to be seen of either of the young ladies, nor was there, in fact, any light in the room they usually occupied, and, taking one thing with another, Susan began to be afraid that some fresh disaster had befallen them. She, indeed, felt confident of it, and was about to enter inn, when the old gentleman, who seemed to have been sleeping in his chair, suddenly rose up, and taking a candle from the table, proceeded up the stairs, which were situated at the further part of the room. Still, however, his face was turned from her, and he passed from her sight, and he disappeared without once turning round, or seeming to take any notice of his companions. Shortly after this, the younger man rose and left the room in the same manner, and raising her eyes towards the window of the chamber that had been occupied by her young ladies, she could see him moving about in it, and, therefore, her fears were confirmed that they were no longer in the house.

By this time she could perceive that the two remaining men were becoming intoxicated, and, being unwilling to present herself before them at that moment, she resolved to subdue her curiosity till the morning, and passing round to the back part of the house, she raised a latch and entered the little room which was usually occupied by the servant girl. To her surprise no one was there, and the fact of its usual occupant being absent raised fresh suspicions in her mind, and she became more convinced than ever that some strange revolution must have taken place in the house during the time she had been away. But what it all meant, or what had became of her young ladies, she was at a loss even to guess, and what made matters still worse was, that she durst not enter the house to make enquiries while the strange men she had seen were present.

In fact, she felt quite convinced that none of the persons she had left here were now in the place; but where they had gone to, or what was the cause of their sudden departure, were questions that yet remained to be solved. And when or how she should be able to satisfy herself upon these points were equally uncertain, for not a word of the language of the country could she speak, and her only hope of solving the mystery rested upon her getting to Paris, which was a long way off, and she knew of no way of getting there as no coaches ever passed along that road, and the idea of going a long journey on foot, with all the difficulties she would have to encounter, was a project that would require a great deal more consideration than she at present had been able to give it.

It struck her, however, from the circumstance of seeing strangers in the house, that it was probable the young ladies' friends had succeeded in tracing them to the place, in which case it was likely enough the host and hostess had been given into custody on suspicion of having been concerned in the plot with the supposed Marquis Valliere and his friend; and in that event, she would be worse off than ever, since she was left behind whilst the others had most likely made the best of their way back to England.

Perplexed with these thoughts, she almost made up her mind to go round once more to the front of the house and endeavour to make herself understood by the persons she had just seen there. If the men were soldiers, she argued within herself, they would be willing enough to assist her in the object she had in view; but then, on the other hand, she could not help thinking of the severity with which she had been treated by some of them during her recent visit to the town, and the thought of this, and the certainty of her present unprotected situation, made her pause ere she adopted this alternative. To be sure she had seen two other persons who might be willing enough to befriend a helpless female when she was destitute of all other friends, yet she was not certain upon this point, and as one of the strangers appeared, from the slight view she had been able to obtain of him, a very young man, her motives for seeking his protection might be misconstrued, and thus lead to further difficulties which it was so essentially necessary to avoid.   Besides, however willing he might be to afford her assistance, he was but one against three, and thus his good intentions would not only be frustrated, but it was likely his own life would be hazarded in any attempt he might make in her favour.

She then thought of retracing her steps to the town she had lately left, but a very little consideration served to assure her that she would obtain no good by doing so, for she was an utter stranger to every one there, and from what little she knew of the world, she felt perfectly convinced that she would only be seeking the assistance of persons who would look upon her as an impostor that was utterly unworthy of being believed.

These various thoughts having been thus disposed of, she once more proceeded with cautious steps to the front of the house, and having placed herself in a situation where she was not likely to be discovered, she again looked in at the window, and saw that the soldiers had risen from their seats, and were preparing to go to bed ; the embers of the fire were carefully raked out, and the bottles and glasses put away in a cupboard, and when all this was done, they bolted the door and proceeded up stairs, leaving the lower part of the house in total darkness.   The lamp they had taken with them was then seen shining in the apartment usually occupied by Madame Deleroix and her husband, so that if she had any doubt as to whether they were in the house or not, it now entirely at an end through the circumstance that had just occurred.   The young ladies, it was certain, were not there, and it seemed as if nothing more was wanted to fill up the measure of doubt and suspense in which she found herself involved.

As the night was anything but a tempting one to remain without shelter, she once more returned to the little detached room that had been occupied by the servant.   She would not, however, venture to undress herself, for fear there might be occasion for a precipitate flight, and merely throwing off her shoes, she laid herself down upon the pallet, more for the rest it would afford her than from any idea of obtaining a respite from her perplexities in slumber.   But fatigue, at length, overpowered her, and after starting three or four times at the horrible visions that crowded upon her brain, she eventually sank into a disturbed sleep, in which the principal incidents that had lately occurred were revived in her imagination with a startling similitude of truth.

How long she had remained in this state she knew not, but at last she was roused by fancying she heard sounds near her.   Anxiously did she listen, in order to ascertain from whence they proceeded, but all became as silent again as the grave, and believing she must have been mistaken in her conjecture, she once more sought the solace of sleep.   Scarcely, however, had she fallen off into a doze, when she became painfully convinced that her first suspicions had been well founded, for the sounds were now nearer and more distinct, and she could even hear persons whispering, but what they were speaking about, or where they were, she could not with all her efforts make out.   She then heard several blows which she felt certain came from beneath the mattrass on which she was resting, and starting up she gazed wildly about her, not knowing whether to flee from the room or remain where she was to watch the issue of an adventure that had filled her with so much alarm.   Presently she could distinctly feel the pallet move beneath her, and then, unable to endure the tortures of fright any longer, she sprung from the bed, and making her way towards the door, was about

The Murder of Mr. Wentford by Gravestow and his accomplices.

to raise an alarm, when the thought struck her that it would be better not to do so till she was well assured that there was real cause for her apprehensions of danger.

Placing herself therefore behind the door, Susan determined to watch the issue of this adventure, and luckily there was just moonlight enough for her to see anything which might pass in the room, without being observed in the retreat to which she had flown. With earnest attention she kept her eyes upon the bed, and two or three times she saw, or fancied she saw, it move as if some person from beneath was trying to raise it up. Scarcely could she refrain from screaming out with terror, and she would have done so had it not been for the thought of the danger she would thus bring upon herself. At last the mattress was raised to a considerable height, and in spite of her wish to believe to the contrary, she could no longer charge herself with having given way to fears that were utterly groundless.

This latter event had the effect of frightening her away from the hiding place where she had been standing, and running outside the door, she was going to alarm the inmates of the house, when reflection came to her aid, and she thought it would be better to remain close at hand and see what it was that occasioned her so much alarm ere she adopted the hasty resolution she had formed.

She listened with breathless attention for any sounds that might proceed from the chamber she had left, and hearing nothing move, she ventured once more to the door. All was as it had been when she left the room, but still Susan could not doubt the evidence of her own senses, for she had distinctly seen the bed moved, and it was quite certain that it could only have been done through means of human agency. Then she thought it probable that the host and hostess might have sought refuge in a subterranean retreat, and that they were now endeavouring to make their escape whilst the darkness of night aided their plans. This notion served to quiet her fears in some trifling degree, and approaching the place with stealthy footsteps, she ventured to look into the room.

"At that instant another violent agitation of the bed was distinctly observable, and after two or three efforts had been made, it was completely turned over, and Susan could see by the faint light of the moon, that there was a chasm in the floor exactly at the spot where the mattress had been laying. This was a frightful incident for our heroine, and terribly alarmed she was, but she contrived to restrain the scream she was about to utter, and having drawn herself up more closely in her hiding place, she resolved to watch the issue of an adventure in which it was possible some important discovery might take place.

For some minutes after this all was still, and Susan began to think more than ever that the suspicion she had entertained before, was correct, and that Madame Deleroix and her husbands having had some intimation that the house would soon be in the possession of a foe, had made this subterranean abode their retreat for a time, and that they were now about to effect their escape whilst the soldiers were asleep. At all events this was the only conclusion she could come to, and so certain did she feel of its being a correct one, that she was thinking of advancing to the edge of the chasm, in order to see if she could render any assistance towards extricating the fugitives from the perils in which they had become involved. But ere she could do this, she saw a head appear above the level of the floor, which, however, instantly vanished again, though not before she had satisfied herself that the countenance was one that she had never seen before till that moment. Under these circumstances she kept close to her place of concealment, determined to ascertain more of the truth before she ventured to discover herself to persons of whose motives she was entirely ignorant.

Presently afterwards she could hear a whispering beneath, and as the persons spoke in the English language, she was enabled to make out the nature of the conversation that was passing between them.

" I tell you it's all right," said one of the men.   " I've just looked round the room, and there ain't a living creature in it as big as a mouse."

" And I say," answered the other, " that I heard footsteps overhead as plainly as could be."

" Then look and satisfy yourself," exclaimed the first speaker.   " There's light enough in the room, and if you see anybody there I'll eat my hat."

At this moment, Susan could perceive a head thrust up through the opening, and as soon as a sufficient survey of the place had been made, it again disappeared as before.

" Well," said the other, " are you convinced now that I was right ?"

" I didn't see anybody," answered his companion ; "but still I know well enough that some one was in the room just now, and I should not much fancy being laid hold of and dragged to a prison."

" Hush !" exclaimed the other ; " don't speak so loud, for fear we should be overheard."

" And if we should," answered his companion, " there's no one would understand the language we are speaking.   Thanks to our knowing a little bit of English, we can manage to speak to each other without fear of betraying ourselves."

" But if our voices should be heard," said the first speaker, " it will be quite sufficient to bring the enemy upon us, and as Madame Deleroix has been taken off to prison, we should be likely enough to share the same fate, if those fellows should happen to get a notion that we are lurking about the place."

" Then perhaps you think we had better stay where we are, till the coast is clear again ?"

" No I don't," answered the other ; " for hang me if I like being stifled in this dark, underground place.   It's all very well as a hiding-place, when there's no other chance of escape, but to stay in it longer than necessary, is like a man burying himself alive."

" Well then," said his companion, " as there's no one about, suppose we make a start of it at once.   It will be easy enough to make our way down to the sea-side, and when once we are there, we have friends enough that will lend us a boat, and if we only contrive to set foot on English ground, we may laugh at the fellows that have been hunting after us so long."

" That's true enough," answered the other, " so here goes ; and remember, if anything should happen, we know what we've got to do."

" Kill 'em, to be sure," replied his comrade.   " We must make short work of it, of course ; and when that's done, our escape must be our first object, or we shall be likely to get into trouble."

There was then a brief pause, after which one of the men crept up into the room, and having looked cautiously round, he beckoned to the other, who immediately followed, and then, having carefully laid the stone over the aperture, one of the men, addressing himself to the other, asked what they should next do.

" What shall we do, St. Ange," asked the second ; " why, seek for revenge, to be sure.   Haven't we been hunted like dogs, and when the enemy is so near, why shouldn't we make short work of it ?"

" Hah !—you would shed more blood, Victor ?"

" Why, what's the odds to men that have never been very particular about spilling blood, whenever our own safety has made it necessary ?   Besides, we have got into a bit of a scrape here, and if it should be discovered that

we are in the neighbourhood, it won't be long that we should enjoy the blessing of liberty."

"And what," asked St. Ange, "do you think of doing before we leave the place?"

"Can you ask such a question," he demanded, "when we know there's a couple of soldiers in the house that are upon the look out for us?"

"You would murder them in their sleep?"

"To be sure I would."

"But there are other people in the house that have never injured us, but who we should be obliged to kill, for fear they should be witnesses against us."

"And what of that, when our own safety depends upon it?" asked Victor Laroche. "We may as well be hung for a sheep as a lamb, for aught I know; and, at any rate, if they all die, the affair will not be found out till we have had plenty of time to make our escape from the country."

"That may be all very true," returned St. Ange, "but for my own part, I think it would be better to get away without troubling our heads about the people that are sleeping here."

"There I differ from you," answered his companion, "for I know well enough that the fellows would be pleased to have it in their power to deliver us up to justice. They are sent out like bloodhounds to hunt after their prey, and as we know them to be enemies, we should be fools to give the fellows a chance of handing us over to the tender mercies of the law."

"Aye, if I thought there was any danger of that," exclaimed St. Ange, "I should think it only right that we take care of ourselves. But as the soldiers are fast asleep, and we have got the night before us, we may get clear off without having more human blood to answer for."

No. 51

"And it has not struck you, I suppose, that neither of us have got any money to assist us in escaping out of the country?"

"I know all about that well enough," replied St. Ange; "but committing another murder won't fill our purses with gold."

"Yes, but it will though," exclaimed Victor; "for there's a couple of travellers in the place, that the soldiers suffered to remain here for the night, because there was no other house anywhere near for their accommodation."

"And you would rob and murder them?"

"I would."

"But," asked St. Ange, "are you sure they have money enough to make it worth our while to do such a deed as this?"

"Oh, yes," replied Victor, "I am quite certain about that, for when I crept out of our retreat three or four hours ago, I went round to the front of the house, and had a look at them through the window."

"What sort of people were the strangers?" demanded St. Ange.

"Why, respectable-looking people enough," replied his comrade, "and just such as at first sight you would say were well worth having a tussle with. One of them is an oldish man, and whilst I was looking in at the window he took out his purse, and began to count over his gold. I could hardly help rushing in to snatch it out of his hand; but, thinking I should have a better opportunity by and by, I let him alone to enjoy the possession of it till we think proper to make it our own."

"And what sort of person is the other traveller?" asked his companion.

"Why, young enough to be his son," answered Victor; "and I've been thinking that if we give him an opportunity, there will be more trouble in that quarter than will be pleasant. However, the thing must be tried, and, to avoid danger, we'll plunge our daggers into their hearts while they sleep."

"And suppose the soldiers should be alarmed by their outcry?" exclaimed St. Ange.

"We must be prepared against that," replied Victor. "By fastening the room-door we shall keep the fellows off for a little time, and if matters should come to the worst, there are two of us against them, and the devil's in it if a couple of desperate chaps like us can't manage the fellows, when we know that our lives depend upon it."

"At any rate," said St. Ange, "they'll not find it very easy to conquer us, for our pistols are well loaded, and if we should come to close quarters our knives will finish them."

"And so you begin to think then," exclaimed the other, "that my proposal is not such a very bad one."

"If it had been possible to have avoided bloodshed, I should have liked it all the better," answered St. Ange. "However, here we are without money to help us in our escape, and so, as there's no way of getting out of it, I suppose I must agree with you."

"And you'll not turn coward when the moment doing the job arrives?"

"I shall be at least as firm as yourself," answered St. Ange, "but if there's any way of getting at the money without killing these people of course you'll not attempt to harm them."

"No, no, we won't hurt them, if it can be helped," said the other; "but if they attempt to stir, or dare raise their voices to alarm the other people, I sharn't scruple to bury my knife in their hearts."

St. Ange knew very well that an alarm would be raised, and he said something more in reply to his companion; but what his words were Susan could not hear, for by that time they had passed the place where she was standing concealed, and she was left to the harrowing reflections that were consequent upon the words she had been listening to. That they were men of desperate resolution, she was but too well aware, for their words had conveyed that much to her, and the arms which she saw about them, proved that they were well prepared to act on any emergency. She thus felt assured that no less than four lives were threatened by the ruffians whose conversation she had heard, and it now become her next consideration how she might most certainly avert a fearful tragedy, the thought of which had so much alarmed her.

There was, however, no time for deliberation, for the villains would be prompt in the execution of their dreadful purpose, and stepping out from her place of concealment, she with cautious but rapid footsteps followed the men whose designs there was so much reason to apprehend.

CHAPTER LV.

SUSAN MEETS AN OLD FAVOURITE.

WHEN Susan arrived at the corner of the house, she peeped round and saw the two men attempting to force open the door, but it was so well secured within, that all their efforts against it were useless, and muttering their imprecations at this disappointment, they next proceeded to the window, which, after a very little time, they were able to open without making any noise that would alarm the people within. This done, they looked about them to see if any persons were within view, and having satisfied themselves in this respect, they held a consultation with each other for some few minutes, and looked towards the upper windows as if to ascertain whether all was quiet within. They then examined their pistols to see that they were primed and ready to use, and when this was done, they stepped in at the window, and Susan lost sight of them.

What to do next she could scarcely tell, for should she follow them to the window, and be discovered, her own life would be sacrificed without remorse by the villains that were in search of plunder, and if she hesitated to run the risk all the inmates of the house were in danger of falling a sacrifice to the murderers. She, therefore, determined to think nothing of personal hazard, and creeping stealthily under the shadow of the wall, she reached the window, and stooping down beneath it, listened with breathless anxiety to hear whether they had left the room. All was silent as the grave, and being thus pretty well assured that no danger was to be apprehended, she rose, and looking into the house, saw that the ruffians had lighted a lamp which was placed upon the table; but they were no where to be seen, and judging that they were searching about the house for plunder, she resolved to follow them, and if possible avert the dreadful crime they contemplated.

Stepping, therefore, into the room, she advanced towards the table on which the lamp was burning, and she then discovered that they had left their pistols there till their return. This was an advantage that she did not anticipate, and removing them to a place where they would be concealed, she blew out the lamp at the very moment when she heard their returning footsteps. It was a moment of extreme peril to herself, yet her coolness did not forsake her for a single instant, and springing towards the staircase, she then stationed herself to listen to whatever passed between them, knowing that from the place where she was she could give an alarm whenever there might be occasion to do so, and at the same time cause the apprehension of the two men of whose blood-thirsty designs she was but too certain.

Thus advantageously situated, her fears had considerably abated by the time the ruffians returned, and she could hear their muttered oaths without experiencing those apprehensions which at any other time would have overpowered her.

"Damnation !" she heard Victor whisper; "who has done this? where's the lamp we just now left burning on the table?"

"I suppose the draught from the open window has blown it out," answered the other, in the same low tones. "But it don't much matter, for with the aid of our phosphorous box we shall soon be able to light it again."

"But the lamp is not on the table," exclaimed Victor, "and though the wind might blow it out, it would not remove in this way."

"Psha! you must be mistaken," replied St. Ange, groping about the table to find the lamp.

"Whether I'm mistaken or not you don't seem to know where it is any more than I do," said Victor. "The truth is it's gone, and now the next thing for our consideration is, how has it been removed?"

"And the pistols have been removed!" exclaimed St. Ange, in a tone of extreme alarm.

"The devil they have!" cried the other. "Then we have been watched by some one who has taken them away during our absence, and it's a hundred to one if we don't fall into hands of the enemy."

"Shall we escape while there is an opportunity?" asked St. Ange.

"No," replied his comrade, "we have our daggers left yet, and desperate as we are, I should like to see who will dare lay hands upon us. Any how we must die, and as I don't choose to perish on the scaffold, they may shoot me if they please, but it shall not be till I have spilt some of their blood."

"Hush!" whispered the other;—"speak lower, or we shall be overheard."

"I care not how soon we see the enemy," answered Victor; "let them come as soon as they please, and take the fate that's in store for them."

"I rather think our fears are unfounded," observed St. Ange, who had been listening with the greatest attention. "I don't hear anybody moving about the place, and, perhaps, after all there ain't quite so much danger as we at first thought there was."

"All's quiet enough, certainly," answered Victor, "but the lamp and pistols could not have been removed without hands, and so somebody must have been watching us, it's only right that we should be on our guard."

"Here's the lamp," said St. Ange, who at that moment found it upon one of the chairs near the table; "perhaps we knocked it over while groping about in the dark. At all events here it is; so set light to it, and when we have had a good search about the place to see if any one is watching us, we'll go and finish the business we have in hand."

Fearful of being discovered when they got a light, Susan proceeded on tiptoe up the stairs, and from thence saw their shadows flit about the room as they passed from place to place in the prosecution of their useless search. At length she could hear one of them propose to the other that they should proceed to the upper part of the house, and finding that no other alternative remained, she rushed into the first room that presented itself, and in terrified accents called upon the sleepers to awake and defend themselves from the assassins that were preparing to shed their blood.

"Who the devil are you, and where do you come from?" demanded one of the soldiers; but Susan understood not the language in which the words were uttered, and pointing towards the lower room, she, by expressive signs, made the men understand that there were robbers in the house. Both the soldiers had thrown themselves down in their clothes, and springing from the bed, they seized their arms, and rushed down stairs. Susan, without knowing what she was about, ran quickly to accompany them, but at that instant another door opened, and the two strange gentlemen presenting themselves before her, demanded of her in English what was the occasion of all the uproar.

"Oh, sir," she exclaimed wildly, "there are assassins below stairs, and the soldiers that slept in the next room have gone in pursuit of them."

"Good Heavens!—assassins!—then we shall all be murdered to a certainty," exclaimed the elder, in a tone that Susan thought she remembered to have heard before.

"I rather think you are safe now, sir," answered Susan; "for no doubt the villains have fled, and if so, the soldiers will soon bring them back as prisoners."

"We will be down as soon as we can dress ourselves," said the younger man, "and if my assistance can be of any service, I will cheerfully give it to rid society of such pests."

"Pray don't leave me, my good sir," exclaimed his companion, "for I should never be able to endure the alarm at finding myself alone in a place where such villany has been going on. For Heaven's sake, sir, stay with me, and if we must perish, let it be together."

"I don't think there's much occasion to be alarmed now, sir," observed Susan; "for I took care to remove their pistols, so that it will not be a very hard matter for the soldiers to make them prisoners."

"Why, bless my heart," exclaimed the elder gentleman, "if I couldn't almost have sworn that that was the voice of my old servant Susan!"

"It is!—it is!" cried our heroine in an accent of delight; "and if I am not much mistaken, you are my old master, Mr. Plumley, of Dalston."

"You are right, Susan," he replied; "so now tell me how you came to this place, and where are my daughters?"

"Ah, sir!" she sighed; "it's a long story to tell, and one that I'm afraid will make you very unhappy."

"Why, you don't mean to tell me that you know nothing of your young ladies?"

"I am sorry to say I am quite ignorant of what has become of them,' replied Susan. "A few days since I went to the next town with some letters to put into the post for you, because the marchioness wanted to tell you something particular. But it was an unfortunate journey for me, for no sooner had I got to the entrance of the town, than some persons seized me, and I was carried before a magistrate. They accused me, I believe, of being connected with smugglers, and after keeping me their prisoner for two or three days, I was set at liberty, and allowed to find my back to this place as well as I could."

"Well, and what happened then, Susan?" demanded the old gentleman.

"Why, sir, I managed to get back here just as it had got dark to-night," she replied; "but the place was deserted by every one that I had left in the house, and what has become of my young ladies I know not. I was afraid to enter the house, because when I looked through the window I saw the soldiers, and yourself,—who I did not know at the time,—and as I fancied that something very bad had happened, I would not go into the house, but went round to the back part, where I knew the servant girl used to sleep, but even she was gone away, and I was left to find out the mystery in the best way I could."

"Well," exclaimed Mr. Plumley, "we may consider it a very fortunate

thing that you did not enter the house ; for, if you had done so, it's most
likely we should all of us have been murdered together."

" I dare say we should, sir," answered Susan, " for I overheard a conversation between the two men, and they had made up their minds to murder all that opposed a robbery they intended to commit upon you."

" Why, where did you hear that ?" asked the old gentleman.

" In the room, where I laid myself down to get a little sleep," answered
Susan. " The mattrass upon which I was lying covered the entrance of a
subterranean vault, and being disturbed by their moving it, I concealed
myself, and overheard this conversation that passed between them. They
spoke of robbery and murder, and in the hope of preventing their evil deeds
I followed them into the house and raised the alarm which has happily been
the means of saving the lives of their intended victims."

Whilst the conversation was passing, the younger gentleman had been
dressing himself in the room, and now taking up his pistols which were
lying upon the table, he was hurrying towards the stairs, when Mr. Plumley seizing him by the arm, besought him most earnestly not to leave him.
The other was, however, resolute in his determination, and as the soldiers
and the prisoners were at that moment heard entering the lower room, he
broke from the hold of the other, and darted down stairs with all the
speed he could.

" You'll be murdered, my dear friend !" exclaimed the old gentleman,
in the greatest alarm. " For Heaven's sake, sir, come back ! Mr. Wentford, come back, or you will be murdered by these ruffians."

" Mr. Wentford ?" cried Susan, in astonishment.

" Aye, that's his name," exclaimed the old gentleman ; " but what makes
you so anxious about that ? Do you know anything of him ?"

" I think it's very likely," she replied, " for my late master had an
adopted son that was known by that name, and he left England to go
abroad, and nothing has since been heard of him."

Having said this, she ran down stairs, where she found the two men in
custody, and the young stranger standing over them with a brace of pistols
in his hands. In an instant Susan snatched the lamp from the table, and
approaching the object of her curiosity she immediately recognised the features of her long absent favourite.

" It is Master Edwin !" she exclaimed in accents of joyful surprise.

" Susan Hoply, by all that's wonderful !" returned the young man ;
and dropping the pistols, he shook her hands with all the cordiality of an
old acquaintance.

" Oh, how glad I am to see you again," she said ; " and how you have
grown since we last parted ! I declare I should scarcely have known you
if it had not been that Mr. Plumley happened to mention your name when
you ran down stairs in such a hurry. But I am glad we have met, for, as
a child, you were always a favourite of mine, and often have I thought of
you, and wondered whether I should ever see you again."

" Well," he said, " I am quite as much pleased about it as you are,
Susan ! so we'll first see to the securing of these two rascals, and when
that has been done, we can set out together and talk of old times."

Upon this the two ruffians, who had been securely bound with cords,
were conveyed from the house to the room at the back of the premises,
which being without any windows, was the safest place into which they
could be put. There they were locked up under the direction of Edwin, and
the two soldiers shouldering their muskets, paced up and down in front of
the building, to frustrate any attempt that might be made to liberate themselves from confinement. This done, the young man returned to the huose,
where he found Mr. Plumley, who by this time had dressed himself and

was gathering from Susan the particulars of all that had taken place with respect to the two prisoners.

Seating themselves round the fire which Susan had kindled, they now began to ask many questions of each other, but the chief anxiety of Edwin was to learn what had become of poor Mrs. Gravestow, and whether she was still living with the husband, whose ferocious temper he had on too many occasions witnessed. This question Susan afforded all the information she had it in her power to give; adding that it was a source of severe disappointment to Mrs. Gravestow, that she had never received a letter from him after his abrupt departure from the house.

"Why, you don't mean to say that she never heard from me?" exclaimed Edwin, with astonishment.

"I am certain she never did," answered Susan; "for often have I heard her regret it; and I rather think she thought you ungrateful after all the kindness you had received from her family."

"And well she might if she has indeed never heard from me," replied the young man; "but I assure you, Susan, I wrote every month, and was surprised at never receiving any answer from her."

"Then this goes to prove a little more of Mr. Gravestow's dirty work," cried Susan. "He was always jealous and distrustful of everybody, and in particular he had a dislike to you, as of course, you very well know. I suppose he opened your letters among others, that were addressed to her, and being aware how much interest she felt in your fate, the letters have been destroyed out of mere spite and revenge towards her."

"I suppose then, by what you say, he is no better than when his tyranny drove me from his house?"

"No, Edwin—I beg pardon, Mr. Wentford, I mean;—he has been growing worse and worse ever since I have known him, and at last his conduct became so brutal, that his wife was obliged to part from him, and live upon the paltry pittance he thought proper to allow her."

"And pray," asked Edwin, "were the murderers of poor Mr. Wentford ever discovered?"

"Never," she replied; "and the foul stigma still rests upon my brother Andrew, that he was one of the persons concerned in that dreadful affair. But I vowed from the first, never to relax my exertions till the whole mystery was unveiled, and though so long a time has passed since the murder, I do not yet despair of being able to bring the guilty parties to justice."

"And has nothing ever been heard of your brother since his disappearance on that dreadful night?"

"Nothing whatever," she replied; "we have, however, ascertained clearly enough that he did not elope with Dolly Pratt, the dairy-maid, as was at first suspected, and that circumstance makes me suspect that he was murdered on the same night as his master, and that his body was concealed for the purpose of making the world believe that he was the assassin. But Heaven will yet reveal the real perpetrators, and my brother's name will at length be cleared of the foul crime with which he has been charged."

"And has Mr. Gravestow," asked the young man, "taken no steps towards a discovery of the murderers of his kind friend and patron?"

"Why he has sometimes pretended to make a little bustle about it," answered Susan; "but it seems to me that he cares nothing about it since he has got the greatest part of the money left by Mr. Wentford. And a very different sort of man he is to what he was when I can first remember him; for, instead of squandering away all his money in idle follies, he has now grown miserly, and all his ambition seems to be that he may become

the greatest man in the county. But money will never make him respected, for, from all that I can hear, he is proud and insolent to his neighbours, and they shun him as a man that they have no wish to make an acquaintance with."

" Well, at any rate, I intend to call upon Mrs. Gravestow, who 1 have
ever regarded as a sister—immediately upon my return to England," said
the young man ; " her husband may also chance to receive a visit from me,
for I have rendered myself independent of him during the time I have been
absent, and as we shall meet upon a more equal footing, there are questions
that I wish to put to him, which he perhaps little expects."

After this, the coversation turned upon more general subjects, and when
at length the morning returned, the soldiers brought their prisoners from
the place in which they had been confined, and some refreshment having
been given to them, they departed for the town which Susan had left the
night before, and where they were to be imprisoned till their trial took
place.

In the same direction Mr. Plumley, Edwin, and Susan went shortly afterwards, for the old gentleman had learnt that a young English female
had been taken away with Deleroix and his wife, and believing that this
could be no other than the daughter he was in search of, he was anxious to
reach the town in order that he might release her from so unpleasant a situation.

CHAPTER LVI.

THE SMUGGLERS' DOOM.

It was about a month after the apprehension of the two smugglers that
their trial was appointed to take place in the town which we have had
such frequent occasion to mention. The interest occasioned by this event
was extremely great, for the men were well known for the desperate characters they had borne ; and though there were some that were glad of there
being a prospect of their being restrained from the commission of further
crimes, there were many others who regarded them as men who had sought
to defraud the revenue, and whose only crime consisted in defeating laws
that were generally unpopular.

On the same day, it was expected that George Ramsden and Morley, the
assumed Marquis Valliere and Major Smith, would be tried for the murder
of the Marquis de Noailles, and far different was the general feeling against
them, since the nobleman who had fallen a victim to their crimes, was be-
oved and respected by everybody. The greatest interest was, therefore,
manifested to bear the trial of these two men, for besides the odium in
which they were held, the story of their treatment of the two English
ladies was generally current, and many extraordinary revelations were expected to take place in the course of the examination that was to ensue. It
was known, also, that they had been extensively engaged in smuggling
transactions, and the utmost curiosity prevailed to ascertain whether they
had been in any way connected with the two Laroches for whom so much
sympathy had been manifested.

The two latter-named personages had long been popular among the
middle and lower classes of society, for songs had been written respecting
them, and portraits published, so that they were known to everybody, and
many were the tales circulated of their prowess in the pursuit they were
engaged in, and which in every case exalted them rather into heroes than

as men whose lives had been spent in breaking the laws of their own country.

It is not therefore to be wondered at that a vast crowd was assembled before the Court-house on the day when the trial was to take place. All present were anxious to obtain a view of the prisoners, whose deeds had made them so notorious, and people came for leagues round the town to satisfy their idle curiosity by obtaining a sight of them.

At length a prison van forced its way through the concourse of persons to the door of the Town Hall, and as a general opinion prevailed that it contained the two Englishmen whose crimes had rendered them so much abhorred, a loud howl of execration took place, which was not interrupted till the two smugglers stepped out, when the cries of vengeance ceased, and loud cheers of encouragement succeeded, till the prisoners were hurried into the Court-house, where their trial was to take place.

Soon after this the doors were thrown open for the admission of the public, and the crowding and squeezing that succeeded would baffle any description we might attempt to give. Numbers of persons were carried fainting from the crowd, and even those who were fortunate enough to force their way into the building, only did so at the expense of torn clothes and bruised limbs. At length, when the place was filled almost to suffocation, the doors were with some difficulty closed, and those who were disappointed of gaining admittance, remained upon the spot, anxious to hear the result of an affair that had created so much excitement.

Shortly after this arrived the carriages containing the witnesses that were required in both trials, from the first of which stepped Madame Deleroix and her husband, the servant girl, and the two men who had been at the inn and taken the smugglers into custody. The next carriage contained Mr. Plumley and his daughter, together with Edwin and Susan, all of whom it was supposed could throw some light on the business, and aid in convicting the prisoners.

There were two charges against the men,—one for the smuggling transactions in which they had been engaged, and the other for having entered the inn during the darkness of night, with the design of robbing the place, and murdering the unsuspecting inmates in their sleep.

Through the evidence that was brought forward there was no difficulty in proving many acts against them of having been deeply concerned in a long and successful scheme, the object of which was to defraud the revenue by carrying on a contraband trade with other countries. All this was made manifest, but the greater part of the crowd betrayed their commiseration with the prisoners by frequent plaudits, which the court in vain interfered to prevent. In fact, there were many romantic incidents narrated which were calculated to excite the admiration of people who were prejudiced in behalf of the prisoners, and when that part of the trial had been brought to a conclusion, it was easy enough to perceive that by far the greater proportion of the auditors were in favour of the men who it was clearly proved had lived by violating the laws which had been made for the protection of commerce.

When this part of the charge against them had been brought to a conclusion, witnesses were produced to prove their having entered the inn for the purposes of plunder and murder. Mr. Plumley and Edwin were the first persons called upon, and the evidence they gave went to prove that the men at the bar were not in the house at the time when they went to bed, and the two soldiers, after giving similar evidence, informed the court that they had been sent to the inn to take the prisoners into custody, but that they were unable to meet with them till they entered the house with the evil intentions set forth in the indictment.

Susan Hoply was the next witness called, and through the assistance of an interpreter, she gave her evidence, which went to prove that she had returned to the house at night, and finding it in the possession of strangers, she was afraid to enter till she knew what had taken place during her absence. She then went on to state that she proceeded to the bed-room of the servant girl, and described all that had taken place,—the noises she had heard,—the moving of the mattrass upon which she had slept, and the subsequent appearance of the two men through the aperture in the flooring. All this began to give the affair a very black appearance, but when she narrated the conversation she had overheard between them, with respect to the robbery and murder they intended to commit, even the most partial of the auditors began to admit that they were desperate characters, and that it was fortunate they had been aprehended before their designs had been carried into effect. All this, together with the fact that they had entered the house by forcible means, was a complete chain of evidence against them, and two or three other witnesses having been examined, the prisoners were called upon for their defence.

"We are both of us quite innocent of all that has been laid to our charge," said Victor Laroche; "and as for what has been said about our entering the inn, I would ask whether it is not most improbable, since we knew the soldiers were waiting there to take us into custody?"

"Till now," exclaimed St. Ange, "our worst enemies have never accused us of robbery, nor have we ever taken taken the life of a fellow-creature, though, on many occasions, we have been hardly pressed by the revenue officers. We, therefore, look forward to an acquittal from this crime, whatever may be your opinion of the other charge."

"You will have strict justice," answered the judge, "and whatever decision we may come to, it will be in strict accordance with the evidence that has been brought forward."

"The female witness," exclaimed Victor, "has spoken of the circumstance of our being concealed in a vault beneath the room in which she slept. I admit that we were so, but we had no bad motive in being there, and so Madame Deleroix could tell you if she thought proper."

"She could, my lord," added St. Ange; "and as an act of justice I should wish the vault to be searched, since it is full of valuable property; and therefore, if plunder had been our object, there was no occasion for us to break into the house to search for it."

"What the prisoner has said, my lord, is very artfully urged," exclaimed the counsel for the prosecution; "but we have fair reason for supposing that the object of these men was to murder all the persons in the house in order that they might be in complete possession of all the vault contained. As we have seen, they had by some means or other discovered the vault of which they have been speaking, and the evidence seems to me quite sufficient to prove that they remained concealed there till the darkness of night came on, and that then they stole out and broke into the house."

"But," said Victor Laroche, "we both of us declare that the English female that was called against us has sworn falsely; for she could not have been present when we came out of the vault, or we must have seen her."

The judge said nothing in reply to this, but called Madame Deleroix and her maid servant,—the latter of whom was required as an interpreter between the court and her mistress. In answer to questions that were addressed to her, Madame Deleroix said that she had no recollection of having shown the subterranean chamber to the two smugglers; but after reflecting a little while, she admitted that she had taken them to it, as she was aware that a pursuit had commenced, and she told them it would be an excellent hiding-place, in the event of their being very closely pressed. She, however, added that she had not assisted them in getting into it, and the fact of their being in the place was a clear proof that they intended to rob her.

As there was no further evidence to bring forward, the trial was now at an end, and the prisoners saw clearly enough that they must be condemned unless they could make an impression upon the court in their favour. They, therefore, determined to assume an appearance of great humility, and Victor advancing to the front of the bar, said :—

"My lord, with all respect for yourself, I must say that the evidence has not been sufficient to prove us guilty of an intention either to rob the house or murder the inmates. And with respect to the other charge, it must be admitted that we have occasionally been concerned in smuggling transactions, which is a crime only because the law has declared it to be one. Yet, even allowing that we have been engaged in the contraband trade, there is no one to come forward to say that we have ever used either violence or cruelty. On the contrary, there are many persons that could come forward to speak in favour of us."

"Are any of them about the court?" asked the judge.

"They are not, my lord," answered Victor; "and the reason of their being absent may be pretty well imagined. In fact, there is danger of their being placed at this very bar, if they were known to have been connected with us, and on that account they have not made their appearance."

"Will you tell me," said the judge, "what motive you had for going to the house of these people?"

"We went," answered Victor, "through a message that had been sent us from Madame Deleroix. The messenger told us that she wanted to see us on very particular business; and as we supposed it was something about the transactions we have been engaged in, we lost no time in paying her a visit, but instead of finding our expectations realized, we were scandalously betrayed, and, for ought I know, our lives were at one time in great danger,"

"In the meantime," said the judge, "I suppose she had given information to the police of your expected arrival?"

"We reached her house," continued Victor, "with considerable difficulty, in consequence of the more than usual vigilance of the preventive men, who, it seems, were on the look out for a couple of Englishmen, who, by means of a dashing exterior and other advantages they possessed, had been carrying on their speculations with a great deal of success. However, we contrived to reach the inn safely, and met with a reception that completely put us off our guard, for Madame Deleroix can play the hypocrite, and upon this occasion she did it so successfully that neither I nor my brother had any notion of the trick she was preparing for us."

"Proceed," said the counsel, as the prisoner abruptly paused. "Finish your narrative, and his lordship will then be able to judge of its truth or falsehood."

"I am telling nothing but the truth, and Madame Deleroix is present to deny it if she can," replied Victor. "She knows that after her husband and an English lady had retired, she came down stairs to us again, and having the servant girl to explain what she meant, informed us that she had got a large quantity of valuable property which she wished us to dispose of with secrecy and expedition. I asked where they were to be seen, and she led us to a place at the back of the house, and removing a bed that was lying upon the floor, and pointing out a stone with a ring in the middle of it, gave us to understand by signs, that she wished us to remove it. We did so, and discovered the entrance of a vault, which was so dark that we were unable to see to the bottom of it even with the assistance of our light. The girl told us the goods we were to see had been deposited in that place for safety and concealment, and we were desired to go down and look at them. Of course we suspected no danger, and descended without hesitation, but no sooner were we at the bottom, than the stone was replaced over the entrance, and we found ourselves the prisoners of the very person to whom we had given our confidence."

"This is a very extraordinary narrative," observed the judge, "but at the same time I am bound to tell you that I cannot attend to it without evidence to support it."

The story, however, was listened to with a great deal of attention, and all eyes were now turned to Madame Deleroix, who was the only person in court that seemed to be unmoved by the words that had just been uttered. Victor fancied he had gained an advantage, and addressing himself once more to the judge, he continued:—

"With some difficulty, my lord, we contrived to escape from the place, and is it likely, I would ask, that, having avoided the danger, we should rush into it again by entering the house? On the contrary, we were anxious to escape, and should have done so had it not been for the gens d'armes, who seized us before we could get away from the place."

"Your story has been very ingeniously invented," said the judge, referring back to his notes, "but the witnesses who have been sworn, declare that you made no attempt to get away till you were discovered in the house. The young woman, too, Susan Hoply, says she overheard your conversation, and that you both distinctly expressed your determination to commit both the murder and robbery. She saw you examine the weapons; was an eye-witness to the fact of your breaking in at the window, and is certain you would have completed the crimes you both meditated if it had not been for the alarm she raised. The soldiers, too, saw you in the house, and with all this weight of evidence this court cannot credit the assertion that you intended to escape without doing any one an injury."

"You have heard the statement made by the prisoner," said the counsel, to the maid servant of the inn, "and I now ask you whether there is any truth in it?—In short, did you see Madame Deleroix take these men to the vault they speak of?"

"I saw nothing of the kind, sir," answered the girl.

"And in your own mind you are positive that your mistress did not shut the men in the place as they have both affirmed?"

"I am sure she did not."

"Now, Madame Deleroix," said the counsel, addressing himself to the hostess,—"are you prepared to deny the story just related by the prisoners?"

Madame Deleroix made signs to the girl, who presently replied :—

"My mistress desires me to say, sir, that they have not spoken one word of truth."

"And this she positively swears?"

"She does," replied the girl, after again receiving instructions from Madame Deleroix, "and she desires me to ask whether it is likely she would send for these men at all when she knew from common report the infamous character they bore? Besides, they are men that are very unlikely to have fallen so easily into the trap they say she laid for them."

"But I say we have spoken nothing but the truth," said Victor Laroche, "and the witness deserves the punishment that I suppose will be inflicted upon us."

"I think, my lord," said the counsel, "there is no reason to discredit the evidence of Madame Deleroix, who seems to have given her evidence in a very fair and straightforward manner. As for what the prisoners may have said, as it is unsupported by evidence, we can only regard it as a story invented to screen themselves from the penalty due to their crimes. Their characters are well known, and there can be no doubt that they entered the subterranean place in order to plunder it, and that they contemplated the crime of murder, so that they might the more readily escape the consequences of a discovery."

"We know very well," said Victor, "that our story is not likely to be believed, but, for all that, it is true in every particular, and Madame Deleroix knows it to be so, though she tries to get us punished, that she may herself escape unharmed. Had we entered the vaults for the purpose of committing a robbery, we could have done so, instead of leaving it as we did without touching even the most trifling article that the place contained."

Again Madame Deleroix made signs to her servant, who, addressing herself to the judge, said—

"My mistress desires me to repeat that she has stated nothing but the truth. She has no ill-feeling towards the prisoners, and would not now have been a witness against them had there been any means of avoiding it. They are strangers to her, my lord, and all she knows about them is from the reports that have been spread abroad."

No further comments were made, and after a brief pause, the judge addressed himself to the prisoners, observing that the evidence produced against them was most conclusive, and remained uncontradicted, in spite of the ingenious defence that had been made. He congratulated them upon the fact that the crime of murder had been prevented, as otherwise it would have been his painful duty to order them for execution. As it was, however, a somewhat milder punishment awaited them, and the sentence of the court was, that they should be imprisoned for the remainder of their lives.

The brothers heard the sentence with the utmost coolness ; but as they were led away, it was observed that they cast a look of fury towards Madame Deleroix, who returned it with one of triumph at the termination of the trial. She, indeed, had good reason to congratulate herself upon the escape she had had, for when first she was taken up, it was upon a charge of being connected with the prisoners in the unlawful traffic they had been carrying on. Her evidence, however, was found to be necessary for the conviction of the two men whose daring acts had rendered them so notorious throughout the country, and she was merely detained in prison to be forthcoming when the day of trial arrived. In this way she escaped punishment; but the property found in the vault was seized and forfeited. to the government, and happy did Madame Deleroix think herself that she had got off so easily.

At the termination of this trial a great number of the spectators departed, and thus the court was rendered more convenient and comfortable for those persons that remained to hear the next proceedings.

CHAPTER LVII.

THE GUILTY MEET THEIR DESERTS.

As the trial of the two Englishmen was next to take place, Mr. Plumley, Susan, and Edwin remained in the court to give the testimony which they knew they should be called on for. There was, however, some little cessation of business, and the judge and counsel had retired to the refreshment-rooms, and taking the opportunity which this circumstance afforded, Susan was about to put a few questions to Edwin, when the two prisoners were brought to bar, in one of whom she recognised the assumed Major Smith, but who she felt quite satisfied was the man she had seen lurking about the gardens of her master on the night he was murdered. She was violently agitated at again beholding him ; but recovering herself, she told Edwin, who sat next to her, the circumstances under which they had first met, and the suspicions she had always entertained that he had had some share in the assassination of Mr. Wentford.

" What other reason," she said, " could he—a perfect stranger—have for lurking about the premises at that hour of the night? I may be wrong, but still I cannot help thinking that he was the murderer of my poor master."

" But he must have had a motive for it," said Edwin.

" Robbery was the motive," answered our heroine, " and he and his companion—for there two of them concerned in it—were sufficiently repaid by what they took away from the house."

" I never heard that any robbery was committed on the night of the murder," said the other.

" It was not gold nor jewels that they sought," answered Susan. " They wanted the will which they were aware the old gentleman had made, and from that time it has been missing."

" Are you sure he made one ?" asked Edwin.

" I am quite certain of it," replied Susan. " Mr. Derwent, the lawyer, and several other persons, can prove that one was made only a few days before the murder, and yet it was not afterwards to be found."

"And if it was as you say," returned Edwin, "how is it that I have never heard anything about it?"

"Perhaps it was my fault more than that of anybody else," answered our heroine, "for I ought to have mentioned it; but you were very young, and I thought it would be useless to say anything about it just then, and just when I was going to mention it, you suddenly disappeared, and I have never been able to hear anything about you till we met so unexpectedly at the inn. Now, however, I may tell you that by the will I am speaking of, Mr. Wentford left you a large sum of money, besides a share in his business, and that in spite of what Mr. Gravestow has since said, the remaining part of his fortune was settled entirely upon his daughter. But, as I said before, it never could be found, and the consequence was that he took the money under his own management, and his unfortunate wife has been turned out of house and home to live upon the trifling pittance he thinks proper to allow her."

"Well," said Edwin, "at all events there is not much doubt about this man's guilt as being one of the murderers of the Marquis de Noailles, and if he should be sentenced to death, it is likely he may be induced to confess all his other crimes when secrecy can be of no further service to him."

"And if he does," returned Susan, "I shall, at least, have the satisfaction of living to hear my brother's name cleared from the foul charges that have been brought against him. That has been the chief wish of my heart, and from the moment he is declared innocent I shall have no other care or trouble to harrass me."

"But it is impossible any one can seriously believe your brother to have been guilty," observed Edwin. "He was always known to have been attached to his master, and would rather have died in his defence than raise his hand against him."

"Aye, so you and a great many others are kind enough to tell me," replied Susan; "but Mr. Gravestow takes care to keep up the prejudice which he was the first to start, and even now there are persons that can find no reason for the mysterious disappearance of poor Andrew. Yet Heaven will discover all in its own good time, and sometimes I am almost tempted to think Mr. Gravestow must have motives of his own for wishing to throw the blame on an innocent person."

Edwin was about to make some further observations, but at that moment the judge and counsel returned to the court, and the usual preliminaries were gone through. The first witness called was Dolly Pratt, who advanced pale and trembling, for all eyes were instantly directed towards her, and she felt that the circumstance attending her connexion with the Marquis de Noailles would place her in anything but an honourable situation in the opinion of all who might hear her evidence. She, however, gave her testimony with great clearness, and proved all the circumstances attending the assassination of the Marquis in a manner so unembarrassed as to impress everybody with a conviction that she had closely adhered to the facts of the case. What her evidence was, the reader already knows, and at the conclusion she retired to another part of the court, whilst other witnesses were confirming what she had been stating.

When the case for the prosecution was closed, a counsel for the prisoners rose, and after an eloquent exordium, in which he entreated his auditors to banish all prejudices from their minds, and to give his statement a fair and impartial hearing, he proceeded to show that his clients, though they might have been guilty of shedding the blood of the Marquis de Noailles, yet that the fact had been committed under such circumstances as would clear them from the most odious part of the charge.

"My lord," he continued, "the prisoners stand before you as strangers in our land, and therefore require more than usual caution and forbearance ere they are found guilty upon the evidence of one witness ; for there is, in fact, but one whose testimony is of any importance, and that witness a person whose character does not stand without reproach.

"And how stands the case as regard my clients? It appears that some few years since there resided, in some part of England, a gentleman and his daughter, among whose domestics was one Dorothea, or Dolly Pratt, a girl of great personal beauty, and possessing a large share of that pride which is too often the consequence of a knowledge of superiority. She had, I believe, many admirers amongst the men belonging to her own class of life, but she rejected every offer that was made to her, and it was supposed that her ambition led her to imagine that she was born to a higher destiny than to become the wife of a rustic.

"At length, however, my lord, one man succeeded in gaining her affections, and that person was a servant in the employ of her master, engaged, I believe, as a footman, and enjoying the confidence of his master, who it seems regarded him with more favour than it afterwards appeared that he deserved. The consequence of this was, that he was trusted and caressed, till at length he was the only domestic in the house that could at all times gain access to the old gentleman, whose kindness he afterwards so cruelly abused.

"I have said that he became the accepted lover of the dairymaid, and the consequences, I grieve to say, were most fatal, for, tempted by her, he at length was prevailed upon to take away the life of the man who had been his friend and benefactor. Yes, my lord, urged by the tempter, he entered the room of his aged master whilst he was asleep, and basely murdered him ! This done, he added robbery to his previous crime, and then fled from the place with the guilty woman that had urged him to the deed. Of course every inquiry was made after them, but all their plans had been preconcerted with consummate art, and though a large reward was offered for their apprehension, no tidings could be heard of them.

"But succeeding as they did in eluding justice, the endeavours of the murdered man's friends never relaxed, and the most unceasing efforts were made to find out some trace by which they might eventually be brought to justice. Amongst the friends I speak of were the prisoners at the bar, who, happening to be in this country a short time since, saw and recognized the female who had prompted the deed, and believing that the person who was with her was the man who had committed the murder, he stopped and would have taken him into custody; a struggle ensued, and, most unfortunately, the Marquis de Noailles, an innocent man and most respected nobleman, lost his life through the suspicion that had been formed against him. This circumstance, my lord, the prisoners deplore, and from the fact of his being with the woman, who they both well knew was the one they were searching for, they mistook him for the guilty wretch that had committed the murder, and hence followed the fatal catastrophe that has deprived us of so esteemed a countryman. He fell, and the woman whose evidence you have just now heard is the person who was once the dairymaid, afterwards the paramour of the guilty domestic of a too confiding master, and finally the kept mistress of the Marquis de Noailles.

"Of course, as was perfectly natural, the prisoners fled immediately after the unfortunate event which has now placed them before this court, to be tried for their lives. They were taken—a strong prejudice was formed against them as having caused the death of a justly-esteemed nobleman,

and it now depends upon the effect of what little eloquence I possess whether they are condemned to perish by an ignominious death, or obtain that acquittal of which I am sure they are in every way deserving. I will now, with your lordship's permission, call a witness who will be able to prove all that I have said, and as his character and respectability are most highly established, I trust his evidence will clear my clients from the foul charge that has this day been made against them."

The counsel urged all his points with so much eloquence and force, that people who went there execrating the prisoners, were soon induced to waver in their opinions, and by the time he had concluded his address, the general indignation was turned from the real culprits to poor Dolly, who became the object of abhorrence and disgust.

Susan Hoply heard this oration with feelings that may easily be conceived, for she had fondly anticipated, that on this day her brother's character would be cleared from the imputation that had been cast upon it, and now she heard him openly denounced as the murderer of his master. On several occasions her feelings so far overpowered her, that she could scarcely refrain from rising to cast back the vile aspersions, but she was prevailed upon by Edwin and Mr. Plumley to remain quiet, and at length found relief in a flood of tears. They then assured her of their conviction of her brother's innocence, and that the prisoner at the bar, or one of them at least, had the crime to answer for, and by this means succeeded, after a little time, in restoring her to a state of tolerable composure.

At that period room was made for the approach of the witness that had been alluded to by the counsel at the close of his address, and what was the astonishment of Edwin and Susan, at beholding Walter Gravestow step into the box where he was to give his testimony!

The evidence given by Gravestow went to confirm all that had been stated by the pleader, and when speaking of the characters of the two men at the

No. 53

bar, he spoke of them as men of irreproachable conduct, and utterly incapable of coolly and deliberately seeking the life of a fellow-creature. Of
Major Smith, as he called him, he spoke in the highest terms, declaring
that they had been friends for many years, and that from his own experience, he could most positively assert, a more honourable, kind, or humane
man never existed.

This had a powerful effect upon every body that heard it, and the general
impression was that the prisoner would be acquitted; but at that moment
a boy in livery made his appearance, and putting a note into the hands of
the counsel for the prosecution, again retired among the crowd. Immediately upon reading the note, the person to whom it was addressed rose, and
addressing himself to the judge, said he had just received some important
information respecting the trial that was in progress, and then turning
towards Gravestow, commenced a close and rigid cross-examination that
made the witness hesitate and stammer in a way that attracted general observation. The counsel inquired of him whether he had not seen the dairy-
maid after her departure from her master's house on the night of the
murder; if, in fact he had not seen her within an hour of the time when
the catastrophe had taken place, and whether he could deny that she had
left the house with him and another companion. He then went on to inquire if he had not seen her in London, where a lodging had been taken,
and whether he had not supplied her with the money which was necessary
to pay the expenses of her journey to France. All these questions were replied to with evident caution; but he denied all knowledge of her after the
event that had occurred at Summerfield; and, gaining more firmness, most
positively swore that it was on the night of the murder that she disappeared, as there was every reason to believe, with Andrew Hoply.

The counsel for the prosecution then desired that the witnesses who had
written to him proffering their testimony in this trial, to come forward,
and immediately afterwards Mr. Derwent and his friend, Mr. Smithson,
made their way through the crowd towards the witness-box.

Mr. Derwent was first examined, and in answer to the questions put to
him, he stated that he had a perfect recollection of Mr. Wentford's murder,
and the suspicions that were entertained at the time that the deed had been
committed by Andrew Hoply and the dairymaid. He then went on to say
that events had recently occurred to throw some light upon the mysterious
affair, and at the same time to reveal a tale of depravity and villany such as
had seldom been heard of. He next spoke of the singular discovery of the
will which had been so long lost, and related the means by which it had been
restored when all hopes of such an event had been given up. This brought
him to the subject of Gravestow's extraordinary conduct, and the suspicions he entertained that he was one of the most active agents in the murder of his friend and patron. He afterwards related his unexpected
meeting with Dolly Pratt in London; the revelations she made—the mysterious disappearance of Amelia Robertson from her home—their journey
to France, and the anxious desire he had to bring home the crime to the
real perpetrators. He then related the singular manner by which he had
been instrumental in rescuing Amelia from the river into which she had
been thrown by Gravestow, in order that he might thus rid himself of
one witness whose testimony he had so much reason to dread.

Mr. Smithson was next heard, and afterwards Amelia, who had accompanied them on their journey to town. She deposed that Mr. Gravestow, or Gayton, as he had always passed himself to her, had prevailed on
her to walk out with him on the night when she was nearly drowned, and
that having taken her down to the river side, he had suddenly plunged her
into the water, then, running off, left her to her fate.

The boy who had been the means of saving her was next called, at the suggestion of Mr. Derwent, and he swore to having seen a man run away whilst the female was in the water, and that he called upon him to stop and give his assistance, but that he hurried off, muttering something tha he was unable to understand, as it was spoken in a language that he was un-acquainted with. This narrative was given with so much mingled sim-plicity and intelligence, that it made a great impression upon all who heard it, and the judge immediately gave orders that Walter Gravestow should be taken into custody. The villain, however, had seen the turn that matters had taken against him, and seizing the first opportunity that occurred, he had slipped out of the court and was no where to be found.

Edwin now rose, and said, that with the permission of the court he would say a few words, and having received permission to do so, he went on to relate the fact of Mr. Gravestow having given him a half guinea a short time after the murder of Mr. Wentford, and that he was able to swear to the coin from the fact of its being marked " April 3, 1781." This he had shown to the housemaid, Susan Hoply, at the time, who had in-stantly known it for one that had actually been seen in his possession on the very night of the murder. This afforded strong presumptive proof that Gravestow must have been engaged in the crime, which he had afterwards sought to throw the blame of upon innocent persons. So apparent did this villany now appear, that orders were given for a strict search to be made after him, and the police were instantly dispersed in every direction for the purpose of securing and placing him in safe custody.

The coin spoken of had been taken from her by the soldiers when Susan was arrested on the first entrance into the town, and the purse containing it and other little articles was now produced and given into her possession. The half guinea was now recognised by Susan as the one that had been given to her by Edwin to keep for him, and was found to be marked with the inscription exactly as had been described. In reply to further questions, our heroine admitted that she had all along expected that it would one day or other be the means of leading to an important discovery, and that no consideration would ever have induced her to part with it except the force which it was taken from her by the soldiers.

The discredit which had thus been thrown upon the testimony of the witness that had been brought forward in favour of the prisoners, had the effect of damaging a cause which it had been intended to bolster up. It was in vain their counsel made a most ingenious speech, in which he en-deavoured to prove that all the witnesses that had been heard since Grave-stow were unworthy of belief, for the agitation betrayed by Walter whilst he was undergoing the cross-examination, proved the alarm he felt at the turn matters had taken, and his subsequent flight increased the suspicion which had been formed to his prejudice.

When the counsel finished, the advocate for the prosecution rose to reply, and in a brief but energetic speech, repelled the slanders that had been heaped upon respectable and innocent persons, who, instead of having any share in the dark transactions that had been divulged, had done all in their power to bring the perpetrators of the murder to justice. That the priso-ners at the bar had slain the Marquis de Noailles was beyond a doubt, and he therefore called upon the court to pass that sentence which the grievous nature of the offence demanded.

A death-like silence followed this address, and then the judge, addressing himself to the prisoners, declared his conviction that the murder of the Marquis was committed under such circumstances, that he could hold out no hope of any commutation of the law in their case. Their guilt was clearly proved, and it therefore only remained for him to order them for execution. The trial being thus concluded, and the prisoners removed to their cells, the parties who had thus met together, proposed leaving the court together, but, ere they could do this, they were detained by a circumstance as unlooked for as it was extraordinary.

From the first moment when Amelia had entered the witness-box, it was observed that Madame Deleroix became excessively agitated, and, springing from the seat, she could scarcely be withheld by those who were placed in the court to maintain order and decorum. Still, however, she kept her eyes constantly fixed upon the witness till the proceedings of the day were over, when, again rising, she found her way through the crowd to the spot where Amelia stood, and, with au exclamation of joy, folded her in her arms. She was unable to speak, but Amelia instantly recognised her as the mother from whom she had been so long parted, and who she had given up as dead. The meeting was in every respect a most affecting one ; but upon Madame Deleroix, as she was now called, it had an overpowering effect, and when they loosened her arms, which had been thrown round the neck of her daughter, it was discovered that she had gone off into strong convulsions. In that state she was carried to a lodging in the town, but she never recovered the shock she had received, and a short time afterwards she expired in the arms of her daughter.

Monsieur Deleroix had, for some time past, sunk into a state of hopeless idiotcy, but he seemed to recognize the features of his child, though no expression escaped his lips that he did so. After the funeral of her mother, Amelia brought him over with him to England, where he passed the remainder of his days with her in a house which Mr. Smithson took for her a few miles from London.

After the trial of George Ramsden and Morley, the greatest efforts were made to prevail on them to confess their crimes, and to satisfy the mind of the public by making a full disclosure of the mystery that still hung over some part of the circumstances connected with the murder of Mr. Wentford. They were, however, obstinately determined to die with the secret in their possession ; and, as they had had an interview with Walter Gravestow the day before their trial, it was supposed that he had induced them to promise that no discovery should be made in an affair in which it was well known he had been deeply implicated. When pressed to declare the innocence of Andrew Hoply, they maintained a resolute silence ; but as they did not again affirm that he had any hand in the murder, it was taken for granted that he was entirely innocent of it. They were next asked if either of them knew what had become of him, and the only reply they made was, that it would be useless to ask any more questions, as they were determined never to answer them.

When the day for their execution arrived, a vast concourse was assembled to witness the punishment of two men whose crimes had rendered them so notorious. The prisoners, however, conducted themselves with the utmost effrontery, and met their death with a stern defiance of its terrors that, had it been exhibited in a better cause, might have obtained for them the credit of having died like heroes.

CHAPTER LVIII.

THE REWARD OF CRIME.

No sooner did Mr. Smithson ascertain that Gravestow had escaped from the town, after the discovery of his villany had rendered his longer stay there dangerous, than he consulted with Mr. Derwent as to what course should next be adopted for bringing so heinous an offender to justice. It was therefore at once suggested that they should pay an immediate visit to the English consul, who would at once put them in the right way to accomplish the design on which they were bent. They accordingly set forth to the residence of the party we have named, and, having obtained a speedy introduction to him, they briefly related the cause of their visit, and the strong proof they had of Walter Gravestow being clearly connected with the murderers who had destroyed Mr. Wentford.

"In fact," continued the lawyer, "we have every evidence against him that can be required; and, had he not escaped with so much dispatch when the disclosures were made at the trial of his accomplices, we should have given him in charge, with the assurance that the French government would freely give him up to the outraged laws of his own country."

"Have you been able to ascertain by which route he left this place?" asked the consul.

"We have not done so at present," answered Mr. Smithson; "but there can be very little doubt that he has sought safety and concealment in Paris. He will probably remain there till this business has blown over a little, and will then, I dare say, escape into some other country, where he may set all our efforts at defiance."

"I am almost afraid your trouble will be in vain," said the consul; "but, whatever service I can perform in the matter, you may freely demand. Perhaps, if I were to write to the commissioner of police in Paris, he would exert himself to aid in the apprehension of the criminal."

"That is exactly what I was going to ask you to do," exclaimed Mr. Derwent. "Both myself and my friend are strangers to the customs and usages of this country; and, if we could procure the assistance you speak of, I think it would not be long before we should have the villain in custody."

"And you are sure he is guilty of the crime you are about to charge him with?"

"Why, of that there can be no doubt," answered the lawyer, "for we have already very conclusive evidence to that effect, and upon returning to England it will be easy to obtain further testimony, which must secure his conviction."

"But had he any motive for murdering this Mr. Wentford, who, it seems, was his best friend?"

"His motive was, I have every reason to believe, to secure a will which had been made by the old gentleman, and, by destroying it, to secure the whole of the property, which, it seems, had been secured to the daughter in the event of her becoming his wife. The poor girl was foolish enough to marry him, in spite of the entreaties of her friends; and, no sooner did he become master of the wealth she brought him, than he commenced a series of cruelties that eventually compelled her to live separate from him. Yet even then the villany of his nature ceased not, for he allowed her a bare subsistence, whilst he was himself enjoying the large fortune that her father had accumulated for the future comfort of his beloved child."

"And was no one else suspected of this murder?" asked the consul.

"Yes," replied Mr. Derwent, "a footman in the family, named Andrew Hoply, was for a long time charged with having committed the deed, and as nothing was ever seen or heard of him after the night of the murder, it was generally supposed that he was really the assassin. We have now, however, every reason to believe that he is innocent, and that he was assassinated while endeavouring to protect his master from the murderous hands of his assailants."

"Is there any chance of proving it?" inquired the consul.

"That I am, just at present, unable to say," answered Mr. Derwent;

" but there was a strange anxiety manifested by Gravestow to prevent the demolition of an old house in the neighbourhood where he lived, and I have a notion that when the place is pulled down, something will be found to throw still further light upon this mysterious transaction."

"Well, at any rate," said the consul, "you shall have all the assistance I can afford to secure the person of this Gravestow, and perhaps when he finds himself in safe custody, he may be induced to confess what share he had in the murder."

So saying he wrote a note, and delivering it into the hands of Mr. Derwent, he continued—

"This will at any rate secure you the aid of the police in Paris, and if he should be lurking anywhere in that city, they will be sure to discover his retreat. Should that be the case, you have only to communicate the fact to me, and I will then put you further in the way of having him surrendered up to the English officers of justice."

Thanking the consul for the kindness with which he had entered into their views, the two gentlemen now withdrew, and returning to their companions, they related all that had passed, and then engaging a carriage, they quitted the town and proceeded with all speed to the French capital. On arriving there, they, without loss of time, proceeded to the superintendent of the police, who, having listened to their narrative, and received a description of the person they were in search of, said—

"I have just been informed by some of our men that a person answering your account arrived here not many hours since. He has taken a lodging in an obscure portion of the city, and if it is your wish, a couple of the police shall accompany you to assist in his apprehension."

"That is the very favour I was about to ask," exclaimed Mr. Derwent; " but as the man we are in search of is desperate and reckless, it will be necessary that every precaution is taken to avoid danger. I should, therefore, advise that your men be well armed in case of resistance, though at the same time I wish him to be taken alive, as it is likely he may make some very important disclosures when he finds that all hopes of saving his life are at an end."

"Your suggestions are hardly necessary," answered the commissioner; " because it is one of our principal objects to avoid danger from the rough customers we have constantly to deal with. However, you may make yourself quite easy on that point, and the men shall be ready to go with you whenever you think proper to require their assistance."

" Then let it be immediately," interposed Mr. Smithson, "for we have every reason to believe he will not make Paris his place of residence, and it would be provoking to lose sight of him after the trouble we have been at to get him into our clutches."

The commissioner summoned one of his men, and having whispered a few words in his ear, the fellows retired, and shortly afterwards a couple of the police entered the room, completely equipped for the service they were engaged in.

"You will, for the present, place yourselves under the disposal of these two gentlemen," said the superior, addressing himself to them. "They are in pursuit of a criminal, and it is my desire that you lose no opportunity of taking him. Once in your hands, I need hardly caution you to see that he has no opportunity to escape from you."

" The gentlemen may be sure of that," said one of the men, "but at present we have not been told in what part of the city he is to be found."

" I have written the address upon this card," answered the commissioner, " and I have no doubt the person you will find there is the one you have to take into custody. Be that as it may, however, you will bring him before me, for, from the report I have heard of him, there is no doubt he has committed some crime or other, and is endeavouring to conceal himself."

"May I ask," inquired Mr. Derwent, "how you know so much about a man that has only been in your city a few hours?"

"Why, the fact is," answered the chief of the police, "it is part of our business to know who comes to Paris, and the business that brings them here. We have our spies in all directions, and at any time when a particular individual is sought for, we know where to pounce upon him, as you will presently have an opportunity of observing."

"And suppose," observed the lawyer, "you take the wrong man, for, of course, your informant is not always correct?"

"It's very seldom we make any mistake," answered the other; "and if we do so occasionally, the man we take is most likely quite as bad as the one we are looking after. On discovering our error, however, we let him go his ways, and a lucky fellow he thinks himself at finding that his time for punishment has not yet arrived. But I'll not detain you, gentlemen, any longer from your task, for my men are now ready to accompany you to the direction I have given them. You will have the goodness to follow them at a little distance, for they may be known, and if a couple of strangers are seen with them, an alarm might be given, and the man escape before you have an opportunity of coming unawares upon him."

By this time the policemen had left the place, and as it was necessary to keep them in view, Mr. Smithson and his friend bade a hasty farewell to the commissioner, and bustled into the street just in time to catch a sight of their guides as they were turning down a narrow thoroughfare some little distance in advance. It was, therefore, necessary to move forward at a tolerably smart pace, and having at last reduced the distance between themselves and the men they were following, they were enabled to relax their speed very considerably.

"Upon my life this Walter Gravestow has given us no little trouble," said Mr. Derwent, as soon as he could recover himself. "Here have we followed him all the way from England, and though we seem upon the very point of laying our hands upon him, it is likely enough the man we are now going after may prove to be somebody else."

"It may be so, certainly," answered his friend, "but I have a notion we are upon the right scent. At any rate there can be very little doubt that he will seek concealment in Paris, as the place most likely to afford him a temporary shelter, and as we have been so prompt in our pursuit after him, he will have no time to guard himself against a sudden surprise. In fact, all I am afraid of is, that he will recklessly defend himself to the last, and in that case one or both the men that are engaged in our service may fall a sacrifice to his revengeful fury on being discovered."

"But," observed the lawyer, "these men know the sort of customer they have to deal with, and depend on it they will be prepared for any rough reception he may feel inclined to give them. Besides, I dare say his spirit is pretty well broken by this time, and what I most fear is, that he will escape the gallows by laying violent hands upon himself."

"Which would at once put an end to all our hopes of discovering the full extent of his iniquities," exclaimed Mr. Smithson; "once get him in the power of the law, and he will be strictly watched to prevent such an occurrence, and I feel satisfied he will be induced to make a full disclosure of the evil deeds, and thus establish the innocence of poor Andrew Hoply, whose name has been branded with unjust obloquy as the murderer of his master."

"I rather think the prejudice you speak of has worn off," answered Mr. Derwent, "for the character of this Walter Gravestow has become so notorious of late, that there are few persons who do not believe that he was guilty of the crime, which, at one period, he was so anxious to attribute to the person you speak of. However, I should be glad to hear of his making a confession, if it was only for the sake of Susan Hoply, whose devotion to the cause of her unfortunate brother has been so exemplary."

"And it seems rather surprising," said the other, "that Gravestow has not, long ere this, contrived to get rid of her by some of the foul means he knows so well how to practice. He must be well aware of her determination to discover the real perpetrator of the murder, and, desperately as he was circumstanced, one would have imagined that his first care would be to rid himself of her."

"And so I dare say he would," said Mr. Derwent; "but the fact is, Susan has always had the good fortune to meet with kind friends, and therefore it would have been rather hazardous for him to follow her among them. Besides, he no doubt thought himself quite secure from discovery after so long a period had elapsed from the tragical occurrence, and under those circumstances it would have been madness for him to trouble himself any further about her. But see, the two men stop before that low-looking house yonder, and by their glancing this way, I suppose they don't care how soon we join them."

With this they hurried on, and reaching the place where the police had arrived before them, they received an intimation, by signs, to follow in silence. The door, which was not fastened, yielded to a slight push, and keeping pretty well together, they were proceeding towards the stairs, when a female, rushing from a room close by, was hastening to intercept their progress, when the foremost presenting a pistol at her head, threatened, in a low tone, to shoot her should she raise her voice or give any other warning signal of their being in the house. This intimidation had the desired effect, and finding that nothing further was to be feared from her, the man inquired whether there was not a lodger in the place who had taken up his abode there but a few hours previously.

"There is," answered the trembling female.

"His name ?"

"That I can't tell you," she replied.

"Is he a Frenchman or a foreigner ?"

"A foreigner, and, as I think, an Englishman."

"His age ?"

"From thirty to thirty-five.

"That answers his description exactly," whispered Mr. Smithson.

"We have him now, then," returned the police officer, in the same low tone; "so do you all remain where you are while I go up and pounce suddenly upon him. When you hear me call, rush up to my assistance, and if he is the man we are in search of, he will have but little chance of escaping from his doom."

With this he crept cautiously up stairs, leaving the rest in a state of fearful suspense as to what would be the result of this attempt to secure a desperate man, who there was every belief would sell his life dearly if he had but an instant's forewarning of the danger with which he was threatened. For some little time all remained as silent as the grave, but at length a sudden outcry was raised, followed by the sound of scuffling as between two men in mortal struggle, and immediately the whole party rushed up stairs to render their assistance. On entering the room the officer and Walter Gravestow were discovered prostrate upon the floor, but the latter was beneath, and with the aid of the second policeman, he was so firmly secured as to present very little chance of his being able to escape. He was then searched, and every weapon taken from him, and this precau-

tion being taken, the officers were about to bind him, when, in a sullen voice, he asked them to leave him unfettered till they took him from the house.

"It is no very great favour to ask," he added, "for you have deprived me of all power of resistance, and surely you can grant me this trifling boon, seeing that I am completely helpless in your hands."

"Heed him not," exclaimed Mr. Derwent, "for he has some desperate design in view, and we shall all repent it if you grant the indulgence he has asked for."

"Indeed!" muttered Gravestow, bitterly; "and so you would carry your resentment against me to the very last. I have been hunted and persecuted for a crime that I know nothing about, and yet you would condemn me before I have an opportunity of proving my innocence and exposing the conspiracy that has been formed against the life of a man that is guiltless!"

"We should not have proceeded thus unless we had strong ground for the course we have adopted," answered Mr. Smithson. "The crimes we charge you with can be clearly proved, and the only reparation you can now make is to confess all, and make your peace with Heaven, which you have so grievously offended."

"I neither ask for your advice nor intend to take it," exclaimed Walter Gravestow, sullenly; "you have throughout ranked yourself among the most vindictive of my foes, and if I have one regret greater than another at being thus captured, it is that I have it no longer in my power to seek the vengeance my heart burns for."

"Come, come, this is no time to talk of vengeance," said Mr. Derwent; "the steps we have taken for your apprehension were actuated by no unworthy motives, for we believe you guilty of the foul crime of murder, and we have, therefore, done nothing more than our duty in assisting to bring you to justice."

No. 54

"What proof have you that I am an assassin?" demanded Walter Gravestow.

"That will be explained at a proper time and place," answered the lawyer; "it is at present sufficient to observe that we have most important evidence to bring against you, and which it is believed will bring the charge completely home; and even should that fail, there is yet a surviving victim who can prove an attempt upon her life, from which she providentially escaped."

"Indeed! and who is this person that you speak of?" he inquired.

"Amelia, the hapless female you betrayed, and would have murdered because you ascertained that she was in possession of a secret that was dangerous to your life. Your attempt against her cannot be denied, and the man who would be guilty of such a crime may surely be suspected of having murdered his friend and benefactor."

"'Tis false!" exclaimed Gravestow, furiously. "Mr. Wentford was assassinated by his servant, Andrew Hoply, and you now bring the charge against me, in order to carry out your revengeful designs."

"I can have no such base views as those you accuse me of," answered Mr. Derwent; "we are nearly strangers to each other, and the only motive I have for adopting this course, is to bring punishment upon the assassin of an old and helpless man. Your denial of having had any participation in the deed is of little consequence; but it has ever been a part of your base policy to accuse Andrew Hoply of the murder, though we have every reason to believe that he fell in the defence of his master."

"This is a vile conspiracy against me," exclaimed Gravestow, vehemently. "I am to be sacrificed for reasons that are yet to be discovered; but let me warn you to desist in time, for I am not to be thus hunted with impunity, and a deep and a lasting revenge will I take upon all those that have leagued together to drive me to this extremity."

"Should it prove that you have been wronged by our suspicions," said Mr. Smithson, "you will find us quite as ready to retract the charge as we were to make it. Unfortunately for yourself, however, it happens that we are not without evidence to support the allegations, and therefore I would warn you to prepare for the defence you will be shortly called upon to make."

"You still persist, then, in believing that I am guilty of the crimes you have named?"

"We do indeed," answered Mr. Derwent, "and as you are now in the hands of the police, it only remains for you to submit quietly, and accompany them before the magistrate."

"And what right," demanded Walter Gravestow, "have I to yield myself to the laws of a foreign country?"

"I know not that I have any business to answer your question," returned Mr. Derwent; "but, for your satisfaction, I will inform you that the assistance of the French police has been granted us, and after hearing a witness or two in confirmation of your guilt, you will be handed over to the officers of our own country, and by them will be conveyed to England for trial."

"That is a triumph you shall never boast of gaining over me," exclaimed Gravestow. "It is true you have succeeded in tracking me to my hiding-place, and I am now in the hands of the officers of justice; but here shall end my subjection to your power, and thus do I dare you to follow me down the dangerous path that leads to my escape!"

As he spoke thus, he made a sudden rush towards the window, and, reaching the parapet, instantly closed the casement, and thus gained time to make sure of the leap he was about to take. This was but the subject of a moment's consideration; and, gently letting himself over the projection, he clung to it for a brief period, and, having steadily balanced himself, dropped down in the garden beneath. Upon alighting on the earth, he felt stunned for an instant or two; but the danger of pursuit quickly recalled him to a sense of his danger, and running onwards, he leaped a wall, and, to his infinite satisfaction, found himself well in advance of his pursuers.

The party he had left behind were struck with amazement at the rapidity with which all this had passed; and, having forced open the window, they saw him beneath unharmed, and running off with as much apparent ease as if nothing particular had occurred.

"By heavens, the fellow has as many lives as a cat!" exclaimed Mr. Derwent, as soon as his astonishment would permit him to speak. "He has fairly escaped us, and the worst part of the affair is, I am afraid, he'll take good care that we don't find him again in a hurry."

"He is gone, sure enough," said his friend; "but I much doubt whether he will be able to elude his pursuers. Our two policemen have scampered after him without loss of time, and he must have nimble legs indeed if he contrives to get out of their reach."

This was the first intimation Mr. Derwent had of the officers having left the room; and, anxious as he was to see the termination of this affair, he bustled after them, followed by Smithson, who was equally desirous that the pursuit of the fugitive should be successful.

In the meantime Walter Gravestow exerted himself to the utmost to effect his escape, for a guilty conscience told him that a death of shame awaited him in the event of his being recaptured; and, with all the energy of a desperate man, he urged his way onwards, in the hope that he might find some place in which to find a temporary shelter till the heat of the pursuit had begun to subside.

All the efforts that he made were, however, in vain, for he had not proceeded any great distance before he heard loud shouts behind, and as these grew louder and louder upon his ear, he became but too painfully convinced that they proceeded from those he had been endeavouring to elude. Urged bp the peril with which he was threatened, he sought, by every means in his power, to increase his speed; but in vain did the wretched man strive to outstrip those who were following him, for he felt that his exhausted frame could not support him much longer, and, dashing heedlessly down the first narrow opening that presented itself to his view, he found himself on the banks of the river Seine, at the very spot where, but a short time previously, he had endeavoured to make away with Amelia, by plunging her into the stream. Gazing wildly round, he perceived a waterman at a little distance; and, hurrying towards him, he earnestly implored to be ferried over to the opposite bank. But the man heard him with apparent indifference, and, pointing towards the spot from whence the sounds of pursuit came, he said,—

"It would be as much as my life is worth to assist the escape of a man when the officers of justice are after him. They are now almost within sight; and, as there's no way of getting from them, you may as well surrender yourself quietly to me, and save all further trouble in the matter."

"I'll surrender to no one," answered Gravestow, resolutely. "I will escape them yet; and, if no other alternative remains, a plunge into the river will serve to baulk yonder blood-hounds of their expected prey."

By this time the sounds of pursuit came nearer and nearer; and, perceiving that all hope of escape was at an end, he took a purse of money from his pocket, and, flinging it to the man, exclaimed,—

"There's gold for you, friend; for I have no longer any need of it.

Leave this place; and, should any one inquire what has become of me,
affect ignorance of my having been near this spot, for I have endeavoured
to shun them when living, and would not fall into their accursed hands
when dead!"

The man picked up the purse that had been cast at his feet; and thinking probably it would be better not to remain where he was, for fear of
being asked questions that might occasion him the loss of the money, he
turned from the place, and in a few seconds he was no longer to be
seen.

By this time the pursuers were close at hand, and not a single avenue for
escape presented itself to the view of the miserable fugitive. He, however,
resolved never to be taken alive; and, urged by the madness of desperation, he rushed towards the bank, and, plunging into the river, instantly
disappeared amidst the gurgling waters.

At length the police, followed by the two Englishmen, and a large concourse of people, arrived at the spot, and a long, though ineffectual search
succeeded. In consequence of the darkness, which by this time had set in,
nothing whatever could be discovered to afford any clue of what had become
of him; and, after some hours had passed away, without attaining their
object, they were compelled to abandon all further thoughts of finding him
till the return of daylight. That he had thrown himself into the river was,
however, pretty certain; but even this was left entirely to conjecture, for
the man who had been last upon the spot, and who could have satisfied
them upon the point, had made the best of his way from the place, lest he
should happen to get into trouble.

On the following morning the search was renewed; and, after some
time had elapsed, the body of the wretched man was discovered floating
among some barges, whither it had been conveyed by the tide. The face
was much swollen and disfigured, yet the features were easily recognized as
those of Walter Gravestow; and, no sooner had it been placed in a shell,
than it was conveyed, under the direction of the police, to the house from
whence the miserable fugitive had so lately effected his escape. There it
remained a few days, and was then interred at the expence of Mr. Smithson and his friend, who, from that moment, resolved to think as little as
possible of the errors of a man whose thirst for wealth had hurried him into
so much crime.

Thus perished the guilty Walter Gravestow, who throughout his life had
never been restrained by a single moral feeling, and who had manifested so
much recklessness and villany towards his fellow-creatures.

CHAPTER LIX.

THE VISION REALIZED.

THE fate of Walter Gravestow was soon conveyed to England by Mr.
Smithson and his friend, who immediately afterwards began to take steps
towards throwing light on the mystery that still involved the death of Mr.
Wentford. Their first care was to see Susan Hoply, to whom they related
the object they had in view, and who heard their determination with a
degree of pleasure that she found it impossible to repress, for she thus saw
her dearest wish about to be accomplished, and it became almost certain
that the foul stain would be at length removed from the name of her unfortunate brother.

"Poor Andrew!" she sighed, "your faithful attachment to a kind master has thus far been rewarded with unmerited hatred; but a period to all this injustice will soon arrive, and I shall yet live to hear your character cleared from the foul charges that have been brought against it."

"An injury has, indeed, too long been done to his memory," answered Mr. Smithson; "but the villainy of the real perpetrators of the murder rendered it impossible to arrive earlier at the truth. Now, however, it is clearly ascertained that Gravestow had the principal share in the crime, and I have little doubt we shall soon be able to establish the entire innocence of your brother Andrew. The mystery of his disappearance may be accounted for; and, as he has never been seen since the fatal night of the murder, I have little doubt that he fell a sacrifice to the blood-thirsty assassins, in order that he might not bring his testimony against them."

"Ah, sir!" cried Susan, "you know not how grateful I feel at your kindness in saying so. You cannot think how much I have suffered on his account, and how mortified I have felt when I knew that people looked scornfully upon me as the sister of a supposed murderer."

"Well, never mind, Susan, they will not have it in their power to do so much longer," said Mr. Derwent, who from the first had taken a great interest in her behalf. "Villany, you know, is sometimes permitted to triumph for a time, but in the end it is sure to come out sooner or later, and you have only to wait with patience a little time longer, when, I doubt not, all will be set right and smooth."

"And poor Mrs. Gravestow, sir," inquired Susan; "how will she be able to bear this dreadful shock, when she comes to hear that her husband was the murderer of Mr. Wentford?"

"I rather think she has suspected it for some time past," answered Mr. Smithson, "and, at any rate, care will be taken that the discovery is made with as much caution as possible. Indeed, I am not quite certain that she need know anything about it, for she lives in the greatest seclusion since her separation from Gravestow, and as none but a few very particular friends are allowed to visit her, she may be kept in ignorance of her husband's guilt for at least some time to come."

"But she must hear of his death, sir," observed Susan, "and when she comes to learn that he made made away with himself, it will naturally cause inquiries to be made that will bring out the truth. And then only think how great her horror will be when she discovers that she has been married to her father's murderer!"

"It will indeed be a moment of severe trial for her," exclaimed Mr. Smithson; "and I almost fear the effect it will have upon her shattered constitution. However, we must consider how the discovery may be best made to her; and you may depend on it, Susan, she will not want all the consolation that can be afforded by her truest friends."

"Ah! I know that," answered our heroine; "and yet, what consolation can be offered to one in her melancholy situation?—Won't she always reproach herself for not taking your advice against marrying Mr. Gravestow? —and how can she ever forget that her own blindness has led her into all the misery that has since fallen so heavily upon her. For my own part, I only want permission to end my days in her service, and then perhaps I might be able to cheer her spirits, when most she needs compassion from an humble but attached friend."

"I rather think that your presence would only serve to remind her the more forcibly of her past afflictions," replied Mr. Smithson. "Besides, if I am not much mistaken, there is another reason why you should abandon such a design as the one you have just been speaking of."

"Indeed, sir!—and what, pray, may that be?" inquired Susan anxiously.

" Why, to be plain with you, Susan," answered the old gentleman, " I have heard that at Summerfield resides a certain miller named William Dain, who——"

" There is," replied Susan, blushing, " but we have not seen each other for a very long time, and I dare say he has been wise enough to forget that he was ever acquainted with such a person as Susan Hoply. Besides, the last time I heard of him it was reported that he was paying his addresses to the sister of Dolly Pratt, and it's most likely he married her long ago, and in that case——"

" You are entirely mistaken, Susan, in imagining such a thing," interterrupted Mr. Smithson, " for the last time I was down at Summerfield, I heard that he was still unmarried, and was likely to continue so, unless a certain person would redeem a pledge that she made when they last parted. I dare say you understand me, Susan, and really, between ourselves, I think his constancy ought to be rewarded."

" Psha!" exclaimed Mr. Derwent, " what occasion is there to remind her of a duty that I dare say is far from a disagreeable one. Susan will never forget her lover, I can answer for it, and I don't know whether I shall not take the pains to tell him, when you and I go down to Summerfield to-morrow."

" Oh, pray don't, sir," cried our heroine, with alarm ; " for William would then think I have grown bold and forward during our long absence, and I wouldn't for the world have him believe such a thing of me."

" Aye, aye, I see how it is," laughed Mr. Derwent, " you would fain persuade yourself that nothing is so easy as to forget this William Dain, and yet, you cannot help being alarmed when you think there's a chance of anything occurring that might alter his good opinion of you. So let me advise you to ask yourself a few questions, and I'll be bound, when next we meet together, you will acknowledge that nothing in this life could afford you so much happiness as to become the wife of the miller of Summerfield."

" Well," interposed Mr. Smithson, " I rather think poor Susan would be obliged to us if we would change the subject, and so now we will take our leave of her, and perhaps when we return from our country excursion, she will have made up her mind what course to pursue. In the meantime, chance may throw us in the way of this William Dain, and in that case it will be easy to discover whether his heart remains constant to its former attachment, and whichever way it may be, we will report faithfully the result of our visit."

After a little more conversation on general subjects, the two gentlemen took their leave of Susan, and returned to their separate homes, with an understanding that they were to proceed by coach on the following morning for Summerfield. This journey was expected to be of great importance, for, with the facts they were already in possession of, they had no doubt that the whole mystery would be cleared up so as to throw the odium of the murder upon those who committed it.

It is unnecessary that we should follow them on their journey, and will, therefore, content ourselves with saying that their first object on reaching Summerfield was to pay a visit to Mr. Snell, the surveyor, who, there was some reason to believe, might have been in the confidence of Gravestow. Snell, however, denied all acquaintance with him, except as far as related to any business transactions, and was much surprised when he heard of Walter's death, and the manner in which it had been accomplished.

" You have indeed astonished me, gentlemen," he exclaimed, " for though Mr. Gravestow was a man that few people hereabouts could understand, I never could have imagined that he had any share in the murder of Mr. Wentford."

" Why of course he was artful enough to conceal such a fact from the world," replied Mr. Derwent ; " but we have at length got a clue that I rather think will satisfy the world that our suspicions have not originated in any vindictive feelings against him."

" I don't know how that may be, sir," replied Mr. Snell, " though it's very certain he was a man that nobody liked as a neighbour. Still, however, I think you must be mistaken, for I have heard it pretty generally reported that the murder of Mr. Wentford was perpetrated by one of his male domestics, who has never been seen or heard of since."

" Aye," said Mr. Smithson, " you allude to a poor fellow named Andrew Hoply, who, as you say, disappeared at the exact period of the murder. But we have now reason to believe that the report was a false and malicious one, and I am much mistaken, if it is not hereafter discovered that the young man you speak of was murdered by the assassins of Mr. Wentford, in order to destroy all proof that might be brought against them."

" And is it possible," cried Mr. Snell, " that you can suspect Mr. Walter Gravestow of having committed the foul deed of which we have been speaking ?"

" I believe there is not the least doubt of it," answered the lawyer, " and, in fact, our present business in this neighbourhood is to investigate the affair to the very bottom ; and now, sir, allow me to ask whether the old manor-house has been pulled down, about which Mr. Gravestow appeared to feel so great an interest ?"

" It has not at present," replied the surveyor, " because I have been in hourly expectation of hearing from Mr. Gravestow, respecting his purchase of it from the proprietor, who, I understand, he followed to France. The commissioners, however, have grown so impatient at the long delay, that I could no further resist their commands, and this morning I sent a number of men to work in order to commence the demolition of the old house."

" We are lucky, then, to have arrived in time," said Mr. Derwent ; " for I shall be greatly mistaken if some important discovery does not take place in the course of the work that it seems is now going on."

" Indeed !" exclaimed Mr. Snell, with surprise ; " and may I be permitted to ask what discovery can be expected to take place from the mere fact of pulling down a building that was just ready to fall of its own accord ?"

" I dare say it may appear rather surprising," observed the lawyer, " but I can assure you we have good grounds for the opinion we have formed. In short, sir, you must have observed how very anxious Mr. Gravestow always was whenever anything was said about pulling down the old manor-house of Summerfield,"

" Why, I certainly have noticed that," answered the surveyor ; " but he accounted for it by saying he had a particular partiality for old buildings, and I believed him, as there was no reason for thinking the contrary."

" Ha !" ejaculated Mr. Derwent, " but we must not take men by the words they utter. The fact is, Walter Gravestow has played the part of a low, cunning cheat all his lifetime, and it now only remains to prove that he had other reasons for wishing to save the old manor-house besides his pretended love for antiquities."

" In a word," continued Mr. Smithson, " we expect important revelations to take place, and as you say the building is now in the course of demolition, it is our intention to remain in this neighbourhood during the progress of the work. Of course, sir, you will lend us your assistance in an affair of such moment ?"

" Oh, certainly," answered the surveyor; " you may command me in any way you please, and I will most cheerfully afford every facility in my power. Yet, though you appear to be so earnest and sanguine in this affair, I must still confess that my own opinion does not coincide with yours. The house, as you are aware, has not been inhabited for some years, and though Mr. Gravestow professed so much regard for it. I never knew him to visit it once during the time he had lived in the neighbourhood."

" Which is a very good proof that he had particular reasons for avoiding it," observed Mr. Derwent. " In fact, sir, I don't hesitate to say that he had guilty motives for shunning that particular spot, and I am most anxious to see the work of pulling down proceed with as much celerity as it may be convenient to use."

" You may depend upon it, sir, there will be no delay," answered the surveyor, " for it ought by rights to have been done two or three weeks ago ; and, as I observered to you before, the commissioners have grown quite impatient about the business. There are now a great many hands employed upon it, and I expect in the course of a week we shall have all the walls down to the ground. You will then be able to satisfy yourselves as to the truth of your suspicions ; but I must repeat, that as far as my own notion goes, I can see no chance of any discovery taking place, because, as a surveyor, it was my duty to examine every part of the building, and surely, if any discovery was to take place, it must have occurred in some of my visits to it."

" There you are mistaken, Mr. Snell," said the lawyer, " for the same villainy that would also prompt Gravestow to commit the crime of murder, would also prompt him to seek the readiest means of concealing it. To be plain, I expect to find the body of his victim buried in some part of the premises."

" You don't say so !" ejaculated the surveyor, with an involuntary start of amazement.

" Such, I assure you, is my opinion, and it will not be long before the justice of it is ascertained."

" But," observed Mr. Snell, " I always heard that Mr. Wentford was murdered in his bed, and that he was afterwards buried in the village churchyard."

" So he was," answered the lawyer ; " but such was not the case of Andrew Hoply, who, there is reason to believe, was also assassinated, and his body concealed to prevent the truth from ever coming to light."

" Upon my word, gentlemen, I don't see what ground you can have for such a supposition," said the surveyor.

" Then I presume, sir," observed Mr. Derwent, " you were not an inhabitant of this place at the time the act we are speaking of took place ?"

" I was not."

" So I thought," continued the lawyer, " and it may therefore be necessary to inform you that Andrew Hoply, of whom such foul slanders have been propagated, always bore an unblemished character down to the period when this fatal transaction took place. It was also well known that he was much attached to his master, and consequently you must admit that it is very unlikely that he should have committed the act."

" But there are hypocrites in the world," observed Mr. Snell, " and he may have assumed an appearance of attachment in order to further his own purposes. Besides, robbery may have been his object, and a thirst for gold has before now tempted men to commit evil deeds."

" If robbery form any part of the incentive," answered Mr. Derwent, " then must we in common justice acquit Andrew Hoply of any participation in this deed, for nothing was stolen from the house, and the only

circumstance that induced people to suspect him was the supposed fact of his flight. But the poor fellow, I have no doubt, perished for his fidelity to his master, and then Gravestow found himself safe from suspicion; and in order to make himself more secure, he himself gave out the report that the murder had been committed by the old gentleman's servant, who had fled to avoid the punishment of the crime."

"Well," exclaimed Mr. Snell, " if your suspicions should turn out to be correct, I must say Gravestow has been the greatest villain I ever heard of. It is true his manners were so repulsive that no one in this neighbourhood would associate with him, but I never dreamed of his having such a crime as murder upon his conscience."

"Nay," cried the lawyer, "we are not certain yet that he has not the blood of more than one unfortunate victim to answer for. We have proof positive that the life of a fellow-creature was thought nothing of whenever he had any particular object to serve, and it is only a short time since that he carried a female over to Paris, and attempted to drown her, because he knew she might be an important witness against him, and he was determined to get rid of her."

"Really," exclaimed the surveyor, " I begin now to think there must have been some such reason for the moody melancholy habits that I have so often observed in Mr. Gravestow. The very children used to run away with fear whenever he came in sight, and I have seen him gnash his teeth, and heard him mutter to himself, as if conscious of the dread his presence was sure to occasion."

" You may depend upon it we are right in our conclusions," said Mr. Smithson, "and so now we will take our leave of you for the present, but shall, no doubt, meet you frequently at the manor-house during the progress of its demolition. A few days, you say, will be sufficient to level it

No. 55

with the ground, and in that time I trust we shall be able to produce sufficient proof of the innocence of Andrew Hoply, and the guilt of the real
perpetrator of the crime."

The two gentlemen now took their leave, and on their way to the inn
where they intended to remain during their visit to Summerfield, it was
arranged that Susan should be immediately sent for, in case her presence
should be necessary to identify anything that might be found belonging to
her brother. A letter was accordingly despatched to London, and then
their future plans were arranged for perfecting the scheme in which they
were engaged.

On the following day Susan arrived by the coach, and was briefly informed of all that had taken place since they had come down, together with
an assurance that they were now more than ever certain that the discovery so
desired would speedily take place. Our heroine listened to them with eager
attention, and when they had finished, said :—

"I also feel more confident than when I last saw you, that the mystery
is about to be revealed, for last night I had a fearful vision, that convinces
me our labours will not have been undertaken in vain."

"A dream !" exclaimed Mr. Smithson, "and pray what may have been
the import of it ?"

"I thought," she replied, "that I was visited by the shade of my
murdered brother, whose melancholy looks seemed to reproach me for not
having brought his innocence to light. He spoke to me in solemn accents,
and said that his body had been concealed behind the wainscot of one of
the rooms in the old manor-house at Summerfield, and charged me to lose
no time in causing a search to be made. This I promised to do as well as
the awe I felt would permit, and instantly afterwards the form vanished
from my sight."

"Aye," observed Mr. Smithson, "it was a dream, and, no doubt, occasioned by your continually thinking upon this one painful circumstance. It
is, however, a singular coincidence, and will appear the more remarkable
in the event of our finding the body in such a situation as you have described."

"Which is likely enough, by the by," exclaimed the lawyer, "for I suppose Gravestow and his comrades had ready access to the house ; and
nothing would be easier than for the assassins to carry the body at night
to the old mansion, and deposit it behind the wainscot for concealment."

"At any rate," cried his friend, "we shall soon put this vision to the
test, and, after all, I should not be surprised if the place indicated proves to
be the very one where the discovery will occur. Such marvellous things
have occurred before now, and I see no reason to doubt that Susan's dream
was something more than the mere effect of chance. However, we will
now separate for the night, and to-morrow commence our task of watching the workmen during their progress, which we will continue to do till
the place is entirely pulled down, or we have made the discovery we seek."

Susan now retired to her chamber, but not to sleep, for her mind was too
full of the task that had been undertaken, and she had, besides, some fear of
a repetition of that vision which had so much appalled her on the preceding
night. At length, when day dawned, she rose, and seated herself at the
window till the people of the house were stirring, and then, descending to
the sitting-room, she waited with impatience the arrival of the two gentlemen who had taken so much pains in her behalf. In about an hour after
they both joined her, and having partaken of breakfast, they all three set
out on their first visit to watch the demolition of the old manor-house.

For some days the work proceeded, and nothing occurred worthy of notice, which served rather to damp the expectation of those who were so deeply interested, and they even began to despair of meeting with the success that had been anticipated. At length, however, as the workmen were employed in pulling down the wainscot of a small apartment that had always been carefully kept locked, they were horror-struck at discovering behind it a human skeleton, lying in a cramped-up position, and evidently placed there for the purpose of concealment.

This discovery naturally occasioned a great deal of wonder and consternation, and immediate notice of it was given to Susan and the two gentlemen, who happened at the time to be in a different part of the building. They, however, hastened without delay to the spot, and if any confirmation of their suspicion of its being the remains of the unfortunate Andrew Hoply was required, it was supplied by the fact of the room exactly corresponding in appearance with the one which Susan had beheld in her late vision.

But the testimony rested upon a better foundation than this, for of the clothes that had been worn by the hapless victim on the night of his assassination, there were sufficient fragments to enable our heroine to identify them as those which she had seen belonging to her brother. The buttons were also all found, and bearing as they did the crest of Mr. Wentford, there could be little doubt that they had once been possessed by Andrew Hoply. Nor was this the only evidence presented to their view, for a ring still remained upon the finger of the skeleton, which was instantly recognized by Susan as one that had constantly been worn by her brother, in consequence of its having been presented to him by a valued friend, and which thus served to add confirmation to the terrible truth, and to identify the remains before her as those of her long lost, and deeply-injured relative.

The shock given to our heroine may be more readily imagined than described, and it was not without much difficulty that Mr. Smithson and his friend could pacify the heavy mental anguish which this event had occasioned. There was, however, at least some consolation in knowing that this discovery would serve completely to establish his innocence of the crime of which he had been falsely accused, and the very fact of his being found concealed in such a place was the most satisfactory and conclusive evidence that he must have been placed there by the hands of other persons, and that he had met his death whilst engaged in defending his master from the murderous ruffians that had made an attack upon his life.

It was also certain that the body had been subsequently conveyed to the manor-house, and concealed in the place where it was found, in order that his disappearance might confirm the report, which was afterwards spread abroad, of his having fled from the neighbourhood immediately subsequent to the assassination of the unfortunate Mr. Wentford.

It was, as we have said, a melancholy satisfaction to Susan that the character of her brother had been thus cleared from the injurious calumnies that had been cast upon it; but she found it impossible to subdue the deep grief that the sight of poor Andrew's remains occasioned, and with some difficulty the two gentlemen at length prevailed upon her to quit the spot and return to their lodging, where, by the soothing language of pity and commiseration, they succeeded in checking her grief, and convincing her that she had good reason to be thankful for the extraordinary discovery that had that day taken place.

" You must not think us devoid of feeling, Susan," exclaimed Mr. Smithson, "that we thus seek to turn your thoughts from this painful subject, for, I can assure you, both my friend and myself have but one object for doing so. It has ever been your most earnest wish to clear the character of your brother, and having affected this, it becomes your duty to bow with resignation to the hapless doom that has deprived you of a beloved relative."

"And that I will do so my future conduct shall prove," answered our heroine. "I have met with friends when I thought myself left alone and unpitied in the world, and it would, indeed, be most ungrateful were I to reject the advice which I so well know is prompted by their anxious desire to see me happy."

"You have judged our motives rightly, Susan," exclaimed the warm-hearted old gentleman; "and I am truly glad to see that our efforts have not been made in vain. It shall now be my last mournful task to see the remains of your brother placed in consecrated ground, and when that is done, you can either return with us to London, or remain here till arrangements have been made for your future maintenance and comfort."

"For a time, at least, I should wish to take up my abode in Summerfield," replied our heroine. "I can then pay frequent visits to the grave of my poor brother, and the tears which I shed over the green turf that covers him will, in the course of a few weeks, serve to mitigate the sufferings I at present endure."

"If such is your wish, I am quite ready to acquiesce in it," returned Mr. Smithson. "To-morrow morning I and my friend go back to town; but previous to leaving this place, I shall give all necessary directions for the funeral of Andrew. And now, Susan, I have one request to make: you will, of course, require money, and in this purse you will find sufficient to defray your expenses here till I have made arrangements for rewarding your excellent conduct as it deserves. Nay, I will take no refusal, girl, for it is the only favour I have ever yet asked, and to reject it would offend one who really desires to be a friend."

Saying this, he placed the purse upon the table, and hastily left the room to join Mr. Derwent, who was busily occupied in throwing together a few notes that would be serviceable towards establishing the charge he was now fully prepared to make against the late Walter Gravestow. It was true the murderer was beyond the reach of earthly justice, but there might be some persons inclined to descredit the assertions that were about to be made, and it was, therefore, necessary that the most uncontradictory evidence should be produced to prove that his was the hand which had slain Mr. Wentford.

CHAPTER LX.

CONCLUSION.

ON the following morning, when Susan Hoply rose, she heard that the two gentlemen had taken their departure for London by the coach, and that they had left a message to inform her that they would write a letter at the first convenient opportunity. She had thus leisure to reflect upon the extraordinary events of the last day or two, and melancholy enough was the impression those thoughts left upon her mind. From this state of despondency, however, she was at length suddenly aroused by the quick opening of the door, and in another moment she was again locked in the arms of Willian Dain, her still faithful lover!

It is unnecessary to describe an interview which it may be readily imagined was mutually satisfactory to them. William, however, refrained from speaking just then on the subject nearest his heart, for he was well aware of the grief that weighed upon her spirits, and even before the interview he had resolved within his own mind to postpone his declaration of continued love till after the interment of her brother's remains. This delicacy did not pass unheeded by Susan, and, appreciating the kindness by which it had been dictated, she mentally resolved to delay their marriage no longer than the usual period of mourning lasted.

At William's request she now entered into a brief detail of all the trials and vicissitudes to which she had been subjected since the period when last they had parted on the day she quitted Summerfield to find friends and a home in the great metropolis. She described the deep anxiety she had endured as month after month passed away, and still no circumstance occurred to aid the one fond wish she felt to clear her brother's memory from the foul stain of crime which had been cast upon it. Nor was she forgetful of the kind friends she had met with among strangers, and the generous aid they had promptly afforded when they learnt the cause of that anguish of heart which all her caution had not been able to conceal. Her narrative then led her to allude more particularly to Walter Gravestow and the many deep schemes of villany in which he had been engaged, and this led her to the sufferings of the unfortunate Amelia, whose hapless acquaintance with him had brought ruin and loss of honour in its train, and had nearly terminated in her murder by the man she had trusted but that he might betray. This part of her recital brought her to the point when she set off to France with the deceived Marchioness de Valliere, and the subsequent apprehension of George Ramsden and his equally villanous associate in crime. The proof that had been obtained against Walter Gravestow was already known to her lover, as well as the subsequent fate of the murderer, and, therefore, she passed over a description which could not fail to give her pain, notwithstanding the abhorrence in which she held the remembrance of the too guilty suicide.

William heard the narrative of her singular adventures with a feeling of astonishment that he could not conceal. He, however, scarcely once interrupted her during the recital, but at its conclusion he congratulated her upon the marvellous escapes she had had, and the successful termination of a pursuit which at one time had appeared so unpromising. In return, he recounted all that had occurred to himself during the time he had been absent, and as slightly as possible of his still enduring affection for her, and the determination he had formed to wait patiently till the moment arrived when he could ask her to fulfil the promise she had given ere the commencement of those troubles which had terminated in forcing her to quit her native village. He, however, forbore questioning her upon the subject any further just then, and at length took his departure, well convinced that his future visits would be no less welcome than this had been.

Overjoyed at the brightening prospects that began to dawn upon him, William Dain became quite an altered man, and, instead of looking sad and melancholy as he had done for some time past, he could laugh and chat with his old friends, and many were the congratulations he received from them upon the subject of Susan's constancy, and the certainty that ere very long he would be able to claim her as his own.

His father, however, still retained some of his former prejudices to the union, for he believed there could be no happiness without money, and as it was pretty certain Susan was not much richer than she was when she left that neighbourhood, he could see no reason for altering the narrow prejudices he had formed. These opinions William endeavoured to remove by arguments, but old people are very seldom to be convinced by those that are younger than themselves; and on one occasion, after a conversation of this kind, he was about to leave the house in no very good humour, when his father, in a somewhat peremptory tone, commanded him to stay where he was.

"I see how it is, William," he said, "you are like all other undutiful sons that think they have a right to an opinion of their own, and now, I suppose, if the truth was known, you are going to Susan to tell her that you will make her your wife in spite of all that I have said."

"You have never known me to be guilty of a wilful falsehood," answered the young man; "and I, therefore, candidly confess that I intend seeing Susan, but not to tell her what you have just now said. In fact, slightingly as you think of her, sir, she possesses too honourable a principle to marry me unless it be with your full concurrence."

"Then, as you are never likely to have it," replied his father, "the most honourable course you can adopt will be to tell her so with as little delay as possible."

"That I cannot undertake to do, father," exclaimed William; "for I believe prejudices may be removed, and I am certain that were I to tell her such a thing, she would yield to the injustice of your demand, even though it might be at the expense of her own happiness."

"In that case I must see the girl, and tell her so myself," answered the old man; "for I have always made up my mind that you should marry a girl with money, and as she has not got any, I have fully determined in my own mind to put an end to this romantic folly, that can only end in your ruin."

"But you forget, sir, that Susan has good friends, and I believe there is very little doubt that she will be rewarded by them for the fidelity she has exhibited throughout her life."

"That would alter the case very materially," exclaimed his father; "and should she ever be able to prove herself the mistress of two or three hundred pounds, I dare say I should no longer offer any opposition to your marriage."

"It seems scarcely possible," cried William, indignantly, "that for so paltry a consideration you can seek to destroy the happiness of two persons."

"You know nothing about the value of money, boy, or you would not talk in this light way of it," retorted the old man. "I, however, have lived a few years longer in the world, and from all I have ever seen or heard, there's no getting on unless a man is independent of his fellow-creatures."

"I suppose then, sir," observed William, "you married my mother more for the sake of her money than for any real love that you bore her?"

"Your mother, sir, was a prudent woman," answered the old man, "and, I believe, would never have married me unless she thought I knew how to take care of her money. Besides, I had saved some of my own, and that was quite proof enough for her to know that I was not one of those harum scarum chaps that spend every thing as soon as they get it. So now, sir, as you have heard my opinion, and can't misunderstand me, I I shall expect that you give up all idea of marrying Susan Hoply till you are well convinced that she has money to make a start in life with."

"And what if I should judge your commands harsh, and venture to disobey them?"

"Why, in that case, you must be content to live in the beggary you bring upon yourself," answered his father. "I have been able to lay by some little money, as I dare say you are aware, but not one penny of it shall ever find its way to your pocket if you choose to marry without my consent."

"You forget, sir, that I am no longer a child," exclaimed William, impatiently, "and that I have some right to have a will of my own in an affair that so nearly concerns my happiness. Susan's character, you must admit, is beyond reproach, and that alone should be sufficient to obtain for her some share of your kindness and regard."

"Aye, aye, there's nothing to be said against her, I confess," replied her father; "but young men are apt to think too lightly of matrimony, and it is therefore the duty of parents to see that their children don't make fools of themselves. Susan Hoply, I dare say, is a very excellent and deserving young woman, and I believe if she had but a small fortune of her own, I should not make much objection to the match."

"And that she may have sooner than you expect," exclaimed William Dain.

"So you would fain have me believe," answered the old man; "but I am not one of those that like to leave anything to chance. If these friends of hers really intend to do as you expect, they had better lose no time about it; and when I know how far their liberality will carry them, I shall be able to make up my mind whether it will be enough to start you in business on your own account."

"But you are aware, sir, that it is impossible to urge them upon such a subject as this?"

"Oh yes, I'm quite aware of that," answered his father, "and you must therefore be content to wait with patience till they think proper to do what they intend for her. Besides, you are not quite sure that Susan may be inclined to marry you after being absent so long, and it's by no means unlikely that she may have found another lover in London."

"Nay, upon that point I am quite certain," replied William, "for I have spoken to her about it, and she has acknowledged that her heart is unchanged towards me."

"Indeed!" exclaimed his father, angrily, "and so I suppose you have arranged all between yourselves, without thinking it worth while to consult me upon the subject?"

"You have entirely mistaken Susan's character if you believe her capable of encouraging me in my opposition to your will," answered the young man. "I, in fact, merely sought an interview to ascertain whether she still regarded me with the same affection that she used, and having satisfied myself upon that point I am content to wait patiently till the period she has named."

"And how long distant may that be?"

"Not till twelve months have passed away from the period of the discovery of her unfortunate brother's remains," answered William. "She was much attached to him, as you are aware; and, though the evidence that had been afforded of his innocence of certain charges that were brought against him was complete, she feels deeply for his unhappy fate, and has resolved not to marry till after the period of mourning has expired."

"Well, you know my determination about it," said the old man, "and for your own sake I would advise you to think well before you take a step that may bring both yourself and the girl to poverty and ruin. She may be, and I dare say is, all very well in her way, but I have a right to have a voice in the matter, and I again tell you the girl must not be your wife unless she can marry you with a portion."

William Dain felt afraid to trust himself to make any reply to this, lest anger should urge him to do so in a disrespectful way, and taking up his hat once more, he left the house without uttering a word, and took his way towards the place where Susan was at present residing. It will readily enough be imagined that he was welcomed with no little joy, but the gloom that had settled itself upon his countenance did not long pass unnoticed, and with much earnestness of tone she inquired what had occurred to make him so melancholy all of a sudden.

" I'll tell you, Susan," he replied, " if you will promise that it shall make no difference between us. The truth is, as you are already aware, my father is opposed to my marrying any one that is not possessed of money, and we have just had a conversation together, by which I find that he is as much prejudiced as ever against our union."

" I feared it would be so," cried Susan, " and it is indeed a source of the utmost grief to me that I should be the cause of an ill-feeling between a father and his son. Under all circumstancec, therefore, I think it would be better that our acquaintances should cease from this moment, and that you should forget such a person as myself was ever known to you."

" That I can never do," answered William, " for that period will ever be the happiest of my life ; and never can I yield to the harsh prejudices of a parent, whose opinions would be so different where he but to know you. Besides, my father is not insensible to the value of a good and virtuous wife ; and I feel assured, that he will think very differently on this subject when he becomes better acquainted with you."

" But," returned Susan, " there may be other reasons that he has not at present acquainted you with. For instance, he may not be altogether satisfied with the proof of my brother Andrew's innocence, and in that case it is hardly to be expected that he will ever be reconciled to our union."

" And do you really think," asked William, " that he can be so unjust as to think so badly of your unfortunate brother when everybody else has been perfectly convinced that the murder of Mr. Wentford was committed by Walter Gravestow and his worthless associates ?"

" I do not say that it is so," replied Susan, " but all people are not to be satisfied alike, and I feared there might be some who would continue to regard Andrew as guilty of that dreadful deed. I may, however, have wronged him, and most sincerely do I hope it may be so, for most of all should I be sorry that the father of William Dain should continue so much prejudiced."

" Believe me, Susan, you have been mistaken," exclaimed the young man earnestly, " for my father has told me over and over again, that his only objection to our union is your want of money. That one obstacle re-moved, he would no longer oppose us ; and I have reasons to believe, that ere long you will not be the portionless girl you are at present."

" And what prospect do you think I have of ever possessing more than I now do ?" asked Susan.

" Why, you have kind friends," replied William, " and I have enter-tained thoughts that it is their intention to make you some recompense for the severe trials with which you have been afflicted. But I trust, Susan, you will give me credit for candour when I declare that I have no desire to see you richer than you are now, except that it will reconcile my father, and render our union certain."

" The friends you speak of," answered Susan, " have been most kind to me, but I have no claim upon their further generosity, and I know not but I should refuse it even if they were to offer me a sum of money, In fact, my sufferings, I trust, have now passed away for ever, and I shall be amply rewarded if the remainder of my days are passed in undisturbed peace."

" But for my sake, I hope, you will not refuse their proffered liberality," exclaimed William ; " you know I want not the money, but if it would procure my father's assent to our union, it would prove the means of render-ing us both happy for the rest of our days. I have heard you speak of Mr. Smithson in terms of the highest praise,—he is rich, and a single man, and

perhaps the sum, however small it may be, would not be bestowed in vain."

"At present," replied Susan, with a smile, "we know not that he has any such intention ; but since you have so urgently pressed me upon this subject, I will promise not to reject any present he may make me, without careful consideration. Besides, we have sufficient time before us, William, for I have already told you that even if our marriage does take place, it will not be till the expiration of a year."

"I am content to wait any time you please," exclaimed the young man ; "so that you do not positively reject my offer. In the meantime I will endeavour, by every means in my power, to soften my father's heart, and as I know he is not unmindful of my happiness, I have little doubt but that, in the end, I shall succeed."

The conversation now took another turn, and having assured himself that our heroine still regarded him with as much affection as ever, he took his departure.

To Susan, the confirmation she had received of her lover's continued fidelity was a source of gratification that served in some degree to mitigate the deep anguish that lacerated her heart. She had, in fact, never ceased to regard William Dain with the same affection as previously to their long parting, and she had often thought of writing to him an assurance that he was not forgotten in his absence, and she anxiously looked forward to the moment when they should once more meet at Summerfield. This, however, she postponed from time to time, lest by taking such a step she might be deemed too bold and forward ; and, perhaps, she was the more induced to do this, as she expected to return to her native village ere long, and in that case she trusted an interview would quickly serve to remove from William's mind any opinion that he might have formed of her having forgotten him

No. 56

during the interval that had elapsed since last they had seen each other. But now she had seen ample proof that his heart remained constant, and, but for one source of grief, she would have been happy. The memory of her brother's unhappy fate, and the wrongs that had been heaped upon his name, could not be easily obliterated, and she still reflected mournfully upon events that had so materially affected the latter portion of her life. Yet the frequent visits of William Dain served gradually to dissipate these thoughts, and when the funeral had taken place she began by slow degrees to recover that cheerfulness of mind that at one period seemed to have fled for ever.

In fulfilment of the promise he had given, Mr. Smithson and his friend paid her an early visit, and acquainted her with all that had transpired since they left her on their departure for London. Every proof had by this time been obtained to satisfy their minds of Walter Gravestow's guilty participation in the murder of Mr. Wentford, and from certain papers that had been found in his house, it was discovered, beyond all doubt, that Andrew Hoply had been assassinated in an attempt to save the life of his master, and that his body had afterwards been concealed for the purpose of aiding a report which was spread about that the crime had been committed by the servant, and that he had immediately fled, to avoid the punishment of his crime.

This intelligence was a source of much gratification to our heroine, as it completely exonerated her brother from the accusation which had been believed by so many persons. Mr. Smithson was one of the first to congratulate her upon the successful result of his well-meant exertions, and having complimented her upon the noble firmness of purpose she had all along manifested, he requested, as a particular favour to himself, to bestow upon her such a marriage portion as would place her and William Dain in a comfortable farm, where they might support themselves in that ease and respectability which they both so well merited. Susan would have refused the proffered gift of her generous benefactor, but he would listen to no denial, and it was eventually accepted, with many expressions of the deepest gratitude for the kindness which had dictated the liberal offer he had made.

Exactly twelve months after the discovery of her brother's remains, and the consequent establishment of his innocence, Susan Hoply gave her hand to William Dain, whose constancy and unvarying love had thus obtained for him the prize which, above all others, he so ardently coveted. Previous to this happy event taken place, a farm was taken near the mill in the immediate neighbourhood of which Susan had passed some of the most joyous years of her early life. The house, too, was situated in a most delightful spot, and even had our heroine been more difficult to please than she really was, she could scarcely have felt dissatisfied with the unlooked for destiny which had at length befallen her.

In William Dain, as might have been expected, she found a faithful and attached husband, whose every thought seemed to be to ensure the happiness of one who he had so long loved, but who for some time seemed to be lost to him for ever. Nor did Susan fail to appreciate the kindness she experienced from the man to whom she had entrusted her happiness, and, as our readers may well imagine, their lives were passed in that contentment which is only to be found among the good and virtuous. Occasionally, it is true, our heroine felt a depression of spirits, that it was impossible at the time to subdue, for frequently her thoughts would recur to the past, and as she reflected upon the one most important event of her life, tears would start from her eyes in spite of every effort she made to suppress them.

But even this sadness wore gradually off in time, for as a family began to increase about her, she had little leisure for reflection, and happy as she felt in the society of her husband and children, she at length seldom looked back to the sorrowful period of her existence, and regarding only the future, she seldom had an opportunity of indulging in those feelings that had at one time occasioned her so much bitterness of heart.

It was not till some time after the suicide of Walter Gravestow, that the widow's good friend, Mr. Smithson, would acquaint her with the real circumstances connected with the death of her worthless husband. Mrs. Gravestow, however, had long anticipated that some such catastrophe would occur, for she had but too much reason to believe him guilty of the violence that had robbed her of a beloved father, and she knew his fierce nature too well to imagine that he would ever permit himself to be taken alive. She had consequently remained for some time in a state of painful suspense, and when she learnt that still further evidence had been obtained against him, and that persons had gone in pursuit of him to France, she anticipated that he would perish by his own hand whenever it became evident to him that no means of escape remained.

For some time past she had been residing in a quiet country village upon the scanty means afforded by her brutal husband, and seldom holding communication with any person who could acquaint her with what was occurring. At intervals it is true, she received letters from Mr. Smithson, but he was silent upon the topic she was most anxious to hear about, and dreading to write for further information, she continued for some time in a state of suspense that she found by no means easy to endure.

Always looking forward to the worst, however, she was more prepared than might have been expected to hear that her husband had at length terminated a career of crime by raising the hand of self-destruction. The suddeness with which the announcement was made, rather startled her at first, but the shock soon subsided ; and as it was necessary for her immediately to proceed to London on law business, her time became so much occupied that she soon recovered from the temporary agitation into which she had been thrown.

The fortune which had been left to her by her father, and which had been taken from her by Walter Gravestow, was now entirely under her own control ; and, having taken a house in the suburbs of London, she again began to mix in that society from which circumstances had for a period driven her. Within three years afterwards she bestowed her hand in marriage upon a gentleman of great worth, whose kindness and regard made ample recompense for the miseries and ill-treatment that had clouded the first few years of her former married life.

It has now become necessary to say something of Dolly Pratt, who has had so much to do in the course of the foregoing pages. Wearied of the false glare of fashion in which she had spent some of her days, she took an early opportunity to leave London, and went to live in a retired part of Wales, where the remainder of her days were passed in ease and competence upon the annuity which had been left her by the Marquis de Noailles. The circumstances that had occurred just previous to quitting France, had served to remove the flightiness which had once been so conspicuous in her character, and in the place to which she now retired, the excellence of her conduct soon gained for her the admiration and friendship of her neighbours, for, though she mixed not much in society, her charity to the poor, and general kindness of heart, procured that esteem which it was her chief ambition to deserve.

For Amelia, it was the particular care of Mr. Smithson to provide in a manner that was most likely to ensure her future comfort. A shop was accordingly taken for her in the neighbourhood of town, and occupied as she was in this, she found forgetfulness of the past; and if occasionally a thought crossed her mind to recal images that she would fain forget, there was yet one consolation in knowing that the man who had sought her life was no longer in existence, and that she had nothing further to apprehend from the malice of secret enemies or open foes.

Of the other personages that the reader has made acquaintance with during the progress of this narrative, there is but one of whom it will be necessary to speak. We allude to Edwin, who, immediately after his return to England, was admitted to that share of the business which had been left him by Mr. Wentford, but of which he had been unjustly deprived by the grasping avarice of Walter Gravestow. With the share of profit which came to him, together with the sum of money that had also been left as a legacy, he was now placed in a situation in life that the excellence of his conduct had so justly merited.

THE END.